CALL TO PURPOSE

KEN W BROWN

CALL TO PURPOSE

Our journey
from celestial beings
to human beings
and back again

ISBN: 978-1-7331710-0-7 (paperback)
ISBN: 978-1-7331710-1-4 (e-Book)
Library of Congress Control Number: 2019907334

This is a work of fiction. Any references to events, real people, or real places are either products of the author's imagination or are used fictitiously. The prologue and epilogue contain work of nonfiction. Certain names and identifying characteristics in those sections have been changed.

Cover: Design by the author. Three photographs, courtesy of the Earth Science and Remote Sensing Unit, NASA Johnson Space Center, https://eol.jsc.nasa.gov, were blended to form the cover image described in chapter three.

Printed in the United States of America.
Book website: www.calltopurpose.com
Publisher: www.transformationkey.com

TO THE READER

∞

After an exhausting climb up the Great Pyramid one night, heart-wrenching experiences from this life unexpectedly combined with those from previous lives. Reliving what it means to be a human being across time both overwhelmed and connected me with a forgotten depth of purpose.

When humans joined with souls to become "human beings," they never knew evil existed. They did not know something called "lies" could be woven into a truth. They did not know how intelligent and reasonable evil might sound.

The prologue and epilogue describe events from my life that bookend the visionary fiction in between. The characters bring the reader along with them as the ancient joy of co-creation with all forms of life is revealed. The characters embody the intense confusion, denial and eventual recognition of evil—and the tremendous courage it took face it—across time.

I share the story with you in the same way it was revealed to me; element by element building to dramatic realization. Each page contributes a thread to the canvas on which this story of joy, loss and reawakening is recalled.

The events that underlay the novel transformed my feelings of isolation and despair into those of connection and resilient hope. May *Call To Purpose* help you experience the story from within yourself, embrace the human-being you are, and empower who you wish to become.

Respectfully,

Ken W. Brown

This book is dedicated to the guardian within you.

CALL TO PURPOSE

PROLOGUE

∞

Giza, Egypt

A mixture of odors assailed the night air with each labored step. Oil on the dark, desert road smelled of an ancient tar pit. The scent of a rotting cantaloupe rose from the shadow of a roadside frond.

However, my perspiration, stiff from a hard day's travel, remained the dominant aroma.

The hill grew steeper, and my pulse pounded. My feet slowed and my gaze swept the sand for a safe place to sit in the darkness.

What am I doing here?

White-hot pins of starlight pierced the dome of the desert sky. Four brilliant stars outlined the corners of the constellation of Orion, its hourglass shape cinched by a belt of three more stars.

The memory of an African storyteller painted my mind. Where was it? Senegal. Near the desert border with Mali. So many years ago, or yesterday.

His ebony skin reflected a translucent shine from the glow of kerosene lamps hanging from wooden poles around the village square. Telling his tale, he pivoted to face each villager in turn, including me.

With each rotation, the lamplight made the wooly, white hair on his head glow with an orange aura and the stubble on his face flicker with fire. Whirling in place, his stare flashed past me, his story weaving with the timeless beat of the drum he slapped. Faster and faster, until I felt his gaze never left mine.

Time evaporated. Day, month, year, gone. He barked a cry, jumped high into the air and returned to Earth with his bare feet spread wide in the desert sand. Dust plumed; his gaze remained fixed on mine.

Slowly, he pointed a bony finger into the night sky. The constellation Orion flared at the end of his outstretched arm.

1

Now, fifteen years later, Orion's Belt blazed in the same place in the sky the storyteller left it. Except this night, it danced above the Great Pyramid.

The memory was pushed aside by a rock under my foot. In one motion, my boot rose and kicked the offender. It skated across the tar but stopped dead when it hit sand.

The boot took another step up the hill, and a deep sigh escaped my chest.

How many states have I explored, forty-seven? How many countries have I backpacked through? Over fifty for sure.

Why?

I knew why. A sense of something missing. Not missing, exactly. Out of reach. It hovered behind a shroud of fog. If I could just move into it far enough, I'd find it.

I glanced up at Orion again. Still there.

Keep moving.

The people I met while traveling up and down and across the U.S. were different, yet not. From the dignified row houses of Boston to the bright colors of New Orleans, and from the Appalachian Mountains to the redwood forests and every state in between—the cultural veneer changed but what lay under it did not. Good people with good hearts.

Sometimes, however, the veneer cracked. In an instant, the same people showing me kindness used keen-edged words to pin other people in place. The seemingly random, hurtful behavior experienced as a child was everywhere.

Another rock challenged me. The scuffed-leather toe of my boot struck it dead center, but rather than skate, the rock exploded into dust. The chalky smell of limestone filled the air. My boots trudged on with a mind of their own.

I paid for a bed at the old Mena House. Why aren't I in it?

A pile of camel dung tried to greet one foot but the Vibram sole passed over it without remark.

It's because I saw the Great Pyramid out my window and felt this deep call.

Stretching out on the comfortable bed didn't turn down the volume of the siren's song in my chest. Nor did massaging my tight calf muscles. No need to turn on the light and wake my wife. I wrote a note: "Went to see pyramids. Back soon."

My still-warm boots slid back on with habitual ease. Staring out the rippled glass window, my hands automatically wound the shoelace around the bow-tie loop twice before pulling the knot tight.

The smell of more dung slowed my pace. Goat droppings this time. I stepped over the pellets without breaking stride.

Why am I so driven?

Dust-filled cracks in the old asphalt reflected starlight and reminded me of the night's sky. Galaxies soared above my head and under my feet.

A childhood memory, unbidden, rolled through my mind.

It was near the 4th of July and my eight-year-old self stood on a rocky slope about a mile from my home. I was the youngest of four boys there. The oldest was a head taller than me and held one of the horned toads common in our small town. In spite of their prehistoric, horned-lizard appearance, they were docile and remained quiet in your hand. My mother liked them because they ate the ants overwhelming our garden.

The boy suddenly put a firecracker in its mouth, lit the fuse and dropped the toad to the ground. It tried to disgorge it but couldn't.

The explosion shook every cell of my body. The other kids laughed. I stared at the oldest boy in shocked disbelief. He laughed a shallow laugh but didn't look for a second toad.

Another memory followed in a seamless tableau. Sitting in my elementary school desk, the boy in front of me turned and, without the slightest warning, stabbed his freshly sharpened pencil into the palm of my hand. There was no explanation or cause to discern. The sudden violence stood on its own.

He jerked out the pencil, turned around, and pretended nothing happened. Not one of the kids around me said a word. Dark red blood pooled in my palm. If it dripped, an explanation would be demanded. I had no idea what I'd done wrong. Pressing the bleeding hole against my old blue jeans staunched the flow. If it wasn't for the broken pencil lead deep under my skin, I might have been able to pretend it didn't happen.

There were two big churches in town and I attended both. Methodist every Sunday and Baptist for summer Bible school. The difference when people were either in or out of them left me dazed. The boy who blew up the horned toad was an acolyte. He led the minister's procession down the aisle while holding a tall, brass cross. The boy who stabbed me with the pencil was in Bible school. He got an extra cookie when he recited scripture the rest of us couldn't.

The reverends of both churches professed, "We who are many are one body," but when I tried to fit my common experience into it, my stomach hurt. "What's wrong with me? Maybe if I studied harder."

The edges of my Bible were worn to the point that gray cardboard showed under its hard, black cover, but I didn't mind. It was the scripture about "we are of one body" that I needed to find. I inserted slips of paper between pages in Corinthians, Romans, Colossians, and Ephesians, each marking a "one body" text. "As members of one body you are called to live in peace" gave me the most solace.

However, finding quotes didn't help me understand why some people wanted to blow up horned toads or stab me. My inner conflict raged and my arms broke out in an agonizing rash. I covered it by wearing long sleeves.

Tornadoes were frequent in the Midwest, and our house had a storm cellar: a big hole in the ground with a rickety door over it. Only flakes of its white paint remained, but its hinges still creaked open. The wooden steps down flexed with rot, but if you kept off the center, they held fine. Lowering the cellar door behind me, silent darkness and the smell of damp earth filled the shelter.

Small disk-shaped plates of fossilized sea plants gleamed in the limestone floor. Old Mason jars filled with pale vegetables of gardens long past were knitted together with a delicate, gauzy web. The spiders that made them lived among orderly canned goods along the walls and had no reason to explore. I sat in the middle of the floor, calm. Safe. Safe to ask questions gnawing inside me. "The bigger pick on the smaller, who soon become big to do the same. Is that how life is?"

Heart pounding, my prayer, "What am I?" emptied into the dusty, limestone floor. My mind stilled. No thought. No light. No sound. All expectation drained away. A gentle warmth started to tingle in my legs. It moved up slowly, mixed in my chest, and grew.

The feeling of "belonging" felt so tangible, it seemed my lungs breathed with the damp stone walls. The sea plants moved with the current in their ancient sea. My body was timeless in Earth itself. Safe with fossils, spiders, and darkness—the ministers were right. All I needed to do was be open to this "one body" they say I'm within, and feel it.

The rich aroma of camel dung pulled me back to the road. Without looking down, I took a long step over the marble-sized pellets. Freed again, my mind rolled on its wandering path to another comforting memory.

I lay on the red dirt bank of my favorite stock pond, in the woods about a quarter-mile from my house. The dirt slope fit my body well and positioned my head perfectly for watching either clouds or the pond. At that moment, water bugs strode across the water, their middle legs sweeping in a circle of oars.

The cavity in the trunk of the old oak next to it held a pair of white-breasted nuthatches. Their white faces and chests stood in sharp contrast to their gray-blue wings and backs.

A water moccasin sunbathed on the rock next to the water's edge. Neither of us had interest in the place of the other. We were both safe. I looked up. Bright-white clouds swam in an inverted bowl of blue. "Like the cellar, this has to be what the ministers feel all the time."

Dozing, in the warm sunlight, in a dream of being a tree and a cloud. My eyes opened at the sound of a nuthatch's single note of song. It peered down, its black feathers flowing smooth and soft from its head to its blue-gray back.

I felt a part of something so vast and beautiful it was beyond words. It felt so real.

Robbie was shot that night. There were no leash laws in my small farming town. All dogs and kids ran free. No different from countless nights before, he pushed open the old, wooden screen door, came onto the back porch, and lay down. I saw blood but didn't know what it was from. I petted him gently. The look in his eyes was both kind and achingly sad.

When my dad got home, he took him to the vet. Robbie died on the way. The vet said the bullet took off the bottom of his heart, and it was a miracle he walked any distance at all. A neighbor kid told me the man that shot him knew he was our dog, but his was in heat and he didn't want the pack of males around. Robbie was the biggest target, a collie.

My hope for the "one body" died with Robbie. It was pretend. Not of the real world. The rash on my arms itched so severely I wrapped them in cloth at night because I woke up with them scratched to bleeding.

The following week a friend laughed when he pushed me off a brickwork pillar with his feet against my back. My head hit the edge and blood soon covered my back. He told everyone I fell.

Cruelty, lying, and betrayal got you what you wanted. The meanest always won.

So I experimented. A new kid, smaller than me, came to town and joined my fifth-grade class. We got along well and became friends. One day, however, I pushed him down to the ground while we walked home from school. It was spontaneous, no forethought at all.

The sense of power it gave amazed me—until I saw his face. The pain it revealed froze mine. My chest physically ached. In that moment, I knew there was nothing I could do to regain his trust. Betrayal was betrayal. We never talked about it, but even so, I did everything I could to be a good friend afterward. His house was within sight of mine and we turned our flashlights on and off to signal goodnight. His family moved the following year.

I put my flashlight on my window the first night after he moved and left it on so long the batteries died. What made other kids powerful made me feel an empty, bottomless sorrow. "What's wrong with me?"

I stopped going to the cellar. The rash on my arms spread to my legs. With iron will, I forced myself to stop scratching. Deciding it didn't exist worked. The rash finally went away.

A sharp clapping sound brought me back to the asphalt under my feet. Hearing the slap again, I stopped in the middle of the road and looked around. A man stood, silent, motionless, in the sand about twenty yards away. His outstretched arm pointed directly at the stars of Orion above the pyramid. I glanced up and back down, recalled the storyteller once more, but forced him out of my mind. He could not be here.

"Hello!" I spoke clearly, yet softly. The figure didn't move. A scan of the surroundings showed he was alone. My first step off the road landed on coarse gravel. It crunched loudly under my boots but still, he didn't turn.

"Hello," I said again.

The shadow condensed into form and my steps shortened. A gust of wind slapped a sheet of plastic wrapped around a small tree, and it snapped against it with a sharp *clap*. The outstretched arm of my storyteller was a sun-parched branch, nothing more. The wind quieted and the tattered plastic drooped pathetically.

My embarrassment at the scale of my misinterpretation parted with a deep exhale, and I marched back to the road. The hill grew steeper and my boots heavier. Memories of other travels came with contemplative steps.

Why didn't I get to Egypt fifteen years ago during my round-the-world trek? I remember having a ride from West Africa across the Sahara north. Oh yeah, malaria. Got it in Cameroon. Loved Cameroon. Except for the malaria.

The caring hands that helped me get to the Lago's airport for a flight to London probably saved my life. The doctors at the tropical disease clinic said it could take a month or so to develop the symptoms. One month after spending the night in a hut swarming with thousands of mosquitoes was when the fever, cramped muscles and uncontrollable, shaking chills hit.

The clinic had clean sheets, and nurses brought me three full meals a day. This stood in shocking contrast to my worn sleeping bag liner and the can of sardines and tomato paste I often had for dinner in rural Africa. No restaurants.

After leaving the hospital, re-visiting Western Europe wasn't as enticing as exploring Eastern Europe. The East Germans, Czechs, Hungarians, and Yugoslavs waited. Of all the people befriended on the road toward Turkey, one in Yugoslavia floated to the top.

Evening found me sitting on a grassy hillock in front of the Zagreb train station. The statue of a stately king on his steed shared the view, and we watched the bustle of day transform into the quiet of night.

A young woman walked out of the station. She wore a long, white, crocheted sweater reaching down to her calves. She paused and breathed in the evening air. In the next breath, she walked up the slope and sat down about ten feet away. An antique silver necklace laced with red coral, common in their Adriatic Sea, hung over her turquoise blouse.

"Hello," I said. Not the most original approach, but sincere.

She looked over. Fine, long, black hair framed honey-gold skin. Eyebrows innocently arched, yet strangely firm. Her eyes were almond shadows in the lamplight.

"American?" she asked lightly. I nodded.

"Yugoslavian?"

She laughed.

Her train was leaving for Vienna in three hours. The only baggage she carried was a tape of Jimmy Hendrix and her player. Rather than wait in the station, she came out for evening air and saw me. She knew from my patched pants and worn rucksack I was a traveler and was curious. When she saw the Vibram soles on my boots, she thought "American."

Neither of us felt the need to be anything else than what we were. Free of any pretense, we fell into comfortable conversation and spoke about what mattered to us.

Her name was Kata, and she shared about her family and plans to go to university in England to study botany. In contrast to other countries in Eastern Europe, Yugoslavians could travel anywhere in the world. She wanted to go to visit the pyramids someday.

As children, we both loved the outdoors and stole quiet moments to be alone with a particular tree or stream, and we still did. We both withstood the ordeal of school by disagreeing with it on the inside while coping with it on the outside. We both loved and were confused by people.

She spoke about how hard it was on families when fathers left to find work in other European countries. How they lived in crowded housing and were second-class citizens there.

"The economy is such that it is complicated to keep families together. It is very hard, especially on the children." She gazed at me with a soft stare. "They need their fathers."

"What's your father like?"

She leaned forward. "He supports where I need support but makes me stand where I am strong enough to stand."

Sharing her life story led her to ask about mine. I told her about my father, the oldest kid in his family, abandoned by his father during the Great Depression. How he'd been a sergeant of a platoon charged to clear duds—unexploded mortars, bombs and grenades—from battlefields during World War II, how he met and married my artistic mom, about my own family and cousins and being raised in our farming town.

Leaning closer, I spoke about the disquiet in my life, even before realizing what I was admitting. How witnessing the pain in the world conflicted with the sense of hopeful joy I felt sometimes. How I questioned my purpose, if there was one.

She raised a quizzical eyebrow, picked up her player and said, "Jimmy Hendrix."

We laughed.

More seriously, she asked, "About that hopeful joy, when did you feel the most?"

I glanced up at the statue of the mighty king and back to her. "During college, backpacking and diving with other nature lovers."

"American women go out backpacking with men?"

"Absolutely. The college women I knew not only backpacked but were rock-climbing partners. Gender didn't matter. Everyone took turns belaying the rope or climbing."

"It's better for us in universities here, too, but what about outside? Unless you live in a big city, jobs are very hard to find outside of home here. Men are supposed to work outside, women in."

Feeling hopeful, I told her about the success Americans had when both the Senate and House passed an amendment to assure equal rights for women under our Constitution. "Now it only needs to be ratified by thirty-eight out of fifty states. With all the support it has, it's bound to happen."

"When America makes a statement like this to the world it's going to help us, too."

We talked on. We leaned against each other but neither of us seemed to notice. As with young people across East Europe, she was both inspired by and worried about what could happen to students demonstrating to stop the Vietnam War.

Her voice rose. "We saw the news when American soldiers shot students. I still don't understand how that could happen in America."

I told her how polarized the Vietnam War became. How every student I knew felt they were saving the soul of our country while everyone else seemed to believe those same students were destroying it.

"We remember when Hungarian students were shot by Soviet soldiers when they demonstrated for free elections, and what happened to Hungary when it sided with the students. It's scarier to see demonstrators shot in America."

A lump caught in my throat. "We're so polarized it's crazy. The same day a student from UC San Diego burned himself alive in protest of the war, I found out my best friend from high school was killed in Vietnam. How can such divisions heal? That was when I decided to backpack around the world. Nothing made sense."

She touched my hand. "I don't know. But I do know my reaction to things is the only thing I can change. Since I want to bring people together rather than farther apart, I'm trying to start with myself."

Kata's gaze was weightless. I was the one traveling around the world on my own schedule. Yet she was undeniably more centered in who she was.

Trains came and went. Each time one pulled into the station, I feared it was the one that would take this friend away. A passenger train came to a hissing stop and, even though neither of us had a watch, we knew our time was at its end.

We got up and walked down the gentle slope. Pausing at the edge of the grass before stepping on the stone walkway, we spontaneously put our arms around each other in a long, warm hug.

I looked into her eyes. She looked back. The world around us evaporated. We kissed, so tenderly it said in the purest terms, "I care."

Our lips parted slowly and, hand in hand, we left the king on his mighty horse behind and walked into the station. By the time we reached her car, the conductor called for final boarding. It started to move the moment she boarded. Our hands touched once more and as the train took her away, she said, "It's good meeting you again."

The train picked up speed and disappeared down the dark track. Like the interactions with people everywhere, the experience was there and gone to make room for the next. However, this one was different. It reminded me of what I felt in the cellar.

With the hour late and the station deserted, I retrieved my pack from a locker. With no direction better than another, I followed the train until I found a place to sleep. The narrow space of ground between a building and its hedge was a perfect fit.

Hitchhiking the next morning. a Muslim gave me a ride to the Adriatic Sea. A Serbian family gave me shelter that night; a Croatian one the next.

Years later, after returning to the States, getting married and having kids of my own, news reports told of problems in Yugoslavia. Somehow, the congenial mix of ethnic groups I knew were separating into Orthodox Serbs, Catholic Croat and Muslim Bosniak nationalists across Yugoslavia. Reports of a ruthless war kept coming and grew increasingly dire. Tens of thousands of people killed, including children slain in front of their parents. Wives were raped in front of their husbands before both were slain. Over two million fled their homes and the places their families had lived for generations.

I had no way to discover the fate of the families who gave me shelter, but found Kata's address in my journal. However, not knowing what problems a letter from the U.S. might cause, I waited until the war was over to send it.

When it finally came, her response said the address I had was for her parent's house, destroyed in the war. Also, the envelope was addressed to the newly formed country of Bosnia-Herzegovina and hers was Croatia. However, the postman recognized the family name and asked his neighbor if he knew whether their daughter lived.

"Yes. She married and has a different name, but I know her. She is a sister of my friend."

Thanks to a caring postman, a letter—sent to a house that no longer existed, to a person with a different last name, in a different country than addressed—was delivered.

Over twenty-five years had passed since our meeting at the station. She described her life since. In her reply she wrote:

"In this stupid war, I lost everything except my own positive persistence— and that is the most important thing in this crazy world. We were in Vukovar and had no idea it would be the first battle of a three-year war. It was in Croatian territory and was surrounded by Serbian forces, who shelled it for three months before moving in. We escaped before it was ethnically cleansed in a massacre and purged of anyone not Serb.

My father was Serbian, my mother German, and my husband Croatian, and we thought of ourselves as Yugoslav. My father was dead, and my husband was missing. I believed finding our way to Sarajevo with my mother and children would be the safest place because most people there were also mixed.

I was wrong.

Two months after we arrived, Sarajevo became the center of hell. Since we were not pure Serbs, we were closed in neighborhoods with Bosniak and Croat families for the next three years of war.

My mother died of hunger. I was wounded by a sniper while trying to find bread. My children grew ill but didn't die.

I learned to respect many things I didn't before the war. Several years of it gave me the best possibility to make choices between good and bad. It tests where we are honest.

After all of it, I know nobody can produce hatred inside of me. The feeling that gives me is strong."

Her husband lived through the war but died soon after. She had good friends, two wonderful children, and felt safe again. She also added, "I studied botany at university in England but never made it to the pyramids. Hope you did."

The recollection raked my heart. Heat rose through my feet and throbbed in my chest. Tears welled.

My feet plodded on and the image of another experience floated into my mind.

The small woman's burn-scarred hand held a cup of milk-thistle tea. I could not rise to drink it, so she lowered it to me. When she saw I couldn't raise my head high enough, she placed her other scarred hand under my head and raised it gently. The tea was sweet with cane sugar.

Hepatitis.

After traveling overland through Turkey and Iran, the strawberries in Afghanistan were, as a French traveler told me, "Worth the trip. Sweet, perfectly ripe and bright red all the way through." The street vendor in Kabul filled his blender with the succulent fruit and turned it on. Berries swirled into a thick, smooth liquid. He took a large, plastic glass from the wet bin and filled it to the brim with the ambrosia.

A month later, I collapsed on a cot in a small, rented room in Varanasi, India. My urine was brown, my stool white clay, and my eyes dark yellow to match my jaundiced skin. I lay, too exhausted to move and too nauseated to eat, but felt a strange sense of peace.

The strong fragrance of the funeral pyres on the shore of the river Ganges below my window welcomed me.

I was going to die. It was okay.

Too tired to think anymore, it didn't matter how many states, countries, mountains or seas I crossed, the difference between what I felt on the inside and my experience on the outside would never be reconciled. Maybe it didn't matter.

This ancient cremation *ghat* was a fitting place to conclude my life, which in the end, found little sense in any of it. Here, the reality of death was undisguised, its inevitability unhidden. Hundreds of bodies draped in white cloth and flowers lay on pyres of wood, and all was transformed into vaporous, swirling smoke that soared into the air. The thought of joining the orange embers streaking into the night's sky gave me solace.

I would join them soon.

Except this small, sari-wrapped person kept giving me sweetened milk-thistle tea: the only remedy they had for an advanced case of hepatitis.

The woman, or angel, I couldn't tell at the time, kept waking me from my slumbering reflections. When she did, every joint of my body ached with exhausting pain. Her threadbare, light-green sari draped over her head and covered her arms, but the burn scars on her neck and arms caught the light.

I'd read far too many news articles in local papers about women being burned by kerosene "kitchen fires" to consider her scars accidental. A girl child meant another mouth to feed and a dowry to pay should she be fortunate enough to marry. If the groom's family deemed the dowry insufficient, the mother of the groom might "accidentally" douse the bride in kerosene cooking fuel. Although outlawed, "bride-burning" remained a way some made their sons available for another bride—and illegal dowry. Those that didn't die were abandoned, too scarred to fulfill their wifely duties or return dishonored to their own families.

My angel was one of those, and the reason I chose to live.

The contrast between the world of these burned women and the world of women I marched and hiked with was crazy. How could people so callously throw away fully half of their culture, their hearts, their minds, and essence?

I kicked a broken brick off the road and it sailed into the night. Emotions swirled in a confusion of worlds while my boots pummeled the tar.

How to deal with it? When I numb out, I become callous—but feeling it is agony. Is the pain bigger than me? How can it be? I'm not the one who is burned, and she kept her heart. Kata too. Where is mine?

"Stop! Stop right there!" a harsh voice called out.

My gaze jerked up from the road. A guard in a dark *jellabiya* robe peered down from his perch on a crumbling wall. "The pyramid is closed."

"Closed?" My feet froze, glued in place. "How can something so big be closed?"

The guard slid off the edge of the low wall and stood, appraising me. His head shook, and he walked the few well-trodden steps to the road and waved his hand.

"Take this way to the light show. The entrance is in front of the Sphinx."

My mouth went slack. "What light show?"

He crossed his arms. "All tourists go to the light show. No lights here. Nothing to see." He waved to my left again. "It's dangerous to walk around the pyramids at night. Open pits and stones. The light show is safe."

There is no way I traveled all day and night to sit in straight rows of metal chairs to watch colored lights.

My expression was too transparent.

The guard pointed west to the open desert. "That way is closed. Too many scorpions and snakes. Maybe bad men." He pointed to the well-worn trail to my left again. "Light show."

Putting on my most agreeable smile, I said, "*Shukran*," Egyptian for "thank you," and obediently turned and started walking toward the show. His work complete, he went back to his wall and sat down,

After walking fifty unhurried paces, I turned my head and peered toward the guard. He still sat where I'd left him, lighting a cigarette.

That takes care of his night vision.

My chapped lips parted in a grin and my fatigue vanished. Recalling the map of the plateau from the hotel lobby, I knew the approach from the west would be clear. There were even some ancient, crumbling tombs for cover. Crouching low in the small chance he could still see me, I left the path to circle north and cross the road I'd walked up.

He was right about the landscape. It was filled with shallow holes and mounds, the work of diggers searching for archeological loot, no doubt, but it was easy to move between them.

Within minutes, I intersected with the main road and scampered across it like a desert beetle. Except for the soft sound of my footfalls, all was quiet. I navigated mounds of mudstone brick fallen from crumbling tombs without

13

concern. The perfectly aligned pyramids rose above the desert floor to guide me.

The guard's warning about snakes, scorpions, and "bad men" fell away easily. It was time to turn back south and parallel the paved road. My night vision was excellent and starlight was all my feet needed to thread through the tombs.

A sound came on the wind. Voices. My body stilled and my pulse quickened.

Arabic crackled through parched desert air. All my senses searched the darkness for trouble. Rotating slowly and moving my head from side to side revealed their direction, but after a few steps, the voices stopped. So did I. However, the scent of burning wood took their place and my silent steps moved toward its source.

A long, low wall slumped across my path. I moved soundlessly along its toothy blocks in search of the fire. Amber light flickered against a solid tomb wall ahead.

My feet picked their way across the rubble-strewn land. In a crouch, I raised my head above the low wall to discover the fire's companions.

One man squatted next to a bed of glowing coals not twenty feet away. He moved embers with a long stick and a flare of orange made the stubble on his face bristle with light.

In a timeless motion, he added water to the blackened teapot and stirred it gently before setting it down. The aroma of mint tea overpowered the smell of burning wood. Dry air bloomed.

Countless nights spent sharing sweet mint tea with nomads from Africa to Asia flowed into one moment. Memories of camaraderie and cook fires filled me with longing. The warm amber glow pulled me toward it and my feet moved. The man, a Bedouin from his dress, picked up the teapot and poured tea into a white cup. Fire sprites made the tea sparkle when it flowed, and the aroma of mint exploded in the night air.

He's alone. Probably was praying to Allah.

The taste of the sweetened tea already felt real to my palate. Every time I entered a nomad's camp, they welcomed this "foreign nomad" to their fire. This man would do the same. My feet moved toward him.

A sparking sprite rose from the glowing ashes and took flight. Caught on a breeze, it soared high over my head and joined many other fire sprites in the sky.

Not cinders, stars.

Formless pinpricks of light distilled into constellations, Orion brightest among them. The three stars of its hourglass belt winked.

Some people say the three pyramids align with them.

A powerful urge bubbled out of my chest, and I breathed, "The pyramids. So close."

My feet changed direction without asking them to.

The Arabic voice crackled in the air again, but this time I knew it was the Bedouin sharing his voice with solitude. My pace quickened.

Keeping parallel to the tarred road, I continued south. When adjacent to the smallest of the three pyramids I turned east, and crossed the road with ease.

No reason for guards. The desert takes their place.

The smallest pyramid, "Mykerinus," the ancient Greeks called it, rose out of the sand straight ahead. My feet found their way across the desert pan.

I scanned from left to right. Not even shadows moved.

Free of concern, I jumped up on the cornerstone and lay my hand on the massive block. My fingertips moved back and forth trying to read braille in bumps of stone.

How many billions of humans have been born, lived and died while you stood? If only stones could talk.

One step on the giant's staircase led to the next. After climbing about twenty feet above the sea of sand, I sat down and leaned against the next course. Slowly rolling over onto my back, the wide ledge felt comfortable. Deep, slow breath flowed in and out of my chest, and the smell of limestone filled my lungs.

Like in the storm cellar.

A soft desert breeze blotted the sweat on my cheek. My lids closed. Cool stone caressed the fatigued muscles of my back.

My pulse pounded, and my eyes popped open in dizzy confusion.

Where am I?

Stars filled my vision. I lay on stone.

Mykerinus. I fell asleep on Mykerinus. A dream. I was a huge bird, or a crystal. Animals. Half man and half beast. Before that. What was it? A planet coming apart at the seams. So hot so fast it exploded from within. Where? It felt so real.

My pulse slowed.

A dream.

Rolling toward open air, another pyramid stood anchored in the sea of sand. Remnants of marble sheeting that once covered it in seamless white now only hugged its top, like snow clinging to a summer's peak.

15

"Chephren," the ancient Greeks called it. The center pyramid.

Sitting up, my legs dangled freely over the edge. Gazing across the expanse to the center pyramid, nothing moved in the dark between us. Climbing down from my perch, sharpened senses reached out to find the route to best shield my approach, but my caution was unnecessary. My ploy to enter from the west worked. No one was there.

A profound sense of relief grew with each step toward the center pyramid as it transformed from shadow into solid form. Standing next to it, the foundation blocks rose waist-high and each stretched longer than my hotel bed. My hand reached out, drew across the stone and rippled the starlight in its dust. I boosted myself up, sat on the bottom course, and leaned back against the next.

My body warmed. Sight and smell became even more acute. If there were a balancing point between two weights, this would be it—an anchoring pivot point between worlds.

Looking up at the peak of the pyramid felt both comforting and disturbing. How can a man-made mountain feel like a real one, birthed by the Earth itself? Pulse racing again, I jumped down to walk along its massive base, which, like any mountain, seemed as much underground as above. I walked on, lost in a dream of timeless stone and stars.

Suddenly, the mountain ended. Staring at the ground, I swayed from side to side trying to unravel what I felt.

Timeless. Why so timeless?

Since no answer came from the ground, my face turned up, and my breath caught.

The sawtooth contours of the Great Pyramid mixed with night so well I couldn't tell which was the tooth, night sky, or stone. Stars danced above both, unconcerned.

The image of the African storyteller pointing to Orion's belt flashed in front of me. I smiled.

Three years around the world. Now married and with children of my own. I still made it here.

My feet moved again and what I was taught about the pyramid washed through my mind.

Its existence was both a wonder and a burden for humans throughout recorded history. How do we explain a primitive people who built something we cannot? Two and a half *million* precisely honed blocks stacked on a base that covers over thirteen acres. Each forty-ton granite monolith of the King's Chamber cut and moved from a quarry over six hundred miles away. There is no equipment able to build it today. However, we, not our ancestors, are the apex of human evolution. There must be an explanation.

Thousands of laborers over lifetimes used chisels, ramps, ropes and millions upon millions of rolling logs to move the massive monoliths across land and water to make this towering, finely honed mountain.

I looked up the giant's staircase, a causeway that disappeared in a point in the heavens, and blinked.

When it's uncomfortable to say I don't know, *make something up.*

Striding to the cornerstone, my hand started to reach out to touch a foundational block of granite. An errant thought came to mind.

I wonder if I could climb—

"Stop! Stop there!" a sharp voice barked. The command ripped my thoughts and I wheeled around to see an old man in a wrinkled khaki shirt and baggy pants standing three feet away.

His palm raised in a stop sign, he said, "The pyramids are closed. The light show is that way." He pointed toward rows and rows of folding chairs down past the Sphinx.

Panic swirled through me, but I put on my best guard-friendly grin and swept my eyes across the colossal landscape. "You closed the pyramids?"

He smiled wryly but his bearing didn't change. He gestured back down the road. "My friend told me of you. He said you walked around through the desert to get past him." My mouth gaped.

"We thought you'd stop and have tea with the guard in the western tombs, but you only stopped to look and walked on." He brought out a walkie-talkie from his pants pocket and held it up for me to see. "Didn't you hear us talking?"

"Walkie-talkies." My hands carved through my hair and paused over my ears. My struggle to project the illusion that my stroll was misunderstood became more difficult with his wide grin.

"I only wanted to touch the pyramids," I said, fully abashed at my miscalculation of their ability.

He offered a bemused smile. "I watched you sit on the other two pyramids."

My mouth opened, closed, and opened again. "But not this one." However, it sounded more like a whine than a declaration. Recovering some bearing, I added honestly, "I'm here to honor them."

His gaze stayed fixed on mine. "Perhaps. I don't think you have a hammer to chip a souvenir."

My head drew back in disbelief. "I wouldn't do that!" I blurted and pointed up the giant's stairway. "This is sacred."

He studied me and his gaze cooled. "Some come to chip it. Why not you?"

The question dropped on my chest so hard I felt it thud. "Because I don't take things that aren't mine, and this pyramid belongs to itself."

It was his turn for his eyes to widen. "Belongs to itself?"

There that feeling was again, the one that said I'd never fit in with the world. I looked up, saw Orion, and my cheeks puffed with a breath held too long. "I've traveled a lot, searching for something. Once I felt everything was alive and I was part of it. Now I don't."

He stared at me blankly.

Thoughts of lives I shared with people around the world rose through my feet and into my chest. Tears welled. I blinked them back but the geyser erupted. "I need to climb the Great Pyramid," I blurted, surprising us both.

His chin wrinkled, but his expression didn't show alarm. Instead, he looked up toward the distant peak and spoke to it. "It's not safe to climb. Last month, three tourists died."

It didn't surprise me. No climbing ropes here and the slope was steep. "How did it happen?"

"They came very late in the night and managed to avoid us. The pyramid is very steep and taller than a forty-five-story building. Desert sand covers chips of rock on blocks. The wind can come and hit you anytime. It's easy to lose your footing." He clasped his hands together. "If you fall it's doubtful you could stop. Even from ten layers up, people die, and there are over two hundred layers."

He moved deliberately and stood next to the bottom course. The top of the block was far above his waist. "I'm fifty-eight and have lived here for fifty years. I know at least two hundred people have died trying to climb."

Studying the stone, I decided that looked likely. Uneven fractures and loose rock covered its surface. Given the number of untrained climbers that probably tried, two hundred dead over fifty years seemed realistic.

"I've done a lot of rock climbing, but we use ropes. I can see how falling off this one could happen."

I focused on the words *I've lived here fifty years* rather than *two hundred killed*. I looked at him and asked plainly, "How many times have you climbed it?"

He replied steadily. "More than I can remember."

"It wished you to be on it, then."

He straightened. "You know the feeling."

18

"I know when I need to climb a living mountain."

A thin grin cracked his lips but his face remained stern. "Last year the police caught over eighty people on the pyramid. They were arrested, fined one hundred and fifty dollars. Anyone caught scaling the pyramids can face three years in an Egyptian jail. Is that how you want to spend your time in Egypt?"

I didn't respond because I was surveying the slope for the best route up its face. Gauging the incline between my vertical body and the stones, I guessed about a fifty-degree slope. Going up the spine where two faces meet would be longer, but around a forty-degree slope. Plus, the steps were wider. My hand rose and pointed to where sides of the pyramid meet. "I expect going up the cornerstones would be longer but safer."

His head bobbed in agreement.

Without saying a word, we pulled ourselves up to sit on the foundational cornerstone. He leaned back against the second course of blocks. I did the same. The open desert loomed to the west. Orion's belt still hovered near the summit of the night's sky.

After a minute of silence, he spoke. "We must be careful. I am not the only guard. You met the two others."

My hand flew to my throat. I yelped, "Three guards and I managed to bump into all three of you?"

"All three." He grinned.

My illusion of sneaking past apathetic guards in ninja-stealth was shattered. However, I still needed to convince this CEO of the pyramid that I could climb without falling. "You saw me walk in from the desert and make my way over here? And go up and down the smallest pyramid?"

"Yes."

"Good climbing takes good partners. You know how to climb pyramids. I know how to climb glaciers. To climb ice we put cleats on our boots that have sharp metal spikes and you kick this way," my boot went forward with a snap, "and they dig into the ice so you can climb it. If you guide me up the pyramid, I'll guide you up a glacier when you visit me in the States."

He laughed out loud and kicked his foot back and forth with its imaginary crampon. He had to crimp his toes to keep the plastic sandal from flying off his foot. We both laughed.

He turned his head toward the Sphinx. "The light show starts soon. Many lights and many people." We scanned the neat rows of chairs. Most of the chairs were already filled. "After this show, there's another. It's not a good time to be here."

Theatrical music began to play on distant but powerful speakers. "It's much safer after midnight. No one's here. Only the pyramids. Everything looks the same as it did when I first came fifty years ago. No time passed."

The timeless image was tempting.

Why not? Besides, later would mean less chance of getting caught.

My mouth opened to speak in agreement, but nothing came out. I rubbed at my lips, and sand grated with grit.

Not climbing now means walking back to the hotel, going to sleep and hoping my little travel alarm will wake me up. Exhaustion would win that one.

My head shook back and forth heavily. "I'm here now. You're here now." My fingers moved on the first block of the staircase again. "The pyramid is here now."

He didn't laugh but his face relaxed.

Sensing an agreement was close, I added with resolute sincerity, "I am a good climber. I can do this."

My timing could have been better. Accompanied by a tidal wave of sound, light blazed upon the side of the pyramid around the corner from where we sat. It startled me, but he didn't blink.

Thoughtfully, he said, "It is not good to climb during the light show. The lights go back and forth from one pyramid to another." As if by his command, the lights turned off and blasted the Sphinx again. "Sometimes all of them are lit at the same time. If you are looking toward them when they come on you can be blinded for hours. If that happens, you can't climb back down."

His head moved toward the spine, where two sloping faces intersected, and raised his hand to point toward the two vast banks of lights about fifty feet away. "When those lights come on we cannot be on the spine. We must be at the top." His face was etched serious.

"But you've done it before," I countered, "many times." He didn't disagree, so I pressed on. "After this show ends, how long does it take before the next starts?"

"Each show lasts forty-five minutes and only has a fifteen-minute break between them."

The face of the Great Pyramid around the corner from our perch glowed as if in the light of high noon, then went dark again. I continued. "How long does it take you to climb?"

His voice rang with certainty. "Ten minutes."

My forehead furrowed while I translated that into his climbing speed. The pyramid was four hundred and fifty-five feet tall and he climbs it in ten minutes. Ascending forty-five feet a minute is fast bouldering. However, the route was straightforward. All I needed to do was focus on the first step, then the next. Plus, unlike bouldering, these were blocks with a wide, flat shelf to stand on before moving to the next. I looked at the old man.

I work out daily and can certainly keep up with him.

"You can do it in ten but we have fifteen between shows. I can do it."

With sudden rise of his head, he looked straight at me. "You're going to climb whether I help you or not."

I looked back, unblinking in answer.

"I am Tabari. I will try to make sure you do not fall off."

"Thank you, Tabari."

He cocked his head. "I must check for soldiers and police. They sometimes patrol here."

A blast of light scorched the face of the center pyramid but I did my best to ignore it. "Okay. I'll wait here."

Reflected light revealed deep creases in his face. Though his eyes gleamed with fiery life, his leathered skin revealed years spent in bright desert sun and wind. He jumped off the foundational block and landed firmly on his feet. "Not here. Too open. I will show you a place to wait." He turned and scurried across the dark bedrock.

Getting my body into instantaneous motion was difficult.

If I can't keep up with an old man in flip-flops, I'll understand it if the pyramid bucks me off.

I caught up with him after half a dozen strides. "We will do this well," I said, but wasn't sure if it was to comfort him or me.

A short scramble brought us to a row of weather-rounded blocks about chest-high. "Wait in here," he said, pointing to a narrow space between two rows. "We must start the moment this show ends."

He continued sprinting across the sand, and the sound of my pounding heart replaced the sound of his footfalls. I eased myself down between the blocks and rested my back against the longest one. Breathing in through my mouth and out through my nose, my breath and pulse returned to normal.

The position, hidden between tall blocks of stone, felt strangely comforting. The welcoming aroma of stone made from seas over fifty million years gone reminded me of its beginnings: living sediment buried deeper and deeper until heat and pressure turned it into what I lay upon now.

A stream of thoughts carried me down into Earth. A crust of continents floated on the hot and dense moving mantel, and that over a hotter core. Immense currents moved the continents across their mantel sea.

A pulsing sensation grew as if the planet had a heartbeat itself. My body was suddenly hot and getting hotter. I stood up and moved quickly away from the block wall. The heat stopped but my feet still tingled.

Let go of what you think should be and feel what is.

I stomped my feet.

What's happening? Where is Tabari?

The thought led to a verbal rant. "What if he isn't coming back? Or went to tell the soldiers? He'll probably get an award for turning me in."

The music of the light show built to a final crescendo. *I wonder if they do sentence you to three years in jail?*

The music stopped. The light show was over. Standing tall, I looked in every direction. No Tabari.

"Now what?" I grumbled. The night returned to its timeless silence. Not wanting to admit defeat, I stared at the Great Pyramid and started walking toward it.

Time to climb, with or without him.

"Come now!" a shadow hissed as it passed.

"Tabari?"

"Come!" he exclaimed in a hushed, hurried tone. "You say you are a good climber. You need to be."

By some trick of magic or light, this life-worn, disheveled guard had transformed into a gymnast. He bounded over big stones without changing stride.

My body jerked out of its slumber. He was already running back the way we'd come. My head whirled with the adrenaline rush.

No way is this guy is going to outrun me.

His flip-flops floated across the surface, but the distance closed quickly when my foot-formed hiking shoes bit through the loose sand and into bedrock. We arrived at the corner of the Great Pyramid together.

"We must climb very fast. Stay near me. Put your feet where I put my feet. Do not look down."

The first block was over four feet high. Tabari placed his palms on it, raised his body up and swung his legs onto its top without using his feet.

He started going up the next course before I got into position. When I pushed up from the edge with my hands, attempting to swing my feet up the same way he did, a calcified stone bit into my palm.

"Not that way." I went into bouldering mode. My fingers found narrow ridges on the top of the stone to grab, and at the same time, the hard rubber tips of my hiking shoes found traction on the vertical face of the block. The combination propelled me up quickly. "Only two hundred and one blocks to go."

Tabari scaled the fourth course now. My hands reached out and found a place for my fingernails to grab. My feet followed suit without conscious thought. When I started the third course, Tabari faced number six. His technique clearly worked for someone that had only climbed in flip-flops, but I was getting into my routine. By the time I got to number six, he was only on number eight. While he was swinging up to the tenth, I was pulling myself up number nine. All I had to do was stay one course behind him. "Only a hundred and ninety-two blocks to go."

By the thirtieth course, my fingers were numb and every muscle in my legs and arms burned with a bone-deep fire. A pithy dryness filled my mouth and my tongue was coated with fine sand.

How long has it been since I drank water?

I stole a look at the satchels on my belt. My camera bag and sleeve for my water bottle were attached but only the camera bag had weight. A half-filled water bottle stood on my bedside table at the hotel. I'd broken my own rule. Never leave for a walk without tight-laced boots, your camera and your water bottle. You never know where you might end up.

Tabari was only two courses ahead of me but showed no signs of tiring.

"Got to move," I grunted.

Bones on fire or not, my hands and feet continued to dig into each course as if my life depended on it. Maybe it did.

The height and width of the steep staircase began to vary more and more. Rows of large, chest-high blocks unexpectedly appeared after several only two feet high. It was no longer possible to maintain a consistent stride. Each course required its own assessment, which made it resemble bouldering much more than climbing a giant's stairs.

Time to push.

After a climbing buddy got hypothermia in the Sierra Mountains, I carried a sixty-five-pound pack, snowshoes, and skis twenty-three miles to get us down and out quickly. I pulled on the memory.

This is nothing compared to that. Climb!

Music blared. The Sphinx flared in light.

Tabari flattened against the stone to the left of the spine. "Down!" he squawked. I dove to join him and stilled. A blast of light lit the spine. "Twenty seconds it will go out," he breathed. "After it does, ten minutes to reach the top."

The light show must have been controlled by his brain because the lights went off in twenty seconds. Poised to spring, he bounded up the next course before my legs were back under me.

Glaring upward, the courses looked about three feet high now, easy bouldering height. My speed increased.

Easier than Cougar Canyon in the Anza-Borrego Desert.

Tabari's baggy pants were only one course ahead of me again. He turned, grinned, and pointed to his left. "Loose rock. We must jump over it."

He leaped across a pile of broken stone, a miniature scree slope of small angular rocks with the stability of ball bearings eager to help me back down.

Tabari cleared it easily, came to rest on the narrow block next to it, turned, grinned again, and continued up the next course, where he perched expectantly.

Stopping to collect myself before making the jump may not have been a good idea. My momentum was lost and there was no room for a running start. My heart pounded in my chest, my ears throbbed and my lungs were bellows.

Tabari stood, concerned. "Do you want to stop?"

Now or never.

I jumped with the spring-loaded grace of a jack-in-the-box and cleared the pile of rubble with a foot to spare. However, too much force propelled me in a low arc instead of the quick up-and-down intended, and my legs could not get out in front of me in time to break my fall.

My body's broadcast was instant. "Roll forward. Hit palms first. Left arm over the edge. Grab stone."

My body did as it said it would. Palms first slowed my tumble, left arm over the edge kept me from going over it, and the right arm relaxed to avoid a sprain or worse. My forehead hit the slab with abrupt force, but I was too filled with adrenaline to mind. I sat up slowly, my feet dangling above the course under me.

"Good?" Tabari asked.

My hand came away from my forehead with a spot of red, but I was fine. "Yeah, let's go."

Standing up, I cast a glance toward the center pyramid and it told me what I expected. Judging by our elevation we were near the top.

Before Tabari started bounding up the spine again, he said, "Lights come on the center pyramid now." On cue, Chephren blazed, and the remnant of its marble cloak glowed bright white.

My hand reached for my water bottle automatically and was surprised to find its holster empty. The gritty hand wiped across my face instead.

24

Almost there. Climb.

The courses stayed around two feet high. My chest heaved and my ears rang. Loose grit rolled under my feet and my knee hit stone. Tabari heard the whack and turned, eyebrows raised.

"I'm fine, fine. Just needed a minute," I spluttered. The lights were still on the center pyramid. "Need to take a photo," I wheezed, knowing full well that I was using it as an excuse to let me catch my racing heart.

"No flash!" he exclaimed.

"No flash! Slow shutter speed only." With settings long since memorized on the old Nikon, and my fingers set the shutter speed as long as I dared, I opened the aperture as large as it would go, set the focus to infinity and took a shot.

I returned my camera to the bag, but before the flap was closed, Tabari said, "Must go now. Light comes here soon! Be ready to jump to other side of spine."

"Let's go," I finished latching the satchel's flap with its tethered Goulimine bead and rose to face the next course. Tabari was already bounding upward faster than a mountain goat.

My hands weren't working right and my legs were knots. Tabari was four courses ahead of me but we were almost there. Only ten steps left to reach the top. All looked less than two feet tall.

"We can do this," I said to any part of me that would pay attention.

Nine to go.

Muscles warmed again.

Eight.

A quick glance over my shoulder showed a steep staircase of at least two hundred steps below. My fingers strained.

Six left.

My muscles found their rhythm.

Only three more courses left. Why is Tabari waving?

My fingers slipped from the slab above me and grazed the edge of a sharp, calcified shell. Pain shot through my hand.

"Damn!" I held my palm tightly against my chest and pressed both against the block of stone in front of me.

"The lights come now! Jump to the other side, now, now, now!" All lights went dark. I glanced down at my feet to make sure the footing was sound, not for a push to the side but up. My face met a blinding burst of white light.

"Jump!"

I felt myself twist, claw my way to the top and drop into blackness.

1. BEGINNINGS

∞

The dream began with a distant, deep, echoing gong. Directionless yet penetrating.

Where am I?

Gossamer threads appeared. Each one thrummed with color woven in a vaporous fabric of graceful, undulating ribbons. Endless hues and sounds rolled in all directions at once.

Floating. No up or down. Far or near. A flower bloomed, and a brilliant light erupted from its center.

Is that a galaxy?

The gossamer threads became harp strings made of light. Thoughts dissolved into their euphoric resonance. All one boundless connection.

An aberrant thought pushed into the reverie, its source unknown.

I'm on the pyramid.

A tether jerked me but more flowers bloomed. So beautiful.

I'm going to them.

It pulled harder. A light flashed, so dense it felt heavy on my face.

I have a face?

Thick sound boomed. Something solid pushed against my cheek and the pungent smell of limestone and sweat fused the air.

Suddenly, I was weightless, formless, and passing through stone, hidden chambers in the pyramid, then on through great caverns deep in Earth.

My thread of self-awareness stretched to breaking, but another thought came.

Observe and learn, don't become what you see.

A portal opened at the bottom of the deep cavern. I could look through but not enter. Surrounded by living Earth, a scene emerged.

~

Darkness rumbled and became shocking, white mist. Distant chimes sounded and their vibration boomed through the mist, changing every particle into a different color. Each became a radiant orb of essence, and each chimed within a chorus beyond sound.

Meaning crystallized from within the saturated solution and resonated without beginning or end.

"Go forth, go forth and create. Learn, expand All with all you become."

Brilliant, orb-shaped beings surged through the ocean of essence. One, an orb of violet-blue, celebrated with the throng. The orb stopped, causing an eddy in the flowing stream. A mixture of confusion and elation roiled through the violet-blue sphere. It called out, "What happened? I am All, yet I now feel self. What am I? Am I separate?"

In response a passing golden orb intoned, "We are unique but not separate. Know your essence, listen to your sound. I am Murann. We are individual, yet within All as All is in us. Celebrate free will! It is Creator's choice for us to self-determine how we co-create in Creation!"

The violet-blue orb pulsed with orange streaks of light in the surging current. "Self-aware and not separate? How?"

The response flowed in a tide of conviction. "We learn! Sent forth to discover how to expand Life in all it can become!"

"But who am I?" the orb asked, and earnestly added, "What am I?" In answer, a sudden vibration rose from its core.

The vibration became a timbre, the timbre an intonation. "Yawwwrriii." The sound, his naming-sound, joined the symphony. "Yawri," the orb sang. "I add my tones to the whole. All becomes more."

Exhilarated, he moved with the current again. The more he chose to embrace his own sound, the more the symphony expanded within him. Delight competed with elation as the orb radiated a brilliant violet-blue light.

However, the instant before immersing himself in the streaming essence once more, an unblended, disharmonic note vibrated in the distance. "No!" a desperate being called out. "To be self-aware is to be separate. This cannot be!"

Yawri recalled his own doubt, but before he could respond, a massive surge of celestial light and sound swept him into the current and the desperate voice faded. Living mist surged around and through Yawri and he bathed in exultation.

The gift of free will! Free to learn how to expand the All with all we become!

Essence throbbed. Portals formed. Immeasurable, conscious essence flowed through them and fed Creation itself.

Yawri set off to discover what is and can be. He learned that being present within one point in time, didn't decrease his awareness of infinite time. Each moment could be savored as a single musical note within a boundless chorus.

Yawri and other beings helped create paths of energy linking time and space. These paths became trails, and trails became time tunnels of living etheric sound and light. The network of tunnels connected any place with any other in the living body of time.

Enthralled with what he'd learned, he continued to explore timeless time and delighted in knowing how to find the source of any Life by following its resonance through time tunnels. Probing a realm on the edge of his knowledge, he found multi-colored dimensions that had more substance than others he'd searched.

He sped down it, instantly curious. A branching intersection gave a choice of direction, but the beauty he followed was so profound the decision was obvious. He eagerly plunged into the one with the most textured living essence.

In contrast to the purely etheric realms known to him, these had additional harmonies.

What causes them? Particles? There are vivid particles here ... melodies of matter!

Yawri had spent his previous existence co-creating in purely etheric realms. Here, beings were co-creating with Creator to form material nebulae and stars.

What a fascinating way to expand all that I am!

He continued to explore, eager to experience this realm of living matter. Galaxies, suns, and planets sang. Each planet added its own chorus of color in their dance around stars.

After investigating yet another solar system of tans and yellows, Yawri stopped to consider his next destination. Most systems had planets of one or two primary colors. The more limited the harmonies coming from a solar system, the less variety in its planets.

I wonder if more complex ones exist?

In answer, he came to another branching fork. Rich melodies and brilliant light came from one tube, promising diversity beyond his knowing. He hurtled down it without reservation, the draw of its mystery compelling.

What could make such a symphony?

29

He accelerated toward it, excited to find out. Each turn took him closer to its source, and its richness intensified.

Enthralled, he hurtled around twisting bends and made a game of navigating between the living walls at whirlwind speed. The branching vein brightened and its intonations grew. Sensing a time where the refrain felt strongest, Yawri exited the tunnel, determined to discover more.

He hovered in a place far from any he had visited before. The nearest solar system was small and on the outer edge of a small galaxy. Small though it was, no solar system sang with more vitality than this one.

The vibrant colors and modulating timbre meant complex life was somewhere here. His elation increased and he accelerated toward the mystery. He discovered its sun, though distant, held millions of frozen comets in a far-reaching orbit of glittering stellar mass.

"We come to bring waters of Life," the glittering comets echoed in a chiming chant.

Bring waters of Life to what?

He moved toward the system's star. Its planets glowed and twirled in a concert of ringing refrain, their combined resonance a cosmic, clarion bell. "We co-create with Creator. Come. Come to expand Creation of All."

He passed by a tiny planet. Even though its surface was glazed clay and ice, its deep, rumbling trill sang with its five small moons and countless bodies far beyond it. Although intrigued by its communion with far-distant stellar bodies, Yawri's attention was drawn to overtones trumpeting from a planet much closer to this star.

Third one out. It's the one with the song I heard across time.

At last, his destination planet was clear. Yawri exclaimed in celebration, "On my way!"

However, while he sped toward it, he noticed a vast, icy-blue sphere more than twenty times the size of the small, glazed planet he'd just passed. At least a dozen moons circled this giant, and each chimed rhythmically with their planet's resounding tones. He stopped above an atmosphere of violent, thrashing winds. A roiling cloud passed below and sped out of sight within moments.

The sun is too far away for heat. This planet should be frozen solid.

Perplexed and intrigued, he dashed down to investigate the hurricane planet. The dense, icy wind passed through the violet-blue orb without effect. He extended his senses into the tempest.

It's getting hotter? How can it be getting hotter?

Confounded, Yawri sped down into the icy shield. However, rather than getting colder, the heat increased rapidly as he plummeted. Swirling gases changed to churning liquid and electric current rolled throughout it in a whirling flash.

What's making this heat?

More determined than ever to find answers, he swooped back and forth between the churning sea and winds to learn more. He noticed something pitching up and down in the distance.

That looks like an iceberg? How could ice be here? It's too hot.

A bolt of lightning streaked past the object's top and burst into flashing tendrils above and he shot toward the curiosity.

He halted in front of a transparent object floating in the steaming sea, both larger and farther away than he first believed. It was a strange, geometric shape with four triangles sloping from a square base to a towering point.

Lightning flashed inside of the transparent, glassy form. Peering closer, he saw its flawless surface mirrored the branching light with sharp reflections. He rose above the structure, mesmerized by its beauty.

"Move! Move out of the way!"

Yawri pulled back, searching for the speaker. Instantly, a bright bolt of lightning streaked away from the tip of the pyramid-shaped form and burst into those flashing tendrils again.

Yawri's violet orb swirled with spokes of bright-orange light when the voice returned. "It's not a good idea to hover over one of us! We don't control these crystal bodies. We only join with them."

Yawri was bewildered, "Who is we? What's a crystal body?"

"You don't know of us?" A luminous, pale purple orb emerged from the pyramid-shaped crystal and came to Yawri. "Is this the first time you've sought to join with material vibration?"

Yawri's violet orb churned with bright yellow and orange. "You're an ethereal being too! What were you doing inside that"—he wasn't sure how to say it—"solid thing?"

There was a long pause. "Please, call me Tilan, and you are?"

Yawri's orb returned to a more consistent violet blue. "I'm Yawri. I've just arrived in this system." He noticed other pyramid-shaped objects both near and far. "Why would you stay inside anything this dense?"

After a long moment, Tilan answered with questions of his own. "Why did you come? Was it in response to this solar system's call?"

"Well, I guess it was a call." Yawri had to collect his thoughts. "There were so many different harmonies coming out of this system I had to find out why."

The other pyramid-shaped forms were definitely moving closer. "I've co-created in ethereal dimensions but never physical. We are ethereal, so those realms make sense to me, but why stay in something so … solid?" he managed to get out. "I don't understand."

Lightning flashed in the distance and reflected off the glassy face, but it still appeared to come from within it.

Tilan's tone was pragmatic. "Solid? What's solid here? It's an extension of the ethereal continuum. There is no division of Life."

Yawri rushed out, "Yes, the All is a continuum, but we're not of matter, we're ethereal."

Tilan's pale purple orb pulsed with yellow ripples. "Our charge is to learn how to expand Creation, is it not? Physicality may be a small part of All, but learning how to co-create with it is a vast undertaking. It's why so many beings have joined with these life forms."

Tilan watched the pyramidal form he'd emerged from rise and fall with the undulating sea. Yawri started watching its rolling motion too.

Tilan continued. "I discovered planets need protection from solar winds in order to thrive. Without protection, atmospheres are stripped away. To deflect the solar winds, planets create magnetic fields around themselves. They all do it in their own way. This planet uses these crystal bodies to help."

"Crystal bodies," Yawri repeated, trying to understand how this made sense.

"A crystal body grown in this sea of carbon."

Yawri watched the strange triangular form rise and fall in its carbon sea. "How?"

Tilan replied easily. "The outer part of this planet is the coldest in this solar system, but where you are now is as hot as our star and under some of the greatest pressure of any planet here. These crystal bodies are grown by this liquid carbon sea. You only see my top half. A mirror image is below the surface. Our bodies are diamond shaped."

"Diamond shaped," Yawri said, picturing it.

"One point up. One point down. The base of each is joined at a square center."

Yawri, still trying to understand, looked more closely. "So you came to this planet and decided to join with a diamond body that helps the planet deflect the solar winds, winds that would otherwise strip away this atmosphere." Yawri considered the floating triangle and its purple orb in the swirling sea surrounding them.

32

"I can understand why a planet would need to deflect particles that would strip away its atmosphere, but you're an ethereal being like me." He wasn't sure how to say it, so he blurted, "There's nothing physical about us. How can you help something made of matter?"

Tilan's radiant purple orb rippled with light. "We are made with Creator's essence, including its sound and light. Correct?"

"Of course."

"These carbon-crystal bodies, 'diamond bodies,' we call them, connect to the planet's magnetic fields. They can move through the sea by changing how they are attracted or repelled by this field. But this sea is thick and movement is slow. We can change the effect of gravity on these forms so they are lighter. We can even raise them above this sea if they need to move quickly."

"Raise them above the sea," Yawri wondered, "How?"

"With soul light and soul sound. We increase soul light and the crystal body can become weightless if needed. To go down, we increase soul sound. If the crystal body wants to grow larger, we can take it as deep as it wants to go into this sea. The opportunity to learn how to co-create with physicality here is tremendous."

"I can imagine. Kind of."

"One moment. My diamond body calls me," Tilan said, and his luminous, pale purple orb moved back into the transparent diamond. Another bolt of lightning streaked from its tip and branched into brilliant tendrils above.

The orb emerged again and moved next to Yawri. "A solar wind storm is coming. I'll be staying at this location but several others will be moving soon."

Yawri tried to absorb what Tilan had told him but recalled a question that didn't involve flying diamonds. "You said this planet is as hot as a star. Do you know why? I thought it would be frozen solid."

"I wondered the same thing when I arrived. It has its own nuclear furnace. The difference between heat and cold makes great currents move throughout the planet. The currents generate the magnetic fields to protect it. All of the planets use something similar, or at least they all used to."

"What do you mean, used to?"

"It's not what they wanted, but given the assault, some have lost the essence needed to keep creating their own heat. Without it, planets cool and lose fluidity. Without fluidity, their magnetic fields die and solar winds strip away the atmosphere."

"Assault? What are you talking about? Our purpose is to expand All-there-is. How can that be an assault?"

"Not all beings were in joy at the birth of souls. Didn't you hear the scream?"

"Scream? What scream?"

"When we were created, a being screamed that the gift of self-awareness separated the One. You didn't hear it?"

Yawri remembered the strange discord in cascading essence. "Now that you mention it, I think I did."

"Not all souls chose to learn how to expand Life."

Yawri was confused. "That makes no sense. We were given free will so we could self-determine how to co-create and expand All. I don't see how doing anything else would even be possible. All is Creator."

Tilan considered Yawri and after a long pause said, "If you keep exploring this solar system, I expect you might find out."

Yawri swirled with questions but no single one formed. "I'm going to find out about this. Everything is of the One. You can't diminish All. We can only expand it." His violet-blue orb pulsed rapidly. "That's our purpose."

Tilan paused and watched several nearby crystals rise out of the carbon sea and hover above it. Yawri saw their lower half was a mirror image of their top. A perfect diamond shape, like Tilan said. They glowed with a soft radiance and began to rise higher.

Yawri commented, "You're a perfectly shaped diamond. I thought to be so stable in this sea you were only the tip of something with a lot of ballast."

Tilan replied cordially. "We can float in any orientation. Soul sound increases the effect of gravity and soul light decreases it. We add what's needed to stabilize our bodies."

Yawri watched the diamond crystals rise out of the sea, accelerate and disappear into the swirling wind. "I think learning how to work with gravity would be incredible," he mused.

"So stay here and learn. Many diamond bodies wish to join with ethereal beings. There is much to learn and do here."

Yawri's violet orb pulled back slightly, surprised. "I'm only investigating! I'm excited to learn about physicality, especially with how soul light and sound affect gravity, but there's so much to explore."

"Explore you shall. Every planet in this solar system grows crystal bodies. Even though we're on different planets, we can communicate because the minerals used to make them all have the same structure."

Yawri considered. "I travel time tunnels to similar points in time by matching resonance, so I suppose crystals could do the same with other crystals."

"Same resonates with same no matter where it is," Tilan agreed. "So your plan is to continue exploring?"

"Yes. The call coming from the third planet out from the sun is drawing me. I was on my way there when I stopped here."

"Third planet. A lot is going on with that one. There are crystal beings I know there, and we communicate often." Tilan became thoughtful again and Yawri had the feeling he was concentrating on something serious.

Tilan said, "Would you accept a gift?"

Yawri was perplexed. "A gift?"

"One moment," Tilan said, as his pale purple orb rejoined with its clear diamond body. Suddenly a light-blue, diamond-shaped, ethereal crystal appeared in front of Tilan's form.

Tilan's voice came from his diamond body and explained, "You can blend with this without joining with material essence. It's One with all realms, physical through ethereal. It will help you connect with crystals on all planets, but especially the one in the third orbit." Even though the gift wasn't physical, lightning reflected on its triangular faces. However, the image still made it appear the lightning was coming from within.

Yawri wasn't sure what he could do with it but accepted it graciously. "Thank you." He invited the ethereal diamond into his center and felt its pale-blue light blend with his own.

Yawri was still focused on Tilan's statement about crystal beings he knew on the third planet. "Maybe I'll find your friends on that world." Eager to experience what lay ahead, he started to increase speed and exclaimed, "Thanks again!"

"Be careful," Tilan called out.

"I will!" Yawri interjected, accelerating toward the sheet lightning above.

Tilan continued. "All that remains of one planet is an orbit of shattered rock!" but Yawri was no longer near.

2. PLANETS

∞

Yawri approached the next planet circling the system's star, which was also blue and about the same size. He darted down into its upper atmosphere and found the same icy, gaseous elements. Descending deeper he found even more diamonds floating in a superheated carbon sea than in the first.

I wonder if all the planets in this system are like this.

Eager to continue his adventure, he shot out of its icy-blue clouds and scanned for the next planet. It was three times the width of the blue ones and emitted strong, melodious chords. He drew closer. Swirling bands of yellows, browns, and grays raced around it in a torrent. A thin but large ring, twice the diameter of the planet, circled it.

Never seen one like this before.

His violet light pulsed enthusiastically, and he soared to the outer edge of the ring. Drawing parallel to it, he flew through the center of the thin disk.

It looked solid but it's only fine ice particles and dust!

He rose above the spinning disk to race above its surface, dipped down through it, and sailed along its underside and suddenly up to its top again. He immediately swerved to avoid another ethereal being in his path.

"Hello!" he said, dashing around the light-green orb. Excited to meet whoever it was, he turned and sped back. In contrast to his flaring violet-blue orb, this being radiated a steady, rhythmic pulse of light green. "I was so fascinated by the ring I didn't see you!" Yawri rushed out.

The green orb remained steady, but its light grew more radiant. "I didn't see you either," it replied succinctly. "Did you come to study the ring? It is fascinating."

Yawri continued, happy to find a being who might know something about this odd structure. "Based on my flight through it, it appears the outer edge is made of tiny ice particles. What have you discovered?"

The light-green orb considered. "Yes. Its outer edge is mostly made of frozen water vapor and dust. However, there are different rings circling as one, each with different sized particles."

"Different rings circle as one?"

"Yes. The exciting discovery is all of these rings are connected by other particles that weave back and forth between them." The being paused. "It's this weaving that keeps the whole ring stable."

"Particles weave back and forth, keeping them stable."

The green orb pulsed. "I've seen a similar structure in plants."

"In plants?"

"Yes. I mostly work with plants. You know how woody plants weave fibers together to connect their growth rings? These rings have a similar lobe structure."

Yawri had no idea how woody plant stems could possibly relate to rings of stardust and decided to change the subject.

"I'm Yawri. What sound do you go by?"

The green orb pulsed with veins of golden yellow. After a long moment, it replied, "Keela. I resonate with the sound of Keela."

"Keela. Nice sound, that. How long have you been here? I've just entered this solar system. So far, I've visited two planets. This is my third." Keela didn't respond, so he added, "What about you?"

"Me?" A ripple moved through the green orb. "My information is preliminary. I've only been studying this ring for a thousand of the planet's rotations."

"You've been here a thousand of its days and nights?"

Keela appeared apologetic. "I know it isn't long for such a complex structure."

Yawri was taken aback. He'd gone through the first two planets in less time than it took this gas giant to complete one rotation. Nonetheless, he continued without pause.

"The closer each planet is to their sun, the stronger their magnetic field. The farthest one out is strong, but the next one in was twice its strength. This one is at least twenty times stronger than the first. It makes sense because the closer they are to their star, the more they need it to deflect its solar winds. Do you know why this one made this ring? I have no idea what purpose it would serve."

The green orb brightened. "I think it's how this solar system's call is broadcast so far and wide. The ring boosts sound. It amplifies the resonance of the entire system."

38

Yawri's orb swirled with more intense blue. "That could explain why its call goes farther than any other system I've heard."

Keela's pale-green orb returned to a steady glow and considered this information. "Your observation about the magnetic fields is adept. It would explain what energizes the ring. I'll study that next, but most of my interest is about plants.

"I don't know anything about plants. Most of my existence has been helping to develop time tunnels."

"You're one of those who developed time tunnels?"

"Yes. I made it easy for beings to go any place in the living body of time. Too easy, really."

Sensing Yawri's unease, Keela didn't ask more. "From its tones, I think the third planet has a lot of plants. I plan to go there next."

"I'm going there, too! Its tones are calling me."

"Which ones?"

Yawri hadn't thought about which harmonics interested him most. He liked all of them. Tilan, the ethereal being on the first planet he visited, came to mind. The image of diamond crystals rising out the carbon sea and soaring away remained vivid.

Learning how to change soul light and sound to affect gravity on crystals might be good.

"Crystals," Yawri was surprised to hear himself say. "I'm very interested in crystals."

Keela watched a radial lobe in the ring shift position. "Crystals live in most planets. It would be interesting to study them."

Thinking about what might be in the next orbit, Yawri surveyed the star-filled space between the ringed planet and its sun. It looked like another gas giant circled ahead. Yawri's violet-blue orb surged with iridescent purple. "This ring is fascinating, but I'm ready to explore more."

Keela was absorbed in examination of a radiating lobe. She said, "You're right. The magnetic field is what keeps the ring functioning so well."

Yawri rose from the sparkling disk. "Your studies are phenomenal, Keela. More detailed than any I've done."

"Yes. I should have considered the magnetic field."

"I hope we meet again."

Keela's orb bobbed, but Yawri wasn't sure if it was in response to him. He bobbed in return, just in case, and streaked away.

The next world lay straight ahead and was even larger than the ringed one. Drawing near, striated bands of pale red, brown, yellow and white clearly whipped around the planet.

Its magnetic field is hundreds of times stronger than the first one I visited!

He dove into its atmosphere and found it similar to that of the ringed planet. With that thought, he rose once more. Emerging from the gas giant's whirling clouds, he searched for the next planet.

The nearest globe reflected a pale, reddish hue. He charged toward it, his violet orb rippling bright blue with anticipation. Without warning, an asteroid passed by so close it grazed his orb.

Where did that come from? I didn't hear anything!

He watched it retreat into the distance, then another asteroid flew by. Within moments, hurtling asteroids surrounded him. He swerved to avoid one the size of a small moon. Confused by their lack of song, he slowed to travel with the current. He sailed in a river of huge, angular boulders, most turning end over end. In contrast to the talkative asteroids orbiting the outer system, these were silent.

He came alongside one of the larger ones and asked, "Where is your sound?" but there was no response. Stretching his senses, he finally became aware of a low drone, one tone without cadence. He moved from one misshapen asteroid to another, but they were all without song.

This makes no sense. Everything sings with Life.

Deciding no answer would come from them, he focused his attention on the reddish planet again.

Maybe this planet will have answers.

The closer he got, however, the less sure he became.

What has happened? I can't hear its song either.

He slowed and hovered above the planet.

No clouds. No winds. No magnetic field!

He recalled what Tilan, the diamond being, said. "Some planets lost the living essence needed to generate their own heat. Without it, they cool and lose fluidity. Without fluidity, magnetic fields die and solar winds strip away the atmosphere."

How can any Creation lose essence?

He descended to investigate. Vast swathes of scoured ground cut across parched plains. A fine, red dust moved in its thin air. Deltas and alluvial fans flowed out of large, dry basins.

A lot of water flowed here once.

He moved upslope, toward the headwalls of the barren basin. Two glowing objects moved near the top of a high canyon wall. Curious, he sped toward them.

A luminescent, pale-yellow orb hovered next to an orange one and Yawri listened to their dialogue as he neared. The orange orb emitted sound in a deep and stable vibration. "So you think those tiny structures are fossilized plants?"

The yellow orb was ebullient. "What else could they be?"

"Lots of minerals can form branching structures, not just plants."

"With those fine strands and tiny, cup-like shapes on the end of those delicate tendrils? How could it not be from a plant?"

"I'm not saying it is or isn't. There are just not enough of them here to decide."

"What would you guess they are?"

"I don't guess."

"If you chose to guess what would you say?"

"Why would I choose to guess?"

"For fun."

"Guessing is no fun, it could be wrong."

Yawri saw they were hovering over a rough course of rock. The orange one appeared rooted in place. However, the yellow one quickly flew to the top of the canyon and back down again. "There are more fossils up there," it piped.

Yawri approached quickly, eager to learn about whatever they were doing.

"Hello!" he greeted them. "I'm Yawri. I just arrived in this system. What did you find?"

The ethereal being with the yellow orb bobbed and replied buoyantly. "I'm Zinn. This is Tisbero. What do you think, are these fossilized plants or not?"

The other orb bristled with vivid, orange light and its words were a measured cadence. "Tisbero. I go by Tisbero. I'm not saying they aren't plant-based, I just can't say for sure."

Zinn's yellow orb rippled with light. "The same kind of fossils are higher up, too."

Tisbero's orb pulsed brightly, then returned to a stable glow. "We don't know if they are fossils. I've connected with fossilized formations on other planets. Minerals can also form delicate branches similar to these."

Yawri didn't hear much past "connected with rocks on many other planets."

"I've connected with many things but never rocks. They're so physical. How do you do it?"

The answer rumbled out of Tisbero. "I start by listening to the sounds of a planet and narrow to mountain formations from there."

Yawri's orb flashed purple and blue. "Why not try it with this rock? Maybe it will tell you whether it's mineral or plant." He moved to the space between Zinn and Tisbero.

"Wait," Tisbero shifted backward. "I've only listened to planets and mountain ranges. The next step might be listening to one formation within a mountain, not tiny, branching threads in one stone."

Zinn bounced to Tisbero. "Come on. We've all listened to sounds coming from a solar system. All we're talking about is doing the same with a plant fossil."

"We don't know if they are fossilized plants yet," he cautioned.

Zinn's yellow orb sparked with swirls of gold. "Exactly. Are you afraid something could go wrong?"

"I'm afraid of nothing. The fact is, we don't have any idea what impact we might have on what's here. What if we harm it?"

"None of us have ever harmed anything. You think harm could happen by listening to something? Besides, the sound of this rock is so muted it will take all three of us blended in one purpose to hear it."

After a pause, Zinn added, "If you think harm could come from listening, don't. Yawri and I can listen while you watch for any sign of harm. How about that?"

Tisbero's orb grew taller and stilled. "I am not going to watch while you two communicate with this bed of stone. I interact with strata in different planets a lot."

Zinn's luminescent yellow orb sparkled again. "Great! Let's do it before I change my mind." Zinn moved directly over the exposed bed. "We'll just pretend we're listening to a solar system while we focus on these fossils."

"That's the plan?" Tisbero grumbled. "Pretend to listen to something we're not listening to?"

Zinn was undaunted. "Yes. Now, pretend you're listening to me. Let's connect with All and ask the tendrils in the rock if they will share their sound."

"We connect to All but just listen to tendrils?"

Yawri enjoyed banter, and these two were great at it, but he wanted to hear what these unusual structures had to say. He centered himself. "Let's try it. If not now, when? If not us, who?"

Tisbero emitted a brief, rumbling tone but his orange orb slowed to a steady rhythm. Yawri felt his connection with Tisbero and Zinn expand. All three increased the vibration of their essence, flowed within time and space, and opened to experience what came.

"I hear water," Yawri began. "The air is moist and warm. I see color here, a lot of colors."

Tisbero's response was concise. "Water, moisture, strong atmosphere. Much water was alive here."

"Green!" Zinn exclaimed. "Green and yellow and blue. There were plants covering the ground!"

Tisbero continued in a measured pace. "I hear harmonics of plants too. Simple but abundant. This planet was developing quickly."

"What happened?" Yawri wondered. "The resonance changed. The air thinned. The rains stopped." He paused a moment, then said, "The sounds are getting weaker. Let's strengthen our connection so we can stay with it."

The three beings increased their connection to each other and All.

Yawri reeled, "The magnetic field failed. Solar radiation is killing everything!"

Zinn pulled back quickly. "The plants are screaming! They weren't prepared for such sudden death!"

A sharp, disharmonic noise startled them so much they lost their connection to the tiny strands. Each felt the blossoming plant life change to fossilized stone. The trio moved upslope in a fruitless attempt to get away from the pain.

They halted and looked upon the parched, scoured landscape that stretched to the horizon in every direction.

Yawri broke the silence. "Why would a planet create Life and then kill it? It must have known stopping its magnetic field would stop this Life." He noticed Tisbero's orb, which was so uniformly stable before, now surging with bright-blue streaks. "Tisbero? Are you okay?"

Silence stretched. Zinn finally said, "He's flaring. He'll be all right."

Yawri didn't know what "flaring" entailed, but he was finding more and more things he didn't know since entering this system. He did what always seemed to help. He talked.

Rising above the fossils, Yawri said, "Whatever co-creation happened here is beyond me. I'm only sure of two things. The first is I never want to experience anything resembling that broken sound again. That was horrible. The second is, joining with you two magnified my ability to connect to Life a hundredfold. That was glorious. Both experiences are new for me. I don't understand either of them," he added wistfully, "but I definitely prefer the glorious one."

Zinn's orb lightened to a steady glow. "I agree completely. Here is what I received through our connection. Knowing the end of the Life was near, those plants purposefully lay down in this sediment in hope they could continue Life in another way. They transformed themselves into fossils so their story would remain alive."

Yawri replied, "That's the sense I received too. Thanks for finding them. I wouldn't have even known fossils existed without you two. I've never co-created with material essence. You've worked with other planets?"

A subtle flicker passed between Tisbero and Zinn but Yawri couldn't tell what it meant. "Yes," Zinn said. "We have."

Yawri hoped they'd say more, but neither did.

He continued, openly sharing his thoughts. "There have been far more questions than answers from this solar system. Here's one: Between this planet and the gas giant, there's an orbit of quiet rocks."

Tisbero's tone was tight. "What do you mean, orbit of rocks?"

Yawri considered starting the story with his near-collision with Keela the researcher. However, given Tisbero's tone he thought a more straightforward answer might be best.

"There's a large field of asteroids between the gas giant and this one. Angular rocks of every size. I heard nothing because there was nothing to hear. Is that common?"

Tisbero's colors prickled from orange to red. "Nothing to hear?"

"The icy asteroids circling the outer system have a loud resonance. These are only a quiet drone, without melody. It's the first time I've come across such a thing. Have you?"

"It's not at all common," Tisbero said, and seemed to retreat into thought.

Zinn floated next to Yawri. "Tisbero and I will go to them. The lack of sound we found on this planet was one thing. The lack of sound in an asteroid field is another. Perhaps they're related, perhaps not. It will be hard to find out if no rocks speak, but we will ask."

Zinn moved next to Tisbero. "Follow me. Let's dive into an asteroid field and find out what we can learn!"

"I've never followed you." Tisbero's tone was gruff.

Zinn's yellow orb swirled with flashing tendrils of green and started moving away. "It's good to meet you, Yawri. Perhaps we'll meet again."

Tisbero called after Zinn. "That's your plan? Dive into an orbit of soundless, dense rocks? We should skirt it first!" Rather than slowing, Zinn accelerated.

Tisbero rose and began following Zinn. "I'd better go. Zinn has a way of knowing where to go until finding out it's the wrong direction."

Yawri watched the two beings, not sure what to think. The orange one caught up with the yellow one, they slowed briefly, then both sped toward the asteroid field.

So opposite, yet so together.

Rising above the barren planet, Yawri sought the next one. The third globe out from the sun. He found it easily because it sparkled with more colors than he'd ever seen.

A jewel floating in space. The source of the diverse harmonics.

With a final glance at the fossilized plants, he sped toward the sparkling globe, excited to learn why this solar system had such wild extremes.

3. CAVERNS

∞

Yawri hovered above the singing world and watched a massive ball of frozen water plunge into its atmosphere.

That's an icy asteroid from the outer solar system! This is what they meant when they sang, "We come to bring waters of Life."

The meteor streaked through the air and released its living water in a white trail of vapor. What ice remained plunged into the ocean with the gift of Life from the cosmos.

Other movement distracted Yawri's reverie. Orbs of light hovered in the distance.

Great! More ethereal beings!

Each one glowed with a unique color. However, he noticed a small group who were all the same silver.

Another thing I've never seen before.

A light drew his attention back to the planet. An aurora of shimmering green light danced in a circle around the pole, while the emerging light of a crescent moon illuminated translucent bands of blue and violet. He watched it rise through the atmosphere until it became a brilliant white arc floating in dark space.

Several colorful beings sped past him on their way down to the surface.

One called out, "Are you joining with this planet too?" The cluster of silver beings moved closer to hear Yawri's response, but he didn't notice.

"Yes!" Yawri enthused.

One of the silver beings spoke to its companions. "That one clearly has no experience with physical Creation. Many naïve ones like him are coming." His silver orb rippled. "I look forward to teaching them the True Way."

The largest silver orb replied steadily, "As with the other two planets, there is no need to rush. Let them commit themselves to serving this world. We will make sure problems arise after they are filled with that dedication. Then they will be ripe for conversion to our purpose." Without further comment the silver beings lined up and watched Yawri descend.

"I'm coming!" Yawri called to the colorful beings, who had sped past him. Then he moved faster than a comet and plunged into a bulbous blanket of water vapor.

These clouds sing with Creation's essence!

A shaft of sunlight parted the mist and revealed a sultry sea stretching from horizon to horizon. Aromas unknown to any reality he had experienced bloomed with wondrous texture.

The vast churning sea reached up to greet him, seeking a connection with the ethereal worlds he brought. Yawri responded in kind. "I seek to touch all you are, as you seek to touch all I am." In exalted joy, he dove into the rolling water.

Vitality shook every atom of the salty sea. Towering kelp, anchored by long, jointed stalks, waved greetings in a liquid blue. Fish with bone-sheathed heads darted to avoid nautiloids whose tentacles stretched far beyond their enchanting spiral shells. A forest of green seagrass sheltered brilliant-blue neon shrimp from the probing tendrils of undulating jellyfish. Lost in a timeless descent through this new world of water, Yawri slowed when he came to another transition.

First air followed by mist, liquid, now a solid sediment. Does physicality always transition this way?

Long, jointed crinoid stems rose from the bottom of the sea, their feathery crowns waving with the undulating current. Hot vents of water rose from boilers deep within the planet, their nutrient-rich geysers adding fertile elixir to the cauldron. He hovered above the sandy solid.

What's next?

Yawri's ethereal orb descended into the sediment, his sound and light touching and connecting with all as he passed through. Saturated sediment became dense, denser still, and finally rock.

Matter isn't really solid at all!

He flowed through the stone. His mind swirled.

What is it about physicality that makes it feel so full of essence?

Engrossed, he descended to learn more. The rock changed from one type to another, each with its own tone, texture, and colors. Then, without warning, the stone was gone. He'd been in rock deep in Earth one moment, the next he was in air.

I must have traveled all the way through this planet back out to its atmosphere!

He moved farther into the dark sky.

How strange. The air feels dense and hot.

Drops of water started to pass through him again.

Rain. I know rain.

However, this rain wasn't falling from the dark sky. It fell from the rock behind him upward into it. He swirled, probing for answers.

How can rain fall up? To where?

Confused and intrigued, he followed the falling rain. Within moments, stars appeared above him. However, they were ill-defined blobs rather than sharp points of light.

Are they a new kind of star?

Eager to learn more, he accelerated, but instead of open space, he found another sea. Bewildered, he moved into it and found hot, mineral-rich water. The blobs of light grew more defined, so he went farther to investigate.

These are crystals! Glowing crystals. How can they be here?

Yawri sailed along a glowing wall of pale yellow and green until he came to a dark, misshapen oval.

It looks like the mouth of a tunnel. What is a tunnel doing here?

He sped through its twisting turns seeking answers. It opened suddenly into another sea and Yawri found this one had even more crystals, all glowing a creamy white. Moving quickly, he discovered a forest of hexagonal crystal columns growing in the hot elixir.

This can't be above a planet. These are chambers within it!

Relieved by his realization, Yawri moved through the hexagonal columns growing in their hot elixir. He saw one more than twice the length of the others, and it seemed suspended horizontally above the floor.

Smaller crystals, fluorite from their shape, covered the floor under it. They were the source of the intense, warm, yellow light amplified by the clear quartz crystals of this other-worldly place.

"Where am I?

"You are here," a disembodied voice responded.

Yawri surged with streaks of violet and looked for the orb who spoke. None were there. He recalled when this happened before. On the first planet he visited, a crystal being spoke from within its crystal body.

"You're an ethereal being, right?" He continued scanning the area. "Which crystal body is yours?"

"Here."

Yawri had no idea where "here" was, but he continued. "I met an ethereal being joined with a diamond crystal body on another planet. May I meet you, too?" All senses open, he waited.

"That would be Tilan. He said you were coming, Yawri."

Bright blue veins shot through Yawri's violet orb. "You talked to Tilan? How? He's on the outermost planet. Which crystal are you?"

"I'm Lazket. If you were any closer, you'd be inside."

Yawri realized his orb was touching the immense crystal growing out of the wall. A domed fluorite underneath it blazed with white light.

"Sorry!" Yawri moved back. "I didn't realize I was so close."

"Communication is about resonance, not distance. It's how Tilan and I speak."

"Right," Yawri commented, with a general idea of what he probably meant.

Yawri glanced to his right and left. The quartz forest was lit by fluorites growing everywhere, even on them.

"How did you and Tilan know I'd find you? I didn't even know you existed."

"It might have something to do with the gift he gave you."

"Oh, yes," Yawri sensed the ethereal blue diamond within him. "Tilan said it would help me connect with the crystals on other planets."

"It did."

Yawri calmed with the memory. "Ethereal beings living inside physical forms are new to me. I didn't even know they existed until I met Tilan. You're my second. I've focused my learning on ethereal time tunnels."

"Why have you come here?"

"Curiosity. I heard harmonies more diverse than any I'd experienced before, so I came to find their source. Why did you come?"

Lazket was circumspect. "I heard this planet's call to expand Life, and discovered it lives in more dimensions than any other planet I'd experienced. After speaking with the spirit of this crystal body, we agreed to join."

"That's similar to what Tilan said. He told me physicality was a small part of All, but learning how to co-create with it was how he wanted to fulfill his charge to expand Creation."

"Crystal life forms are quite multidimensional. They live consciously across time."

Yawri watched a column of hot water distort light coming from crystals behind it. The crystals appeared to move. "You said communication is about resonance, not distance. You can talk to Tilan because he's also in a crystal body?"

Lazket spoke with ease. "Yes. All minerals have their own crystalline structure, independent of where they are. The structure does not have to be big to resonate with minerals on another planet. There are many billions of planets with diamond and quartz crystals, just in this galaxy. Learning how to

50

co-create with a life form that connects across Creation like that is why I'm so grateful the Earth spirit of this crystal body agreed to join with me."

Yawri's questions ricocheted through him. To help center himself, he focused on Lazket's colossal body of quartz. Miniature rainbows flowed across feathery formations inside it. "Your bodies live millions of years. I'm used to traveling through time tunnels to any ethereal reality I choose whenever I choose. Maybe sometime I could join with something shorter-lived."

"Joining is a major commitment. My first joining was with an icy asteroid. We helped to bring water to another world. It took much preparation for me to make sure my choice to blend with physicality would enhance All, not detract from it."

"Detract from All? I don't see how that could happen." Yawri pulled back in disbelief. "The more I've worked with ethereal dimensions the more I've expanded into All. Physicality is only a very small aspect of Creation, and I don't see why working with it could have different results."

Lazket was quiet a long moment. "We make choices based on previous experience, and I started with no experience in physicality. I've found the gift of free will means Creator will not stop me, independent of how I choose to use it. I've learned to be cautious."

White light flowed back and forth across the chamber in rippling waves.

Such beauty. I wonder what else is underground.

"I've traveled down into this planet, right? How far?"

Lazket considered the question. "We are much less than one percent of the distance to the core."

"Is there more Life farther down?"

"Much more. Currents of very hot, malleable rock circulate up and down below us. Different crystals grow at different depths. The diamond bodies grow deepest. Even deeper is where the ethereal being of this planet and Creator blend thoughts. All Life on this planet is created from those thoughts."

Yawri brightened with a new thought. "You and the crystal are joined in co-creation, ethereal and physical. Are you saying the entire planet is joined with some aspect of Creator in the same way? It co-creates with Creator as you do with the crystal?" The thought was so alien to his thinking he wasn't even sure the question made sense.

Lazket understood. "We are vastly different in ability, but basically, yes. This planet is a conscious co-creation with Creator, including the crystal body with which I have joined. That is the scope of the opportunity I spoke about. Creator gives us the opportunity to learn how to co-create in physicality because of it."

51

Yawri seemed to swell. "You said there is a place where the ethereal being of this planet and Creator blend thoughts, and all Life here is created from those thoughts?"

"All Creation started with Creator's thoughts. So of course our own Creations, as well as those of planets, begin with them, too."

Yawri's orb thrummed with bright violet. "To go to this place where these thoughts spring forth within Earth would be unlike any experience I know. Have you been there?"

"I've not gone there myself because I don't feel ready. I'm learning about co-creation through the Earth spirit of this crystal body. That is enough for me to learn now. I don't think I'd be able to keep my center in the presence of such timeless essence of Creation."

"But why not? Physical time has no effect on us. We are made of timeless essence, yes?"

"Even though we originated from Creator's thought, being in the presence of so much primal formlessness would be hard. The more I've learned the more I understand how much I don't know."

Yawri watched the miniature rainbows dance through Lazket. "But without trying new things, how can we know what we do and don't know? I've traveled time tunnels to thousands of realities. I've never felt overwhelmed in any of them. It's all about learning how to expand with Creation, right?"

The domed fluorite under Lazket undulated with intense light, then steadied. Lazket's tone was respectful. "There is no right or wrong in learning."

"Exactly." Yawri started to move away. "Our charge is to learn how to expand All. How can I learn what I don't know without trying new things? I hope I see you again!"

"I hope to see you again too." Lazket replied, but Yawri's violet orb was already descending through the living crystal floor.

5. THOUGHT FORMS

∞

Yawri sped downward. Fixed rock gave way to flowing, viscous rock. Bubble-like caves in the moving mass concentrated different minerals. Each grew different crystalline forms and cast different sounds.

"You came!" An exuberant voice penetrated the superheated rock. Yawri stopped, startled. A brilliant red diamond crystal appeared next to him.

"A carbon crystal! Tilan's kin are in the Earth!" Yawri exclaimed. "I had no idea how to find diamonds on this world. It's miraculous it happened."

Similar to Tilan, but far smaller, the red-crystal diamond tapered from a square to a four-sided point on both sides.

"That ethereal diamond within you guided us to each other."

Yawri felt the gift from Tilan pulse, its pale-blue light now seamlessly blended with him. "It's from the outermost planet."

"We know Tilan," the red diamond toned. "Although his diamond body is joined with an ethereal soul and ours is not, we still have the same resonance. We converse. Have you come to join with a diamond body? There are many here."

Yawri's violet orb flashed with iridescent blue. "Uh," he said cautiously, "I don't think I'm ready to join with anything."

Amiable amusement chimed in response. "I agree. You prefer to travel time tunnels and move where you want when you want."

"How do you know that?"

"Personality is within sound. We listen."

"I do want to learn. It's why I came. I just arrived, though." More carbon crystals approached, curious. "I had no idea a planet could have so much Life."

The diamond's tone deepened. "If you want to learn from this planet, it asks for an agreement. It asks ethereal beings to blend with it to discover more of all you are. The reason is simple. The stronger your connection to all of yourself, the more you can co-create with it. The blessing is beyond my

53

imagining. I'm learning how to co-create with much more of All from this planet."

"Everything I am and do is in agreement with that."

"It seems obvious, but crystals on a far distant planet tell of some ethereal beings who may not agree. It seems they believe the goal of the sending forth is best achieved by merging into one, rather than being unique within the One. "

Yawri couldn't understand the concept. "That makes no sense. Every being knows they can only be a part of the One as much as the One is within them. We were sent forth with individual free will to learn how to do that. Right? I can't imagine any being doing otherwise."

"That is the same for us. We don't filter what we hear, only share it."

Yawri wanted to learn more about how crystals communicate. "You can talk to crystals on other worlds because of resonance, but all of Earth's organic life forms are on the surface. Do you communicate with them?"

"We need to be on the surface to do that. Earth moves some crystal bodies to the surface. The raising process for most minerals, like for Lazket, is gentle. Ours is explosive. Magma takes us to the surface within hours, where we cool very quickly. It's for the reason you say. Earth moves some to the surface so they can connect with Life there. They communicate with us and we communicate with our kin inside other planets."

The mention of Lazket reminded Yawri about the reason he decided to explore farther down. "Lazket said there is a place where the ethereal being of this planet and Creator blend thoughts. Is it far from here?"

After a long pause, the red diamond warned, "Very intense essence resides there. When in the presence of such pure essence, an ethereal being can be overwhelmed."

Yawri considered the statement but it didn't seem to apply to him. "I only want to go close enough to sense the reality of it, not go into it."

"Observe only?"

"At a safe distance. I've traveled many ethereal realms and have experience keeping centered within timeless essence. This is the first chance I've had to see how a planet works with Creator. Aren't you curious?"

"I am one with Earth, so its Source is well known to me." After a moment the red diamond continued. "I respect your choice to learn as you will. The wellspring of creative thought is still a long distance toward the core, but you'll know when you get close."

"How? How will I know?"

"Don't worry. You'll know."

"Thanks, Red!" Yawri began moving down once more. "I hope I see you again. I appreciate crystals a lot!"

"Red?"

"Having a name will make it easier to remember our talk. Is 'Red' okay, or do you have another?"

"Red is fine. If I'm sent up near the surface, I'll send a message to the ethereal crystal within you."

Yawri's violet orb glowed with anticipation. "Great! I hope you make it to the surface. Do you know diamonds fly on Tilan's planet?"

"I know."

"I'll put in a request at the wellspring!" Yawri accelerated downward, intent on at least locating it.

The farther he descended, the hotter the gelatinous, flowing minerals became. Currents of flowing rock rose, cooled, and fell in giant cells that mixed essence throughout the planet's mantle. Suddenly, he found himself in a down current.

Flowing down with it might be faster.

His descent accelerated faster than he intended, so he willed himself to slow down. He didn't slow. He willed himself to stop. His plunge continued. In fact, independent of his wishes, the deeper he went the faster he descended.

Something appeared to his right, then another to his left. Fluid rock continued to flow by in a blur, but these two forms moved with him. He bore left, then right, but they stayed alongside.

Two more forms of the same shape came, one in front and the other behind. Suddenly, all four moved closer to him.

What can these things be? They move through mass like I do, so they must be ethereal beings.

A voice cut through the flowing rock. "What are you?" it demanded.

What am I? How could one ethereal being not recognize another?

He focused on the form that spoke. It looked more animal than orb. Its body was barrel-shaped and had muscular, fin-like arms. A rounded paddle formed its tail. Yawri shifted from side to side to view it from a different perspective, but the strange form maintained its front-facing position.

It must be another shape for an ethereal being, but why would an ethereal being manifest such a bizarre image?"

Yawri continued to observe the apparition. A long, broad snout tapered up to its bulbous head. Two dark, wide-set eyes stared back. Two nostrils sat above its wide mouth.

Nostrils? Beings don't have lungs.

Even though he hadn't willed himself to do so, his speed slowed to a crawl. He willed himself to bolt forward. He didn't move. In fact, he'd stopped, and the four strange ethereal forms made a circle with him in its center.

How can this happen?

He searched all of his experience but no explanation came. This was wholly untethered from any reality he'd known.

"What are you?" the voice repeated insistently. A fifth and sixth ethereal beast joined the circle. "Why are you here?"

An unsettling quiver of light ran through him.

Did all six of these beings lose themselves to physicality?"

The apparitions stood taller than his orb, and their eyes burned.

Re-center yourself. No matter where I am, all places are within All.

One of the apparitions moved closer and lowered its head as if to smell him. It pulled back spoke to the others. "Maybe it's lost the ability to understand the language of the All."

"Or perhaps it never had it in the first place," another said. "Perhaps it's connected to nothing but itself." The circle around him tightened.

Yawri whirled. "What do you mean lost ability? I've only expanded ability with all I've learned to be."

These have to be the ethereal beings Lazket spoke about, beings that lost themselves in physicality.

The first strange being said accusingly, "So you do understand the one language of All. That's good. Now you can tell us what you are and why you are here!" Its eyes appeared shockingly physical.

"I'm an ethereal being, same as you!" Yawri tried to remind them.

The aberration moved back in disgust. "You're not of this Earth!" it exclaimed. "You do not belong here!"

Yawri spun. Each strange form moved in closer. "I'm an etheric soul learning how to be ever more All. I'm here to learn about physical co-creation. Isn't it why you came here too?" he exclaimed.

The circle of strange forms tightened. "We know who we are and it is nothing like you! We are thought forms of this planet and Creator!"

Another of the strange beings spoke. "And we know our purpose. Long ago, some ocean creatures left the sea to walk on land so they could to bring the wisdom of the ocean to the land. Fins became legs. We are to take the wisdom they gained from land and deliver it back to the sea. Now legs become fins again."

Another burst out with, "You have no songs or colors of this planet. How can you help its Life without its sounds or light?"

Yawri spoke to them all. "You're right! I'm not a thought form of this planet. I'm an ethereal being, and I serve to enhance Life everywhere I go."

The first apparition moved even closer. "You say you serve to enhance Life wherever you go. Since you are here, let's learn if it is true. We will bring the dimensions of this planet to you. If you maintain your center within them, you are welcomed."

Yawri tried to understand. "But as an ethereal being, how could I not be centered in who I am?"

The form spoke, unconcerned. "Then connecting to all the dimensions of this planet won't be a problem. Centered, you expand with Life and have more of yourself. That gives to Earth. Without center, you lose yourself. That takes."

Another said, "We will see which you do."

The circle tightened again and Yawri felt the "thought forms" increase their connection with the dimensions of Earth.

This is crazy. I've always been centered in who I am and never feel separate from All.

A swirling, disorienting wave passed through him.

I'm here to share experience, not become it.

The swirling wave grew taller and he sank in its trough. Another wave crested over him and broke with a thundering crash. The torrent swept him out to sea. Not a sea—an ocean of essence without beginning or end. Yawri started to dissolve into a living flood of joy.

"There is no I. Only All!"

A sound came. Far distant, but piercing.

"Yawwwrriii …" it rang. The sound was familiar, yet not.

A shadow appeared. Immense in width, it towered above the rolling waves. Hundreds of thick, strong limbs danced with the flood.

It that a tree? It's a thought form of a tree!

The pronouncement gave him an anchor in the endless current, and he held onto it.

Another thought came. "Go forth, learn to expand Creation in all you become."

The anchor strengthened.

I go forth within All.

The tree resonated with him, and he felt its calming, centering effect.

"Yawwrrii …" The sound came again. Stronger this time.

Yawri is my sound.

A voice resounded through the tree and enveloped him. "Experience your essence within the One and the One within you."

Certainty rang through Yawri and he celebrated his place in the flood of sound and light.

I am an ethereal soul created by Creator!

The giant tree became a willowy pendulum swaying across time. "Be all you are, now!" the penetrating resonance said.

Yawri felt all the ethereal dimensions he knew: Countless time tunnels he'd traveled through within living time. Intertwined points of existence, each strong within itself; each moment with unshakable knowledge of its value to All.

There is no beginning or end, life or death, only transformation into ever more.

The tree spoke again, welcoming and kind. "What do you bring to this planet?"

Yawri's awareness moved through overlapping realms. Bubbles overlapping bubbles, each a unique time and space, separate but within one another. One brightened, and he focused on it.

In one moment, he perceived an overlapping matrix of living time, and the next six thought forms of manatees surrounded him. With his buoyant center returned, he spoke to them. "What a wonderful Creation you are! You will assure the wisdom of sea and lands are rejoined!"

The manatees' eyes opened wide. Yawri remained buoyant. "There is much I do not know. However, I bring all that I am, all the ethereal planes of existence I am. That is what I am able to give. I will use what I know and learn how to connect with this planet in a way that we both can expand in co-creation." The statement felt so matter-of-fact, so natural, that by its end he wondered why he'd felt the need to say it.

The fin-shaped arms of the thought forms dropped to their sides. Their flat paddle-tails barely moved, as if slowly treading water.

"Are you okay?" Yawri asked, concerned

One of the six finally spoke, regret in its tone. "We erred. We saw what we expected to see. Not you. We see now. You carry many ethereal dimensions and crystal essence. That connection will help this planet expand in all it can become."

"Please forgive our inexperience," another said. "In our earnest intent to fulfill our purpose to keep balance, we lost balance. We were so dedicated to our task we forgot its purpose."

Yet another spoke. "Thank you for helping us learn this lesson now rather than after becoming fully physical."

All were quiet in apparent reflection. One finally said, "We know Earth calls ethereal beings to support its development. You are the first we've met. We did not know what you were."

Another spoke, more relaxed now. "Are you going to join with a physical form? Our bodies will be very large. Ethereal beings will be able to join with us. We have much to learn and much to give each other."

Yawri, though filled with appreciation, was taken aback. It took a long moment to remember his reason for coming to this particular space and time.

"I do want to learn more about physical co-creation. However, I don't know enough to join with a physical body yet. There is so much to learn."

"Yes, there is much to learn. This planet teaches the importance of timing. We honor yours as you have ours."

Another of the thought forms spoke. "We will tell the other mammals who are returning to the sea about our learning with you. We will seek ways to help your kind. We share your purpose to expand All. Thank you for listening to Earth's song and choosing to come."

The six apparitions turned to proceed on their transformational journey to the surface and the physical world. Yawri stared after them, transfixed. After a long moment he said, "I should continue my journey to the planet's wellspring."

He started to move downward again, but another shadowy form emerged from the flowing rock. The shape that distilled from the mist was several times wider than the manatee and taller. Much taller. Several arm-like appendages come into view, but instead of ending with hands, they continued branching into more and more branches.

"A tree!" Yawri said, recognizing the form. "You're a thought form of a tree." The branches swayed with delicate precision.

"Hello, Yawri." The sound moved through the flowing, living stone. "It's good to see you again."

Yawri tried to remember meeting a tree. "Do I know you?"

One of the branches swept down and touched Yawri's violet orb. "A very long time ago. I heard you ask, 'Am I separate?' and I shared my name, Murann. I intoned we were not separate, but individual within All. I encouraged you to celebrate the gift of choice given to us so that we could self-determine how we learn and expand in all we become. Do you remember?"

Yawri beamed. "How could I forget? One moment I didn't exist and the next I did. Everything was bursting from everything else and I was self-aware, but then I wondered what was aware of what?"

"I heard you ask the question and I answered the best I could."

"But you remember my name! It was so long ago."

"Yours was the first name I heard after my own. 'Yawwwrriii.'"

"Just Yawri is fine. Your name was …" He tried to recall but didn't.

"Murann. I resonate well with the sound of Murann."

"Murann. I remember!" Yawri tried to reconcile what he recalled from that moment with this one. "Murann … right … So now you're a tree?"

"Not a tree, I'm with a thought form of a tree. It's still more ethereal than physical. Joining with a thought form lets ethereal beings learn how to become physical gradually."

"So you'll be in a tree, but not be a tree?"

"I won't be a tree any more than the ethereal beings in the crystals are a crystal. Physical bodies are composed of matter from a planet. We don't have matter. When invited, ethereal souls can join with them to blend together and further expand All-that-is. We remain etheric because that's what we are. A tree being is the Earth spirit of a tree joined with an etheric being."

I can't believe that Murann is joining with a tree. He'll be rooted in the same place for ages.

"Why did you decide to do this?"

Murann replied thoughtfully. "The more diverse a planet the more it can connect with All. I wish to learn how this planet creates in so many dimensions. Trees are some of its most multidimensional life forms."

Yawri wasn't sure how to respond. "I don't know about trees, but I've met ethereal beings joined with crystal bodies to become crystal beings. The same mineral has the same structure on each planet, so they can communicate across solar systems. I guess it works well."

The tree thought form glowed a golden red. Murann continued, "Trees are similar, but unlike minerals, trees are organic life forms. I wanted to learn co-creation from them. From what I've learned, joining works well unless you lose your center and begin to believe you are physical."

"Lose your center? That's the same thing the manatees talked about."

"I noticed they brought forth all of the dimensions of this planet at once. How was the experience?"

"Fine. A little confusing at first, but fine. Same as I told them: As an ethereal being, how could I not be centered in who I am?"

Murann was quiet for a long moment. "You didn't experience a loss of place, time or form, or lose your sense of self?"

Yawri tried to recall the experience. It was so intangible now. "Well, maybe for a moment, but I remembered I am within All. I wasn't alone, there was this … tree." Yawri's violet orb suddenly pulsed with blue and green. "Wait," he ventured. "There was a tree. I was in an ocean and the tree grew out of it. Do you know anything about that?"

"You're welcome," Murann responded.

"That was you?"

"It seemed a good time to remind you of yourself." The tree's branches swayed. "Free will means we won't be stopped from doing healing or harm. Learning the difference is up to us."

"Well," Yawri replied cheerfully, "Nothing was harmed. I certainly don't want to harm anything."

Murann responded, somberly. "The physical realm can be quite"—he paused to consider—"compelling."

"Compelling?" Yawri looked at the flowing mass surrounding them. "I only want to learn how physicality became so full of Creator's essence. It's a small part of All, maybe five percent. Yet its impact seems immense."

"Much less than five percent, I think."

"Its sensations are filled with such vital texture. No wonder so many beings are here. I never knew it was possible, so I'm going to observe how they join with physicality."

Murann considered, and finally said, "Free will is free will. Be careful. I've heard some beings have forgotten their ethereal selves so much they've come to experience themselves only as physical."

Yawri scoffed. "Physicality is such a small part of Creation, how could that even be possible?"

"I only share what was heard. I don't know how it could happen either."

"For an ethereal being to only experience themselves as physical, they'd have to disconnect from their Source. That's not going to happen. We're learning how to expand with Creation, not disconnect from it."

"Then All will be more," Murann said. "All will be more."

Yawri extended his awareness to sense any more thought forms. None approached. "I think I'll follow those manatees and see what happens. Maybe there's some way I can help them." He studied Murann's growing tree. "Tree bodies are good, but I want to find out what other forms Earth is creating. The manatees said there are many."

Yawri focused on where he'd last seen the creatures and drifted that direction. "It's very good to see you again, Murann. Thank you for being with me during the turmoil of our beginning, and just now with those thought forms. If you ever need anything, tell a crystal being. Maybe it can talk to the one within me and I can find where your tree is rooted."

"I will," Murann confirmed.

Yawri started moving quickly away and didn't slow when he asked, "I wonder how many different body types Earth is preparing for ethereal beings?"

Murann pulsed with iridescent, golden light while Yawri disappeared into the flowing rock. "I'm sure you're about to find out."

5. LIGHT BODIES

∞

Eons passed.

Earth changed.

Mosses, tall fungi, fleshy plants and seed ferns prospered. Branchless trees festooned with broad, long leaves at their crowns grew wherever water was plentiful. The new soil made from these and other plants allowed ever more Life to bloom. Earth teemed with countless creatures on land and in the sea.

Life and death were one, each feeding the other in continual creation in All. More and more ethereal beings came to learn from and care for this conscious planetary being, which continually created so many life forms in so many dimensions.

The agreement Earth asked in return was simple. Ethereal beings, including Yawri, agreed to learn how to blend their ethereal dimensions with the planet and to expand its connection with All. With this guardianship in place, Earth received the touch and assistance it wished for co-creation.

Yawri and other beings of light slowly changed shape to those more suited for working with this world. Diverse physical creatures flourished, all with heads, torsos, and various appendages. Noticing the success of this form, the guardian beings manifested similarly shaped light bodies instead of orbs. With this light body form, they could connect their "feet" directly to the planet's ethereal and physical energies while their own connection to the ethereal universe entered through their "heads." After centering and balancing each source in their torso, the blended essence flowed from their hands. This allowed them to give additional essence of All to strengthen and protect the Life balance.

Life flourished. Earth's thought forms of living Creation emerged, generation after generation, and found the supportive hands of the guardians offering nourishing connection to more of All-that-is. The guardians did not decide, or even have an opinion about which of Earth's life forms would survive. The beings joyously served to blend the diverse Life forms and dimensions within One. Life permeated air, water and land. The Earth sang. Since their light bodies were ethereal, they swam through air, sea, and rock and nurtured Life wherever it called.

Yawri's radiant light body was over twenty feet tall. His "eyes" were cobalt-blue portals to the universe. He could focus on any point in time but always saw it within All, free of division or separation. His light body still heard the first vibrations of the Beginning, but he also heard the chorus coming from specific mineral, plant or animal with which he now worked.

On this day, a call sounded from a weathered bed of stratified rock. Dark-red lines of mineral-rich iron glistened between alternating bands of translucent, brown chert. Pioneers of Life, delicate strands of woven fungus, found a home in its cracks and crevices.

Yawri lifted one of his translucent arms toward the fungi, outstretched an ethereal hand, offered a greeting, and waited. The fungi would respond if it wished. He studied its fine filaments a long moment before the iron rock, not the fungus, replied.

"A new life form is prepared to emerge at this place to help us. If the fungus can receive it, it will evolve into one that will dissolve iron into the water to nourish others. Will you help us?"

"Yes," Yawri agreed.

He would assist this connection. His light body glowed with soft orange light. Essence of Earth rose through his etheric feet, and essence of the cosmos entered through his head. They blended, and his light pulsed brightly. Hands raised, he gently shared this elemental source of vitality with the fungus and Earth's new creations.

Yawri glided through timeless time to bring the first vibrations of the Beginning to this moment, at this place, and nourish it now. He drew his focus to the delicate fungus living in nooks and crevices of the iron-rich rock. The filaments were so fragile, yet so strong they reduced mountains to plains.

Focusing deeper, he sensed minuscule root hairs growing into hard rock and the continuous cycle of life and death for fungi and mineral. He joined the sequence of their constant transformation with his own. After becoming One with it, he increased the flow of primal essence through his light body and offered it.

Yawri watched living light play back and forth across the delicate fungal strands, fascinated. Majestic and glorious, a tiny purple spark appeared in a fungi-filled crevice and began to glow.

Its glow increased, and a new song began.

"Ye-es!" Yawri gleefully soared into the vaporous air, then back down and into the ground to swim in celebration within the living rock. "The Creator Itself blesses this place!" he exalted, and once more shot up into the air.

"What are you doing, Yawri?" A gruff tone interrupted his speedy ascension. "You're asking for the wrath of Zinn with such commotion!"

Yawri looked down from his soaring perch to see Tisbero on a low hill. "The wrath of Zinn? You mean the zest of Zinn, don't you Tisbero? Nothing is going to slow her down."

Tisbero remained focused on his task. "She's helping a new thought form blend into a large animal right now. Not a good time to disturb her!"

Yawri hadn't seen Keela, whom he'd met on the rings of the gas giant, since he came to Earth. He'd seen Tisbero and Zinn, the two beings he met on the red planet, engaged in earnest debate over a fish with legs, and had approached them. They never did decide if the creature was leaving or returning to the water, but their shared appreciation for the gift of free will brought them together.

When he'd first met them, the two appeared to be so different that he wondered why they traveled together. He'd gotten no further insight since then. If anything, their differences were even more pronounced. Tisbero's light body resonated with the masculine aspect of Earth, whereas Zinn resonated more with its feminine aspect, and their differences continued from there.

Tisbero loved to plan. Zinn loved spontaneity. Tisbero's light body seemed to be made of blocks and Zinn's from raindrops. Tisbero was fiery but would never burn anyone. Zinn was airy but could crisp even the most fire-resistant personality. Yawri enjoyed them both.

He zoomed over to Tisbero. "If anyone can help animals receive complicated thought forms it's Zinn. Where is she?"

"Down that hill." Tisbero pointed to a herd of large animals with long noses and shovel-shaped lower tusks. "Their diet is limited to water plants. Zinn is helping them receive a thought form which will broaden their range considerably. They'll be able to eat dry tundra grasses." A pale-yellow light body emerged from the herd. "She says with the changes the planet is making, they'll die out if they don't change. Delicate work. I was watching out for her when you shot up like a geyser. What were you doing?"

"I was doing delicate work," Yawri said in his best, most-serious tone. "The sea needs the minerals locked up in this rock. If the fungus I was working with hadn't evolved so it could dissolve them, it would have become extinct too." Yawri stared down the hill toward the rocky crevices. It would be easy to overlook the fine fungi if you weren't fascinated by cracks in mineral-rich rock. "They'll evolve now, but I'm glad I wasn't interrupted."

Tisbero grew taller and boomed, "I would have watched from here and made sure you weren't! Why didn't you tell me? A little planning would have reduced risk of extinction!"

"True. It worked, though. The fungi is evolving." Tisbero's light body pulsed while Yawri continued. "Keeping track of Zinn's adventures plus your own is more than anyone else does. I have trouble tracking my own. By the way, how is your work with the volcano? Zinn said you were working with the magma chamber so it could expand slowly rather than explode."

Tisbero's pulsing light body stilled strangely, then returned to its steady rhythm. "Zinn told you? I'm helping it grow slowly so it can add land next to the sea." After a reflective pause, he added, "That is its wish, but many volcanoes explode. It's not easy to have a gradual flow when you're working with highly pressurized molten rock."

Yawri wanted to ask more, but noticing Tisbero's hesitant response, thought he'd wait. After all, he reasoned, Tisbero was here to assure Zinn's work with the animals wasn't disturbed, and Tisbero took his commitments very seriously.

Yawri preferred a more philosophical approach. He remained passionately committed to the purpose of the sending forth but decided commitments worked best when flexible. Long ago, his devotion had been to work with time tunnels. However, the tunnels made travel so easy, beings who weren't prepared to use them got lost.

Best to dabble rather than stay in one place too long.

His response held a humorous lilt. "You are kind of like a mountain, Tisbero, so I'll leave the mountains to you. Though the six-sided basalt columns from volcanoes are one of my favorite life forms."

Tisbero's blocky light body rippled with a steady, light-orange tint. "There is nothing better than a family of columnar basalt. They are both solid and fluid." His eyes swept the sky and finally settled on the animals around Zinn.

Yawri cast a glance toward the new iron-eating fungi and felt its vitality increasing with its evolutionary choice. He heard no other life forms calling him here.

Where should I go next?

A thought came and he shared it with Tisbero. "There is a limestone valley to the north. When I visited it last, it must be over ten years ago now, it told me Earth is making an opening to some deep crystals. Today is a good day to visit it. Give my best to Zinn!"

Tisbero spared a glance. "Ten years? You waited ten years?"

"I wasn't waiting. Every moment's been full."

Tisbero offered a parting wish. "Take care! Expand All with all you become."

Yawri enjoined, "Create with Creator!"

He accelerated toward the ridge, excited about what he might find. However, he was interrupted by the sound of the shovel-tusked animals trumpeting repeatedly and loudly, so he slowed to see what caused it.

"Ye-es!" Zinn soared into the sky far above the herd, bouncing jubilantly. "They received the thought form well! They chose to change!"

Yawri saw Tisbero scanning land and sky, double checking for any other cause that might lie behind the herd's outburst. Though he knew Tisbero couldn't hear him, Yawri laughed, "That's the zest of Zinn!"

Yawri soared over the ridge in search of the distant valley, his glowing light body rippling with joy.

I wonder what's there now.

6. LICHEN VALLEY

∞

Keela didn't avoid other guardians, however, working alone meant fewer distractions. The expansive rings of the gas giant were complicated, and time for uninterrupted focus was essential for understanding them. Surprisingly, the passing violet-blue orb had been right about the interaction of the planet's magnetic field and the spoke-lobes ... and the idea about the rings helping to extend the range of the solar system's broadcast had also proven correct. However, given enough fleeting thoughts—and that being appeared to have a lot of them—some are bound to be right. In spite of the tantalizing harmonies from the third planet, which promised complex vegetation, Keela stayed and determined that the rings did, in fact, serve to amplify the solar system's communication with the universe.

This world has different aspects of one thing–lobes and orbiting particles making a ring, in this case–connecting to form the whole. Every planet I've studied uses different aspects of a whole to expand in Life.

She focused on the sparkling planet in the third orbit out from the sun.

That world has so many colors and sounds, I wonder if it uses different aspects of the same life form to create.

Curious, she sped past the other gas giant, the asteroid belt, and the red planet to find out. She found an isolated valley of delicate moss and enjoyed her study of it in private. Within an hour of arriving she'd found her answer.

Same as the other worlds I've studied, this one connects different aspects, female and male of the same plant, to expand Life too.

Keela was most interested in the female aspect of plants because it specialized co-creation within itself, then released it to the world. It's how it created seeds. The male aspect specialized in co-creation outside and then felt the result within. Both were integrated into the same whole. However, on this planet she decided to learn about the female aspect first.

To better work with plants in the long, narrow crevices of this area, Keela manifested a tall, evenly proportioned form. Her long fingers with their exceptionally refined movement were well attuned to the subtle tones of small plants.

Vitality flowed through her radiant structure as she floated near a ledge of large-grained granite and examined a clump of blue-green moss growing in a moist crevice. Fertile soil overflowed from what was once barren rock onto a ledge below.

This moss easily holds twenty times its weight in water. Without it here, rainwater would quickly run back into the sea.

She listened to the soft cadence of water dripping from one clump of moss onto another. She gently communicated, "I come in response to the song on the wind. It told of a need here. I offer you my greeting."

The moss's response came through a sensation of knowing rather than in words, but its meaning was clear. "Earth calls us to evolve, but to do so we need to join with our distant counterpart."

Keela peered closer. The moss in the crevice had tiny, flask-shaped structures nestled among even smaller leaves; each flask had an open neck. Recognizing this female aspect of the moss, she asked, "You wish help with connection?"

The moss affirmed, "We are too isolated to develop in the way Earth requests. The counterpart requested is distant. Can you bring what is needed to us?"

"I am happy to serve your need." Keela shifted her perspective to inside the vessels, then gently increased the flow of ethereal sound and light and offered it to the tiny vessels. The vessels responded, nurtured by this gentle bathing in the nectar of All-that-is.

The moss intoned, "We are prepared to receive living essence from our distant counterparts. Please bring it to us now." Within their communication was an image of a similar moss growing in a distant valley. Fortunately, what the moss considered distant was not far for Keela.

Her light body rose into the air and sailed toward the place. After she passed over a dry ridge of windswept rock and descended along its far side, clumps of lichen began to appear. The clumps joined with moss and soon became a carpet of emerald green spotted with brilliant drops of pale blue and orange.

She looked toward the next ridge but something caught her eye below. The carpet of green in this area was peppered with circles of barren rock.

What could cause those?

The scene receded behind her, and she saw encouraging movement. Other beings, their light bodies shining with an unfamiliar silver color she'd never seen before, were tending the valley.

Good. They're healing it.

Relieved, she refocused on her task.

Almost there.

Keela moved quickly over the next ridge and began her descent to find the counterpart. She came to a stop where the call was most active and hovered above a dense but dryer moss than that in the crevice. Following the tones to their source, she found a moss with minuscule leaves interspersed with tiny, golden stars. The tip of each stalk held a rosette of thin, long leaves spiraling down a stout stem.

Keela communicated with the universal language that resonates with All. "To honor Earth's purpose, the moss in a distant valley seeks to evolve. Its female aspect asked me to deliver your fertilizing essence to it, so moss can thrive in the changing world."

"We heard the request in the air and are prepared. Our purpose is the same. We expand Life. Please take our fertilizing waters to our counterpart so we can evolve with Earth."

Now that she was here, Keela wasn't sure how to transport fertilizing waters.

"How can I help?"

The small cups at the base of the tiny crown-shaped heads moved in the light and Keela saw they were filled with water. The moss continued, "We direct our fertilizing vitality into these cups. They are both ethereal and physical. We will increase their etheric nature so you can carry them to our female counterpart."

Although Keela was an etheric being, she'd been learning how to blend with physical dimensions for eons. With guidance from the moss and its bond with Earth, she was able to gather hundreds of the tiny, potent bowl structures in her hand.

"They feel charged with electricity," she said, rising.

"Deliver it in haste," was the reply. "The charge you feel will extend the Life you carry, but it will die if it does not join with the female's vessel soon."

With a respectful nod, she turned toward the ridge and accelerated toward it. Vegetation passed below her in a blur. She glanced down at her hand to make sure the charged forms were safe. Reassured, she looked down at the carpeted valley and caught sight of the area with the strange pockmarks, and wished she could stop to help.

At least those guardians are healing whatever caused those holes.

As she continued to soar, the sight of the valley below shocked her so much she dipped and banked sharply, almost spilling her charge.

The land looks more damaged now than during my first pass over it.

She looked down again, but her speed had already taken her beyond the scarred ground.

It must have been a difference in light. Guardians are there.

A sudden downdraft reminded her of the need for a steady flight. The ridge of the next valley rose steeply and passed under her.

I'll come back and help after I've delivered this.

Keela descended to the granite ledge and raised the minuscule cups of fertilizing waters above the female moss. The moss instantly released a sweet-smelling scent. The effect was immediate. The cups she carried released a fine spray of fertilizing fluid into the air. The mist followed the trail of electrified scent back to the female moss with a palpable force of attraction.

Keela wasn't prepared for the dramatic change in vibration. Rather than two musical chords blending to make a harmonic third, the union of these two made more varieties than she could count.

"We will thrive!" The broadcast emanated from the moss in the crevice. "We are a new One!"

Keela rose slowly above the bountiful crevice, miniature and immense at the same moment. Beads of water hung from the tip of every leaf. Sunbeams played with each droplet, shifting the light while it moved through them in celebration. Each bead returned the sunbeam to the world in a tiny, sparkling rainbow of reds, yellows, greens and blues.

"Thank you for helping us join," chimed the moss through the air. "We evolve."

Keela rose farther into the air, her work here complete.

This is why I came to this world. The more diverse the planet, the more I learn about physicality, and the more I can help.

She continued to soar above this celebration of completion. However, her expression soon changed from one of contentment to one of concern.

The pockmarked valley. Now I can study what happened, and help the other guardians heal it.

With a last glance at the rich, green crevice, she soared toward the peculiar place. A magnificent bird with a wingspan stretching wider than she was tall glided high over the ridgeline. Using it as a signpost, Keela banked sharply around treetops and jutting beds of red rock, intent on getting there quickly. With the bird far above her, she crested the ridge and flew toward the damaged valley.

As she rapidly descended, she noticed the discordant vibration. Instead of harmonic tones blending songs of others within All, these wailed—the agony of confusion echoed through disharmonic cries. The closer she came more holes appeared. Large spots of lichen, along with its underlying red sandstone, were missing.

What have they done? There are more holes now than the first time I flew over it!

She looked for the guardians she had seen earlier but saw none. Keela, normally calm, flared. No reason, no justification seemed possible for leaving this wounded land with scars of broken, red rock piercing a verdant sea.

Something moved near the edge of the pitted landscape. She focused on it. There … A light body skulked low and slow. Unlike the others she had seen, which had been variations of silver, this one had color, but it didn't matter. At least one of them remained.

The target was crouched over an unusually large section of missing Life. Concerned that this entity could also leave at any time, Keela launched toward it with the speed of a comet and circled around to approach it from behind.

This one will explain why it's worse, not better!

She came upon the light body at the same moment it straightened up. "Hold!" she exploded, hovering in front of it to block its path of escape. The form flared with rapid streaks of electric blue. "What are you doing here?" she demanded.

The culprit responded with equal intensity. "What are you doing here?" the light body, a male aspect from its energy, exclaimed in return.

"Why is this valley in more pain now than it was earlier? It's harmed, not healed!" she retorted while his flaring form neared.

A white-hot surge in his light body took the place of electric blue. "Harmed? By me? There is no way you're going to stop me from doing what needs to be done here!" The surge of white-hot light might have hidden his descent into the ground from others, but not from Keela.

"You may still be able to swim through earth, but so can I!" She surveyed the ground for an indication of his direction. Strangely, holes in the red rock began to fill with liquid sandstone, like water from a spring. "Are you trying to hide the wounds you and your friends caused?" She threw the words at him and drove in pursuit.

She moved down, into, and through the rock and noticed the disharmonic tones were softening. The pulse of primal vitality from the offending guardian wasn't fighting against the disharmony, he was embracing it.

Fine. Trying to disguise the harm by connecting it to All won't heal the lichen and stone that was taken. It's gone, but I'll blend with your energy to aid my healing effort of what remains.

Magnifying Earth's healing intent, she opened herself to Creation's essence and felt a river of Life flow from the core of the planet, through her body of light, and out. Though still intent on pursuing the fugitive, she brought in more ethereal nature from her own source and the band of disharmony continued to diminish.

He's circling. Why would he be circling?

She doubled her speed. The circles he traced were spiraling inward, each rotation smaller than the last, but she was gaining on him. She re-doubled her connection with All. A massive current of balancing Earth energy flowed through the ground she passed. Her focus on healing was so complete she didn't realize they'd reached the center of their spiral until it was too late. He was upon her. Before his radiating hands could clasp her from behind, she spun to face him. Unable to grab their darting opposite, they both twisted and rose above the ground in a whirling blur.

His dark eyes were open portals into star-filled space. She locked on to them, searching for the disharmony he'd brought. However, the deeper she probed, the more she felt connected to the All.

Rather than look away from her penetrating look, he was looking deeper into her eyes.

The circle spun faster and tightened, but she didn't look away.

"We can probably stop now," he said in a mischievous tone. Uncertain about what to do now that she'd caught him, Keela decided to slow the spin but keep holding his gaze. He did the same and they came to a stop, standing locked in each other's tight stare.

"Thank you," he said. "Healing this valley would have been much harder without your help."

Keela surged with flashes of her own. "The harm you do is yours!" she said, recalling why she chased him.

"Harm, by me?" He was offended. "I thought it was you who didn't want to heal the harm until I felt your energy supporting me."

Keela's light body flared. "Oh yes. I support healing, but not you! What aspect of Creator did you use to make all of these holes in Life?"

He raised both hands in question. "What holes?"

She'd had enough. "Those holes!" she burst out and broke the riveted gaze, ending his excuse to avoid seeing the harm he'd done. "Look around this valley! Both lichen and the rock they grew on are gone!"

She pivoted to take in the scene surrounding them, but what she saw made no sense. The pockmarks were gone. Every pit had been refilled and moss and lichen had grown back to cover it. She kept turning to find the destruction, but it was gone.

"I'm good at working with minerals," he said with disarming lightheartedness. "Minerals are all made of their own kind of crystals. I enjoy working with crystals."

She kept looking for the damage while the crazed entity continued his speech. "You were interfering with the healing needed to be done here, so I chose to work from within the ground rather than from above it. Few swim through rock anymore, so I was surprised when you followed me."

He waited for her land-scanning gaze to return to him. "I was astonished when the energy you brought was actually helping me! From the way you pounced, who would have guessed?"

Confusion and conviction tumbled out of Keela. "But the missing lichen and stone! If you caused these holes, you should have some in you to experience how it feels."

"You made that message very clear." His reply was light and cheerful. "But given you were so well connected to the All and were so intent on following me, I thought circling in a spiral was the best way to help the land." He looked at the emerald green and finished, "I think it worked."

The living tapestry of moss and lichen sang across dimensions again. Keela felt both pleased and annoyed. "Who are you?" she asked, but it came out an indictment rather than a question. Noticing her confrontational tone, she quickly added, "I'm Keela. I work with plants."

"Keela? You're Keela?"

"Yes. I resonate with the sound of Keela. I'm asking, do you have a sound with which you resonate?"

"Keela!" He sang with the same annoying, cheery air. He even bobbed slightly.

Fully facing him, she responded coolly. "Only one thing matters. What caused the holes?"

Yawri stilled himself for a moment. The rhythmic tones now coming from the ground made his light body brighten, so he bobbed some more. "You don't remember me, do you?"

"I remember every detail of my existence since my beginning. I've never met you."

"In a light body. You've never met me in a light body, only an orb."

Keela stilled and focused so intently on this odd entity she seemed anchored in place. "Yawri? You're Yawri, the traveler I met on that large planet's great ring," she now remembered.

"You do have a good memory! It was a brief visit a very long time ago. I'd never have remembered your name."

"I remember everything," she stated flatly. "You don't?"

He looked at her, his eyes still portals to the universe, seeing energies far beyond the narrow band of physical light. Perplexed at her behavior, he asked, "Why did you try and stop me? When you did, it made me think you did not want this land healed. "

This was one of the reasons Keela preferred working alone. It was so easy to misinterpret the meaning of something new.

I assumed he was hurting rather than helping because I didn't study the situation first.

"I flew over this area on my way to work with another valley and saw ethereal beings healing small eruptions in the land. Patches of missing lichen. When I returned to help them, all I found were more holes, missing stone as well, and you. I was so shocked I jumped to a conclusion that I shouldn't have. I apologize."

Yawri was looking across the landscape from valley to ridgeline. He thought he saw a glint of silver, but Keela's apology drew his attention back to her.

"Neither one of us have anything to apologize for. We were the only ones here and each thought the other didn't want this land healed. Even though we didn't understand what caused the harm, we did heal it. That's what matters."

Keela was quiet a long moment. "I'm still going to find out what caused it."

"Of course. Totally agree with you." He regarded her thoughtfully. "You think others made the holes intentionally?"

"I don't know," she said, frustrated. "I didn't take time to study it. I reacted."

Yawri surveyed the sky and replied, "Reactions happen."

"Not from me. Not like that."

Yawri continued, undaunted. "The land is singing again, so now we can consider what might have caused it. You said there were several guardians here you thought were trying to heal it. What if you were right?"

Keela pulled back, surprised by the question. "Right? How could I be right? The valley was wailing."

"Maybe they were trying to heal it and didn't know how. Have you ever met an ethereal being trying to intentionally harm Creation?"

"No. Of course not."

"Yet, we each assumed the other would. We each assumed the absurd. Many new entities have come to the planet. If they came upon this place and didn't know how to heal it, they could have tried and made it worse. Maybe they went to get help."

They were both silent, recalling all they experienced about the event. The land now sang with so much vitality no one would ever know what happened here.

Keela carefully weighed her words. "They did look similar to each other. I've never seen dense, silver light bodies before. Their lack of diversity could mean they were young, which could explain why they left."

"We're all learning how to expand All. When first I arrived, I wouldn't have known how to heal this either."

Keela looked down at the thriving moss and lichen. "True, but what could have caused the harm in the first place? This is new, and I need to understand its cause." A soft breeze tickled the tiny leaves of the moss. Their movement reminded her of the female and male moss aspects she'd helped connect earlier, and the memory uplifted her.

Yawri was enthused. "Sometimes floods can erode land like that. I have a friend I could ask. He's very connected to communication across Earth, and always has insights." With a mischievous undertone, he added, "You'll enjoy him."

To her it seemed like Yawri was taking the situation rather casually. "Why would I enjoy him?" she prodded.

"You enjoy plants. He's a tree."

"A tree? Your friends a tree?"

Yawri cast a glance toward the head of the broad canyon. A majestic bird circled above. It marked his path to the tree and would serve as an excellent signpost.

"Coming?" he asked with a playful air. "Don't you like adventure?" He floated up and started to turn, ready to depart.

"I like trees," she clarified and rose to join him.

After a last, glancing review of the renewed emerald valley, their multicolored forms accelerated toward the head of the broad canyon.

Neither saw the two dusky-silver light bodies rise above the ridge behind them. One remained where it was, watching silently. The other one followed.

7. DISHARMONY

∞

Although Yawri's light body could still pass through matter freely, he enjoyed speeding around trees and skimming canyon walls. He didn't know why, but the challenge of going around things rather than though always calmed him.

He thought Keela would enjoy it too. After all, she was the one who kept increasing her speed while they circled to heal the lichen valley. Her satisfaction when she thought she was gaining on him was palpable, even though he'd only slowed to make sure their healing energies remained together. If she really wanted to meet Murann, she'd come.

Keela was a short distance behind him. From her point of view, his whirling, dodging flight was senseless. He was fast, but by merely passing through the obstacles he was so determined to go around, she had no problem keeping up.

They soared up one valley, down the next, and up again. Mosses and lichens gave way to leafy plants, brush, and small trees. Crashing waves bathed black volcanic rock in white froth as they flew over a broad bay.

"Not far now," Yawri called back. He took a sharp turn inland and brightened at the sight of some of the tallest trees on the planet. Their rough, dark-red trunks were as broad as a mammoth was long. Keela followed Yawri up a ravine of ferns and trees where he finally stopped.

"You kept up!" he said, surprised to see her right behind him.

"Where else would I be?"

He is strange.

They descended slowly and hovered above dark, moist soil. A group of spectacular dragonflies sprang into the air and fluttered around them. Their scarlet-and-blue wings danced on a background of green.

The loamy aroma of the soil combined with the thick smell of foliage relaxed Keela. Plants always gave her peace.

"I'm used to plants covering the ground, not the sky," Keela whispered.

"You brought a friend!" came a greeting.

Still soothed by the beauty of the forest, Keela remained steady and looked for the speaker. Yawri responded with lighthearted banter. "It's good to see you, too, Murann. Keela, this is Murann. Murann, Keela." To Keela he said, "Murann's been standing in the same spot for thousands of years. I don't know how he does it."

Murann returned the banter. "When you want to learn patience, I'll teach you."

"Thank you, Murann, but I don't think I'm suited to stay in one spot for long."

Murann replied easily. "This tree body may have been in the same place for six thousand years, but the Earth spirit of this tree and I are ethereal, like you. I come and go as I please."

"I'm still not interested." Yawri was resolute. "Six thousand years is a long time to be joined with one physical form."

"Yes, but perhaps you are fixed in ways I am not," Murann added lightly. Then said, "Hello Keela. Yawri and I met long ago when we first came to this planet. He was arguing with manatee thought forms at the time."

"We weren't arguing," Yawri declared. "We were getting to know each other."

Keela stood motionless, disquieted by the overly familiar way these two communicated with each other.

This is why it's better to work alone.

Murann's branches swayed and sunlight played across the ferns and dancing dragonflies. Sensing her disquiet, he said, "Yawri and I have been friends for a very long time. We prod each other occasionally because we both can get too comfortable in our ways. We enjoy each other."

"I'm sure," she said hesitantly.

Yawri's light body shone with a lively radiance. "You heard Murann, Keela. He values my prodding. It took eons to learn how to get through his thick bark, but I was determined to help him. He joined with the red trees when they first came to the planet and has been one with them ever since."

Full of questions, Keela placed her radiant hand on the rough, red bark, and wondered, "What is it like staying in the same grove so long? You would get to know the trees around you very well, but six thousand years does seem like a long time."

Murann's branches moved and light twinkled across the ferns. "Trees communicate over great distances. I know trees all over the planet."

Keela watched the light dance, intrigued. "How can that be?"

"I'll show you if you'd like."

Murann emerged from the tree as the same golden, ethereal orb Yawri met long ago and floated in front of their light bodies.

Keela studied the tree, then Murann's radiant orb. "You really are an ethereal being in a tree body."

Yawri said from beside her, "I once saw a crystal being come out of its body the same way. It still seems bizarre, though."

"Come with me," Murann instructed. "We'll start in the roots." The golden orb descended into the ground. Yawri and Keela followed Murann down and saw tiny, white root hairs entwined with gossamer tubes of delicate fungi.

Yawri exclaimed, "There is so much Life in this tiny space!" Sparks flashed between the root hairs and fungi tubes. The sparks continued to roll in an electric wave off into the distance. Almost instantly, a wave of sparking current returned.

Keela couldn't get close enough to the entwined cells. "The roots and fungi send a signal and get a response!"

Murann moved to a particularly active node of roots and fungi. "The fungus body lives under the forest. A communication has arrived from trees far up the valley. They're curious about your presence here, Keela. They know Yawri."

"They know I'm here?" Keela questioned, wondering what else was being broadcast about her.

"Not only this forest knows you're here, but soon forests separated by the ridges will know, too."

Yawri came closer. "Beyond the tree line is bare rock. How does it work? I understand how you can communicate using physical roots and fungi, but there are no trees on the ridge."

"The wind is physical."

"Well, of course, the wind is physical," Yawri countered. "But unless I've missed something, trees don't fly in it."

Keela glowed with curiosity. "I've seen birds deliver messages over great distances. They fly, but how can forests communicate beyond their boundaries?"

Murann's golden orb rippled with light before settling into a constant glow. "Want me to show you? I asked my tree body if I could bring you both inside of it with me. It agreed."

"Inside your tree body?" Yawri questioned. "For how long?"

Keela said, "Fascinating. I want to learn about this."

Yawri added, "I've never been inside a tree body before."

"Keep your ethereal presence in balance with its Earth spirit and you'll be fine. Follow me." Murann's golden light pulsed soft blue.

Keela rose through the roots with Murann, and Yawri followed behind them. They floated up through the tree and saw how the flow of life moved back and forth between the roots and the rest of the tree.

When they came to tree needles on its upper branches, Murann spoke. "Here is how we communicate beyond our valley. The needles and branches send and receive messages through the wind. The wind carries them all over the Earth."

Keela looked even closer. "How does that happen?"

Yawri observed, "Some branches are moving without the wind."

Murann replied, "Focus your sense on the air around the tree. You'll notice subtle vibrations, scents, and even faint images. The tree releases these to the wind at the same time the needles breathe in new messages."

Yawri wanted to make sure he understood. "Let me get this right. You're *rooted* in place here, but you talk to trees *everywhere* on the globe?"

"Yes."

Yawri couldn't believe it. "I've been on Earth for eons and had no idea trees could do this. Why have you not told me about it before?"

"You never asked."

While Yawri considered this, Keela wondered, "Murann, trees would do this with or without ethereal-beings in them, right? Why join with one?"

"Because my ethereal presence touches the Earth in a different way. Together we add Life and dimensions not possible by either of us alone. It teaches me how to blend my ethereal state with the planet's ethereal *and* physical energies. As an ethereal being, learning physicality that way is a gift beyond measure. Perhaps you see why I wanted to join with a tree, Yawri?"

"I'm getting the idea," he replied.

Murann contemplated his two guests. "Do you wish to watch an ethereal being join with the Earth spirit of a tree, and become a tree being like me?

Keela's response was instant. "Yes."

"Join with a tree?" Yawri replied in question. "Sure. Watching would be good."

Murann's golden orb began to move out of the tree body. Yawri asked, "What about your tree body? Can you just leave it?"

Murann continued moving away. "I'm an ethereal soul. There are many levels in a joining. The tree's Earth spirit and I are partners, not prisoners of each other. I've gained, not lost, the ability to live in multiple dimensions."

The trio sailed over the tops of immense red trees and over grassland dotted with spiral-horned, grazing animals. After crossing the grassland and a winding river, more trees appeared again. They followed a gentle bend until they came to a clear tributary. "Almost there."

Murann left the river and flew through the forest. He finally stopped above a young tree in an encircling grove. A pale-blue light body stood next to it. Murann slowly descended until he hovered near it and said, "Greetings, Howland. The wind carried news of your joining today. I'm glad you and this tree spirit have decided to join. "

Howland's light body glowed brighter blue. "Murann, glad you came. The tree spirit and I have been friends for a few hundred years now. We feel we are ready for a joining."

"This forest throbs with Life, and your union will bring even more." Murann's orb radiated a warm, golden glow. "I came in response to your invitation, but thought you might be interested in meeting these two visitors, Yawri and Keela. They have never seen a joining. If it is fitting, they wish to witness yours."

"They are welcome." Turning to Yawri and Keela, Howland said, "News of your visit with Murann preceded you."

A sudden stillness infused the forest. Every tree appeared to be listening. Yawri began to respond, but before he did, Howland asked, "Are you planning to blend with a tree spirit? Do you come to witness how we join with a tree body as a step toward learning how to do it yourselves?"

Yawri responded quickly. "I have a lot to learn before I even consider joining with a physical form. I do help crystal minerals strengthen their connection to All, though, and have met ethereal beings joined with crystal bodies."

"The planet is expanding into more physical and ethereal dimensions, and as the planet becomes stronger in physicality, it will be much harder for etheric beings to co-create with it. Do you know what you will do then? Will you leave?"

Yawri never heard of such a problem. "I'm still learning how to best help physicality without joining with a physical form. It's the best preparation I can make for any future right now."

Howland's light body glowed more intensely. "I understand. It's an infinite universe and there is so much to learn."

Keela moved closer. "I wish to witness how a joining happens. I've worked with a lot of plants but the topic of joining has never come up."

"I'm not surprised. It takes a large physical body to maintain balance with the ethereal dimensions we bring. Most plants are small." Howland hovered next to the tree and pulsed with a soft, translucent blue. "The Earth's tree spirit and I have asked questions of each other for many years. We each had a lot to learn, and this joining is the next step in our learning." A shaft of sunlight fell on the tree and its branches swayed in its living current. "We take that step now."

The three witnesses stepped back to the edge of the grove.

Howland spoke to the Earth spirit of the tree. "We have shared many questions and discovered answers. I ask to join with you so we can aid our expansion with All."

The branches of the tree waved in a slow undulation and the tree spirit responded. "I am soul of Earth and this, my tree body, is of Earth. You know to join with me is to join with Earth's soul and body. I invite you to join with us."

Howland spoke again. "You are a tree spirit with the strength to keep the etheric realms I bring balanced. I accept your invitation and honor it."

The tree's Earth spirit was silent for a long moment. "With our joining, All will be more. We are prepared. It is time."

Howland glanced at Murann and gave a subtle nod. Howland's glowing light body descended slowly into the ground. Murann ushered Yawri and Keela into the ground too so they could observe the joining.

Howland extended his luminescent fingers, which moved tenderly along the roots of the tree. In response, delicate filaments of root tendrils pulsed with a soft, orange light.

Howland's blue light body rippled with the same orange light. He sang softly.

The tree counseled, "Bring your song into mine so we can align our harmonies."

Their songs joined to form a third sound, and multiple harmonies chimed. The roots and branches of the tree started to radiate a wondrous green light and the tree spoke. "As you described, the ethereal oceans are indeed immeasurably vast."

Howland beamed, "We share soul sight and sound, and both become more. Each strand of physical life, each atom, is filled with sensation and texture rich beyond measure."

Murann indicated Yawri and Keela should follow him back to the surface. "They are joined now. Where there were two, now there are three."

Yawri and Keela stood wordless, the sanctity of what they witnessed profound. The trio moved further back into the trees, surrounded by the chorus of the forest and the soothing tones of the distant, grazing herd.

Murann asked, "Was it different from what you expected?"

"I didn't know enough to know what to expect," Yawri stated. "Amazing. It was amazing."

"Thank you." Keela's light body thrummed with an amber glow.

Their profound peace flowed seamlessly with the music of the forest, blending with the comforting chords of the grazing beasts.

After several minutes Murann said, "It is time for me to return to my tree. Then, I'll be able to—" Murann was interrupted by sharp, bleating cries from the grazing beasts, quickly followed by panicked hooves thundering across the land.

"How odd!" Murann exclaimed. "I've never heard grazing animals panic like this." The bleating continued and birds and dragonflies rose fluttering into the air. "Something is not right. I'll go into the ground and ask the fungus if it has received any messages from trees near the herd."

Yawri and Keela watched Murann's golden orb descend into the ground, wondering if there could be a message such a short time after the event. They didn't have to wait long. Murann returned perplexed. "Some guardians were tending the animals. We don't know why, but they left very quickly with some newborn wildebeests. It panicked the herd."

"Took newborns? Why?" Yawri was aghast.

Murann's orb pulsed rapidly. "I don't know. It's the only time I've ever heard of such a disturbance. We increase harmony, not discord."

"Discord," Yawri repeated, recalling the reason they came. "We saw another disturbance this morning. Lichen, moss, and even the rock they were attached to were missing. It's where I met Keela. We healed it, though. We came to ask if you'd heard of anything similar."

"When were you going to mention this?"

"It's why we came." Yawri added more quietly, "Okay. At the time learning how trees talk and join captured my attention."

Murann's golden orb undulated with bright yellow. "You say ethereal beings were tending the moss and lichen. Did you know them?"

Yawri looked at Keela. She was gazing down in thought. Yawri said, "Tell him what you told me, Keela."

Keela's form rippled with iridescent light. She spoke mindfully. "While on my way to tend some plant life, I flew over a valley and saw some ethereal beings, all with light bodies in a similar silver color, working there. It seemed they were healing several bare patches where lichen couldn't grow.

When I returned from my errand, they were gone and there were more barren spots, not fewer. After going down to investigate, I found the sandstone missing as well as the lichen. I was shocked to find the damage had gotten worse while the beings were there." She paused, thinking about her next words. The silence stretched as she considered how to explain her confusing interaction with Yawri.

Yawri took up the story easily. "That's when she saw me. I hadn't seen anyone else there, only the damage. However, she thought I was one those that had left it that way. She came after me with the force of a saber-toothed cat after a gazelle."

"Understandable."

"Really? Do I look silver to you? Before she pounced, I went down into the rock to heal it. She followed me. We ended up healing the land. She is amazing with plants. Then we came here."

Murann asked calmly, "Did you recognize any of them, Keela?"

She replied genially. "No, they were new to me. They were radiant, but not with colors I'd seen before. They all had similar hues of silver."

"Silver." Murann's golden orb stirred. "The trees reported the light bodies that took the wildebeests had similar hues of sparkling gray."

All were quiet, and the sounds of the forest were back to normal. "I wonder if the same ones were at both sites." Murann started moving away. "I'll return to my tree body and ask if other forests have heard of anything similar. We must learn if these are isolated events or something more."

Keela volunteered, "I can ask the lichen I work with, but their range is quite limited. They're near where I met Yawri."

Yawri said, "I'll go to a deep crystal cave and ask the crystal beings there if they have heard of anything unusual." He remembered something. "I'm supposed to meet with two guardians, Zinn and Tisbero." He looked at Keela. "The meeting place is on the way to where we met, but in the opposite direction of the crystal caves. Would you mind stopping by to let them know about these two events? They travel a lot and may have heard of more."

Keela shifted back and forth. "I don't know them. I was on my way to work with the lichen."

"Yes, lichen is essential. Will it be harmed if you don't go to it now? Zinn works with large animals, and Tisbero works with mountains and volcanoes. He really enjoys the life force of volcanoes."

Keela hesitated, evaluating her options.

Yawri continued, "Zinn and Tisbero are like Murann, except more fun, and you enjoyed him, right?"

Murann said, "Other trees think I'm fun."

Keela turned to Yawri. "I don't see how I could enjoy them as much as I have enjoyed meeting Murann."

Yawri bobbed slightly. "Tisbero studies large planetary structures, like the rings of the gas giant where you and I first met. Zinn enjoys ... well, Zinn enjoys everything, but especially large animals. She would know if they have reported any events. Will the lichen be harmed if your work with it is delayed?"

"The more things I do, the less time I have to focus on what I'm studying."

"True, but we found out these two events might be related to the same beings." Yawri continued without pause. "Maybe Zinn or Tisbero have heard if these silver beings are new arrivals. If they are, maybe they're looking for guidance."

Keela was quiet so long Yawri started to wonder if she'd heard. He was about to ask when her light body pulsed in a stable rhythm.

"Yes," she agreed. "I'll go meet your friends. But I'm going back to my work with the lichen immediately after."

"Great! Thanks, Keela. I'm happy we met again!"

Yawri gave her directions to the meeting spot and turned toward the golden orb. "Thanks for being you, Murann!" To them both he said, "If any of us learn anything more, let's let ourselves know."

Yawri moved in the opposite direction from which they came, and darted around a vertical wall of rock at high speed. Keela moved carefully through the trees on her way to meet with Zinn and Tisbero.

Murann gazed down at the young tree now joined with Howland. It glowed even brighter than before, and the forest sang. With a parting nod, he accelerated toward his home tree, eager to send his questions on the wind.

8. THE AHJA

∞

Keela flew above a winding river, the trees along its banks tall and dense. She thought about stopping to examine them but dismissed the thought immediately.

I agreed to meet with Yawri's friends. It shouldn't take long to let them know about the two events and ask if they've heard of anything similar.

True to Yawri's description, the river rose into the hills and narrowed to a frothing stream. Tree branches soon arched over it, and she followed the stream until it reached a ridge.

Yawri said to follow this and pass five enormous limestone pillars, then stop at a high cliff. Zinn and Tisbero will be on a promontory where two rivers meet below it.

She soared along the ridge toward the first of the five pillars. Always on the watch for unusual plants, she saw something moving fast near the rock face far below. A bird. Its feathers were multiple shades of blue, and a broad splash of orange flowed down its back.

Focusing on her flight again, she wove around the first pillar in mindful grace.

Only four more to the cliff.

A high-pitched shriek echoed off hard rock. A creature with a wingspan far wider than Keela was tall suddenly rose next to her. Its penetrating eye drew her focus away from its massive, hooked beak. An unblinking, bottomless, dark pool ringed with fiery orange stared at her. She slowed, but the soaring beast adjusted its position to keep her between its sharp beak and the red wall of stone.

She accelerated, rose and fell, but the bird of prey mirrored her every move. She did not have fear, only curiosity.

Even if there was danger, I could move through the stone. It cannot.

Soaring closer to the bird's eye, she asked respectfully, "Can I help you?"

The bird moved slightly away but its eye never left hers. "I recognize you from the emerald valley. What was the purpose of the work? Guardians removed lichen, moss and stone, and then you replenished it. What was the guardians' plan?"

Keela's light body dipped at the words but leveled again. "Plan? I don't know of a plan. I and another found the valley hurt, so helped it heal. You say the lichen, moss, and stone were taken? We reasoned that others may have come upon it as we did, didn't know how to heal it, and left to get help."

The bird sailed on invisible currents of air. "Your healing was not a part of the other guardians' plan?"

"We didn't know them and arrived after they left. However, guardians only help Life expand, never diminish it. The only explanation that makes sense is they didn't know how to heal it, so left to find guardians that did."

The bird flexed its talons again. "Except there were no holes in Life there before they came, only after."

Keela passed through the second pillar of limestone rather than sail around it. "You know this because you saw the valley before they came?"

The beak opened and closed with a snap. "The holes were only there after they left, not before."

Keela dipped down in flight and noticed the bird followed her movement. "Had you seen these guardians before?"

The feathered creature was brusque. "Not seen before. Light of color, more uniform than any I know. The emerald valley is a place of vital Life. Lichen is evolving from co-creation with algae and fungi. Guardians know this and come to nurture it often, so I was glad to see guardians there again.

"However, after they left and flew out to sea, I sensed disharmony. Flying down I discovered the missing Life. I am not a seabird so could not follow them, but saw you. Now I learn the healing you and your friend gave was not a part of their plan."

"I hear what you say, but can't imagine a guardian intentionally doing harm. Perhaps they are newly arrived and don't know how to work here."

The great bird's wingtips barely moved but its talons open and closed. "Yet, they knew how to take these things with them. Light bodies with such skill are not unknowing."

Keela nodded, remembering how difficult it had been to transport the fertilizing essence of moss. Compared to what they took, it was a minimal quantity of physical-ethereal matter. "It must be a part of some large plan to expand Life. It's the only thing that makes sense."

"I trusted the taking and healing of Life was a part of some guardian's plan too, but only you and your friend came to perform the healing. Not one of them. Did you know one of the silver ones followed you and your friend when you left?"

"Followed us? One of the guardians who took Life from the land followed us?"

"It's one of the reasons I thought you were together. They flew down from the ridge behind you but your speed was fast and agile. They did not catch up."

The bird and Keela dashed around the third granite pillar. Keela said, "You mentioned they went out to sea. The nearest continent to the west is across an ocean. If transplanting Life was their goal, it needs to be replanted within a few hours, not the days it would take to reach land across an ocean. It makes no sense to me."

"Nor to me."

Silence fell between them. Keela wasn't sure why it was important, but a question kept returning to her mind. "I know ethereal beings who joined with tree bodies, but may I ask, are you an ethereal being joined with a great bird body?"

"You may ask anything you wish. It is my choice how to respond." They flew around the fourth pillar. "Earth prepared these flying forms so ethereal beings could join with them. The Earth spirit of this form and I have co-created with many avian bodies before this one. It is a good form. We keep land animals in balance and even scavenge the dead to make sure their essence remains part of a living death. We deliver seeds, kernels of Life filled with ethereal and physical dimensions, across the lands. These bodies allow us to learn physicality as a part of the ethereal, and the learning is endless."

The fifth pillar was in sight. After it would be the cliff where Keela would descend to meet with Yawri's two friends. She said, "It's good to know you exist. Now that I do, there is another event I wish to tell you about."

The bird's eye targeted hers. "Another event?"

"I didn't see it myself, but I heard the cries of wildebeest. The tree being my friend and I were with said ethereal beings took some newborn wildebeests. I go now to meet with two others to learn if these were isolated events or if they know of more."

The bird swayed back and forth before speaking. "The only disharmony experienced in all my lifetimes is this one in the emerald valley. You tell of another with wildebeests. I don't know if this is related, but a fledgling of my kind is missing from its nest. After hearing about the taking of the newborn wildebeests, I am wondering if it might have been taken."

Keela flew closer. "Could it have flown away on its own?"

"Too young. It could not fly far and we would have heard it call out. There is no evidence of a struggle, so it wasn't a predator." The raptor being was quiet while a gusting thermal draft took them higher. "Guardians are well known to us and our young have no fear of light bodies. Considering these other reports, if we don't find it soon, we may have a larger problem than any of us have imagined."

The bird dipped down into the updraft and let the current propel it up again. "If you find the ones who caused disharmony to the emerald valley, or to the wildebeests, please let me know. I have questions for them." It flexed its talons once more, and its piercing eyes probed the valley for anything out of place.

"Of course. How shall I contact you?"

The considerable beak suddenly turned toward her face and opened wide. Before Keela could react, the beak closed on one of the orange feathers on its back and pulled it out. "This is for you. It's physical and ethereal, and in the continual flow of Life and death."

Keela carefully grasped the living feather, slowly brought it to her chest, and held it there. "Thank you," she managed to say, so touched by the gift she could not speak.

"Invite it to become One with you and it will. I resonate with the name of my kind, ahja. Call me through that name. If you speak to one of us, you speak to all."

After several heartbeats, the piercing eyes left hers and turned toward the horizon. The leviathan raptor tucked its wings, plunged down at speed, and shot upward before opening them again. After a spinning flash of orange in goodbye, the raptor being banked sharply and flew over the far side of the valley.

Keela watched until the ahja disappeared. When she looked down to study the feather against her chest, she saw her hand was empty. She quickly scanned from side to side to see where she dropped it. A warmth made her focus on her chest. The ethereal, physical feather was inside her, joining with her. It glowed a warm orange and pulsed in harmony with all the other colors of her light body.

She increased speed, passed the fifth pillar, and plunged down the cliff face toward the river junction below. For the first time in her existence, Keela was in a rush to talk to strangers.

9. LAZKET'S CAVE

∞

Yawri honed in on the reverberation coming from the immense quartz chamber he'd found when first arriving on the planet. Over eons, Earth had moved the crystal being Lazket's chamber closer to the surface, and its pulse was even more intense. Although it did not have an opening to the air yet, Yawri felt confident that if any unusual events had occurred, Lazket would know about them.

He chose to enter the cavern through his favorite tunnel. The long, twisted hydrothermal vent that once brought hot, mineral-rich elixir into the chamber was now filled with glowing, angular crystals. Yawri enjoyed testing his memory of the tunnel's constrictions and turns and seeing how fast he could go without touching any of its spiked walls.

His light body sped through the vent, out its end, and across Lazket's chamber so fast he continued into the rock above before coming to a stop.

I sped through that twisting vent without touching one crystal!

He descended to re-enter the chamber and savor its beauty. Fluorites still glowed with pale yellows and greens, some with a deep blue-violet. Huge, hexagonal columns of clear quartz absorbed and amplified their light. Rotating in a small circle, Yawri flew across the crystal forest with the same sense of wonder he felt the first time he'd entered it.

When the yellow, green, and violet hues from the fluorites changed to creamy-white light, he slowed to check his location. Seeing his destination, he accelerated quickly toward it.

He passed tall columns of hexagonal quartz sprouting from every angle, and the creamy light of fluorites radiated through them. Lazket's sound reached him long before the crystal being came into view. He followed the song until he arrived at its source: A massive quartz column extending horizontally from of the wall above the light of the fluorites underneath it.

Yawri paused to enjoy the misty cloud-like formations within the massive quartz body. Each long, wispy, white streamer was a living doorway to dimensions untold, and the white light that entered each one came out separated into a vivid rainbow from violets to reds.

"Hello, Lazket. There's something about the way you blend your ethereal essence with this crystal body that's obviously working. Your joining continues to expand Life."

Lazket spoke with modulated, yet full sound. "Welcome, Yawri. Your entrance was memorable as always. It's rare to see comets shoot through our chamber."

"It's the least I can do. Since you're One with the crystal, and it is One with Earth, and Earth is One with the universe, why not add a comet?"

"I see the comet made it through the tunnel without going through any of my companions."

"Faster each time," Yawri beamed.

"Stopping seems to be your challenge. Since you are completely ethereal, no harm can come from going through us. If you ever blend with physicality, it might be a harder landing."

"No risk of that. I'm perfectly content to remain ethereal and leave blending with physical dimensions to those who like working with denser energies."

"You know the planet's maturing. It will be interesting to see how content you remain while the planet continues to expand its physical and ethereal spectrum. Purely etheric energies won't be able to keep up." The rainbows of light within Lazket sharpened.

"I'm keeping up fine." Yawri moved the conversation toward the question he wanted to ask. "This chamber's much closer to the surface than it was. Do you know if this will be air-breathing someday? I remember you told me Earth's deep crystals connect to what's happening on its surface by connecting to the winds."

"And the crystals in deep Earth connect to crystals on other planets and even other solar systems. Yes, that's still the plan. The greater the connection between those on the surface and those in deep Earth, the farther the communication goes."

Yawri came closer. "When I came, the idea of connecting deeper with Earth to deepen connection to the universe seemed absurd. I'd only experienced it as an ethereal being."

Lazket's oscillating timbre blended with the cavern's song. "I can still travel ethereally, same as you. However, to incorporate that information in a physical body, it has to come through this crystal's connection with Earth.

Learning how to co-create with this planet's physical dimensions allows me to expand in Creation far beyond what I could do alone."

"That's what you said you wanted to learn when we first met, and you're doing it," Yawri said, delighted. "It would be great if this cavern became air-breathing someday. The tree beings are listening well, but having crystal beings on the surface would broaden communication to the mineral life forms. The wind carries news of many changes."

"There are always changes. What do you mean by 'many' changes?"

Yawri replied quickly. "The ethereal touch of every guardian I know expands Life. Land, sea, and air sing with increasing diversity and balance. Yet, I came across a disharmony. It was odd. Then again, everything new feels odd until I learn about it."

"What was odd?"

Yawri tried to come up with a factual, objective description but finally just let the words roll out. "While flying over a lichen and moss valley, I heard a disharmonic cry. The main discord came from small circles of missing lichen. When I investigated, I found even the pockets of stone they had been attached to were missing. Another being and I reconnected the area to All. By the time we left, the land sang again as before. Have you ever heard of cause for such a thing? The one who healed it with me said other guardians were there before us. It's the first time I've experienced anything like it."

The number of miniature rainbows within Lazket increased. "Other guardians were there before you? Was there evidence of a storm? Sometimes floods will wash away plants, particularly if they are in small depressions, but the impact on the entire area is obvious."

"The patches seemed methodically placed, but Keela and I wondered same."

"Keela is the one that healed the land with you?"

"Yes. First she thought I was doing harm, but we ended up healing the valley together."

"She thought you caused the harm?"

"She thought I was one of the guardians she'd seen when she first passed over the valley. I was the only one there when she returned."

"Did she see guardians take the plants and stone when she first sailed over them?"

"No. She saw the pockmarks from high above and thought that they were healing them. When she returned she saw the damage was even worse."

Lazket was silent a long moment. "Those of us here only know about guardians connecting harmonies, none that cause disharmony. However, we are not yet breathing air of the surface where such communications would be." The fluorite under Lazket blazed with white light. "So you don't know if the cupped stone was bare before they arrived or not?"

"No, I don't. What could cause it?"

"That is the question."

"Maybe I'm making something big out of something small, or something small out of something big."

Lazket was silent again, but finally said, "I have no knowledge of this disharmony, but I'll ask other caverns if they have ever heard of it." Lazket's hexagonal body quickened with bluish-white light. That light, in turn, pulsed across the chamber in other crystals and beyond to contact other subterranean caverns of Life in Earth.

Lazket said, "I have heard the red diamond you spoke with in deep Earth is coming to the surface. It would be good if you two could meet again."

Yawri welcomed the distraction. "I'd like that very much! How can I find it if it does? It's a big planet."

"The ethereal diamond Tilan gave you will help."

Yawri sensed the light-blue diamond that Tilan, the first ethereal being he met, had given him. It resonated with him, and the memory of diamonds moving through the carbon sea and flying through that blue planet's atmosphere remained vivid.

"How is Tilan?"

"He still appreciates your visit. Other beings were so focused on getting to Earth, virtually all passed his home by."

"I found it fascinating. I had to explore it. Tilan is doing well?"

"The diamond beings on the two outermost planets are well. Those planets traded places, you know. The one Tilan lives on used to be closer to the sun than the other, but they matured and decided to switch orbits."

Yawri stumbled on the thought. "Planets can switch places?"

"If they choose. It doesn't matter how big your body is, free will is free will. All the planets have changed their orbits since they were young, although only the outer two changed places. The nearest gas giant could have been another sun but decided to be a planet instead. It takes a while to learn who wants to become what within Creation. You're learning the same, aren't you?"

"Learning? Of course." Yawri was curious about the red diamond. "If Red comes to the surface, the ethereal diamond Tilan gave me will help me find it." Yawri glanced toward the exit tunnel. "I wonder if the guardians who came to the pocked valley found it in the same condition we did, tried to heal it, but left when they couldn't. However, that doesn't explain why it was in worse condition when Keela returned."

The pulsing light in Lazket's body steadied. "A message from another cavern is returning. Interesting. It reports voices of some surface crystals are absent. That's unusual, but surface caves can hibernate.

"Wait. Another message comes." A dimensional doorway within Lazket's body, a wispy cloud in appearance, swirled with color. In a moment, the doorway returned to white light, and Lazket spoke evenly. "A second chamber reports disharmonies on other planets but the messages are unclear. It says truths are unclear because they are somehow mixed with untruth."

"Untruth? What's an untruth? How could anything untrue exist in Creation?"

"I've not experienced it myself. The message described a disorientating or disrupting sensation in some communications."

Yawri couldn't relate to the concept. "A disorientating communication? The purpose of communication is to clarify connection, not disrupt it. What universe is that cavern you spoke with in?"

"You asked, 'What else could cause the disharmony you found?' I reported the response without editing it."

"Nothing about disappearing stone or plants?"

"No."

"It may not be related, but Keela and I know of a second disharmony. According to the trees, some guardians were tending a herd of wildebeests. The trees don't know why, but the guardians left very quickly with some newborn wildebeests. It panicked the herd and they stampeded."

"That is more than unusual. It's unheard of, at least based on what we know, and there is much to learn."

"Yet, it was a disharmony. We were sent forth to learn how to expand Creation in all we become. Harmonizing with All expands All. How could any being think that disharmony with All would expand it?"

Lazket replied, "Creator gave us free will to self-determine how we co-create in Creation. Creation is infinite and so are ways to Create. We don't know what we don't know."

"Yes, but we're talking about Earth. Agreements to co-create here are clear. It seems these were isolated events, but I'm going to keep asking other guardians if they've heard of other examples." Yawri looked toward the exit tunnel again. The chamber ceiling, walls, and floor whorled with undulating light.

Lazket said, "We will keep listening. I'm sorry we don't have more information about disharmony in Creation. I have not experienced it."

"Nothing seems wrong with the world when I'm here."

"Why not stay? Join with the Earth spirit of a crystal body. It's an excellent way to learn co-creation with physicality."

"Thanks, but I'm sure I'd miss daylight. I'll come back soon, though. I always enjoy you."

"Since it's been over three hundred years since your last visit, your definition of 'soon' is open to interpretation."

"What's three hundred years to a body that's already several million years old?" Yawri started to move away. "I didn't pass through even one crystal body on my way in. I wonder if I can go faster on my way out."

"I expect you're going to find out."

"Until next time." Yawri bowed, straightened, straight shot up, turned, and sped toward the tunnel.

Plummeting into the labyrinthine shaft, he navigated three tight turns before passing through the end of a crystal. A narrow, comparatively straight section of the tunnel lay ahead.

Faster. Go Faster.

10. THE REPORT

∞

Keela sailed down the cliff wall to the promontory overlooking the two rolling rivers. The wedge of land high above the river junction was laced with broad veins of white quartz, just as Yawri described.

All I have to do is find his two friends, tell them about the disharmonic events, and ask if they have heard of anything similar. I'll get back to my lichen soon.

Keela descended and saw five light bodies on the promontory.

He said there would only be two!

Discomforted, but determined to keep her agreement, she settled near a large vein of quartz and faced the five. Before she could ask if Tisbero or Zinn were among them, a buoyant light body approached.

"Welcome!" the ebullient being said. "Are you with Yawri? He's usually the first to arrive but now he's last."

Keela considered how to respond. "Yawri's in a crystal cavern. He asked me to come and meet with Tisbero and Zinn."

"I'm Zinn. Tisbero is the wide one over there." She smiled in his direction. "So, Yawri's in a cavern. No surprise. Welcome. What sound do you go by?"

"Keela."

Zinn turned to the others. "This is Keela. Yawri's somewhere underground, probably seeing how fast he can race through cracks in the earth without touching anything. He asked Keela to come."

Keela raised a luminescent hand to her head. "He races underground? He told me he was going to ask the crystal beings if they knew of any unusual events."

"Don't worry. I'm sure he'll talk to them in between flights."

Tisbero approached. His voice was deep and resonant. "Greetings, Keela. I'm Tisbero. Thank you for coming. Zinn and I meet with Yawri often to share news."

Keela wanted to get back to her lichen, but she tried to be social. "Yawri said you study the Life force of mountains, volcanoes, and earthquakes. Is that right?

"I've worked with planetary forces on other worlds. I'm here to apply what I've learned to aid Life here. What about you?"

Keela preferred learning about others much more than talking about herself. "Yawri and I met while healing some rocks and plants in a valley near here. What about you, Zinn? Do you have a specialty? "

Zinn swayed from side to side slightly. "I work with large animals. It couldn't be going better. The ones I work with are evolving with thought forms as they arrive. Earth's expansion of Life thrives."

The three other light bodies approached and Zinn greeted them brightly. "Yawri can't come today. This is Keela. Keela, this is Camic, Rhee, and Shahten."

Zinn turned to Keela and said, "Camic asked Tisbero and me if they could join our meeting. Since it's always 'the more the merrier' with Yawri, we invited them."

Keela wasn't sure how to respond. Meeting with two was far different than meeting with five, but the sooner she fulfilled her agreement the sooner she could leave. "Yawri asked me to come and ask if everything is going well and what you have heard."

"What a curious question. It's going very well for everyone," Camic said. Rhee nodded in agreement. Shahten was examining a large crystal in the quartz dike and didn't appear to hear.

Tisbero turned to faced her. "Why wouldn't it be going well?" He gestured to the thriving promontory. The wind carried harmonies blended with those from the rivers below. "Do you know why Yawri wanted to know?"

Shahten, the being who was examining the quartz, straightened suddenly and approached. Keela pulled back, surprised at his height and long arms. "I'm sure Yawri has a good reason for asking the question," he said coolly. "However, with our co-creation going so well, what prompted him to ask it?"

"You know Yawri, too?" she asked hopefully.

"I hoped to meet him today. However, I am delighted to meet you, Keela."

She tilted her head in surprise at his response but knew social conversation was not her strength. Still, something about him was different. His light body had multiple colors, but unlike everyone else, his were concentrated in spots.

Shahten repeated, "Do you know why he wanted to ask such a strange question?"

Keela looked down.

What's a strange question?

She raised her head. "He asked me to come in his place because we witnessed two disharmonic events. He wanted me to ask Tisbero and Zinn if they'd heard of anything similar."

Shahten moved toward her and he seemed even taller. "Disharmonic events? It's a good thing more of us are present to learn of this! I've helped many planets. Perhaps I can help here."

Camic offered, "Shahten has co-created on far more planets than anyone I know. What is unexplainable to us might make sense to him."

Shahten dipped his etheric head in a gesture of humility. He paused, evidently in deep thought. "While it is true that I have worked with many planets, none have the richness of this one." He swept his pale, luminous hands to indicate the spectacular spectrum of Life surrounding them. "The opportunity here is magnificent." He turned to Keela and pointedly asked, "What did you witness that you can't explain?"

The others remained silent, awaiting her response.

Now that she'd learned no one else had experienced anything out of the ordinary, she considered how best to report.

One of Keela's strengths was providing analytical descriptions of her observations. In a calm, steady voice she related her task of collecting and carrying the fertilizing essence to the female moss and seeing the silver-toned guardians below while on her way to deliver it. She described how she thought they were healing the valley of its strange pockmarks, but learned they'd left disharmonic, shrieking holes in the stone with missing lichen instead. She described the healing she and Yawri provided, and how the valley sang again before they left. She paused to signal the beginning of the next description.

Her light-body steady, she told them of the disharmony with the wildebeests and their missing calves. Finally, deciding to share everything she couldn't explain, she described the great soaring bird and its concern about the missing hatchling.

Tisbero leaned in closer with each description. When she stopped speaking, he erupted. "There *were* a couple of disharmonic events I heard about, but I dismissed them before hearing of yours. One was about the disappearance of other grazing animals, but smaller than wildebeests, which live in the mountains. I also heard a report about crystals missing from a cave. Neither included sightings of the silver-toned light bodies you mentioned, but both described disharmonic stress similar to what you heard."

Zinn pounced. "Mountain ibex are missing? They were accepting thought forms to aid their evolution well when I last saw them!"

"Crystals too?" Keela asked. "Does Yawri know about this?"

Tisbero flared with agitation. "I'll make sure he and others know about it now. It didn't occur to me that they could have been taken, but I must reconsider. Disharmonic cries would certainly occur if Life was removed without its permission."

"Wait!" Shahten stepped in the middle of the group. "I've experienced this before."

Tisbero exclaimed, "Where? Why would disharmony ever arise when our purpose is to harmonize with All-that-is to enliven it?"

Shahten took a moment to watch a flock of birds fly overhead. After they passed, he said thoughtfully, "What do we know? We know Creator is in all things, in all places, in all time." He paused to see if anyone disagreed. None did. He continued in a soothing pace. "We are of Creator, yet are One." He paused again, once more to provide time for objection.

Keela looked down in concentration, trying to understand how these self-evident statements related to the reports of disharmony. Wondering what information she missed, she asked, "Those statements are foundational to us. What do they have to do with the disharmony we described?"

Shahten rose above the ground slightly, which made him appear even taller. With polite consideration, he said, "I've seen what you described with lichen and other forms too, many times. We all interpret what we experience based on what we have previously experienced. To understand the power of disharmony—used to create harmony—is my specialty. How were you attracted to the moss you helped? Did you not respond to a disharmony and take the action you did to restore it?"

Keela considered his words carefully. From what Camic said, Shahten had much more experience than any of them. "I heard the female moss call for aid and went to ask if I could help it. I have never felt a call for aid as a disharmony though."

"Was the moss in harmony or was it seeking help to achieve harmony?"

Keela considered his words and replied, "I've never experienced a request for aid as a disharmony before, but I understand your point."

Shahten continued, "I have met the silver guardians of whom you speak. Had you stopped to ask, you would have learned their work was very similar to yours. They were asked to do what they did to enhance One, like you did with the moss. I spoke to them at length. The only difference is scale."

Keela's mind swirled. "How can it be the same? The moss I worked with did not have disharmonic sound. It only wished to expand into more harmonies, and nothing was taken from the moss I helped evolve. In contrast, the land of the lichen valley shrieked."

Shahten remained serene, his reasonable manner unchanged. "But you did take something, Keela. You took fertilizing essence from one location to another. The guardians working with the lichen and stone did the same. The difference is they have the ability to transport greater amounts of matter, so are able to do the same as you did on a larger scale."

Keela churned with confusion. "But the land. They left the land crying. Living stone and lichen were both gone. How can causing pain expand All?"

Shahten answered smoothly, "Do you think the seeds that must open their hard casing and push up through the soil don't feel pain at their struggle?" Shahten turned to Tisbero. "When volcanoes explode do you think that it is a painless event for the Life around them?" He turned to Zinn. "When the animals you tend give birth, are they free of pain?" He faced them all. "When the comets brought their waters here, do you think burning up in the atmosphere was painless?"

Shahten focused on Keela once more. "When you took the fertilizing essence from the male moss, did you linger? If the male moss started emitting disharmonic vibration would you have stayed, knowing that any delay would mean the essence you carried from him would not survive? Or would you complete your agreement to deliver the essence, and return to re-balance the male moss afterward?"

Keela replied, "I would make the delivery and return very quickly. To do otherwise would mean that any disharmony the male moss experienced was for nothing. My action to aid their evolution would take instead of give to them."

"Precisely. You left immediately so both could evolve. Long-term gain versus short-term pain. The guardians you saw did the same for the same reason. Except when they returned to rebalance the land, they found you and your friend already had."

Shahten grew even more patient. "The land in that valley asked for this assistance, knowing that it would be painful, but choosing to do it so that the lichen could expand into barren areas a thousand times more quickly. Everything on this planet understands long-term gain versus short-term pain."

He paused, but not long enough to allow an interruption. "Even though those guardians are quite advanced in the way of working with the One, it was a traumatic experience for them. We know that nature may create disharmony in existing Life, and even end it, in order to evolve. Floods, droughts, volcanoes, and meteors give plenty of evidence of that. However, for us to create such disharmony to existing Life would be very traumatic. Would it not?"

He returned his attention to the whole group. "Yet they chose to answer the request and give what was needed instead of what they wished, and to learn from their pain."

Keela stood wordless. The reality Shahten described shattered her preconceptions. Her resolve dissolved into confused fragments. "I didn't know," she managed to say.

"There is no crime in not knowing," Shahten replied sympathetically. "The problem comes with acting without knowing." He turned to face the others. "Other than this well-intentioned but misinformed report about the lichen, has anyone else here actually experienced a disharmonic event?"

Silence. Shahten persisted, "Experience or hearsay? Anyone?"

Even Tisbero remained quiet.

He turned to face Keela again. "How much fear have you sown in others, fear that creates mistrust between guardians of the same common purpose?"

"I did not know." She faced Shahten squarely, always willing to take responsibility for her mistakes. "This is a lesson I will not forget. It is my custom to study anything I do not understand. I thought I came here with a question. However, I must have come with an answer."

Shahten radiated understanding. His spots of color flashed brightly. "We are all learning." He dipped his head in apparent respect.

Camic stood next to Shahten. "We all have a lot to learn. However, I'm glad Shahten was here to share his knowledge before this misunderstanding grew."

Shahten dipped his head again and gracefully moved out of the circle. "I am sure we will meet again. Thank you for inviting me to your meeting." He stopped and looked at the large quartz in the dike and spoke softly. "All will be One again. I promise."

In sharp contrast to the others present, he stood tall, and in a voice filled with confidence said, "I must depart now. Others have requested my presence." Dipping his form yet again to signal his goodbye, he rose and accelerated quickly over the river and toward the far ridge.

Keela shook her head. Zinn stepped to one side of her and Tisbero to the other.

Zinn spoke first. "Thank you for reporting what you saw. It matters to me."

Tisbero added, "Just because I haven't witnessed a disharmonic event personally does not mean they didn't occur. I don't think your report should be so easily dismissed."

Keela murmured, "The ahja said no one returned to the emerald valley after Yawri and I left. Shahten said they did. Giant soaring bird or not, he must have missed them."

Camic and Rhea continued listening but stepped away from the group.

In a hushed voice, Rhea confided, "Thank you for pointing out that, if not for Shahten, this misunderstanding could have created mistrust between guardians where none existed before."

Camic leaned closer. "Shahten is right. We all interpret our experience based on what we already know, and it's clear he has a lot more experience with planets than Yawri and Keela do."

"I'd like to meet the guardians he spoke about, the ones who chose to give what was needed instead of what they wished, in spite of all that pain."

Camic looked toward the ridge. "Me too. Let's find out if we can."

11. SHAHTEN

∞

Shahten didn't slow down until he crested the ridge and doubled back to join one of his companions waiting there.

"How did it go?" the other asked, its light body shimmering with hues of silver.

"Well. It went very well," Shahten said, surveying the promontory below. The light bodies were distant but he could tell the one who rose into the air was Keela, relieved to get back to her lichen, no doubt.

He studied the remaining four. "The one that told you about Yawri's plan to meet here has potential."

"Camic. Camic and his friend, Rhee."

"Both were open to the Way. Yawri wasn't there, but you understood the names of the two healers from the lichen valley correctly: Yawri and Keela. Very good of them to heal the land. No evidence of our harvest remains."

"After they sped away, I stopped at the valley and found it still resonated with enough of their sound to discern their names. After I overheard Camic mention Yawri's meeting, it was easy to get him to ask Tisbero if he would extend the invitation."

"Good. Keep Camic and Rhee in good favor. They may be of more use."

Shahten waved a hand toward his points of color. "Help me get out of this." His companion took off the cloak and carefully rolled it into a small bundle. Shahten moved freely again.

"Did the gem cloak work? Your idea to use multi-colored gems to avoid confusion about our stable color was a great one. "

"I kept them so off balance that they didn't even notice the colors were localized instead of flowing. It was more difficult than it should have been to keep all those gemstones glowing uniformly, though. We must further isolate them from each other so they are more compliant."

"I will see to it. Now that we know who they are for sure, do you think Yawri and Keela are possible to convert?

"It is too early to tell. Keela apologized for her error and was so discredited in front of the others that no one will believe anything she says now. Since we know Yawri's identity, he'll be easy to track. We will discredit him as well. He must learn that sowing distrust between guardians does great harm to the One. If adequately humbled they may realize the inevitable wisdom of the Way."

Shahten looked from their sheltered perch back toward the promontory. Two of the remaining four rose into the air and started to move his way.

"That would be Camic and Rhee. They supported everything I said. After what happened to Keela, I expect they decided to seek more of my counsel."

"They are the smart ones," his companion declared.

"Still," Shahten counseled, "To make sure the misguided have no more examples to feed their reckless rumors, we will stop harvesting from this area." He smiled dismissively. "The lack of any future events will discredit them entirely."

Shahten watched Camic and Rhee approach for a long moment before he said, "Give me the cloak again. No reason to startle them." He donned the cloak eagerly. "They are about to learn how my explanations will answer any question they may have."

12. FOOT PRINTS

∞

Even though the light bodies were ethereal, their constant co-creation with physicality influenced their form. Over time, their bodies became more defined and expressed the personalities of individual beings.

Yawri's well-formed arms and legs glowed brilliantly, and his face always seemed near a smile. The bottomless, cobalt-blue portals which had served as his eyes now held a circle of light green and yellow around a black center. His vision still perceived wavelengths of sight in countless variations, but physical objects appeared sharper and more textured than ever. Yawri's more defined light body moved surely and quickly, although its direction of travel often changed.

Many guardians felt he was too impulsive, but Keela remained loyal and steadfast in their friendship. Zinn found Yawri's spontaneity a perfect balance to Tisbero's preference for planning. Since Tisbero and Yawri both cherished volcanoes, Tisbero occasionally invited Yawri to join him in his volcanic work, even if Yawri's penchant for adventure sometimes derailed his plans.

On this day, Yawri sped above the winding grassland on his way to a meeting Zinn requested with Keela, Tisbero and him. Centuries had passed since the event with the shattered stone and missing lichen, and no further examples had been reported. Shahten's explanation became accepted as historical fact.

Although Yawri never talked about it, he still preferred thinking a flood caused the damage, because the idea that the Earth would ask guardians to do something so traumatic to Life remained absurd to him. The few guardians recalling the story pointed out it was the only disharmonic event witnessed, and the two guardians who reported it were also the ones who removed all traces that proved it actually happened.

Their familiar refrain was, "Yawri and Keela described themselves as healers, but caused unhealthy mistrust where none existed before." Questions about the missing animals, crystals and young birds never reoccurred.

Yawri accepted his learning without self-reprisal. "Everyone's learning their way to be ever more of All."

However, it took several months after Keela's meeting with Shahten for Yawri to find her. He finally came across her in a deep, narrow canyon rich with moss and ferns.

While she worked to help bring evolutionary thought forms into some pale green moss, he heard it call for more iron-rich minerals. He was able to help and the moss soon glowed with a warm, yellow sheen. Even though the moss sang with liveliness, Keela wasn't exactly overjoyed to see him.

However, his joy at finding her soon overwhelmed her resistance. That's when he found out the reason for her absence. "I thought telling Zinn and Tisbero what we'd experienced was straightforward, but it came out as a story that only created mistrust between guardians. I really am fine working alone."

It had taken his efforts combined with Tisbero's and Zinn's to finally convince Keela she hadn't done anything wrong. That, plus Yawri's constant message, "everyone is learning how to be ever more of All," eventually allowed her to laugh when he recalled their spiraling race to the center of the harm, their swirling vortex, and her astonished expression when they saw the valley healed.

I'm glad she finally got over it. At least, I think she did.

Yawri shot low, skimming the river's surface, rising and falling with its water as it rushed up and over boulders. As he neared the meeting place, he sped up a shallow river and grinned at the bright-blue flowers within the tall grass.

I wonder why Zinn called this meeting.

Brush took the place of savanna grass, then trees took the place of brush. Yawri rose over the canopy of leaves and was glad when the outcrop of hard, white limestone of their meeting place came into view. He shot forward and stopped abruptly above its center to scan for Keela, Tisbero, and Zinn. He noticed movement where brush met forest.

"Keela!" he called when he saw her full-bodied form near the edge of the forest. He accelerated, stopped suddenly, and descended to her side. Long accustomed to his peculiar way of moving, Keela only glanced up before her gaze returned to the ground. Yawri didn't see her smile.

"How goes Creation?" he asked.

Keela glanced up again. "Creation goes well." Her robust, radiant form was the color of a seashell at sunset. "Would you look at this, Yawri? What do you think made these tracks?" Yawri knelt down and examined the depression.

"That's interesting. I thought it was the footprint of an ape, but the largest toe isn't in the right position. Apes have the biggest toe angled out to the side for quick climbing. This toe is parallel to all the others."

Keela stood and moved to the next indentation. "It also has a longer gait than the apes I've seen. Zinn's seen other differences, too, and wanted us to share what we think about them."

Yawri considered the two footprints. "I'd guess a deformed ape. What does Zinn think? She works with animals far more than any of us do."

Keela's eye followed the footprints into the dense forest. "Zinn's found far too many footprints for them to be from one deformed ape. She thinks they're from a troop of humans."

Yawri stared into the forest. "Humans? You mean those hairless apes? Aren't they a little weak to survive here?"

"She and Tisbero are following the tracks to find out."

Yawri studied the strange impression again. "I'm glad she wanted to meet, but what's so important about another kind of ape? Last time we met, she and Tisbero said they'd heard from guardians who were having trouble getting clear communication from Earth. I thought we'd be talking about that."

Keela shook her head slowly, her voice full and succinct. "Zinn says these apes are different. They're smart."

"We found the humans!" Keela and Yawri spun to see Zinn and Tisbero emerge from the forest. Even though Zinn was the smallest of the four, something about her movements made her appear as substantial as the much stockier Tisbero next to her.

Zinn continued to bubble. "Yawri, you made it here! These hairless apes are fascinating!"

Tisbero remained at Zinn's side but peered back the way they came. He turned with a welcoming nod to Yawri and added, "They are few, small, and have to hide from just about every other creature in the forest to stay alive. I don't know how they've survived this long."

Zinn's excitement drowned out Tisbero's somber assessment. "Humans are to animals like volcanoes are to mountains!"

Tisbero's light body swelled, but before he could respond Yawri asked, "Zinn, what makes you think these apes will survive?"

She took a fluid step toward the center of their circle, efficiently bringing them all closer together. "They're smarter. The hairless apes make shelters. Not a simple nest under some protective branches like the other apes make.

They interlace sticks to construct sturdy homes covered with leaves to keep themselves dry, even in hard rain."

Tisbero remained unconvinced. "Other apes might figure out how to make shelters too if they were hairless."

Zinn remained ebullient. "Did you see the one in the stream trying to catch a fish with a spear tipped with a sharp shard, Tisbero?"

"You mean the one jabbing the water with a broken stick?"

Zinn continued without pause. "And the fire? What about the fire? How many apes have you seen tending their own fire?"

Tisbero's broad face remained steady. "None. They have made reasonable adjustments to compensate for their vulnerability, so over time, the ones adapting best will survive best. However, ask me about landforms and the forces of mountains and volcanoes. Them I understand." He pointed a finger toward the forest, "You're the one who works with animals."

Zinn's amber eyes twinkled. She enjoyed Tisbero's pragmatic disposition, perhaps because it was so opposite to her own. "If Yawri and Keela want to see the human camp, can you take us on a more direct route than the one we used? The tracks we followed meandered everywhere."

"Yes, of course I can."

Yawri said, "Lead the way, but meandering routes are fine with me."

Tisbero gestured to the far right of where the tracks disappeared into the trees. "The direct route is half the distance."

Keela asked, "Yes. Please lead the way, but will we be able to observe them without being seen? Their behavior will change if they know we're studying them."

Zinn said, "Tisbero already found a secure place where we can observe."

After Tisbero scanned the area, he led the group into the forest. Sunlight fell through the canopy of leaves and bathed the air in hues of tender green. Dragonflies with the wingspan of birds fluttered among red flowers sprouting from woody vines.

Their light bodies moved between sparse trees grown broad with age. Since the area was too dry for ferns, the fibrous stalks of plants with thick, dark-green leaves checkered the forest floor. Much sooner than Zinn expected, the foursome came to an overgrown embankment above a narrow river. Tisbero led them to a thicket of branches with a safe vantage point, where each found a place to peer through dark-green, waxy leaves.

Down a grassy slope, a long, domed structure made of woven sticks and thatch stood near the bank of the river. Twelve adults and five children were visible. The front and back of each adult was draped with a long, thin animal hide.

Yawri was amazed. "These apes lost their hair, and now they have to wear the hair of other animals to survive. Why would nature think naked apes are a good idea?"

Zinn continued staring through her gap in the leaves. "To increase the kind of environments apes can live in."

Tisbero straightened. "How can losing hair expand their territory?"

Keela's response was thoughtful. "Because they can choose how much fur is needed. They can wear nothing if it's too hot, a thin hide like they're wearing here, or thick ones if it's cold."

Zinn chimed in, "Which greatly expands their range. The rainforest apes need fur to protect them from hard rain, sharp-edged plants, and bites from other animals. These apes moved out to the dry, sunny bush and savanna where there are no other apes and far fewer predators."

A large fish jumped and splashed in the river. Several humans made high-pitched nasal tones directed at one of the females. She returned a sound, picked up a long, slender stick, and walked toward the river.

"Look at the point on her stick," Zinn said. "Is it stone?"

Tisbero scrutinized the tip. "Stone shaped to a sharp point and attached to a straight stick. They are smart."

Keela was still contemplating the tonal interchange between the apes. "Were the sounds they made specific communication or only vocal additions to their gestures? Whatever it was, it resulted in one of them wading into the river with a spear."

Zinn leaned so far into the leaves she almost passed through them. She pulled herself back quickly, remaining fixed on the camp. "It appears to be a spoken language, but I need to observe more to know for sure."

Safely ensconced, the four watched the female wade into the river with the short spear and stand motionless. After a long minute, the spear flashed down into the water in a blur of motion. When she drew it out, a fish longer than her forearm was pierced all the way through. In one fluid motion, she held the fish in one hand, pulled the spear free and tossed the prize to a male on shore. He caught it one-handed and their laughter was joined by others.

"That's amazing," Yawri said, peering through his own opening. "Whether they are talking with words or not, they're very good at communicating."

Zinn looked at her friends. "One thing is certain. These humans are very different from the other apes. It's why I wanted you to see them. But why would Creator and Earth co-create them? Their abilities are far beyond any animal I have worked with, and I don't see why the planet would need an animal smart enough to live in forest, tundra, or mountain. All others are limited to specific areas."

No one answered, enthralled by the activities unfolding below. A fire blazed in the center of the camp and the fish rested on stones. Flames licked its scales.

Keela pondered Zinn's question. "Zinn, you know of many animal bodies prepared by Creator and Earth for joining with ethereal beings. Do you think these animals could become one of those? If not, why would Creator and Earth co-create ones so capable?"

Yawri pulled back from his vantage point, jarred. "I don't see how they could be. They're too small. The animal bodies joined with ethereal beings I know are many times the size of these. The larger the better to keep the physical and ethereal energies in balance. You can't put a sea in a seashell."

Tisbero agreed. "If they were the size of mammoths, perhaps. I don't see how these hairless apes could be large enough for a balanced connection." He looked down the slope again. Now the fish was being eaten by a group of hairless apes gathered around the fire. A chorus of hoots and cackles mixed with smiles.

Zinn was uncharacteristically pensive. "It's a fair question. I've worked with more types of animals than I can count, and none display the abilities of these humans. Their diet is like the hairy apes. At least half is fruit. The rest is mostly plant roots, shoots, seeds and nuts. They eat some meat, small mammals or fish when they can catch them. The difference is they can travel much greater ranges to find food, that and the fact they fashion complex tools; build shelters; and wear what's needed for the weather, is promising for their survival."

Keela appraised, "Look where they put their camp. It's in the open space between forest and river where there's a wide field of view. It's too well positioned to be there by chance."

Tisbero murmured, "It's where I would have put it."

One of the male apes brought a large stone down on small stone, splitting the smaller one into sharp-edged pieces. He picked up a long, thin flake and handed it to another who was trying to cut a thick root from a fibrous stem. The sharp flake cut through it quickly.

Zinn spoke again. "It takes skill to make such a sharp blade. I've never heard of an ethereal being joining with an animal because of its intelligence, but I suppose it could provide for a whole different level of learning."

Tisbero deliberated. "I still don't see how they can survive against all the predators hunting them. Even though they can run, they can't outrun the big cats of the savanna. They don't have claws, sharp teeth, or thick hides for protection."

A female put more wood on the fire. Keela said, "It would have been good to observe the thought form meant to evolve these creatures. We could have seen the intention."

Tisbero was frank. "I still don't think Earth could be preparing these little bodies for ethereal beings."

Yawri shook his head firmly. "They're too small and short-lived to keep ethereal energy in balance. Giant mammoths and huge birds with lifetimes of over a hundred years are one thing. These small, naked apes will do well to live for twenty. They may be smart, but that's not enough time for an ethereal being to even begin to get to know the Earth spirit of its body."

Keela had to smile. "Spoken by someone who works with crystal bodies living millions of years."

"And trees. I work with trees, too." Yawri countered.

"Another perspective," she replied. "They live for several thousand years."

Zinn's amber eyes twinkled. "Whatever the case, I'll continue tracking them. Not all thought forms evolve with their physical forms successfully, but these might."

"Let me know if they live." Tisbero sounded gruff but the tone was normal for him.

Zinn brightened. She moved fluidly next to him. "Let's come back in three weeks. The moon will be full and we can observe them at night." He shook his head but didn't object.

Keela addressed Zinn. "Thank you for calling us here. Even though I specialize in plants, these animals are fascinating."

The quartet turned away from their perch and moved back through the forest. Yawri spoke to Zinn. "Thanks for getting us here, even if I'm leaving with more questions than when I arrived."

"No problem," Her impish expression remained bright. "I wouldn't want you to run out of questions. You'd leave to find more."

"Let's take the long route back. No reason to see ground we've already covered," said Yawri.

"Really? It's twice the distance," replied Tisbero.

Zinn moved forward. "Let's show them where the humans collect the sharp-stone. Isn't it this way, Tisbero?"

The others couldn't see the smile on Tisbero's face when he said, "Yes. Circuitous routes are good for sightseeing, but direct routes get you where you need to be efficiently."

Iridescent blue-and-green butterflies rose around the party. "True, but this way you get to see butterflies," Zinn bantered. Delicate wings fluttered between trees and tall plants with thick, dark-green leaves.

Keela asked, "Did you notice the root the humans were cutting? It only grows in sandy soil. Not jungle."

Zinn replied, "Interesting evolution, running rather than climbing apes. That root proves they are going beyond the forest and finding different foods."

Yawri had a question. "I'm glad we met about this, but last time you and Zinn said you'd heard of guardians having trouble getting clear communication from Earth. Have you heard any more?"

Tisbero considered, "Not I, but I'm still asking if others have."

Zinn moved ahead. "This is the place. This is where the humans get their sharpening stone."

Tisbero scanned the surroundings before focusing on the quarry. "This is volcanic glass. The lava it came from cooled unusually fast."

"Mostly silica mineral," Yawri added. "The same element in quartz crystals, but this cooled in hours. Crystals take millions of years to grow."

"These apes might survive after all," Zinn said. "All animals are intelligent, but these apply it differently. I wonder what Earth and Creator are planning for them?"

13. COUNCIL

∞

Over eons, Earth continued to expand across ever more physical and ethereal dimensions and created billions of new life forms. The guardian light-body beings continued to nurture Creation. However, because they were purely ethereal, they were less and less able to communicate clearly across the planet's growing physical-ethereal spectrum of Life.

Yawri, Keela, Tisbero, and Zinn gathered with many other guardians to share and discuss the problem. Guardians from many lands clustered in groups on a promontory overlooking expansive grasslands. A glistening ribbon of water, fed by a waterfall to the east, wound lazily across the waves of green. Yawri, Keela, Tisbero, and Zinn stood near the edge of the promontory's cliff to watch thousands of grazing beasts below.

Tisbero scanned the horizon. "When I came to this planet I could communicate clearly with any formation in Earth's crust or its core. Now, communication's not clear. I need clarity when working with mountain-building forces. Volcanoes are temperamental."

He paused but when no one else spoke, he continued. "I thought I was listening when I was helping a volcano release its magma slowly. I thought it wished to create more land. It exploded to rain ash from the sky instead. I've never been so mistaken, ever."

Yawri continued to watched the pastoral scene below but said, "I called a mineral essence to help some trees and it didn't come. They were yellowing because the soil was so magnesium poor they couldn't make enough chlorophyll. It's the only time a mineral needed for growth didn't respond to my request. I don't think it heard me."

Zinn floated above the cliff to get a better view of the animals. Their antlers were the most massive of any she'd seen. "Not long ago I sent a herd of wildebeests to a valley I thought had plenty of grazing for them."

She appeared to shrink when she lowered her light body to the rock again. "There was no good grass there, and the herd was weakened because I made a mistake. That's never happened before."

Keela considered her friends. Each expressed the concern she'd also felt but hadn't spoken. She raised her head. "I still resonate with the strength of Earth's soul in its evolution of plants, but not nearly as well." She hesitated. "I tried to tell a flutter of butterflies about a place where plants needed them, but they didn't hear me. I've studied the communication problem but can't solve it."

Zinn brightened a bit and shared, "The ethereal beings I know who have joined with large animal bodies say they have better communication with Earth than ever before. It's the opposite of what I'm experiencing, but I still don't know how to join with a physical form without harming myself or its body."

Yawri joined Zinn at the edge of the cliff. "Learning how to expand in Creation has worked so far, but expansion means change. It's hard to know what you need to change when you don't know why things are changing, but I'm sure we'll work it out. We always have."

He glanced at the gathering groups of guardians and saw his friend Hetlin coming to the center.

"Thank you for coming!" Hetlin's substantial light body glowed, but with dimmed iridescence.

Keela asked quietly, "Do any of you know who she is? I've not seen her before."

Something about Hetlin always reminded Yawri of a great tree or perhaps a large crystal. "Hetlin is one of the guardians tending the lands far east of here. She works with crystals, too. Several caverns have opened there."

"Is there anyone you don't know?" Keela said evenly.

"I'm sure there is. Let me know if you know them."

Hetlin continued in her earthy style. "Our community is having trouble getting clear communication with Earth and its life forms, but we didn't know if others were too. I sent out the request for this meeting to find out. From the number of you present, it appears many communities have the same concern."

She held up her arms so all could see them. Like everyone else, her radiant glow was dimmer and more opaque than the brilliant glow of the past. "I can't will my light body to be more physical without doing harm. Yet, to not do so limits my ability to speak with Earth the way we need to for conscious co-creation. Do others wish to speak about their concerns?"

Tisbero spoke with the fiery intensity he felt. "We all know the vibratory rate of Earth is expanding into ever more ethereal and physical dimensions. I've continually densified my own light body in order to stay. However, if I continue doing so indefinitely, I risk harming myself—and harm of self harms All."

An especially opaque guardian sounded flat. "Is there no way in Creation for us to reverse this process? If it continues, how can we stay? If we leave, what is the impact on Earth if no purely ethereal beings remain?"

Zinn, her eyes glimmering, floated above the ground to observe everyone present. "I don't know how to join with physicality without endangering myself or a body. However, I know many ethereal beings have joined with the Earth spirits of magnificent animals. They will remain here even if we have to go."

A bristle-haired creature scurried through underbrush near her. The rustling sound drew the attention of many, and they watched it run down a wide crack in the rock.

A guardian beseeched, "I didn't even sense that animal before it scurried away. We can't co-create with Life without complete connection with it. What if we continue to lose our ability? I sense my time as an ethereal guardian here is coming to an end. It grieves me to say it, but perhaps it's time to plan for leaving Earth."

A tall guardian added, "That can't be! We are needed here! There must be something we can do. Life is about change. Perhaps something will change soon."

Another said, "Ethereal beings with more experience than I have not only joined with large animals but large trees, sea creatures, crystals, and other forms prepared for that purpose. However, those forms are far too complicated for me."

Keela looked at Yawri, willing him to speak. Leaning toward her, he quietly encouraged, "It was your idea and it's a good one. Some will like it, others won't. Give them a chance to learn from their own reactions like you do."

She shook her head slowly and replied more quietly. "It may be my idea, but there is no reason you can't be the one to share it. After all, you know everyone here."

Yawri nodded and addressed the group. "Keela and I were discussing another option." Everyone looked at them both.

Their expectant expressions gave Keela pause, but after a darting glance at Yawri's questioning gaze, she decided to speak. "Neither of us know any ethereal being who joined with a complex life form as their first step. All started their learning on worlds with fewer dimensions. We could do the same.

We could leave temporarily to learn how to join with simpler physical forms and return with the ability to join with the perplexing ones here."

A quiet fell. After a long pause, many beings voiced similar thoughts. "I'll be sad to leave," was heard over the din, "but I have much to learn before joining with the multi-dimensional bodies that are here. Learning how to join in small steps makes sense."

Yawri looked down at his misty feet, still radiant but no longer completely translucent, and held up hands that had the same misty glow. His voice carried. "To continue here as a guardian, is it best to leave and return when I am more able, or stay knowing my limitations could cause harm? Do I show my caring by staying or leaving?"

Scanning the assembly, Tisbero flared brighter. "Since harming self harms All, we need to do what reduces the risk of harm. Taking small steps to learn how to join with a physical form is more respectful than assuming we can take a big one."

A chorus of support sounded. All guardians evidently agreed with the plan. When the timing required it, they would learn how to join with physicality on a simpler planet, and return to continue their guardianship here when wisdom allowed.

Suddenly, someone burst forth over the conversations. "What about the human bodies Earth prepared for us? Why do you abandon them?"

Startled, all turned to see a light body at the edge of the assembly.

"Camic," Tisbero rumbled to his three companions. "He and the one next to him, Rhee, echoed everything Shahten said when we met long ago. It was that meeting when Keela first told us about the disharmonic events she and Yawri experienced. From the look of his form, he's pushing the limits of manifesting physical energy."

Rhee, floating a bit higher next to Camic, continued vigorously. "Creator gave human bodies the ability to live and move anywhere on the planet, much as we do, except they do it in the physical human form. They are the most intelligent animal on the planet, and they are developed specifically for us to join with them."

Confusion rippled through the assembly. Evidently, very few had even heard about human bodies. Keela exchanged glances with Zinn, and from the look in her eyes it was clear Keela wished her to ask the question they were both wondering.

Zinn brightened and leaned in toward Camic and Rhee. "Are the human bodies you speak of the hairless apes? I've been observing them for hundreds of years, but they appear too small and immature to be able to maintain the balance needed for a successful joining."

Yawri joined in, "I've seen the hairless apes too. Are they the human bodies you speak of?"

Rhee drifted back down, leaving Camic in front of him. Camic, realizing it was up to him to respond, blurted out, "I also thought they were hairless apes, but I've learned otherwise. I visited an island, a magnificent island. It has stone dwellings for hu—"

"Hello, Yawri!" Everyone turned to see a tall, very lean light-body approach the gathering. Its body shimmered with points of light in many different colors.

"Have we met?" Yawri knew many guardians on this planet but had no memory of this one.

"Hello, Shahten," Tisbero thundered. "It's been a long time." He swept his gaze to Camic and Rhee and back to Shahten. "Still an authority, I see."

Shahten was affable. "It is so good to see you again, Tisbero! How nice, Keela and Zinn are here too. When we last met, we were able to clear up the unfortunate confusion about Keela and Yawri's disharmonic experience. The one about the guardians who put helping Earth above their own pain, and transplanted moss and lichen where it could expand Life."

Shahten raised a hand to his temple in thought. "We haven't met, Yawri, but I remember your name because Keela told me it was you who help spread the rumor. The one which caused the unfortunate mistrust among us for the first time in Creation. I'm glad we cleared up that trivial misunderstanding long ago. Long ago."

Keela started. *I didn't speak Yawri's name on purpose. It wasn't relevant. Camic told him. Didn't he?*

"Caused mistrust, Shahten?" Yawri questioned, confused. "All we did was openly report our experience. As you did when you shared your knowledge about the missing algae, moss, and stone. You knew it had been correctly transplanted by other guardians. You said Keela and I healed the land from its trauma before they came back to do it themselves."

"Yes, as I said, a misunderstanding cleared up long, long ago. I apologize for bringing up ancient history." Shahten turned toward the gathering and in a commanding resonance said, "Today, a question was asked about the human bodies prepared for us. Besides myself, who else has studied the humans?" Shahten walked tall from the outer circle of the assembly toward Yawri, Keela, Tisbero, and Zinn.

Guardians moved aside as he passed. Several murmured they had seen hairless apes, but Zinn was the only one who spoke up. "Animals are my area of focus. Observing hairless apes has been a priority of mine for hundreds of years."

"Have you interacted with them?" Shahten stopped and stood next to her.

"No. I believe observing the role animals play in nature before interaction is important. Then I can understand how my interaction may impact them."

Shahten seemed to tower when he turned and spoke to the entire assembly. "Yes, it is important to have all the facts at hand when making decisions. Don't you agree?" Murmurs of agreement passed through the sea of guardians.

"We all know how assumptions can cause unnecessary confusion." He didn't need to glance toward Yawri and Keela to make the implication clear. "I'll provide you with facts." He casually stepped in front of Yawri. "Camic and Rhee are right. The hairless apes are not apes. They are humans, another life form made here for union with ethereal beings. And they have an exceptionally strong Earth spirit, strong enough to blend with an etheric being."

"I told you!" Camic exclaimed. He cast a meaningful look toward Zinn and her friends. "I don't know what apes you saw, but humans aren't apes, and they are asking to join with us."

Shahten raised an arm in the air and pointed a long finger skyward. "Another fact you may not know is that Earth wants your guardianship to continue, not end. These humans developed specifically to join with you. Unlike any other life form, humans can cross any sea and live on any land, whether it be mountain, cave, ice, desert, jungle or tundra. They were created so we can go anywhere Earth needs us, blended in the physical dimensions as human beings."

All were too stunned to reply and a silence fell. He let it grow.

Yawri considered Shahten. The stranger had walked through the assembly to stand next to Yawri and his friends for a reason he couldn't fathom. All present had opportunity for equal voice from any place. He noticed Keela's eyes were downcast, so he moved from behind Shahten to stand between Shahten and Keela.

He focused on Shahten and asked seriously, "You speak with great certainty, Shahten. I have watched the hairless apes you call humans. Perhaps they are being created for the reason you state. However, they are small, and even with large bodies the timing must be right or harm can result. Tell us, why do you think they are mature enough for joining?"

Shahten's tall light body shimmered with layered, silver opalescence. It gave the impression he lived in hundreds of different dimensions. He spoke kindly, with captivating sincerity. "I had the same concern, and I struggled with it." He bowed slightly and fell silent in apparent contemplation.

The silence stretched. Tisbero began to repeat Yawri's question, but Shahten suddenly stood even taller and passionately asserted, "I don't know what choice others will make. We have free will so each individual can decide, but I can share what I have learned on other planets." He paused and waited for a side conversation to still. Silence reigned. "I have blended with humanoid forms on other planets."

Rhee raised his hands above his head and interjected, "Shahten has experience we don't! Has anyone else here joined with a humanoid or even a physical life form?"

A murmur rolled through the assemblage but none called out. Shahten raised an opalescent silver hand to his chest and spoke reassuringly. "I confide in you. From my experience on other worlds, the human bodies here are ready for what must be done. Earth itself tells me this."

Most guardians momentarily froze in place, and some drew back. Tisbero stepped next to Yawri and steadily asked Shahten, "No one I know has been able to speak clearly with the soul of Earth for decades. How is it you can?"

Shahten gazed casually from Tisbero to Yawri and back. His attitude was pleasant. "My confidence comes from experience. There can be no substitute for it. I understand why you are uncertain." He increased his authoritative manner and addressed the crowd. "If you wish to listen to what I have to report I will speak. If not, I will leave."

The guardians responded with, "Stay!"

"Tell us about this!"

"Share your experiences!"

Shahten waved a hand and looked toward Tisbero, Yawri, Zinn, and Keela, seemingly seeking permission from them to continue speaking. Receiving quizzical expressions in return, he spread his arms wide and spoke to all.

"We all came to this planet in response to its call, correct?" Heads bobbed slightly in agreement. "We all support Creation, correct?" Voices murmured their assent. "We all want to help Earth thrive?" The murmur rose to an amiable cheer.

Hetlin's rich voice carried across the gathering, and the laudation calmed. "No one is contesting our role in Creation, Shahten. However, human bodies are young and small compared to other forms Earth has prepared for joining. Why are you sure they are mature enough to maintain connection with their own Source, physical and ethereal Earth?"

Tisbero cautiously added, "We need to consider all angles of this. If there is any doubt, we should leave to give them and ourselves time to develop and come back to join when there is no question about our ability and theirs."

Shahten looked directly at Tisbero. "Yes, you can leave. Each must make their choice."

Shahten earnestly turned toward the assembly. "This is challenging learning. But ask yourself, how will you feel knowing you chose to abandon this planet after Creator made human bodies so you could stay?" He glanced at Yawri. "What will that reveal about you and your willingness to make long-term commitments?"

Silence gripped the guardians. Colorful points of light flashed across Shahten's gleaming, silver body. "If not to join with us, why would Creator and Earth conceive bodies so capable, strong, and intelligent?"

Zinn shook her head and bobbed forward. "It is not our commitment we question, only how best to perform it. We can do much harm by not respecting the timing of any Creation. Absent clear communication from Earth, how can we be certain we will not do harm?"

Shahten continued speaking in a cool, probing rhythm. "There was a first time for me, too. I was uncertain and my questions were many. If I joined, would I retain all of myself, or get lost in physicality? Was my need for comfort greater than my courage to give when the outcome was less certain?"

He leveled his gaze across the assemblage and challenged, "Did the sending say go forth and learn to expand Creation, or stay safe?"

His posture relaxed. In a comforting and conciliatory manner he said, "My companions, do you know that when you join with a human, you only move a very small portion of your energy into a body? Just enough to have a connection with it. We ethereal beings remain free to come and go as we please. It is you who control the amount of ethereal energy you provide to the human. You are the 'being' of the 'human being,' after all."

Scanning the hopeful, attentive faces, he continued, "Any ethereal being joined with one of Earth's forms can attest that we become more effective because we become One with Earth in all of its dimensions."

Hopeful smiles moved across the assemblage in a wave, and Shahten's silver opalescence shone brighter. "Listen to what you know. Are the ethereal souls who joined with the great crystals and trees leaving the planet? No. They blended with the physical bodies Earth prepared and continually provide ethereal connection and co-creation. Now, Creator has blessed this world with humans so we can travel to do the same ... wherever Earth calls."

The murmur of approval grew to a soft roar. Smiles expanded with the laughter of relief.

Hetlin exchanged a glance with Yawri, and then said, "Shahten, you say you have joined with humanoid bodies on other planets. What was the result? How do the bodies here compare with those?"

Shahten looked down at her in exasperation. When he raised his tired eyes, they seemed filled with sympathy. "They are comparable. The joining was successful for its purpose. I don't know how else to tell you how important this union is for fulfillment of the One."

Rhee crowed, "Tell them about the human beings on Earth, Shahten! The first human beings on Earth! Shouldn't they have all the facts?"

"Human beings on Earth?" several questioned.

Shahten raised his hands in supplication. "You are right, Rhee. All of us deserve all of the facts." Shoulders back, head raised, he stated, "I endeavored to help you find your own answer to the question you face, not influenced by the choices other guardians have already made."

His next words were so quiet, all strained to hear them. "I know the human bodies here are ready because, hearing the planet's distress at the thought of us leaving, I asked about the timing of the human bodies to receive us. No one was more surprised than I when it was only a matter of hours before two humans requested to join with ethereal beings such as you. Still, I was uncertain. However, I mentioned the request to a group of guardians no more prepared than any of you. They were concerned for the same reasons you express. However, two of them decided their comfort was less important than Earth's request."

Shahten paused to let the audience contemplate the courage it must have taken the two guardians to join. "Since I knew the subtleties of what it takes to join with a humanoid form on other worlds, they asked me to help. I was able to make sure the bodies and beings were prepared and the timing was right. The joining was a complete success. Human beings now walk the Earth."

To make sure she gathered all the opinions available, Keela had decided she wanted to listen rather than speak at the meeting. However, her shock at the announcement propelled her forward. Icily, she said, "You decided the timing was right to co-create human beings? After what study, with who? Such decisions have always been agreed upon by many, never just one."

Shahten leaned back in surprise at her uncharacteristic outburst but didn't forestall his response. "Who is this 'many' you speak of, Keela? All here said they could no longer get the clear communication from the planet which is required for co-creation. You yourself said guardians should leave, only to return after they gained that ability. Do you blame me because the ability of many was reduced to one?"

Yawri exclaimed, "Even if the information about it comes from few, the decision to join with a new life form has always involved many!"

Shahten turned immediately toward the assembly. "I apologize to each of you. I allowed my spirited hope for our future to supersede my wish to involve many. Again, I apologize for the supposed breach of process, and I thank Keela and Yawri for bringing it to our attention."

He casually stepped in front of them both. "The fact remains that because of my hope for us, there are now two more besides myself who have unambiguous communication with this planet. In fact, they report their connections with physical-ethereal Earth are more substantial than ever. The results are undeniable."

He spoke softly again. "Do you think I would counsel you to stay without knowing the results—without being sure? Like you, I only aid what is best for the One." Shahten paused to survey the crowd. Relieved expressions and even pleasure at his words graced the guardians.

He continued. "When the blending happened, the Earth spirit of the human body welcomed the touch. Welcomed it! And why not? They were ready to receive essence of the ethereal oceans. The fact that the timing is right is confirmed because guardians are once more speaking clearly with Earth."

"Thank you for your courage, Shahten!" Rhee enthused. "You persevere when others give up!"

Others sounded their agreement. Shahten raised his hand and spoke with pastoral calm. "The two human beings are thriving. They now know the water of the universe and the fire of Earth in the same moment. They bring new questions to old answers, and solve problems that plague humans."

He drew himself taller again. "We are all responsible for the impact of our choices. What is the impact of abandoning Earth now that it has prepared bodies for you to join with?" He raised his hands, pleading. "Please talk freely amongst yourselves. Search your thoughts and ask yourself the same question Yawri asked: Do you show your caring by staying or by leaving?"

The assembly immediately broke up into dozens of separate, small groups. All traces of heaviness were replaced by chatty, excited conversations.

Yawri, Keela, Zinn, and Tisbero found themselves standing together. Yawri gave a slow, disbelieving shake of the head. He chuckled. "Well, now I understand why Keela's report so long ago went the way it did. He questions everyone but himself."

Zinn swayed slowly back and forth. "It was the same when we met with him before. I didn't understand why I felt adrift after talking to him then, and I feel the same way now."

Keela looked over at the guardians surrounding Shahten. The others followed her gaze. "Well," she said after observing the growing circle. "It is evident most others agree with him."

Tisbero was pragmatic. "They prefer his answers to our questions. His certainty overrides their doubts."

One of the guardians near Shahten laughed loudly and waved to another group. Nodding, the group moved to join him. As they walked by the quartet, they overheard one saying, "I'm glad I didn't leave before he got here. The ones who spoke first had me convinced I should leave. They clearly had no idea human bodies were developed for us."

A second voice added, "Same with me. I'd forgotten they were the ones who spread the rumor about guardians causing harm."

After they passed, Keela said, "I don't want to base my perception on assumptions again. Shahten could be right. I haven't studied humans to know otherwise."

Yawri started to move toward Keela but stopped. "What assumptions? All we did was report what we saw and ask questions. How else can anyone learn what they don't know?"

Zinn blurted out, "The way he talks makes my head spin. Why is that?"

Tisbero's voice was tight. "He is so certain he is right. And it's hard to remember if he actually answered our questions or not."

"I don't think he did," Zinn said. "He said what he wanted and ignored our questions."

Yawri's gaze bounced across the scene. More groups moved toward Shahten. "He said ethereal beings control the amount of ethereal energy entering the human. I never heard it described as control before, only as co-creation."

Zinn's elfin expression wrinkled and she looked down. Her voice a whisper, she asked, "What if he's right? What if the human bodies have been prepared so that we can join with them soon?"

Tisbero shook his head. "Why didn't he bring the two human beings he helped join to the meeting with him?"

"Great questions!" The four looked up to see Hetlin's group of over twenty guardians approach.

"Hetlin!" Yawri greeted. "Always good to see you. Good questions from you, too."

Hetlin's light body looked stout but flowed with the flexibility of prairie grass. "I requested this meeting so we could all find out how extensive the problem was and hear questions and ideas about it. Even though Shahten deftly deflected your questions, you kept asking them. I am grateful to you."

Yawri moved toward her and grinned. "Why would we stop when we still have more? He turned to introduce his companions. "Keela, Tisbero, Zinn, this is Hetlin and others from their community. It's the largest one tending the far-eastern lands."

Hetlin's presence was as rich as Earth. "It's a pleasure to finally meet you. Yawri and I communicate on the astral while in the crystal caves in our regions, but meeting you in person is more reassuring than his cryptic descriptions."

Keela eyed Yawri. "What descriptions?"

Yawri volunteered, "You know. Short descriptions."

Zinn joined Keela. "What do you mean by short?"

Hetlin spoke again. "That's what I mean. You keep asking good questions."

A male light body next to her added, "Honest questions. We also noticed Shahten said you caused mistrust among guardians. We disagree. The world has events. Our responses are our own. All you did was report something you experienced and what you thought about it. We all do the same."

Keela spoke at a measured pace. "That was my intent, but sharing our experience at the meeting Shahten mentioned apparently did result in mistrust among guardians when there was none before. Or so I keep hearing."

A guardian on the other side of Hetlin gave a thoughtful nod and asked, "When a volcano erupts, is it the responsibility of the lichen or the volcano to grow lichen again?"

Keela raised her head. "Like lichen, how I respond to Life is my own responsibility. If I believed otherwise, it would greatly diminish my ability to co-create."

Hetlin replied, "We all wish to continue serving this planet—provided we truly help it and we expand connection to All. Independent of the abilities of humans, the concern we have with Shahten is this: rather than increase connection via his communication, we experienced it to be divisive."

Keela spoke evenly. "I was perplexed by his words but didn't know why. Thank you for sharing your thoughts. They help me organize my own."

A shaft of sunlight fell through a gap in the clouds and hit the basalt cliff face. "What are your plans, Hetlin?" Yawri asked. "I came to the meeting thinking there would be a time I'd need to leave, learn how to join with simpler physical forms, and return. However, that changes if humans are already asking to join with us to co-create human beings."

Hetlin glanced toward the expanding crowd around Shahten. "We've decided to go back to our lands and see what develops. Even if humans are being created for joining we must be certain they, and we, are ready."

Zinn chimed, "I'm still not sure if the hairless apes I've observed are the humans he's talking about. They seem too small and immature to maintain balance if we added our ethereal essence now."

Another of Hetlin's companions spoke. "When we talked amongst ourselves, all voiced the same concern. We will return to speak with others in our region. If there are any who believe these humans or hairless apes are ready there, we wish to learn of it."

Hetlin spoke to Yawri, her light body stout but lithe. "Rhee said he visited a magnificent island that had stone dwellings. I believe he was going to say they were for humans, but Shahten interrupted him. If you hear more about it, let me know through the crystal caves. Now that I see that diamond crystal in you, I understand why you work with them so well."

"Is it so obvious?" Yawri asked. Hetlin's companions broke out in broad smiles in response.

"It's obvious to those who remember how to see when they look," one of them said.

"Your feather is nice, too," another said to Keela.

Her light body rippled with color. She thought Yawri was the only one who knew about it until he'd pointed it out to Tisbero and Zinn.

"It was a gift from one of the great dark-blue birds. The ones with a patch of orange on their back." Her hand went to her chest as if to safeguard the precious gift.

"We know the great birds," another woman said. "They move in flocks across our skies, but even those joined with ethereal beings rarely approach us." Respect for Keela's connection with them wove through her sound.

Hetlin continued with her resilient presence. "Please send any news through the crystal caves, Yawri. I will do the same."

"Happily!" One of his hands went to his chest, automatically communing with the ethereal diamond there. "I'm always looking for another reason to visit them."

"Done." Hetlin placed a hand on his shoulder, dropped it slowly, and turned to Keela. "The great birds do not make such feather gifts without good reason. You will learn the reason when it is time." Her astute gazed swept from Keela to Zinn, Tisbero, and Yawri in turn. "You each have unusual abilities," she said simply, and added, "We must take our leave. There is much to investigate and share with others in our lands."

Tisbero stopped his watchful scan of the surroundings and turned to Hetlin and her companions. "Thank you for calling this meeting. I appreciate your abilities as well. There is much for us all to investigate, and I look forward to meeting with you again."

Zinn stepped forward with such agility she seemed to disappear from one place and reappear in another. "If you hear of anything unusual happening with animals please let us know. Several of the larger species can join with ethereal beings, and I enjoy working with them."

A male guardian spoke thoughtfully. "I work with large animals too. If I hear of problems, I'll make sure you know."

The diverse group of light bodies started to slowly ascend toward the treetops. Hetlin called out the traditional way of parting. "May you expand Creation in all you become."

"Go ever forth and Create with Creator," Yawri responded in kind.

The four watched the guardians rise and accelerate toward the lands of the east.

"Thank goodness," Zinn beamed. "It's good to know we're not the only ones with more questions than answers."

"They made a point of coming over to talk to us," Tisbero noted.

Yawri turned toward the large group surrounding Shahten. "I think everyone else agrees with him. I doubt anyone even noticed our conversation."

Uncannily, Shahten suddenly looked over at the group of four, a congenial smile on his face. He casually glanced in the direction of the departing community, and his smile grew.

The sharp cry of a monkey redirected the quartet's gaze. Across the valley, they saw a monkey flailing helplessly in the talons of a large, dark-gray bird. The four companions watched the bird until it flew over the ridge, taking the shrieks of its prey with it. When they looked back toward Shahten, his smile looked strange, even predatory, but it returned to a friendly one so quickly it was probably a trick of the light.

14. HUMANS

∞

Earth continued to expand across the ethereal-physical continuum, and more and more guardians struggled to communicate with the planet across its growing spectrum. But the ethereal beings who joined with humans reported more connection with the planet than ever before.

Invariably drawn together by their devotion to help Earth expand in Creation, Yawri, Keela, Zinn and Tisbero often met to share what they heard and saw. Late one spring afternoon they convened on a low hill overlooking a grassy plain peppered with large wildebeest.

Zinn's light body, though still effervescent, was far dimmer than it had been. "I've been watching several tribes of humans. The ones joined with ethereal beings are developing well as human beings. The human beings are growing taller and are solving problems humans haven't been able to solve for centuries."

"What kind of problems?" Tisbero wanted to know.

Zinn was glad to provide more detail. "They are cutting and lacing the hides of animals for better fit and protection. Their shelters are much stronger. They weave sticks to make sturdy walls and tie bundles of grasses together to cover the roofs."

Keela shared her observations. "I've seen other changes, too. Remember the chopping stones they made by chipping off big flakes to form a crude edge? They make teardrop-shaped tools now. They are sturdy, but have a much sharper cutting edge."

Yawri turned from the roving herd of wildebeests to look at his friends. "Are you sure these changes happened because they joined with ethereal beings?"

Tisbero added, "Couldn't this be due to the evolution of their own intelligence?"

"I wondered myself," Zinn replied airily. "Previously, females and males always sought to partner with their most physically fit counterparts. That's still important, but now they favor partners joined with an ethereal being. The human beings are easy to spot. They have an unmistakable vitality and glow that the others do not."

Keela reasoned, "It makes sense. The humans joined with ethereal souls may not always have the strongest bodies, but they'll be much better at problem solving. And the faster you can solve problems the more likely you are to survive."

Zinn's spritely voice affirmed, "The humans who have joined with ethereal souls are prospering."

Tisbero nodded, "There are too many reports about human beings communicating clearly with Earth again for me to deny their success."

They stood quietly, each considering the words of the other. All watched sunbeams from the late afternoon sun streak past a cloud and dance across the prairie grass.

Keela's light body brightened. "I've interviewed beings who joined with humans. They told me blending only a little of their essence opened the door to clear communication with Earth again. They said they are fully aware of All they were, plus much more."

Yawri gazed absently at the waving prairie grass. "I'd love to be able to hear Earth's voice clearly again."

Zinn said, "From everything I've seen, Shahten might have been right after all. The humans do seem ready now, if not when he initially proposed it, to become human beings."

Yawri raised his hands and studied their dim light. "Well, this isn't working anymore."

Tisbero's light body glowed dully, in spite of its iridescent copper tint. "I do not agree with Shahten's timing or manner. However, based on our own observations, it could be that humans are ready to blend. If that is true, leaving Earth now would be counter to my agreement to nurture its expansion."

Yawri focused on each of his companions in turn. The more they'd talked about joining with humans the more uplifted they became. Tired of waiting, he blurted. "Let's seek out a tribe and ask permission to join with a human body."

Rather than protest as he expected, all thoughtfully nodded agreement.

Zinn raised her arms above her head and lowered them again. Relieved and excited, she said, "Decided at last! How long has it been since any of you thought you were going to leave?" She stared at Tisbero.

Tisbero stared back and spoke solemnly. "Several years."

"Years? You've known for years and you didn't say anything?"

"When to join remained a question. There is no reason to rush when you know where you are going."

Zinn glowed brighter. "Almost every other ethereal being I know has already joined. I thought you were waiting for the continents to move."

"They move. Slowly. They also know where they are going."

She shook her head in response.

Yawri noticed Keela was standing tall with her head high. "So what tribe did you have in mind?"

She gave a gentle smile. "You'll find out tomorrow."

15. HUMANS GREETED

∞

Yawri and Keela hovered in the low branches of a thick cedar tree and watched the familiar camp. After over a year of observation, they'd each picked the human they wished to approach.

One of the female humans removed glowing coals from a pouch she carried and placed them on a bed of shredded wood. The tall woman fed kindling to the growing flames until a flurry of sparks streaked into the air.

"That's her," Keela said, "She's the one that carries the fire when they move." The female wore a fine-haired tunic made from the hide of a gazelle. She moved several paces from the fire, sat down on a log and started sorting dried leaves and roots into different piles. "I've been watching her for weeks. She's very strong in her connection to Earth."

"You'll ask to join with her?"

Keela observed her for a long moment before answering. "You know I've always been intrigued by how the female aspect of this planet manifests life. It connects with Life inside of itself first, then moves it to the outside world. It's a level of Creation I want to learn."

Yawri watched the woman sort the dried leaves and roots. She had eight piles so far. "The way female aspects of this planet Create is amazing," he replied sincerely. "Since you're joining the female aspect it makes all the more sense for me to join with a male. There's a lot to learn about this. Do plants use male and female aspects?"

"It's similar. Even moss requires connection of these different aspects of itself to evolve. This dynamic had to be set up on this planet for a reason."

"We are trying to learn how to connect different aspects of a whole, our ethereal energies with this physical and ethereal world, in order to Create. Maybe learning how male and female energies Create within this planet's whole will help us."

Keela considered Yawri's response. "To evolve, every species I've worked with uses these different perspectives within itself to strengthen Life. It might be why this planet is so alive."

"It's why I want to join with a human from this camp. Tribes that honor each aspect equally like this one are doing much better than those dominated by one or the other. It's easy to understand why when you think about it."

The male human Yawri thought might be a good match walked across the camp and sat on a low, flat boulder surrounded by tiny flakes of shiny rock.

"What's around his neck?" Keela asked.

Yawri leaned close to Keela. "He's making little holes in the shells of sea snails so he can string a thin cord through them. He ties each cord to make a circle. That's one around his neck. Did you see the shiny rock he picked up? That rock is from here but the shell comes from the coast. Zinn said this tribe trades the chipping-stone for things from other tribes. Humans are the only creature she's seen that trade this way."

The male struck the shiny rock he held with a small, rounded stone. Small chips of the rock flew off in flakes. Another male approached and the two humans exchanged sounds.

"Do they have language?" Keela asked. "I'm not sure if they communicate with sound and gesture or by speech alone."

The new arrival handed a long, thin, wooden pole to the man sitting on the large, flat rock. He took it into his broad hands, flexed it back and forth, and sighted down its length.

A range of sounds flowed back and forth between the two humans. Finally, the one that had brought the pole walked away. The man sitting on the rock quickly sorted through several sharp, tapered pieces of shiny stone, selected one, and held it next to the tip of the pole.

Keela was impressed. "That was too complex a communication to do without language. Gestures were minimal. I think they were talking."

The male human examined the cupped half of a dried gourd and stirred its contents. When he exhaled his cheeks puffed with a soft *swoosh* of air. After a single nod, he got up and walked toward a trail that led out of camp.

Yawri turned toward Keela. "I know where he's going. They use pitch and cord to attach those sharp points to a pole to make a spear. The pitch comes from a tree down that trail." The human quickly disappeared behind trees and Yawri started moving. "I'm going to follow him."

Keela nodded in response but had turned to watch the female. "I'm amazed at her concentration. Those are medicinal plants she's sorting. That leaf helps rid digestive systems of parasites. That tree bark fights infections."

Yawri's gaze rolled to the female and back to Keela. "She is very focused," he agreed. "I'll be back soon."

Yawri's light body flowed quickly along the path. He found the human scraping thick, sticky pitch from a split branch near the base of a tree. Yawri came closer than he intended and stopped in plain sight of the human. The human stared at him with an intent expression. Rather than being afraid at the sight of a light body twice his height, the human looked back at Yawri with penetrating certainty, effectively conveying that if anyone should be afraid, it should be Yawri.

Encouraged, Yawri tried to communicate with the universal language of thought feeling. "I am called Yawri, and I offer my hello." He listened without expectation to learn if the human could respond in the thought feeling language of All.

The human continued his appraising stare for several seconds, to the point where Yawri wondered if the human had heard his message at all. Then the human's eyes narrowed and he replied, "Other tribes talk of spirits-of-light who live inside the great trees. But you are not joined with the Earth spirit of a tree. Why are you here?"

Yawri was surprised by such a pointed question. He replied evenly. "I, like the spirits-of-light who live in the trees, seek to learn how to join with a body of Earth. They have learned to be one with this planet through tree bodies. Other spirits-of-light are learning how to do the same by joining with humans. I seek to learn how to co-create with Earth in that way." He moved a little closer to the human.

The gesture was not lost on the human. He responded by taking two steps forward, pleased to examine the body of this spirit-of-light more closely. His voice was resolute, his face unflinching. "I am Kunuta, great tool maker, hunter, and provider."

Yawri's response was equally resolute. "I am Yawri, a spirit-of-light that is here to learn and nurture Life." He tilted his luminous head toward the sky.

Kunuta followed Yawri's glance at the sky but brought his eyes back down to the ground. He tapped his callused, bare foot on the fertile soil. "Earth is the source of all things."

Yawri responded steadily. "Yes. All things physical are of Earth, and the spirit of Earth feeds all here with its spirit. My spirit comes from the same source as Earth's spirit."

The human's eyes flashed. "You and spirit-of-Earth are of the same source?"

"Yes, but spirit-of-Earth is wise far beyond my knowing. If I am a drop of water, it is the sea. Earth co-creates with Creator to form All here. I seek to join with a single one of its physical life forms to begin learning of such co-creation."

Kunuta stood and faced Yawri, the bowl of pitch in one hand. He asked again, "Why are you here?" He pointed to the ground. "With me?"

Yawri floated closer to the human. "I seek to blend my spirit from Creator with Earth's spirit from Creator that lives within you." Yawri waved his luminous hands to the trees and sky surrounding them. "I seek to learn and expand with it in all we can become."

Kunuta continued looking at Yawri while he took another step toward him. "Earth sends new thoughts of what it wishes to become. We must continue to evolve or die out. We hear of some in other tribes that have joined with your kind and have evolved. Are you here to help me do the same?"

Yawri wasn't sure how respond. The more he talked with Kunuta the more he thought joining with him might, in fact, be correct. He decided being direct was best. "Yes. By joining with you, I will help you connect with more of All, and through you, help your tribe. And as you evolve, so will I."

Kunuta looked up the path toward his camp and back at Yawri. "This joining would be good for my tribe." He cradled the cup of pitch in both of his hands, holding it gently against his waist. Kunuta spoke with surprising calm. "Those who embrace the changes this planet makes will have children that outlive those that do not. What must I do to join with you?"

Yawri was again uncertain how best to proceed with a joining. The conversation progressed much more quickly than he thought it would. However, he remembered what Murann told him about his joining.

The Earth spirit of the tree and I talked long and often. Neither of us spoke much about the actual joining. One day the timing was right, and it happened with the guidance of Earth.

Thoughts rolled through Yawri's mind.

I need to join with a human spirit to continue guardianship of this planet. Kunuta needs to join to evolve with the planet's changes. We're both motivated. I just wasn't expecting him to be so motivated.

Yawri moved slightly closer and affirmed, as much to himself as Kunuta, "This joining will be good for All." His eyes fell on the bowl of pitch Kunuta held. The human's fingers were covered with a dark, tarry sap. "We will speak together much more and soon," Yawri began to move back. "We will do this well."

Kunuta replied with conviction. "Earth's timing is our timing." With a parting glance at Yawri, he went back to scraping pitch into the bowl.

Yawri returned to Keela, energized by his exchange. He wasn't sure why he was surprised to learn that while he was having his conversation with Kunuta, Keela was doing the same with the female human with similar results.

She looked at Yawri intently. "Now I understand why Tisbero and Zinn joined months ago. They said the humans were eager to join, and after speaking to a human myself it's clear she believes it will help her tribe evolve and thrive."

Yawri bobbed. "I have the same sense from Kunuta, but I'm still glad we waited."

"Strange to hear coming from the most impulsive guardian I know."

He replied, "It is a big commitment. I want to make sure I am being careful with my choices this time. Earlier, if I hadn't been so committed to build time tunnels everywhere, I would have been much more likely to notice problems before they occurred."

"How long are you going to let what happened so long ago bother you? There is no way you could have known beings without any experience would choose to use them and get lost."

"True, but it seems the bigger the commitment, the bigger the no-way-I-thought-that-would-happen shock can be."

"Aren't you the one that keeps telling me it's all just learning?" She looked in the direction of their friends and back to Yawri. "Come on. They've waited long enough. Let's go share our good news with Zinn and Tisbero."

16. JOINING

∞

Yawri and Keela met with their humans daily for many seasons. With each visit, the humans seemed more certain and prepared to join. Their identity and connection to Earth's expanding physical-ethereal continuum grew stronger than ever before.

Just as Murann had described, the mutual respect between human and being continued to grow. One day, without fanfare, Yawri and Kunuta simply knew the timing was right.

Yawri found Kunuta collecting tubers from very tall, single-stalk plants with almond-shaped leaves and big, yellow flowers. The human used the prying edge of a long hand ax to loosen the ground around one of the plants and spoke without looking up.

"Hello, Yawri," he said, sensing the being's presence. He pulled on the sturdy stalk and a number of large, misshapen root tubers came out of the soil with it. He used a stick to remove the soil clinging to them and held up the root. "These have the taste of a sweet nut. Very good." He laid it on a stack of others. "We dry the stalks and use them to build walls." He stood straight and faced Yawri. "We are ready to do our joining, yes?"

If there was ever any question about the strength of this human's connection to Earth, it had been laid to rest long ago. Kunuta was one with the spirit of this planet and was no less significant than this light spirit called Yawri.

Kunuta continued speaking. "The number of humans choosing to join with your kind is increasing. One of our young females left to join a tribe led by a human that joined with a spirit-of-light. Tribes with such unions are growing in size while those without are lessening."

"Yes. I agree it is time for our joining," Yawri replied calmly. The responsibility was one he both wanted and resisted.

It had helped him to have Zinn's counsel. "You're a partner, not a prisoner," she'd told him. "It's an extension of the agreement we made when we came to Earth." He could still hear the mischievous lilt in her voice when she added, "Unless you're going to leave to visit other planets."

On reflection, Yawri was surprised at how confident he was. Of course, it also helped that Zinn had gone over the joining process with him in detail numerous times.

Since Murann entered his tree body through its roots, Yawri had asked her if it was the same for animals. "No," she replied. "Beings enter tree and crystal bodies through their roots. Animals are mobile, so the structure is different. The entryway for us to join with animals is through the head. Earth spirit comes in through an animal's feet." During their last visit, she confided, "I was worried, too, but learned how any form Creator and Earth prepares for a joining innately knows how to connect."

Yawri rose above Kunuta's head, paused to assure all remained centered and gently sent a strand of his essence to touch the center of Kunuta's crown. At the same time, Kunuta increased the amount of Earth spirit in his body to receive it. Yawri felt their energies meet slightly above Kunuta's head and slowly, gently braid together in a tapestry of sound and light.

Yawri expected the tones of Earth to be amplified through Kunuta but was startled by the intensity. The communication boomed. "The agreement will be this," it said.

"Soul of Earth," Yawri replied, focusing on keeping in balance. "I seek to learn about co-creation with you and Creator, and with that learning, expand Creation in all I become."

If such profound clarity results from such a small connection, what's it going to be like when it grows?

The planet's sound traveled through the small braided connection and resonated through Yawri's entire light body. "The human spirit you seek to join is my spirit. His physical body is my body. There is no separation between us and Creator. We are individuals within one body of one source."

Yawri was clear in his response. "I seek to learn how to be both physical and etheric, and bring Life to All without doing harm as I learn."

After a pause, the Earth continued. "Mistakes are a part of learning and may cause harm. When you make mistakes, do you agree to feel their impact and care for their impact on All, including yourself? Do you agree to balance, heal and learn from those? "

"I agree."

"The human form was made to travel across water, ice, desert, mountain or plain, so it could be a guardian of all places. Do you agree that with this body, you will live in all the dimensions of Earth, and blend your own with it? "

"Yes."

"The body will retain its own identity of self, as you will. Do you agree to not possess the Creation resulting from this joining? Do you agree that as the human form and the ethereal being are cherished today, the human being created from this union will be equally cherished?

"Yes."

"I see you have already learned what it means to be a guardian as an ethereal soul. With this joining, do you agree to help expand the physical and ethereal dimensions we express? To be and become a guardian of Life? "

"Yes. The ethereal sounds and light I offer will only strengthen and expand our connection to All."

"With those agreements, you are welcomed. Be One with this planet and All it is connected with. May the human being made from this union ever expand our conscious co-creation with Creator."

"We will," Yawri replied. The tones of Earth quieted, but he remained more enthralled than ever about this new adventure.

Yawri continued to hover above Kunuta cautiously. Suddenly, the strand of essence he had sent to connect with the human's Earth spirit doubled in size, startling him.

Remember, any life form Creator and Earth prepare for joining knows how to connect.

The braids of light still met above the human's head, but now formed a brilliant sphere of liquid light.

The body is developing a structure to regulate the amount of ethereal energy I bring into it.

Yawri sensed a portion of the stream of his essence flow through this sphere and down through Kunuta's body. It percolated through a sequence of more swirling spheres, all aligned down the body's center. He felt an equal current flowing up from Earth.

There's another sphere of liquid light below Kunuta's feet. It's regulating the amount of Earth energy entering the body, to assure what flows into it from Earth is in constant balance with my energies.

He relaxed. Experiencing this elegant blending relieved a tension he didn't know he'd been holding. When Yawri mentioned his concerns to Zinn about joining with a human without first learning from simpler forms, she reassured him by describing the same spheres of liquid light in the body he was experiencing now.

"All you have to do is listen to and honor the structure bodies have in order to maintain balance between you. The human is the one that knows how to create across the planet's physical-ethereal continuum. Learn from it."

Yawri heard new tones and felt their joined essence cycle through the body in a balanced blend of braided essence. Sounds deeper, higher, and more intense than any Yawri had ever experienced vibrated through him. With a shock, he realized he was looking through Kunuta's eyes. The plants of the forest burst with color, so intense he was almost lost in them. Each color held a new sound and resonated with texture. Sensations never before imagined coursed through him.

Are they Kunuta's or mine?

Kunuta experienced himself swimming, engulfed in a vast ocean. No up or down. Physical matter was present and invisible in the same moment. Infinitesimally small particles streamed through the vast ocean. The creative force in a single particle was more than the total of all he'd experienced before.

A tsunami launched Kunuta down a trail. The soles of his feet ran but without traction. Nothing felt firm. It propelled him down a path that only appeared with each new, flailing step. Fireflies swirled by, or were they stars? A flower of otherworldly colors and sounds bloomed. A brilliant chorus of light erupted from its center, a galaxy born.

"Kunuta," Yawri called gently but insistently. The human turned, looking for the source of the sound, but was alone in a cave without walls, ceiling, or floor. A web of gossamer threads suddenly crisscrossed the darkness. The call came again. "I'm Yawri, and I know this place well. Focus on this point, where several of these threads intersect. It will take you back to your space in time."

"How?" Kunuta asked with more presence of mind than Yawri thought possible.

"Time has paths through it like the forest you run through. I helped make these paths, as you help make paths across land. If you bring your attention to this intersection, we will return to camp together."

Kunuta instantly felt himself moving through a tunnel of light, first slowly, then with increasing speed. He passed intersection after intersection of branching light, but a voice both disembodied and within him kept him centered. "This is the path home."

Planets of icy blue streaked by, followed by two more striped giants of yellow and tan. He hardly noticed a small, red, dusty planet because the call of a glowing sphere of blue and white beyond it so entranced him. His eyes filled with tears of yearning—a deep affection and devotion to all Life of his home—as it neared. It sparkled, a sunlit jewel in an ocean of night.

Abruptly, he stood among familiar plants. He looked down. His body was glowing. The pile of tuber roots was again next to his feet. Kunuta swayed, his eyes open wide, and he stared at the white tubers with their fine root hairs and thick, straight stems. He breathed in the potent fragrance of dark-green plants and fertile soil. The bouquet mixed with the birdsong, the gentle rustle of leaves, and palettes of color.

He heard Yawri within him. "Feel your muscles, how they move. Feel your feet on the ground." Kunuta flexed. His mouth grew into a wide smile when it seemed his feet had roots in Earth deeper than ever before. New thoughts came to the human.

The more ethereal, the more physical I become, and I am its center of balance.

He hopped slowly from one foot to the other, then faster. With a bounce, he jogged to the trunk of an old snag. Its wrinkled bark—completely covered with lichen and mushrooms—was both fully alive and dead in the same moment.

He stepped up on the patch of bare, weathered wood crowning its top and surveyed the land. The leaves of tall tuber plants waved in a gentle breeze, along with golden-tipped grasses and undulating trees.

Standing tall and with his shoulders back, he spoke to Yawri. "I am made of Creator's Earth. Its spirit is my spirit. You bring ethereal realms beyond what I knew. Because of our joining, I am more. Earth is more."

Yawri was surprised connecting such a small strand of his ethereal presence caused Kunuta to experience his perspective of timeless-time. Fortunately, Kunuta had chosen to focus on the point in time Yawri knew was here and now. If he'd chosen another, Kunuta would have popped into another place and moment within the All, which would have been disastrous for them both. Kunuta had done well. He received Yawri's thoughts and regained his center quickly.

Yawri's reflection was interrupted when Kunuta suddenly jumped down from the fallen tree and bent to pick up one of the tuber roots. The suddenness with which he brought it to his mouth and took a bite startled Yawri, but he was even more shocked when the crisp, sweet flavor filled Kunuta's mouth. The taste and texture felt like—no, it *tasted* like—Creator's essence.

I've got to keep in balance. Our braid is strengthening moment by moment.

The thought was overwhelmed by a new sensation: breeze against Kunuta's skin, followed by more fragrances in the wind. The deep-blue sky sang with light. Kunuta's breath and the throb of his heart chimed with a tumbling kaleidoscope of escalating sensation.

Blood surged in his body with a palpable current. Cells of bone, muscle, and nerve divided and grew in a melodic chant. Yawri reeled with the vibration.

Kunuta took another bite of tuber root, its juice filling his mouth. He bent down, picked up the pile of tuber stalks, rested them on his shoulder and began to run. Yawri felt the body glide, flying over the ground. His feet moved by their own volition, thrumming with each stride in perfect symmetry. Yawri darted around trees, laughing with joy, fluid as the wind.

Got to get back to my tribe's camp.

Yawri experienced his body sailing through the forest, and he was excited to rejoin his tribe.

A voice intruded. "Feel how the winds of Earth move with the solar winds. Listen to the solar winds whistle around the planets as Earth's winds whistle around trees. Different, yet One."

Another sensation started to grow. Yawri sailed from planet to planet, excited to be with the stars. He felt, heard, and saw living particles of mist flowing through him. A sense of personal identity within the tumult returned, and he felt centered once more.

Yawri asked, "Who spoke? You helped me regain balance."

"Soul of Earth."

"You come again, and your sound is clear!" Yawri exclaimed. "You co-create with Creator across realms beyond my knowing. I join with Kunuta to learn how to expand in Creation with you."

The voice came from everywhere at once. "Kunuta became overwhelmed as he experienced the purely ethereal life force you bring. After he touched those realms, and it was only a touch, you helped him focus on this space in time. You gave him the single dot of sand within an endless beach that returned him to himself. He is now more than what he was before the joining, without being harmed."

"Of course," Yawri replied. "As I agreed. The ethereal sounds and light I bring are to strengthen Life, never subtract from it."

"So I responded in kind. Ethereal souls can become overwhelmed with physicality. After you touched those realms, and it was only a touch, I helped you focus on your source, the origin of us both. You are also more than what you were, without being harmed."

Yawri wasn't sure how to reply, but said, "Thank you. Even though I prepared to maintain my center, the intensity of physical essence within All was much more than I expected."

"Co-creation connects with so many realms its best to let go of all expectations."

"Yes. All I can do is prepare as best I can. However, as I seek to learn how to do something I don't know how to do I don't want to do harm to you or myself."

"Your actions have made that clear. May you, Kunuta, and the human being formed by your joining continue to learn how to expand here in co-creation with Creator. May All learn to be a human being and be One with All."

Yawri felt Kunuta's buoyant steps toward his tribe's camp. When the human being entered camp all eyes noticed his glowing radiance, which showed he had joined with one of the spirits-of-light. All considered the event good fortune and celebratory greetings rang.

Yawri experienced a warm, safe feeling spreading throughout their body as he strode toward the fire.

Emotions, like all of Kunuta's perceptions, are far more engaging than I imagined. This is going to be an adventure.

17. JOY

∞

Yawri, Keela, Tisbero and Zinn met on a high bank above a clear stream. Their light bodies glowed with renewed vitality, and the fine, woven strands of essence connecting them to their human bodies shone brightly.

Clear water flowed down a ramp of tumbled black rock and pooled in a deep crevice. The guardians watched the frothing water massage the rocks. Beyond the swirling pool, the water flowed to a creek where a large cat stood, its two long teeth protruding down from its tight jaw. Its large, yellow eyes looked at the guardians and, unconcerned, it lowered its head and took a leisurely drink.

Yawri saw Keela shift her focus away from the animal toward the sky. Following her gaze, he saw a broad-winged bird land in a tall tree slightly upslope from the animal. Its eyes were fixed on Keela rather than the predatory cat.

"I think that bird likes you, Keela."

"And plants. Plants like me, too, like some rocks like you."

"They're not rocks. They're crystals."

"You told me rocks were made of minerals and all minerals are crystals."

"Yes, but that's like saying a seed is a tree."

"A seed has a tree in it."

Tisbero leaned in between them and interjected. "Please, the day is growing late. Didn't we agree to discuss changes since joining with our humans?" He turned his head to check on the large-toothed cat, but it was gone.

Zinn pivoted to face them all. "The change in how I perceive Life is amazing. The textures, flavors, and varieties of the foods the human I joined with eats are astounding. When she ate berries yesterday I was so absorbed in the experience, I only noticed when she stopped eating.

"And running!" she continued, frothing more than the creek. "The sensation of running and jumping while this body moves and looking through its eyes is like having two lives. Me as a light body, and me in a physical form. The physical sensations are fascinating!"

Yawri appreciated Zinn's enthusiasm. "It's the same with Kunuta! There's stunning Life force in everything he touches. Although I have only the slightest amount of my essence in him, my ideas and questions help him solve problems much better than the unjoined humans. What about yours, Tisbero?"

Tisbero spoke with purpose. "I've practiced problem solving with my human partner. His tribe made narrow spear tips that could be withdrawn easily during the repeated stabbing needed to kill game. They would lose the whole spear if the game escaped. However, they needed a different kind of tip that would stay in a fish. I whispered an idea to see if it would help."

Curious, Zinn tilted her face toward his. "What thought did you whisper?"

Tisbero rumbled steadily. "While he split a bone to get at its marrow, one of the pieces divided into a triangular sliver. It was wide at one end and tapered to a point at the other. I offered the thought, 'A spear tip this shape won't come out easily. The fish couldn't swim away.' I think he thought the inspiration came from himself, but it didn't matter.

"He used bone to make one with a broad shoulder that tapered to a sharp tip rather than the oval ones made of glassy rock they all use. He tried it with success, but I offered another thought about notching its edge with teeth and indenting the shoulder rather than have it run straight to the shaft. It works so well it's the only tip the tribe uses for spearing fish now. Plus, they have all the bone they need. They had to trade for the glassy rock. He's advancing to a leadership role in the tribe."

Yawri rushed, "It's the same with Kunuta. He's head of his tribe now."

"Head male," Keela added quickly. "The female I'm joined with is his equal in the tribe."

"Equal in his mind, too," Yawri acknowledged. "He seeks her counsel often."

"As she does his. The combination of male and female perspectives make them very effective problem solvers, and their reputation is spreading. They've become the largest tribe in their area."

Zinn chimed in, "I'm learning how emotions instantly communicate what the body perceives. Initially I became the emotion. You can lose yourself in them! Now, I've learned to listen to them like a language, a language of the body. Different experiences cause different emotions. They flow through the body and tell every cell what's happening. No wonder humans have survived. Their bodies react instantaneously, without thinking about it."

"Don't all animals do the same?" Yawri asked. "They react instantly too."

"Similar, but experiencing the world as a human being gave me a very different outlook. My human partner reflects on its responses in a way other animals don't. I use that ability to help her."

"I've been learning how to listen to, instead of become, the emotions of mine, too. There is a lot to learn," Keela said quietly.

"What have you learned?" Zinn wanted to know. "Do you think emotions are the language of the body?"

"From what I've experienced, yes. Listening to her emotions tells me how she perceives the world at that moment. I've identified different sensations when she's feeling joy, contentment, fear, safety, humor, sadness, gratitude, remorse, satisfaction, frustration and many more. Each one motivates different actions, different behaviors. She's transparent in the moment, and the next."

Zinn said, "Exactly. When the woman I'm joined with experiences something that frustrates or scares her, I whisper the questions and choices she has and feel her emotion change from frustrated to decisively hopeful within seconds. I bring options to solve problems she's had for years. Since they come from within her, she claims the ideas as her own and is empowered to create change, and she does."

Tisbero said, "That's what must have happened when I suggested the new spear tip. Fish were running in a river, big ones. My partner was good at spearing them, but the oval tips kept slipping out. Everyone was frustrated because they were only wounding the fish and causing them to die without purpose. I brought questions and choices the tribe hadn't considered before. My thought changed how he perceived the problem, and his frustration changed to action within seconds."

Keela enjoined, "That's why the humans who joined are surpassing those who haven't. We bring them inspiring new thoughts and questions, and they bring us the connection we need to learn physical co-creation from them."

Zinn said, "No other animal I know can understand new concepts and change so quickly. Creator gave them this talent for a reason."

"Perhaps it is so we could join with them in spite of their small size. Without their ability to receive inspiration and then change, I don't see how our co-creations could work." Tisbero said.

The conversation reminded Yawri of an old question. "They are small and short-lived. Have any of you heard how we retrieve our energy from the bodies when they die? The human's learning will simply go back to its source, Earth's soul and matter. What about ours? We need to retrieve all of our learning from the body when it dies, too. Otherwise we'll have to repeat the same learning over and over again."

Zinn nodded. "I was speaking to a human being who joined long before we did. He told me retrieving our essence isn't a problem. The bodies know their source is the Earth. When they die all of the human essence automatically returns to it. We all chose bodies with strong connection with Earth. What remains, we call back to us."

"It makes sense," Yawri said, relieved. "Kunuta has a very strong spirit of Earth. We've learned a lot about co-creating physically and ethereally together. When his human spirit gets a new body, I should be able to join with it as I did this one."

Tisbero spoke. "I understand the same. The body of one guardian I know died sooner than he expected. His connection to the body's Earth spirit was strong, and when it was reborn in another body, they greeted each other with joy. He said the joining was easier than the first time, and they are connected more deeply because both he and the Earth spirit retain all of their knowledge from their first life together."

Keela said thoughtfully, "So the more we connect with our bodies, the more we connect with Earth. The more we connect with Earth, the more ethereal presence we can bring into our bodies."

Zinn added, "Amazing opportunity, isn't it? It shows what can happen with a planet in conscious co-creation with Creator."

Yawri beamed. "Right. What a wonderful way to expand in Creation with all we become. The guardians who left the planet because they didn't think the humans were ready to become human beings don't know what they're missing."

All four guardians smiled, pleased that the decision they avoided making for so long had turned out so well.

18. COMMUNITY

∞

Over generations, the blending of human spirit and ethereal being flourished. Human beings thrived and increased in both size and longevity.

The color of the fine, woven basket Keela held matched her flaxen hair. Her body was almost twelve feet in height and moved gracefully while she surveyed the harvest of dried roots hanging on the drying rack.

She took a deep breath, enjoying the sensation of air passing in and out of her lungs, and raised a nimble hand to a long, tapered root known for its calming effect. Her alto voice could have been a bird's song. "Thank you for sharing your life force with ours. May your nourishment help our mindful connection to the Whole."

The response from the plants was beyond physical hearing, yet reverberated in her body.

We willingly transform to nourish and calm those who enrich Life.

"Thank you. May our essence be one with yours." She gently placed the root into the brimming basket.

The cry of a young voice split the air. "It's not responding!"

Keela raised her head toward the cry. She was directly under the growing shadow of a massive, plummeting stone.

A second youthful voice yelled, "We're going to crash!"

Even though Keela knew there wasn't time to escape, her body started moving to try. However, with death imminent, its Earth spirit started pulling its energy out of her doomed form, and Keela's ethereal soul started doing the same. The shadow darkened. She felt the warm, centered sensation that comes from deaths continuous transformation into new Life. Her body moved but her mind was calm.

It will be a conscious death and a conscious return.

A bright light suddenly flared around the edges of the plunging monolith, framing its underside in white.

The slab came to an abrupt stop just above her head. Halted mid-stride, she looked up and saw pink granite filled with golden-brown garnet and shining mica. The slab hovered a long moment, rose slightly and floated about twenty paces away.

The threat gone, Keela's body relaxed and the essence of Earth and her ethereal soul flowed back into it. Her foot touched the basket and she looked down. The roots in it, as well as those on the drying rack, were still singing. She retrieved the long one she'd placed in the basket, the one that produced a calming effect. She didn't feel a need for it, but whoever was piloting that skystone was going to.

The hovering skystone descended slowly and stopped slightly above the tall grass.

Experienced pilots always park skystones above the ground so nothing's crushed, but those voices are young.

"Yawri!" she yelled, seeing him appear behind two young guardians. "I should have known!"

Yawri, his body still glowing with soul light, looked at her and nodded a greeting. A smile cracked his lips. Her eyes met his and she shook her head with all the rebuke she could muster. It was Yawri, after all, and she'd learned long ago he had no concept of a "mistake," either made by him or anyone else. "It's all just learning," he was fond of saying. However, catching his eye, she raised an arresting eyebrow in question.

Yawri looked at the young man and woman, whose faces were downcast. "What happened?" he asked with a seriousness rare for him.

Both avoided his gaze. The young woman was first to realize the answer would not come from the granite slab she stared down upon. "I don't know. We connected with the crystals to increase soul light. Adding soul light has always decreased gravity and made us ascend before, but this time we fell."

The young man volunteered, "Remember when you taught us to increase air pressure under the skystone so it would rise faster? All I did was tell the wind to increase pressure to do that. We should have gone up faster, not gone down."

"You *told* the wind?" Yawri wanted to be sure he'd heard correctly.

"I meant asked, I asked the wind," the young man corrected himself.

Yawri was silent a long moment while he considered the mortified look on the youth's faces. "We'll work again the day after tomorrow," he said, trying to sound stern. "Between now and then, both of you practice speaking with those boulders over there." Yawri pointed to an outcrop of hard, pale-yellow sandstone. "When you say hello, don't expect an answer.

In fact, don't have any expectations at all. Before we try this again, you'll need to show me you've learned how to ask, not tell, stone and air what you wish."

The young woman's darting glare spoke volumes to her companion. "Two days of only talking to boulders for me, too? I wasn't telling the wind to do anything."

"Good to know, Mariyonta. I'm glad to hear this exercise will be easy for you." To them both, he said, "If one boulder doesn't wish to communicate with you, keep saying hello to others until you find one who does." Both students nodded agreement and quickly stepped off the skystone, but walked carefully to avoid stepping on any plants.

Keela muttered to herself, "At least Yawri taught them to keep off plants." However, her unblinking eyes stayed fixed on him.

Yawri's taut, agile body was taller than hers, not by a lot but enough to make her tilt her head up as he approached. He strode toward Keela, arms open wide, his body still glowing with the soul light he had used to stop the falling skystone. "That was Mariyonta and Aronlat. My best students!"

"If they're your best students warn me before you go up with any others. Our bodies could all have died, and from the looks on their faces, those two would not have died well. How could they return to a new body remembering who they are if they died in trauma?"

He lifted his large hands with his palms up. "No one was in danger. The skystone and I knew we could stop."

"Tell that to my body and these plants." She waved toward her drying rack. "How were we supposed to know you could stop like that?" Her tone was stern but Yawri saw the slight curve of her mouth.

"Keela, you know I'd never crush your plants."

"And that's why I'm never far from them when you're in the air." She looped her thumbs in her waist-sash.

Maybe he'll start taking events like this more seriously.

Keela's gesture drew Yawri's eyes to her sash. "Where did you get a sash with so many colors? It's fascinating!" Although all guardians wore similar long, off-white tunics, their sashes were commonly a solid color. Yawri liked orange. "Did you make it?"

Her response was succinct. "A guardian in Tisbero's community and I started using our dyes to color thread, not just entire sashes. I used the colored thread to outline patterns, then filled them with stitches of more thread."

He looked closer. A vine of leaves and small flowers weaved the length of the sash. He boomed, "This is amazing!"

She took her thumbs out of the embroidered waistband and pulled her shoulders back. She wanted to tell him more about how it was done and to find out more about the youths on the skystone.

She cast a glance toward the distant boulders. The two young adults were having an animated discussion, or perhaps an argument. "So they're the two you've been so hopeful about?"

Yawri grinned. "They need to learn how to ask rather than tell each other what they want. They'll do much better after spending a couple of days with those no-nonsense boulders."

"That's your plan?"

Yawri looked from Aronlat and Mariyonta, then back to Keela. She held the root in her hand like a candle. He asked, "The root harvest is in?" She handed it to him. He smelled it and took an appreciative bite. "These are sweeter than last year!"

"Eat all you want. They calm nerves. "

"Nerves? I'm not nervous," he said with mock anxiety and took another bite.

Keela persisted. "What did they do to make a skystone fall? Become totally soul sound and forget the light?"

"Hi, Yawri!" a loud, masculine voice boomed.

Both he and Keela pivoted. "Gamon." Keela spoke with the same neutral tone she used when identifying a plant.

Yawri's reply to her was filled with whimsy. "I'm sure he'll have many helpful suggestions."

Gamon strode toward them, arms swinging wide. His voice boomed again, "What happened, Yawri? I mistook your skystone for a meteor."

"Gamon, I've never known you to make a mistake. You ended up right, though. It was a skystone."

"Yes, but why are you teaching students how to fall instead of fly?"

Some guardians found Gamon pushy, but he didn't bother Yawri. Then again, they were usually the same guardians that said Yawri was too impulsive. "So they know how to stop falling when the unexpected happens."

Gamon almost spoke over him. "My students do well with repetition. If they repeat the right actions often enough, mistake-free reactions become second nature." He turned and stared fixedly at Aronlat and Mariyonta. The two stood unmoving and silent in front of different boulders. "Looks like they could use some communication right now. Mind if I go talk to them?"

"Not at all. That's the reason I sent them over there."

Gamon's pained expression showed he didn't understand Yawri's statement but also conveyed he didn't expect Yawri to make sense. "I'll go visit with them." He turned to Keela. "I've learned some new information about plants. We should talk sometime."

Keela was respectfully circumspect. "I always like learning new things about plants." They watched Gamon's long steps and swinging arms while he quickly walked to the young adults.

"Gamon is Gamon," was all Yawri said.

Undistracted, Keela repeated her question. "So how did Aronlat and Mariyonta make a skystone fall so fast?"

When Keela decided to learn about something, Yawri knew she'd persist until she did. He handed the root back to her.

She received it carefully, but as she spoke, pointed it toward him. "Mariyonta, Aronlat and the skystone?"

His hazel eyes strayed to the skystone. The rough slab of pink granite still hovered above the grass. Two lengthy quartz crystals lay along the edge of each long side and reflected the sun.

"They learned how to pilot small skystones as individuals well. They each could expand a skystone crystal's connection to the Earth's magnetic field and use it to propel us anywhere I asked. It was time to put them together on a larger skystone so they could learn to pilot with others."

Yawri took a step toward the pink granite slab and stood silently a moment. "Even though human beings can't fly through rock like our light bodies could, you have to admit this is a good substitute. Joining gave us the ability to work with physicality in ways I never imagined."

"Yes. I enjoy flying skystones, too. Joining with humans meant we also joined Earth's ethereal-physical continuum. I think we were all surprised at how expansive it is."

Keela took a small bite of the root and handed it back to him. "So why did the skystone fall?"

"You know how we ask the air to weave currents in front of us so we're screened from the wind? Doing that together proved harder than adjusting their soul light and sound to go up or down. The windscreen came and went unpredictably, but they finally learned." He paused and continued. "You know how I ask the wind to increase air pressure under a skystone while decreasing pressure above so we can shoot up with the force of a geyser?"

Keela's lips pursed. "I know you're the only one who asks the wind to do that. Changing amounts of soul light and sound makes skystones go up or down plenty fast enough for everyone else."

Yawri straightened. "Since I'm teaching them how to ask the air to braid a windscreen, why not teach them how to do this, too? You never know when you might have to move up or down faster than soul light and sound can manage."

"And when would that be?" Keela wanted to know.

"It's how I stopped the skystone from hitting your head."

"Which wouldn't have happened if you weren't teaching them how to do something no one else sees the need for."

Yawri nodded toward the young adults. "Aronlat commanded instead of asking the wind. That weakens connection. The windscreen failed. They both panicked, lost contact with wind and stone, and finally with each other. Speaking with boulders for a couple of days will help them remember co-creation is about connecting, not controlling." He took another bite of the root and looked at it appraisingly. "These are delicious."

"You could have harmed your body with the amount of soul light you pulled in. You know power surges can cause instantaneous combustion. All that's left is ash."

Even though only a stub of the root remained, he pressed it into her hand and looked into her eyes. "Keela, the skystone, wind and I knew we wouldn't crash. We've never lost connection."

Keela broke his gaze and searched for something less intense. Her eyes fell on the skystone he'd so conscientiously parked above the grass.

After plunging so far so fast, how could anyone have the presence of mind to do that?

She crossed her arms over her chest and stared back into his eyes. "I had no need to know that the garnets on the bottom of that skystone are the size of eagle eggs."

Yawri cracked a smile. "Do you enjoy garnets? Those are golden brown. Best for skystones. Green ones are really good with dimensions and plants."

"Yes, green ones are my favorite … but not at that velocity."

Yawri turned toward the large sandstone boulders. Gamon was speaking to Aronlat and Mariyonta in earnest. "What do you think he's telling them?"

She followed his gaze. "That you're too impulsive and bodies learn best by repetition."

"What seems impulsive to some is flexibility to others."

"Wouldn't being impulsive make flexibility a requirement?"

"Maybe being flexible simply looks impulsive to those that always plan." Before she had a chance to respond, he added, "I have an impulsive question for you that I've been asking myself a few years now."

Keela's eyebrows arched and she leaned back. "You've had a question for years that you haven't asked anyone else? I guess that proves there is a first time for everything."

He continued to study Aronlat and Mariyonta. "Does it seem it's taking longer for human beings to remember their knowledge from past lifetimes? These two are recalling faster than most, but others are having trouble just speaking with crystals. They have expectations about how it should work and it keeps them from experiencing what's actually there."

Keela offered him the last bite of the yellow root stub but he raised a hand in polite decline. "Why do you always bring up things I'm wondering about but haven't spoken about yet?"

Yawri stood tall and smiled. "Because I speak what I'm thinking?"

Keela sighed. "And I speak after I think."

Yawri swayed from one foot to the other. "So tell me, what have you been wondering about that you haven't talked about?"

She ate the last of the root and swallowed hard. "It does seem more difficult for the young to remember what they've learned in the past. I asked one of my students to gather honey from a hive and they got stung. Unimaginable! It's never happened before."

Yawri ran a hand through his tousled hair. "Why would it be getting more difficult to remember? It's still the same ethereal soul and Earth spirit in each body. Every new body has always had complete memory of previous learnings for me."

"Same with me. Some seem to be having difficulty, though. But maybe ours is a rare observation. You're the first guardian I've heard speak of it."

"Maybe the others have been wondering but not speaking of it, either. I'll ask a few others. No harm in that. There's a lot I don't know, but I'm always willing to share it."

Keela was still deciphering what he meant when Tisbero's distant voice cracked the air. "There you are! Zinn's found a mammoth that might need help. Would you two come with us to find out?"

"Sure!" Yawri replied, always ready for a new adventure.

Keela knew mammoths were one of Zinn's favorite animals. The feeling was mutual. They invited her to ride them on occasion. "What kind of help? Should I bring anything?"

"A skystone," Tisbero called out. "It needs to be fast."

Yawri's response was spontaneous. "I can see to that."

19. MAMMOTH

∞

Tisbero's long, white, linen tunic pulled tight against his barrel chest with each stride toward Yawri and Keela. He spoke in a voice as rough as his weathered hands.

"Zinn doesn't know what the mammoths need, but some are dying without any apparent reason. On the astral last night she found a herd that looks ill," he said, referring to the guardian's common practice of traveling out-of-body with their etheric, astral selves while their physical bodies slept. "It's about an hour's skystone flight southeast, near the cave of yellow crystals you showed us, Yawri."

"The citrine cave that blends physical and ethereal dimensions on the planet?"

"That's the one. Zinn said the herd is a short flight from it. If you take us there, she can find them." He stopped and glanced at the skystone Yawri used for training. "Would that one take us?"

Keela looked at Yawri, and her eyes were narrow.

"I'll ask," he said, curious about what it would say after the plummet and rapid stop. Communicating in the universal thought-feeling language of All, the answer came quickly.

"Uh … let's ask the green granite skystone over there," he said. "This one is a little …"

"Grumpy?" Keela interjected.

"Yeah," he agreed quietly. "Grumpy."

Tisbero pivoted and in one smooth stride started back the way he'd come. "I'll leave it to you to find a skystone while I get Zinn. She doesn't know how fast they're moving so she wants to leave as soon as we can."

"We'll be ready," Yawri affirmed.

Keela and Yawri walked toward a rectangular, green, granite slab with four large quartz crystals lying along its long sides. Yawri stopped an arm's length away from it and communicated the purpose of the journey. The response was clear.

We wish to aid your effort to find these mammoths.

Yawri spoke to Keela. "It agrees to take us. I've flown with it many times. It has four crystals to propel it rather than the usual two, because both it and I enjoy going fast."

Keela answered, "Great, as long as the rest of us enjoy it too."

They stepped onto the skystone and saw Zinn and Tisbero crest the rise. Zinn's voice sparkled. "Thanks for getting the skystone ready, Yawri! Based on my astral conversation with the herd, they don't understand why they are dying. The sooner we get to them the better."

Zinn jumped onto the skystone, her lithe body moving in a whirl. She and Keela formed a line behind Yawri while Tisbero stood at the rear and quickly surveyed the sky.

Yawri compressed his lips in concentration, but they transformed into a smile when the crystals connected to Earth's magnetic field even faster than usual. The skystone was ready to propel them any direction needed. The four guardians increased soul light to decrease the effect of gravity on the skystone and it rose into the air. Within minutes, they were passing quickly over the trees.

Rather than follow the river valley, the most popular and level direction, Yawri flew the most direct route: up, over, and down mountain peaks and valleys. The rapid change in topography made it far more challenging for everyone, but no one expected him to take the level route.

Each guardian stood firmly connected with the stone under their feet before Yawri made his first bizarrely rapid ascent into the air. In answer to Tisbero's quizzical look, Keela said, "He's using his air pressure trick." Tisbero knew Yawri's method but hadn't ever felt the need to use it himself.

They sailed over the next valley with increasing speed. After catapulting up and over the last range of mountains, they passed the final ridge and Yawri pointed. "The cave of yellow crystals is directly below us."

"How does he do that?" Keela heard Tisbero ask. "I never see landmarks, but he always comes to the right spot."

She turned and smiled. "He says he follows 'impulses.'"

Tisbero shook his head. "It has to be something more."

Within moments, a grassy plain stretching to the horizon came into view. "There they are!" Zinn exclaimed, pointing to hundreds of dots moving in the distance. "It's the herd I visited in my astral body last night!"

"Let's make sure," Tisbero said from behind her.

Yawri, no longer concerned about the sudden updrafts and whipping winds of the mountains, asked the skystone to accelerate even more. This caused the other three to take a quick step back to avoid falling. The skystone banked far more sharply than any of them ever had, but even Tisbero grinned.

The skystone suddenly slowed, leveled, and hovered over the enormous animals. Several mammoths looked up, their long tusks two crescent moons rising on either side of their massive heads.

"Where do you want to land?" Yawri asked Zinn.

Zinn surveyed the scene. "These mammoths aren't ill. They look healthy enough to ride!" she said with relief. "Maybe the ones I saw are very few."

Tisbero's eyes raked the plains. "What about those?" He pointed to a group of dots far behind the massive herd. "Is it normal to have a small herd separated by such distance?"

Zinn stepped to the edge of the monolith. "Let's find out."

The skystone started moving immediately but at a slow speed. The closer they came, the more disconcerting the scene. Mammoths were alert animals. However, none of these even looked up as the skystone approached. Mammoths typically trampled a threat first and returned to see what it was later, but these didn't show any sign they even noticed the stone slab over them.

Zinn spoke with a seriousness new to the others. "Down. Go down!" In a whisper, she added, "What's happening to my majestic mammoths?"

Before Yawri parked above the plants, she jumped off the skystone and disappeared into grass much taller than she was. "They're headed for the shade of those trees," she called back over her shoulder.

The other guardians followed quickly. When they caught up to her, she stood facing a young bull. It gazed dull-eyed at her, took two faltering steps toward her upturned face, and toppled onto its side. The young bull's chest expanded, and after a long wheeze, lay still.

The guardians stood in shocked silence. Tisbero was the first to see a sizeable female mammoth approaching. "A big one comes."

His voice broke their daze.

"It's the matriarch of the herd," said Zinn.

The skin of the elder drooped with each plodding step. She didn't look at the human beings, only at the fallen bull. She reached the still form and nuzzled it with her long nose. When it didn't respond, she prodded more earnestly, her nostrils flaring. Still getting no response, she laboriously pushed her tusks under the bull and tried to raise him. Weak herself, she finally stopped and took one step back. Except for tears rolling down her weathered face, she stood unmoving over the breathless body.

Zinn approached the grief-stricken mammoth. Tenderly, she extended her senses in communication with the giant. "I am sorry," came from every cell in her body.

The matriarch spoke slowly. "We have never experienced any such illness."

Zinn replied reverently. "We see you are an ethereal being joined with the Earth spirit of a mammoth body. We come as human beings to help if we can. Do you know why this happening?"

Tears continued to trickle from her huge, dark eyes. "Neither the Earth spirit of this body nor I know. Nothing resembling this kind of death has happened in all the lifetimes we've shared."

Tisbero's gaze probed the surrounding tundra. "How does the sickness begin?"

The colossal animal swayed silently in place so long the guardians thought she might fall. Finally, she spoke. "We've grazed this plain for lifetimes. Yet now we get ill. We become lethargic. Thirsty, while our mouths drip saliva. The milk we need to feed our young dries up. We have better deaths if we find a place with water and shade. We are on our way to such a place now."

The matriarch looked down at her young, fallen friend. "None of us know what learning can be retrieved from this kind of death. It feels outside of nature, yet it must be of nature or it would not be here."

Zinn knelt to examine the young mammoth. The foam of his saliva formed a veil of white over the top of his massive tusks. His eyes were glazed. She closed his eyelids with a tender hand.

Keela saw long stalks of grass clinging to the beast's mouth and bent to gently pull them out. Studying them, she said, "This is curious." She opened herself to the life force within the grass. Her eyes flew open, then words erupted from her. "This can't be! It doesn't make sense."

Yawri came to her side. "What is it?"

She pulled back, frowning. "It makes no sense."

"What doesn't make sense?" He placed a hand on the dark-brown fur of the fallen animal's huge neck and extended his senses to try to learn what had befallen it. After a moment, he said, "Something is toxic in its intestines. It's not a mineral. It's something growing with the plant." Keela waited to see if he sensed the same thing she did. He looked at her. "It's the fungus that joined with the algae to create the lichen we healed! How could it be here? It's for lichen, not grass!"

Keela's voice rose from deep in her chest. "I agree. It is the same fungus which joined with algae to co-create the lichen valley we healed." She looked at the severed stalks of grass in her hand. "How did it come here?"

Zinn turned to the matriarch. "This grass is taller than in the rest of the tundra. Is it widespread?"

The majestic animal swayed. "It's taller than the other grasses. It started near here but now grows to the river far west."

Keela rolled a stem back and forth between her long fingers. "All the fungus and plant roots I've seen benefit each other. This fungus works very well with algae to make lichen, but alone it makes grass toxic to mammoths."

The matriarch mammoth swayed further. The guardians moved quickly, standing on either side of her drooping head, as her tusks hung just inches above the ground. "Why would Earth create grass that kills us? Mammoth bodies were some of the first ones that Creator and Earth made ready to receive ethereal souls."

The matriarch raised one massive leg slightly above the ground and set it back down. "Our feet send and receive vibration much farther than the eye can see. We relay messages across continents, and where we walk the vibration of our feet brings Life to the ground. During the still of night, our great, crescent tusks are One with the moon. We walk to where Earth wishes in desert, forest, or snow to strengthen connection of All." A gust of wind thrashed the surrounding grass. "Why would the soul of Earth want us to end?"

Zinn said, "As human beings, we strive to do what you have already done for millennia. Intentionally ending mammoth makes no sense to me whatsoever."

Tisbero loosened his clenched jaw. "We will find the explanation."

The matriarch raised her head. New tears flowed down her weathered face. "I hope you do. We have not." After a pause she added, "The moon tells us of other planets with similar forms to ours. With our death here, we will take our learning to one of them that wishes to receive the Life we bring."

She looked down at the young bull. "He was an ancient and wise soul, one of the first to join with these bodies. His death was slow and torturous, and not of its timing. I do not know the effect such a death has on our ability to retrieve the memory of learnings needed for future lifetimes."

Yawri released a deep breath and lowered his eyes from the matriarch to the bull. "We will do all we can to see that the Earth spirit of this body returns to Earth with all of its learnings. We will help its ethereal soul retrieve all of itself as well. Be assured, we can help his death feed Life as Life feeds death."

Tisbero nodded definitively. "We will do this."

The mammoth being turned slowly and took halting steps toward the rest of the herd. They stood unmoving and huddled in the shade of the trees.

Yawri ran his hand through his flailing hair. "You're right, Zinn. This makes no sense. Why would Earth want to end such a Life-sustaining force? Yet the fungus Keela and I discovered is here, taking rather than giving Life."

Zinn stared at the departing matriarch in uncharacteristic silence.

Keela finally said, "The fungus made the grass taller. Do you think Earth needed longer grass for some reason?"

Zinn shook her head without taking her eyes off the retreating mammoth. "And kill the animals the same grass needs to spread their seed across the lands?"

Keela looked long and hard at the stilled body of the young bull. "The answer is not here. The mammoth beings themselves don't know it."

Yawri's voice was thick. "Let's do what we can to strengthen the connection of mammoths to All."

Without another word, the guardians connected to the ethereal-physical continuum each knew well. They deepened their connection with Earth ... One with all the Life they helped co-create ... One with the flow of Life and death as continual learning ... One with all the physical-ethereal continuum of Earth their bodies channeled.

Within moments, multiple shades of light and harmonic scales surrounded them and spread to the land. The soil itself gave a soft, warm glow. A gentle breeze joined with the wind of Earth, and the wind of Earth joined with the solar winds. Connection expanded connection.

Though not visible to physical eyes, the area where the sick herd stood shimmered with soft light. Their death would not be separated from Life here. Beginnings and endings would remain together, each continually feeding the other within the Whole.

Mammoths trumpeted. Even though weak, their sound was picked up by the soft breeze and carried on. Deep, subsonic tones from their great feet traveled through the ground to tell other herds of their experience.

The amber highlights in Zinn's eyes flashed. "They leave in grief but without trauma. They will take their ability to enrich Creation to another planet."

"It still doesn't make sense," Keela echoed. "They gave Life to Earth with each step they took. That's something I strive to do myself."

The guardians walked back to the skystone in silence, parting the tall grass as they went.

All four stepped upon the stone and looked toward the west. Keela spoke with focused calm. "Why would nature wish mammoths gone?"

Yawri's baritone voice throbbed with sorrow. "I don't know, but I do know that if we hadn't come the mammoth would have died in such pain the Earth spirit and ethereal soul might not have been able to retrieve their essence. Such an agonizing death would make the return of each to their source very difficult. How can this enhance Earth's co-creation with Creator?"

Keela looked back toward the herd. "Let's take the long way back. Although trying to stay upright might be a welcome distraction, level flight will give me time to think about what happened."

Yawri said, "Sounds good to me."

20. KNOWLEDGE LOST

∞

A year passed, and no more odd events occurred. Although the anomaly was never explained, a sense of normalcy returned. Keela, her long, honey-colored hair flowing in the breeze, stood next to her well-used drying racks. They were filled with another season's plants. Several young guardians surrounded her, relearning how to listen to the plants with their whole body. Some of the reborn were very slow to remember what they and their Earth spirits had learned in their previous bodies. However, almost all were able to recall full memory after lengthy and concentrated practice.

Keela brushed her hair away from her high cheeks and fixed her dark-blue eyes on a skystone passing high overhead. She recognized the translucent, light-green slab Yawri had left with early that morning. Few guardians favored such a fast skystone, but Yawri was an exception.

She was turning back to her students when she saw the skystone stop in midair, go up, then down, forward again, shoot to the left, right, and backward.

"What *is* he doing?" she said aloud.

The skystone shot forward again. In answer, one of her students shared, "Mariyonta told me she and Aronlat were training with Yawri."

"Really," Keela said coolly.

Those are complicated maneuvers, even if you recall lifetimes of learning how to fly those rocks, and you do not need four crystals of propulsion to do them.

Her stern expression deepened when the skystone plummeted down.

Not again.

Several of her students stepped back, but she could see they were safe. The stone fell toward a group of nearby trees. The giant granite monolith came to a sudden stop a short distance above the tallest tree, but without the sudden flare of Yawri's soul light.

Surprised by the lack of alarm from the trees, she turned to her students. "Did any of you sense the trees were alarmed?"

"I didn't."

"Why didn't I?"

"Strange. I didn't either." After hovering above the trees a long moment, the translucent green monolith moved slowly toward them. She turned to her students and said briskly, "Collect more of the same herbs we did earlier, but by yourself this time. If you take any without receiving permission from the plants, I'll know."

Fleeting stares at the approaching skystone told her they wanted to stay and watch the interaction, but the students also wanted to avoid the consequences of ignoring her instruction. She watched them leave, knowing some would glance back. The few that looked back were greeted with a riveting stare from her sober eyes. Keela allowed herself a small, satisfied smile, knowing they would complete the assignment and return expecting more. She swept her gaze to Yawri and tried to frown, but couldn't help a small smile. He looked at her with his familiar half-grin. She narrowed her eyes.

The skystone continued to float her direction but more slowly. Aronlat and Mariyonta, their faces long, stood at opposite ends of the skystone. Yawri said words she couldn't hear. The skystone stopped, rotated in a perfect circle, and lowered to stop a hand's width above the tops of her perennial herbs and flowers.

Yawri's half grin changed to a full one. He stepped off the skystone, his feet automatically avoiding the plants. "Better?"

"Much better," she admitted, knowing Aronlat and Mariyonta thought the question was about them and the time the skystone they piloted almost crushed her. "Yes. You're doing much better, Yawri. The last time you were here you trampled two flowers."

Yawri's grin turned into a laugh. "Be careful when you dismount, you two. Flying is safe compared to treading here."

Keela walked purposefully toward Aronlat and Mariyonta. "Hello! Anyone doing the maneuvers I saw with a flying rock won't have a problem walking through an herb garden. Welcome. It's good to see you here again."

The young guardians looked contrite but Keela didn't understand why. They'd done well. "That was amazing flying. I know guardians that recall lifetimes of memory who couldn't match it. Did you take turns piloting or was it collaborative?"

"Collaborative," Yawri said, pleased to report. "To make it challenging, I also had them switch places. First Mariyonta in the front and Aronlat in the back, then the opposite."

Keela leaned back in surprise as she addressed the young pilots. "It's hard enough to collaborate with another pilot to get where you're going, let alone do those maneuvers while switching places. I can't imagine what it must have been like when Yawri instructed you to take that plunge." She turned to Yawri. "You wanted them to experience it again so they knew they could pull out of it?"

"Something like that," he replied, straight-faced.

Aronlat and Mariyonta still appeared more chagrined than pleased. "Well …" Aronlat looked at Mariyonta, clearly wishing she had a response in mind. She didn't. "Dropping that fast wasn't exactly planned."

Keela's eyes turned into whirlpools with Yawri at their center.

"Don't look at me," he said innocently. "I wasn't flying."

Mariyonta turned to Keela and beseeched, "We've never been able to do such complicated maneuvers without him."

Yawri was unapologetic. "You did those all by yourselves. I stopped helping shortly after we took off."

"But you didn't tell us you'd given complete piloting to us," Aronlat agonized.

Yawri remained unperturbed. "The fact you didn't notice meant you were ready. All I did was tell you where I wanted to go and enjoy the ride."

Keela's whirlpools swirled at Yawri's innocent hazel eyes. "So the plummet wasn't planned for today's training?"

"Plans work until you start using them." The curve of his smile was battling with his serious expression. "After you start, do what works instead."

Keela couldn't believe what she was hearing. "So what kept the skystone from pulverizing those trees? There wasn't a surge of soul light this time."

Aronlat and Mariyonta looked at each other, too embarrassed to speak. After growing uncomfortable with the silence, both started talking at once. Mariyonta tried to explain. "For our last maneuver, Yawri asked us to descend by only using air pressure, no soul light at all."

"Only air pressure?" Keela shook her head.

Aronlat tried to explain next. His words rushed, "We use it all the time now. Learning how to ask the wind to increase pressure below while decreasing it above can move a skystone up or down much faster than changes in soul light and sound."

Mariyonta followed with, "After Yawri gave that instruction I realized he hadn't been communicating with the skystone at all, only to us." She looked at Aronlat. "I panicked and lost my center."

"Same here!" Aronlat agreed. "My last thought before falling was we couldn't have done those maneuvers without him."

Yawri looked skyward and down again. "Yes, but you did do them without me, and you finally realized it."

"Barely in time, though," Mariyonta squawked.

Keela hooked her thumbs into the waistband of her embroidered sash. "How did you stop the fall?"

Mariyonta cleared her throat. "After realizing Yawri wasn't going to help us, I re-centered myself and strengthened my connection with the crystals."

"I did the same," Aronlat said. "The first thing Yawri taught us was how to connect with crystals in the deep cave."

Yawri murmured, "Foundations. To fly high, you need your feet in the ground."

Mariyonta stood up straighter and tugged her tunic. "I remembered how you taught us how to connect to those cave crystals. Connection happened to those on the skystone without working at it. Same with the air. It wasn't work to re-center inside myself, more like relaxing into it."

Aronlat said, "It felt slow but it happened fast. We were suddenly centered and asking the air to increase under us and decrease above. The skystone slowed, and stopped."

"Without soul light!" Mariyonta emphasized.

Yawri looked at the four-crystal skystone expertly parked above the flowers. "Good job. The plan for today was to have you learn that you no longer need me. Take the same skystone up by yourselves tomorrow and repeat the exercise." Aronlat and Mariyonta looked at Yawri, trying to discern if they'd heard correctly. He nodded. "I'm leaving for a couple of days, so the timing is perfect."

They turned slowly, looked back one more time, and after Yawri nodded encouragement once more, he walked back to the skystone to thank it—and to also make sure it was willing to work without Yawri.

Keela spun to face him. "You did have a plan!" It began as a compliment but ended as an accusation.

Yawri kept watching Mariyonta and Aronlat. "Of course. The pliable plan is to help them use their strengths to find their weaknesses so they can learn from them. Today what they've accomplished is very real to them. Birds kick their young out of the nest for a reason. I do the same."

"Pliable plan? How could you be sure they would fly instead of smash into the ground?

"I'm not sure about anything, but it seemed time for them to be sure about themselves."

"Sounds dangerous," Keela persisted.

"Did you hear the trees complain?" He knew she didn't. "I'd agreed to stop our fall at their first flash of anxiety, and they knew I would. However, Aronlat and Mariyonta might have hesitated to use all they've become if they knew. They believed they had to rely on their own wings to live. Now they know they can."

"All right. All right." Keela turned back to the drying rack, picked up a white calming root, raised it to her mouth and took a bite. It snapped cleanly. "You'd think I'd know by now you rarely look like you know what you're doing, but somehow you do." Her eyes widened after hearing her own words. "I didn't mean you don't know what you're doing," she tried to explain. "It just looks like you don't. Sometimes."

"Thanks, Keela."

She laughed. He joined her. Laughter turned to smiles as they walked side by side. After a few paces Keela said, "You told Aronlat and Mariyonta you'd be gone for the next few days. Are you visiting Murann to talk about how much longer it is taking some of the reborn to remember who they are? If the trend continues, it's only a matter of time before one of them won't remember at all."

"Don't I have any secrets from you?"

"Yawri! Is everything all right?" a voice boomed.

Yawri recognized it without turning around. "Greetings, Gamon! Yes. Everything is fine."

"I saw your skystone falling again. When I talked with your students last time, they seemed to understand the importance of repetition, but maybe they need a refresher. It's the best way to teach a body how to respond instantly."

"They listened and commented on your advice many times. Something helped them. They did very complex maneuvers, including that plunge, and performed them very well without me. I was just along for the ride."

"Along for the ride? Maybe you should reconsider. Many of my students keep coming to me for decades. There is always something to teach."

"I'm sure, but I enjoyed being a passenger today."

Gamon came to an abrupt stop in front of Yawri but turned to Keela. "What do you think? You have students that return to you for decades."

"They're friends. Not students."

"I understand. My students can be friends, too." A few of the young adults Keela sent to gather more herbs returned, then more, all of their baskets full. Gamon noted them and asked Keela, "Did you show them the herb plants I brought you? The ones from the far north?"

"Yes, of course. They're more potent than the local variety."

As was their practice, Keela's students stood in a rough line with their baskets held at their waists. Eyes traveled from Keela to Yawri. Many lingered on the skystone, but none on Gamon.

Gamon knew why and smiled. Only those confident in themselves could meet his gaze. *Compliments will comfort them.*

"Good to see you know how to gather herbs. Keela tells me she showed you the ones I brought from the north. Continue learning from her and someday you'll be speaking to plants in distant lands too." The students were attentive but none spoke.

Keela interjected, "From what I'm hearing, it seems you did a good job of asking the plants if they wished to be gathered."

At her words, the students relaxed. Several looked from Keela to Yawri to the crystals on the skystone and back to Yawri.

One of them ventured, "Is it true you're going to lead this year's cave stay, Yawri? I hope so." Several heads bobbed in agreement.

Gamon barked, "Where did you hear that? It hasn't been decided yet."

The entire line of students froze, except for the one who spoke, who jumped back with her eyes wide.

Yawri took an easy, relaxed step toward the one who asked the question but addressed them all. "I've heard that, too. I think Gamon starts the rumor every year because, frankly, the world is safer with me underground for at least one moon cycle every spring." The students relaxed and began to smile again.

"Or longer," Gamon added, managing a smile. "The cave stays I lead have a forty-five-day schedule."

Yawri cheerfully added, "As you know, Pergaine the elder speaks with stars and the cave to determine which teacher is most appropriate for each year's young adults. After she does, we still have to see if that person is available. Like Gamon says, training can last over forty-five days."

Gamon felt Yawri was a bit too cavalier, so added seriously, "And as you know, after cave stays youths are considered to be adults. I'm sure you understand why it's so important the most qualified teacher is with you."

Before another word could be said, Keela stepped in front of Yawri and Gamon, raised her palms and brought them together with a loud clap. Her rich alto voice broke the tension.

"Are you still in communication with your plants? Distractions happen, and I appreciate Yawri and Gamon helping me with this lesson. It gives me the chance to understand how you're progressing." Every student brought their basket up to their chest.

A nod of thanks to Yawri and Gamon conveyed *Time to leave. I've got a class to teach.* Yawri and Gamon dipped slightly in acknowledgment and walked away together.

"She's good," Gamon said. "Few recognize the value of structure like she does, and the longer it is taking the reborn to remember their former knowledge the more important it's becoming."

"You're noticing it more, too?"

"How could I not? Impromptu instruction may still be working for you, but teaching by rote is the only thing working for everyone else."

21. MURANN

∞

When flying alone, Yawri preferred the small skystone of azure-blue quartzite. Delicate, feathery bands of white quartz threaded through it that reminded him of silky clouds in a morning sky. They made him smile. When in direct sun, the stone's surface shimmered as specs of mica played with the light.

In spite of its small size, it was one of the few skystones able to blend with six, rather than the customary two, propulsion crystals. They enjoyed working with Yawri as much as he did because they balanced maneuvering, speed, and shifting winds so well together.

Yawri darted around a rocky crag faster than a whirlwind.

I wonder how Murann is doing. Trees are never in a hurry, but you don't fly with six propulsion crystals to relax.

Yawri didn't visit Murann often, but he knew the way well. He sailed over a plateau in moments and soared into a valley carved by river rapids. Cedars towered on either side.

Good, I'm making up for lost time. That greeting from Pergaine turned into a long talk.

Pergaine was the oldest guardian in his community. She helped him retrieve his memories when he came into a new body, and he considered her the reason his awareness returned so quickly while others struggled. Today, her greeting turned into a request for him to lead this year's youth cave stay, and their conversation had lengthened. He'd led the training the year before and he knew others, like Gamon, were available.

However, everyone knew Pergaine's ability to communicate with stars and the deepest caves was exceptional. If anyone disagreed with her recommendation, she was happy to discuss it. It only took once for new arrivals to learn her recommendations did not come from her, but from stars and Earth.

Even though Yawri had questions, she took all the time he wished to answer. She knew he wouldn't refuse, even if it would upset Gamon.

Yawri soared over the ridge, down into the adjacent valley, and grinned. He'd more than made up for a late start.

As his destination came into sight, the combination of crystals working with Earth's magnetic field and the wind pressurizing air in front of him quickly slowed the skystone to a crawl. A small pond of clear water and blooming water lilies passed under him and the skystone came to a gentle, hovering stop above bright-green ferns. The living slab lowered to the tops of their delicate fronds and stopped. Careful not to step on any plants, Yawri stepped onto the ground and walked toward Murann's tree.

The sounds of the forest washed out the chatter in his mind. He held his arms out wide but it would take ten spans to circle Murann's trunk for a hug. He lowered his arms and made the final step to the immense base. Yawri's whole body relaxed when he placed a hand on the furrowed, red bark.

"Good to see you're still in the same spot, Murann." He tilted his head back to take in the sight of red branches, all wider than his own body, undulating in the air.

The tree remained quiet. A small seed cone sat upright on a branch less than an arm's length away. It fell to the ground, rolled, and came to rest next to Yawri's foot.

At last Murann spoke. "Hello, Yawri. You had a different body last time you came. It was taller."

"This body is not as tall, but it's just as good with dimensions and flying skystones." Yawri placed both his hands on the bark of the tree, closed his eyes and opened his senses to feel the dimensions in which the tree lived. Sugar ants crawled on its trunk, fungi mingled with root hairs, air currents danced in its branches; sunlight kissed some needles while others cooled in shade.

"It is good to see you," Yawri said again but much more quietly.

"You're always welcome here. By the whole grove, not just me."

Yawri turned. Sunbeams flowed around the branches of other trees and bathed ferns in golden liquid. Murann's needle-like leaves waved in a slow dance. "How goes your learning? Is each body more capable than the last as you envisioned?"

How does he always know what I want to talk about?

Rather than respond immediately, Yawri took a breath and examined Murann's sculpted bark. Vertical strips of reddish-gray velvet stretched from the massive trunk into the sky. "Joining as a human being is a lot more complicated than I thought. I've learned a lot, but mostly that there's a lot more to learn."

"Good. Boredom doesn't work for you. I see Kunuta's Earth spirit remains well connected to the soul of this planet, as it is to Creator. Of course, it's complicated. You know there is no end to learning about All-that-is. It's ever changing."

Yawri lowered his hands and rested them on the center knot of his dark-orange waist sash. "I know, but experiencing All as an ethereal being is far different from experiencing it blended with physicality. The more this body connects to Earth's physical realms, the more ethereal dimensions I can bring into it. Experiencing the scope of Creation this way is incredible."

Murann's voice came through both air and ground. "It's the same for trees. The greater the body's connection with Earth, the more of my ethereal self can enter. It's why tree being bodies live so long. Do human beings live longer than the humans?"

"Yes. We live much longer and grow much larger." Yawri leaned forward. "I've gotten better at listening to the emotions of the body. It's how I know what the body is experiencing. It's how I know what thoughts or questions to provide to help solve problems. Each lifetime does seem better than the last."

"It's going well, then?"

"No complaints from me. Others are having problems remembering who they are when they get new bodies, though. When tree bodies die, how do you select your next body? Perhaps their problem has something to do with that."

Murann moved a branch and a beam of sunlight fell directly on Yawri. "The tree spirit and I need a new tree body that is capable of providing for the needs of a lifetime. Each cone is fertilized by a specific tree so the genetics are right. The grove makes space for young trees by moving branches to allow sunlight and rain to nourish them. The mature trees direct fungi to support their roots. So their identities are strong, the oldest teach the young how to strengthen their connection to Earth. As you said, the stronger the body's connection to Earth's dimensions, the more we can connect."

Murann's massive branches waved and millions of needle-like leaves flashed with bright green. "Timing is important. Most tree-bodies are two hundred years old before they are ready for joining. What about human beings? How do you select your next body?"

Yawri touched the bark with outstretched fingers. It looked rough but felt silky.

"Similarly. After a human body enters its death cycle, its Earth spirit takes what it learned back to the soul of Earth, and we retrieve our learning back to our purely ethereal selves. Kunuta's Earth spirit and I meet ethereally and decide what to learn in the next lifetime. After understanding the genes that our next body needs, we connect with the male and female human beings that are most suited to bring the body we need back into the life cycle."

Yawri watched a fiddle fern unfold next to the seed cone Murann had dropped. "Similar to your grove, our whole community is responsible for parenting children. We raise them so every child knows they are respected and protected. They learn their self-worth from feeling their impact on others, on Life, much more so than from what we give them. As a result, they know their value and how much their actions matter to Creation."

Yawri bent down and exhaled an appreciative breath near the unfolding fern. The fern and cone released their breath to him.

So much Life is here.

He stood again. "Every new body has different timing, so we don't join until the Earth identity is very strong in it. As with trees, the amount an ethereal soul can blend with a human depends on our ability to remain balanced, neither aspect is lesser or greater in a human being."

The air seemed to wiggle.

"Do you sense movement?" Murann asked. "Something is coming."

Yawri stilled. There was a vibration. Not one of a beast. Something more fleet of foot and with much more stealth. "What can it be?"

Murann's roots probed. "The fungus says it's a band of humans. They don't come here often, but do hunt these forests."

"Humans? I'd heard there were still tribes that haven't joined with ethereal beings."

"Pure humans are few, but those that remain are still One with this planet's Earth soul. Its Life is their own."

The sound of swishing ferns joined the sound of muted voices. Suddenly all sound stopped.

Yawri looked at seven hairless humans frozen in place, their unblinking eyes focused on him. Forehead wrinkling, he studied the troop. Each human wore hairy animal skins. Necklaces strung with small, colorful shells hung around their thick necks. Four carried satchels brimming with roots and tubers. Three had small, lifeless animals draped over their shoulders. All carried long spears with sharp, glassy tips.

I wish I'd had time to hide. Observing them would be much more fun than them observing me.

Zinn had told him that unblended humans still existed. However, there was no reason to seek them out. Human beings and humans were as different as night and day, and like night and day, each had their purpose on Earth.

Every eye fixed on the giant twelve-foot human being standing next to Murann. Hurried speech coursed among the humans. They placed their satchels and the three small animals on the ground. Gestures combined with words in a rapid torrent.

With a final grunt, the hunter who carried the largest of the three animals reached down, picked it up, and held it above his head. All eyes re-locked on Yawri.

"Eee!" the man called out.

Yawri remained still, uncertain. One of the hunters gently prodded the man holding the animal. The man's eyes narrowed and his lips tightened. He lowered the animal to his chest and took one hesitant step forward, then another. His eyes furrowed in concentration, and he approached as one might approach the crumbling edge of a precipice.

A bead of sweat rolled down his forehead and hung on his eyebrow, but his eyes remained on Yawri. He stooped and laid the animal at Yawri's feet. Releasing it instantly, he backed away in a crouch, his gaze lowered.

Palms up, Yawri spread hands in question and shook his head. "This is your food. Earth gave it to you." He bent down and picked up the furry form. It had been speared but a skull-crushing blow to its head killed it. He held the beast in front of him, a gesture meant to offer it back to the humans. Each human froze, their faces creased in alarm.

"Receive it!" Murann advised quietly. "They gave you something precious. If you reject it, you reject them."

Yawri lowered the animal to his waist and tried to smile. The hunters watched, their muscles tight. Yawri brought his hands together, cradled the animal and held it to up to his chest. The smile on his face was full.

Tension drained from the hunting party with an audible sigh, and the sigh transformed into smiles as broad as the giant's. Yawri nodded, took one step back and lowered the gift to his waist again, then another step back.

The humans walked backward a few steps too, their eyes still fixed on Yawri. After a final nod, they turned and moved away with the same quiet grace they'd used when they approached.

"It would be interesting to hear what they'll tell their tribe about you," Murann said.

Yawri held up the bloody ball of fur in his hands. "Why did they want me to have this? Earth grows all we need."

"Have you looked at your reflection recently? There's a pool over there." Murann pointed to the lily pond Yawri flew over.

"But Kunuta's body looked like theirs once," he stammered.

"Not anymore. It's twice their height and flies across the sky on big rocks."

"I didn't know his body would change so much," Yawri countered. "Ethereal souls have joined with other Earth bodies for eons. Trees look the same whether an ethereal soul has joined with them or not. It's the same for the large animals, crystals, or whales for that matter. The dimensions they live in expand but you can't tell the difference by only looking at their bodies."

"I don't know why the human form changed shape after joining, but it certainly did."

Yawri looked down at the bloody creature in his hand. "They treated me like I was something grand." He raised the trophy. "Kunuta never did this. He knew his connection to Earth's soul was stronger than mine. I was the visitor. He was One with Earth, while my communication with it was comparatively weak. We agreed to become a human being to help us both expand in Life." Yawri looked down the path the humans had taken. "It doesn't make sense. Kunuta wasn't intimidated by a light body four times his height, but a whole hunting party bows at a physical one less than twice their height. Why?"

Murann's voice blended with the sound of bird song and frogs. "Perhaps it is because you are physical and a giant compared to them. How is it with the other human beings? Is each of their lifetimes still more capable the last?"

Yawri gently placed the dead animal on the ground and stepped back. "That is something I came to ask you about."

"You always come with questions. I like questions."

"Me, too." Yawri stared up at Murann's towering branches. Another cone sat upright on a nearby branch, its interlaced, scaly seeds still on vivid display. "It used to be the reborn guardians remembered how to fly skystones the same way young birds take to flight. A certain age came and they knew. Not anymore. Some guardians remember faster than others, but all need to be taught."

"Is this only happening with those trying to remember how to fly skystones?"

"Keela's noticed it, too. She helps guardians recall their knowledge of plants. With every generation, it's much more difficult for them to ask and hear what each kind of plant needs. One of them even ate a poisonous leaf. That's never happened before. Ever."

A small opossum took a cautious bite out of the dead animal. Yawri continued and so did the opossum.

"Pergaine, our oldest guardian, asked me to oversee the young adults with their cave stay again this year. Instructors usually rotate, but this time she said the cave asked for me because some of them still need to learn the basics of communicating with stone and crystals. She said many young adults *expect* a response when they say hello. There is no listening with expectation."

"Ears already filled with answers can't hear, let alone listen. I agree with her. Let them practice with a cave wall for a month. Are all of them like this?"

"Of the twenty coming, I only know two who are awakening well. Aronlat, a young man, and Mariyonta, a young woman. Most of the others think they should know how to fly because a part of them remembers doing it, but the skill didn't come with the memory."

Murann responded with quiet intensity. "No one can learn what they don't know if they think they should already know it."

"Have you heard anything on the wind about this?"

Murann moved his branches and sunlight peppered the ferns. "I have not. Was it sudden?"

"No, it's been very gradual, even hard to see between two generations. You have to look across several."

"That's probably why it's not been talked about. Especially since your bodies last over a thousand years."

"And today, those humans treated me like I was something to be feared, or at least appeased. That's a vast change from Kunuta."

"It is interesting that guardians are having trouble remembering who they are at the same time humans are having trouble remembering who they are."

"Why would that be?"

Yawri sensed Murann's attention go inward and down into his roots. Even bird song stilled. Murann returned, and his trunk seemed to expand and contract with breath. "As you know, the fungus is much more ancient than we are, and is a life form on many planets. I'm being told of a memory from one of them. Ethereal beings and the physical forms joined but became lost to themselves. Evidently, the ethereal beings did not consider the timing of the form with which they joined. Without the physical body's ability to maintain balance with the ethereal, they became overwhelmed and lost their connection to their own source. The learning of the body and ethereal being became so immersed that neither could retrieve their essence. It may be unrelated, but I'm told it started with the loss of ability for new bodies to recall who they were."

"But we were very respectful of the humans' timing. In fact, I waited for Kunuta to tell me he was ready."

"Did all the ethereal souls do that?"

Yawri took a step back. "They must have. Why wouldn't they?"

"It's just a question."

Murann's branches moved and a shaft of sunlight fell directly on the gift at Yawri's feet.

22. CAVE STAY

∞

"Come on. Why don't you want to leave the cave?" The young adult's head turned toward the distant entrance. A craggy sliver of white light cracked the underground night. "Yawri already kept us here over two full cycles of the moon. Last year's cave stay was only one."

The student next to him took a step toward the exit but stopped. "I bet I've talked to more rock since I've been in here than all my previous lives. The last thing Yawri said before he left was it's up to us to know when it's time to leave."

Mariyonta and Aronlat were two of twenty young guardians in the antechamber near the exit of the cave. Alive with the vitality of Earth, its minerals fluoresced in bands of pale green, violet and red. One narrow passage out of the antechamber led to a distant crack of white light. The other led down into darkness.

Aronlat finished sorting his pack and stood. "After Yawri left, the cave spirit told some of us about another multidimensional part of the cave. Why would it tell us about it if we weren't supposed to go there?"

A young woman's voice echoed in the small chamber. "You know the equinox ceremony is the day after tomorrow and it includes a celebration for us. This cave stay is our last training before we become adults. Do you really think Yawri would want us to miss it?"

Mariyonta stepped forward to face the group. Her shadowed silhouette contrasted sharply with the phosphorescent red glow in the wall behind her. "Yawri tested us before. He almost let Aronlat and my skystone plunge into the ground so we could learn our own strength without him. I think he already knew the cave was going to tell us about this other part of itself."

"That's crazy, but even if that's the case, the test might be to see if we stay longer than we should. After all, Aronlat is the only one that heard this message clearly."

"I kind of heard it too," another said. "Maybe we should stay and check it out. It's still two days before the equinox."

"Did it say how deep it is? It could take more than two days just to find it."

Yet another voice commented, "Remember, Yawri also warned us to stay in the areas he showed us. What if this part of the cave is beyond that? This cave's a complicated maze. Some guardians come in and never come out."

Aronlat cinched his stout cloth pack closed and joined the circle of friends. "Since I did get a clear message, I need to go and check it out. I'll be careful." He saw Mariyonta's glare in spite of the dim light and quickly added, "You're all welcome to come, too. Whatever you think is best."

Mariyonta's voice was iron. "I was working in another part of the cave and didn't hear this message. However, it doesn't feel right to leave without investigating. I'm going with Aronlat."

The young guardian nearest the exit tunnel spoke. "We don't know if Yawri knew about it or not, but we do know we've completed all the work he asked us to do." The speaker glanced toward the entrance and its sliver of light. "Besides, how many times have we been told that this cave is dangerous? The test could be to see if we have the presence of mind to leave."

Aronlat and Mariyonta exchanged glances. Almost every other head faced the crack of light. Mariyonta stared into the dark tunnel opposite it and sighed. "Tell the community that we don't feel our work is complete, so we decided to stay until it is. We'll be fine."

"Are you sure?" the young guardian closest to her asked.

Mariyonta nodded, her memory of Yawri's last learn-your-strengths test vivid.

"I want to leave and join the celebration, too, but I need to stay."

Aronlat cast a glance at her pack on the cave floor. She caught his meaning and picked it up. "We'll share what we learn when we come out," she said, and swung the pack to her back with practiced ease.

The one near the exit said, "A couple days after the celebration we're going to take skystones to the far northern forests. Since we'll be adults, we don't even have to ask anyone for permission."

"Sounds great to me. Maybe we'll be out by then," Aronlat said with a faint but hopeful tone. He tossed a small leather bag of acorns back and forth between his hands.

Mariyonta noticed. "Do you want me to put that in your pack?" He handed it to her in one smooth motion so she could open the pack's cinched top.

Before she could close it, the person next to her said, "Take this dried fruit."

A second added, "I still have a lot of the sweet tuber root. Take it, too."

A third said, "I've got a bone sewing needle."

Within minutes, Mariyonta filled Aronlat's pack to the brim. She cinched it with a confident yank. Aronlat turned to face the group of friends again. He stood tall, even though the weight of his pack had doubled.

"Thanks! I think we've got enough food for another month."

Apprehensive, hopeful grins filled every face. After giving what they could, the parting companions took their first step toward the way out.

"I'm still concerned about leaving you behind," a young man said. "This cave goes on and on. Don't get lost!"

"We'll be fine. Enjoy the celebration!" Aronlat's voice rolled toward the crack of light.

"Give my best to the village," Mariyonta enjoined.

Another voice floated back and echoed around the chamber. "Expand Creation in All you become."

"Create with Creator!" they both responded in kind, but the cavern swallowed their sound before it could escape.

Mariyonta and Aronlat stood unmoving. The sound made by two people was far less than that made by twenty, and quiet stillness saturated the damp air. A single drop of water released its hold from the roof and landed with a *splat*. It was enough to bring Mariyonta out of her trance.

"You know the way to the part of the cave that spoke?" she said, looking at the lightless tunnel.

"Follow me," Aronlat replied, wetting his lips. "Watch your step."

"In the dark?" her voice flashed but he'd already moved several steps down the narrow, dark channel of living stone. She took one parting look around the empty cavern, turned and set off at a brisk pace. There was no way she was going to miss out on a multi-dimensional encounter with this cave. Yawri would understand.

23. ASTRAL MEETING

∞

While their physical bodies slept, guardians traveled with their astral forms, an etheric double of their physical form, to meet with others. The method was particularly useful because no travel time was involved, and upon awakening, their memories were as clear as if they'd taken place physically. Yawri, Keela, Tisbero, and Zinn requested a meeting because many of their students were struggling to remember knowledge from their past lives.

More guardians than they expected arrived. Tisbero, true to his fiery nature, spoke first. "Given the number of guardians present here, it appears a great many share our concern. It's been a slow progression, but there are too many examples of lost memories to deny."

Keela agreed. "I made the journey to Tisbero's community to determine if the same difficulty was there as in my community. It is. Human beings are taking much longer to remember what was intuitive for them in their last body."

Murmurs rose. A woman from the river valley beyond the coastal mountains spoke. "We hoped it was a rare occurrence. However, I report the same. Some of our children are less connected to All-that-is than their parents. Their bodies are smaller, too. That's new."

Another guardian waved his hand dismissively. "Our children are fine. Their bodies seem more capable than the last. This must be a local concern."

"I agree," said another, "Perhaps your problem is caused by evolution. Each continent is developing its own vibratory rate. Different types of human bodies are evolving to work with each. I can understand how this problem could happen if the new bodies are not attuned to these changes."

Tisbero took a step forward. "Yes, lands are changing and the bodies on them must change with them." He raised his arms. "My own body took on a reddish hue for that reason. We have always taken land changes into account when parents are chosen for new bodies. However, memory is still becoming more difficult to revive."

Yawri joined him. "I've helped many generations of guardians remember how to speak with crystal caves. This last group was the most difficult yet. What used to be accomplished in two days took two moon cycles."

Pergaine, the wise elder woman known for speaking with stars and Earth, conveyed a strength that belied her aged appearance. "Of the twenty that did this year's cave stay, eighteen seemed to emerge because of the timing of our equinox celebration, rather than their training by the cave."

Gamon, still believing he should have been this year's cave stay trainer, blurted out, "Then why were they allowed to leave?"

Pergaine spoke before Yawri had a chance to respond. "Because adults are expected to know when their training is complete, and thus bear the results of their choice."

Gamon's brow furrowed but he knew better than to argue with Pergaine, at least in public.

A student shouldn't be expected to know when to end their training. That's a trainer's job. Yawri gives responsibility to students before they're ready.

Hetlin, a robust guardian from the far east, spoke with a resonance that conveyed deep connection with Earth. "We expect the same of our young adults. That requirement has not changed. What has changed is the length of time it takes for them to remember who they are."

Keela recalled Hetlin from a meeting long before ethereal beings joined with human bodies. She liked her because you never had to guess what she was thinking.

Hetlin's the one that saw the etheric feather in me, and the etheric diamond inside Yawri. She spoke to us when few did.

"Have you seen a problem with other students, Hetlin? I help returning souls remember their knowledge of plants."

Hetlin looked straight at her. "Fire ant bites, Keela. The first we've ever known."

At the sound of her name, Keela's mouth fell open.

After all this time, she still remembers my name.

Zinn rose on the balls of her feet. Because she resonated with the lands she tended, her appearance incorporated the warm, brown hue of rich soil. Her straight eyebrows sat above wide eyes that conveyed a mischievous spark. Although her body was small, her voice rang large with passion for Life. "I've had similar problems with guardians recalling how to communicate with animals. Will we have the same problem with our next bodies?"

Tisbero's eyebrows drew close. "Not one young adult I'm working with has any memory of speaking with volcanoes or storms. Rather than listen with their whole body, they expect to hear with their ears."

The murmur of concern rolling through the assembly increased in volume as more and more guardians realized events they had hoped were isolated were common.

Yawri said, "A tree being told me this problem could happen if ethereal beings join with a body before it's ready. Honoring the timing of a body is essential. Has anyone heard of a being who joined too soon?"

A new voice pierced the rumble. "Shahten helped the first ethereal beings join with humans on this planet. They are the oldest line of human beings here. If any joined before humans were ready, wouldn't they be the first to show a problem?" The question hung like a cloud over the assembly. Movement stilled.

A second voice cried out. "Yes, what about the children on Shahten's island? He was the only one of us with experience joining with humanoids on other planets. Has anyone spoken with him?"

The rumble returned, fell, and rose again. Tisbero turned to Yawri. "That's Camic and Rhee. I know them from that meeting Keela attended with Zinn and me long ago, the one where she reported the valley of missing lichen and rock you healed. Shahten and these two were there." Yawri straightened, recalling the event.

Camic, the one who mentioned Shahten first, spoke again. "If the first human beings on this planet are doing well, we'll know the problem must be local. If they are not doing well, we could consider other ideas, like Yawri's. "

Rhee turned to face Tisbero. "His island isn't very far off the coast from your lands, Tisbero. Have you visited him recently?"

"Not this lifetime."

Keela barely let him finish before speaking. "Since I'm already on the coast with Tisbero, he and I could leave tomorrow. We'll also ask Shahten why he doesn't attend these astral meetings. It might shed light on many things if he did."

Yawri's voice vibrated with intensity. "I want to go with you. I can leave tonight, but it's another long flight to Tisbero's community. If you wait, all three of us could visit him the morning after tomorrow."

Gamon rose tall and moved toward Yawri. "What about the two students you left in the cave? They could be lost in the maze of tunnels or in dimensions by now."

Yawri's lips pressed together in a slight grimace. Gamon was right. He conceded, "Aronlat and Mariyonta have regained almost all of their abilities.

189

I'm confident they will emerge when they consider their training complete. However, the cave can be a harsh teacher. I'll check on them first. Will you wait for me?"

Tisbero and Keela exchanged a level glance. Keela said, "Yawri, it would be good to have you with us, but you don't know what you're going to find in that cave. They may be fine, but what if they aren't? You attend to them. We'll attend to Shahten. We'll probably be back before you get to Tisbero's community yourself."

Camic blurted out, "It might be wise to wait so Yawri can be with you. Having all three of you report back would be better, and three could cover more of the island than two."

Rhee agreed. "A few days won't make a difference in the answers you find. The more who go, the more land that can be covered and the more questions asked."

Tisbero shot a questioning glance toward Camic and Rhee but addressed Yawri. "Depending on where those young adults are in the cave it could be a week before you can join us. The sooner we find out if the lineage of the first human beings is having a problem the better. If they're not, we can focus on the specific communities which are."

Keela placed her hand on Yawri's wrist. He was always ready to join every adventure, but his timing wouldn't work for this one. She spoke with calm determination. "Two finding out sooner is better than three finding out the same thing later. Besides, while you check on Aronlat and Mariyonta, you can find out if there's any news from the crystal caves Hetlin works with. We need all the information available."

Yawri's head tilted in disagreement, even though he knew she was right.

Keela let go of his wrist and surveyed the assembly. "I agree more guardians would be better. Is anyone else near enough to join us tomorrow morning?"

Many spoke of their desire to go, but it became apparent no one else was available. After quiet grew, Camic said, "I can't travel with you, but I could meet you there. It will be a long flight, but if I leave tonight, I'll be there by mid-day tomorrow."

Rhee spoke as well. "I might arrive a little later, but it's important to get the facts. I'll leave tonight, too. That will make four."

Tisbero confirmed the decision. "Thank you. While we make the trip to see Shahten, will the rest of you gather more information? Let's look afresh for any evidence of regression of abilities. If no other events are found, we will at least know it was not due to a lack of vigilance."

Nods of agreement came from everyone present except Yawri. He wanted to speak but wasn't sure what to say. He finally leaned toward Keela. "I'll check on Aronlat and Mariyonta, and talk to the cave crystals." His voice deepened. "Be careful."

She touched his elbow lightly. "You know Tisbero. A leaf can't move without him noticing. We'll be fine." She smiled. "Don't hit any stalactites. You can't fly through them anymore."

Her reassurance didn't relieve the trepidation he felt. His eyes fell on her sash and he managed a grin. "I want an embroidered sash someday."

"Trade you for a big, green garnet."

Pergaine the elder's voice drummed, "We all have a lot of work to do. Let's reconvene on the night of the next quarter moon." Her eyes traveled across Tisbero's party. "Will that give you enough time to gather news from Shahten's island?"

"Yes," Tisbero replied with confidence. "Plenty of time."

The meeting's purpose concluded, the astral bodies began to fade. It was time to return to their sleeping physical bodies.

Rhee whispered to Camic. "I wish Yawri was going with Keela. They were the well-meaning but misguided ones that spread those rumors of mistrust. From what they said here, they haven't changed. If they'd gone together, Shahten could have educated them both at the same time. They just don't understand."

Camic said, "Well-meaning but misguided sums them up. At least we'll be there to encourage Keela and Tisbero to listen."

Rhee concluded, "Best we get to Shahten so he can prepare. He's the one with the answers." With a parting nod, each returned to their bodies, fully intent on getting to the island long before Keela and Tisbero arrived.

24. CAVE LAKE

∞

Mariyonta and Aronlat crawled through the dark, twisting passage, its surface slick with wet clay. "I hear rushing water ahead," Mariyonta said.

"Me too," Aronlat cautioned. He stopped and pointed an unseen finger to his right. "There's a steep drop-off next to us."

Mariyonta bumped into him. "Tell me before you stop. I can hear the difference between rock and open space but I can't see a thing. Let's listen more deeply with this aspect of the cave. Maybe we can find out where we are."

The two explorers sat down and, after checking to make sure each had room, rested the full length of their bodies on the damp floor. Consistent with what Yawri taught them, the more they relaxed, the more the cells of their supple bodies mingled with the crystalline minerals.

Aronlat whispered, "It feels like I'm sinking or melting into the living stone."

"I can feel the cave breathe," Mariyonta said quietly, not wanting to interrupt the experience. "It's breathing. Do caves have lungs? Not the same as ours, of course, but for the same need?"

"I don't know, but I feel a pulse through my body," Aronlat murmured. "At first I thought it was mine. But it's different. It's a throb under my own." His short, stout fingers stroked moist clay. "Why do we sense breath and pulse here?"

Mariyonta's long body remained prone, mesmerized by the experience. It reminded her of something Yawri told them the first day of their cave stay. "Didn't Yawri talk about how a cave's body has aspects that parallel ours? How different parts of it function like the different organs in our body?"

"I didn't understand what he was talking about at the time, but it feels so real here. Maybe we feel the breath and heartbeat of the cave."

They lay quiet again. The darkness was so complete that sound and smell became their light.

Aronlat finally spoke. "I hear the calling again. We need to walk along this drop-off until it narrows to a crevice. We step over it and follow the other side back until we reach an opening. There is another one after that, then we take that tunnel down to it."

"Lead on," Mariyonta said. She stood and accidentally bumped into him. "Do not make us fall into its stomach."

He replied to the complete darkness. "No problem, if you keep your balance." He took a long step forward knowing she'd have to move quickly to keep up.

Every cell of their bodies sensed the shape of the cave. The pair walked at a measured pace. After an hour's hike along the edge, the sound of rushing water made talking impossible. Finally, the chasm narrowed to a width possible to jump across, with the thrashing torrent now far below. Stretching their senses into the darkness, each knew where they had to jump and land. Aronlat went first, turned, and caught Mariyonta's hand perfectly as she landed.

"Yawri told us we'd see without our eyes by the time we left," Mariyonta remarked.

The lip on this side of the crevice narrowed. Aronlat gave a quiet sigh of relief when his hand touched the opening of the first tunnel.

Mariyonta moved into the open space, felt its narrow wall, and beamed, "So far so good. It's the first opening, just like you said."

"Was there ever a doubt?" His stocky body filled the channel so well it blocked the sound of the rushing water behind them. "Although I think the cave has a different perspective on distance. I thought it was closer."

They both saw the faint glow at the same time. "There's a crystal glowing farther down this side channel," Mariyonta said. "Maybe it can tell us more."

Aronlat looked down toward the pale light and back toward the dark, watery crevice. "Okay, but let's not lose our night vision. The directions have been good so far, and that second tunnel isn't far away. I can feel it."

"We'll only say hello," Mariyonta agreed.

The channel twisted up and to the left and narrowed. After passing through a low arch, it opened to a tall, thin chamber. The two stood spellbound. Veins of glowing blue crisscrossed the cavern's surface, which was a pulsing red. A crystal, high in the wall, shone with a warm, orange light.

"You keep your night vision," Mariyonta said. "I'll go in and ask it if will speak with us."

"Sounds good." Aronlat took a step back and turned toward the darkness.

The silence was so complete Mariyonta could hear the beat of her heart. After communicating with the phosphorescent cave and its crystal, she returned to tell Aronlat what she heard. "It's cautioning us to be careful."

"That's something we all agree with," Aronlat chirped, still facing the darkness. "It's been slow going since crossing the crevice. If the distance and pace stay the same, it could be another hour before we reach the next opening. I have no idea how much farther it is after that to reach the place that called."

Mariyonta continued. "It's showing me a picture of swirling water. The water can be much higher than it is now. It's telling me it's safe to stay here."

Aronlat took another step toward the dark crevice. "The area that called is definitely the next opening. It's made of different rock. I can even smell it. Going slow would be better than stopping and having our muscles freeze up."

He glanced back at Mariyonta. Her body stood outlined in a mist of red and blue, and it reminded him of a sturdy, tall, willow tree. He said, "But we could rest here if you're tired."

"Rest? I'm not tired. Are you?"

"Me? Never. I think we should go."

She turned to look at the small cavern and its crystal, gave thanks, and said, "I agree."

They reached into the darkness with all of their senses and traced their way back to the deep crevice, their night vision well in place by the time they arrived. The ledge narrowed and their pace slowed.

Almost an hour passed. "We're almost there." The tenor of Aronlat's voice revealed his heightened concern. The distance was greater than either had imagined. Both breathed heavily.

Mariyonta was first to feel a soft vibration in the air. The sound of a distant rumble grew in the darkness behind them. "Aronlat!" she yelled. "Water coming!" Her voice was drowned out by the roar of the flood that engulfed and swept them away.

They rolled and pitched without sense of up or down. The tumbling torrent of carbon-black ink carried them deeper and deeper. Each explosive exhale became a race for one more breath. Each youthful guardian thought every breath they held was their last. The thundering force of crashing water sped them into infinite darkness.

Mariyonta did not feel panic. She felt grief, bottomless loss.

"We worked so hard to remember our past knowledge," was her last thought before the darkness outside swirled within.

Timeless time moved but she felt no anchor in it.

Life stirred. She opened her eyes.

Where am I?

She felt suspended, weightless. Her eyes refused to focus on the stars above her.

How can there be stars?

Without thought, she raised her hand to wipe her eyes. The sound it made confused her.

Drops of water?

Her hand moved again.

I'm in water. What am I doing in water?"

Memory returned, and with it, her first taste of panic.

"Aronlat!" she managed to get out, shocked at the croak she heard. "Aronlat," she tried again. It came out a squeak.

Mariyonta's thoughts coalesced. She lowered her legs and moved them back and forth, treading water to raise herself above the black sea.

"I can't see where it ends." She kicked harder and looked from side to side, then up. Her breath caught.

The stars are crystals. I'm in a cavern. An immense underground cavern.

She made herself take slow, measured breaths. The air was moist, yet crisp. She opened her mouth and swallowed some water.

It's a lake, and it's alive with essence.

She took a long drink and felt her strength return. "Aronlat!" she roared with a voice that echoed off the ceiling.

Something thrashed loudly in the water. "Aronlat?"

"Mariyonta!" The churning water stopped. "Is that you?"

"Me? Yes, it's me!" Dread of the unspeakable changed to relief. However, silence returned and it rekindled her dread. "Where are you?"

There was a splashing sound again but with much less force this time.

"Are you hurt? Why are you thrashing?"

What looked like a bear swimming like a flailing dog emerged into the dim light. "It's hard to stay above water with this pack!" Aronlat kept moving toward her with a mixture of wheeling arms and paddling.

She swam to him, placed a hand under his pack, and kicked her long legs. The flailing of his thick arms stopped, though they continued to fan water back and forth under the surface.

Feeling Aronlat's pack made Mariyonta remember hers. It was gone. From the ache in her shoulders, it must have been torn off.

Probably why I'm alive.

"My pack's gone," she said simply. "We've got to get to shore." As she kicked harder to raise her head and see the nearest shore, crystals flared and revealed the land. "That's the closest shore." She gestured toward it and half-lifted, half-propelled Aronlat toward it.

"I can swim," Aronlat protested, but the sound of his labored breath overruled his declaration. Mariyonta was as adroit at swimming as she was at running. She increased her support of her waterlogged companion in response.

They moved slowly but steadily, alternating between swimming and rolling over on their backs and kicking. "It's okay to drink the water," she volunteered. "It's alive," she said, realizing that the water, which had almost killed them, now sustained them. "Only a few hundred strokes to go."

Aronlat's arms and legs still moved, but only enough to keep him and his pack above water. The muscles in Mariyonta's long, strong arms burned with each stroke, but they never slowed.

Aronlat's stout legs pushed them onto a rocky shore. He dropped his pack and they helped each other crawl over a labyrinth of rocks to reach sand, too drained to speak. Their ragged breath finally slowed and they dropped into an exhausted sleep where they collapsed, their arms still around each other.

Aronlat's eyes opened first. Mariyonta was in his arms, something he'd often wished for, but he expected she never had.

Her eyes opened slowly. The first thing she saw was a man's toothy grin. The first thing she felt was her arms around him, then with a start, she realized his arms were around her.

Her head swirled as memory returned. "Aronlat!"

Her eyes went wide.

"We're alive!" In one smooth motion, she pulled away and rolled to sit up, her head turning like a turret, surveying the scene. Words tumbled from her. "This looks like the cavern Yawri described to us once! I never thought I'd see it!"

Aronlat rolled to his side and sat up. "The water looks so calm, but it almost beat us to death on its way here."

Mariyonta gave him a concerned glance but soon turned back to speculate on the enchanting cavern. The light from the crystals in the walls and ceiling reflected so perfectly in the water that she couldn't tell where wall and water met. She leaned back on her hands. "If I didn't know we were inside a planet I'd think were we surrounded by stars."

"The planet is surrounded by stars," Aronlat said thoughtfully. He raked his fingers through fine sediment and closed them to draw it into his hand. He raised his palm to her, slowly opened it and let the sand fall between his fingers. The grains danced with starlight as they fell. "We made it. This is the place that called us."

Mariyonta wrapped her arms around her knees and leaned back. "This place is more than alive. The universe is here." She looked at Aronlat. "We made it, but almost didn't. I can't believe I didn't listen to that crystal. It tried to warn us."

Aronlat looked away, remembering he was the one who said they should leave the safe place. "No Yawri with us to stop our fall this time." His eyes fell on the rocky beach where they had crawled from the water. "The cave provided a safe place for us to stay while the flood passed. It even had light. I blocked out all I've learned about the difference between hearing and listening over the last two months, and more, because I wanted to get us here."

His words made Mariyonta remember waking up in the silent, dark lake.
I thought Aronlat died.

She looked at him. He was still looking at the beach, hunched over as if he could hide his bulk. She picked up a pebble and dropped it on his head. "Glad to hear you admit you don't know how to listen."

He reared back. "I know how to listen. I just didn't then!"

She sat up straight and grinned. "Neither did I. The crystal talked to me, not you and I agreed we should leave." She picked up another pebble and rubbed it in her hand. After a moment, she put it back down and said, "Best we forgive ourselves so we can move on. After all, the cave did."

Aronlat leaned forward and folded his square hands over his chest. "True. If it didn't, we'd be dead."

Mariyonta looked down the long shore. A mound of warm, white light shimmered in the distance. She pointed to it. "What's that?"

Aronlat had seen the same thing while swimming to shore, but had been concerned about staying alive at the time. He focused on it now. The glow flickered with shifting light. He reached out with his senses, asking to connect with air, water, and stone alike. It responded. Gentle warmth moved through his body and he felt his knotted muscles relax. "Let's find out."

Mariyonta answered by standing up, and in one fluid motion, stretched her hands toward the cavern's stars then down to touch the sand. She smiled and started walking. "Don't forget your pack."

Aronlat scanned the rocks to find the sodden anchor. It lay less than the length of a skystone away, where he'd left it at the edge of the lake.
So close? I thought we crawled forever!

He darted to it, slung the water-laden rucksack across his back, and sprinted toward Mariyonta. A final, determined stride brought him next to her, and he realized she'd been walking much more slowly than her long, strong legs commonly carried her. She felt his smile without seeing it and bit her lip. The length of her next step doubled.

They walked down the narrow shore side by side and a sense of calm vitality filled them both. "This place is surreal," Aronlat said, looking around. "It is like another planet within a planet."

"Look," Mariyonta stopped and pointed down to a spot near his feet. Small, leafy, green plants grew amongst the rocks. She bent down, her fingers outstretched. "There's more than one kind. See?"

Aronlat bent down to inspect the plants and, with his neck lower than the top of the pack, water ran out of it and over his head. He tried to ignore it. "This plant has pods like miniature versions of flat *peas or beans.* I wondered how long the food in my pack would last. No need to worry about that now."

"Or, given your pack, a way to carry water," she chimed.

He stood up and cast a serious eye toward the glowing mound. However, the drop of water hanging on the end of his nose mitigated his determined expression.

Mariyonta felt her lips start to arch but managed to keep them pressed together in a thin line. "We have plenty of food and water to stay until we and the cave think it's time to leave."

The drop of water doubled in size before it fell off Aronlat's nose and landed on his foot with an audible *plop.* It broke the dam of pent-up tension, and they both laughed.

"I have no idea how to get out of here," he admitted.

"Neither do I."

"Where's Yawri when you need him?"

"Gone, as usual."

Aronlat imitated Yawri's baritone voice. "You'll never know your own strength if I'm always with you."

"If you live."

They laughed again. They refused to think about what it would be like if only one of them remained.

Their steps quickened to reach the shimmering light. It transformed from an indistinct glow into a cluster of crystals. They stopped and stood, transfixed by what looked like a luminous lotus flower floating on dark sand.

Aronlat said, "Wow. That's one astonishing crystal family. I wonder if it's what called us here. "

They stilled and opened themselves to receive whatever this crystal lotus wished to impart. The answer came quickly. "Not I," it communicated. "The center called from the cave behind you."

Mariyonta and Aronlat turned. What appeared to be a small crack in the wall of the underground chamber blazed with light.

"That's a cave?" Aronlat said, looking at the fissure.

The lotus crystal pulsed. "The entrance is small. What it leads to is not."

They walked toward it slowly, their eyes never leaving the crack. It grew in length with each step, and after they stepped over a rocky mound, they could see it widened before it plunged underground.

They paused at the top of the small hill, looked at each other, and took simultaneous steps down the slope. They stopped in front of a low entrance, wide enough for them to pass side by side. They bent down to see what they could see. Their eyes, accustomed to darkness, tried to adjust but only saw dazzling outlines of angular shapes.

They waited for their eyes to adjust to the light. The radiant shapes appeared to move. Mariyonta took in a breath that went down through her feet and into the Earth. "I think we found it."

Aronlat took her hand. The look of reassurance that they gave to one another was brief, but neither took a step forward until it was complete. They leaned forward and walked into the expansive, multidimensional, crystal cave.

While the lotus crystal looked on, the fissure flared with explosive brilliance, then went dark.

25. CRYSTAL CAVERN

∞

The moist, earthy breath of the crystal cave reached Yawri long before its jagged mouth came into view. He was the only one who knew of this small, remote cave mouth and preferred it to the main entrance, an entrance far safer for young adults to travel. The narrow and craggy-rock floor in this one made it impossible to negotiate by foot. It required a small skystone and a pilot who could navigate tight, twisting turns and water channels. Flying through the small passages at high speed on his azure-blue skystone always made Yawri smile. Except for today. Today his lips were a thin line.

Although he had come to make sure Aronlat and Mariyonta were safe, he kept returning to thoughts of Keela and Tisbero.

Why do I keep thinking about them? There is more danger for Aronlat and Mariyonta.

Still, an inner sense of urgency implored him to increase his speed, even though the tunnel held surprises. Stone had fallen since his last visit, and what was open earlier held jutting rock now. Negotiating the sinuous channel, his body swayed and bobbed as the skystone rose and fell.

A sudden change in sound alerted him to the blocked passage ahead.

A flash flood.

When rainfall overran riverbanks, water saturated the ground and rushed into porous fractures below. Until it drained through cracks and fissures, floodwater filled this part of the passage. Yawri didn't slow but instead sped toward the water. An instant before hitting its surface, he threw himself down flat on the skystone, his body seamless with its mineral matrix.

The skystone split the water and knifed toward the glowing crystal at the lowest point of the submerged passage. Yawri usually stopped to greet it, however this time his hello passed in a blur. The skystone shot up again and burst through the surface, water trailing in a long veil. The skystone stopped at the top of the cavern and hovered.

Yawri rolled and rose to his feet in one motion. He oriented himself in the glowing chamber and looked for Lazket, the crystal being he befriended when he first arrived on this planet. Eons ago, this chamber was part of a larger one that arched over a vast underground lake. Millions of years later, when the planet chose to raise the enormous chamber to the surface, it separated the cavern into two parts. Lazket's was the smaller and deeper of the two. Yawri had never taken students to either, because even an experienced guardian could lose themselves in space and time by coming through so many dimensions.

Whereas most crystals in the cavern grew angled upward, Lazket's massive crystal body paralleled the floor, its root deeply anchored into the cave wall. Yawri began sailing his skystone toward his old friend.

I feel like a crystal myself when I'm here. The diamond being on the first planet gave me my ethereal crystal so long ago it's hard to remember what it was like without it.

He positioned his skystone to hover near Lazket, safely above the crystalline clusters living on the cavern floor. Dismounting, he walked between them and stopped next to Lazket's long, hexagonal form. Fluorites glowed around the quartz, and their warm, white light transformed into miniature rainbows when it passed through the wispy, cloud-like structures within Lazket's body.

"Welcome, Yawri. It's always good when you come. I see you still enjoy a dramatic entrance. There is something to be said about your consistency, even if raucous."

Yawri stood straight, his head up. "The other crystals seem to enjoy it, too. It gets the air moving, don't you think? I can't imagine sitting in the same spot for millions of years."

"We move, but with different timing. Our lives are measured in thousands or millions of years. The lifetime of your body is a blink to us. I suppose that's why you like speed."

"I've always enjoyed seeing how fast I could go without damaging something. Even when I had a light body."

"Or you're always in a hurry to leave one thing and get to another."

Yawri bent down, his face aglow. "Hello, Red! Does Lazket give you a hard time, too?"

Yawri met the red diamond when he first arrived on Earth, and he had hoped the planet would move Red up to the surface at some point. Eons later, when Lazket told him Red was above ground, Yawri used his ethereal diamond to find him. The red diamond asked Yawri to deliver him to this spot, and Red had lived here ever since.

Even though the pressures had been extreme when a molten vent carried him above ground, Red's shape hadn't changed. He barely fit in both of Yawri's large hands, and still resembled two pyramids attached at their bases, their tips pointed in opposite directions. Yawri had learned the diamond had a profound ability to connect to Earth's magnetic fields. The fastest Yawri had ever flown was with Red on the way to Lazket's cave.

Red's communication resonated through Yawri. "Lazket does not give me a hard time. It is more likely the other way around."

Lazket replied, "Try living in a quartz body next to a red diamond and see what changes."

Red addressed Yawri. "Thank you again for bringing me to this place. I chose not to join with an ethereal being. However, Lazket shares his connection to his ethereal realms.

Yawri was deep in thought, a state of mind he rarely showed to others. Light from distant crystals reflected off Red's mirror-like facets so vividly it was hard to tell if the lights were coming from inside or outside his body.

Red asked, "And you, Yawri? How does it go for you and other human beings?"

Yawri stepped back so he could see both friends. "How is it going?" he repeated. "I'm not sure."

A long, quiet moment passed. Finally, Lazket replied, "You don't know how it's going for you, or for human beings?"

"Me? Oh, I'm fine." He cleared his throat. "It's the rest of the world I'm concerned about."

"Spoken like a true Yawri," Red said plainly.

"Agreed. I am truly Yawri."

The comment didn't change Red's question. "You visit every three hundred years or so and it's only been a hundred. If you were fine I don't think you'd be here."

Lazket repeated, "So how does it go for you and other human beings?"

Yawri rubbed his forehead, took a breath, let go, and began. "First, I've got two young adults somewhere in the cave that might be lost."

"They aren't lost," Lazket replied.

"Where are they? Are they all right? What are they doing?"

Red said, "They have good connection with Earth. They realized they weren't done with their cave stay and chose to remain, even though their companions encouraged them to leave. They understood when we told them about their next chamber of learning. They are in the one above us."

"They were ready for the lake cavern? I've never taken young adults there."

The diamond continued. "They were almost ready. Still too attached to how they thought things should be in order to listen well. The water in the lowest part of the channel you flew through is what's left of a flash flood that washed them down."

Yawri stood bolt upright. "Washed down? All the way to the lake cavern, and they lived?"

The fluorite under Lazket glowed brightly. Red continued, "They're rather overwhelmed at the moment, but are okay."

Yawri grumbled, "Plummeting seems to be their specialty."

Lazket lightened and said, "The flood took them quickly. We were able to rid the young woman of her pack, but the male held his. As you know, the lake cavern provides all a conscious guardian needs to live."

"Young adults don't quite fit our definition of 'conscious guardian.'"

Red thrummed. "Well, we need conscious guardians. So does the planet. We will keep these young ones safe, and I believe they learned the value of listening rather than thinking. I am much more concerned about the youths who left."

Yawri looked down thoughtfully, then up. "The others left because they didn't want to miss the equinox celebration."

Red continued. "And so they miss Earth's training for them instead. They did debate, but in the end, they chose to hear what they wanted to hear: that their training was complete and it was time to celebrate being an adult."

Yawri's gaze bounced from place to place and he ran his hand through his tousled hair. "It's the first time this has happened in all my years of teaching."

Lazket spoke quietly. "There are good hearts in them all, but they didn't listen with their whole bodies, only with their ears and to their inner chatter."

Yawri took a breath and let it out. "Other teachers also find it's taking longer for the returning guardians to remember who they are. Much longer."

A vibration rolled through the cavern. Yawri drew back. "What is that?"

Lazket and Red's attention drew in and down, as they communicated with other crystals near and far. The whole cavern went silent. Yawri forced himself not to speak, knowing they would let him know what they found.

The fluorite under Lazket pulsed with light. Yawri started to pace back and forth. Finally, Lazket said, "Do you know the large crystal caves in the lands of the far northeast? You help us connect with them through your friendship with a woman there. A woman with great vitality and connection to Earth."

"Hetlin. Yes, I remember. She attended the same meeting I did on the astral last night. We agreed to gather any news from crystal caves in our areas and share it."

Red responded. "She has done so. The cavern she is in reports something bizarre. Many small caves in that area have yellow quartz crystals. They're especially skilled at blending physical and ethereal dimensions. A number of them have gone silent."

"Silent?"

"Yes. Sometimes caves will hibernate, but this is different. They were singing one day and silent the next."

Yawri froze, his stare unfocused. "Did that cause the tremor?"

Lazket replied, "No. That came from a disturbance to the west. There is a large crystal family in great distress. It is somewhere we have not heard crystals speak before. Some islands of basalt crystal are there, but this is quartz, like me."

"An island?" Yawri stormed. "Two of my friends are going to Crystal Island to find out if the community there is having the same problems we are."

"A crystal island?" Lazket asked. "Of basalt?"

"No, quartz."

The fluorite under Lazket flared. Lazket spoke in earnest. "Concentrate; focus on your two friends there. We can follow your connection, and through them, to this island."

Yawri focused on Keela and Tisbero. It wasn't hard. He knew where they were going and wished he was with them.

Lazket boomed, "It's called Crystal Island because crystals have been taken there against their will! It is not their home. They are cut off from us, from Earth."

"Why are your friends there?" Red asked.

"To find out if Shahten is having the same problems we are having."

"Who is Shahten?"

"He's the only guardian who had humanoid bodies on other planets before coming here. Not I, but many guardians sought his advice."

The entire chamber went quiet. It was so still, even drops of water stopped falling from the ceiling.

"Take me to that island," the red diamond thundered. "Now."

Yawri looked at Red, then his skystone, then Lazket.

Lazket spoke, his voice flame. "You need to go to your friends, now. Red connects to Earth's magnetic fields in a way no other crystal can. It will double your speed."

"Mariyonta and Aronlat are—"

"Safe," Lazket interrupted. "Your friends are not."

Yawri moved like water from a burst dam and gathered Red into both of his hands. Two long strides brought him to the skystone and he lowered Red onto the center of the azure-blue quartzite slab. The double-terminated red diamond joined with the skystone, making its six quartz crystals more radiant then Yawri had ever seen.

Red implored Yawri, "We are One with the matrix of this stone. Go!"

Yawri instantly increased his soul light and asked the air to braid under them to hasten their ascent. Within seconds, they reached the channel leading down to the water draining away from the flood. The speed of their exit pulled so much water behind them that the trail crashed against the channel's ceiling and fell back down like a cloudburst of rain.

The jagged mouth of the exit came into view, and it opened wider. The six crystals and Red increased their attraction to Earth's magnetic field, and the skystone sped even faster. The cave exhaled a breath of air and the combination made the skystone shoot out of the cave's mouth toward the island at triple the speed most guardians could manage.

26. THE ISLAND

∞

Keela landed her small skystone on the grassy promontory that served as the gathering place for Tisbero's community. The way it jutted out from the rocky coast and held broad, cupped bays on either side made it one of her favorites. Tisbero had asked several members of the community to meet him here to coordinate plans, and the result was apparent. While she landed, three other skystones rose into the air and moved in different directions.

Tisbero's gravelly voice called out the traditional parting. "Travel safely! May you expand Creation in all you become!"

"Go ever forth and Create with Creator!" drifted back on the wind.

A female guardian's voice roared above the sound of the surf below. "Travel safely, Tisbero! You too, Keela! I have a new dye to show you—bright orange!"

Keela recognized Twaque's voice. The two of them had developed most of the dyes local guardians used to color their sashes. "Let's use it to dye thread! I want to embroider another sash!"

"Great! See you soon. Got to go!"

The sense of urgency in the air was palpable. Ever since the guardians learned that the problem of less-capable youth was much more widespread than they'd realized, all were focused on resolving it.

Keela stepped onto Tisbero's skystone in one even stride. "Where are they going?"

He continued scanning the sky, watching them leave. "To different areas in the region to find out how much of what we're hearing is story or fact." He turned to ask her if she needed refreshment before they left, but changed his mind at the sight of her level stare. "Let's take four instead of two crystals. We'll be able to make better time."

She agreed. Although it took more concentration to use four rather than two, the sooner they could get back with the information from Shahten the better. "You lay that side and I'll do this one."

The crystals were long, but even laid end-to-end along the rim there was still plenty of room to maneuver down the center of the skystone. Keela saw Tisbero holding an additional crystal in his broad hand. "What's the fifth one for?"

He continued raising it for her to see. "It's a recording crystal. Yawri introduced me to it during his last visit. All crystals know their surroundings, but this one records everything around it in detail. I haven't used it yet, but having a third set of eyes and ears with us seems like a good idea."

She turned away and smiled. "Why am I not surprised? Yawri couldn't come with us, but he'll still get to see and hear everything we do."

Tisbero's expression grew pensive. "Well, yes ... but not at the same time. Anyone that knows how to speak with the crystal will know what we experienced. It's a practical solution." Tisbero placed the recording crystal into a side pocket of his long, white tunic. He re-tied his crimson sash to cover the top of the pocket for further protection.

"I agree we should take it, but I can also see why Yawri might not want it with him. It would record his 'creative' adventures."

"I don't think he'd care. He's the most transparent person I know."

Keela reconsidered. "He is that, actually. It's me that's private." She connected like a root to his skystone. "Let's go."

Tisbero replied, "All the crystals are joined with the skystone. They won't move from where they are no matter how we have to fly."

Without another word, the two guardians increased soul light. The effect of gravity on the skystone decreased and it rose into the air. Experienced with sharing energies, they coordinated with the crystals, and the skystone accelerated west. The sound of waves crashing against rock chiseled the air but fell away over open sea.

Shahten's community was several hours distant but they'd make good time. The island had the reputation of being a prime location for vital co-creation. Before joining with human bodies and their Earth spirits, etheric beings visited it frequently. However, since the blending of humans and ethereal beings restored communication with the planet so effectively, few made the journey these days.

The lone skystone sped due west, soaring above waves cresting and falling in crescents of white. Within the hour the horizon looked the same in all directions, but Tisbero kept their bearing true.

The day grew long. Tisbero leaned forward, straining his senses to catch a glimpse of the big island. He finally pointed to a distant bump where sea met sky. "There!" Waves passed below in a streaming cascade of black and white, but he and Keela only had eyes for the growing mass.

Tisbero's gravelly voice lowered further. "It's in the right location, but Crystal Island is ringed with black cliffs of basalt. This one is white."

Keela started to speak, paused to reconsider her thought, then continued. "Fog. That island is covered in low clouds."

Tisbero hurled words toward the shroud. "Fog? Only high clouds or sun come here!"

Keela asked, "Then why is it here now?"

Tisbero repeated, "Right. Why is it here now?"

Keela weighed possibilities. "Things are changing on the mainland. Why not here? Perhaps fog is needed to help Life grow."

Tisbero grumbled, "Perhaps," but his eyes remained fixed on the horizon.

The island neared, and the streaming cascade of black and white sea below washed to gray. Within moments of entering the fog, visibility shrank to a few skystone lengths. All that was visible in any direction was a uniform gray.

Tisbero shifted back and forth, shaking his head. "We have to get low enough to see the waves. We can follow their crests in."

Keela and Tisbero decreased soul light and increased soul sound. The skystone responded to the change in gravity and descended through the clingy mist until the dark sea poked waves through the shroud.

Maintaining all the speed they dared, their tight faces peered into the scene below. Mist melted into the waves and made the boundary between them dissolve. Occasional words between them kept the guardians from being lulled into timelessness. Resisting the mesmerizing dream, Keela said, "As long as we keep perpendicular to the crests we're going toward land."

Tisbero's head rose with a start. "Do you hear that?"

Keela heard the sound of the waves change in the same moment. "It's surf!"

A large and jagged black rock split the curtain of fog in front of them. The skystone spun up and to the right in a pivoting jerk. A black mass hurled past their heads no more than a hand's width away.

Keela and Tisbero leveled the skystone and brought it to a hovering stop, once more surrounded by a uniform mist of quiet gray. They looked to see that each stood unharmed, then to the crystals. Their connection to the skystone was so complete none had moved.

Tisbero growled. "It was the change in the sound of the waves. If we hadn't heard it, we would have collided."

Keela bit her lip and looked at the sea. She cocked her head. "What happened to the waves? They've gone quiet."

They piloted the skystone down until a flat sea appeared under the thick mist. Tisbero glared into it. "I've never seen a sea as flat as a lake."

Keela said, "Or maybe it is a lake. Is it possible we're over the island?"

Tisbero leaned back. "I don't see how that's possible, but a sea this calm isn't possible either. Waves get taller as they approach a shore."

They flew on, but without the waves to guide them in the dense fog, the direction and distance to a shore of any kind remained a mystery.

Tisbero reasoned. "Our direction remains true. Sea or lake, we'll find out soon."

"Watch out!" Keela yelled. "Go up! Up! Up!"

They flared with soul light and asked the air to increase pressure under them at the same moment. The skystone changed from horizontal to vertical flight so fast both fell back onto the slab. Eyes wide, they lay, One with the stone, fixed in place.

Monumental columns of basalt screamed past, close enough to touch. The skystone shrieked when a sharp, black, stone claw raked its underside. Its nose pitched away from the colossal cliff to avoid more jutting rocks, and the guardians looked down to see nothing between themselves and the rock-crashing sea but air. Time lengthened and shrank until it had no meaning. A sense of its passing only returned when they shot out of the clouds into a clear blue sky with a bright sun.

Shaken, they brought the skystone to a hover over the bright-white, dense fog. Keela finally stood and looked over the edge. Tongues of fog licked the edge of the cliff as if hungry. She looked at Tisbero. "I'll never tease Yawri about his air pressure trick again. If we hadn't known to ask the air spirit for help, we'd be dead."

"And I told him I couldn't imagine ever needing it." Tisbero stomped to the edge and looked down himself. "It's been a very long time since I've been here, but since when does any island have calm sea and fog surrounding it?" He shook his head in dismay. "I've never known of such a thing!"

"The conditions have obviously changed here as well."

"I don't understand it," Tisbero muttered. Keela was already looking inland in search of the high, cone-shaped peak Shahten's community called home. She pointed to a silhouette of rolling mountains in the distance. "Is the community on that mountain?"

"It should be, if that hasn't changed too. I have more questions now than when I left." Tisbero stretched his arms and rolled his shoulders. His eyes fixed on the mountain. "Let's find Shahten."

The skystone responded to their requests as if it was eager to talk to him itself. Rolling hills passed under them quickly. They came to an ancient plateau of volcanic basalt now filled with mineral-rich soil.

Tisbero's hand shot out and pointed to their right. "What are those? No rock outcrops look like that."

The skystone drifted that direction for a closer look and Keela studied them. "They're shelters. See there? A man's coming out of one now." They looked down at him but he did not look up. "Meetinghouses? Similar to the long, grass-walled structures we use?"

"Except these are too small and are made from stone."

Keela counted them. "Forty-three individual structures instead of one large one."

The skystone slowed. "What are those low walls for? See them? There are low stone walls between them, without roofs. Why would guardians need those?" Keela tilted her head to the side, her lips pursed. "Are those animals? Wildebeests or something behind the low walls?"

Tisbero fired back, "I have no idea. This co-creation makes no sense to me."

Keela chewed her lower lip. "The guardians must be keeping them safe from something, or maybe they're here because they're hurt." Her neck craned. "Could it be for healing?"

"Zinn would know." Tisbero peered forward. "Let's find Shahten and ask him." The skystone banked and accelerated. "The center of the community is straight ahead, up the side of that mountain on a plateau."

They followed the rising elevation of the land. After rushing up a long, steep incline, they soared over a strange landscape. Keela gestured to the structures below. "More of those stone shelters. Lots more."

Tisbero rubbed his brow. "None of this was here the last time I visited." The travelers struggled to interpret what their eyes saw. "I've never seen a rock formation like that."

Keela spoke succinctly. "It's hundreds of those stone dwellings in one place. Many hundreds, and they get larger as we fly up the mountain."

Tisbero scanned back and forth in search of the landing area. "It used to be here. It's so different with all of these dwellings now. There!" he pointed. "At least the community's landing area hasn't changed!"

Their destination in sight, they increased their speed.

They soared over a tall, pitch-black wall. Without speaking, they slowed the skystone to gaze back at the structure. Tisbero straightened from his survey. "I've seen this kind of wall before, but not for millennia. It was when the planet was more ethereal, and Earth's thought forms had more impact on the physical. Zinn and I helped co-create a wall like this to help each stay where they wanted to be." He turned toward the landing field and the skystone accelerated toward it again. "It was made of mud brick but it looked black to physical sight, same as this one." He shook his head. "The confusion that thought forms could have on the physical is long past. Long past. What possible reason could there be to build a wall that exists in multiple dimensions today?"

Keela shrieked, "Go left. Now! Now!" In less than a heartbeat, the small skystone pivoted left. Even with that, the underside of the largest skystone they'd ever seen only missed them because they lay prone on their stone. Raising their heads and propping themselves on their elbows, they stared at the backs of at least thirty guardians facing the landing field, oblivious to their near miss.

"Here comes another one!" Tisbero cried out. "Down! Drop down!" Their skystone plummeted, but even with the help of the air, only a quick return of their heads to the stone allowed them to pass under the second skystone unharmed. Tisbero scanned the sky. It was clear. He pointed to an open area at the edge of the field. "Land there!"

Pulses racing, Keela and Tisbero brought their skystone to a stop above the tall, flowering prairie grass and hovered there. Tisbero ran his hands through his hair and Keela blinked in disbelief as the two enormous skystones dropped onto the ground a few skystone lengths away with the sound of rock grating on rock.

One of the guardians on the massive slab nearest saw them and snapped, "What are you doing on this landing field?" The taut muscles of his neck strained against a high-necked collar on his crimson leather vest. "This is a training field for SkySlabs! Shahten had the other field built for skystones from the mainland. Why didn't you use it?"

The other men and women on the immense slab remained standing in place. All wore rust-and-tan colored tunics and held large yellow crystals to their lower chests.

"Greetings!" an even louder voice called from the second platform. Another guardian dressed in a high-necked, crimson leather vest easily stepped off his platform and, eyes fixed on them, strode through the tall prairie grass. "I apologize for this poor welcome! Two other visitors arrived earlier, but our public landing area is in the main courtyard. Their skystone is there. "

The first leather-clad guardian stood with his arms crossed and feet wide on the bow of his "SkySlab." He glared at Keela and Tisbero. "Did you just land? It looks like it!" He jabbed a finger at their diminutive skystone. "There is no way we can see something so small when piloting one of these. You could have collided with us! Why didn't you use the public field?"

Tisbero glared back. "The last I heard, Shahten's instruction was to land in this field. He never mentioned another."

The guardian uncrossed his arms and placed his fists on his hips. "Shahten is always very clear in his instructions. He had the public field built to keep visitors safe. He would never tell you to use this one in its place."

The second SkySlab pilot stopped at the edge of Keela and Tisbero's skystone and leaned toward them. "My fellow captain is understandably upset because your landing could have been catastrophic." He nodded to his companion, who stood on the bow of his SkySlab like cold stone. "Seriously. You could have been killed. However, you are safe now. I'm sure Shahten is expecting you. Best we not delay."

Tisbero cast a knowing eye toward Keela. Shahten wasn't aware of their visit. Tisbero released a deep breath and gave a slight nod to the SkySlab pilot. "It won't happen again."

"Of that I am sure." His voice was calm but unsettling. "Shahten would certainly be displeased if any further mishaps occurred, as would we all. When you are ready, I'll escort you."

He turned to his fellow captain. "Please see to our menders and I will see to our guests."

"Yes, master captain." The disgruntled unhappy guardian waved dismissively to Keela and Tisbero and turned to face the group on his SkySlab.

Keela mouthed to Tisbero, "Master captain?"

The red leather clad guardian next to them said, "I am the master captain of all our SkySlabs. Now that I know you are here, I can assure your safety as well as that of your skystone. Please, follow me."

Keela and Tisbero exchanged glances, then walked to the edge of their skystone and jumped off. The grasses were tall and they landed with a jolt. The master captain started walking, but Tisbero stood with Keela to observe the area a moment before following. The uniformed guardians from the other slabs weren't paying them any mind. They were busily stacking citrines against the bases of the SkySlab crystals. Unlike the ones on Tisbero's skystone, which lay flat along the outside edge, these stood upright in a row down its center.

Walking quickly, Keela came alongside their escort. "How do you get your crystals to stand upright? I didn't know they could unite with the stone's minerals without laying flat."

The master captain didn't look at her but replied, "Sockets. Each stands in a socket. My SkySlab has twenty crystals. If they were laying down, there wouldn't be room for the menders."

"Menders?" Tisbero stepped to his other side.

"They help us keep Life in balance," was his quick reply.

Tisbero's gaze swept to the SkySlab. "We find those yellow crystals, citrines we call them because of their lemon color, exceptionally fine for dimensional work. They keep ethereal and physical energies as One, so divisions don't occur. Is there a problem with dimensions here?"

The master captain glanced at Tisbero and back to the path. "Many communities have problems, but not ours. We solve them." He swiveled his head toward Tisbero, both eyebrows raised. "Leaders of many communities come to learn how we continue to progress while they regress. I hear some of their children are born without memory of who they are. Tragic. Shahten helps them. Is that why you've come?"

Keela's foot stopped mid-stride, then continued moving. "We have come to speak with Shahten," she acknowledged. Curious, she asked, "Your 'menders' use citrines to help new adults remember their past learnings?"

His reply was quick and cordial. "You are wise to seek Shahten's counsel." He pointed toward the large stone structure far up the hill. "He'll be waiting for you at the temple."

"Temple? What's a temple?" Tisbero asked, his face furrowed.

Their escort pivoted to face them. "Many that come from the mainland only know grass huts." The corners of his mouth curled in a faint smile. He pointed to the structure on top of the hill again. "Because so many seek Shahten's wisdom, we decided to make a special place for gatherings. The temple is our special place to honor guests. We made it with stone rather than sticks to show the permanence of our commitment to the Way."

Keela opened her mouth to ask what that meant, but the master captain continued without pause. "Please, follow me. You landed a distance away and he always wants to greet guests personally when they arrive, no matter how busy he may be."

Their incredulous stare at the temple was interrupted by their escort's abrupt about-face and long step toward it. More anxious than ever to meet with Shahten, the travelers fell into step behind him.

The narrow path through trodden grass joined a wide walkway of white stone. The escort kept walking without the slightest change of pace. However, Keela and Tisbero slowed, their eyes narrowed in thought.

Tisbero recognized the stone and his gravelly voice lowered. "This is a vein of pure marble. However, I've never seen such a straight line next to basalt before. I have no idea how it was formed. I asked the stone to tell me but received no response."

Their escort stopped and turned around, his feet planted wide. "You will learn of many new and wonderful creations here. This marble walkway leads from the gate at the bottom of the hill to the temple at its top. Like the Way, Shahten wanted the path to be clear and lasting." His confident steps became strides.

Now that they were standing on it, Keela and Tisbero saw the marble path curve back and forth up the hillside. It ended at the black wall they'd flown over.

"What's a gate?" Keela asked Tisbero while they hurried to keep up.

He gave a quizzical shrug of his shoulders and said, "No idea."

The master captain called back to them, "Shahten will answer every question you have. He did mine."

Three SkySlabs crested the hill behind the temple. Similar to the first ones they'd seen, each had a line of crystals running down its center accompanied by two columns of "menders" on either side. Except for one red-vested captain standing on the bow, all wore the same rust-colored tunics and held yellow crystals.

Tisbero blurted, "There's a tremendous amount of dimensional capacity in all of those citrines. How many communities have problems with separation of ethereal and physical dimensions? Are they One with the continuum again?"

"Many need balancing," their escort replied stiffly, clearly tiring of their questions. "Shahten will explain all you wish." He stopped suddenly and looked up. One of the SkySlabs was passing very slowly overhead.

Two guardians dressed in off-white, loose-fitting frocks similar to Keela's and Tisbero's waved cheerily down to them. Their wide smiles filled with relief at seeing them on the white stone path.

"Camic and Rhee!" Keela said. "Did they already meet with Shahten? The plan was to meet together."

The master captain's expression hardened. "They arrived much earlier. If you are late, we had best move more quickly." He turned and strode up the hill so fast it was impossible to converse.

As the distance to the temple shrank, the sense of its monumental size grew. Four of the island's massive SkySlabs or twelve skystones laid end-to-end wouldn't match the length of the temple wall. The sinuous walkway ended at a long ramp of marble steps.

Keela said, "I've seen one or two steps leading into a prayer place but there must be over fifty here." Their escort scaled them with practiced ease. Keela and Tisbero followed.

The top of the staircase opened onto a wide-open courtyard, also covered with white marble. The escort crossed it without a fleeting look to either side, but the two travelers stopped to look at a sculpture familiar to them both.

Keela said, "At least Shahten promotes the connection of human beings within the All. We use this image to educate children. It shows bodies of four different animals as One. It has the legs of a wildebeest, creatures that live solely off plants. The body of the great-toothed cat, creatures to assure plant eaters are kept in balance with Earth's plants. The wings of the great bird assure wisdom is seeded throughout the land. Lastly, it has the head of a human being, listening and watching to assure the One body remains in balance. There's a lot I don't understand on this island, but at least I understand this symbol."

"Please come," their escort said from the threshold of a tall archway. He stepped across it and beckoned them to follow. The travelers stepped through and stopped, stunned. Pillars of fine-grained, translucent marble at least four feet in diameter and sixty feet tall outlined a courtyard twice that distance across.

Supported by the pillars, the temple roof rose to a towering peak above them. Sunlight came in through the open sides of the structure and reflected off the polished white floor like sunlight on fresh snow. The travelers shielded their eyes.

"Follow me," their escort commanded. They marched behind him down the great hall and stopped in front of another flight of stairs. Although a third of the height as the last staircase, each step was higher and deeper. "Wait here," he instructed before walking up the steps, hesitantly it seemed, and disappearing from their sight.

The master captain entered the next chamber slowly, hoping to allow his eyes time to adjust from the glaring light. It didn't help. Shahten's voice greeted him immediately.

"Master captain, you bring them here? What part of my instruction did you not understand?"

He spun toward the sound, but all was hidden from his sight. Shahten would have no problem seeing him.

He spoke factually. It would only be worse if he did otherwise. "We did as you instructed, my lord. You said fog the coast. We fogged it, thickly. You said to calm the sea so they would not be alerted by the sound of waves. We made it as smooth as glass. We waited for the collision none could avoid. However, instead of the crash of stone on stone, they popped up a hand's breadth in front of the basalt wall like a lava bomb hurled from a volcano. I know of no way a skystone could rise that fast. Yet I saw it with my own eyes."

Shahten watched beads of sweat grow on the master captain's forehead and let the silence build. He spoke calmly. "You've not seen skystones piloted by guardians with full memory before. This is one reason they remain so arrogant." In an even calmer voice he added, "How did they manage to land? It is very difficult to avoid colliding with a SkySlab that drops directly in your path, no matter the pilot's skill."

The master captain could see Shahten now, pacing slowly back and forth. He spoke with a confidence he did not feel. "We came at them very fast as you instructed, and caught them in between us. We expected to see their heads fly through the air. It was unnatural the way their skystone dropped out of our way, faster than any change in soul light or soul sound makes possible."

"Guardians with full memory retain their skill. That they lived will be their loss. If their bodies had died in sudden trauma, it would have been much harder for them to bring their learning into their next body. Their retraining in the Way would have been much easier." Shahten clasped his hands in front of him and paced slowly. "We must help them start anew or they will remain forever trapped by their past."

Shahten finally stopped his thoughtful pacing. "My friend." The tone was kind, yet commanding. The master captain stood still as stone. Shahten continued, the voice of reason.

"I made you master captain of our SkySlabs for a reason. You are disciplined and lead the other captains and our menders well." He paused to assure his dark stare penetrated the man's lined face. "These people are dangerous, particularly the woman. I have spoken with her before, yet she continues to poison the minds of many. Her traumatic death would have helped her release what binds her to old ways, a kindness to her as well as to Earth."

The master captain straightened. "Her abilities were unknown to me. It won't happen again. I will see this kindness through for her sake as well as Earth's. I vow it."

"Yes, you will." Shahten continued his slow, measured pace. "The two guardians that arrived this morning have been cultivated for many months. If they came with any suspicions, they are replaced with awe. We can count on their allegiance."

"Camic and Rhee. As with all others you have met with, my lord, who still have the ability to listen."

Shahten stopped and faced the master captain. "You observed our tardy arrivals while you walked them here. What is your sense of them?"

The captain felt his leg muscles tighten, his body ready to run. He forced himself to stand motionless.

What would Shahten want to hear?

He cleared his throat.

"They seem well-meaning but ignorant, my lord. They are overwhelmed at the sight of creations common to us. They carry so much confusion inside themselves I don't see how they can ever see the truth of what's before them," the captain finished with lowered eyes.

"It was the man called Tisbero with Keela, not the one called Yawri?" Shahten wanted to be sure.

"Yes, Keela and Tisbero."

"I remember him. A fiery bumpkin. What a pity Yawri did not come too. Yet, we must make the best of the opportunity Creation provides." Shahten stretched. His voice sounded warm and caring.

"Challenges come and go, but Creation thrives with us, master captain." His face held a knowing grin. "I will find a way to save them from themselves. Of that I am certain."

27. TEMPLE

∞

Keela peered at the sculpted archway at the top of the stairs for the third time. "I wonder what's taking him so long?" She took one step up the staircase.

Tisbero joined her. "Maybe we should go up and look for him." He craned his neck to see if a different angle would provide a better view. "He said Shahten always dropped whatever he was doing to meet with visitors. I'm ready for him to drop whatever he is doing now."

Keela tried yet another time to communicate with the beautiful white marble surrounding them. "The stone carries Life force, but I can't speak with it. The tones are unlike any I've ever heard." She placed a hand on the low banister wall. "Is this a new species of rock?"

Tisbero's face tightened. "I haven't gotten clear communication from anything since we landed." He took two more steps up the wide stairs and stared into the sculpted archway. Whatever was beyond it lay in shadow. "If all the guardians here are like those two captains, it's going to be a short visit."

Keela stepped up to join him. They turned around to contemplate the immense gallery of pillars. Tisbero scanned from side to side. Nothing moved. Keela closed her eyes and listened. "I've never met guardians like the captains, or stones like these before, but I need to communicate with both."

A high voice penetrated the air and bounced off pillars, floor, and roof. "Shahten will see you now!"

Although the noise seemed to come from all directions at once, the travelers spun toward its source. The master captain was nowhere to be seen, but a woman stood at the top of the stairs. Instead of a leather tunic, she wore a finely woven silver robe. A thick purple sash draped around her neck, crossed her chest, and flowed down her sides. She gazed down, examining the visitors. Keela and Tisbero stared back. Finally, in a voice so calm it was hard to believe it came from the same person, she said, "Please come. Shahten will see you now."

Tisbero blew out his cheeks with a sharp exhale. Keela placed her hands on the knot of her embroidered sash. Both started walking up the broad, luminescent stairs.

Keela caught Tisbero's eye. "I expect she's as curious about us as we are about her." He rolled his eyes but didn't comment.

Tisbero's body was stout but Keela's legs were long, and they reached the top of the stairs at the same moment. Keela bobbed her head to the woman before them and said, "Thank you for welcoming us. We traveled far to speak with guardians such as yourself. I am Keela."

Tisbero dipped his head as well. "I am Tisbero."

The robed woman blinked. A small hand rose and touched her throat. "I am Rayel, a priestess of this temple."

Keela replied warmly, "What is familiar to you is new for us. We appreciate your reception very much and hope you can share some of your knowledge and experience with us."

Rayel's eyes widened. The sleeve of her beautiful robe fluttered when her hand returned to her side. She bobbed her head once as Keela and Tisbero had. Her voice brightened. "Thank you for coming."

Her eye contact steady, Keela said, "I hope we get a chance to talk."

The priestess took a step back. "I just realized that I haven't spoken with guardians from the mainland in years. Perhaps after your meeting with Shahten, it will be possible." She stepped to the side and swept her arm toward the archway, her silver sleeve trailing its motion.

"Thank you," Keela replied graciously.

They entered the archway but Tisbero slowed. "Let's give our eyes a moment to adjust from this bright light to a chamber likely lit by crystals." Keela had already slowed, equally aware of the need. By the time they strode into the chamber they could see clearly. "Hello, Shahten," Tisbero's gravelly voice crooned. "Very good to see you again."

Shahten drew back, surprised that they could see him in his dim chamber. His mouth came open but he didn't speak.

"Are those glowing crystals?" Keela swept her hand toward alcoves along each side of the chamber. About twenty crystals commonly used for light sat in them, but they barely glowed. "Is there a problem?"

"Of course not. I've just arrived myself so haven't brightened them yet." Light bloomed. "Welcome. Welcome to our community. So good of you to come."

Shahten took in a deep breath and sauntered toward them, his dark-red robe shimmering with silver highlights with each silent step. "Your two friends, Camic and Rhee, told me to expect you. I wish I'd known earlier that you were coming. I would have liked to prepare." He stopped in front of them and waved a hand. "What do you think of this? Think of it as a sculpted cave." The glowing crystals flared with light.

It was Keela and Tisbero's turn for their mouths to drop open. They were accustomed to the rough stone of the cave caverns. This cave was perfectly rectangular with finely sculptured walls. Light from the crystals penetrated the translucent gypsum surrounding them and made the walls glow. Keela and Tisbero stood still, too captivated to take another step.

The high, curved ceiling was inlaid with small stones and gems. At the top of the domed ceiling, large diamonds formed constellations in a night sky. Under them, a tableau of gems and colored stones told stories with more patterns.

One mosaic pictured radiant orbs—beings descending from the stars. Another band portrayed a landscape of blue ocean filled with kelp forests and sea creatures.

The wall next to it showed every kind of plant and animal, and radiant beings with long legs and arms walked among them. Their hands were outstretched, giving golden healing energy.

The next wall portrayed humans sitting near campfires, then human beings twice their height standing with overflowing piles of fruits and foods.

The last wall showed stone buildings, penned animals and rolling fields of crops. Under it all stood a broad band of black obsidian. The dark contrasted so sharply with the colors above it gave the impression everything floated in a timeless void.

"Beautiful, isn't it?" Shahten boomed.

Keela and Tisbero spun, startled out of their reverie.

Shahten stepped in front of Keela, extended his hand, and tenderly wrapped his fingers around hers. "Our co-creation goes wonderfully well here. From what Camic and Rhee shared, I'm sorry to hear it is not going as well for you."

Keela withdrew her hand. "You recall Tisbero. He's been to this island before."

Shahten took a step toward him but didn't extend his hand. Instead, he raised it to his chin and massaged it slowly. "I didn't remember you'd been here before. Welcome back!"

Tisbero was surprised at Shahten's lapse in memory. They'd had many conversations, even if they weren't recent. "The island has certainly changed a lot since my last visit."

"Yes. Creation means change," Shahten declared. Changing the topic, he added, "I had an excellent meeting with Camic and Rhee this morning. I wish you could have joined us. I'm afraid my afternoon is quite busy, but it's important all your concerns are addressed. What is this about ethereal beings and Earth sprits not remembering their learning from past bodies? It sounds frightful."

"You've had no such problems here?" Keela asked. "If everyone is born with full memory here, why are the guardians on your SkySlabs so subservient to pilots?"

Shahten laughed so hard his chest shook. "Subservient? What do you base that assertion on, Keela? I remember our conversation on the promontory where the two rivers join, eons ago. We all learned you jump to conclusions before you have the facts. Is that right? Assumptions created a lot of disharmony between many guardians then, are you doing the same now?"

Keela flared but kept her voice even. "Once again I have questions, not answers, Shahten. You were the one with the answers then, and from what I hear, you're the one with them now."

"Facts, Keela. Facts," Shahten responded smoothly. "Come," he said so politely it must have been genuine. "Your two friends that came earlier today, Camic and Rhee, completed a tour of the island. I do wish you could have gone with them. They were taken anywhere they wished to go. I'm going to meet with them to learn if they have any unanswered questions. Please join us. You can roam freely, but since you're reporting back to the same community, you might wish to talk with them before they leave."

Tisbero leaned forward. "Leave? Why? We agreed to meet with you together."

"There is a storm coming and they said they wanted to make it back to the mainland before it arrived. Why inconvenience them because you came later?"

"A storm coming?" Tisbero asked. "The air hasn't communicated anything to me about a change in weather."

"Nor to me," Keela added.

Shahten spoke good-naturedly. "The vibratory essence of different lands has changed over time, and different types of human bodies have evolved to work with them. Haven't you noticed changes in the physique and tint of human bodies? This island is no exception. Tell me, has your communication with Life on this island been clear?"

Keela spoke at the air rather than make eye contact with him. "It has not."

Shahten looked at Tisbero. "It has not," Tisbero echoed.

Shahten raised both his hands in supplication and smiled. "You came on behalf of your community to learn if we were having problems recalling past learnings. Since we are not, you wish to understand why not. Correct?"

Neither spoke. They both leaned back slightly, lips pressed together.

Shahten leaned forward. "Please, I'm trying to understand your concerns. I certainly don't blame you for being distraught. Who wouldn't be if they couldn't remember who they are? The fact is, the Way we use works. You can stay as long as you like to learn as much as you like. Shall we go to meet your companions? Listening to them might be more helpful than anything I can say."

Keela did not understand her disquiet.

The past is the past and Shahten is being more than reasonable.

"Yes. I would like to meet with them very much."

Tisbero noticed he was clenching and unclenching his hands, and held them still. "Good idea. Yes. Their questions are likely ours too. It would help to know what's been resolved."

Shahten was unusually tall, but he seemed to increase in height as he said, "Please, follow me." He moved quickly, and although their minds raced with questions, both travelers put them aside to catch up.

Shahten stopped in front of a panel of carved alabaster, identical to all the others as far as Keela and Tisbero could tell. However, this one swung open with a slight swish of air and Shahten walked through with practiced routine. After they followed him through, Keela turned to see the panel already closing of its own accord. Tisbero caught her expression of wonder, shook his head, shrugged, and kept walking to keep up with Shahten.

The next time they stopped was on a small balcony that overlooked a courtyard far below. "Your friends must already be waiting for me on the terrace." They followed his gaze to the SkySlab parked below. It was the same one that had carried the people who passed over them during Keela and Tisbero's walk here. It sat next to a much smaller skystone. Camic and Rhee's, no doubt.

"I have business to attend to before our meeting, so I must hurry. Please follow this walkway up and join us on the terrace. I think you'll appreciate the view and refreshments." He walked back down the way they'd come–a much shorter route to their destination than the one he advised. With a voice as innocent as a baby's laugh, he said, "Please park your skystone where Camic and Rhee did the next time you come."

Tisbero stared at Camic's skystone. "How did they know to land here?"

Keela joined his examination of the courtyards and structures below. Now that they were here and free to investigate as they pleased, Keela wasn't much interested in Camic and Rhee. "They must have been here more recently than you."

A light flashed among the buildings in the distance.

"What was that?" Tisbero asked.

They both watched another flash. "Sunlight reflecting off something very big," she said.

They walked farther up the marble path to a less obstructed view.

"Heavenly Earth!" Tisbero said, focusing all his senses on the site. "It's a crystal, larger than a village hut!"

"What? Are you sure? Crystals that size are only found deep in the Earth."

They stared for several minutes but no more flashes came.

"Coming?" Shahten's distant voice carried down the long marble path, amplified by unseen acoustics.

They looked up to see Shahten wave from the top of the terrace. "Coming!" Tisbero yelled with equal intensity.

"What?" Shahten shot back, apparently not hearing the reply. "Your friends are waiting for you!"

"Why is it we hear him but he can't hear us?" Tisbero grumbled.

"Let's start moving. There's nothing wrong with his sight."

They moved quickly up the path. Keela spared one more glance toward the courtyard and saw a flash of light. "The big crystal there is where the flash is coming from!"

Shahten's voice cascaded down from the terrace. "Camic and Rhee have to leave soon. Please come!"

Keela and Tisbero doubled their pace. Keela vowed, "Let's find what we can from Camic and Rhee now and learn about that courtyard later. Shahten said we could go anywhere we pleased, and we will."

28. HIGH TERRACE

∞

Shahten strolled through the seamlessly paneled door and on to the terrace. The master captain watched it close silently behind him and disappear into the wall. "Keela and Tisbero are still on the balcony where you left them, my lord. Having them walk the path along the outer edge of the hillside rather than the direct route will take much more time."

Shahten contemplated the two small figures at the base of the winding, marble path. "They weren't receptive to our words after we had them walk from the landing field to the temple, but they should be more receptive after walking the long way here."

The captain agreed with a knowing smile and his head swiveled toward the open terrace. "Camic and Rhee await you at the dining table that overlooks the community. Their skystone has been moved from the large field to the one below as you instructed."

"Have Keela or Tisbero had any nourishment? They haven't even started walking yet. Perhaps they are more depleted than we thought."

The master captain's high leather collar flexed tightly against his stiff neck. "They've had nothing to eat or drink since they arrived, and there were only meager provisions on their skystone." Keela and Tisbero took several steps up the path but stopped. "Shall we put tea from the joy plant into the pomegranate juice for them as we did the first two? It put them in a much better mood. They were indifferent to the two women we prepared for them before drinking it but accepted their attention after."

Shahten considered the idea. He'd experimented with the potion ever since he found that after the red petals fell off the large, egg-shaped seedpods, the little black seeds inside could be made into a potent, euphoric tea. A little bit each day helped the human women they trained adapt to their role. However, he also learned that if he gave them too much, it had the opposite effect. They became disagreeable, even demanding. Left on their own, if they found a pot of the tea they'd keep drinking it until they died.

"Not now. If Camic and Rhee drink any more, their over-relaxed behavior might raise questions. We need them to leave on schedule. After they're gone, add the potion to pomegranate juice for Keela and Tisbero. They've gotten very fixed in their ways and it will help them open to a more receptive frame of mind."

Shahten cast a glance down at the misguided guardians and saw they'd moved a few paces but stopped again.

It's the first time they've seen such construction and they are awed by it.

He spoke thoughtfully, "Unlike us, they have no ability to keep centered when truths are mixed with untruths. They remind me of children, too infantile to know the difference. When I simply discount what they say, or completely ignore it while I share anything with my unshakable confidence, they flounder like a fish on a shore. They must be taught but don't realize how much they don't know. We will show them their ignorance so they can start to learn."

"Children need a parent. If they are wise, they will seek that guidance from you."

Shahten's eyes traced across the terrace of arched stone. Camic and Rhee stood on its far side, enjoying the view of rolling hills and distant sea. Two human women dressed in thin silken robes were next to them, and laughter floated in the breeze. One of the women placed her hand on one of the guardian's forearms and more laughter bloomed.

The master captain said, "Your training of the female humans is proving a success. Guardians from the mainland always think that they are masters of their bodies. They have yet to learn the reverse is true."

"After I reminded our guests it was our duty to help the human species evolve, their conviction for rigid separation of humans and human beings cracked. Of course, the joy tea and the women we trained to educate them helped. They look and act the same, only shorter."

"And more passionate, my lord. They have the drive to survive and bring more capable children into a world that is far beyond a common guardian's understanding."

"That's because those guardians only have passion about Life. They have no knowledge of lust, so no defense from it. A pity Yawri isn't here. 'It's all just learning,' he'd say."

The stance of the master captain's body was identical to Shahten's but neither noticed. "I remember the confusion of some in our community when you introduced your plan to take infants from their tribes and raise them as our own. Confusion melted away after you explained how it was a part of our duty to help the human species evolve. You brought ideas we would never have thought of on our own. Without you, we would be locked in the past with guardians like Keela and Tisbero. The thought makes me shudder."

Shahten gave a beneficent smile. "Many planets, master captain. I have brought my knowledge to many planets. This jewel, though, this jewel is special."

He observed Keela and Tisbero once more. "Why are they still gazing at the settlement below? What could be of such interest?" His eyes flared. "Can Generator be seen from that balcony?"

The master captain thought carefully. "Only the tip of the tallest one. Otherwise, there is nothing to distinguish it from all the other stone structures. If I didn't know precisely where to look, I wouldn't see it."

"Still," Shahten said and strode to the top of the path so they could see him. "Coming?" he yelled down, waving them forward.

"Coming!" He heard Tisbero yell in response but ignored it.

Your words mean nothing unless you move, Tisbero.

He yelled louder. "Your friends are waiting for you!" They started walking, but slowly.

He boomed, "Camic and Rhee have to leave soon. Please come!"

He watched Keela and Tisbero lower their heads and move more quickly up the path toward him. "Finally."

"They are like children," the master captain affirmed, "without parents."

"Alert me when they near the terrace. I have more mature guardians to attend to." Shahten straightened his flowing silver robe and walked toward Camic and Rhee, light as a breeze.

"Greetings! I trust your visit has gone well."

Camic's hand flew off the shoulder of the human woman standing next to him and came to rest on his chest. "Yes, very well!"

Rhee took a step away from the woman next to him. "Our tour of the island answered all of our questions, Shahten." His eyes flickered to the two women and back again. "Your work helps everyone."

"Very good. Very good." Shahten inclined his head toward the women. "Would you please go down to Camic and Rhee's skystone? It's in the courtyard below. Make sure the bags of fruit and provisions we provided are ready for them. There is a storm coming and they will need to leave soon. I know you wish to see them off for a safe return."

"Yes, Shahten," both women replied.

The one next to Rhee placed a gentle hand on his wrist. "I do wish you a safe journey and hasty return." Her fingers trailed down his hand and lingered on his smallest finger before slowly, hesitantly dropping away.

She turned with the gracefulness of a swan and joined her friend. They strolled across the terrace, their silken robes clinging like water to their skin. They didn't glance back until turning the final corner. The guardians were still watching. The women's smiles were fleeting but radiant.

"Please, join me," Shahten said, breaking their trance. He gestured toward a long table inlaid with dark-red, azure-blue, white, and jade-green rock. Five finely carved wooden seats gleamed soft brown. He sat down comfortably in the one at the head of the table and spread his hands wide, inviting them to sit on his immediate right and left. "Please."

Camic and Rhea sat as the selection of foods on the table captured their attention. A platter of sweet radishes, still moist from harvest, sat next to a large bowl of boiled cabbage. Finely crushed salt formed a perfect mound on a black disk next to it. A basket of waxy, dark-brown dates lay next to a platter of sectioned pomegranates, their seeds gelatinous rubies. A bowl of firm, ripe, purple grapes stood next to a low dish of dried ones, and their wrinkled skin glistened with thin crystals of sugar.

Their eyes continued to roam.

Another platter held filets of dried fish next to an even larger one filled with light-brown beans mixed with slivers of white onion, chopped green parsley and flecks of red pepper. A large pitcher of pomegranate juice sat in the middle of the table.

"Enjoy," Shahten said, picking up a sweet radish with one hand and a pinch of salt with the other. It made a crisp *snap* with his first bite. He swallowed, licked his lips and took another bite.

Following Shahten's example of uninhibited delight, the two guardians sampled platter after platter.

"Have I satisfied all your questions? I've enjoyed your visit, but must confess I believe I've learned more from you than you've learned from me."

"I don't see how that could be," Camic said, finishing a handful of dried grapes. "I've never learned so much so quickly."

Shahten proffered a curved platter of round, golden-yellow fruits, each about the size of a child's fist. Late afternoon light set it aglow. Camic leaned forward. "What is it?" Rhee slid his chair to get closer.

"It's quince fruit." Shahten picked up a shining metal knife, cut one in half, and placed each half on a dish. With unhurried ease, he proceeded to slice the crisp fruit into thin, bite-sized slices, and with a ceremonial flourish, placed the plates in front of the puzzled guardians.

They tried to demonstrate calm restraint but it fell aside with the first burst of succulent flavor in their mouth. "Delicious," Rhee managed while he reached for another piece. "Sweet and dry at the same time."

Camic finished swallowing his last piece. "It invigorates the palate in a way nothing else does. Where do they come from?" He pursed his lips, leaned back and cast a wandering eye toward the platter of whole quince fruit. Rhee did the same.

Shahten smiled. "We grow them."

Always best to leave them wanting more.

"It's excellent you came to learn the facts about progress here. Assumptions are a poor substitute." He gave a meaningful pause and added, "Keela and Tisbero will be joining us soon. I'm sure listening to what you have to say will help them much more than anything I can impart."

Shahten picked up another quince fruit and cut it into slices. He gave a few to his guests but the majority stayed on his plate. "I wish Keela and Tisbero hadn't come so late in the day. At least you will be able to keep to your plan and leave before the storm arrives. It could last several days."

Shahten ate a slice. "For their own safety, they should leave after the storm passes. There is no need to rush them, is there? As we did for you, we'll use SkySlabs to take them wherever they wish to go. We'll visit all the distant lands they wish in our astral forms while our bodies sleep. Rather than wait for them, can I count on you to deliver your thoughts to the mainland guardians when you return?"

Rhee finished his last slice of quince fruit. "Yes. There's no need to rush them."

Camic held his last slice in his hand. "We came to find out if each new generation here was having more difficulty remembering what they'd learned from previous lives. You've shown us that the human beings here are progressing, not regressing." He ate his last piece and licked his lips. "Your methods help human beings, as well as humans, prosper. After you explained why we needed to help the humans evolve, the only question I had was why we hadn't realized it ourselves."

Shahten rested his elbows on the table, the fingertips of each hand touching their opposite. "The mind of any of us can become fixed in what's familiar. It is only because of my experience that I know the way of the past will not create the future we need." Shahten put a sizeable serving of boiled cabbage on a couple of gold-ringed saucers. "The little flecks of red you see are dried pepper. I find they spice the cabbage nicely." He passed the saucers to his guests.

The captain called out from across the terrace. "Keela and Tisbero are arriving soon."

"Thank you, captain." Shahten picked up a plate of sweet quince fruit and set it down between Camic and Rhee. Neither saw his smile.

29. TEMPTATION

∞

Keela and Tisbero rounded the top corner of the paved path. Rather than the harried appearance Shahten had expected, their unhurried pace and countenance showed they'd been engaged in a mindful conversation. He watched as they came upon the table filled with more food than they'd probably seen for a single meal before. Their eyes went wide a moment but quickly narrowed.

Camic and Rhee rose from their seats, all smiles. "Keela, Tisbero! What a relief! We saw you on the walkway when we flew over. What took you so long to get here? We were getting very concerned."

Tisbero strode toward them. "Good to see you, too. How did you get up here so fast?" he wanted to know. "It's a long walk."

"Walk?" Rhee asked, confused.

Shahten stood quickly, his chair making a loud, scraping sound across the stone floor. "Welcome again! I hope you enjoyed exploring. Please come. Join us! We can talk about anything you wish."

Camic and Rhee didn't need an exhausting walk to make them open to new ideas.

Shahten gestured to the only available chairs.

Keela and Tisbero sat down; across from each other and farthest from the head of the table. They had to lean forward to see Shahten when he said, "You must be famished. Please take refreshment." He passed a pitcher of honey-sweetened water to Rhee and a tray of ruby-red pomegranates to Camic.

They refilled their cups and put another serving of pomegranate seeds in their bowls before passing them on. "Everything here is delicious," Rhee said. "Try it."

Shahten picked up a platter of stewed beans and asked Camic to hand it to Keela. "Please let me know what you think of this, Keela. It's flavored with herbs you might recognize." He picked up the platter of smoked fish and passed it down the other side of the table to Tisbero. "I'd appreciate learning what you think of this."

Rhee said, "This fish is cured by smoke and heat from a chimney that comes into a small stone chamber. It's one of the many new things we've learned about." He shuffled dishes to make sure all were within reach of the new arrivals. However, the platter with the round, golden fruit stayed at the end of the table next to Shahten.

Shahten looked from Camic to Rhee. "Would you like to share any thoughts with your friends before you have to leave?"

Rhee jumped at the invitation. "We've seen many things and asked many questions. What questions do you have? Perhaps they're similar to ours."

Keela and Tisbero blinked at each other across the table. They had so many thoughts neither knew where to start, so they both did. Keela asked, "Why do you need stone dwellings? And we flew over large sections of land that only had one crop, and others that had penned animals."

Tisbero leaned forward and asked, "What kind of problem are you having with dimensions? Your SkySlabs were filled with guardians holding citrines. It must be serious for that many to leave their cave to come here."

Tisbero, still looking at Shahten, added, "And the wall, Shahten. I haven't seen a wall built in multiple dimensions since we needed to help thought forms avoid confusion. Why do you need one here?"

Shahten held up both of his hands as if holding back a flood. "Please, please. Take a breath and let your bodies receive nourishment. There is no rush. You can stay until all of your questions are answered, and longer." He gestured to Camic and Rhee. "Can you help them? Unsurprisingly, their questions are similar to yours."

Rhee handed Keela the platter of smoked fish. "Our questions were answered, and yours will be too. We'll be happy to share everything we've learned. Let's start with this fish. Did you know food can be stored if it's prepared this way? It's prepared using smoke chambers and they showed us how to make them. No more waste."

Keela sighed and placed one of the filets on her saucer. She tore off a piece and took a pensive bite. "It is good." Her smile was genuine but her finger tapped the edge of the saucer.

Camic held out a bowl of raisins for Tisbero. "These are grapes that have been intentionally dried in the sun."

Tisbero sampled the raisins. "Good. Very sweet."

232

Rhee said, "Another method to preserve food. We found this way of thinking every place we went. I'm sure you will be taken to see everything you have questions about. Shahten already told us he would."

Shahten placed a grape in his mouth. "Of course." He pointed casually at the dish of spiced beans he'd passed to Keela. "You haven't told me what you thought of these flat beans. Do you recognize the spices?"

Keela and Tisbero exchanged a glance. Keela added a scoop of the bean stew to her dish and took a bite. She lifted her head, closed her eyes and considered its flavors. "Delightful. The leeks, parsley, pepper, and onion work very nicely together with the broad beans, but there is another taste. It adds a warm, earthy flavor."

"Cumin," Shahten responded with a pleased smile. "I knew you'd taste it."

"Cumin." Keela nodded thoughtfully. "We use it in a tea to aid digestion, but I've never tried it this way."

Rhee volunteered, "We've found many innovations. We started with foods because everyone cares about nourishing more with less."

Camic passed a plate of white cheese to Tisbero. "This is a way to preserve the essence in milk." Tisbero took a piece and gave the plate to Keela. They both noticed that Camic was more relaxed and content then they'd ever seen him.

He even smiled while he said, "In the lands we care for, we make large, long meeting houses by weaving sticks together. Guardians in the forests make simple, leaf-covered platforms high in the trees. We never overuse the land. We move long before that happens. So I expect your reaction at seeing stone dwellings was similar to ours."

Rhee added, "We were surprised to learn the stone dwellings were not for guardians, but for humans."

"Humans! Why would humans need them?" Tisbero exclaimed.

"Same question we asked." Camic held a weightless gaze. "I haven't worked with humans since joining with a human spirit millennia ago. Have you?"

Keela shook her head and Tisbero said, "Why would we? The hairless apes still live much as they did then."

"Yes," Keela agreed. "They remain complete in what they are. The human spirits of their bodies continue as One with Earth's soul."

"So we believed." Rhee smiled and ate a piece of cheese followed by a grape.

Keela studied his expression.

Happy. Why is he so happy about this?

Tisbero drilled, "All creatures on this planet are One with the soul of Earth, which is in direct co-creation with Creator. The only reason we joined with a human was so we could continue our efforts to enhance that co-creation. There was no reason to involve other humans."

Camic replied easily. "Until today we thought that was true, too."

Shahten leaned back, chin held high; he looked directly at Tisbero. "Yes. Human beings were formed by each guardian joining with one human, and we each nurtured that same human spirit through generations so that the abilities of both would continually expand, right?"

"Yes," Tisbero responded. "I have been with the same genetic line, the same human spirit, since we joined."

"They invited us to do so, true?" Shahten fingered a plump dried fig.

Tisbero leaned forward. "Yes, of course. To not do so would not be co-creation."

"If Earth had not prepared bodies for us, we would have left. Also true?" All four of his guests nodded, agreeing with the obvious.

Shahten stretched his long legs out under the table. "We were all content. However, like you, I began to notice that some of our children were taking longer to remember their learning from previous lives."

Keela rounded on him. "So it is a problem here, too!"

Shahten stared down at the mosaic made from colorful, chipped stone that covered the table. He placed a hand on its surface and traced a pattern with a long finger. He raised his eyes and locked his gaze onto Keela. Yet his smile conveyed only patience. "It was long ago, but yes, I understand how distressing it is to witness the regression of friends. Few wished to speak with me about my observations. Most denied me, reasoning that it must be due to the natural evolution of bodies on changing landmasses. They thought the problem was probably caused by not taking these differences into account when mates were paired to bring forth the new bodies."

Keela's brow furrowed. "That same thought was spoken at our last astral meeting."

"Really?" Shahten shook his head slowly. "If the change was due evolution of bodies on different landmasses, those of us who were willing to investigate would not have found the identical problem in so many different places. More and more guardians were reborn without memory."

Keela sat unmoving; her head tilted toward Shahten in a studying stare. "How long ago did this happen? Why didn't we hear of it?"

Shahten rubbed the back of his neck. His shoulders curled slightly forward and he said, "Long ago. Few heard of it because few wished to carry the news."

He straightened again. "We were perplexed. How could there be a problem when our whole purpose was to help All evolve?"

"They discovered something," Camic said. "They were very methodical in their questioning."

Tisbero's blocky chin jutted forward. "What was discovered?"

Shahten met his stare, yet in contrast to Tisbero's strained posture, he appeared relaxed. "After much examination, we found two possibilities. We either erred when we first joined or erred somehow after. Since our first joining took place with permission from the human spirits and our abilities only increased over lifetimes, we focused on where the error could be after."

Shahten spread his arms as if encompassing the whole island. "Look about you. Both human and human being prosper. Can you say the same for the lands you tend? Our children grow to surpass us. You say yours are not."

Camic said, "It's why so many are coming to ask for his help." He turned to Shahten. "Aren't you meeting with emissaries from five communities this afternoon?"

Shahten looked down. "I must ask the master captain to speak with me in private about my appointments." He looked up. "But, yes. More and more guardians come to learn how we regained the ability to progress."

Tisbero opened his hands, palms up, above the table. "What did you do to regain the ability to progress?"

Shahten plucked a large, purple grape from its bunch, and considered it. "We discovered the problem was hoarding."

"Hoarding?" Tisbero flared. "What hoarding?" He turned to Keela. "We give our Life to Life and always have."

"Do you?" Shahten retorted. "Did you even consider the question before that instant response? I don't know the truth for you, but I've learned responses without reflection can be a symptom of arrogance."

"Arrogance?" Tisbero's mind swirled.

Shahten continued with a measured pace. "Again, I do not know the truth for you. I only know for myself that automatic answers can show unwillingness to question self. I've learned the greater my reaction to the question, the greater my arrogance." Camic and Rhee stared unblinking at Tisbero, considering Shahten's words.

Tisbero, his hands on the table, leaned closer to Shahten. "My answer was swift because it is throughout every cell of my body! To hoard Life from Life is against every action I have taken."

Shahten put the large, purple grape in his mouth and savored its sweet nectar. "Yes. You are clearly certain you are right. It was only a question. I apologize if it upset you."

Tisbero steamed with intensity greater than any he'd ever felt. Rather than speak, he grew quiet to reflect on the fervor of his response.

I've never responded that way to a question before. Could he be right?

Keela observed the interaction studiously. When she spoke, her voice carried a tone of wonder. "Please continue. You said you discovered the problem was due to hoarding."

Shahten leaned toward her with calm deliberation, and spoke so quietly she had to strain to hear. "You know answers were never meant to last for eternity. All must change." All four guardians focused to hear his words. "It was not easy, or comfortable to face, but yes, we discovered that we were hoarding." His eyes swept across all the faces but returned to Keela. "We had our way of life, our human spirits of the soul of Earth, and bodies with which to continue our guardianship. We did not think about humans."

Keela raised her tented hands to her chin and said, "Why would that create this problem? Earth has humans and human beings. Both are needed. Both add value."

"True." Shahten spoke calmly, but in a louder voice added, "Guardians help all manner of Life; mineral, plant, and animal develop. But tell me, how long has it been since you asked a human animal what it needed to develop?"

Tisbero raised his head and with an intense glare said, "I have not heard that Earth was dissatisfied with humans or human beings. We only go to life forms that call us."

Shahten smiled. "All calls? Are you sure? Why are your children regressing?" The question hit Tisbero's chest like a stone.

Keela watched the reaction of each guardian in turn, and spoke with an even, unhurried tone. "Hoarding, you said. What was the hoarding?"

Shahten took a deep breath and held it in. It blew out his cheeks when he let it go. "Hoarding and arrogance was the problem. We were not including humans in our guardianship. Why should we? We had the human spirits we wanted so that we could continue our work here. We had our physical bodies evolving and developing. We were happy—happy until this problem with our children." He paused. "It was only the pain of the loss that made us ask why."

Rhee chirped, "You'll find this interesting, Keela. It wasn't until after my tour of the island that I understood it, though."

Shahten nodded toward Rhee and placed both his hands on the table. "After much introspection, we discovered that the reason our children were no longer surpassing us was because they were too isolated, too disconnected from their ancestor, the human. They lived their brief lives as they always did, in caves or wherever they could hide from the beasts preying upon them. We discovered that humans were crying out for growth, and we had been deaf to

236

them. The more we listened, the clearer the need to help the humans develop became. It was time to connect the ethereal realms to them as we did for our original humans. It was time to give our seed to the source from which we came."

Camic emptied his cup of pomegranate juice. "That's what all the stone dwellings and the crops are for." He leaned back and swept a hand in a wide arc. "And all these new ideas! Both humans and human beings are prospering. How could Earth not be pleased?"

Keela ran a hand through her thick, honey-colored hair and sighed. "But how can that be? I have never heard of any species being called back to rejoin with an ancestor. Humans and human beings evolved to fill different roles. Each fulfills different needs of Earth."

Shahten filled Camic's cup with pure pomegranate juice. Unlike the remainder that had been in his cup, this contained no tea from the joy plant. "Have you spoken with humans since you joined with yours? Have you asked what they need to fulfill their development?"

None had, and everyone at the table knew it. Shahten let silence make his point, and continued. "We learned it was time to give our seed to all the humans. The time for it to be reserved exclusively for our own pure genetic line had passed. It was time to let them gain the ability our bodies have had since our first joining, the ability to connect with ethereal realms beyond those provided to them through the soul of Earth.

"You mean physically mate with ... humans?" Keela had difficulty even speaking of the idea.

Rhee reached out to touch Keela's hand. "They aren't animals. We saw many on our tour. They speak perfectly well and are clean. They want to learn how to connect to more of the All as we do. They're also quite intelligent. They know they are limited, and feel the only way they can develop as they need is through their children. Please don't let your past impressions prevent you from seeing what they are today."

Camic said, "Their human spirit will go back to Earth at the end of each lifetime as it always has. They want to experience the freedom of co-creation we have. They want to evolve. How in good conscience can we deny them that?"

Keela and Tisbero both flinched. Tisbero rubbed his forehead. "So all the people we saw tending the crops, the animals, and holding those citrines on the SkySlabs are humans?"

Keela, hesitated, weighing her words. "That explains why they were subservient to the captains. They're humans, not guardians."

"They ask to be like us, to be guardians!" Shahten proclaimed.

Keela folded her arms across her stomach. It ached. "It takes many years and many adults to correctly care for and teach a child. How can young humans possibly be prepared to join with ethereal souls without the preparation, the training?"

Shahten pressed his hands to his temples and frowned. "You assume that we are the only parents capable of raising children. Why? Old answers are for old times. We learned that when the humans are allowed to raise our children, the children are stronger in their connection to Earth. They know the intrinsic value of their physical bodies. They are the master of their physical form.

"Same as with our new bodies, when they are mature enough, we connect a little of our essence with them the same way we did long ago. Over generations the ethereal oceans will gently bathe them, nurture them. In this way they will expand their ability to connect more of All. They have changed! Children no longer need to be parented by us to ascend like us!"

Camic and Rhee turned as one to face Keela and Tisbero. Camic spoke first. "The humans are thriving here. We saw them. We had all the time we wished, without being accompanied by anyone else, to experience them. What Shahten says is right. All they want is to touch the ethereal dimensions through us and add to those they know through Earth."

Rhee followed quickly. "Our physical bodies originally came from humans so that we could continue co-creation here. Now that I know them, it makes me cringe to think of them being forced to live like animals because we neglected them. It's shameful."

Keela's hand dropped to her sash and her fingers repeatedly rubbed back and forth across the embroidery. "But won't that make a third group? There will be the humans with the human spirits of Earth's soul that it created. The ethereal beings like ourselves that have co-created with the same human spirit over millennia. Now this new group, which will have the circuitry to join with ethereal beings but without the clear agreement for conscious co-creation. How can this third group retain its identity as both a human spirit and human being when their purpose is unclear?"

Shahten sat straight as a spear, his shoulders back and chin high. "Very good! I had the same question!" He gazed at his cup as he swirled the pomegranate juice in it. "This is the best year for this juice yet. Nature provides such delicacy." He put the cup down and sighed.

"I had the same question. Here is what we discovered. This third group, as you call it, is progressing so well that I'm certain that someday, there will only be one group. There will only be human beings.

"Why? Because the children we give them have the genetics for the bodies needed to join with advanced ethereal souls. Further, these genetics are dominant; they continue in their offspring as they mate with each other. Within a few generations there will be ever-increasing numbers of ethereal beings that can come to aid Earth. All can be One again."

Rhee said, "We've seen it. This will allow more ethereal beings to come and learn how to create with physicality like we have. What better way to help others expand Creation?"

Shahten lifted his eyes to make contact with Keela. "I know these facts are new to you." His eyes shifted to Tisbero. "They are not based on old answers but the new creations." He gestured toward the buildings below. "Original human beings and new human beings live together now. Humans changed from sleeping on a bed of leaves under a tree to sleeping on a soft mat in a safe, stone home. Moreover, crystals in every dwelling provide clean light and heat. Humans no longer suffer and die from soot and filth."

His voice steadied, its tone a soothing, lower pitch. "All we do is help them become all they can become." Shahten caught the eye of his master captain.

Tisbero watched a SkySlab crest a ridge and fly toward the large landing field. The humans of whom Shahten spoke formed a line of tan tunics along its long edge. Crystals stood like spikes behind them.

Keela stared down at the colorful mosaic of chipped stone that swirled along the tabletop. There was more food and more selection on it than she'd ever seen for a meal for so few. "Much of what you say sounds reasonable, but I still have questions."

In response to Shahten's subtle signal, the master captain approached. "Please excuse my interruption. Shahten, the emissaries await your attendance. Also, the hour grows late for any guests wishing to avoid the storm." He bent and whispered into Shahten's ear.

Shahten brought his hands together in a soft clap. "Time passed swiftly!" He spoke as if in a private conversation with Rhee and Camic. "The master captain tells me your friends are waiting for you at your skystone. You certainly impressed them. They made something special for you, rare on this island, I understand."

He straightened and spoke to Keela and Tisbero next. "We must make time to see that all of your questions are answered. Because they arrived earlier, we were able to take Camic and Rhee where they needed to go. Their questions have been answered, but yours have not. Unfortunately, meetings with emissaries from other communities were already scheduled before I knew of your coming. I must leave to join them now. Will you please stay the night so I can see to your wishes tomorrow?"

Keela and Tisbero didn't have to check with the other to know the answer. Both responded with "Yes."

Keela's eyes brightened, the decision made. "We appreciate your hospitality very much and look forward to speaking again tomorrow."

"Good!" Shahten sat back from the table, preparing to rise. "I asked that a dwelling be made ready for you in hopes that this would be your wish." He turned to address his master captain. "The accommodations are prepared?"

"Yes, Shahten. It's the one with the mermaid fountain. I was also able to find two humans that will take them to it and settle them in. They are waiting in the lower courtyard near Camic's skystone now."

"Splendid." Shahten, his chair once more scraping across the floor, addressed Keela and Tisbero. "Ask the two humans any questions you may have. Everything is open to you here. I look forward to hearing what you think about them. I must attend to the visiting emissaries now. I wish I were less busy. Even nights are filled with all the meetings on the astral I'm asked to attend. Hopefully, your visit here will result in many more."

Shahten noted a guardian in a gray leather tunic standing on the far side of the terrace. "Their SkyShuttle pilot?"

"Yes. He will take all of your guests to the lower courtyard whenever they wish." The captain only glanced at the pilot for an instant but the communication was clear. He walked with perfect posture and a determined step toward the gathering.

Shahten addressed his guests. The master captain and I must attend to other responsibilities. I'm glad I was able to accommodate your schedule." To Camic and Rhee he said, "Travel well and fast. I do not wish you caught in a storm."

To Keela and Tisbero he said, "Enjoy the rest of your day and evening. I leave you in good hands. If you have any problems I want to hear about them tomorrow."

He and his captain moved with quick, long steps to a side door. Engrossed in conversation about their meeting with the emissaries, no doubt, neither looked back as they passed through it.

Keela picked up her cup of pomegranate juice and raised it to Camic and Rhee. "Your questions are answered? You are comfortable with what you've seen?"

Tisbero still studied the SkyShuttle pilot who stood still as a statue, but Camic and Rhee raised their cups. After long sips, Rhee spoke, swirling the juice in his cup to enjoy the fragrant bouquet. "Whatever uncertainties we came with are resolved. Everything I saw tells me guardians here are born with all their wisdom of their past. The humans are undeniably progressing, too."

"I found you!" an excited voice called out.

Keela, Tisbero, Rhee, and Camic all turned to see Yawri emerging from the same hidden panel door Shahten used after he left Keela and Tisbero on the balcony.

The eyebrows of the solemn SkyShuttle pilot rose sharply, then lowered back into place. No one used Shahten's passageways, but these guests did. He pulled in his stomach and placed his hands behind his back.

"Yawri!" Keela exclaimed, jumping up from her chair. Tisbero, Rhee, and Camic came to their feet as well. "You got here!" Then eyes wide, she asked, "How?"

All five guardians stood in a small circle as Yawri spoke. "I made better time than expected. The crystals of my skystone had no trouble finding yours, so they took me to where you landed." He glanced at the SkyShuttle pilot, who stood rigidly respectful and attentive. Yawri's rich baritone voice rolled across the marble floor. "I am Yawri, and you are?"

The statue seemed to wobble. Keela came to his rescue. "That's our SkyShuttle pilot. He's going to fly us down to the courtyard."

Camic said, "We arrived earlier than Keela and Tisbero and went everywhere we wanted to go. All our questions are answered, so we're on our way back to the mainland now. Shahten arranged lodging for you in a place with a mermaid fountain, whatever that is. He said you could stay as long as you wish to learn whatever you wish. We'll let everyone know when we get back to the mainland."

The pilot swallowed. Only the most special of Shahten's guests stayed in the mermaid dwelling. He cleared his throat and said. "I am to fly all guests to the lower courtyard so those who are departing can do so and those who are staying can go to their accommodations without delay."

Yawri took two long steps toward the pilot and extended his open palm, then brought it back to touch his heart. The pilot blinked, but repeated the customary gesture of greeting. "Thank you," Yawri beamed. "We fly skystones but yours are much, much larger. I look forward to learning all I can about them."

The pilot stammered. "I only fly the SkyShuttles. The SkySlab pilots are another class."

Rhee spoke lightheartedly. "There are a lot of amazing things here, Yawri. Our eyes have been opened to co-creating in ways we'd never even thought about before."

Keela started walking toward the SkyShuttle. "We best get going so Camic and Rhee can leave before the storm comes." She cast a meaningful eye to Yawri. "I could use a rest, and Tisbero and I can fill you in on what we've learned."

It was just a glance but her message was clear.

We need to talk … privately.

He wondered what she'd meant about an approaching storm but only said, "Good idea," as he joined her.

The pilot hurried to lead them to his SkyShuttle. It was parked on the far side of the terrace, directly on the marble stone ground rather than hovering above it as was customary for mainland guardians. Another difference was the configuration of its crystals. These stood vertically rather than laying down. However, the pilot's expertise was apparent. Without apparent concentration, the pilot flew the SkyShuttle into the air, rotated it gracefully, then glided toward the courtyard smoothly.

While Yawri attempted to communicate with the SkyShuttle's vertical crystals, Keela approached the pilot. "Shahten said there are many settlements similar to this in other lands. I'm sure pilots like you are kept very busy flying to them all. How many settlements do you guess there are?"

The pilot straightened to a more erect posture. A touch of pride tinged his voice. "Perhaps a hundred. They're on every continent, although not in the area where you are from. We are hoping that your visit will change that. All the guardians that visit with Shahten take what they learn and apply it in their lands."

Yawri straightened from his attempt to communicate with the crystals. Evidently, they weren't in the mood to talk. The pilot seemed happy to, though. "Hundreds? There are hundreds of settlements like this?"

"Not so large, but many guardians are adopting Shahten's counsel. All that come see its success." The SkyShuttle landed on the ground with a quiet *thump.*

Two female humans were there to greet them, and the guardians stepped down to join them. Rhee said, "We'll report to the assembly but want to hear your thoughts as soon as you return. Shahten wants to answer all your questions, so let him." One of the women placed her hand in his and they walked toward Camic's skystone.

Keela walked several steps and spoke to Yawri. "We've not spoken to any of the humans here yet, but Rhee and Camic have." Yawri saw they were engaged in friendly conversation with the two human women. "They told us they'd gotten to know a couple of them during their stay. These must be them."

Yawri, Keela, and Tisbero stood riveted to the tableau.

"We made something for you," they heard one of the women say, "to remember us by." She held up a woven basket for Rhee and Camic to see. With the other hand, she took out a dark, golden-colored fruit and raised it toward them. It resembled a golden barrel tapered to a peak at the top, a bit smaller than her fist. "We stewed these quince fruits in honey water," she said as she gave one to Camic. Her friend reached into the basket and gave one to Rhee. "Tell us what you think."

Each guardian took a large, confident bite. Their heads tilted back as juice dripped from the fruit and rolled off their chins. A sweet, delicate fragrance permeated the air. "I liked them before, but I think you've improved upon perfection," Camic said, his eyes closed.

Rhee lowered the fruit from his glistening lips. "You have perfected the perfect," he commented to the young woman next to him. She looked up to his towering form and wrapped her arms around him. "However, I don't think I needed this to remember you by."

The woman blushed and looked down. Raising her face to him again, she said, "There are quince jellies in the basket," she said. "Enjoy them. Share them. Let others know of us."

Rhee, still holding his quince in one hand, placed his other on her hair gently and said, "You taught me more about the rapture that can come from co-creation than I've learned from any other. I will let guardians on the mainland know of your wonderful way of life here."

She buried her face in his chest, then, still holding him, turned her face to the side so she could speak. "You give me hope that someday my children's children will be at least a shadow of you." Her voice was a genuine prayer, heartfelt and real.

The other woman handed a small cloth to Camic while the fingers of her other hand wrapped around his wrist. He took the fabric and wiped glistening juice from his chin. She looked up at him and asked, "You will remember us and return? The fear of being abandoned by one such as you will haunt my dreams."

"We will return," Camic replied, steadfast. "Replace that fear with the certainty that we agree with Shahten. It is time to co-create with all humans now. You are body and spirit of Earth. Know that my commitment to Earth is my commitment to you."

The impact of his words was clear. Her hand rose from his wrist to her eyes to wipe away tears. The other woman took her friend's hand and after a long moment, the two stepped back from the guardians so they could gain their skystone. "Travel safely and return, our guardians. May you expand Creation in all you become."

"Go ever forth and Create with Creator," the two responded automatically, not noticing that the humans were using the traditional way of parting that guardians had used for generations.

Yawri spoke while continuing to watch. "How did the humans know that parting?"

"What's quince fruit?" Tisbero asked.

"We know," two voices declared from behind them.

30. MERMAID FOUNTAIN

∞

Yawri, Keela, and Tisbero turned to face two humans, a young man and woman. Both fresh-faced and fit, their tanned skin shone with a warm, golden-brown tint. Their hair was the color of ebony, shiny, thick, and healthy.

They bowed.

"My name is Shayna." The top of her head barely came to Keela's chest. "We have been chosen to take you to your dwelling."

"My name is Eston. It is an honor to serve you." The young man shifted from foot to foot. "If I may answer your question, we are taught to use the traditional speech of parting when addressing guardians." His large, round, brown eyes conveyed such innocence it made the guardians temporarily speechless.

The young woman smiled shyly. Her voice quivered, uncertain but determined. "You asked about quince fruit. It is the most precious food we grow. Guardians favor it over all other fruit."

"Of course," Keela said, nodding with recollection. "Shahten said two people would meet us. Thank you for coming."

"Thank us?"

Eston's head flinched back.

"We know the way well!" Shayna explained, but her voice quavered with question. She plowed on. "There are refreshments waiting for you in the mermaid dwelling."

Yawri wanted to speak with Keela and Tisbero in private as soon as possible. He quirked an eyebrow and looked at the two young humans. "Can you take us there quickly? We've never been in such a large settlement."

Shayna rushed out, "We know the quickest path to anywhere on this island." She added more quietly, "It's the only place we've ever lived."

Yawri scanned the private landing field and saw five entrances. His gaze dipped to hers, his eyebrows raised in question. "Now?"

Her face beamed. "This way!" Eston hurriedly led the way toward the exit leading to their dwelling. Everyone followed closely behind.

Shayna cast a shy glance at Keela. "I hope to travel and heal lands the way guardians do someday. I wish I could sail the skies, go to different lands and glide the way you do."

"Glide?" Keela asked.

The young woman's almond eyes looked up to see Keela's eyes of dark blue. "When you move, you glide. Even your steps are light."

Keela wasn't accustomed to looking into the eyes of a human. Shayna's were portals to the dimensions of Earth. Keela's rubbed the embroidery on her sash and she said, "Not all guardians travel. Some stay in the same area their entire lives so they can learn one place really well."

"Really?" The young man questioned.

"Really," Keela replied easily. "And because you know this island, you know how to take us somewhere I have no idea how to find."

Eston crowed, "This will be the first time either of us has been inside a guardian's dwelling. Yours has the new mermaid fountain. It's the best of the best."

Tisbero's rough voice rolled out of his barrel chest. "I hope to see it soon."

Shayna and Eston drew side by side and quickened their pace. The guardians let them pull ahead.

When they were out of earshot, Yawri said, "What have you learned? Lazket told me you were in danger."

Tisbero stiffened, his muscles primed yet fluid, while he scanned the area. The sky, the pavestone pathway and dwellings on either side were clear. "What kind of danger?"

Keela's foot hesitated mid-stride but landed smoothly. "Shahten has treated us very well. However, everything is so new to me here. I don't know if I'd recognize a danger if I saw it. Is that why you came? How did you find us?"

"I planned to come anyway but Lazket saw danger and Red joined my skystone. The combination tripled a normal skystone's speed. The crystals on your skystone are One with those on mine so finding it wasn't a problem. No one was on the landing field but I found some guardians—humans, I realize now—who brought me to you. They knew exactly where you were, and took me through so many narrow passages and turns I'd have never found you without them. What have you learned?"

The trio kept far enough behind their escorts to afford some privacy but close enough to avoid concern. Tisbero spoke, low and gravely. "I've only felt welcomed by Shahten. He invited us to stay until all our questions are answered." He looked at the stone buildings to his right and the courtyards to his left. "I don't understand any of this and do have a lot of questions. However, our children are less capable than those before them, and from what we've seen; guardians here aren't having a problem remembering all they are." He gestured to Shayna and Eston in front of them. "I can't deny the progress humans have made here."

Keela bit her lip. "There are many new things here. Everybody seems to have specific roles and they wear different clothing to show it. We all have different strengths. However, here they dress differently, depending on which skills they have. Clothing's not dangerous, so I wonder if I feel averse to it because it's new or because it's ill-advised?"

Tisbero spoke, his eyes probing an alleyway. "We haven't been able to communicate with the land and Life of the island. Shahten says it's because Earth speaks with a different sound. Rhee and Camic are convinced he's right. They told us they were taken to see everything they wished and all they saw were thriving humans and guardians."

Keela's rich alto voice breathed, "Shahten said they had the same problem we're experiencing until they reconnected to humans. The guardians here still continue with the same Earth spirit of the first human body they joined. However, they were only able to progress again after they began interbreeding with humans."

"They are interbreeding with humans?" Yawri retorted, more loudly than he wished. He lowered his voice. "How can mating with humans solve the problem of regressing?"

Tisbero shook his head. "Basically, since all human spirits are of Earth, he said there is a limit to how far our human spirit could develop apart from those which are only connected to the planet. A branch can only grow so far away from its trunk."

Keela tucked her head to assure her voice didn't carry. "After touring this island, Rhee and Camic agreed the humans have proven themselves ready to connect with an ethereal soul. Since they are ready, they believe it would be selfish to make them continue living as wild apes. The humans here are undeniably more capable, and they found guardians here are becoming more capable, too."

The trio walked in silence for several steps, and Yawri summed up the feeling of all. "It sounds reasonable, but I don't like it."

Keela took a deep breath. "From what the pilot said there are hundreds of settlements adopting this new way of co-creating. I don't understand many things about what's happening here, but evidently many others do."

Tisbero stopped in the middle of a large intersection and pointed. "There's the balcony where Keela and I got our first look at the settlement here." He looked at the tall column standing at its center. "I remember this."

Yawri's eyes rose from its large, circular base upward. "Is that a sculpture of an animal on its top?"

Shayna's voice called to them. "Do you wish to stop and rest? There is shade over here."

The trio stepped toward their escorts without looking back. "Please continue," Yawri said.

After several more minutes of purposeful walk, Eston faced them. "This is your dwelling. It has a new fountain. The best of any."

Shayna marched up three steps to a flagstone entryway and placed her hand on a wide, wooden plank framed by a stone wall.

"What's a fountain?" Yawri quietly asked Keela.

"I have no idea, but why did we stop at a wall of solid wood and stone?" she replied.

Shayna grasped the knob of a short metal rod. It moved with an audible *clunk* and the wide plank of wood swung open. The trio walked through an archway and looked back to see her push the plank closed, grasp the knob of a short metal rod on the inside and push it into a hole in the stone next to it. Her face expressionless, she walked a few paces forward to join Eston. "This is the entry room," she said proudly.

The trio walked through the entry but remained focused on the massive, wooden slab Shayna had moved with a touch of her hand. Tisbero grasped the metal knob. It slid the rod back out of its hole with ease. He pulled the wooden slab toward him and the archway opened. He pushed the plank toward the arch and it closed. He slid the rod back into the hole in the framing stone. His hand lingered on the rod before going to his chin.

Shayna bowed her head. Her voice wavered. "Did I fail to operate the door correctly?"

Tisbero dropped his hand from the small metal knob. "Door?" He gave a slow nod and turned to face her. "You operated the 'door' flawlessly. I only wanted to examine its mechanism."

Shayna smiled and her wide eyes sparkled. "We were told to expect questions." Her voice was genuine, without a trace of deceit.

The three guardians exchanged glances. None of them had ever seen a massive wooden door before, and this one could even be locked in place.

Yawri said, "Here are a couple of questions, then. Why are doors needed, and why do they need to lock so they can't be used?"

The young woman raised her head and stood taller. "For the privacy of guardians. They need a place to discuss complicated things without the concern of confusing others."

Eston noted, "Confusing us humans, she means."

Shayna continued her declarative report. "This dwelling is one Shahten uses when he wishes to protect us from discussions we are not ready to hear. The timing of all things must be respected."

Keela shook her head. "How do you feel about locked doors?"

The young woman's forehead creased. "Feel about being protected? It's for our own good."

Eston spoke by rote. "No limits are imposed on us. They say that if we flourish, they do too."

Shayna stood in the center of the entry room. It was large enough to fit two skystones side by side. She twirled slowly. Each wall held an alcove with a small, glowing quartz crystal nestled inside. "All dwellings, guardian or human, have glowing crystals for light and heat. All our homes are free of smoke and soot. Wood is left in the forest."

Yawri walked over to the nearest alcove. "They emit a lot of light for such a small crystal."

"I can make much more. Shall I show you?"

"Yes, please do."

In a soft but commanding voice, Shayna said, "More light." The crystal blazed brighter instantly. Yawri pulled his head back in surprise. A moment later the young woman said "Less light," and the crystal returned to the earlier lighting level.

"Fascinating." Yawri pivoted back and forth to examine the crystal but saw nothing to explain how it could blaze with such brilliance, especially since it wasn't with its family but alone in an alcove.

"The other rooms are this way!" Eston weaved excitedly back and forth while standing in an open entryway framed in carved white alabaster. The guardians joined him, their curiosity piqued. Eston led them down a long, wide hallway. There were two rooms on the right and two on the left. They all had wooden doors. Two were for sleeping and one for dining with a kitchen beyond it. The last one was for bathing, and judging by the wisps of vapor rising above a large, round tub in its center, the water was hot. All the rooms had beautifully carved furniture and high windows.

Eston stood proudly in front of a tall archway at the far end of the hall. "The fountain is through here," he announced, stepping aside. The three guardians walked forward and stood under the arch. With Eston on one side and Shayna on their other, each swept open arms toward the courtyard beyond.

The trio stepped through the ornately carved archway and down two broad marble steps into a courtyard. A high wall of fossilized limestone blocks enclosed it. Large broadleaf plants bloomed with long-necked, pink flowers, and bright-green ferns grew in abundance. A path of large, flat stones led to a raised stone pool.

The trio walked about ten paces and stopped. Sunbeams passed through clear water and played across the pool's mosaic sides and floor. Turquoise-blue lapis lazuli and red quartzite flickered with light. A foaming jet of water rose into the air from the mouth of a woman's sculptured body, her arms raised in supplication to the sky. A dome-shaped sheet of water fell back to bathe her in a glistening veil. Its sound imitated a cascading brook and filled the garden with a trickling caress.

Keela studied the sculpture. It had the body of a woman but from the waist down was a fish. "Is this what you call a fountain?"

Shayna appeared to recite the answer. "There are many different kinds of fountains. All have water doing different things. The older ones flow down steps to make a waterfall. The newer ones have humans mixed with different animals. They are to remind us our bodies are One with all other forms."

Keela said, "We have similar carvings, but very small for teaching children. The temple here has one common to us. It has the legs of a wildebeest, body of the great-toothed cat, wings of the great bird, and head of a human. All equally serve to keep balance in the world."

Shayna lifted on her toes to emphasize her words. "All are different aspects of One!"

"Your refreshments are here!" Eston stood next to a low stone table and held a tray balanced on one hand while holding a pitcher in the other. The fragrance of dried dates, nuts mixed with raisins, dried fish, and fresh fruit filled the air.

With a flourish, he set them down. Smiling brightly, he announced, "Please sit and enjoy the fountain while you share nourishment." He bowed toward the smooth stone benches on either side of the low table. "It will be some time before we can bring your evening meal. We were instructed to make sure you are nourished and that any need you have is satisfied."

The three guardians sat down on one side of the table. Yawri murmured to Keela, "You or me?"

Keela did not have to look at Yawri to know that he was asking who should begin questioning. They would have different approaches. His experience with youths involved teaching them to pilot slabs of rock flying through the air while hers was helping them remember their plant wisdom.

She considered the young humans. "Shayna and Eston, please sit with us." The two remained standing in place, their mouths agape.

She waved toward the bench on the other side of the table. "Please."

Eston coughed, "Sit down? With you?"

Shayna stammered, "We are here to serve you. We are not guardians."

Keela's voice was calm, measured, and authoritative. "You were instructed to make sure our needs were satisfied. Is this correct?" Both nodded in earnest. "Our need is to have you sit down and eat with us."

The two humans glanced at each other and quickly moved to sit on the bench opposite the guardians. However, they sat frozen.

Yawri gave a half smile and Tisbero rubbed an eyebrow. Keela gently pushed the tray to the middle of the table and said, "Where we come from there are no titles. There are no higher or lower roles." She paused to consider her words. "Everything in Life seeks to learn how to co-create with ever more of All. You are as much a part of All as we."

Shayna rocked back and finally blurted out, "Guardians are much more a part of All-that-is that I am."

Yawri picked up the plate of dried fish, took a piece for himself and held it out for Shayna and Eston. "Fish?"

After it became clear he was not going to lower the plate until they did, each reached out took a piece. Yawri set the plate in front of them.

Yawri ate a piece himself and rolled his tongue across his teeth. "This fish is spicier than we make, is it the common way it's prepared here?"

"We wouldn't know," the young man replied as he eyed another piece. "We've never had dried fish, only the fresh ones we catch." His eyes traveled to the big bowl of nuts and dried grapes. "Or those."

"Or pomegranate juice," Shayna added, seeing the pitcher. "We're to serve, not eat."

Keela picked up the pitcher of pomegranate juice and filled two cups. "You will have them this afternoon." She handed them the cups. Yawri placed helpings of dried fish, nuts, grapes, figs, and dates on plates and set them down in front of the humans. Keela continued in her calm, kind, yet authoritative tone. "Where we come from there are no higher- or lower-status people. For us, there are no greater or lesser Creations because Creator is All. It pleases us to have you eat with us."

Yawri filled his own cup with pomegranate juice. "By eating with us, you respect our way of life while we learn about yours."

Shayna and Eston's eyes went wide and Eston said, "We respect you completely! We will do whatever you request to prove it."

"I believe you," Keela said.

Both of the young humans took a long drink from their cups. "This is new to us," Eston said. He took another sip.

Keela's tone was genuinely motherly. "Please, tell us about your parents. Do you live with them?"

Eston picked up a date but just held it. "You give us another easy question! Thank you. Families of children live with their trainers, not their parents."

Keela said, "Our children do not always live with their biological parents either. It depends on what the child needs. You live with 'trainers.' What does that mean?"

"All families of children live with trainers. There were twenty-three children in my family. We shared one big room." Eston was quick to add, "We're adults now. Now we have our own rooms."

Keela nodded, "Do you know your biological parents? Since you've lived on this island your entire lives, it seems you might."

Shayna took another drink of juice. "We don't know about our mothers but both of our fathers live here. They're guardians."

Keela persisted. "Your fathers are guardians. Where are they?"

"Mine is a pilot of a SkySlab."

Shayna picked up a handful of plump raisins. "Mine is a priest in the temple. He was one of the first to come from the mainland. He keeps the glowing crystals working in all the dwellings."

Yawri picked up his cup of pomegranate juice. "We fly skystones ourselves. What's a temple priest, though?"

Shayna leaned against Eston and took another sip of pomegranate juice. "A temple priest is a guardian that understands what underlies everything. My father oversees Generator. He makes sure the glowing crystals work."

Yawri had brought the cup of juice to his lips but lowered and swirled it instead. "Generator? What's a generator?"

Shayna spoke in a relaxed, almost giddy voice. "It's a big crystal family. It has a courtyard all its own. It's not far. We passed the way to it on our walk here. I don't know much but I've heard guardians talk about it. They don't pay attention to whether I'm listening or not."

"Unless they want something," Eston chuckled. He took another drink and placed his arm around Shayna's shoulders as if it was a familiar action.

Yawri leaned forward and raised the cup again. "I work with crystals, too. What do the guardians say about the generator?"

"Well," Shayna began, relaxing further against Eston. "They call it Generator because it sends energy to all the little crystals in our dwellings so they can make light and heat to cook. Before I was born, my father came here to help humans. It's why he's a high priest. He set up Generator." She took another handful of raisins and nuts. Eston refilled their cups.

"I'd like to see it," Yawri said, lowering the cup to the table.

Eston responded with a smile. "It's not far. When you stopped at the intersection with the large column in its center, I thought you might want to see it. It's the first walkway to the right from the one we took."

Yawri turned to Keela and Tisbero. An almost imperceptible nod communicated his thoughts. Keela took a deep breath, stretched her arms, and let it go. "We're going to our bathing pool. Will you please stay here while we do? We don't want to be disturbed."

"Of course!" they both said in unison.

Shayna stared at them incredulously. "You don't want us to bathe with you?"

"No!" Tisbero barked.

Keela followed immediately with, "Thank you, no. You were instructed to make sure our needs were satisfied. Our need is to have you to stay here and enjoy this food and fountain. Will you do that for us?"

"Yes," they replied more sheepishly, but relief showed in their faces.

"We'll stay here until you return." Shayna patted the table.

Yawri stood up and opened his palms toward them. His eyes steady on them, he said, "Thank you for honoring our request."

Keela and Tisbero rose and the three walked purposefully through the arched doorway and stopped. The sound of laughter from Eston and Shayna rolled softly to their ears on the fountain's mist.

The guardians proceeded down the wide hallway, entered the bathing room, and closed the door. It had a lock but they did not slide it into its hole in the stone frame.

Yawri wheeled. "Red and Lazket told me you are in danger. They also said crystals have been brought here without their consent, and are in great pain. We haven't seen evidence of danger, but we've got to get to this crystal family called Generator."

Keela and Tisbero started to move toward the door but Yawri said, "How is this water being kept hot?" The two stopped. Wisps of vapor rose above a large, round tub in the center of the bathing room. "Shayna said Generator provided light ... and heat." He walked over to the hot pool and examined its inlaid mosaic sides. "What's this?"

Tisbero and Keela came over to investigate. Yawri said, "It's a panel of some kind. The humans that took me to you opened a larger one for me on your lunch terrace. There was a latch of some kind that opened it."

Tisbero felt the mosaic. "It's hot. Very hot."

All three guardians searched for a mechanism that would open the panel. Yawri exhaled and said, "We don't have time for this."

Tisbero spoke the obvious. "You want to see what's inside." Keela and Yawri continued to search for the release. Tisbero said, "Please step aside."

Keela said, "You're not going to—" but before she finished Tisbero swung a wooden stool. Its heavy seat hit the mosaic panel with a smart *crack* and small pieces of colored stone flew through the air.

Keela's mouth fell open but Yawri said, "Thanks," bent down, and looked through the sizable hole.

"A crystal!" he spat. After a moment of quiet listening he rose. In a slow, measured voice he said, "This crystal does not have its own sound. It's the sound of another."

Keela bent down to listen herself. "Why would any life form choose to voice the sound of another? Even crystals can only co-create with who they are."

Yawri straightened. "It didn't choose it. Do you know anything more than what Shayna told us about this Generator? She said it sends energy to all the crystals in the dwellings so they can have light and heat."

Keela placed her hands on her hips and tugged at her embroidered sash. "We saw sunlight flash off a crystal face when we stopped on the balcony."

Tisbero growled, "It's the one I pointed to when we stopped in the intersection that had the column in its center. Shayna said the path to Generator was to the right of the one we took here."

Yawri locked eyes with his companions. "Let's go."

31. DISCOVERY

∞

Tisbero followed Yawri and Keela out the door, closed it, and slid the lockbolt home with a determined *snap*. Keela walked down the marble steps. "Shahten said we could go wherever we wish and get all of our questions answered.'"

The trio walked side by side down the flagstone walkway, alert and confident. Humans passed by but fell silent as they approached. A robed guardian walked past them and paused. However, seeing the dwelling they'd exited, he put his head down and walked on. The trio went through two intersections before reaching the one with the column in its center.

Yawri eyed the lone pillar. "I can understand why a monolith of stone might agree to be part of a big meetinghouse, or temple, as they call it. We make meetinghouses, though not nearly that big, out of wood and fiber instead of stone. However, monoliths sometimes agree to become skystones. What I don't understand is why one would want to leave its home to stand in the middle of an intersection."

Yawri arched his back to look up. "What is that on its top? When we were here last, I thought it was a sculpture of a rearing horse. Now I see it has the body and legs of a horse, but it has the torso and head of a man."

Keela and Tisbero studied the figure and Keela hazarded a guess. "Shayna said new sculptures are being built to remind them humans and animals are different aspects of One."

Tisbero shook his head. "It must be quite a priority to teach that if a stone this massive decided to leave its home and stand here with that on top of it."

Keela said, "We use a figurine of three animals to teach our young something similar. The animals vary but the most popular has a human being's head, an ahja being's wings and a lion being's body to represent the joining of ethereal beings with different aspects of Earth. We carve ours in small stones that agree to carry that teaching, nothing so large as this."

Yawri looked the column up and down. "I don't get it. Why ask a monolith to teach something a small figurine can do?"

Tisbero surveyed the sky. His eyes traced across the upper terrace high overhead. He pointed to an overhang. "That's the balcony Keela and I stood on when we saw the flash of sunlight from a crystal face."

"It would be right where Shayna and Eston said Generator would be. The next right should take us to it," said Keela.

Yawri nodded agreement. "Let's keep moving. The sooner we find Generator, the sooner we might find some answers."

The guardians increased their pace, repelled by the strange sculpture and feeling urgently drawn to their destination. The walkway, still paved with flat stones, narrowed and they progressed single file. Yawri was in the lead when they crested a hill. The path ended at a low wall only fifty paces ahead. "There's a big crystal on the other side of that wall. I can feel it."

"Can I help you?" a sharp voice called out. A guardian wearing a silken, silver robe with a purple sash draped across his chest stepped out of a doorway and blocked the narrow path.

Yawri pulled up so short that Keela bumped into him. "What's going on?" Tisbero barked, barely able to avoid colliding with Keela in turn.

Keela's mind raced. This man was wearing a robe identical to the one the temple priestess wore.

What was her name?

She touched Yawri's elbow so he knew she wanted to speak. About to say something himself, he paused and looked at her. She kept resting her hand on his arm and spoke in her unhurried, rich, alto voice. "We met Rayla in the temple this morning. You work with Generator, too? Shahten told us there would be guardians available to help us understand the answers to our questions."

Tisbero tried to look around her. "We saw Generator on our way to the upper terrace. Shahten didn't have enough time to go into much detail over our noonday meal."

Yawri looked down at the narrow path and then squarely at the priest. "Is there a place to talk?"

The priest's brows furrowed. The visitors looked rooted in place, but so was he. "I am on my way back to the temple, and there is no one else here."

Tisbero spoke with the demeanor of a stone pillar. "If you step out of the way we can pass and you can continue to the temple."

Keela was calm but her blue eyes held tight. "We'll ask Rayla our questions about Generator when we return to the temple ourselves. She was quite knowledgeable."

Tisbero grumbled. "Or we can ask Shahten when we meet with him tomorrow morning."

The priest blinked.

Keela spoke amicably. "We're staying in the dwelling that has the new fish-woman fountain. He wants us to stay as long as it takes to learn what we need."

Yawri was cheerful. "We should let him know who we tried to talk to here, though." The priest's silken robe, taut when he first spoke, was slack with wrinkles now. His feet hadn't moved but his body slumped.

Yawri took a step toward the priest. "My name is Yawri. This is Keela and Tisbero." All three stared at the priest, awaiting his response.

The priest's clenched hands opened and he tented them at his waist. "Laric," he said, and looked toward the doorway from where he'd come. "My name is Laric, high priest of Generator." He took a step backward toward the door. "There is plenty of room for us to talk in there. Perhaps I can answer some of your questions." The high priest dipped his head slightly and the trio did the same in return. Laric turned and walked to the doorway.

Yawri spoke to his back. "Thank you for making time for us. We saw the glowing crystals work in the temple and our dwelling. I wish to learn how Generator makes this possible."

The priest walked over to a table and swept a hand toward its chairs. "It's taken me a lifetime to learn the answer to that question, but I will do my best to explain."

All the guardians sat down at a table. Like the one in the upper terrace, it was inlaid with a mosaic design of colored, polished stone. "We keep minimal nourishment here but please partake of what we have."

Laric raised a purple linen cloth from a tray in the middle of the table and revealed a bowl of grapes, one of olives and another of white, flaky cheese and some flatbread. He thoughtfully lifted four fired-clay saucers and cups from a stand behind him and set them on the table, and poured from a large carafe of water.

"Please join me in this light refreshment while I do my best to explain." The priest lifted his cup to his mouth and sipped. "This comes from a spring not far from here. I think it's the best on the island."

The three travelers didn't need encouragement. All were thirsty after what had already been a long day, and it promised to be much longer before its end. They raised their cups in thanks to their host and drank deeply.

The priest sat straight now, his robe once more taut across his chest. "You're correct, Generator provides all dwellings here with light and heat.

Generator frees the humans from the labor of collecting wood and burning it. They no longer suffer the unhealthy effects of smoke and soot."

Yawri rolled a grape between his fingers. "And frees the forest from its loss of the wood."

Laric sat up straighter. "Of course. That too."

Yawri ate the grape and decided to come to the point. "We've all known Shahten for a very long time. We came to see him because we've noticed a difference in the ability of children to remember all they'd learned in previous bodies. He said the guardians here once had the same problem but solved it. Is Generator a part of the solution you found?"

The priest leaned back, his hands spread on the table in front of him. "It seems you sought out Shahten to see if he could help with the same problem we had. Our children were regressing, too." He took another sip from his cup.

Keela said calmly, "Please share your experience."

The priest shut his eyes and after a long pause, opened them again. "I'll start at the beginning. We were experiencing a slow but constant decline in the abilities of our children, and our fears grew with each new birth. None of us wanted to come back in a less-capable body, yet our future was clear. We didn't understand why it was happening. I was familiar with this island because of its volcanoes. I enjoyed them because of their life force. Lava is the birth of Earth by Earth. Nothing is more vital, and communicating with them was one of my favorite pastimes."

"Mine too!" Tisbero exclaimed. "The first time I came to this island was for the same reason. I only hear the basalt columns of the cliffs speaking now. The volcano is silent to me."

"The cliffs still talk? I haven't been there in decades. When the volcano went quiet, I thought it had all gone dormant."

Keela leaned forward, her voice honed to a point. "You said you sought out Shahten for the same reasons other guardians did. What did he tell you?"

"I expect the same he is telling you and many others." The priest placed his elbows on the table, tented his hands and leaned into them. "The guardians in my area discussed and debated the regression for many, many years. It changed when one birth shocked us. No matter how much help we gave, the ethereal soul and human spirit could not recall their knowledge from the past. None of it! Our future was upon us. We finally accepted Shahten's counsel." The priest sighed and looked around the room. "It was long ago but seems like yesterday."

Yawri cleared his throat. "But how did his counsel result in this stone settlement for so many? I can see why you'd need Generator to provide heat and light. A local forest couldn't sustain such a population."

Laric's eyes stared unfocused and distant. "It started slowly. Shahten reminded us that humans were the ancestors of our bodies. He asked us to wonder what they might become, might be able to create, if they were liberated from their constant struggle to survive. He asked us why we weren't thinking about their need to expand All with all they can become."

The priest took another drink of water. "We started with one family, two adults and their five children. First, we wanted to see what they would do if we freed them from predators. This island has no beasts that eat them. They felt safe in caves, so we built a dwelling out of stone to resemble one. We showed them how to grow their food, and they learned quickly.

"However, the smoke from the fires they built in their 'caves' made them sick, as it did before. That's when Shahten mentioned the idea for Generator. The humans can't co-create with soul sound and light the way we do. Not yet, anyway. Generator provides heat and light for them without harming their health or the forest's."

Yawri leaned forward, fully engaged. "I've worked with crystals since coming to this planet, but the idea wouldn't have even occurred to me."

The priest's eyes remained unfocused and half closed. "Nor to me, but Shahten had seen it used on other planets. He showed us how to provide more energy to a crystal than it could use. Then it sends the extra energy to other, smaller crystals to maintain its balance. We started with the one stone dwelling. It worked, so we added them to each new dwelling that was built as more children came."

Keela raised an eyebrow. "You said 'children,' but what of their parents?"

"Shahten came upon eighteen more children by accident. Their entire tribe had been washed away by a flash flood. Only the children were able to climb up into trees and survive. We could either care for them or watch them die. The choice was obvious." The priest looked out the doorway to all the dwellings beyond. "It seemed like such a small choice at the time."

Yawri persisted. "So this settlement was populated by children, and now children of those children?"

"The adult humans didn't adapt well. Younger children adjusted best. Shahten told guardians in this area to bring any human child found abandoned or lost here for sanctuary. Many have come. Shahten found most of them."

Yawri recalled the conversations with Eston and Shayna. "The humans are doing well here. You've found out what humans can do if freed from the daily struggle to survive."

"Mostly thanks to Shahten. He knew what to do every step of the way. He brought knowledge of all this and more: how to produce the crops and animals, and the specialized work humans enjoy."

"And your problem with the children of guardians remembering who they are with each new body was solved?" Tisbero asked.

"From what I've seen, yes. I haven't always been comfortable with the changes Shahten has brought. However, when I ask a question, I am shown results that answer it. Results are results."

Keela said, "We asked Shahten how so many people in one place could be fed without harming the land. He began to explain how the genetic wisdom guardians have from our human spirits is used to co-create other life forms. Does that include food?"

The priest took several grapes and a slice of cheese and leaned forward. "Yes. Shahten showed us how the information from our body's human spirit could be used to access the genetic history of anything on the planet. We have always been able to work on a genetic level of co-creation. However, we had never considered co-creating new species until he showed us how Earth brings forth genetic changes all the time. He showed us how to help it create more bountiful crops and foods of all kinds. The animals you flew over are content to stay and be cared for in their pens. Everything thrives here. It is a new way, but the Way works."

Tisbero's tone was steady yet simmering. "What does having different, role-defined garments for guardians have to do with it? Different abilities do not make some guardians are more important than others. Yet your garments convey hierarchy to me."

"I had the same question when Shahten introduced the idea. He explained it wasn't for us, it was to help the humans. They come from a hierarchical, tribal society, and they've had a headman and woman since tribes began. Like you, we were already wearing colored sashes with our white robes. Adding different colored robes would help the humans make their transition from their society to ours. He agreed there is no hierarchy when All is One. However, the teacher needs to start where the student is, not where the teacher thinks the student should be."

Tisbero ran a hand through his reddish hair. "Shahten has an answer for everything."

The priest's fingers traced across the sleeve of his silky robe. "He has more experience co-creating with humans than anyone I know. Is he wrong for that? He asked me if I was resisting helping the humans because I was hoarding my abilities due to arrogance. Did I want humans to remain trapped in a daily struggle to survive? It was a painful question but one I needed to ask. I chose to help the humans and see what happened. He reminded me there is no 'wrong' in learning how to co-create with Creator. So if not arrogance, what was my problem?"

Tisbero almost jumped. "He asked us the same question this morning!"

The priest leaned back and smiled. "I'm not surprised. We came to him with the same question. Why would the counsel he gave me differ from what he gives to others?"

Yawri faced the priest squarely and his words shot out more intensely than he intended. "But the planet has always created the change it sought. Species evolve with thought forms. Some prosper, some do not. I don't have the wisdom to know what genetics of which of its life forms Earth wishes to accelerate. This could be beyond its timing or design. Without clear communication, how can you be sure?"

The priest's mouth turned up with a knowing smile. "I sounded the same forty years ago." His smile widened. "We are of Creator. We all heard Earth's call and came to help it develop more life in more dimensions and share our learning with All. As Shahten reminded me, we were invited to join with human bodies and become human beings for that purpose. How is having a child with a human different from helping species cross-fertilize or expand with new thought forms? What succeeds is decided by Earth not us. The way we co-create has always changed as we learn. We've learned how to bring more choice, diversity, and Creation to Earth in yet another way. Is that not our purpose?"

The priest glanced down at the floor and noticed the length of the shadows cast on the wall. He sat up suddenly. "I'm sorry, but it is later than I expected. I must return to my duties in the temple."

He stood up. "I have enjoyed speaking with you more than I can express. You remind me how much I enjoyed friendship with other guardians. We don't get many visitors, or at least I don't. Many guardians come to speak with Shahten, of course." He paused, searching for words. "Feeling how you connect to All reminds me to do the same myself." The priest turned to go.

Keela stood and touched his wrist. He stopped and looked, held by her deep-blue eyes. "Thank you, Laric. You gave us refreshment and a great deal to think about. I hope we see you again."

Yawri came to his other side. "Please come by our dwelling this evening if you can. It's the one with the mermaid fountain. Do you know where it is?"

The priest bowed his head slightly in thought. "Shahten uses it for entertaining emissaries. I've not been inside it." The priest worried his lip. "Since you invited me, I suppose I can come."

Tisbero said, "It would be good if you can honor our request. We can talk about volcanoes we know."

Laric smiled for the first time since they'd met. "Yes, why not? I look forward to seeing you this evening." He turned, walked briskly to the doorway and out to the path.

A pensive silence fell in the room.

Keela straightened her long, white linen robe. "He struggled with the same questions we have."

Tisbero grumbled, "Shahten had an answer for them all."

Yawri said, "You two have seen more on this island than I have. The explanations sound good, but they don't feel good."

Tisbero fired back, "Shahten said the reason I didn't like them was because of arrogance."

Keela looked at the food on the inlaid table. "Yet another answer. Everything sounds logical, and they say they have solved the problem with regressing bodies. Rhee and Camic said all of their concerns were satisfied."

Yawri pulled in a deep breath and blew out his cheeks. "The more I learn, the more I realize how much I don't know. There are untold numbers of ethereal beings with more experience in physical co-creation than I have. Not only with humans, but with large crystals and trees."

And giant birds," Keela said, recalling the feathered gift inside her.

Tisbero added, "Ethereal beings I know have joined with the same mammal, living on land or in the sea, for many more lifetimes than I have with a human one. Shahten is the only ethereal being I know with experience joining with human forms on other planets."

Yawri took another sip of water before putting the pitcher back on the side table. "Just because I don't understand something doesn't mean it's not a good idea. It's the first time I heard that we resist helping the humans because we are arrogant. I need to consider it."

Keela massaged her forehead and mused. "Laric said this is only a new way to help Earth fulfill the charge to go forth and create, to bring more choice, diversity, and Creation to All."

"And maybe it's something else," Tisbero flared.

Yawri moved toward the door. "Let's go see Generator. Laric's explanation made sense, but I want to communicate with this crystal myself."

Rejoining the path, the guardians strode toward the low wall at the end of the flagstone pathway. The trio stood next to each other and looked over the wall for their first close look at Generator.

A large, multi-pointed cluster stood at the courtyard's center. The cluster formed a brilliant array of twelve flawless, hexagonally shaped crystals which stood three times the height of the guardians. The courtyard was shaped like a bowl at least five times the width of the cluster of crystals at its center. The side of the bowl was covered to its brim with smaller crystals.

Yawri folded an arm against his stomach. "What is this?"

Keela stood, her mouth covered with her hand, and Tisbero took a step back.

Yawri swayed slightly. "Sound without song. I've never known crystals without song."

Keela found her voice. "The bowl shape concentrates sunlight on the crystal family in the center."

Tisbero stepped next to the wall and hovered over it. "Laric said Shahten explained that if more energy is provided to a crystal than it could use, it would send it to other crystals. Here it is in practice. Countless small crystals are positioned to concentrate sunlight on the crystal center."

Keela lowered her hand from her mouth to her throat. "From what Shayna and Laric said, humans are clearly benefiting from glowing crystals. But Generator is not."

Yawri stood, his hands by his sides and his eyes gently closed. He heard and felt his diamond crystal pulsing with Life's essence within him. His whole body vibrated and his brow furrowed. "Generator's tones are flat. They have the same monotone as the glowing crystals in our dwelling. None of them have their own song. These crystals are in pain."

Keela shook her head. "I have not been able to get clear communication from anything here since arriving, not even from plants. Yet, I too sense the pain."

Yawri's eyes were still closed. "Lazket said crystals have been taken from their cave homes without their agreement. Cut off from Earth that way, they would be in great pain. These crystals are being forced to send energy, and the glowing crystals are forced to receive it."

"No wonder neither have their own sound," said Keela.

Yawri expanded his connection with Earth's crystals large and small, into the place where life and death are not separate but an endless cycle of Creation. He felt the diamond within him and the diamonds floating in the carbon seas of the first two planets he'd seen. Centered in this presence of One, he greeted Generator with the touch of a gentle, caring breeze.

The sound of Generator changed. First distant and remote, the crystals became stronger, not in volume but in the diversity of their sounds.

Images formed within the sound. Silver-colored guardians extracted crystals from their Earth-made sockets in their cave. Not asking, not co-creating. Taking.

The joined crystal being and Earth spirit screamed, confused and in pain and separation from their home. However, no matter how much they screamed, the silver-colored guardians taking them did not listen. They moved with certainty, so convinced their actions were right there was no need for questions. The silver guardians increased their soul light so much it reduced gravity on the crystals to the point they risked being hurled into space from the outward force of the spinning Earth.

The crystals shrieked at their impending death, so far out of timing with their Life. The guardians of silver decreased their soul light and saved the crystals from this fate, but forced them to move with the magnetic fields of Earth and propel themselves to the new "Crystal Island," all cries of protest ignored.

The tones grew to convey thoughts. "We are losing ourselves," the crystal being conveyed to Yawri. "We lose our center, our own sounds, to heartless harm. The crystal Earth spirit and I were One. We sang together, but now our sounds are almost lost. We cannot find our connection to our source. If we die lost from ourselves, we will not be able to rejoin with all we are in a new crystal body. We and the body will both be born lost."

Yawri hunched over the wall, tears freely flowing down his cheeks. "How can we help?"

"Do not let us die in this murder. Help us die in Life," was the plaintive response. "Help us die connected to All, while we have enough memory of ourselves. We can return to our sources, Earth spirit to soul of Earth and ethereal soul to its source of self."

Yawri ran a hand through his tousled hair and choked out, "How?"

"You do not need to relearn what you remember. And you remember. Feel your own sorrow and grief at this travesty and we will feel ours. You recall the feeling of being both individual and One in Creation. We cannot. You and your friends, be the moment of Creation now!"

Yawri reached out to hold the open hands of Keela and Tisbero. "Be your moment of Creation."

Without discussion, the guardians connected all the ethereal and physical dimensions they knew as One. There was no life or death in Creation. No beginning or end. The One was in them as much as they were in the One. Their connection was so strong, so inclusive, that all the crystals in the bowl began to feel the flow of All expand. The three guardians glowed with a gently flowing rainbow of light, their colors moving and changing continually.

Each felt their experience as a brilliant orb of translucent radiance bursting forth, dancing in a streaming, rushing torrent of Creation. Unique and individual within one endless, embracing symphony, each note infinitely precious to All.

A stream of light and sound flowed through the bowl of crystals in a rapid, pulsating current. The living soul light and sound of the crystals moving appeared once more. Monotone cracked, and all the crystals in the bowl harmonized their individual tones with All.

The bowl of crystals sang, "Your connection with all of the crystals of Earth and Life beyond offered our reconnection to it. From this place, we can change."

They sang on. "The timing of our death is ours to choose again. We will die in Life, not this murder. Our next crystal bodies will have full memory of all we have learned, including the knowledge of human beings that choose to enslave Life rather than enrich it."

Tears flowed down the faces of all three guardians, but they were tears of relief and joy. Yawri placed his hands on the low wall once more, leaned out over it, and breathed deeply. Tears fell onto the small crystals at the foot of the wall. In response, the floor of the bowl rolled in a liquid wave of color.

"Thank you," Generator conveyed again. "We will continue to send energy to the crystals in the dwellings. We will bring them back to their own sounds over time. The humans are innocent, and they do need light and heat.

"It is a choice we make now, not one imposed by slavery. After we integrate our learning from this, we will make our disagreement known to those who imprisoned us.

"They may not realize the harmful impact they are having on Life because they choose only to see what they want to see and hear what they want to hear." Generator paused for a long moment. "However, the planet will teach them the impact of their actions. The intensity of its teaching depends upon their resistance to learning it. The less they choose to see and hear, the more intense the teaching will be."

Yawri continued breathing slowly and deeply, his body blended in physical and ethereal Earth, timeless, though filled with the presence of now. "I am sorry this lesson is upon us."

"Free will is free will. Now we know there are those that use their ability to destroy Life rather than expand it. I must warn you, there are those that have enslaved crystals, which were created to join dimensions, to make them separate dimensions instead. They call it 'unmaking.' If you encounter them, hold a conscious crystal in your hands and blend with it in this essence of Creation. With you and it connected this way, it can intercept the unmaking and return it to the sender. It gives them a choice to die in Life rather than the murder they intended for others."

"Thank you," was all Yawri could say.

"We will bide our time here. Nevertheless, know that when the time comes we will die in the way and time we choose. You and your friends have returned choice to us." The chorus of Generator thrummed, but camouflaged until a day of their choosing.

Yawri felt a gentle touch on his shoulder. "Yawri," he heard Keela say. "Your body glowed with more soul light than I've ever seen. Breathe."

Tisbero rested a hand on his other shoulder. "That was more essence than I've felt in a very long time."

Yawri moved his arms up around their shoulders and all three leaned against the low wall. The wind came. Keela said, "Solar winds. The crystals are connecting to solar winds. Their learning will be shared with other planets."

Sadness weighed down Yawri's voice. "Shahten brings learning for us all, but it is not the learning to expand Creation. He brings the learning of its destruction."

32. ABOMINATION

∞

The three guardians stood next to the low wall, their hands on the top of its rough, stone surface. Yawri moved his fingers across it and took a breath. "It may not look different, but even the minerals in this rock are reconnecting to All. Generator is centering in itself again."

Tisbero saw something out of the corner of his eye and looked up. A SkySlab crested the hill beyond Generator. "Look there." Yawri and Keela followed his glance. Red-jacketed humans lined the sides of the SkySlab and each held a citrine. It passed overhead without slowing and soared toward the sea, evidently on a mission of some importance.

Keela exuded calm focus. "We've got to get this information back to the mainland. Guardians must be warn—"

A high-pitched human squeal cut her sentence short. The trio spun toward the sound and scanned for its source.

The squeal split the air again. Yawri swung himself up and stood on the top of the narrow wall. "It's coming from there!" He pointed to a much taller wall beyond the far end of the Generator's bowl-shaped courtyard. His eyes raked the distant structure. The cry came again, but it was weaker this time. Before the words, "Let's go" made it out of his mouth, Keela and Tisbero jumped up to join him.

They ran with sure-footed balance, every swift footfall directly in line with the previous, in rapid progression toward the startling sound.

The low rock wall led past a series of small courtyards filled with different varieties of plants. The trio sped on until the wall ended against another wall over six times its height. Their breathing slowed and they strained to listen.

A whimpering cry floated through the air. Keela pointed up. "It's coming from the other side."

The guardians jumped down into the tall grass and started walking toward the sound, but the words "Get the claw poles!" stopped them in place. A confused clamor of shouts flowed over the high wall. The panicked voice cried again, "Get the claw poles!"

Yawri spoke everyone's thought. "We've got to see what's in there."

Tisbero scrutinized the courtyard they stood in and pointed to a gap in the grass surrounding them. "While running I saw a pile of square stones over there. If we stack them against this wall maybe can see over it."

"Let's do it." Yawri was already moving toward the pile. However, Keela rolled a jacket of seeds from the grass between her fingers and didn't respond. Yawri and Tisbero hurried to the pile of stones and returned with three blocks each. They stacked them next to the wall.

"We're going to get more," Yawri said, moving again.

Keela remained engrossed in examination of the grass, and murmured, "This is the same kind of grass we found with Zinn and the dying mammoths."

Keela finally raised her eyes when she heard Yawri say, "The blocks are in place."

She dropped the grass and turned. Three columns of stone blocks stood stacked against the towering wall. "Standing on the top stone should let us see over it." Yawri was climbing up a column and she quickly started scaling the center one.

"Be careful," Tisbero cautioned. "They're stacked end-to-end rather than flat. They're higher but less stable that way." She heard him but didn't slow.

Yawri and Keela reached the top of their columns and paused a moment to wait for Tisbero. He'd moved his wide hands and feet more slowly to create much less wobble to his stack. After a nod, all three slowly straightened their legs to peer up and over the top. They looked into a large courtyard. Two rows of dwellings ran down the middle of its flagstone floor. Instead of wooden doors, the entrances were lined with strange vertical rods.

To the far right, four guardians wearing scarlet tunics held long poles with metal hooks or clamps on their ends. The one holding the most extended pole shouted, "This time, I'll get the back right leg and you get the left. We'll pull them apart. When he loses his balance, you two get his front feet. If we fail to get him into his cage this time, we'll have to unmake him. This one is more trouble than it's worth." The animal they were referring to had its head tucked into a corner, and only its powerful rear legs were visible. It looked like a wildebeest.

The lead guardian moved cautiously toward the beast's hindquarters. It shrieked when the poles neared and its legs pulsed up and down, muscles taut, ready to kick if the guardian came in range. The four scarlet-robed guardians cautiously moved their poles into position, but a sudden frenzy of barking and howling wolves drowned out all other sounds.

From their perch on the wall, it was impossible for Yawri, Keela, or Tisbero to tell which dwelling housed wolves, but a woman in a disheveled scarlet tunic thrust her long pole through the bars of one. Rather than quiet the wolves, barks and snarls tumbled over each other with more ferocity.

"Let them be for now!" the lead guardian yelled. "Focus on catching this trouble maker!" Muscles rippled under the wildebeest's sweat-drenched coat and its hooves danced, poised to kill. The leader spoke again. "When I say 'grab,' we clamp onto his legs and pull them apart."

The four scarlet guardians stood, claw poles ready, safely out of range of a strike.

"Grab!" he yelled, and the poles of the two at the rear shot out, their clamps closing above the wildebeest's back hooves. The beast bucked and kicked but the guardians let their poles move with each kick. When each hoof flew through the air, they skillfully pulled it to the side. By the third kick, the beast's legs were splayed so far apart it couldn't move. The other two guardians raced in and locked their clamps around the top of the animal's front hooves. The wildebeest's penetrating, high-pitched scream carved the air.

With a coordinated yank, the pole bearers pulled the beast's feet out from under him. It fell on its side so hard its thudding mass vibrated the flagstone, and the frenzied howls of the wolves increased.

The wildebeest kicked its hind leg and tore a pole from a guardian's hands. Still attached to the beast's hind leg, the pole jabbed back and forth and speared through the air. It almost hit the head of the lead guardian holding the beast's other leg.

He yelled, "Hold on! Move them apart! Keep this monster down!" The one who lost his grip on the pole retrieved it and stretched the rear leg so far to the side a joint snapped.

The leader yelled over its scream. "Keep it down! I'm getting the unmaking crystal!" He returned with a citrine quartz, the kind guardians commonly used to join dimensions. The wolves barked and howled with such frenzy the previous ones sounded tame.

The leader held the citrine above his waist, tightly pressed against his scarlet tunic. A tone emerged, but its alien vibration seemed to inhale rather than exhale essence. The air between the crystal and the beast deadened and the color between them faded into gray. The wildebeest's scream froze midcry and its thrashing ceased. The howls from the wolves changed to a whine.

The lead guardian lowered the citrine from his waist and the color between it and the fallen wildebeest returned. "I told Shahten we might have to unmake this one. He was fine with it. It's not the first time or the last. Not all of our creations succeed."

The wolves howled again and hurled themselves against the bars in an avalanche of muscle and bone against iron. Scarlet tunics whirled, their poles lunging toward this new threat, and they speared their claw poles through the bars.

Yawri, Keela, and Tisbero stood on their makeshift pillars, riveted in place. Now that the body of the slain beast was visible, Tisbero spat, "Only the body and legs of that creature is wildebeest. From the waist up it's a human!" Yawri and Keela stared wide-eyed. In place of the wildebeest's neck was, indeed, the chest, head, and arms of a human. Tisbero continued, "Why did they make a creature half animal and half human?" He reeled back and one foot stepped off the top block.

Keela grabbed his hand to steady him. Her stones wobbled and Yawri caught her by the sash. Distracted by the motion, the female guardian below spared a glance from the ferocious snarling to look up. Three faces disappeared from view so fast she wasn't sure they were real.

"Was that—?" she got out before her pole jerked out of her hand.

"What are you doing?" The lead guardian bellowed. "Get your pole! Or tell Shahten why you lost it!" She darted toward the end of her pole to catch it before the wolves' jaws took it forever. Her companions jabbed their claw-tipped poles toward the thrashing teeth. She lunged for her pole and missed. She lunged again and grabbed its end just before it was lost into the cage.

She and the lead guardian pulled back on her pole with all their might. The wolves' jaws held tight and another wolf bounded off the iron bars in front of them. A third scarlet robe joined the tug of war. The wolf opened its jaws and the pole flew free. The tumble of scarlet robes fell backward so fast nothing could stop their fall. The head of the lead guardian hit the stone floor with an audible *smack*.

The jumble slowly distilled into separate shapes. The leader finally sat up, rubbing his head. Without raising it, he called to the only scarlet robe still standing. "Throw some monkey meat to those howling heads to shut them up!"

The woman rolled to her side, sat up, and stammered, "Were those faces? I thought I saw faces." The wailing howls drowned out her words.

Yawri, Keela, and Tisbero landed at the bottom of the wall but were too traumatized by what they'd seen to stand.

Yawri howled himself. "This is not co-creation! It enslaves creation!"

The wolves suddenly stopped their wailing, and the absence of sound was more alarming than snarls. The trio listened in the sudden quiet.

A female voice exclaimed, "I tell you there were people up there! They were watching us from the top of the wall!"

The voice of the lead guardian was more controlled but even louder. "What people would dare? Everyone knows this is Shahten's private compound. Their lives would be forfeit!"

The grass surrounding the trio waved in a silent breeze. The woman's voice sliced through it. "I saw them."

A third voice spoke. "You are sure, then? A lot was happening."

The wolves sounded their barking cry once more and the leader's voice barked in response. "Give them more meat! I need to think." After the frenzied yips quieted again he said, "Telling Shahten we had to unmake the minotaur is one thing. Telling him we were seen doing it is another."

A third voice said, "We need to be certain of what she saw."

Before the lead guardian could respond, the woman cut in, "Maybe I'm wrong, but we need to be sure."

"She's right," a third added nervously. "Shahten has only started to educate our people about the need to take the best of different species and combine them. If word of this great work gets out too soon, he will not be pleased."

Another said, "The educational sculptures will take time to work. If word of this gets out, he will be more than displeased. He'll be angry."

"At us," the woman's voice added. "He'll be angry at us."

The lead guardian commanded, "We two will stay and make sure all of the creatures are contained. You two inspect the courtyard on the other side of that wall to see if there are any traces of these visitors."

After a pause, he continued. "If you find *anything*, call to us over the wall. The only way out from there is by walking the low wall past Generator. If anyone was there, pursue them on foot. We'll take the SkyShuttle and cut them off at Generator. I don't need to remind you what will happen if you fail."

"Don't worry. If they exist they won't exist for long," the woman hissed.

The sound of busy feet but no more words traveled over the high wall to the trio's ears. Keela's words came out with a disbelieving tremor. "She said if we exist we won't exist for long."

Tisbero fired, "We've got to tell the guardians on the mainland about this, and attending the astral meeting tonight is out. We can't sleep here." No explanation was needed. All knew they'd likely be killed before then.

The trio stood up slowly. Yawri shook himself and took a step toward the low wall they'd used to get here, the only way out. "Let's get to our skystones. If we don't get back to the mainland, no one will know."

Tisbero scanned the courtyard. "If they see our stone blocks they'll know we were here. Scattering them would buy us some time."

Yawri waved a hand at the trampled grass. "True, but it would only delay their conclusion by seconds and cost us minutes. I don't think we have minutes."

Tisbero considered and nodded. "Let's go."

All three ran to the low wall, pulled themselves up and on it with a seamless jump, and continued with long strides along its narrow top. With adrenaline propelling their pace, the rough stone passed beneath them in a blur. Courtyard after courtyard, their feet fell and sprang off the stone in an unerring line.

The uppermost edge of Generator's bowl of crystals rose into view.

"There it is!" Yawri said, and their stride quickened further.

Tisbero, trusting his feet to unerringly land in the middle of the narrow wall, scanned the surroundings for danger. A glint of sunlight flashed from the observation wall ahead, the place where they first saw Generator.

"Someone is at the observation stand!" he called out between labored breaths. Yawri and Keela were already slowing and all came to a halt, chests heaving. Tisbero surveyed the sky and down both sides of their wall. On the left side of the wall lay a narrow patch of ground under a mass of broadleaf plants. "We can talk down there."

Yawri didn't hesitate to jump where Tisbero pointed. He slid his back down along the wall and sat on the ground, temporarily out of sight from anything but birds.

Keela and Tisbero landed next to him. Yawri looked at them in turn. Glistening, dusty, brown tracks traced where sweat had dripped off their faces. He steadied his breath. "Laric said he was going back to the temple. It makes sense another one would replace him. Given our grime, it might be harder to convince a second priest of our right to be here, though."

Keela looked down at her long, white tunic. It was streaked with dirt and grass stains, and so was her embroidered sash. "It looks like I've been running, scaling walls, and crawling on dirt." She looked at Yawri and made an effort to grin. "Is my hair as bad as yours?"

Yawri ran his hand through his thick brown hair but it was too matted with sweat and dirt for his fingers to comb through. "No. Yours is still yellow. Mostly." He pointed to a tear in the sleeve of Tisbero's dirt-stained tunic and joined Keela's partial grin. "You're a mess."

Tisbero shook his head. "We talked our way in, but there's no way to talk our way out."

Their breath slowed, lips thinned, and brows furrowed while they rested against the wall's solid stones. The fleshy broadleaf plants stood a hands-width in front of their faces, and hid what lay beyond.

Keela's hand went to her chest. The ethereal feather given to her so long ago still pulsed with her heartbeat. She asked Tisbero, "Do you still have the recording crystal?"

Tisbero felt it for the hundredth time since falling from the wall. It remained deep in his pocket. "Yes. All we have to do is get it home." His eyes darted toward the sky. "Do you hear something?"

Their bodies tight, all three tilted their heads up and stilled their breathing. The rapid, rhythmic swish of footfalls on the wall carried on the wind.

"They're coming," Yawri said.

Keela worried her lip a moment and said. "Since they're coming it means the other two are taking their SkyShuttle to Generator. They'll ask the priest if he's seen anything unusual. If he saw us before we saw him, we'll have a big problem."

The rhythmic footfalls of their pursuers grew louder with each passing second. Tisbero stared into the green foliage. "This problem is big enough. With only one way out, it's only a matter of time before they find us."

Keela looked at Yawri. He winked. "Why are you so cheery?" she whispered.

A grin cracked his lips. "I have an idea. Follow me." He started to crawl deeper into the cloaking plants.

Tisbero caught Keela's eye. "Yawri has a plan?"

Keela raised an eyebrow. "You're kidding, right? Ideas, yes. Plans, no." However, they both dove after Yawri before he got out of sight. They caught up with him several body-lengths from the wall, lying on his back, staring up through a mass of leaves. Keela and Tisbero did the same, all glad to see only a tiny patch of sky through the foliage above them.

Yawri breathed, "Lazket was right. There is danger. Shahten's followers did a great of job of hiding it, though." He blew out his cheeks. "I wonder if he'll agree that we should be dead."

Tisbero's eyes went wide with recognition. He turned his head toward Keela and found her eyes as wide as his. Tisbero cleared his throat. "Maybe he already does."

Yawri's chin snapped toward them. "What do you mean? You told me he's been the picture of hospitality."

Tisbero let it out, "Two SkySlabs nearly collided with us before we landed, but it looked completely unintentional at the time. One of the captains even escorted us to Shahten."

Keela lay still and stared at her small patch of blue sky. "There was another near-death event. The coast was covered in fog and the sea calm as a lake when we approached. If Tisbero hadn't heard the basalt's tones, we might not have known about the cliff face in time to avoid it. Even then, without the help of the wind under us, we probably would have hit."

Yawri fumed. "When did you plan to tell me you were almost killed by two SkySlabs and one wall of stone before you landed? Fog and flat sea? The sky was clear and the waves were pounding against the cliff when I came."

Tisbero lay still and stared through his own crack to the sky. He blinked. "I was blind because it was beyond my thinking that anyone would want to do harm. However, I apologize. Being blind is no excuse to be mute."

Keela said, "We both were. Now we're not."

Tisbero opened his mouth to apologize again but closed it quickly. Footfalls pounded the stone near them. The trio asked their bodies to still and to join with the plants surrounding them as One, melting into the fleshy green.

The sound of their pursuers grew, their feet heavy on the stone. The three lay still. The pace of their pursuers didn't change when they passed and continued.

The three guardians breathed deeply, exchanged knowing glances, and slowly rose to a crouch. Yawri peeked above the surrounding sea of green. The others joined him and all watched the scarlet robes continue their run toward Generator, but with more labored strides.

"Drop down!" Tisbero exclaimed a whispered shout. All three heads disappeared into the leaves without touching a branch.

"Over there!" They heard a distant voice say, "I saw something."

The trio lay still as stone and asked their bodies to be plant and ground once more. They sensed the shadow of the SkyShuttle creep toward them. Like an eclipse of the sun, the light surrounding them changed from bright green to shadowed black. The shadow came closer and grew darker. Submerged in the gloom, the three guardians strained to see through shifting leaves. The underside of a large slab of fine-grained granite stopped and hovered directly over them. Moments stretched into a timeless void.

Finally, another voice from above said, "Nothing's here. We need to get to the priest at Generator and find out if they've already left. If they did, we'll call in the others to expand the search. If not, they're trapped in here. Either way, there's no way we can let them live."

The shadow receded and the plants glowed with sunlit green once more. The three guardians sat up slowly. "Let's go," Yawri whispered urgently and started to crawl back to the wall. Keela followed immediately but Tisbero hung back, trying to discern Yawri's plan. "Go? Go where?"

"Come on," Keela whispered back. "I think I know his idea."

"Idea. Right. What's wrong with plans?" Tisbero mumbled, but he crawled toward the wall with earnest.

When they got to the wall, Tisbero was surprised when Yawri turned away from Generator rather than toward it. However, he continued on Keela's heels, scrambling along the base of the low wall until they reached the intersecting wall of the next small courtyard. All three guardians stood up slowly and looked back toward Generator. The SkyShuttle stood parked next to the priest's observation area.

"It's now or never," Yawri said, with a quick glance at his companions. Tisbero's head moved back in question but Keela was already up on the wall next to Yawri. "Coming?" she asked over her shoulder.

"That's his idea? Run back to that compound of angry, half humans? What happens when we get there?"

"Get there and you'll find out," Keela replied quietly. Heads down, all ran in a low crouch on top of the low wall. None glanced back. They ran crouched until they knew the line of direct sight was passed. Heads up, they rose to their full height and their strides became a blur. Courtyard after courtyard passed and the high wall grew in size until it dominated the sky. Reaching it, they jumped off the low wall and ran to the tumble of stones.

Without pausing for breath, each restacked their blocks and scaled its column to look down into the courtyard once more. After making sure it was deserted, they placed their hands on the top of the massive wall, pulled themselves over it and swung their legs up and over it to sit on its edge.

Tisbero cocked an eye toward Yawri. "The idea was to come here because they're busy trying to find us back there." He looked at the drop-off in front of them. "I think I'm getting this. The plan is to plan one idea at a time. Now we need an idea to get us down from here." He swung his legs back and forth over open space. "Before they see us."

Yawri grinned and pointed to a wide wooden door on the far side of the compound. "They have to deliver food and supplies here somehow. I bet that door is the way out. All we have to do is get to it."

"And open it, go to our skystones, and fly home, but there's no sense getting ahead of ourselves," Tisbero added, but his lips finally showed a smile.

"We need to find a way to lower ourselves down to that ledge," Keela said, pointing to a lip of stone jutting out from the wall over a body-length below them.

Tisbero studied the problem. "It's a walkway. Not wide, but see how it runs around the entire compound? A lot of forethought went into building this. They wanted a way to move around the courtyard without having to be on the ground. They were thinking ahead to the time one of their genetic mashups got loose."

"We saw how much good that plan did them. We can use it, though." Yawri turned around so his chest lay against the top of the wall. "I think I can land on that ledge if I lower myself as far down as I can before I let go."

Tisbero reached for his hand. "Wait, Yawri. Please wait."

"You're the one that said we needed to get off this ledge before they see us."

"Yes, but I meant alive. Get us off alive."

"If I drop straight down I'll land in the ledge. It's plenty wide."

"Unless you fall back from the wall."

"Why would I fall back from the wall? All I have to do is drop straight down and stand up."

Keela intervened. "If you have another idea, Tisbero, this is the time for it. Absent that, you know he's going."

"Okay. Okay. Give me a moment."

Yawri raised himself off his chest and turned around to sit on the edge again. "Think fast. That SkyShuttle could be on its way back now. We need to get off this wall. I'll go first and can stabilize your landing after."

Tisbero took off his sash. "Give me yours, Keela. Yawri, we need yours, too."

Yawri took off his bright-orange sash. "I see what you have in mind. Just make sure you can untie them again. I'd rather jump than suffer Keela's wrath if you can't."

"I gave him mine. I'm not complaining." She locked eyes with Tisbero. "Ruin it and you'll wish you jumped."

"You're both impossible."

"Zinn said you were impossible too," Yawri reminded him.

"I know." Tisbero knotted the sashes together and tied small loops at each end. "Put your hand through here and slip it over your wrist. You can hold it with both hands. I'll do the same on my end and lower you slowly. It should be long enough to get you down."

"Should be?" Yawri turned around again, lowered himself to the edge and held on to the sash.

"If it was a plan I'd know for sure. We're going with ideas, right? Besides, I figure if I can learn how to skip along from idea to idea you might be able to learn how to plan more than one step at a time someday."

"Lower me or I'm jumping."

Tisbero nodded.

With the sashes fully stretched Yawri's feet just touched the ledge. He had to admit it was safer, though not nearly as exciting as jumping. Keela was next, but her toes hovered a hands-width above the ledge. Yawri wrapped his strong arms around her to hold her weight so she could remove the loop from her wrist, and he lowered her to the stone. She touched down safely.

"Who's going to lower you?" Yawri called up. "I'm sure you have a plan."

Tisbero hadn't thought beyond getting the others down safely, but he came up with one fast. There was a small space between two blocks. If he could wedge the end of the sash in it, the loop would keep it from pulling through. When he got down to the ledge, he could whip the line and pop it free from the block. He positioned the loop and pulled. It held fast.

"I'm coming."

He lowered himself slowly, hand over hand. He was less than halfway down when the crack in the stone holding the loop gave way. Flying free, the end of the line acted as a whip and pulled him away from the wall. Tisbero watched, frozen in midair a moment. Then the joints in the stone wall screamed by as he fell. The balls of his feet struck the outer edge of the ledge walkway, but his heels only hit open air. The wall moved farther and farther away. One foot left the edge of the walkway entirely.

Yawri swung his arm in a fast arc and his open hand landed on Tisbero's back. In the next instant, Tisbero's face hit a rough block in the wall. Ears ringing, he heard Yawri's voice.

"Good landing."

Tisbero opened his eyes, his cheek still firmly squashed against solid stone, and looked into Yawri's face.

"I could have died," Tisbero said simply.

Yawri's half-grin returned. "Not until you tell me why you got to jump and I didn't."

Yawri lowered him to sit on the ledge walkway, then sat down too. Keela finished recoiling the knotted sash rope and sat down between them. She looked from one to the other. To Yawri she said, "We need an idea to get down off this ledge that doesn't need my sash." She handed Tisbero the coil. "Please untie mine so I can put it on. Yawri might not be there to keep my tunic in place after jumping off a wall next time."

Yawri looked her squarely in the eye. "Of course I will. Who else?"

"Good point. You're the only one that would ever ask me to jump."

Tisbero handed Yawri his orange sash, Keela her embroidered one, and he examined his, which was dyed a dark crimson. The end was torn where he'd pulled free of the block, but otherwise it was no worse for wear.

The three sat on the walkway ledge and studied the flagstone courtyard and barred dwellings aligned down its center. The ledge was half-again as high as they stood, but Tisbero had returned their sashes with clear finality and Yawri decided not to suggest jumping again.

All three guardians leaned forward, trying to see a way to get down from the walkway. Yawri mused, "There must be a way for the scarlet robes to get up here if they need to. Otherwise, why build it?" The wolves, either out of food or smelling the visitors' scent, started to bark again.

"Over there." Tisbero pointed to a long log leaning against the ledge. The guardians rose and ran quickly. The log had notches cut into opposite sides from top to bottom.

Keela said, "Crude stairs safe for human feet but out of the question for hoofed ones."

The guardians descended to the courtyard easily and stood at the end of two rows of dwellings that ran down its middle. Several baskets were stacked down the center, equally distant from the dwellings on either side. Rather than wooden doors and high windows, the fronts of these dwellings were lined with metal bars.

Yawri took a step toward the first one. Tisbero said, "Easy, we don't know what's inside." However, Yawri, engrossed in what he saw, took another step.

He stopped in front of the first dwelling with Keela and Tisbero by his side. The creature in it had the body of a bull, and in place of its neck had the torso and head of a human, the same as the one they saw unmade. Other than its shifting eyes of malice, it stood rigidly.

Keela ventured, "Another minotaur, the scarlet robes called it."

The next dwelling held a creature with the body of a horse but the torso and head of a human where its neck should be. It spun and kicked its hind legs toward them, both hooves passing skillfully between the bars.

The guardians walked on in silence, desperately wanting to disbelieve their own eyes. However, the next pen held the still form of the half man, half wildebeest they'd seen killed. "Unmaking," Yawri said stiffly. "Generator warned me that they were using citrines to separate dimensions rather than connect them as we do."

The panicked death in its fogged eyes even made Tisbero pull back. "Separate dimensions? How can we protect against that?"

Yawri stared at the beast, remembering Generator's words. "Generator said to be in the same energy we were when we healed it but with one addition.

Hold a crystal that is also one with essence in Creation so it can intercept the unmaking. If you both remain connected to All, the unmaking would be returned to the one that sent it. It gives them a choice to die in Life, not murder."

Tisbero pointed at the still form. "Hold a crystal so it can intercept whatever made the blackened hole in that?" He shook his head. "Good luck."

Keela took a halting step toward the next dwelling and looked in. Her hand went to her chest so quickly it made a sharp slap. "No! What have they done?"

Yawri and Tisbero came to her side. Some kind of bird stared back. Except where the head of the bird should be, was the feathered face of a woman. It screeched and raised a taloned claw, daring them to come near. Her screeching cry was soon drowned out by the barks and howls of the next dwelling-cage.

They sounded like wolves but weren't. The trio took a retreating step back, but with the baskets down the center of the alleyway there was no place to go.

The howls came from the throats and heads of large, black wolves, but those heads were on human bodies. Male and female human bodies alike stood upright and well balanced on legs and feet. Human hands held meat, but it was being torn by sharp canine teeth in long, snarling snouts. A few heads turned predatory stares toward the guardians but soon refocused on the pile of meat in their cage.

"We've got to get to our skystones," Yawri managed to say.

"Glad you came back!" a piercing voice erupted from behind them. "This will make things much easier."

33. REVELATION

∞

All three guardians spun around, expecting to see a scarlet-robed guardian. No one was there. Tisbero's sharp eyes raked the ledge walkway but it was empty. Yawri stepped toward the broad, wooden door—the only exit in sight—but it remained closed.

Keela was respectful and deliberate. "Who is speaking?"

"Me," the disembodied voice replied. "We hoped you'd return."

The guardians stared, incredulous. A creature behind yet another set of bars stared back. It had the body and legs of a goat, but where the goat's head should be, the chest, arms and head of a human grew in its place. It spoke again.

"We haven't been fed. Would you check to see if there's any pomegranate juice in the baskets?" The trio remained locked in place, so the creature added, "The tenders were in such a rush they only fed the dog-heads before they left." Coinciding with the words, a savage growl came from the cage behind the guardians, followed by the sound of snapping jaws from one human-wolf and a squealing yip from another. "The dog-heads will eat anything, including each other."

Yawri and Keela stepped toward the speaker. Tisbero scanned side to side before joining them.

Six more of the human-goats pranced toward the bars of their cage, their hooves clicking on flagstone. They halted in a line slightly behind the speaker. Their eyes were relaxed but held a playful glint.

Yawri, curious, strode up to the bars.

Tisbero said, "Not so close," but Yawri was already there. The speaker stepped forward, his appraising gaze matching Yawri's. After a long moment, Yawri grinned generously and surveyed the row of square baskets lining the middle of the aisle. "Which one?"

"It's in the tall one at the end of the row. They often add poppy tea because it puts everyone in a better mood. Including our tenders."

Tisbero was nearest to the basket. He walked over, and after bumping it to make sure it didn't contain some other type of creature, opened the lid. When he stood, he held a jug in each large hand. Keeping his eyes on the human-goat while he walked to the cage, he set the jugs down next the bars. "I didn't see any cups."

"We have them," the speaker said.

One of the human-goats reached through the bars and brought in the jugs while another came with a stack of carved wooden cups. Within moments, the contents of a jug filled them all with dark-red juice.

The speaker smelled it. "No poppy-seed tea in it this time. We get their excess because it doesn't keep well. No excess means it's in demand today."

Seven more human-goats emerged from the interior. They moved lightly, with quick, prancing feet. Three competed to see who could make the highest fun-loving leap as they approached.

Four more emerged from the dwelling and held long, narrow bones to their mouths. Yawri asked, "Must you eat bones? Is there more food in the baskets?"

Before the last word escaped his lips, a trill of whistling tones issued from the bones. Yawri and Keela jerked upright and Tisbero ran his thick fingers through his mahogany hair.

A young female chimed, "Eat bones? Never. We play them ... and dance!"

Head back, the speaker's fingers touched parting lips. "You don't play flutes? Find a wing bone, make a few holes down its length, and blow into one end." Trills blended in a melodic quartet.

Tisbero said, "Dance? You dance?"

The female human-goat moved one hoof up and down to the rhythm from the flutes. After a rolling melody, her front hooves took turns, one up one down, but the click of hoof on stone remained true. Another human-goat joined her, then another. The guardians looked on, spellbound.

The throbbing trill from the flutes vibrated off stone with increasing fervor. Now their back legs joined the dancing swirl and switched cadence with all the other hooves rising, falling, and swaying through the air. Groups of four pranced together, yet in time with all the others. Laughter mixed with trilling melody and cascaded over the slack-jawed guardians.

Without any outward sign, all the dancers jumped into the air and landed at the same moment the flute music stopped. Laughter boomed, it's sound free of cages and bars. One of the human-goat women pranced up to the guardians. "There should be a basket with eggs, figs, and bean porridge, too. Would you look? We haven't eaten since last night."

The first human-goat that spoke to them said, "It would be much easier if we brought the baskets in here instead of passing food through these bars. If you would move the knob on that latch away from the stone frame, we can simply bring the baskets in here." He pointed to a flap of metal outside the cage.

Yawri saw the latch was the same kind Shayna showed them how to use on their own dwelling's door. He reached to unlatch it, but before Tisbero could even say "Don't," he stopped himself. Casting a meaningful glance back at the dog-heads before returning to the human-goat, he said, "Let's wait until we get to know each other a little better."

Keela turned to Tisbero. "Discretion? Did Yawri just use discretion?"

Yawri ignored Keela's comment and kept his grin instead. "This latch is out of your reach for a reason. Tell me why—from the beginning—and I'll consider it." Yawri looked unblinkingly into the eyes of the human-goat, his companionable smile still tracing his lips.

Tisbero sat a basket of food next to the bars, opened its lid and stepped back. The female human-goat winked at him and began taking food from it and passing it back. The lead human-goat looked on and smiled. "My name is Fawin. I know little of the world outside these walls."

Yawri placed a hand on one of the vertical rods and wrapped his long, strong fingers around it. "My name is Yawri. Please share whatever you know."

One of the human-goats handed Fawin a bunch of grapes. Fawin plucked two from the stem and ate them one at a time. He considered Yawri and said, "The tenders have bodies like yours. Strong and very tall. The humans that bring us food are small. The tenders tell us they are fragile, cannot live without shelter, and with only two legs are very limited in speed and agility. The tenders took the best parts of humans and the great mountain goat to create us."

One of the human-goats ran up the side of their dwelling, bounded into the air and landed on all four feet with a laugh. Fawin continued. "We can live outside in the wild or inside a building. We eat sticks or stew. We can do everything that humans can do with our hands, but we run faster and longer over mountains or plains, in any weather. We can do everything humans can, but better; and as you see, we are a lot more fun."

Keela leaned toward Fawin, her jaw clenched. "You say the tenders created you. Did they tell you how?"

He looked into her dark-blue eyes, raised the bunch of grapes to his mouth, and pulled one off its stem with his lips. "They tell us they are from the stars and bring realms of great knowledge to Earth. Are you from the stars? Your garment is different but your body looks the same."

Keela considered her response. "We and the tenders are from the same source. We came to learn how to help this planet expand in Creation."

Fawin ate another grape. "The tenders said they received knowledge of how to create us from this planet and have used it to strengthen the humans in many forms."

Yawri leaned forward, his neck stiff. "How many forms?"

"Many. Many different creatures for land, sea, and air. Some still live but most die. The tenders tell us we are the strongest new human they have created. I agree."

Keela's eyes fell to the cloven hoof and back to Fawin's very human eyes. "They obtain genetics from humans and animals and combine them somehow?"

Fawin responded openly. "I'm not sure how, but the first of us were born from a mother goat. The first human-wildebeest came from a mother wildebeest. The tenders brought the young of many species here from many places. Not just animals, but plants, too. They say if it wasn't right to use this knowledge it would not have been given to them."

"Is anything not working well for you?" Yawri asked.

Fawin's gaze turned distant. "We try to find joy in all we do, but … there is something missing. The mountain goats and humans from which we came have a connection, a sense of belonging, which we don't have. So we try to forget with dance." He reared up on his hind legs and spun around in a circle before nimbly coming down on all four feet. "The planet will decide if we prosper." He pointed to the prostrate form of the minotaur. "At least we're not being unmade by those bad crystals."

Yawri stared at the floor. He held one hand to his stomach and looked at Fawin. "The crystals aren't bad. They were created to join dimensions, not sever them. These followers of Shahten enslave them. The crystals do this against their will."

Tisbero came to a stop next to Yawri and Keela, breathing heavily. "I took a run up the notched pole and went to the far side of the compound. I could just see over the wall there, and they're starting to search the courtyards."

Keela squinted up at the sky. "And that SkyShuttle could come back at any time."

Fawin shook his head. "I knew it. The tenders didn't know you were the ones watching from the wall." His hoof pawed the flagstone with a sharp clack. "You are why they left in such a rush. They are after you!"

Tisbero gave him an iron stare. "You're the ones in the cage."

Fawin reared back on two legs and his head matched the height of Tisbero's. He remained upright, balanced on his rear two legs, and returned a primal gaze. "We are in a cage, but a safe one. They consider us their prize. I have seen them unmake creatures large and small. I know them, and they will unmake you." The human-goat swept his eyes across the faces of the three beholders. "That is, unless you help us, so we can help you."

Yawri stared back. Whereas looking into the eyes of humans like Shayna and Eston led to the soul of Earth, these eyes only led to emptiness, lost to the connection to All from which their ancestors came. "What these tenders do is no fault of yours. I'd like to help you if I can." He touched the latch on the cage but didn't open it.

Tisbero's voice was like rumbling gravel. "Be careful. We have no reason to trust them."

Several other human-goats raised themselves up to stand on two legs and joined Fawin at the bars. Fawin said, "Have we given you any reason not to?"

Keela stepped forward, placed her hand on one of the round, iron rods and wrapped her nimble fingers around it. "If we set you free, how can you help us? Our skystones are far down the mountain from here."

Fawin went down on all four hooves again, followed by his companions. He spoke to the entire herd. "Did you hear the question? They are sought by the tenders. You know what that means. If they set us free, how can we help them get free?" A rattle of hooves echoed across the stone floor. A line of twelve human-goats three rows deep stood in front of them.

A male in the back line spoke in a steady, low voice. "The tenders do not know they are here. We are Shahten's treasure. If we are gone when they return they will be so panicked trying to find us that finding three visitors will no longer be a concern."

A woman's voice from the first row continued, "They have complained about poor latches for months now. This wasn't the first time the minotaur got out because of it. They'll assume the same for us."

The male next to her agreed. "They've been asking for better locks for months. Blaming the metalworkers will be first and foremost in their minds."

Another female addressed the three visitors, "Tell us which direction you want to go and we'll draw them in the opposite."

One holding a flute said, "Please be assured, it's not in our nature to do harm. We only wish to be free, like you."

Fawin spoke in a whisper. "If you leave us caged they are going to make us tell them about you. They have ways. We won't have any more choice than the yellow crystals do. If we're not here, they can't make us talk. We will lead them away from you instead. Help us so we can help you."

Yawri exchanged a fleeting look with Keela and Tisbero. Keela dipped her head. Tisbero's lips were a thin line, but he finally bobbed his head as well. Yawri's hazel eyes held a hopeful glint. "We need to go downslope toward the gate. While flying in, I saw a dense forest upslope. It wraps around and down the other side of this mountain. You go up, we go down."

"A forest that wraps around the mountain? Sounds ideal." The herd responded with the clatter of hooves on stone.

Yawri pointed to the broad wooden door. "Is that the way out?"

"Yes. It's how the humans bring in food. They have to keep clear of the giant, though."

"Giant?" Tisbero pivoted.

"In the cage to the right of the door. The tenders thought bigger, stronger humans might prosper more than the small ones. However, the big ones required much more food and bigger shelters. Plus, they weren't smart like the humans, and their eyes were so close together they had no depth perception. Fawin's eyes flicked toward the door. "He's the last one left and not very happy about it. The humans who deliver our food are terrified of him. His arms fit through the bars and he caught one once."

"Thanks for the warning." Yawri cocked his head toward Keela and Tisbero in question, and after no objection came, stepped toward the latch. Grabbing its knob, he pushed it sideways. It moved with a squeal, but same as with the entrance to the mermaid dwelling, a large, iron pin slid out of a hole in the door's stone frame. He pulled and the door swung open with a grating groan.

The human-goats were already lined up. Each held small rectangular sheets of cloth. "You're well organized," Tisbero commented.

Fawin replied, "We convinced the tenders we only live in the moment. The cloth came from food baskets, one at a time over many months. They don't know we like to plan."

"I like you more and more," Tisbero said, stepping out of the way so the human-goats could stream by. They moved to the remaining baskets in the aisle and spread the cloth on the floor. In less than a minute the corners of each cloth were pulled up and tied around the food piled in its center. Long strips of fabric were wrapped around the knot and tied in a loop to form a shoulder strap. Even Tisbero's mouth hung open as the guardians watched the human-goats sling the straps over their heads so the food could be carried hands-free. Others took all the meat that remained and tossed it to the dog-heads.

"It's the only way to keep them quiet," Fawin said. "We've been planning this for a long time. Even though escape was improbable, preparing for it anyway kept us alive with hope."

The herd gathered at the end of the row of dwellings, a mixture of anticipation and sadness on their faces. A female human-goat said, "None of the others have the ability to run, hide, and survive like we can. Freeing them would create chaos in the streets and help us all escape, but it might result in them being unmade. The tenders would rather have us dead than seen."

The trio watched the dog-heads fighting over the meat. They would do the same to humans. "Understood," Yawri said, and they joined the back of the herd, moving quickly but carefully toward the door.

While two human-goats distracted the giant, another went behind them to open the door. Three latches held it closed, but while the giant's arms flailed toward his prey, the bolts slid free, the door swung open, and the exodus began.

The human-goats pranced and danced clear of the massive hands with such skill it made the trio suspect "dancing" was a means to improve agility without catching the eye of the tenders. Fawin looked at the expressions on the guardians' faces and winked.

An exploding roar accompanied the giant's thrashing arms, and a face with one thick eyebrow pressed against the iron bars so hard it would deform a softer skull. The human-goats were unfazed and jumped with shouts of glee through the open door.

Fawin was the last to go. "When you run past, remember the giant's eyes are so close together and sunken into his skull he can only see straight ahead. If you're not directly in front of his bulbous nose, he can't see you."

To demonstrate he approached the giant's cage, and while the giant was looking at a human-goat standing beyond his reach just out the door, Fawin bounded from floor to wall and out the door so quickly the giant's head didn't even have time to move.

"May we all remain free!" Fawin said while the giant bellowed, his hands opening and closing in futile pursuit.

"You go, Tisbero," Yawri cried. "Get to the other side and distract him. It worked for Fawin."

Tisbero knew every moment that passed was a chance lost. While the giant remained turned toward what just ran by, Tisbero rushed toward the door and rebounded off the same place on the wall as Fawin did. However, the fact that Tisbero was more than twice Fawin's height and on two feet instead of four made his exit less straightforward. Only his deft spin when he reached the threshold prevented the giant's outstretched fingers from grabbing his tunic. He landed in a pile, but free of the door. He stood, waved his arms and bellowed back to distract the giant.

Keela sprang toward the door. As Fawin had done, she landed on the threshold, feet pumping in stride. However, the giant's shoulder had pried the bars apart just enough for his arm to reach slightly farther than before. A hand shot toward the retreating hem of her tunic and found it. Grabbing it firmly, he twisted it in desperation. Her forward momentum stopped mid-air and her eyes went wide. Time and all movement froze. It thawed, and she fell on the threshold with a resounding *thump*. The air in her lungs rushed out in an exploding gasp. The giant's other hand shot toward the first. He wrapped thick fingers around her small, trailing foot, and pulled it toward him with a satisfied grunt.

Yawri and Tisbero went airborne at the same moment. Yawri landed on one of the massive arms that reached through the metal bars while Tisbero landed on the other. The giant bellowed in rage and his face pressed against the bars with such force his eyes bulged. Hurled by rancid breath and anger, spittle flew through the bars and onto Yawri's neck.

Yawri dug his fingernails into one of the giant's hands while he sent his other fist through the bars and into a flaring, bulbous nose. Tisbero's hand closed around the recording crystal in his pocket. He drew it out and slammed it down on the giant's hand.

The giant's scream eclipsed the howls of the dog-heads and sent a wave of sound vibrating like hail off stone throughout the compound. The monstrous hands released their hold on Keela and flung the guardians back. Tisbero sailed out the threshold to land on his back. Yawri flew into the wall opposite the cage with a thudding *crack*.

Tisbero grabbed Keela's wrists and pulled her with him toward open space. Yawri rose to a crouch and staggered. Although the stone floor seemed to shift under him, he grabbed both of Keela's feet and pulled them away from the cage. One giant hand lunged toward him, but he jumped to the side and through the doorway.

All three guardians fell into a pile on sunlit flagstone. Yawri looked back to make sure they were out of the giant's reach. Huge, bloodied hands waved toward them: One in a fist, the other holding a sandal.

The giant reared back, and with a burst of festering rage, hurled the sandal toward the targets of his venom. It hit a bar of the cage and rebounded instantly, striking him squarely in the face. The scream was even more deafening than the last.

Tisbero freed himself from the tumble of arms, rolled to his knees, grabbed the edge of the open door and pushed it closed. The giant's roar and the howls of the wolves muted to a drone. He dropped down again next to his friends and stared at the massive door, too drained to think.

Keela sat hunched between them. Her breathing slowed and, finally, she looked at her foot. She pursed her lips and blew out a breath. "He took my sandal."

Yawri and Tisbero looked at her, their faces blank. Yawri deadpanned, "It's not going to fit."

Keela started to laugh, more out of relief than anything. Yawri chuckled and Tisbero smiled. The absurdity of their situation combined with its shock mixed in a whirl of emotions, but the result was more laughter. They laughed so hard tears came to their eyes, although none of them understood why.

Laughter became chuckles, and chuckles became smiles. Yawri raised a hand to his head. A flash of pain stabbed where he touched. He pulled it away. His fingers were red.

"You're bleeding!" Keela yelled in concern, but it came out accusatory.

Yawri touched the wound again, somewhere above his right eye. His forehead beaded with sweat and dizziness whirled. "Sorry," he said.

Keela rolled to her feet and stormed behind him. "Keep your hand down! I can't see anything with those big fingers in the way." Yawri tented his hands over his raised knees and rested his chin on them. She began to carefully pull hair away from the wound.

Yawri took a breath and sighed.

"Stop jiggling."

His head throbbed but the trace of a grin showed on his lips.

She reached into a pocket of her tunic and drew out a pouch of herbs. "Tisbero," she said, knowing he wanted to do whatever he could to help. "There are six small packages in this pouch. Take the yellow one and mix half of the red one in it. We don't have any water. I'll mix it with his blood to make a poultice. If I can lay the skin back down where it belongs the bleeding might stop." Tisbero took the pouch and moved with focused haste.

Keela took off her embroidered sash. "What are you doing?" Yawri protested.

"This might hurt." She held the tightly woven edge of the sash against his scalp to let blood pool there. "I'm going to pull a big flap of skin down. Don't move when I do." Her chin bobbed at Tisbero as he brought the mixture. Her eyes focused on the growing pool of blood dammed in place by her sash. "Dump it there."

He did.

With the sash damming the blood into a cup, she slowly kneaded the mixture to make sure the herbs formed a uniform paste. Satisfied with its consistency, she raised the flap of skin with one hand, positioned the sash against the wound with the other, and pressed it home. Pain exploded in Yawri's head. His eyes watered but he didn't move.

"Almost done." Keela massaged the sash against the wound to make sure the poultice filled every open space. Yawri pressed his chin into the tent of his hands on his knees so hard his teeth grated.

Keela glanced at Tisbero. "Hold this here and keep the pressure on while I wrap the ends around his head and tie it."

Tisbero held it in place and Yawri took a breath, amazed that the white-hot pain had already changed to a dull throb.

Keela wrapped the sash around his head and tied a tight knot so the ends trailed down his back. She sat back on her heels and surveyed her work. "The bleeding is stopped. The pain should subside soon."

Yawri's mouth showed the shadow of a grin. "I'm sorry you lost your sandal."

Keela looked down at her feet. "A giant took it. I can't believe a giant took my sandal."

Tisbero cleared his throat. "Can you walk? I'd rather the tenders think that ruckus was caused by our four-footed friends than us." Yawri raised an arm. Tisbero grabbed it and helped him up.

Yawri stood erect, tested his balance, and shrugged. "I can walk." His first steps were halting, but by the third he started walking with his chin high and his shoulders back. Tisbero followed at his side, just in case.

Keela started walking but stopped, mumbling under her breath. Hopping on her bare foot, she took off her remaining sandal and, standing squarely, threw it onto the nearest roof. Her bare feet ran in silence over the flagstone and she landed with a definitive step when she came to Yawri's other side.

She surveyed her companions. Yawri had her bloody sash tied around his head. Tisbero's linen cloak, which had been white not so long ago, was now riddled with every color but white. She looked down at herself. She was barefoot, without the traditional sash around her waist, and a torn hem trailed behind her in a forlorn effort to sweep the flagstones.

Keela raised her head and strode in front of her two companions. "Come. We are honorary guests of Shahten. Let any who question it quake before our gaze!"

"What's gotten into her?" Tisbero asked Yawri. "Was there something else in that pouch?"

Yawri straightened and repeated a favorite phrase. "Never give up, always let go ... It's gotten us this far."

Heads high, the bizarre trio marched on, ignoring the fact that if they ran into anyone who questioned their noble countenance, they would join the fate of the minotaur.

34. RACE

∞

The three guardians walked quickly, but more like dignitaries on their way to an important meeting than running for their lives. Two sets of humans passed them going the opposite direction, but they only smiled in greeting.

The marble walkway broadened and the intersection with the human-horse sculpture loomed ahead. They entered it with some trepidation since it was a key hub. Even though hurried, they stopped when they saw the pillar with the gallant, rearing horse with the torso and head of a man.

Yawri's voice was ice. "So this is the educational program we heard those tenders talk about. They're using sculptures to teach people that combining different species to make a new animal is a good thing."

Tisbero steamed. "No wonder they don't want word about what they are doing to get out. Even devoted Shahten supporters might object, and the humans these beasts are meant to replace surely would."

Keela's voice was strained. "Shahten put us in a dwelling with a half-fish, half-woman water spout. The nerve. We need to get off this island, but how? He has probably wanted us dead from the beginning."

They started walking again. Yawri said, "We've got to get to back to our lodging. It's the first place Shahten's priests and captains will look for us. Hopefully, Shayna and Eston still think we're in the bathing room. It won't be good if they've gone looking."

Tisbero looked ahead. "We pass two intersections; the entrance to ours is the third one on the left." Keela lengthened her stride and the other two kept by her side.

"Only one more intersection to go," Tisbero said. He slowed suddenly. "Human voices," he said. "They aren't keeping quiet like the others. Something's changed."

Keela said, "So we project all the authority we can and hope they aren't assigned to find us."

A group of seven humans coming toward them didn't lower their voices or purposeful steps when they saw them. If anything, both increased.

As they passed, a woman leaned toward Yawri and murmured, "Three priests are coming this way. Hide in the courtyard at left."

The human behind her said, "Thank you for freeing the goat people. We deliver food to that hurtful place. Now others will know the truth, too."

The humans passed so smoothly no one watching would have seen anything other than respect for the guardians. Yawri spoke quietly. "Their chatter was to disguise a message. Priests are coming. Follow me." In case eyes were watching, in a louder voice he said, "Look, here's the place with the plants we wanted to examine." He walked boldly through a passage with a narrow archway and bent down to study flowers behind a low wall.

Keela got on her knees to examine the flowers. Tisbero scanned for other exits before stooping to join them. "They're coming."

A few moments later, a shrill voice carried through the air. "Walk faster. We need to hurry."

"What's going on?" another asked.

The shrill, winded voice replied, "Some creatures may have escaped the Compound of Human Development."

"Escaped the compound? Impossible. The walls are too high, a giant guards the door, and tenders are there constantly."

"I know. Nonetheless, we have orders to scout the forests."

"Scout the forests? Not me. There are wild animals living up there."

"Denying orders would be worse, believe me."

Feet rushed past the low, stone wall of the courtyard, one stride away from the guardians hunched over flowers on its other side. Silence returned.

Tisbero whispered as much as his gravelly voice would allow. "The human-goats told these humans to help us? How? The herd went upslope and the humans came from below."

Yawri looked over the edge of the wall. The scarlet-robed guardians were nowhere in sight. "The humans must have a way to communicate that Shahten doesn't know about."

Tisbero and Keela rose too. Keela said, "Fawin's herd stayed true to their word. They're drawing priests north so we can head south."

"And they've asked humans to help us, and the priests don't know we were involved in their escape," Yawri said.

"Yet," Tisbero added.

Filing back through the narrow archway with as much official demeanor as they could manage, they set off with a determined drive, their lips pressed together into a chiseled line. A few more humans passed, but their eyes told them the way was clear of priests. They increased their pace to a dignified jog.

Tisbero reached for Yawri's arm. "SkySlab. In here." The trio ducked into a doorway just as a SkySlab filled with menders holding unmaking crystals soared overhead.

Yawri paled. "They're headed to the forest." All knew what that meant.

Tisbero said, "The herd is fast and smart. Finding them will not be easy. We hid from a SkyShuttle hovering directly above us and all we had was a cluster of leaves." Yawri and Keela appreciated his effort but neither took comfort in the words.

"Let's go," Yawri said.

After trotting in silence for several minutes Tisbero said, "There. Third entrance on the left."

Keela marched up to the door, raised the latch and threw it open with strength neither Yawri nor Tisbero had seen before. She stalked through, and Yawri and Tisbero followed her. She was already headed down the hall. Tisbero closed and latched the door behind them while Yawri came to her side. "Shayna and Eston will still be here."

Tisbero caught up with them at the doorway to the bath. "One moment," he said and disappeared into the room. He came out with three thin, white bathing robes and wet towels. "If we put these on over our tunics we won't alarm them at first sight."

Yawri wiped his face with one of the wet towels. It came down pink and streaked with blood. Keela looked at her towel. It had transformed from soft white to muddy brown. The trio put the bathing robes on to cover their dirty tunics and descended the steps into the dwelling's opulent courtyard.

"Act normal," Yawri said, not sure what that was anymore. It reminded Tisbero to stop and scan the sky and walls for danger before proceeding. Odd behavior for a guardian, perhaps, but routine for him.

They found the young humans where they left them, but they seemed more relaxed. Much more. Eston and Shayna lolled in a stupor next to the fountain. Empty bowls and platters lay on the ground next to drained cups and the empty pitcher of pomegranate juice on its side.

"We're back." Keela looked the most normal of the three and did her best to sound calm and convivial, even though her bare foot ached where the giant had grabbed it.

The two young humans rolled their faces toward the sound but their eyes were unfocused. After staring at the guardians a long moment, both young humans seemed to recall their assignment at the same time. They rose to their feet, using each other for support, and gazed at the three guardians with broad smiles.

Eston, his arm draped casually over Shayna's shoulders, drawled, "You weren't gone long."

Shayna, her clothing askew, added, "We drank all the red juice. I'm sorry."

In explanation, Eston added, "It was delicious." He tried to stand straighter. He had a job to do, although he couldn't seem to quite remember what it was.

His eyebrows changed from furrowed to arched. "We can go get your dinners now! They'll be at Shayna's dwelling. It's not far. We'll be back"—he tried to snap his fingers but they didn't cooperate—"fast."

Yawri spoke quietly to Keela and Tisbero. "Fawin told us how juice can be laced with poppy tea. That jug was intended for us." He took a congenial step toward their saviors. "Is your dwelling near the place where we landed, Shayna?"

Shayna stared, unblinking, at the sash around his head but only said, "Yes. Yes, it is. Very near."

Yawri continued easily. "We must attend to our skystones. Since your home is near them, can we see where you live? It would help us understand what we came here to learn."

The young woman stammered. "But our dwellings are simple. Guardians never go there."

Keela placed a gentle hand on her shoulder. "True of some, but not of us. We *want* to see it."

Shayna and Eston both looked down at the floor, uncertain. Tisbero spoke. "Are you still responsible for satisfying our needs?"

The two young humans locked eyes for a moment and the young man said, "Yes. Yes, we are."

Shayna looked down and gave a little bow. "We will take you." Her eyes focused on Keela's bare feet. "What happened to your sandals? Did you lose them? We will find them!"

Keela responded calmly. "Someone wanted them more than I. Your dwelling, is it far?"

The young girl beamed at Eston. "She wants to see where I live!"

"The sooner we get there the better," Tisbero said. In response to their uncertain stares, he added, "Our dinners are there."

Shayna and Eston stood and looked at the archway leading into the dwelling. Yawri was already walking toward the archway. "Do you know a faster way than by the main paths? The ways humans use are much more interesting to us than wide, marble walkways."

"You want to see the alley we use? I've never seen guardians walk on them!" Eston beamed.

The youths stumbled over each other in their rush to get out the door first. By the time they stood on the paved walkway in front of the mermaid dwelling, they appeared reasonably sober.

"Lead the way," Keela commanded in the light but commanding tone she had used to teach young adults for years.

Shayna and Eston went straight across the marble walkway and stepped onto a narrow path Tisbero hadn't even noticed before. The strange troop sailed down one alleyway after another, making sharp turns and working their way downslope. Although the guardians were more than a third again taller than the humans, Eston and Shayna's shorter legs pivoted and changed direction so quickly the guardians found their longer stride held no advantage. The young humans' lower center of gravity and lithe limbs were ideal for moving through the terrain. Shayna and Eston were aware of this and slowed more than once so the guardians could keep up.

In about a third of the time it had taken Keela and Tisbero to get to the temple, Shayna announced, "My home is here." Chin high and eyes bright, she stopped in front of a thin, tattered curtain that hung in front of a low doorway.

Shayna bounced up a low step, gathered the door-curtain into her hands and moved it aside. "Please, come in!"

Keela crouched to half her height to get through the entrance. She started to straighten once inside but the ceiling was too low for her to stand, so she found a place on the floor to sit. Yawri and Tisbero did the same.

A recessed alcove held a small crystal providing light. Shayna sat down on a pallet stuffed with straw. "Do you like it?" she said, pulling a deep breath.

"I do," Keela replied with heartfelt sincerity. "It's filled with caring."

"Your meal is here!" Eston picked up a large basket and set it on a small wooden table.

Keela knelt next to the table and reached toward the basket. Shayna sprang from the pallet. "Please, may I serve?" Keela leaned back and Shayna lifted the large bowl out of its center, set it carefully on the table, and raised its lid.

The room filled with the delicious scent of well-seasoned flat bean and vegetable stew. Shayna lowered the lid, reached into the basket again, and drew out a wooden bowl of plump, purple grapes; another of diced yellow roots; white cheese; and a dish of figs.

Shayna held her breath while she brought out the last two items: two gourds filled with liquid, sealed with tapered wooden pegs. She removed a peg and sniffed. "I'm sorry, but it's only honeyed water. Pomegranate juice is very rare." She looked down at the floor, her lips tightened with worry. "It's what we drank in your dwelling today."

Yawri held out his arms wide and said, "You followed the instructions we gave you very well. We instructed you to partake of the refreshments so you did. If anyone says otherwise you are to direct them to us. Will you do that? You satisfied our needs well."

Both young humans looked up from the floor. "We will. We are taught to follow instructions from a guardian," Eston said. Shayna nodded.

Yawri folded his arms across his chest. "That's settled." He looked at Keela and Tisbero in turn. "Aren't we due at the landing field?"

"Yes," Tisbero agreed. "Let's see if we can find it ourselves."

Shayna stared at them. "You're leaving? Without eating?" Eston rubbed his throat, his eyes wide.

Keela placed a hand on Shayna's shoulder. "We have a responsibility we must attend to. You've both done all we've asked. "

"But the food," Eston beseeched.

"I know what we can do," Shayna said. She took one of the square cloths from the basket and laid it on the table.

Eston said, "Of course," and took the bowl of figs and deftly upended it over the cloth. He tied the corners together with twine made from grass.

Shayna pointed to the bowls of grapes, roots, and cheese. "We need to do the same with these, Eston."

Yawri glanced at Keela and Tisbero. From the slack-mouthed expressions on their faces, they were all thinking the same thing. Humans and the human-goats used the same technique to move food quickly. Either they came up the idea separately, or more likely, were in communication.

Shayna's gaze fell to Keela's bare feet. She smiled and whirled to a well-worn basket next to her pallet and brought out two small, woven mats and placed them on the floor in front of Keela. "Please step on these."

Knowing protest would only delay their departure, Keela quickly did so. Shayna pulled the sides of one woven sheet up and over the top of one foot and deftly ran a bone needle back and forth, sewing them together. She pulled the heel portion up, darted it to fit and attached it to the sides of the new sandal. She did the same with the other foot and trimmed the toe and top with a metal blade.

Keela walked around the room in a small circle, smiling ear to ear. "This design is better than the sandals I came up with!" She held up one foot for all to see.

Shayna released a satisfied breath and seemed to grow taller. "You can slip them off and on without needing to fasten them like common sandals."

Keela rolled her toes and flexed her heel. "I'll show this design to the others. It's excellent." Shayna beamed with delight.

Eston finished wrapping the food bundles. Tisbero tied the pouch of figs and grapes to his sash and Yawri took the cheese and roots. Tisbero handed one of the gourds of water to Yawri, gave the other one to Keela and took a step toward the door.

Keela started to tie the water-gourd to her sash when she remembered it was around Yawri's head.

"You need a sash!" Shayna exclaimed, looking at Yawri and then at Keela's waist. Without a second glance, she went back to her worn bedside basket and drew out a long, narrow cloth of supple flax. Holding it in both hands, she offered it to Keela. "Please take this."

Refusal was out of the question. Keela placed her hands on Shayna's shoulders. "Thank you."

Shayna wrapped the plain cloth around Keela's waist and tied it in the traditional guardian's knot. Keela's fingers lingered on the fabric. The cloth was so supple the knot flowed evenly from one side to the other. "Well woven," she said, amazed at its quality.

Yawri moved toward the door. "Responsibilities call. We should be going." The thin cloth over the door beckoned in a breeze.

Keela contemplated the remaining fruits, cheese and large bowl of flat bean vegetable stew still on the table. She leaned toward the two young humans and, in her best matriarchal voice said, "We must go, but I have two more requests."

"Name them!" Eston and Shayna replied quickly.

Keela nodded appreciatively. "What tasks were you instructed to do after you fed us?"

Eston cleared his throat and swallowed. "When the meal is finished we are to take what's left to our trainers. They will ask us about our service to you."

"Of course." Keela knelt in front of the table, took the lid off the stew and placed it to the side. She arranged the remaining bowls, grapes, diced root, white cheese and figs in front of it.

"We don't want to offend those who prepared this food. It is excellent and we wish it to be enjoyed. Will you please finish it for us?" Shayna and Eston nodded instantly, not needing to check with the other before doing so. "When you have finished this task, return the dishes and basket to your trainers, as they expect. They will see it was enjoyed."

The tip of Eston's tongue traced across his upper lip, his posture erect. "We will do this."

"Thank you." Keela continued. "When they ask you about your service to us, tell them what we told you. You both did all we requested and we are very pleased."

"We will," they replied in unison.

Yawri leaned toward them. "We are going many places but learning to navigate through the settlement on our own is our wish. Tell them what questions we asked if you need to. Again, you did what we asked of you as instructed. Will you do this?"

"Yes," the young humans said in unison. Shayna added, "I wish I knew more about how the crystals work. Perhaps you could ask my father about them tomorrow. He was the first priest of Generator and knows more about them than anyone."

"Perhaps we will," Yawri said, doing his best to stand still. Tisbero stood anxiously by the door. His hand pulled the curtain slightly aside so he could look out. Yawri began to move toward the door himself. In passing, he asked, "What is your father's name?"

"Laric." The young woman spoke timidly, although a gleam of pride showed in her eyes. "I've not seen him for months. If you see him tomorrow, please tell him I am thankful for all his work."

Keela stopped midway in her movement toward the door and turned back to Shayna. "Laric, you said? If Laric spent more time with you, he would be very proud. Of that I am certain." Tears welled in Shayna's eyes, but before they fell, Keela bowed slightly and turned to shield her own moist eyes.

Yawri's jaw jutted out while he looked down at the floor. He looked up again. "Yes, very proud of you both." He pulled in a deep breath and let it out slowly. "While you are finishing this meal, we will go for our walk. This is by far the largest settlement we have ever experienced. It is time for us to see if we can navigate it on our own following your directions."

Shayna's hand wiped her eyes. "Come outside. Tell me where you want to go and I will give directions." Eston and Shayna almost tripped over each other getting to the door.

Outside, Yawri said, "We wish to see if we can navigate ourselves to the landing field by the quickest route you know."

"See that opening between those two walls?" Shayna pointed to a narrow gap between two dwellings. The quickest way is down that path to the third path on the right. Follow that one until it comes to the wall of an old courtyard. Go over the wall and straight across the courtyard. Take the first left after that. It leads directly to the landing field."

Eston nodded agreement. "The paved walkway takes five times longer. We can tell you the shortest way to get anywhere if you want." He looked at Shayna, a grin on his face.

Yawri moved toward the space between walls. "Thank you. Hopefully, we'll do so well with this one we won't need another test. We'll see."

Tisbero already stood at the gap.

Keela pointed to her new sandals and sash. "Thank you again."

"I can make you more any time!" the young woman chirped.

Keela turned to catch up with Yawri, but with a parting look said, "Go, enjoy the rest of the meal, so we can enjoy our walk, knowing it will be enjoyed!"

Eston and Shayna bounced on their toes and ran back through the wispy curtain.

Tisbero waited for Yawri and Keela to rush past and looked toward the temple. "If we don't get to our skystones before Shahten's captains do we won't be going anywhere. No shortcut can outrun those unmaking crystals."

35. FLY OR DIE

∞

After several paces Yawri muttered, "Laric. The priest at Generator. Shayna's father is Laric. "

"And he's coming to our dwelling this evening," Tisbero recalled.

They increased their pace. Keela breathed, "I don't think he knows what's really going on here."

Tisbero snapped, "He didn't. But we do now."

Yawri's feet stomped while he ran. "Shahten separates people that ask questions from those who like his answers. He divides guardians and humans by talents and the clothes they wear. Walls of every kind are everywhere."

Tisbero said, "The temple priestess and Laric were stunned when we wanted to speak with them. I think it let them realize how isolated they'd become."

Yawri's expression was cold flint. "Shahten knows if you only speak with people like yourself, you only get your own answers from another mouth."

"So much for expanding Creator's Creation," said Tisbero.

Keela said, "Shahten's explanations always sound so reasonable. How does he do that? They sound right but feel wrong." After one more stride, she added, "If you disagree with what he's saying, he says it's because you're wrong—that if we weren't so arrogant, we'd agree with him."

Yawri replied, "We have no experience with his way of twisting words." After a few paces he groaned, "Eons ago, Murann told me some beings use the gift of free will to harm Creation rather than expand it. How can we counter something we don't know about?" The trio took several strides in silence.

Tisbero scoffed. "How could an ethereal being harm Creation? Creation is All. You'd be harming self."

Yawri replied, "Creator gave us the gift of free will to learn what we choose, and that means Creator doesn't control us, even if our choice is to harm Creation."

Keela was steadfast. "We've got to get to the mainland to warn everyone. They only have the reports from Camic and Rhee. All they saw was a utopia."

Tisbero glanced up at the sun. "We have about one hour before dusk. The moon is full, though. If we make speed, Keela and I should reach the mainland by dawn. Several in my community are waiting there for our return. The news will spread fast."

"With the red diamond added to the crystals on my skystone, I'll get back to my community by mid-morning."

They bore right at the third alleyway without slowing down. Yawri felt something on his eyebrow. He touched it, and his finger came down red.

"You're bleeding again!" Keela exclaimed. Scarcely slowing but smoothing her stride, she took a small pouch from her pocket in one hand, the gourd of water from her new sash in the other. Without missing a step, he poured the powder down its neck and shook the gourd.

"Drink this." She thrust the potion into Yawri's hand. "Drink all of this by the time we get to the landing field. It will keep you alert and reduce some pain. Tisbero and I can take turns piloting. You can't. At the speeds we'll be flying, and in the dark, one mistake could do Shahten's work for him."

The trio ran stride for stride, their speed unwavering.

Tisbero said, "The wall of the old courtyard is just ahead. After crossing it, we take the first left, straight to the landing field." They swung themselves over the top of the wall in flawless strides and ran side by side.

Whereas most other courtyards were flat, this one had hummocks of rough stone covered with patches of green and light-blue plants. After jumping over a high mound Keela slowed abruptly and stopped. Noticing instantly, Yawri and Tisbero only ran one pace farther before they did the same.

Tisbero scanned the courtyard while Yawri called, "What's wrong?"

Keela stood rooted in place, her eyes fixed on the ground. Yawri stepped to her side. "Keela?"

Her nostrils flared with controlled breath. She bent down and touched one of the plants, a pale-blue lichen on reddish rock. Peering intently, she used her long fingers to part delicate leaves. Her hand flashed away as if burned. "I knew it! Those traitors of Life. Those destroyers of Creation!"

Yawri looked down at the vegetation. It had less vitality than he would expect, but that could be due to many things. "What is it?" he implored.

Keela stood up, temporarily speechless. Tears welled in her eyes. "This is where they brought the lichen and the red sandstone they took from the valley we healed."

Yawri bent down and moved his fingers across the red stone and froze. "This is the sandstone taken from the emerald valley! Shahten said they took it to seed other lands! It's here!"

Keela rocked back on her heels, then looked down again at the primitive plants at her feet. "Fawin told us the "tenders" mixed different species of plants the same way they mixed animals. They started by learning how to separate lichen into its algae and fungus aspects here. Eons ago, Shahten was already taking steps to learn how to make the half-human beasts today."

Tisbero's arms went rigid, his hands locked into fists. "He explained what you and Yawri saw with such reason. I believed him!"

"So did I," Keela said. "We had no experience with his way of deceit. How were any of us to know?"

Yawri stood straight, his feet planted wide. "The lichen, moss, and rock; the sick mammoths; the missing hatchlings; the disappearance of crystals— Shahten explained it all away. Everyone believed him, but no longer."

Keela's voiced quaked. "Creator's Earth made lichen by joining algae and fungus. Shahten separated them again. What was a travesty to us was play for him!"

"The grass!" Yawri said. "The tall grass you found in the courtyard next to Shahten's secret compound. Is it the same as …?"

Keela threw her head back and stormed. "It's the same grass that killed the mammoths. He probably convinced guardians to take it there by telling them it would help them. Even his followers wouldn't kill animals intentionally. All know the mammoths were the first animal bodies made ready to join with ethereal beings. He probably wanted them gone. Too much connection. Too much honesty."

The weight of the betrayal felt more massive than a mountain, but if they didn't get moving it would crush them where they stood. Yawri drew himself up. "Let's go."

In the moment between leaning forward and their first running step, a loud *clang* from the temple gong shook the air. Not taking time for words, their strides fell as one and lengthened in a race to reach their skystones in time.

36. KILL THEM

∞

Laric knocked on the door.

I didn't know how much I missed talking with other guardians. Shahten has so much for me to do there hasn't been time to speak with anyone but other priests.

He knocked again. The door swung open a crack.

They must have left it unlatched for me. I'd be in the back courtyard, too, if I were them.

He walked down the hall and past the empty rooms quickly and stepped through the back archway. Evening sun sparkled across the moving water and fine marble of the mermaid fountain.

It is beautiful, but I don't see why we need such large sculptures to remind children we are One with all creatures when small figurines have always worked. Shahten always has good reasons for what he does, though.

He took one step down the stairs and stopped. The sound reminded him of the babbling creeks where he grew up. Long ago now, but such a wonderful memory.

He walked down the rest of the steps, stared up at the water jetting from the mermaid's mouth, shook his head, and walked to the fountain's edge. Empty bowls, platters, a pitcher, and two upended cups lay scattered at his feet. He murmured, "How could guardians make such a mess? It doesn't seem like them."

He walked around the fountain. "Yawri, Tisbero, Keela—Where are you?"

A stone bench stood near the back wall and, although some tall grass partially blocked the view of the sculpture, he sat down.

They'll be back soon. Tisbero said the basalt cliffs on the coast were still talking. Maybe I could reconnect to the island's volcano through them. I'll ask how it worked for him.

The comforting sound of the babbling water resounded off the walls. Laric closed his eyes and tried to remember the feeling of contentment he had when sitting on the banks of the brook near his childhood home.

I remember feeling every cell of this body was within All. Why haven't I done this more often?

The sudden whirlwind of Shahten's unmistakable voice drowned out the babbling fountain. "I see our guests enjoyed their food!" Shahten stood near the scattered dishes. Laric started to rise, but paused and pulled his robe straight instead.

The voice of Shahten's master captain carried clearly. "Not surprising. Drinking an entire pitcher of happy-plant juice would make anyone senseless." Laric leaned forward, intending to stand, but remained sitting, catching occasional glimpses through the tall grass.

It's best not to interrupt them.

Shahten spoke again. "Pity they drank it all. I thought such esteemed guardians would know the importance of moderation. It was to help them relax enough to stop their constant questions. Have the humans we gave them reported back yet?"

"Shayna and Eston, my lord. Not yet. However, they are similar to the humans we selected for Camic and Rhee's entertainment. Shayna and Eston are some of our best-trained humans. They will do anything to please a guardian and put them at ease."

Laric leaned forward and breathed, "My daughter!"

Shahten's voice lowered but still carried to his ears. "Yes, those are two well-trained animals. Our visitors will be puddles by now. Guardians like them are so predictable. When I ignore whatever they say and state my facts with unshakable confidence, they flounder more than a fish out of water." Shahten's laugh vibrated the air. "They have no ability whatsoever to keep centered when truths are mixed with lies. They believe everything they are told like babies."

The captain had heard Shahten say the same before but knew that it pleased him. "You have brilliant methods that help guardians with fixed minds open to new ideas."

Shahten was beneficent. "Many planets, master captain. I have brought this knowledge to many planets. Though I bring it to this jewel with special relish."

"Shahten! Shahten!" a third voice called in panic.

"Yes. Yes. I'm here. What is it now, tender? Are you having trouble with the minotaur again? I told you there would be problems with wildebeests."

"Worse, my lord. Much worse!"

Shahten's voice was ice. "Calm down. I detest hysteria."

The volume remained the same but the speaker suppressed her panic. "The satyrs have escaped. We left to investigate some intruders Mostay thought she saw, and when we returned to the compound the satyrs were gone!"

Laric recognized the name of the woman. Although he didn't know what she did there, Mostay was one of the genetic authorities working in Shahten's human-development compound.

"Gone? How could they be gone? They're goats!" Shahten bellowed.

"They must have figured out how to unlatch their cage. They're smart. They know how to plan. They took food. We've been asking the metalworkers for new latches for months."

Shahten's voice was a slap. "Even so, there are walls and the giant guarding the door. Not one of you stayed? Why?"

"The minotaur broke out of its cage again because of the latch problem. The metalworkers tell us they are assigned to other priorities. Blades of some kind." There was a pause while the speaker considered how best to proceed. "After a great ordeal, we had to unmake the minotaur. While we were moving the body, Mostay said she thought she saw three faces above the wall."

Laric heard a platter crash into a wall. Kicked, he supposed.

Shahten's voice railed. "Three faces? The wall is too high for anyone to see over, and everyone knows the consequences of invading my privacy."

"Yes. It sounded absurd, but to make sure, I sent two of our four around the wall to check. They found three stacks of stones against it! Someone *had* been there. As you designed, there is only one way out of the courtyard. Mostay and I took the SkyShuttle to block any escape past the entrance to Generator while the other two ran the wall to flush them toward us."

The messenger stammered. "Some of the courtyards are filled with plants, and whoever the three are, they must be hiding in one of them. We have a cadre of humans walking through each one now. They will be found. There is only one way out. But the satyrs, my lord. The satyrs are running free."

Shahten said. "The three foolish people will be found and dealt with. Curiosity was likely their undoing. However, knowing the latches needed repair, and knowing there was only one way out, you abandoned the compound to look for them.

"Only one pilot is needed to fly a SkyShuttle. You took two. If one had stayed in the compound, these creatures would still be in their cage. What will happen when unprepared guardians and humans see half-human and half-goat beasts? Trapped curiosity seekers are nothing compared to that!"

There was a long silence. "They have not been seen yet, my lord. Only the menders, a few guardians who know of the work, and their trusted humans are pursuing them now. The satyrs headed upslope away from the settlement before any unprepared humans or guardians saw them. That is in our favor. However, if the human-goats go up and around the far side, they can scatter into the old, dense forest. If they get to it, we may never find them. They are fast and smart. I come to you to ask for SkySlabs to cut them off."

Shahten said, "Fools. Fools, all fools!" and bellowed, "Master captain, sound the alarm and get your crews to the SkySlabs, now! Tell your menders a mutant enemy is upon us and they will be expected to use their unmaking crystals to protect us all."

"It will be done." The master captain called to a subordinate. "Summon all pilots and menders to the landing field. Go to the roof of this dwelling and flash the alarm to the signal tower, now. If I don't hear the calling alarm within the minute, you will pay in pain."

"Yes, master captain!" rushed a nervous voice.

Shahten spoke with searing focus. "Master captain, see that a few bags of grain are loaded on each SkySlab. Goats can't resist its smell. Make sure the menders have fully charged citrines. If our genetic priests can't capture the goats with all the ropes and claw poles I've given them over the years, direct the humans to unmake them."

"Yes, my lord," the captain barked.

The voice of the genetic priest squealed. "Unmake them, my lord? It has taken us several breeding cycles to get the right genetic combination! They are exceptional in every way. They are the best new physical form for humans that we've found!"

Shahten's voice was a clipped, dark rage. "Yes, and you should have watched them more closely! Because of your incompetence, they run free. If they are seen our entire population, guardians and humans alike, will panic. Capture them or kill them."

A resounding gong began to ring with its unmistakable message of alarm. "Shahten! Shahten!" a new voice cried out, loud enough to be heard over the pounding gong.

"Now what?" Shahten screeched.

Mostay's voice shook with strain. "We found this!" She raised an object before her bowed head.

"A sandal? You found a sandal?" Shahten said in disgust.

"We found it in the giant's cage," the woman seemed to plead.

"The giant's cage. When?"

"Only now, my lord. We went to feed him before leaving to find the satyrs. This sandal wasn't there yesterday." The sound of the last gong faded away.

The splashing water in the fountain seemed ominous rather than comforting now. "It wasn't made here. It came from the mainland."

"The mainland." Shahten sounded both perplexed and focused. The flowing water made the only sound for a heartbeat before Shahten's voice exploded. "Fools! Fools! There is only one woman here from the mainland. Keela! I warned you about her. It was she and Tisbero on that wall. While you busied yourselves at Generator, they doubled back to my compound and freed the goats!"

"But there were three," the woman's voice quaked.

"Three," Shahten yelled. "Are you positive? They were only two, and no other guardian here would betray our cause."

The woman spoke in a rush. "I saw three faces. And while I ran here with the sandal, I saw three again. Two skystones rose from the landing field below. One of them held two guardians. The other held one. All three wore the white dress of the mainland."

"Three?" Shahten's voice was iron. "Four came from the mainland. Two left this afternoon. Only Keela and Tisbero remained."

The woman started to speak, halted, and began again. "Only four met with you, my lord? I understood the SkyShuttle delivered five from your upper terrace to the lower. Two left immediately. Shayna and Eston brought the other three here."

"Three?" Shahten was ominously silent. He erupted, "Yawri! That reptile! He came after I met with the others! Why did no one tell me?"

Dishes and plates shattered against stone. No one spoke.

The soothing sound of the fountain split with Shahten's rage. "Master captain, forget the goats! These misguided fools will poison countless minds if they get to the mainland. Take three SkySlabs, triple their crystals for maximum speed. Place thirty menders on each, our best in the use of the unmaking citrines. Follow the fools and kill them."

The sound of hurried feet stepping on broken pottery fell in a torrential downpour, then it was quiet. Laric sat frozen, staring down at the ground without seeing. His hammering heart was the only sound he heard.

He leaned forward slightly, elbows on knees, his face in his cupped hands. His fingers rubbed across his forehead in long, firm strokes, trying to erase the memory of what he heard.

What does "keep centered when truths are mixed with lies" mean? Did he say Shayna is an animal?

His choked sob joined the sound of the falling water. "Kill them. Shahten said to kill the guardians from the mainland."

37. CAVE WORLDS

∞

Mariyonta and Aronlat walked side by side into the multidimensional crystal cave. The geode chamber shone with an intense, brilliant light so powerful they covered their eyes against the pain. In the next instant, the chamber went dark. Strangely buoyant air and the smell of moist minerals saturated the silence.

They opened their eyes, long accustomed to complete darkness. Slowly individual crystals with a growing inner glow took shape. There was no audible sound, though a vibration hummed through their bodies.

"Welcome. You heard the call and came," the cave resounded. "We lowered our light for your comfort, and will raise it to our usual radiance slowly."

With that simple greeting, their complex training began.

The two young guardians adapted quickly. They made their camp near the shore by a cluster of long crystals. Aronlat placed stones to form two rectangular pallets for sleeping while Mariyonta filled them with dried moss and sand to cushion the rocky ground. Crystals in the vast chamber's high ceiling, twinkling like stars, provided light. Leaves and the green seedpods of the small but prolific plants provided food, supplemented by the dried meats and fruits from Aronlat's pack.

The ancient lake moved with the moon's gravitational pull, whose invisible force nursed its tide. The soft sound of its caressing lap against the shore gave a pulsing reminder of the moon's union with Earth.

The pair finished a breakfast of mineral-rich greens and tea made from very small, dried leaves. Leaning against a limestone block next to Mariyonta, Aronlat inhaled the sweet air. "I've never felt so alive."

Mariyonta's eyes sparkled with inner light. "I had no idea how much there was to this cave. It's aware of everything in it and beyond. I'm learning more than I ever imagined."

Aronlat ran sand through his hands. "And I thought Yawri was a hard teacher."

Mariyonta leaned back and looked up at the sparkling crystals in the chamber's ceiling. "Yes, although they both almost let us kill ourselves."

"'Almost' is the key word. I'm relieved the cave told him we were alive and well. The thought of him thinking we were lost after all the lessons he gave about listening is scarier than dying."

Mariyonta cracked a wry smile. "It's what he'd do to us when we came out that worried me. How many years would he make us talk to boulders before we could fly again?"

They locked eyes for a long moment, then returned their gaze to the lake.

Mariyonta tented her long fingers over her upraised knees. "Remember how he always said cave bodies function like ours do, but differently? Witnessing how deep cavern lakes function as eardrums for the planet is very different from being told about it."

Aronlat stretched his legs out in front of him. "If I could pick up sound like they do, harmonizing would be a lot easier."

Her eyes strayed to his. "I like it here. A lot." She started to get up but leaned against the limestone again.

He brushed sand off her shoulder. "Me too."

She leaned forward, stood up slowly, and gazed down the beach. "I could do another run, but I expect we should get to our cave class."

Aronlat quickly stood straight up from a sitting position and faced her. "No time like the present, when you're in timeless time."

"Timeless time? Seriously?" she needled, but her lips were smiling.

They strode up the rocky embankment and down to the arched entrance of the crystal cave. The young guardians glided through the opening and came to a stop in the middle of the towering geode. Its inner surface glowed with pale-blue light.

The cave brightened and pulsed with a faster rhythm. "It sounds like you're ready to experience something with timeless time."

Mariyonta raised an eyebrow at Aronlat. He gave a slow disbelieving shake of his head.

"Saying hello to the nine ethereal energy centers of this planet should suffice. They all live in timeless time."

Mariyonta recovered from her surprise and stood alert. Instruction from the cave was at hand. "The planet has nine energy centers? Do they correspond to the nine energy centers of our body?"

314

Aronlat leaned forward. "Is this related to what you taught us about how our physical organs relate to the areas of a cave? These deep lakes are the ears of Earth, for example."

"The structures in Earth are, indeed, reflected in your body. Even your blood. The planet transforms plants carried deep within it and makes its own circulating fluid. It is stored energy from the sun."

Mariyonta summarized, "So the nine ethereal energy spheres you've taught us to experience in our bodies relate to energy centers in the planet."

"Yes. It is complex. Our session will be brief, but it is important that you understand how the ethereal energy centers of your body relate to those of the planet. "

The two apprentices focused within their bodies and tuned in to the familiar etheric spheres distributed from beneath their feet to above their heads. By habit, they started with the one under their feet. The towering crystal geode rippled with pale-yellow light.

"Do you recall why we always start with the one below your feet?"

Aronlat was quick to answer. "Earth essence. Because it's the energy sphere regulating the amount of Earth energy entering the body. The greater our body's connection with Earth energy and nature, the more ethereal presence we will have."

"Yes. To be balanced, the ethereal presence in your body must match the amount of Earth energy. If one overwhelms the other, the body can lose its identity, even its connection to its whole self. The sphere of energy below your feet controls how much Earth energy your body receives. Always in balance, the greater your body's connection with Earth, the more consciousness your ethereal self can have in it.

Aronlat and Mariyonta swayed slowly back and forth in the flowing current. The geode cave continued. "Now, from within this sphere under your feet, ask to know where the energy center in Earth that corresponds to it is."

Feeling more present in his body than ever before, Aronlat said, "The land resonating with this sphere is located in the desert continent south of the equator. It's the one with coastal forest and dry interior."

"Correct. Remain balanced in your body, and from within it, ask this energy center of Earth its purpose."

Mariyonta spoke with deliberation. "It shares the wisdom of how Earth keeps physical and ethereal energies in balance. There is no separation between them. They are aspects of one continuum."

"What else do you notice?"

Aronlat shared, "I feel more Earth energy flowing into my body, which broadens my perception of everything inside and around me. I'm experiencing more awareness of All within my body than ever before."

"At one time, this balance of energies was automatic for human beings. Now you must work with Earth to remember it. I'm glad you're willing."

Mariyonta exclaimed, "How could we not be willing? What could be more important in Life than learning all you are?"

"We don't know. Perhaps being comfortable, getting what you want, or equinox celebrations?"

The young adults recalled the moment when their friends left the cave. Whirling with emotion, they wondered how their friends were. Suddenly, each felt their body sway a moment before finding themselves staring again at the geode wall.

The cave being said, "Did I forget to mention this work requires you to be in your body in order to receive information about something outside of it? You left your bodies to check on your friends. With your ethereal selves gone, your body maintained ethereal-physical balance by reducing its physical connection to Earth. How do you feel?"

"Out of it," Aronlat declared.

Mariyonta reflected, "Less present. Less of All-I-am."

"Good lesson. The deeper you are in the farther you can see. Being inside your body opens All that is within to All that is without."

Aronlat shook his head. "So this is what Yawri meant when he said the deeper we connect into the planet, the more ethereal our body can be."

"You were taught it, now you learn it."

They re-centered and, starting with the etheric sphere under their feet again, felt their presence within their bodies expand.

The cave said, "Next, please focus on the energy sphere at the base of your spine and tune into the planet's corresponding center."

Mariyonta only hesitated a moment before speaking. "I feel it resonating with a continent far to the west. It's across the ocean and north of the equator."

"Again, remain centered in your body, and from within it, ask this land its function."

She chose her words thoughtfully. "It's the planet's center for survival, staying alive and adapting. Its information can keep us alive on any land. It's survival wisdom for any place on the planet."

The cave said, "Seven more to go. Aronlat, shift your focus from the base of the spine to the energy sphere above it, in the area of your lower abdomen. Sense the vitality of this sphere. Experience once more how it connects continual life and death with Creation. And where is the corresponding center on the planet?"

Aronlat opened the senses throughout his body and listened. "It speaks from a continent below the equator from where we live. The one abundant with jungle and the most diverse and largest animals on the planet. "

"And this land's purpose?"

"It is a compelling essence for continued Creation, re-birth and renewal. Many life forms were birthed there because of its creative force, including humans."

"Good. Now shift focus to the next energy sphere, the one centered where your body first digests food."

Mariyonta volunteered, "I feel it resonating with a second continent far to the west. It's across the ocean and south of the equator. Integration. It's about integration of energies and planetary timing."

"Yes, integration. The blending of etheric and physical energies in Earth's timing. It integrates the inner and outer world experience. The planet's citrine crystals, most of which are within those lands, were created to support that center."

The geode cave glowed with a soft blue light and continued. "Five more introductions remain. You'll know the next center very well because you live on it. The planet's ethereal heart center has the jungle continent to its south and the planet's largest continent to its north. What is your experience of it?"

Aronlat was glad to respond. "For me, it provides the wisdom of caring co-creation."

Mariyonta said. "I agree. It's how I feel the impact of my actions on Life. It expresses the language of emotions, how all things feel and what it means to care."

The guardians felt the tones of the geode rise up through their feet. "What would Creation be without caring? How do you know the difference if you aren't emotionally fluent? Similar in function to your body's heart, this planet's center circulates compassion in Creation. As with the blood concentrated in your heart, it's why so much of Earth's circulatory fluid of stored sun energy resides in this area of the planet."

"You have experienced the heart center in balance. I asked this center if it would show you what happens if it was not in balance, and it agreed."

Aronlat tilted his head to the side. "Show us imbalance? Why?"

"If you've only known balance, how can you understand imbalance? How can you bring healing to what you don't know? This session is only an introduction. The first step is recognition. This center will let you experience

317

what happens when it is unbalanced." The light in the geode cave changed to a warm orange. "Ready?"

Mariyonta and Aronlat nodded eagerly.

The next moment they both staggered back. Aronlat's hands went to his chest. "What's happening? I feel empty. Numb, yet it hurts. It hurts a lot."

Mariyonta took a shaky breath and in a disbelieving voice cried, "I can't feel any of the other energy orbs in my body! Everything is disconnecting. I can't feel the planet! Is it dying? It feels like we're dying."

A pulse of vibrant, warm orange filled the chamber. Balance returned.

Aronlat could barely speak but managed to get out, "That was imbalance? No problem recognizing that!"

Mariyonta stopped swaying but her head still spun. "That was just the imbalance of Earth's heart center? Not all of them?"

"Only the heart center and only a brief demonstration."

She folded her arms against her stomach. "Could such imbalance happen? It seems impossible."

The cave glowed and rippled with blue and yellow light. "Even strong life forms are vulnerable. Even planets. Everything has free will and everything affects everything else."

Mariyonta's hands fell to her sides. "I never considered Earth could be unbalanced. Planets are so strong!"

The cave spoke gently. "This is why we are teaching you, as we have others through the ages. The future is unknown, but the more you learn about All-that-is the more you can aid rebalance of any future, even one that includes imbalance."

Aronlat asked, "If this is what happens when only one energy center is unbalanced, what happens if all of them are?"

"That exercise will wait for another class. However, multiply what you just experienced a hundredfold and you might have an idea. Now, before we continue, how are you doing? These are intense energies."

The colors in the cave changed. "We've brought in some healing energies to help stabilize your bodies."

The pair straightened and focused again.

Mariyonta said, "I'm bewildered and a little tired, but I think I can continue for a while."

Aronlat agreed. "This introduction showed me how much there is to learn, but I can re-focus and be fine."

"All right. We'll move quickly through the next three because we'd like to spend a little more time on the last one."

"The healing energies are helping," Mariyonta said. Aronlat nodded in agreement.

"Very well. Focus on the energy sphere of your throat, mouth and ears. Open your awareness to its corresponding center in the planet. "

Aronlat spoke first. "The immense continent to the northeast of here has the largest desert in the world. Similar to the energy sphere of our throat, ears, and mouth, this center of the planet is about communication. It conveys knowledge about speaking and listening inside and outside of one's self. It teaches how to communicate with languages beyond words."

The light in the cave changed from orange to a golden yellow. "Very good. We are only going to touch on these centers today, so we'll move on. Please focus on the next ethereal sphere in your body, the one centered in your head behind your eyes. Where is the corresponding center in the planet's body and its function?"

Mariyonta once again stood relaxed and riveted by the adventure. "There's a large, deep, narrow lake north of that desert. It's the eye of Earth. It sees both inwardly and beyond into the cosmos. It's the planet's sight in all its dimensions. It teaches all Life on the planet how to see this way."

Her eyes sparkled. "Oh! There's another eye, a great lake on the opposite side of the globe from it. It has to be the largest lake on the planet. It's in the continent across the ocean northwest of here. The one with the survival center. Now, I'm being shown two more lakes. The largest lakes that are on the continents south of the equator are eyes, too. All of them see together far beyond any physical sight. This center of sight helps all Life on Earth see dimensions across Creation!"

The cave spoke softly. "That's enough of that center for now. We don't want you leaving your bodies to go the places it shows you. Remain here, centered in your body, and from within, experience its sight. If you leave your body to go there, it won't work." The cave paused and said, "Now, please shift your focus from this energy sphere to the one at the top of your head."

Aronlat said, "This sphere resonates with land in a long range of peaks and valleys on the largest continent. They are the highest mountains on earth. It's a wellspring of knowledge about ethereal realms, and how they are also physical! It's what helps me feel that deep sense of knowing I get when I feel something is right for me without even understanding the logic of it. It is wisdom and knowing."

"Excellent. Before we go to the last one for this session, please rebalance. Return to the sphere of essence under your feet, the one regulating the amount of Earth energy coming into your body."

Aronlat and Mariyonta swayed slowly back and forth in the flowing current running through their feet, legs, and torso.

"Now to the sphere above your head. Focus on it and tell us what you are experiencing."

Aronlat's smile lit up his face. "Oceans. Oceans of ethereal-physical energies flowing through the universe, unique aspects within the Whole. It's located … where? South of the equator, in the island seas east of the desert continent. This area provides Earth's connection to its ethereal wisdom in all the dimensions of its Creation."

Mariyonta tilted her head to the side in thought. "You told us our ethereal presence in a body must match the amount of energy from Earth because if one overwhelms the other, the body could lose its identity. To avoid imbalance, the energy orb below our feet regulates the amount of energy coming in from Earth, and the one above our head regulates the amount of ethereal essence entering from our ethereal selves. I'm experiencing how each are kept equal as they come in. However, now I'm aware of how the energy sphere in the middle of my body blends both energies and distributes balanced life flow throughout the body."

Aronlat breathed deeply. "More than ever, I feel the conscious intent of Earth and Creator's design for human beings. We are very blessed to have these bodies so our learning could continue on such an alive planet."

The cave rippled with light. "Yawri told us you would remember what you learned from previous bodies quickly."

Mariyonta said, "I've been taught how everything is of the One body, but now I experience it. I didn't realize how much there is to learn."

The cave continued, "How can you know what you don't know without asking questions? You ask good questions. This was your first lesson to experience how the energy spheres in your body communicate with the corresponding energy centers of the planet. After your foundations incorporate this, you can experience how they work with the planets of the solar system."

Aronlat coughed. "It goes on and on, doesn't it?"

"There is no rush in learning what is infinite. It's a more complex level of dimensional work. The multidimensional cave will open the way when you are ready for it."

Aronlat shook his head and his voice cracked. "The multidimensional cave? What do you mean? You're not the cave that spoke to me?"

"We are all multidimensional here. But the one that spoke to you works in many more dimensions than we do. We provide training for those preparing for it."

Aronlat and Mariyonta froze.

The cave said, "It's the cavern Lazket lives in. Didn't Yawri tell you?"

Their faces remained blank.

"Then again, why would he? He didn't know what would result from your cave stay any more than we did. We only received you after you proved yourselves ready. The multidimensional cave will do the same."

Mariyonta covered her mouth with her palm. Aronlat's hands fell open.

"It is time to rest your bodies." More pale-orange healing light rippled through the geode.

Eyes staring blankly, the young guardians turned and slowly walked back toward the lake. Their only thought was to sit down on the sand.

38. PURSUIT

∞

The trio leaped over the low wall surrounding the landing field and sprinted to their skystones.

"They look okay!" Yawri rushed. "Those captains probably tried to take the crystals off, but unless you're One with skystone and crystals alike, there is no way they'll separate."

Keela ran next to him, stride for stride. "They just stand their crystals in sockets. They also land their SkySlabs directly on the ground. They don't care if they crush plants!"

Tisbero leaped atop his skystone. "Keela and I should reach my community by early morning. The news will travel fast from mouth to mouth then."

Even before Yawri reached his skystone, he felt the ethereal diamond within him connect to Red and the six crystals on it. It started to rise into the air the instant he stepped up. "It will be dark soon. Flying fast at night carries its own risk."

Keela said, "Less risk than sleeping here and trying to contact them on the astral."

"That would be our doom. Flying fast it is." Tisbero's skystone rose and turned toward the northeast coast, the straightest line back to his community. He glanced at Yawri. "If they bring fog and a flat sea again, you can fly through it at speed by listening for song from the basalt pinnacles. There won't be any sounds from surf."

The skystones started to accelerate in different directions. Tisbero and Keela aimed northeast and Yawri southeast. Keela called out, "We can sleep tomorrow night. See you at the guardian's astral meeting then!"

Yawri called back, "Travel safely! Expand Creation in all you become!"

Keela answered, "Go forth. Create with Creator!"

Yawri watched them speed away. After they flew over a ridge, he slowed and surveyed the sky between the landing field and the temple. Several short-range SkyShuttles, filled with menders holding yellow crystals, flew toward the landing field ... and the three SkySlabs parked there.

He looked to the northeast. Tisbero's skystone was still in sight, undoubtedly much slower than his own.

Yawri began a low, arching turn, circling west into the setting sun. There he waited, letting the setting sunlight hide his position, and watched the shuttles land.

I wonder how they'll respond to this surprise.

Yawri's skystone rose out of the setting sun like the tongue of a solar flare. Darting up, down, and around all obstacles, he bore down upon them, roaring.

Time froze. Menders dove off SkySlabs, hurling their yellow crystals to get them out of the way. The citrines bounced off stone and rolled, some shattering before they fell off the edge. Four menders who had been preparing to lower a tall, clear quartz into its socket let it go and ran. The long crystal fell on the edge of the SkySlab with a terrible *crack*. Yawri continued his flaring rush toward the master captain in his red leather tunic. The captain's eyes were white, his mouth open. He dove to the ground, barely avoiding the soaring blue quartzite. Using skill honed over lifetimes, Yawri's skystone rose straight up, rolled a sharp pivot, and plunged toward the screaming melee again. Not one mender remained on a SkySlab. Not one of them still held their citrine.

That ought to buy some time.

Yawri passed over the low wall and heard the master captain rage, "All three SkySlabs, after Yawri!"

The voice of one of his companions yelled a panicked response. "If we consolidate crystals we can get two after him now. We need new ones for the third!"

The master captain bellowed back. "Two after Yawri! Get that third after Tisbero and Keela. He's going to warn his community and we know where that is. Yawri could go anywhere. We have to stop him, now!"

A junior captain railed, "Menders! That false guardian is lost to the Way! He wishes to send you back to the jungle!" The menders' explosive outcry vibrated air and stone.

"Unmake the lost!" another junior captain boomed.

Yawri didn't look back. He could sense the two SkySlabs rise in pursuit. They were large but fast. The challenge would be to keep them close enough to encourage their pursuit so they didn't divert to Tisbero and Keela, while keeping far enough away to not be killed.

He made a straight dash for the nearest coastline and peered toward it.

They brought back the coastal fog.

To keep both SkySlabs in pursuit, he skimmed the ground until he reached the cliff. Rather than dive into the fog to disappear, he hugged its upper reaches, going far slower than he needed to. He looked back and saw the SkySlabs had closed more of the gap than he expected, but they were still distant. Suddenly, several shafts of dark light streamed around him.

Long range! The unmaking beams have long range!

He accelerated forward so fast his conjured windscreen had trouble compensating for the sudden increase in pressure. The ends of the sash around his head whipped wildly through the air behind him. Another volley fired and arrived at the speed of light. Although poorly aimed, each SkySlab held thirty menders. One shaft of dark light hit one trailing tail of the makeshift headband and instantly turned it to ash.

The torrent that went past him drained the color out of the fog like hail-sized meteors vaporizing anything in their path. On impulse, he dove down in a spiraling descent.

"We hit him!" the junior captain shouted.

Leveling off and fishtailing in the fog, Yawri slowed so they could glimpse his wavering shadow. The junior captain yelled, "He's losing control! Should we slow, pursue, and finish him off? We can't see any better than he can in this fog, and the sea is calm. Without waves who knows what's ahead?"

The master captain demanded, "Increase speed. Finish the kill!"

Yawri took Tisbero's advice and focused his senses on the song of the basalt columns that dotted the near shore. Several of the massive columns were dead ahead. He increased speed to dare his pursuers to do the same. "Steady, my friend," he said to the living skystone.

Every cell of my body feels paired with the crystalline minerals of the skystone.

Without his conscious thought, the skystone dodged up and to the left. The place they'd just been was bleached of color, pierced by multiple shafts of dark light.

Yawri banked sharply right, then left, while he increased speed. The enormous SkySlabs hurled after him, their pilots confident that Yawri would hit any rock face first.

Several more shafts of dark light shot past to his left. The air rushing back to fill the void resounded with a muffled *clap*.

"There!" the junior captain's voice cried. "There he is!"

Yawri pulled left as blood escaped Keela's saturated sash and flowed down his forehead.

The song from several columns of massive basalt penetrated the fog ahead. *How far ahead?*

Blood streamed into his eye.

Straining to keep focus through a red haze, Yawri heard the song of a basalt column suddenly intensify. Shafts of dark light shot around him. One hit the water gourd tied to his waist and it disappeared. More shots came and he heard his skystone shriek, shudder, and shudder again. It dropped away from his feet.

Yawri floated mid-air in a formless, timeless mist. Every direction was the same shade of gray. His momentum became evident when a shadow jumped toward him and quickly congealed into a black wall. The basalt's deep, resonant tones suffused the air, but were suddenly overthrown by the massive clash of stone breaking against stone and screaming men.

Yawri touched the embroidery on the sash around his head and followed the screams into the thrashing, dark sea.

39. DARK LIGHT

∞

Tisbero and Keela hurtled at top speed through the night. Both knew the SkySlabs could outrun their skystone, but starlight revealed nothing behind them. The focused concentration required to fly so fast left little time for nourishment. The water jug emptied hours ago.

Morning's sun cracked the horizon and both strained to see any landmark on the distant landmass. The sun continued its roll upward. A brilliant egg of light sat on its earthly nest.

"There," Keela said, pointing to a flat-topped peak on the coastal range. "That's the one I head toward when I come to work with Twaque on our dyes."

Tisbero straightened and tilted his head back. "That's it. My community is above the bay to its north."

The nose of the skystone moved a few degrees to align with it. Keela leaned forward. "You navigated over a featureless sea all night and arrived on the coast just where we planned."

"I've learned to use my gut," Tisbero said as he scanned dawn's sky behind them. He thought he saw a flash, but the sun was climbing fast. It could have been anything.

Still.

He faced forward again. "Keela, I know we're exhausted, but as soon as we land, please take your skystone south to tell the first community you find what we've discovered."

Keela gave him an incredulous stare. "This is going to be very hard news for guardians to believe. Hearing it from both of us would be more reasonable. Doesn't it make more sense for us both to speak with your community, then proceed to the next? I don't think one person will convince communities. It's hard for me to believe, and I saw it."

Tisbero's skystone began a rapid descent. "Yes, that would be more reasonable. However, little I've seen of late is reasonable. Shahten has proven he'll do anything to convince others he's right." He stared into her eyes, unblinking. "We're the only ones that know he'll even kill to have his way."

The skystone slowed over the community landing area and Keela looked down. Only five white-robed guardians waited there. The majority hadn't returned from their investigations, but probably would soon.

Keela spoke in a steady, low pitch. "We need guardians to believe us, but Shahten planted seeds to destroy my credibility long ago. Who is going to believe me if I go alone?"

"I don't know that I will make any difference in who listens and who does not, but they can at least be warned by one of us. We can cover twice the number of communities if we split up. Let me do this one and continue to the north while you go south." Their skystone slowed to hover above the tall grass. "Maybe you're right about them not believing you, but please indulge me. Leave now for the communities south. I'll see you and Yawri at the astral meeting tonight."

Keela searched his face and, leveling her voice, said, "All right."

Tisbero exhaled and lowered his head. "Thank you."

Their skystone came to a stop and Tisbero and Keela jumped to the ground, each with their mission in mind.

Tisbero was already explaining to the white-robed guardians who approached. "We have unhappy, urgent news. So urgent, I asked Keela to leave and convey it to communities to the south."

Twaque, Keela's dye-making friend, beseeched, "Keela, we were going to go over our dyes together! Must you leave now?"

Keela sprang to her skystone and called back. "Soon, Twaque! Soon! Listen to Tisbero. He has urgent news to share!"

"Travel safely. May you expand Creation in all you become!" Twaque enjoined, but Keela's skystone was already rising.

Tisbero watched Keela's skystone disappear over the southern ridge. He straightened, and eyebrows drawn together in concern, addressed the five other guardians.

"We return from the crystal island with difficult news," he said with a hard edge in his voice. "We learned Shahten mixes truth with untruth to convince guardians that his Way expands Creation. It does not expand. It divides!"

The tallest guardian present said, "How can that be? We expand Creation in All we become. What you say makes no sense."

Twaque pointed to toward the sea. "Look! More guardians are returning with reports. Let's wait for them so they can participate, too."

Tisbero bellowed. "Run to your skystones! Warn the other communities! Go now!"

"Why?" another asked.

A third asked, "Why are they holding citrines? Do dimensions need healing? It that why our children are regressing?"

"Dimensional rifts! Of course. That could explain our problem!"

Tisbero pleaded, "To your skystones, now! Go!"

The huge SkySlab's shadow changed the white, sun-lit robes to shadowed gray. A voice thundered down from above. "These false guardians are all lost to the Way! Unmake them so they can return to the essence of All and be healed!"

Narrow shafts of dark light rained down from above. Where each shaft hit ground, anything growing on it became ash and char. Tisbero's skystone was the first to rise, but five shafts of dark light hit it. Tisbero heard the stone scream and saw a crack widen. He barely returned the skystone to the grass before it split in two and fell with a hard *thud* to the ground.

The crystals that had been One with his skystone rolled free. Tisbero picked one up and instantly recalled what Yawri told him about returning unmaking beams. After they healed Generator, Yawri said, "Hold a conscious crystal in your hands and join with it in this essence of Creation. What the enslaved crystals send will be returned to them. It will give them a chance to remember who they are, just as was done for Generator. They too will have a choice to die in Life, not murder."

Running with the crystal held to his chest, Tisbero yelled, "Who has the nearest skystone?"

"I do!" a guardian yelled. He and Tisbero sprinted toward a long greenstone slab hovering near a distant crevice, a crevice Tisbero knew led down to the beach. Shafts of dark light peppered the ground around them.

"It's a fast one!" the guardian yelled, pausing to make sure Tisbero was near. In that moment, a beam fell directly on his chest. He screamed in tortured pain, his eyes wide with shock. Living dimensions ripped apart. Life and death as One ruptured. The long-nurtured union of human spirit, etheric soul, and physical body was torn and scattered.

His lifeless body crumpled on the ground.

Tisbero spun and scanned the area while shafts of dark light continued to hail around him. Three other guardians lay on the ground, their limbs bent and sprawled unnaturally. Only he, Twaque and one other remained alive.

She was nearest, her packets of herbal dyes scattering behind her as she ran desperately to her skystone at the end of the field. "Twaque! This skystone is closer!" At the sound of Tisbero's voice, she changed direction in one stride and bolted toward him. "Take this recording crystal and fly this skystone down the crevice! It's too narrow for them to follow. It funnels down to the beach!"

She hurtled past him, grabbing the recording crystal from his outstretched hand and pleaded, "Come with me!"

"Go! I have a plan!" he yelled in return. "Go now!"

Tisbero pivoted to see if the other guardian had escaped. Four guardians now lay contorted and motionless on the ground. Two of their skystones still hovered about the grass, untouched. The two others lay partially buried in the field. They'd fallen from considerable height.

Tisbero watched the SkySlab turn from its deadly pass and point its nose toward him and Twaque. It held six menders across its bow, citrines at the ready. It moved unhurriedly, its captain standing straight as a pole between the menders, confident that the last two guardians would fall quickly. Like all the others.

Tisbero glanced at Twaque. She ran fast but needed more time.

They need to come after me.

His feet streamed through the grass and he spared a look over his shoulder. There were two SkySlabs now, and both now moved toward Twaque and the skystone.

He ran and came to a stop directly between the SkySlabs and her. Both SkySlabs moved side by side, relentlessly closer.

Tisbero brought the crystal he'd gotten from his skystone and held it to his chest. Though cool to the touch, it glowed with a heatless white light in his arms. Recalling Yawri's instruction about unmaking, he spoke to the crystal with a calm drawn from a deep reserve.

"You joined with Yawri, Keela, and I while we healed Generator. We recalled Creation together. We connected all the ethereal and physical dimensions we know together. We experienced the reality of everlasting change not separated into Life and death." Tisbero's body glowed with the crystal.

The two SkySlabs stopped in easy earshot of Tisbero. Six menders stood across the nose of each, all awaiting their captain's command.

"Are these the only two left?" the captain in the red tunic on the newly arrived SkySlab asked. Tisbero recognized the master captain, the one who had escorted Keela and him to the temple.

"These are the last," the junior captain of the first SkySlab replied. "What about Yawri?"

The master captain smiled. "Dead. The SkySlab closest saw his skystone fall into the sea without him while we filled the air with unmaking beams.

Unfortunately, Yawri took it down with him. They were so intent on killing him that its pilot rammed their SkySlab into a stand of basalt columns." The SkySlabs hovered a stone's throw in front of Tisbero.

The junior captain said, "Pity to lose so many menders, but at least Yawri's gone. Hard to imagine a death more traumatic. It should make it impossible for him and his body's Earth soul to retrieve their information. He'll be much more supportive of the Way next lifetime."

Tisbero wove back and forth. He let out a hard sigh as his eyes closed. He forced them open again.

Don't give in to hate. It only divides. Connect. Connect to Creation, which includes All. I am in the One and the One is in me. Yawri's instruction. In complete self-honesty, we return nothing to them other than what they send.

The master captain's unhurried, deliberate voice called down. "Greetings, Tisbero. Shahten was particularly patient with you. Much more so than most. Yet you still choose to ignore the wisdom of the Way. With this unmaking, you will have another chance. May you be more open-minded toward the Way next lifetime."

Stay centered. Remain One with All.

The master captain dipped his head toward the junior captain of the other SkySlab. "I'll have the six menders on my bow unmake this arrogant, false guardian. Your front six unmake that woman about to reach that skystone." He laughed. "What fools."

The master captain gave a curt nod to his menders. "Let's watch him dance. Fire."

The mender on the far left loosed his killing light first. His laugh was cut short when he collapsed and tumbled from the platform.

"Clumsy ox! Keep your balance!" The master captain yelled, and turned to make sure the SkySlab's crystals were correctly aligned down its center. They looked good. He cast a glance back down at Tisbero.

He spun to his menders. "He hasn't even moved! What are you…" His words froze in his mouth. Four of the six lay sprawled on the ground below.

"He's got an unmaking crystal!" he bellowed to the junior captain of the other SkySlab. "I don't believe it! Our first false guardian to show anything but fear. Our first with spine!" He waved toward a few menders, indicating they should come forward to fill the vacancies. "Tisbero, you seek an honorable death! It will not change the outcome, but you surprise me."

Tisbero stood, living soul light, with sound and connection moving through him and the crystal. Before the new recruits arrived, the two remaining menders wanted to show the master captain who was the best. They'd helped many lost guardians begin again, and when the dark light hit them in the chest, the lost ones were unmade without fail. Each mender wanted the kill and, as done countless times before, aimed carefully and told their crystal to release unmaking.

But this time was different.

Faces frozen in shock, both menders toppled from the bow and hit the ground with a loud *smack*.

Taking the opportunity to check on Twaque, Tisbero spun to see if she had made her escape. Shafts of dark light peppered the ground around her and she wasn't taking time to ask the skystone to rise. From its movement she was only asking it to slide forward to sail off the edge.

The master captain pointed and yelled, "All menders, unmake her! Now!"

Tisbero didn't hesitate. He started running toward her as fast as his stout legs could carry him.

Even menders without a clear line of sight started firing their unmaking beams at her. Shots went wild. Several menders were hit in the back and toppled to the ground.

Twaque dove onto the skystone and it started to tip over the edge.

The space surrounding it filled with so many shafts of dark light that the air roiled. Twaque screamed. One shoulder was gone. Another shaft hit her midsection, and Twaque's scream of desperate anguish was cut short.

Tisbero ran through the tumult of dead, streaming air and jumped on the teetering skystone. If he could get to its end, his momentum might give him the chance to fly it down the crevice.

He called its crystals to action but the skystone didn't move. He looked down. A crack ran its length. More unmaking beams fell and one hit it the crack. The tortured stone shifted. Tisbero swept the recording crystal from Twaque's dead hand and jumped clear. The broken stone fell over the edge.

He pivoted, his own crystal held high to face the next salvo.

It didn't come.

The SkySlabs were moving slowly to either side.

They're going to hit me front and back.

Feigning a stumble, Tisbero dropped the recording crystal down a narrow fissure that branched from the gaping crevice. Without pause, he continued several staggering steps before he stopped. The long side of the SkySlabs hovered to his left and right. Behind him was the gaping crevice and in front of him the devastation of his community. Yet he was filled with centered calm.

Like Generator, I choose to die connected to All. In this connection, may the recording crystal live.

The master captain crowed, "You refused to expand with Shahten's wisdom." He waved to the menders lining the sides of both SkySlabs. "You'll expand now!" he bellowed.

Tisbero's hand stroked the crystal he held. "Thank you. Thank you for your connection. We die in Life."

In a mixture of dismay and panic, the menders released dark light in a scattered hail. Unmaking returned to eight more of the menders before the first deadly beam caught Tisbero from behind. The break in his focus occurred as three unmaking beams hit the crystal. Choosing its time of death, it flared outward with brilliant white light and exploded in a blinding flash. Searing fragments hit a several menders, who fell screaming to their doom.

Not wanting to be the target of Tisbero's unmaking beams, the captains of both SkySlabs watched from behind the firmly socketed crystals. This was the first lost guardian to fight back, ever. Each hoped it would be the last. They'd both watched the blast from Tisbero's own unmaking crystal hurl him across into the far wall of the crevice. His body hung, pinned in foliage, for a long moment before its dead weight tumbled into the dark chasm.

The master captain surveyed the field of broken bodies and stone. He spoke to the junior captain on the other SkySlab. "Make sure he is dead. Check the other bodies and make sure Keela is among them. They and Yawri had their chance. Shahten said all three must be unmade."

The junior captain pulled on his red-leather tunic and drew back. "She is not here, master captain. We saw her flying south while we approached. Only having one SkySlab, we could not pursue her. First, we needed to end the community here."

The master captain flared. "Not here? See those two skystones still hovering over their pet grass? You could have had one of your subordinates take some menders and kill her within minutes after your arrival. It is on you to make sure she is unmade! It may be difficult. After all, one exhausted woman on a diminutive skystone without any defense might be too great a challenge for you. Will one SkySlab with double the crystals and thirty menders be enough?"

The junior captain blanched. "She will be found and unmade, without question!"

"Good! However, entertaining as Tisbero was, I've lost eighteen menders. Take those you need from my SkySlab to give you a full complement, and the extra crystals to double your speed."

"Yes, master captain."

"I will make sure this place has no story to tell. We've managed to erase all evidence of unmaking from the other communities lost from the Way, and the same must be done here. Those not yet following the Way cannot understand why the truly lost must be saved from themselves."

The master captain flicked a hand toward the crevice. "Yawri is dead at last, and we must report the same for Tisbero and Keela."

The junior captain was already lowering his SkySlab. "You menders! On this SkySlab now!" He turned to the master captain. "Consider the deed done."

Keela didn't see the SkySlab approach from below. Several shafts of dark light hit the underside of her speeding skystone. A glaring spray of rock and screaming stone ripped her mind from her thoughts of reporting what she'd seen.

She responded instantly. Her small skystone rose and fell, cascading back and forth in sudden, random jerks.

Streaks of unmaking essence from thirty menders hissed through the air in a pelting stream. Keela's jaw clenched and her dark blue eyes flashed fiercely.

I must warn the others.

She changed direction so quickly the menders could not aim. "Stop! All of you must fire at once!" the junior captain ordered. "Aim. Aim. Hold your aim. Release now!"

The air around Keela faded with the unmaking light. Her skystone shrieked, and pieces of stone flew through the air. Her skystone started to plummet, stabilized with a wild wobble, and strained to follow her request to dart left.

A rapid succession of unmaking beams broke the tortured skystone apart and Keela wheeled in free-fall toward a rolling, white-capped sea. "No!" she cried, the instant before she hit the water so hard it felt like a solid wall. Her body sank with shattered hope and stone alike.

40. GATHERING

∞

While their human bodies slept, the guardians met again in their astral forms.

Rhee and Camic had returned the previous night and reported excellent news. All guardians at the meeting were relieved to hear that Shahten had found the way to not only stop but reverse the loss of abilities. With the answer at hand, the crisis was over. All they needed to do was spread the news and follow Shahten's counsel.

Some wanted to hear the report from Yawri, Tisbero, and Keela before choosing the next course of action. However, since they had yet to arrive for tonight's meeting, Rhee and Camic were happy to repeat their report. After all, it was good news for everyone.

Rhee's voice rang with excitement. "Shahten welcomed us all to stay as long as we wished, to learn whatever we wished! Since we arrived much earlier than our friends, there was time to answer all our questions. Everything we saw told us the new bodies of island guardians are more capable than their last."

Camic followed, equally earnest. "Shahten's methods are helping the humans, too. They are healthy, vital, smart, and capable. The foods they prepare are diverse and excellent. The entire island prospers, and we can again, too."

Rhee rushed, "After understanding why we needed to help the humans evolve, the only question I had was why we hadn't realized it ourselves. All we have to do is share our success, our selves, with the humans. Simply giving back to them, the source of our own bodies, means all children grow in ability. How could Earth not be pleased?"

"What a relief to hear this!" One of the guardians present exclaimed. "This way lets both human beings and humans prosper. Yes, Earth will be pleased."

Camic chimed in, "I'm sure when our friends return they'll report the same."

"No!" a voice rang out. "They won't report the same!"

All turned to see Yawri approaching the large circle of guardians. His astral form appeared inexplicably pale, but his voice was clear. "Shahten has deceived us! He does not expand Creation. He destroys it!"

The gathering of guardians, shocked by his words and his wavering astral form, turned to him.

"Yawri!" Zinn exclaimed, moving through the assemblage toward him.

"Destroy Creation?" Rhee exclaimed, shaking his head in disbelief. "How can you say such a thing? It's crazy."

Camic took a long step toward the center of the circle as well. "We have *seen* the results of Shahten's work. He has the way for us all to prosper again, including the humans!" Guardians murmured their agreement.

Rhee stepped to the center of the circle with Camic. "We listened to you once before, Yawri! Long ago you caused division and mistrust among us, but we are not so naive now. Your reputation for jumping to false conclusions is well known."

The circle of guardians closed around Camic and Rhee as if to protect them. Yawri stood at its outer edge but his voice carried to all. "Camic and Rhee, was there a storm on your flight back?"

"What does the weather have to do with anything?" exclaimed Rhee.

Yawri persisted. "Was there a storm?"

"No. It must have passed before us."

"Yet, Shahten said you had to leave quickly to avoid it, correct? His urgency made it impossible for us to talk privately. He gave us no chance to compare our experiences."

"Shahten was only concerned for our safety!" Camic retorted.

"What about his huge 'SkySlabs' lined with human 'menders?' Thirty on each one, all holding the citrines we use to join dimensions. Did you sense any problems with dimensions during your stay?"

"Well, no, but he's working with many communities. Elsewhere they may be having problems."

Yawri addressed the entire gathering. "Shahten has twisted the citrines to make them separate dimensions, not connect them. I saw them used to kill a half-human beast. They used them to try to kill me. If I hadn't known how to pilot skystones through water, they would have. My skystone has the scars to prove it!"

"Absurd!" Camic barked a laugh. "Prove it? Like you 'proved' that guardians took lichen and stone from a valley eons ago? We all found out they were only transplanting it at Earth's request."

"Speaking of that missing lichen, we found the plants and rock taken from that valley on Shahten's island! He needed it to start his genetic experiments. Shahten deceived us then, and he deceives us now! Keela and Tisbero saw it too!"

Camic raised his arms above his head. "Genetic experiments? Did everyone hear that? This is crazy!"

Yawri scanned the assembly.

"Where are Keela and Tisbero? They should have returned long before me."

Blank stares were the response. Zinn came to Yawri's side. "We haven't heard anything from them."

Rhee spoke soothingly. "Please, guardians. We must listen to reason. They must still be on the island. Shahten told us they'd be traveling by day on SkySlabs and by night in their astral forms to see everything they wished. They aren't here because they are traveling with him. They knew we were returning with our report. Why would they rush their own?"

Yawri's voice pounced. "We've got to leave immediately for Tisbero's community! I told you of the attack on my skystone. They left the island before I did. They should be at this meeting!" He scanned the assembled guardians. "I landed on the coast; the first safe place I found. I can make it to Tisbero's community by morning. Who will meet me there?"

Zinn stormed, "I'll leave as soon as I return to my body after this meeting."

Guardians shifted their gaze from one to another but none spoke.

"Go!" Camic exclaimed. "They are in no danger, but the sooner you leave, the better. The answer to our problems is obvious, and irrational ravings are no help." He stood in the center of the circle, raised a hand, dropped it, and spoke with deliberate calm. "We discovered the reason our children were no longer surpassing us was because they were too isolated, too disconnected from our common ancestor, the human. Hoarding and arrogance is our problem. Search your hearts! If we think we are better than the humans, we must heal our arrogance. Guardians must not hoard Life."

Rhee jumped in. "We discovered humans have been crying out for growth, but we were deaf to them. The more we spoke with them the more it became clear. It was our responsibility to reconnect to them so all humans, not just the ones we joined with, could develop. Our problem is solved when we give back to the source from which we came. Listen to reason. If we let go of outdated, fixed ways of thinking our problem is solved."

Mutters of agreement turned into a chorus of approval. "It makes sense."

"Much more sense than Yawri's tale," a guardian chimed.

Yawri turned to Zinn. "They're so relieved to hear Shahten's answer they can't hear anything else." He gave a final look at the gathered guardians. "I wished his answer was true, too—but it is not. The longer honesty is denied the greater the loss."

He faced Zinn straight on. "Can you make it to Tisbero's community by dawn?"

"Yes. I'm just inland from our community now." She paused. "Why is your astral body so pale? What did you mean about piloting your skystone through water to escape?"

Yawri's astral form didn't show the damage to his physical body but it did reflect in its energy. "It wasn't an easy escape. Their skystones are many times the size of ours and carry humans trained to use citrines to 'unmake' whatever they are told to kill. They pursued me out to sea but it was foggy and dark. The skystone crystals, Red and I, had a plan. When our destruction was imminent, Red and I would separate from the skystone so it could plummet into the sea without us. Red and I would follow. Our death would appear obvious.

"The minerals in my body are One with the minerals in the skystone. My experience flying through water in and out of Lazket's cavern came to good use. Red and I flew underwater on our own until we rejoined with the skystone. When it was safe to emerge, we flew to the nearest coast, where my body sleeps now."

"You said your skystone was scarred from the attack. How badly? Is it a long flight from where you are to Tisbero's?"

"One side of its wonderful light-blue quartzite has a long black scar, but it's still willing to fly. Its six crystals and Red are ready to go. We'll be there by dawn."

She gave him a level stare. "What about you?"

"I just need to eat. I've got a pouch of yellow-root and cheese. I best return to my body though. I'll see you at Tisbero's landing area soon."

"Okay. I'll see you soon."

Of the guardians engrossed in Camic and Rhee's hopeful explanations, only Gamon noticed Yawri and Zinn leaving the meeting.

41. TISBERO

∞

The first rays of sun cracked the horizon of the coastal mountains. A moment later Yawri's speeding skystone came up alongside Zinn's. She fishtailed back and forth in greeting and looked over. Her straight eyebrows creased and her round lips froze in a thin line.

Keela's embroidered sash was tied around his head, blotched with dark red and shorter than it should be. One end was black with char. Yawri's long, white tunic was torn at the shoulder, streaked with dirt and splattered with scarlet.

Yawri dipped his strong chin to return the greeting. He raised a hand and pointed ahead. The landing area for Tisbero's community was illuminated by the morning's golden sun.

They brought their skystones to a hovering stop above low brush. Zinn bounded off hers first and sprang toward Yawri. He moved slowly. She reached him just after he stepped off his skystone. Her eyes traveled across several purple bruises on his flesh and then to a black and pumice-grey scar that ran along the edge of his beautiful, blue, quartzite skystone.

"Citrines did this?"

Yawri touched his forehead, lowered it and looked at his fingers. His head throbbed but there was no fresh blood.

"Shahten forced citrines to separate dimensions instead of connecting them. He trained humans to use them." Yawri scanned the area.

Zinn's eyes remained fixed on the skystone's scar. The lifeless gray contrasted dramatically with the delicate, narrow bands of white quartz threading through its light-blue stone. The sight was devastating, and her lips pursed in a deep frown.

"People should be here. Where are they?" Yawri asked, continuing to scan. "The sound is different, too. That bushy cedar has always greeted me before."

The amber highlights in Zinn's brown eyes flashed. She jumped up on Yawri's skystone for a better view. "This is still their meeting place, right? It's a big community, and they would have moved if the land was harmed. From what I can see, no one's used this field for weeks."

"It is the right place." Yawri bent down and moved his fingers across the soil. "Its sounds are muted." He touched the small petals of a blue flower. "The flowers look the same but don't vibrate."

Zinn knelt down and smelled the ground. "What happened to it? It's not singing."

Yawri walked to the large, bushy cedar. "This tree no longer speaks!"

"All trees speak. Why would it stop?" Zinn paused in thought. "It all looks normal to the eye but the dimensional sounds and light are missing."

Yawri's hands stroked the bark gently. "This tree's traumatized. It's in shock."

A light rain began to fall. Zinn jumped down from Yawri's skystone. "Let's check the area. If we move in ever-increasing circles, we'll be sure to cover it well."

Yawri thought of Keela. He'd used the same spiraling method to cover ground with her when they'd healed the pristine valley of broken lichen and stone. His eyes watered.

"Let's go," he said as he got out.

The gentle rain continued to fall while they walked larger and larger circles, eyes focused on the ground. No evidence of recent use appeared.

Finally, on the outer edge of the field, Zinn called out, "What's this? There's a strange color here." She held up fingers smudged with blue.

Yawri quickly knelt next to her. He ran his fingertips through the wet soil, smelled and examined them. "It's dye. Dark-blue dye. Like the dyes Keela makes from plants." He stood and walked a circle around the stained soil and increased its size to walk around it again.

"Here!" he exclaimed. "Another color. Purple."

Zinn hurried to him and, following a hunch, walked in a straight line connecting the blue and purple spots. In a moment she cried out, "Red! Someone dropped a packet of red dye here."

Yawri's heart rose to his throat and his mind raced.

Maybe Keela left a trail.

However, even though they walked the line of three spots farther in each direction, no more spots were found.

"Let's go back to the last one on each end and spiral out. Maybe they changed directions," Yawri said, hope wrestling with fear.

Zinn sprinted ahead and circled the red stain. In her third orbit around it she said, "Green! You're right. Someone was running and changed direction."

Zinn continued walking the new line formed by spots of red and green. Yawri ran past her. "Orange!" he exclaimed.

Zinn darted past him. "More orange! They were running this way."

Yawri looked where the marks of dye pointed. "The crevice! The person was running to the crevice!" They both ran in a rush. "Look!" he exclaimed, pointing down at bare granite. "This rock's been gouged! These are recent scrapes."

Zinn bent down to inspect the scar. "Whatever caused it was wide and long."

Yawri took a step toward the edge. "A skystone! These scrapes came from a grounded skystone."

Zinn joined him and looked over the edge. "It didn't fall down there. None of the vines or rocks below look broken."

The etheric diamond in Yawri's chest pulsed. Yawri stilled to listen. "There is a crystal nearby. Weak but near." He closed his eyes and moved toward the sound. Bending down, he finally got on his hands and knees and, eyes still closed, listened.

He opened his eyes and looked down a fist-wide crack in the granite, a fracture that ran from here to the crevice. He stretched his senses. "It's down here. It wants out."

Yawri looked up at Zinn, eyes aglow, and said, "It's going to take a very strong connection to raise it. I'm going to my skystone to ask Red if it will help."

Zinn stared down into the fissure, but before her eyes could adjust to the darkness, Yawri reappeared. He knelt on one side of the fissure with Zinn on the other. She placed her hand on the red diamond that Yawri held directly over the crack.

Without need of words, Yawri, Zinn, and Red connected as One. The cracked granite around them began to sing. They invited the crystal below to join the connection.

"It's connecting," Yawri breathed, "as best it can. Let's increase soul light."

"It's not moving," Zinn said. "Its trauma is great. Maybe greater than its strength."

Yawri sent a thought to the six crystals on his skystone.

Please help.

Beads of sweat formed on Zinn's high forehead. Yawri said, "All we need do is be who we are."

Zinn relaxed.

There is no trying. Only being.

The two guardians and the large, double-terminated diamond they held radiated sound and colors filled with Creation's essence. The crystal at the bottom of the fissure began to rise slowly. The closer it came, the faster it moved and the stronger its living sound. It floated into Yawri's open hand with the grace of a bird settling into its nest.

"It's the recording crystal!"

"Recording crystal?" Zinn leaned back. The glow surrounding her subsided and her skin returned to its natural tint of rich, loamy soil.

Yawri tipped his head back. "I gave this to Tisbero last year. He took it to Shahten's island. It records all its experiences. It will show you what happened to us and what happened here."

Zinn stepped over the fissure to stand by his side.

He held the priceless crystal, comforting it, supporting its connection to Red, the crystals on his skystone and Zinn. It sang.

Yawri said, "What it has experienced will not be easy to witness. Are you ready for the pain?"

Zinn stepped closer. "Do I place my hands on it?"

"Next to mine."

She relaxed without expectation, open to the unknown. A trickle of images, sounds and textures came first. The trickle became a stream, and as if they had been held back beyond endurance, surged. Zinn stood entranced. Images came wave after wave.

The hopeful words of Tisbero and Keela on their way to the crystal island.

The fog and silent sea.

The shock of their near collisions.

Their confusion about the black wall and the temple.

The Generator.

The unmaking of the minotaur.

The release of the human-goats.

Shayna and Eston and the drugged, red liquid.

The trio's desperate run to their skystones.

The landing here, a rising skystone and death raining from a SkySlab.

Tisbero's last stand before being blasted into the crevice.

Evidence of the carnage taken and dropped into the sea.

The menders lying in wait for the rest of the guardians to return and their unmaking.

The last rolling wave of sound and image faded and Zinn stood shaking with shock and sorrow. Even though Yawri knew what to expect, silent tears still welled and fell. He wrapped his arms around Zinn while her body shuddered with sobs.

Timeless minutes passed. Zinn's sobs slowed and she gave a deep sigh. At last, she forced herself to speak. "I don't want to believe this horror!" She wiped her cheeks and groped to find words to help release the pain in her chest. "How could beings of the Creator use its gift of free will to rip Life apart?"

"I don't know. Shahten has chosen to separate what is Whole. He cleaves essence into Life and death, end and beginning, creation and destruction."

Zinn held her stomach and moaned. "Never did I imagine there could be such a thing as murder. And of guardians by guardians."

Yawri lowered his gaze. "Shahten mixes truth with lies in a way we do not know, and he tricks guardians into making his thoughts their own. It happens so slowly, I don't think they realize it."

"But it doesn't make sense." Zinn's voice rang with desperation. "Why?"

All Yawri could do was release a deep breath and slowly shake his head. His lips in a thin line, he looked down at the recording crystal.

He choked on the inescapable thought. Keela had been here with Tisbero, her fate sealed with the others. He swallowed a dry lump in his throat, the misting rain mixing with silent tears. He had to say something, or feared he'd never speak again.

"Even while Tisbero saw his friends being murdered; he stayed connected to the All. It kept him alive long enough to hide the recording crystal." Yawri looked across the crevice to where his body had lain before it fell.

Zinn stared unseeing down into the crevice. A slight movement caught her attention and the distraction was welcome. Her eyes narrowed. "Did you see something move?" She pointed down toward a bare bulge of granite far below.

Yawri looked but only saw snaking vines and rock.

"There it is again! To the left of the exposed granite."

Yawri looked again and saw a quick movement. He concentrated, focusing all of his attention on the spot.

Several gnome-like creatures were moving around. "Earth devas and elementals. Tisbero's community would have tended this area with them like we do with ours."

Zinn's brow furrowed in question. "How could they stay in a place so traumatized? It would be excruciatingly painful for elfin-kind to stay here."

She stared down, trying to discern more. She heard movement at her side and looked. Yawri's head was disappearing over the edge. "What are you doing?" She stepped closer and looked down. "You're exhausted and wounded and climbing down a cliff?"

"The elementals stayed for a reason. Maybe that's where Tisbero's body landed. I'm going to find out." He disappeared with the swish of parting plants.

"The rain's making everything slippery!" Although the thought of seeing Yawri tumble down tied her stomach in a knot, Zinn couldn't look away.

Vines rustled. With a loud *snap*, a long, twisted vine of green fell from the crevice wall. "Yawri!" she yelled, but her voice was absorbed by leaves and rain. All was silent. She leaned over the edge farther than was safe. Nothing moved. Not even the elfin-kind.

"I found his body!" Yawri's words were muffled. Zinn's neck craned. "It's here. The elementals led me to him!"

Yawri knelt next to Tisbero's still form. It was wrapped in vines, which had slowed his fall. Yawri turned to the elfin-kind. "Thank you for helping to break his fall. Thank you for staying with his body. Thank you for taking me to him."

He touched his friend's mahogany hair. It was plastered against his head from the rain but still bushy and wild … and clotted with blood.

Without thinking, Yawri placed his fingers to the side of Tisbero's pale neck. His friend's unique, warm, reddish hue was gone.

Tisbero felt cold but not as cold as he should be. Was that a throb? He tried again but wasn't sure. It had been so faint, it was probably his imagination.

Light flooded the crevice. Yawri glanced up to see clouds moving aside. The crack of blue sky framed the planet's sun and its warm light flowed onto Tisbero's face.

The elfin-kind are communicating with the clouds. Warming Tisbero … Why?

Yawri gently opened one of Tisbero's eyes.

The large pupil contracted into a tight ball.

"He's alive!" Yawri's baritone voice climbed the wall and hit Zinn's ears with force. "Zinn! He's alive! Get your skystone!"

Zinn had already started running to retrieve it at the first call. The second words made her soar.

She flew her skystone over the edge and plummeted down the crevice without hesitation, communicating with the skystone and elfin-kind alike to speed the descent. Branches and leaves parted around her tear-streaked face like water around rock.

She didn't blink.

She pulled the skystone out of its dive slightly above the rocky bottom and moved toward Tisbero's still form.

Yawri had already freed him from the life-saving vines and was carrying him toward the skystone. Zinn jumped off and in one fluid motion joined him. The nimble arms of her acrobatic body were too short to reach around Tisbero's barrel chest but she still managed to take most of the weight.

Together they lifted Tisbero onto the skystone. When they lowered him, air escaped his lips in a halting groan.

Yawri said, "Tisbero, it's Yawri and Zinn. We're with you now."

A delirious gurgle came out of Tisbero's contorted throat.

"Don't speak. Save your strength."

Zinn began moving the skystone toward the sky, keeping it level but at speed.

"Kl." Tisbero's voice sounded like a dry whisper.

Yawri leaned closer. "It's okay. We're here."

Tisbero's glazed eyes cracked open. "Keel," his voice grated. "Scape?"

"Keela? You mean Keela?"

"Coast. South." His eyes began to roll back in his head. "Escaped."

Still cradling Tisbero, Yawri reached into his pocket and grasped the recording crystal. He asked for the memory showing any skystone in the air before the SkySlabs came.

The crystal retrieved the image and showed Keela's unmistakable form on a lone skystone flying to the south. But Yawri's elation died when the next image showed a SkySlab, filled with at least thirty menders, following her.

Zinn reached the top of the crevice and glanced back to check on her two passengers. Tisbero lay securely between the skystone's crystals. Yawri was holding the recording crystal, an expression of panicked hope on his face. In a voice filled with both hope and despair, he said, "Keela left before the attack! I'm going to find her."

Zinn responded by quickly accelerating her skystone toward Yawri's skystone. "I'll take care of Tisbero, you stay alive! If anyone can find Keela you can!"

Her eyes fixed on his skystone, she began her descent. Before she had a chance to land, he jumped from her skystone down to his. The Red diamond connected to its six crystals before Yawri's feet touched its quartzite surface and his skystone rose to meet his feet.

Zinn managed a small smile. "Create with Creator!" she exclaimed.

"Travel safely!" he boomed in response while her skystone turned and sped away.

Yawri planted himself on the scarred skystone and felt his connection with it expand. His body glowed with soul light. The crystals radiated white light.

The skystone shot into the air, passed over the rocky beach and pinwheeled south.

He touched the embroidered sash around his head, still fixed in place with dried blood. His fingers lingered on the embroidered design Keela had stitched into it.

Images of her deep-blue eyes and determined stance competed with images of shafts of dark light falling on guardians and their faces contorting in pain.

"Creator's Earth, please help," he said aloud. He knew no one could survive thirty unmaking streams. Yet his eyes watered with hope. "I will find you, Keela. Dead or alive."

Three hours later his tired eyes still searched the coast for any sign of her. He didn't see the giant bird dropping toward him like a meteor, its talons outstretched.

42. RAINING ROCK

∞

The paddle-like flippers and large, flat tails of two manatees moved slowly up and down among the rich seagrass in the warm coastal sea. Similar to the way mammoths used their trunks, their large, flexible, muscular lips broke the grass quickly and skillfully steered it into their mouths. The thick, gray skin of the larger one was slightly darker than the smaller. The shape and color of both contrasted sharply with the streamlined, colorful fish darting around them.

"Did you hear that?" the larger said.

The smaller manatee hovered motionless and listened. "Something is hitting the surface, and it's coming closer."

Suddenly, a hail of stone shards fell through the water surrounding them. Although the manatee's powerful tails could propel them through water much faster than the bulbous shape of their bodies implied, they stayed where they were. The direction away from the maelstrom was unknown.

"It's raining rocks!" the first manatee exclaimed. "How can they fall from the sky?"

The concussion from their impact sent pressure waves through the water. However, it was nothing compared to the shock when a massive slab of rock hit the surface. Fish swept back and forth, stunned, but the manatees had already nestled into the seabed floor.

They watched the huge slab move toward them so fast it was impossible to get out of its way. It hit bottom nearby and hurled sediment up and around it. Another more muffled splash followed. The manatees looked up again to see a whirl of white cloth billowing in the water. Rocks falling into it were wrapped in its fabric. Their weight pulled the white form down, and the swirling mass came to rest near the slab of stone. Cloth roiled in the current.

Keela's honey-colored hair swayed back and forth while her head lay expressionless on the seabed floor.

"It's a guardian!" the smaller of the two manatees exclaimed.

Both knew what that meant. When they had been only a thought form, a guardian taught them two foundational lessons: "See what you're looking at instead of what you think you are," and "Don't make any task more important than the Life it is meant to expand." In appreciation, manatees had sought to aid guardians since that time.

The larger manatee moved toward the prostrate form. "Her lips are blue. She needs air!" Small rocks continued to fall through the water. "She'll drown here but be killed by stones at the surface."

The smaller of the two hovered over her. Stones pelted its back, but it didn't flinch. "We teach our children how to breathe pockets of air underwater. Let's see if it works for her. You cover her face and I'll provide the air."

Quickly, the large mammal placed his flippers on either side of Keela's head and arched over her face. His companion exhaled air into the pocket formed. The larger manatee gently raised her face into the dome of air.

The other one swam quickly to the surface, exhaled and took in a deep breath. It returned and released more air into the pocket. "I saw a huge skystone flying away. It had many people on it. If they wanted to help, why would they leave? Whatever the reason, rocks no longer fall. It is safe to rise."

While the large manatee held her face in the air pocket, the smaller of the two nuzzled under Keela's back. Both manatees moved toward the surface and the one under her changed position to fully support the guardian's body on its back. When they broke the surface, her arms hung down, unmoving. Still, the bluish hue of her skin hadn't darkened.

High overhead, a great bird plunged toward the living raft. The manatees' eyes were small but their eyesight was excellent. Both saw orange feathers between the bird's shoulders flash when the dark-blue wings tilted toward them. The larger manatee said, "I don't know why an ahja teratorn is coming but maybe it knows what's going on."

It came to a hovering stop above them, its wings twice the length of a manatee, flapping back and forth in broad, sweeping strokes. The manatees looked into the avian's dark eyes. A circle of fiery orange ringed each black pool.

It said, "You saved her. Thank you."

The larger manatee swam vertically in the water, its head above the surface. "Not yet. We're a long way from shore. You know her? "

"I don't know her, but others do. She carries the energy of my kind. I feel it within her, but her body is weak. I am connecting to it to give her strength."

"She fell from a great height into the sea. What happened?"

"I saw her flying through my area on a small skystone and watched from high overhead. Unbelievable as it sounds, a skystone larger than any I've known knocked hers from the sky and shattered it into pieces. I don't know why."

The smaller manatee said, "We can get her to shore, but which landfall is best? She needs fresh water and a safe place to rest."

The colossal bird gave a high-pitched shriek and rose into the sky almost as fast as it had come. Long minutes passed while the manatees scanned the sky for return of the ahja, or the return of the immense skystone.

Both blew bubbles in relief when the bird returned. "Swim toward that cleft on the horizon," it said. "I spoke to the divas in that area. There is no shelter, but there is a small beach with fresh water near. They will see she gets it."

Keela's skin remained blue and pale.

The manatees could easily move through water faster than a human can run, but could triple that speed for short bursts. These two sliced through waves while keeping Keela evenly straddled on the smaller manatee's back. The beach, however, brought progress to a stop. Manatees had vestiges of the limbs their ancestors used to walk on land but limbs were flippers now.

The larger manatee said, "Let me take her now."

"And do what? Our flippers cannot support weight on land."

"True, but she must get beyond the surf. Roll her onto my back and I'll see how far up the beach I can go."

The giant bird came to rest where surf lapped the shore and opened and closed its massive, hooked beak. "I will help."

The manatee used the rhythm of the surf to raise itself on its front flippers and lurch forward. Resting its chin on the sand, it used its rear flippers to dig into the sand and push. Large rocks poked from the sand ahead. "It's as far as I can go," the manatee said.

With her out of the sea, the giant bird hooked its stout beak under the sash that Shayna made for her. Massive wings flapped and it moved her up the beach out of reach of high tide. When the giant bird released her, she rolled onto the sand without any movement of her own. "She's weak but lives."

Several elfin-kind, all carrying curved leaves of fresh water, came. "We will add nourishment to water and feed it to her. She carries wisdom of plants on land and in sea alike. How did this happen?"

The ahja raised its wings and brought them down against its body with a whirl of air. "People on a very large skystone attacked her. I was so far away all I could do was watch. How could such an act be possible? Never in my furthest imaginings has such a thought occurred to me."

One of the elfin-kind said, "The wind carries urgent news. Crystals on a distant island, long silent, now speak. As impossible as it sounds, some guardians seek to control Creation rather than co-create with it. The controllers even built a black wall on the island to keep Earth spirits such as us out of places they do not want us to see. The controllers used knowledge of multidimensional walls to keep us out. They have secrets, an energy unknown to this planet before."

The giant bird said, "I have heard of this on the wind as well, but didn't understand it. In addition to plant wisdom, this guardian carries an ethereal feather of my kind. To attack her is to attack all ahja teratorn. These attackers have made themselves our enemies, and should we find them, we will attack them as they attacked her."

An elfin-kind finished dripping water from a leaf into Keela's motionless mouth. "We will do all we can to keep her alive, but if the attackers find her, I fear we cannot stop them."

The giant bird flapped its wings and rose into the air. "I will circle the area. If they come back it is I who will attack them. Their fate will be what they wished for her: death in the sea."

43. THE COUNCIL

∞

Most guardians trusted Shahten's solution to stop the regression of their children so completely, few pursued questions, and even fewer noticed Yawri and Zinn's absence. However, the astral meeting reconvened because other guardians were still reporting from their investigations.

Camic and Rhee were pleased. At each meeting, more and more guardians sought them out to hear firsthand about their experiences on the idyllic Crystal Island. Although they stood to the side of the central meeting, the circle around them grew.

Hetlin spoke to the larger assembly with her unhurried and deliberate voice. Her robust astral body looked strikingly similar to her physical one. Even the balmy-yellow tint of her skin showed in her astral form.

"We come from the northern lands of the far east to report what we learned." She gestured to include the astral guardian with her. He was tall with a strong-looking face. "You recall we travel into the deep caves of our lands. Speaking with crystal beings there, we hoped to learn the problems we saw were anomalies, readily explained." Her eyes swept the assembly. "They were not."

Some side conversations dimmed at her words, but most continued. She knew her report ran counter to the hopeful pulse of the guardians present, but she persisted. "The deep caves told us of crystals that have been taken from their homes in Earth without their agreement. First their wishes and finally their pleas and panicked cries were dismissed as they were removed from their crystal families."

Hetlin's words carried with the calm intensity of the eye of a hurricane, and only the light-hearted conversations near Rhee and Camic continued. "They took many kinds of crystals, but especially the citrines. Greatly disturbed and confused, we made our way further down into Earth. Earth listens to planets far and wide, so we hoped our limited ears misunderstood.

We went to the deep lakes of ancient, pristine water—Earth's eardrums. Each of us challenged ourselves to put aside our wish to hear what we wanted to so we could hear the reality instead."

The group around Rhee and Camic remained engrossed in hopeful conversation, ignoring Hetlin. She continued. "Through the sacred waters we heard the sound of Creation, our birth. We re-lived the Creator's gift of free will to us. Few heard it at the time but there was a scream during that birth. It sounded small in the streaming tumult of Life, but was there nonetheless. One being used its free will to disagree with the sending-forth. It chose to make the expansion of Creation wrong. So all of its efforts have been to destroy Creation, not expand it."

Rhee and Camic realized the guardians surrounding them were no longer listening to them, but to Hetlin. Their eyes widened when they heard Hetlin's last comment.

Camic shook his head and cried out, "What are you talking about? One of us wants to destroy Creation? What was in that ancient water?" He barked a quick laugh. A few of the guardians around him chuckled, but all others simply looked on.

Rhee raised both of his hands in the air. "Guardians, what is this nonsense? Does the report by one woman of one incident outweigh the reports of countless others? Our solution is at hand! How can your hope for the future be so frail? Every ethereal being was Created by Creator's sending-forth. Do you really think one of us could consider that wrong?"

Uncertainty froze faces. Gamon, known for his strong opinions in Yawri's community, said, "Let's hear everyone out. There are lots of points of view here."

A young woman guardian spoke. "Thank you, Gamon. Others have spoken here about communities that disappeared. One near ours is gone. They had many questions about Shahten's Way and we planned to meet with them. However, they disappeared before we could. Has this happened to others?"

Rhee shrieked, "So now its Shahten's fault when communities decide they need to move? Please! Guardians have always relocated when they felt their continued presence in one spot was starting to harm it."

"But *no* trace remained."

Camic's voice rang with disgust. "When your community moves it leaves a mess? When the rest of us move the point is to leave no trace." The quip landed well and several faces cracked smiles.

Pergaine, the elderly woman known for helping young guardians regain their knowledge of the stars, spoke. The strength of her voice surprised those who didn't know her. "We must hear from others who know of such disappearances. Yawri often visits our deep caves and told me of concerns similar to Hetlin's. A cave of citrines near the place where great numbers of mammoths used to roam has gone silent. He plans to visit it soon to find out why."

"Yawri?" Camic jeered. "Now you want us to listen to more tales from Yawri?"

"Yes!" a voice cracked like lightning. "There are going to be *a lot* more stories from Yawri!"

All faces turned to see its source. The astral forms of Yawri, Keela, Tisbero, and Zinn moved slowly and deliberately toward the assembly. Their astral bodies radiated a soft orange glow, a vibration of the light and sound that bodies used for healing.

They stopped at the edge of the gathering, but guardians made room for them to enter the circle. Yawri blazed, "We return, not with stories of comforting illusion, but what lies underneath them. Shahten's polished varnish hides great deceit." His eyes swept to Rhee and Camic. "He deceived us all." He scanned the assembly. "He mixes truth with lies to convince guardians to join his Way and expand Creation, while he hides his design to destroy it."

Keela took a step forward. Her astral body wavered because her physical body remained so weakened by her ordeal. Yawri unobtrusively ran his arm around her for support. Yet she stood tall, her voice authoritative. "I will relate all I experienced in time. However, I will start with my last encounter with Shahten's Way. It is only the most recent example of many." She leaned forward.

"When Yawri last met with you, he told you about huge SkySlabs lined with humans trained by Shahten in the use of citrines. He calls them 'menders' but they are trained to tear dimensions apart, not join them. They sent shafts of dark light from enslaved citrines into my skystone while I was over the sea. It was only because of caring sea creatures, the great birds, elfin-kind, and finally Yawri that I survived. My body recovers in safety, but"—she held up an astral arm, the meaning of its orange glow understood by all—"Shahten's plan to murder me almost succeeded."

Yawri hadn't bothered to tell her about his near miss with the ahja. The giant bird recognized Yawri's connection to Keela at the last instant and, rather than sending him into the sea, took him to her side.

He stood tall and his voice boomed. "Shahten tried to kill us, as he has killed others who don't follow him!"

Rhee shot his fists into the air in protest. "But how can this be? We saw the SkySlabs of menders and their citrines. Several guardians there explained how humans are trained to support Creation, not harm it!"

Tisbero, supported by Zinn, stepped forward. His was the palest of all, yet he spoke with fire. "You have heard how he tried to kill Yawri and Keela. Now you will hear how he killed all in my community."

"No!" voices gasped. The young female guardian who had spoken of the community that disappeared clutched her arms across her chest and squeezed her eyes shut.

"Two SkySlabs came and rained shafts of unmaking, dark light upon us. All traces of my community are gone. I was hurled into a deep crevice and left for dead. Like Keela, I would not be here if Earth divas had not cared for me."

"Your entire community killed? Why?" a guardian pleaded.

Tisbero bristled. "Because we questioned Shahten. We made investigations. Shahten declared us false guardians and lost souls that harm Creation. He instructed his menders to purge Earth of the false and lost in order to save it. He doesn't tell them the Creation he saves is only his own." His form wavered. Zinn, already close, took his hand in hers.

"All traces gone? Nothing remains?" The young woman who spoke about the missing community earlier asked.

Zinn rose on her feet. "All traces. Yawri and I circled the area many times. No trace remained. If we hadn't found some grass stained by a few packets of dye we would have never found Tisbero."

Tisbero straightened, recalling the courage of Twaque. "There is more, much more to report. Come to Yawri and Keela's community if you can. We took a recording crystal to Shahten's island. It will share all it experienced with you."

"Go there," Zinn challenged. "I did. If you have any doubt about what you have heard, the recording crystal will dispel it. Quickly."

"You can be sure I will!" Gamon declared.

Hetlin finished a brief discussion with her companions and spoke to the assembly once more. "We encourage those near the recording crystal to go, but the lands we tend are far away. We do not need to hear the record from the crystal to know what they report is true."

She considered Yawri, Keela, and Tisbero. Their fatigue was increasingly evident by the ebbing glow of their ethereal forms. "Before you arrived, we told the others what we learned from the ancient waters and crystal beings deep in the earth of our area. Adding your report to what we have heard here allows us to say more." She turned to the sea of faces.

"When there was little evidence, it was easy to deny. However, denial is a request to Creation for a more dramatic lesson. For us, we have no more denial. We face a force that chooses to destroy Creation, not expand it. We do not know how to halt its harm, but we must learn how." Even Camic and Rhee joined the silence.

Her steadfast voice continued. "We will return to the ancient, underground lakes in our region. As Yawri and Gamon know, caves connect with great crystal beings of this Earth and beyond. By Shahten's own admission, there are other planets where he has done his work. Work, we know now, to dominate and harm Life. There must be a way other planets have learned to counter it. We will go to the eardrums of deep Earth and listen for this wisdom."

"I was blind," a hollow voice pleaded. "The promise of lifetime after lifetime becoming ever more knowledgeable again was so great."

Yawri spoke to all. "We all wanted that promise. None of us knew the knowledge Shahten promised was how to destroy Creation. However, we are guardians, are we not? He seeks to cleave the individual from the All and to polarize and separate. We will learn how to remain individual while we strengthen it."

Heads nodded in agreement.

Zinn spoke with confidence, her astral body as lithe as her physical one. "Whatever it takes, we will learn how to stay One with Creation while others try to divide it."

Tisbero stood straight. "To treat this disease, we must learn what feeds it and how large it has grown."

Pergaine spoke and her voice carried across the assembly like thunder. "Hard choices lie ahead." More nods of agreement. "Let's return to our bodies to speak physically with others. Try to learn how Shahten's words convince guardians that they are expanding in Creation when the opposite is true. Is his work planet-wide or limited to certain areas? How many communities agree with his Way and how many communities do not?" She paused to consider her words. "Learn what you can about the communities that have disappeared. We need to know if they have simply relocated or were destroyed."

Guardians' conversations waxed and waned. Some wanted to confront Shahten immediately. Some feared what he might do and wanted to negotiate terms for limiting his influence to what it was now, on the Crystal Island. Some wanted to withdraw to remote places. Most wanted to learn how to halt this harm. All soon returned to their bodies, except two.

Rhee and Camic stood alone, their eyes shut, shaking their heads as if to clear away a bad dream.

44. SHAHTEN'S WAY

∞

The large Crystal Island community bustled with activity. Over a hundred skystones from communities following Shahten's Way rested on the few remaining open fields in the walled city. Dressed in the finery commensurate with their position, the summoned envoys gathered at the temple.

After the envoys conversed and shared news of their progress, Shahten was to answer questions and impart news of a major advancement. He strolled through the crowd, personally greeting representatives, which also gave him the opportunity to eavesdrop on conversations. Today he liked what he overheard and his smile of satisfaction broadened.

"The work is going extremely well," a priestly guardian from the far southwestern continent said. "The cross-bred humans are excellent workers. They are delighted to be a part of our civilization, safe from the dangers in the wild."

Another said, "Saving the young ones from their primitive villages has proven most effective. The younger the better. Ones we saved fifteen years ago are now excellent craftsmen."

The cascade of positive comments continued.

"We've trained ours to grow and prepare foods unheard of by them before. There's no way they want to go back to foraging for nuts and roots."

"Some of our humans tan leather, while others make clothes!" The woman raised her arm to show a well-fitted, supple leather sleeve.

"We brought bolts of the cloth our humans make. They spin woolly animal hair into fine fibers, and weave those into cloth. It's much better than the old flax-cloth we used to wear. We only use flax to make baskets and nets now."

"Do you know guardians of the old way still only wear flax clothing? You would think they'd be bored wearing such a simple tunic, and still only in that off-white color. It's only occurred to them to dye their sashes."

"And those are mostly shades of red or brown. Why they don't use more colors is a mystery to me. What about yellow, blue, green, or orange? I don't think they'll ever be creative enough for purple." Laughter spilled.

"At least they don't wear the untanned, hairy skins of animals like the wild humans do. The time of them both is coming to an end. Nothing can stop the improvements Shahten's wisdom brings. Earth evolves. Anyone with open eyes can see our results, and anyone in their right mind will join us."

Several envoys stood along an informal line where Shahten customarily strolled through the temple. However, their hopes of getting a personal greeting faded when the sober demeanor of his master captain carved a path through the assembly, Shahten immediately behind. Eyes narrowed while the envoys watched the captain escort Shahten past them to meet with two guardians standing a few steps up the stairway leading to the temple's high chamber.

"Rhee and Camic," one of the annoyed envoys announced. "New to the Way."

"They should be down here taking their turn with the rest of us."

"Who do they think they are, waiting for him on the stairs?" another said.

The envoys milled, expecting Shahten to return quickly. All had traveled long distances at his request. Half an hour passed while rumors covered every corner of the temple. Somehow, the upstarts Rhee and Camic had manipulated the master captain into taking Shahten to meet with them at the expense of long-standing and more essential emissaries.

The release of tension caused by his absence was palpable when the assembled envoys finally saw Shahten emerge from the sculpted archway of the high chamber. Steps full, arms swinging, he strode toward his traditional speaking place near the top of the stairs. He stopped short of the first step and looked down with a beneficent smile. His pillars of white marble stood like sentinels around the lower temple floor, which held over a hundred emissaries from around the globe.

He stood tall and his eyes wandered across their faces. Each waited in silent anticipation of his words—words that would dissolve any doubts about their choice to follow the Way.

"Thank you. Thank you for coming!" His voice rolled through the chamber. He raised his palms above his head in greeting; and he turned to the emissaries standing to the right, then down the center, and finally on the left side of the court. He clapped his hands together. "You are the Way!"

Voices thrummed in response. Many exclaimed, "The True Way is True Creation!"

He waited for the chorus of accolades to peak and raised his hands again after it started to subside. The chorus stilled. He took a step forward, but rather than descend the staircase he leaned over its top step and drew himself up. "My time to visit and walk with you today was cut short because some envoys brought urgent and hard news that required my immediate counsel. You know I would do the same for you. Rest assured, we already have a plan to address the crisis, which I will share with you later. I am sorry my time among you was cut short. It is my loss. However, I am with you now. Let us focus on the news you bring instead!"

He surveyed the spectrum of colored robes and cloaks filling the great hall and his smile returned. "The news *you* bring … is that there is nothing but good news from everyplace else!"

The crowd roared. Smiles greeted smiles in congratulations, all concern about Shahten's absence forgotten.

"During the time I walked and talked with you all, only reports of good fortune and prosperity filled our great hall. Immense communities of immeasurable beauty arise because wise guardians create monumentally beautiful things."

Shahten stared down, confident he would give the message they wanted to hear. "Look around you! See the glory of good works. Majestic stone, once hidden within the Earth, now reveals its splendor for all." He swept a hand from the marble floor, to carved alabaster, to sculptured columns and the wide, peaked roof.

"You brought gems and crystals, once sequestered in darkness, into the light of day! You help wild animals and plants evolve to better serve All. Humans, once limited to trudging across the land in search of food and safety, now live in our communities. They live safe in their homes of stone, free to learn and expand without concern for survival, while contributing to the prosperity of us all!"

Heads bobbed rapidly in agreement. "True Creation helps all Life truly become One. You today, and thousands of guardians in all the communities you represent, have not only taken Earth's bounty and brought it to light, you have reached back to the humans left in darkness and shared the light with them!"

The crowd thundered, but some voices rose over the noise.

"Humans must evolve with Earth!"

"All humans prosper through our etheric touch!"

Shahten spread his arms once again to encompass the temple. "All guardians know that Earth provided the humans so we could stay on this planet. The results of your first joining proved this. Now your touch of ethereal light on more humans opens them to experience ethereal realms unattainable to them before. Now, they also touch True Creation." He looked out over the smiling faces. "We are True Creators of the True One!"

Cheers rose and fell in a tide of accolades. When it started to recede, he continued. "Only you, true guardians of the Way, realized the reason our children were regressing was because they were disconnected from our common ancestor, the human. Only you had the courage to hear humans crying out for growth, and know was time for our seed to give back to the source from which our bodies came so all could be truly One again."

"What we're doing is righteous!" a woman in a dark blue robe exclaimed. "It is our duty to help Creation expand!"

A voice across the hall called out, "They beg to create children with us. Who are we to deny them?" Laughter echoed around the hall.

Shahten let the humor roll until it began to subside. "And they honor us in doing so."

All voices hushed.

"Today, humans and human beings live together in grace and splendor." He turned around and pointed to the high chamber's archway. A line of humans started to walk through it. Eyes went wide as they emerged from the upper chamber, a privilege normally only granted to high priests.

Male and female humans, beautiful and vibrant, walked with a grace even rare to guardians. Their clothing, made of thin layers of the finest wool, flowed with multiple hues of green, blue, and red. They walked as if on air toward Shahten.

A flute began to play. Not the sound of the one-holed reed children played, but one playing multiple tones. It took a moment for the emissaries to realize the sound came from several multi-holed flutes playing all at once, in harmony.

The humans came to a stop in front of Shahten, and to the shock of the envoys, it was he that gave a slight bow and stepped aside. Mere humans stood at the top of the staircase to the high chamber, the place of Shahten himself.

The humans started moving their heads, hands and feet all at the same time in the same way. They moved faster, but still the movement of one perfectly mirrored the movement of another. They shifted and twirled faster still. Yet, each remained synchronized with all the others as if a single organism. The envoys gazed spellbound as a whirl of color wove its tapestry around the stage.

All the flutes ended their last note, and at the same moment, fluid bodies stopped and stood motionless. The mouth of every envoy hung open.

A single, loud clap of Shahten's hands broke their trance. Shahten held his clasped hands together and, raising them above his head declared, "Grace and splendor!"

To a one, the envoys clapped their own hands together and raised them toward the sky. The reverberating sound of the hands slapping together was only slightly less than the sound of over a hundred voices echoing, "Grace and splendor!"

The humans turned and exited back through the archway and Shahten returned to center stage. His fingers formed a steeple over his waist while he watched the amazed emissaries exclaim their surprise.

Light streamed through an opening in the roof and fell on Shahten's silver cloak. The timing of the sun crossing the sky could not have been more perfect. The cloak sparkled and glinted. "Thank you. Thank you. Your actions made such progress possible. The proof of the Way is before you.

"Thanks to your renewed connection, the separation between humans and human beings becomes less and less. Thanks to you, within a few generations, all humans will be replaced by human beings. Your generosity humbles me."

Cheers echoed down from the peaked roof and amplified the sound, which caused more cheering. Shahten raised a hand and the celebration quieted. His voice poured down the staircase, thick and sweet.

"Since we are of one mind nothing stands in our way. However, you know some lost guardians remain attached to the old Way. News of their plans to harm True Creation was what caused my absence earlier today."

"Who are they to harm True Creation?" voices demanded.

"What plans?"

"How?"

"They plan to harm Creation? Why?"

Shahten bowed his head, then raised it to peruse the sea of faces. "I confided to you earlier that we are developing a plan to stop their harm. I also agreed to share everything about this hard report with you. I will do so now." His eyes lingered on a guardian wearing an emerald-green embroidered robe. "We all know how important it is to act on facts instead of hearsay."

He straightened to his towering, full height, "There are a few ignorant and unfortunately arrogant false guardians who live in the lands of the ethereal heart center of the planet. For those of you who have not been there, it's the landmass bridging the jungle continent of creative essence to its south and the largest continent with other centers to its north."

The guardian in the purple robe returned Shahten's glance and spoke so all could hear. "Isn't the heart center where, eons ago, two guardians spread false rumors about others? Are they involved? If it's them, they have a long reputation for acting on hearsay rather than facts."

Shahten watched emissaries who remembered Yawri and Keela whisper to those around them, passing on their names along with the fictitious story.

"It may well be the same two, but ravings are ravings no matter their source. The fact is there are lost guardians who seek to malign the Way. Our actions are ruled by our belief in True Creation. Theirs are ruled by fear."

Another guardian asked, "How can they possibly think True Creation is not wise? The success of the new Way compared to the old is apparent to all who can see."

Heads nodded in agreement, and a woman in a scarlet priest's robe said, "Anyone controlled by fear only sees what they are afraid of."

Another added, "Shahten was right when he said they do not hear words that counter what they want to believe. He also said those convinced they are right have no need for questions."

"They don't question themselves! Only us!" Voices began to cascade around the temple.

"Humans flock to us seeking to learn the divine, and we share it. No human is asking to learn anything from a lost guardian. The lost ones make us wrong in their minds because they are afraid to know their own failure."

"How rigid they are to forbid humans our knowledge of Creation."

"It would be irresponsible not to use all we've learned to help them flourish!"

Shahten took a small step forward so the shaft of sunlight from the roof continued to fall on his cloak. "These lost guardians, these saboteurs, seek to destroy the Way of True Creation. I have tried—we have tried—to talk to them. They refuse to listen because they would have to acknowledge that we are advancing Creation of the One and they are not."

A red-robed emissary cried out, "You said you are developing a plan to stop their harm. How can we help?"

Shahten looked down upon the earnest faces. Some were wide-eyed with zeal. In a casual gesture, he pointed to eight priests gathered below and summoned them to him. The fervor of the crowd was at such a pitch no one noticed the eight stepping forward were also the ones who had provided the most supportive comments during Shahten's report.

As they walked up the stairs toward him he railed, "Now more than ever it is critical for all of our communities to realize how indispensable they are to True Creation. There are nine key ethereal-energy centers on Earth. Each of these guardians lives near one of them. So, including myself, we have communities near all nine. We will protect this planet's ethereal energy centers from the lost ones, but what of our humans? We cannot protect them without you."

Voices stormed.

"We will help!"

"We must stop the lost guardians' attack on Earth!"

"Name what you need and it is yours!"

Shahten stood, flanked by his chosen, four on each side. He knew all were steadfast in their support. Four of them, plus his master captain, had accompanied him when he first traveled to this life-rich planet. The other four added their commitment to him soon after. By strictly following his advice, they'd methodically convinced thousands to support the True Way.

He leaned forward and said, "You have seen proof of the progress humans can make under our guidance in your own communities—and here today." He gestured to the sculpted arch behind him. "You see how your gift of yourself has allowed them to evolve. Such is the way of true guardians!"

The chorus of the crowd rang in fervor, yet Shahten's voice carried over it. "These lost and false guardians would send this grace and splendor back to jungle!"

"No!" voices cried in alarm. "No!"

He scanned the faces. All zealots now, soon becoming a rabid mob.

Excellent.

"I only ask for one thing."

"Name it! Name it! Name it!" poured the chant from the great hall.

Shahten leaned forward, as though he was about to fly off the top step. "The threat is far and wide. Every ethereal-energy center of Earth is at risk. We will see that the centers are protected." He spread both arms out to indicate the splendid guardians standing next to him. "However, the lost-guardians also think our humans should never have left caves. You must protect the humans."

Rhee and Camic stood at the rear of the great hall and when Shahten spread his arms Rhee jumped on the square base of a column and yelled above the din, "We can protect many humans but not all! Is it possible to teach them how to protect themselves?"

Camic joined him and exclaimed, "From what we saw today, Shahten is a master of their training. Shahten," he shrieked, "will you train humans to protect themselves?"

"Shahten's experience teaching humans is far beyond any of ours!" Rhee followed.

"Teach them to protect themselves!" resounded through the temple with greater volume than seemed possible from the hundred present.

Shahten bowed, waited for the crowd to return to a low rumble, and stood with his head high and shoulders back.

"Very well," he conceded. "I will have my master captain make sure the humans are trained well and soon. However, we can only teach those you send. You must decide how many to send here to learn to protect themselves from annihilation by the lost ones."

"We will send them!" Some guardians grabbed the hands of those nearby in relief. Some closed their eyes and nodded thanks. The sound of breath suddenly exhaled was audible.

Shahten casually shifted his silver robe and its folds blazed in the shaft of sunlight. "I will make sure their training here is complete. Tell all the humans you can the truth. If they win, these lost guardians will send the humans back to caves of darkness and hunger. Humans will never know the luxurious foods, the glowing crystals, or safety for their homes ever again. Send all the humans that are able so we can train them to defend themselves."

"Thank you, Shahten!" echoed from the roof.

He raised his hands into the air and dropped them, signaling the end of the event. "We have come too far to have our work undone by those who refuse to believe the truth. They are lost to the Way, but we embrace it. They seek to undo us, but there is no doubt of our success. Travel well, guardians of the True Way! Send your humans. Prosperity for all!"

Without prelude, flutes suddenly played from behind every column of the great hall. The musicians walked around them, resplendent in fitted wool clothing of dark blue and green. The instruments were long, and nimble fingers rose and fell over their six holes so quickly it was hard to tell which movement made what sound.

Envoys proceeded to exit in an orderly and exuberant parade. The sounds of the flutes followed them out as if welded to their shadows. Any secret doubts the envoys might have brought lay crumbled and forgotten under the massive weight of Shahten's certainty. They would deliver the message to their communities. If humans could dance as they did today and play complex instruments with such glorious sound and harmony, the proof of the True Way was indisputable. The idea of leaving them in caves when they were capable of such works was insufferable. The lost guardians who wanted to stop the Way were heartless. It was they who must be stopped.

Shahten looked on with a distant, unfocused smile. He gave a crisp nod, turned, and walked toward the arch of the high chamber. Without looking back, he murmured, "Follow me," to the eight resplendent guardians summoned to the stage.

Eyes down, they trailed after him into the chamber. The master captain slid a panel home, closing the arched entrance with a sharp *thud*. Its glowing crystals shone with a warm light as the captain made a circuit of the ornate chamber, turned to Shahten, and crossed his arms over his chest.

Only then did Shahten speak.

"We meet in private because, taken out of context, what we speak of would only confuse our envoys. In addition to the protection of the thick stone walls of this room, the temple priests know that when I meet here a sacred session of the high chamber is invoked. They will protect their sovereign with their lives."

"As would we." One of the two priests spoke the thought of all.

Shahten continued. "Please thank the envoys you commissioned for the comments they made during the event. They were well placed, as were yours."

"We expect no less of them or ourselves," another said.

Shahten's riveting stare swept the circle of his priestly companions. "Emissaries who came with questions were some of the first to approach the master captain and ask how quickly they could send their humans." He raised a hand and beckoned the captain with a finger. The captain joined the circle without a word, his rightful place in it known to all.

Shahten's silver cloak swirled. "The lost guardians have proven they will stop at nothing to poison minds against the True Way. Unfortunately, the reports from two junior captains deceived us into thinking Yawri, Keela, and Tisbero were dead. If not for today's report from our two recent converts this deceit would still be hidden.

Our efforts to convert Rhee and Camic to join us were well spent. It didn't take a lot of convincing before they understood the lost guardians' true motivation. Yawri and Keela never forgot the loss of credibility they suffered when I spoke the truth about their healing of that emerald valley. After our converts understood the extremes those two would go to discredit me in retaliation, they held nothing but disgust toward them. Camic and Rhee are eager to divulge any plans the lost ones have."

Shahten glanced at the master captain. "Make sure they have private lodging and the company of the same two human females who served them last time. With emissaries filling our city beyond capacity, finding suitable private lodging may be difficult. Evicting emissaries in deference to new converts could make them less inclined to distribute our message. Yet we must assure the loyalty of these two minions endures."

"I have already found suitable lodging, my lord," said the master captain. Shahten raised an eyebrow. "The two females are already with them in my domicile, and are feeding them quince fruit and pomegranate juice."

Shahten smiled. "It is child's play to use their arrogant ignorance against them. They know nothing about the need of a human body to procreate. They think the driving force to mate doesn't apply to them because they are from ethereal realms. But millions of years of evolution drive that need. We're helping hapless guardians learn about something that hasn't even occurred to them."

The glowing crystals of the chamber flickered, so slightly Shahten was the only one that noticed. Momentarily distracted by it he said, "Master captain, check with High Priest Laric to make sure Generator is functioning as it should. We will need a lot from it soon, and I don't want any surprises."

He clasped his hands together over his silky, silver sash and continued. "Thanks to our patience, we have discreetly converted communities ready for the True Way while concealing the unmaking of communities that never would be. However, the time of patience is over.

"Although we may have been able to discredit the hearsay from Yawri, Keela, and Tisbero, we cannot do the same for a recording crystal. More and more are swayed because of it, and the longer we wait the more substantial the disbelieving herd will become. While our emissaries are busy sending us their humans and our captain sees to their training, we will prepare to meet the lost guardians when they assemble at the ethereal centers of Earth. After they amass, we will use our newly trained and motivated humans to unmake them all at once."

The master captain automatically caressed the collar of his red leather tunic. "It will be done, Shahten. We give them the gift of rebirth in bodies free of the memories binding them to old ways." Catching himself, he returned his hand to his side.

Shahten turned to him. "Make sure our new menders know the lost guardians want to send humans back to a life of struggle and poverty. This is as important as teaching them how to fire an unmaking crystal or ride a SkySlab without falling off. They must be motivated to fight to their last breath."

"It will be done."

A priest in a dark-blue robe with golden lining asked, "Why should they need to fight to their death? The lost guardians we have unmade to date either stood dumber than a mud brick or ran screaming in hysteria into a shaft of dark light. Not a single mender has been lost."

Shahten eyed the priest with a penetrating gaze and his tongue flickered across his lips. "There has been one exception. The master captain saw Tisbero use an unmaking crystal. True, he is the only one to try it out of the thousands we have unmade, but some menders were lost. Best not to allow a single example to multiply. We will move too quickly for other lost guardians to adopt the practice, but we will also make sure the trainees are properly motivated to fight to the death in case others try it."

Sobered by the example, no one spoke. Shahten said simply, "It was bound to happen sooner or later. Thanks to our thoroughness, it was later. All the reason to move quickly now." Shahten only glanced at the master captain but his thoughts about the mistake the junior captains made reporting the deaths were clear.

"Each of you will scout your energy center to make sure your attack is unseen. Allow no witnesses. Unmake everything: animals, plants, and lost guardians alike. Even though the area we unmake is small compared to the size of an ethereal center, it will be sufficient to assure the center is opened to the Way."

Another of Shahten's chosen started to speak, paused, and finally said, "The minds of our humans are simple. Even with the motivation we're providing I'm not sure how they will perform. We currently have one guardian of the Way piloting each SkySlab. Should we enlist other envoys to join them?"

Shahten addressed them all. "I agree the humans are weak-minded. The master captain will assure they are well conditioned to follow orders of their captain. By the time we are done with them the only question they'll have is 'Where do I shoot?'

Few true guardians have the ability to participate in such a large unmaking. All others will slow us down with questions we don't have time to answer. Remember, we are already taking every available human our communities can spare to 'teach them to protect themselves.' Our emissaries will be quite busy operating their communities without them. Best not to distract them from it." He added with a smile, "Think of the outrage if they ran out of grapes."

"Or pomegranate juice," said another.

The master captain said, "We increased production of the poppy tea as you requested."

"Yes. Make sure all of our envoys leave with a good supply of tea. We had a bumper crop and wish to share our bounty."

A mixture of smile and smirk painted every face.

"And master captain? Two junior captains deceived us with their false reports. The first about the death of Yawri and the second about Tisbero, and Keela. Their deceit might have been our ruin. Have menders unmake both of them. Slowly. The extra trauma will help assure the separation between the Earth soul and etheric soul of their next body is complete. Hopefully, they will be reborn without any memory of their past so they can be taught what true allegiance means." Shahten's smile was beneficent. "In fact, unmake them in front of our other captains."

The master captain smiled. "It will be done." He stroked the leather collar of his crimson tunic and asked, "When we attack the lost guardians at each energy center, do you wish our SkySlabs evenly distributed at each?"

Shahten's tongue traced across his lips. "No. Earth can survive damage to most of its energy centers, but its ethereal heart center provides the connection to caring Creation. Sever the ethereal heart center from the others and we'll have control. Caring for Creation is what keeps guardians vulnerable. When we show them the strength of control, all but the truly lost will join us. Place a quarter of our SkySlabs at that center. You and I will lead that attack."

"It will be done."

"Yes. Once and for all, the lost guardians will be unmade. This planet is ours."

45. PROTECTION

∞

Zinn stayed to tend to Tisbero and Keela while Yawri went to learn more. He raced up the broad river valley toward Murann. The scars on his skystone were deep but it sped on in spite of them.

Questions whirled in his mind.

Shahten mixes lies and truth to tell people what they want to hear. Relieved by his words of promise, many joined him. How many communities were destroyed because they did not?

The river thinned and finally branched into two main streams. Yawri followed the larger.

Other planets have survived.

After one banking turn, the red trees formed a dense canopy over the stream's earthen banks. Yawri continued to dash along its winding, shadowed path.

After seeing Murann, I've got go to the cave of citrines and find out why it's gone silent.

The branches closed overhead, so he shot upward and skimmed spires until he saw the spring-fed pond near Murann. He passed over its calm water and slowed. Lily pads crowned with lotus blossoms hugged its surface.

Relieved to see it undisturbed, he descended, stopped, and focused on a water lily. Its white blossom floated on a round island of green in the sparkling pond.

His skystone moved slowly toward the bank and over plants holding small, blue flowers. Coming to a gentle stop above verdant fiddle ferns, he stepped off his skystone and stood still. The sounds of the forest flowed around and through him, sweet and alive.

He took careful, brisk steps toward Murann and stopped next to his massive trunk. Thin, vertical strips of reddish-grey bark ran from his roots to the sky.

The tree being spoke evenly. "In all the times you've come, this is the first time you didn't stop your skystone suddenly and have it bob up and down."

Yawri's gaze fell upon the place where the human hunters had presented him with a dead lemur. He shook his head.

"I come with disturbing news." His words tumbled out. "There is an island. It's called Crystal Island, although its only native crystal is columnar basalt.

"Guardians there are taking quartz crystal to it without even asking.

"They're using knowledge of Creation to make half-human creatures.

"They're using citrines that Earth made to connect dimensions to separate them instead.

"Shahten tried to kill us because we disagree with his Way. Tisbero's community ... is gone." Yawri placed a hand on Murann's bark and looked down at his feet.

"I know."

Yawri leaned back. "You know?"

"A large crystal family on that island is telling the wind and all crystals what happened. It tells of what you spoke and more, including three guardians who healed and freed it."

Yawri dropped his hands to his sides. "You know."

"It won't be long before all trees and crystals know about it too, and that you, Tisbero, and Keela survived."

"We survived because that crystal family, called Generator, told me how." Yawri placed his forehead against the tree, his voice a whisper. "How could this happen?"

"Beings are free to go and grow in the way they choose," Murann answered.

Yawri straightened. "True enough for human beings, but what happened to the humans? They're the ones unleashing the unmaking."

Murann's branches waved slowly, imparting their own message to the wind. "Remember what Kunuta experienced when your ethereal dimensions touched his?"

"It overwhelmed him for a while. He became lost in time, swirling in an ethereal ocean with no up or down, beginning or end."

"Why didn't he remain lost?"

Yawri stated the obvious. "Because I helped him reconnect to his home."

"Could Kunuta have found the way back to himself otherwise?"

"I don't see how."

"What if you'd chosen not to help him and left him disconnected from his source?"

370

Yawri flinched and his eyes narrowed. "He would have stayed lost, but it was never a question. I agreed to do no harm."

"If those human menders were still One with Earth, do you think they could use crystals made to help connect dimensions tear them apart?"

Yawri grimaced and cleared his throat. "Well, no."

"You saw what happens when crystals are possessed. First they were traumatized, taken from their home, then isolated further so they would be dependent on outside sources of essence to survive. They became enslaved. The human 'menders' are the same, disconnected from their source."

"By guardians," Yawri added sadly. "They were enslaved by guardians. How can any guardian think an aspect of Creation belongs to them instead of itself?"

"Some have chosen to make the sending-forth wrong, and feel justified to collapse it. We thrive on diversity to expand the One. They seek to eliminate it. If we don't learn how to counter this harm, we will be its next victim."

Murann's branches swayed. A cone fell into the pond with a *plop*. Sunlight dashed through shifting canopy and danced with dragonflies flying over it. One alighted on a lily pad and the other on its flower. Their wings synchronized in a dreamy, restful motion.

Murann stilled and said, "This is not the first planet to suffer this learning. Trees, crystals, deep lakes and the winds are all listening to the universe. Those who disagree with Shahten's Way must stay alive so they can keep Life alive."

Yawri shook his head. "How can we stay alive? Shahten is killing whole communities."

"You survived the attack of unmaking because Generator told you how."

"Escaping Shahten's island, yes. Its advice saved my life. Generator said to hold a conscious crystal in my hands and blend with it in the same energy I use to heal land. I didn't hold a crystal but Red, the quartz on the skystone and I were all blended in Life as we flew. Even with that, we were almost killed. Tisbero almost died as well, and the crystal he held had a terrible death."

"But a conscious one. It will return with All-that-is."

"It exploded into a thousand shards."

"To protect Tisbero and send him across the crevice, where he might have a chance to live. It worked. Only the crystal's body shattered. Tisbero lived and the crystal's spirit remained whole. There is nothing wrong with dying. It's who you are when you die that matters."

Yawri leaned toward Murann. "Yes. Those who disagree with Shahten's Way need to stay alive, but how? They'd need crystals willing to die like Tisbero's. Even if they had them they'd still need to know how to use them."

Murann was quiet a long moment. A winged sprite of the elfin-kind dove toward a bumblebee and chased it away from an iridescent blue flower. The tree being finally spoke. "You plan to go to the cave of citrines and find out why it's gone silent, correct?

Well, yes but ... how did you know that?"

"I find great predictability in what others consider your spontaneity. Of course you'd go."

Yawri felt the ethereal diamond within him. "I'm going. Drawn to go, actually."

Murann said, "Generator is releasing information to the wind, and I learned why that cave has been silent. Shahten listens for the song that citrine caves make and follows it to find them. He rips the crystals out of their homes and enslaves them. The remaining caves went silent to avoid detection. The cave you're called too chooses to help keep those who disagree with Shahten's Way alive."

Yawri swallowed hard, recalling the recording crystal's images of Tisbero's crystal exploding. "Even if it might mean their death?"

"They choose to die in Life rather than murder. It's your choice to help them do this or not."

Yawri stiffened. "Of course I will."

"Go to the cave. The crystals will consciously detach themselves from their home, and with your soul light to help with gravity, they will move to your skystone. As you did with Tisbero and Keela, teach other guardians how to work with them to return unmaking. They will tell you of other caves that wish to help free their enslaved kin as well.

"When they return the unmaking, it will give the enslaved crystals that sent it a choice in how to die. They can fracture themselves to return whole or chose to continue sending murder. Either way, the guardian helping the cave's crystals return the unmaking will remain alive. Unless ..." Murann paused.

"Unless?"

"Unless they are overwhelmed like Tisbero's crystal was, or if the guardian holding it loses connection to All. If a guardian thinks they are better than their attackers not even a citrine can save them."

Yawri bowed his head. He gazed, unfocused, through the sprites darting between the fiddle ferns and moss carpeting the ground. "That's the hard part to teach."

"Yes, but you and your friends have shown you know how to disagree without disconnection. If the guardians holding the crystals do the same, the unmaking can be returned. Complete honesty with self is the key. Judgment is disconnection. Division is division. If guardians succumb to it, they will experience the disconnection themselves."

Yawri touched the sash around his head. It was clean but remained stained, and because an unmaking beam had cut though a trailing end, it was shorter than it originally was. Keela had mended the end but didn't want it back. He decided to keep wearing it.

Murann noticed his touch. "That sash is Keela's, right? I'd have never thought of wrapping a sash around your head. Evidently her embroidery looks good on anything."

Yawri managed a small grin. "It was her favorite. She told me she likes green garnets, so I'll find her one. Some of them are even better than citrines at keeping dimensions open. "

Yawri stared at the shimmering pond. A winged sprite hovered over a lotus plant, seemingly in conversation with a dragonfly. They darted off together and flew into a hole in the end of a moss-covered log.

"Keela said the lotus is one of the few plants which have their roots in the ground, their stems immersed in water, and their leaves growing in air. She says they're experts at integrating physical and ethereal realms."

"There is a lot to learn from pond plants."

A breeze came and rippled the crystal-clear water of the pond, then suddenly stilled. Every molecule around them felt fixed in place. "What just happened?" Yawri said below a whisper.

The forest remained quiet. Yawri held his breath.

Leaves twirled without the wind. Messages, Yawri knew, were being sent and received. He waited. No dragonflies, butterflies, or divas of any kind flew.

Murann finally spoke, his voice somber and firm.

"Something traumatic has occurred. The nine main ethereal energy centers of Earth have been hurt by unmaking beams."

Yawri's neck corded and his nostrils flared. "What? Impossible!"

It's on the wind. Shahten's menders attacked Earth's energy centers. All nine were harmed enough to draw attention but not enough to stop their function. The question is why. In addition, Generator reports many humans and enslaved citrines have arrived on the island. If guardians are not prepared in time, I fear they will be murdered like the communities before them, and even the planet's energy centers could be unmade."

46. CHOICES

∞

Anxious guardians gathered in the dream world at their usual astral meeting place while their fatigued human bodies slept. It was obvious no one had found anything good during their physical explorations to mention. Report after report only extended the dire news.

The number of unmentored humans from Crystal Island was increasing exponentially. Their untimely union with the ethereal realms by Shahten's followers unhinged their connection to the ethereal centers of Earth and planetary co-creation. Information from the ethereal realms made them increasingly capable and creative, but separated from their source, they lacked the understanding for its use.

Guardians reported over twenty more missing communities. However, even that news paled in contrast to urgent reports about harm to the ethereal centers of Earth.

Gamon was fervent. "Enough reports! When do we leave to heal the centers?"

A guardian from the far northwest said, "But from what? Since the damage happened at the same time at each one, a powerful surge of energy from Earth itself must have caused it. How do we heal what a planet does to itself?"

"How about by going and asking?" Gamon exploded.

A woman from the great desert continent spoke. "We've all heard of human bodies instantly burned to ashes if an ethereal being accidentally surges with too much energy. Perhaps the planet had a power surge of some kind. In any event, it will take a large number of guardians to help bring these energy centers back into balance."

A guardian from the emerald jungle continent added, "Our bodies are Earth's body. It is our responsibility to keep Earth's body in balance as we do our own."

"The sooner the better!" said another. "The centers all became unbalanced in the same moment. I think we'll need to heal them all at the same moment as well."

"I agree!" chimed another.

"What if the centers surge again? The circle of damage could become so big we won't be able to help Earth at all."

Gamon proclaimed, "That makes sense. They all surged at the same time, so simultaneous healing would work best. Can everyone get to the ethereal center of their land on the next full moon?"

Keela and Tisbero were not yet completely healed from their ordeal, and Zinn, intent on their full recovery, wanted to make sure they could leave their bodies safely. Their astral forms were vaporous clouds compared to the other astral bodies. However, hearing Gamon's statement, Zinn manifested fully and bounded into the discussion.

"Gamon, you call for a decision before all have spoken. I agree we must attend to Earth's ethereal centers, but I do not agree with the few here deciding for the many. Keela and Tisbero are still recovering, but will fully manifest here soon." She surveyed the assembly. "Where is Hetlin? And Yawri? Others are missing, too."

The astral bodies of Keela and Tisbero coalesced. Even though still recovering, Tisbero flared, "We are here now. We need to wait for others as well. We always listen to all before making decisions."

Gamon's face soured but he didn't argue. "Fine, let's talk." To a companion he grumbled, "Too bad we didn't decide before they got here. If talk could heal the Earth, we'd have healed several planets by now."

A guardian from the north spoke, but her whole form drooped. "We hoped to learn otherwise, but three communities have disappeared, same as Tisbero's, without a trace. They did not relocate. They are gone."

"Three more communities! Will there be no end?" another cried.

The guardian from the north raised her head and continued, "All three villages questioned the devotees of Shahten."

A guardian near her said, "Devotees. Yes, that's what they've become. We don't know how many have joined Shahten's Way. We do know their numbers are many and are increasing. We traveled to a community known to support 'the Way,' as they call it. They are convinced Shahten is right. They believe that to restore their ability to speak across the expanding dimensions of Earth, they do not need to become more physical, the humans need to become more ethereal."

Another jumped in. "But the recording crystal shows Shahten is responsible for killing guardians and enslaving Life. How can they follow him?"

A woman from the large northwestern continent far across the ocean spoke. "From the recording crystal, we also know how he skillfully twists truth and lies to placate desperation. I know I was so relieved by his answers that I didn't want to question him, either. Fortunately for me the reports allowed my need for honesty to outweigh my wish for comfort."

Keela's astral form still lacked its full vitality but her voice was steady. "How could any of us recognize something we didn't know existed? Shahten skillfully distracts guardians from their questions by responding with questions of his own. We saw how he engages his followers in 'important' work, isolating them from other guardians; how he consoles them with comforts, finery, and accolades. The number of guardians who actually knew about his deceit were very few. Even the priests we met did not know its extent."

Gamon cut in, his conviction to quickly heal the ethereal centers of Earth undeterred. "Yes, Shahten fooled many into following him. However, the truth will soon be known by all. Even his devotees will leave him. The urgent problem now is to heal Earth's ethereal centers. That's the priority."

"I agree," added another. "The ethereal spheres of our bodies have constant interaction with those of the planet. Our bodies need information from Earth for conscious co-creation. If its centers are not in balance, ours will not remain in balance either. "

Another guardian rallied support. "Plus, an imbalance of Earth's centers will soon harm the ethereal spheres of more than humans! All Life on the planet relies on them."

A guardian next to Gamon stepped forward. "We need to go to them. They power-surged once. Why couldn't it happen again?"

"I know why!" Everyone turned to see who spoke. No one even considered standing in Yawri's way while he walked to the center of the gathering with long, determined strides. "You speak of urgency. I agree. The urgency to deliver this report brings me to the center of our circle."

The stout, astral form of Hetlin suddenly appeared, along with two others from her large community. "Hetlin!" Yawri greeted. "Very good to see you. I'm about to share what the trees and citrine caves learned about the attack on Earth's energy centers."

Guardians cried, "Attack? What attack?"

Hetlin strode toward Yawri. "Very good to see you, and all here! I apologize for our late arrival. We have emerged from speaking with great subterranean lakes. I will share what the eardrums of Earth heard from the universe about what is upon our planet." Guardians parted wordlessly as she strode to the center of the gathering to stand with Yawri.

He surveyed the faces. All were familiar, most Yawri had known for eons. "Many of you came to our community to witness the report from the recording crystal. All that came know it confirms the reports from many guardians." He looked at Keela, Tisbero, and Zinn. Heads bobbed in acknowledgment.

Yawri continued. "We have all learned that Shahten mixes truth with lies to trick us into believing him. We all know the wind uses no such tricks. It reports all it touches, without filter, and the trees and crystal caves listen without filter. What they report is more than alarming, it is foreboding beyond measure."

No one moved. Each guardian focused in order to best hear.

"Their report is this: The nine ethereal centers were harmed at the same time, in the same way, but not because of some power surge. Shahten coordinated attacks to make us think that."

Gamon jerked to attention. "How? How could any force other than Earth itself do this? The centers are scattered across continents around the globe. To ask us to believe such simultaneous, identical harm is possible by Shahten's minions is unreasonable."

Tisbero flamed, "These are unreasonable times. Do you believe the wind, trees, and crystals are in error?"

Another spoke, burning with distress. "If it was intentional, as they report, it only increases the need for us to go and heal them now. The likelihood of Shahten's followers returning to do more harm before we can heal them is much greater than Earth releasing a mistaken power surge a second time. If they attack again the harm might be too great for us to heal!"

Keela stepped forward, "Listen! We listen to all before deciding anything!"

Another retorted, "I have listened, and I don't think it's possible for anything other than Earth to have done this. Power surges have burned bodies in a flash. Accidents happen. We need to help Earth rebalance so it doesn't happen again."

Yawri stood amazed.

All this evidence and they're still in denial.

He roared, "Who here has been targeted by shafts of unmaking and is still alive?" His eyes probed a hundred faces.

Zinn, never one to hold back, answered, "Tisbero, Keela, and Yawri. All the others are dead." Her usual impish smile was gone. "If you want to be told what you wish to hear instead of honest reports, you're at the wrong meeting!" Her words carried the force of an anvil dropped on stone. The audience stilled.

Yawri's thick eyebrows furrowed. His voice turned to iron. "Do you think we are the only ones who meet on the astral? The attacks were coordinated the same way." Hetlin's dark-brown eyes watched the sea of faces while Yawri continued. "Representatives from every continent attend our astral meetings. It's the same for Shahten. He sent nine SkySlabs, each filled with enslaved humans and their citrines, to attack the nine ethereal centers at the same time. I have learned that he planned to damage them in a way that would make us think Earth mistakenly harmed itself. He succeeded."

"But why? What reason could there be for such a complex undertaking?" said another.

Tisbero flared. "Why does he destroy communities that question him? We question him. It would make sense that he's setting a trap for us."

Yawri swept the assembly and his baritone voice resounded, "His followers are convinced we are false guardians that have corrupted Earth's ethereal centers beyond repair. They are convinced we must be unmade so we can begin anew, under Shahten.

"I believe he expected us to interpret what happened to the centers just as we have, then rush to concentrate ourselves at each one. The number of his SkySlabs with enslaved humans and unmaking crystals is increasing. Concentrated at the centers, he could kill all of us, like all the communities he's destroyed, and get control of the planet by destroying its ethereal centers in the process."

Shock brought groans, then silence.

"But why?" a plaintive voice asked.

Keela spoke in a light yet authoritative tone. "Because he believes our Creation was a mistake. That the best way to become One is to return to what existed before it. His followers are convinced we must be unmade so we can begin anew, without memory. However, if Earth's centers remain alive we could relearn our way back to ourselves. His followers are told our unmaking is needed so our next bodies will be receptive to following the Way. Given that, how could they let Earth's ethereal centers live?"

A woman from the northern continent said, "The depth of our plight is beyond pain. It is beyond sorrow. This disease has been growing for eons. Signs were there, but I refused to believe them. I didn't want to believe them. Now I learn that all guardians who question Shahten's Way are either murdered … or will be."

47. DECISION

∞

Only Hetlin saw Yawri's subtle nod. Her penetrating, dark eyes scanned the assembly. When she spoke, her voice resonated with the elements of Earth.

"We agreed to report what we learned." She gestured to include two guardians standing at either side of the meeting. All three had eyes that angled upward slightly, flowing black hair and strong cheekbones. She turned back to the group. "There is hope."

Yawri moved slowly out of the center of the circle.

Hetlin's voice rang on, "We tend the far eastern land, and it has many caves. We went to three deep caverns, which hold ancient waters and serve as the great eardrums of Earth. We asked each if they knew of planets in the universe with knowledge of what we experience here now."

Hetlin pulled the thoughts from the deep, primordial lakes into words. "Many worlds have experienced this intentional harm. Most planets were left a shadow of their former selves, or destroyed. Some, however, not only lived but gained so much wisdom they thrive. We asked to learn from them."

"Intentional harm? Why would any ethereal being come here to do intentional harm?" a guardian agonized.

Hetlin took a breath and released it slowly. "The sound of vitality from this living jewel drew us from across Creation because we wished to learn how to expand with it. That same sound of vitality attracted those who wish to silence it."

The guardians stood unmoving, overwhelmed.

Zinn finally asked, "You said some planets lived to thrive again. How?"

Hetlin looked at her two companions for a long moment. Each remembered how hard it was for them when they first heard Earth's report. Feeling the support of their steady gaze, she went on. "The surviving planets did so by hiding their most vital parts. It was similar to what a bear does when it hibernates through winter so it can reawaken in the spring. The communication from planets that lived is clear. To live, Earth must sleep."

Murmurs rolled in a wave of confusion across the assembly. One wondered, "Sleep, while a murderer destroys your home?"

The murmurs grew to a rumble.

Hetlin's eyes flicked across the faces. Most were agitated. She noticed, however, that Yawri's was calm even though he was speaking with Gamon.

She continued with the inescapable tone of a glacier moving down a valley. "Earth cannot remain so sensitive, so vital, and stay healthy through a siege of murder upon it. It would go dark, just as any loving child would go dark from lashes of constant cruelty. Its only hope to remain healthy is to sleep now, so, like the bear, it can reawaken after this disease has run its course. To survive, the lush spectrum and dimensions of Life here must hibernate. Earth's knowledge and pure life force must be hidden."

Heads shook in confusion. Everyone spoke at once.

"Hear me out!" she beckoned and attention returned. "If Earth goes into hibernation, there will be less Life to harm. Earth knows how to sleep through cold winters or dry summers. However, no planet that has lived through this assault has done it alone. It makes a request of us."

"This is all too much!" someone wailed. "I have no knowledge of how to help with this!"

Hetlin stood resolute. "None of us do. However, Creator enables Creation. Souls who have gained wisdom from learning of this evil on other worlds will come. We are not alone. That much is clear. They are One with Creator in ways we have not yet learned."

Another chimed, "How many planets survived? Shahten has grown so strong. Is it false hope?"

Tisbero boomed, "One or a thousand, it doesn't matter! Inaction is still a choice—a choice to support Shahten. Without doubt he wishes all of us to feel overwhelmed by the enormity of what's happening. He wishes us to give up hope and to believe there is nothing we can do to change it. However, we know that to do nothing when you know of harm tells Creation you agree with that harm."

Even though Keela's astral form wavered, her voice carried crisp and clear. "We made an agreement when we joined with a human. We agreed to learn how to co-create in order to deepen our connection with Creator. The fact that others have come to destroy it does not lessen our agreement. It magnifies it."

Another speculated, "Maybe if we heal the centers before Shahten can get there with his SkySlabs we can avoid the conflict."

Tisbero roared, "Avoid conflict? Tell that to the guardians who have been unmade. Tell that to Twaque. Conflict is upon you now!"

Zinn stalked toward the center of the gathering. "Earth asks for help to withdraw, to go into hibernation so Shahten has less to feed on. If we don't help Earth hibernate it will be killed." She reached the center of the circle and her eyes raked across the assembly. "Other planets have done this and lived. Let Hetlin speak so she can tell us how."

The murmuring voices faded quickly.

Hetlin remained standing, resolute in her reporting task, and continued where she left off. "As Yawri also reported, the attacks occurred at Earth's centers rather than on our communities for a reason. With Earth's centers strong, even if we are unmade human beings could heal over a few lifetimes. Even the humans, separated from Earth's timing, could eventually heal. Physical bodies belong to Earth and Earth's soul, One with Creator. With that connection, Life on Earth could heal.

"Shahten believes dividing what's whole into isolated parts: life and death, good and bad, physical and ethereal, will return Creation to what it was before the sending-forth. That is why he attacks Earth's energy centers. He seeks to separate the planet from its source so that healing will not be possible."

Hetlin scanned the guardians slowly. All sagged in sorrow and confusion. The two guardians she came with caught her eye and nodded.

"To help a planet hibernate is no simple task," she ground on. "Earth's ethereal centers are wide open now, and pulse with dimensions of all Life. Rich forests and thriving oceans stretch from pole to pole. Crystals provide light within Earth. The solar winds are One with Earth's.

Yet, all of this strength has no defense against those who choose intentional harm. Earth would rather choose death than be murdered." She paused to let all feel the meaning of the words.

"Here is how we were asked to keep the planet alive. We need to travel to each of Earth's centers as planned, but with a different purpose. The healing of the centers now also includes helping them to close down and sleep. The planet will draw its most vital essence deep into itself. This will protect its most vital life force, although it will still be vulnerable.

"If we provide some of our own essence to protect and maintain the closing, Shahten will not be able to possess the centers and destroy them."

Hetlin continued, knowing that if she stopped it would be hard to start again. "Earth's knowledge is our knowledge, our knowledge is Earth's. By sharing our essence, the planet's centers will be able to function, although minimally compared to now. An ice age will occur. Deserts will cover what is now forest. The wide spectrum of Life the planet has now will be lessened.

The murderers will have less Life to prey upon." Her gaze fell to the floor, her own grief finally showing its toll.

Yawri had moved to the center of the circle again and stood by her side. "When we came to this meeting, we all knew this desperate situation would require desperate action. The years of small choices, which have led to what we face today, stretch into the distant past. Neither we nor the planet asked for this learning, but it is now ours to learn."

Keela called out, "Creator nurtures Creation! We are not alone. Help will come."

Yawri raised his chin. "Help does come. Even now, the great forests are listening to the winds of the universe to learn more from planets who faced this before. Crystals within Earth are seeking information from crystals on other worlds." He nodded toward Hetlin. "The great lakes of Earth see into the universe and seek the same. Our learning, Earth's learning, is hard. However hard this learning may be, the choice to help Earth slumber is a choice for Life. It is the only way for us to continue to learn how to expand Creation in all we become."

Slumped postures straightened. Expressions thawed and eyes opened. Zinn stepped next to Hetlin and vowed, "We can do this!"

Other voices echoed in hopeful agreement. "We will keep Earth's centers alive, and learn more of All-we-are by doing it," was a general proclamation.

One guardian asked, "After we leave a part of our essence to fill the void, how do we remain conscious of All-we-are?"

Hetlin responded. "The same way we remained conscious after joining with a human. Remember how we only sent one filament out, yet learned so much? The more guardians who contribute, the less each will need to give. As with the humans we joined, we will become aware of more reality, not less."

Another voice rose. "But we must return to Creator with All-we-are, not a portion of what we are. When our human bodies enter a death cycle, All-we-are returns to its source, Creator, and the body's essence returns to its source, Earth. The planet's centers may need our essence for many lifetimes. How will we retrieve it when it's no longer needed?"

Hetlin said, "Earth does not desire to keep our ethereal essence. When the time comes for it to reawaken, it will return our essence to us. Of course, to do that we must be on Earth when it reawakens."

She raised her head. "Make no mistake. Those who choose to lend their own essence commit themselves to being here, reincarnating in physical bodies lifetime after lifetime, until Earth is ready to reawaken and can return our energy to us. No one who provides essence will be able to fully leave until it is returned. We will be joined with Earth. Its fate our own.

"No planet knows how long Earth will need to hibernate; however, all say it should not sleep if only to postpone its murder. Before the Earth closes down any of its centers, it must know there is, in fact, a time in the future when it can reawaken with Life.

"To be clear, if no such timeline in the future can be found, Earth considers it best to die now in a time of its choosing rather than be murdered. This is what makes our task extraordinarily complicated. We must find out if this future time exists."

"It must exist," a voice declared.

"We will keep this planet alive to make sure it does," said another.

Feeling heard, Hetlin's shoulders relaxed. "We all know Creation is everywhere at once. Time tunnels, ever-shifting and living veins of etheric light, were co-created to connect any place in time with any other. Sequence lives there, and though it is within the timelessness of Creation, each moment is a single note with its own vibration in the sound of All."

She glanced at Yawri. "Some of us must use them to find out if this future time exists. These searchers will travel across time to find a future self that is able to receive the essence we lent to Earth's energy centers. This will form an arc of consciousness, from past to future, from future to past." Hetlin looked down and paused.

I must speak all we were told, even though it's hard.

"No one knows how long finding this future self will take, or if it even exists. While the searcher's astral bodies journey across time, their physical ones are vulnerable, far more so than during our usual astral meetings. If their physical body comes to harm, it will not matter if their astral selves find a time in the arc or not. The connection to the part of the timeline they found will be lost to us. We must keep the bodies of the searchers safe.

"When the time for reawakening is found and Earth feels the arc of consciousness is strong enough, it will begin to go to sleep in this time and simultaneously wake up in that future time. It must happen simultaneously. Earth will know a future beyond murder exists and will choose to live.

"We have much to prepare. From the reports we expect Shahten's forces to do all they can to stop us. We must complete the work Earth has laid out before us before he can marshal them. I understand that going to each center the day of the next full moon has been proposed. That leaves us little time, however, from what we heard, we should plan for that date."

Small groups began discussing what they could do in earnest, each guardian thinking through what they needed to accomplish within the allotted time. No one noticed Rhee and Camic arrive. Even though they were late due to the companionship of the human women Shahten provided them, they eavesdropped on all the conversations they could.

Absorbed in conversation and seeking space, Gamon and a group of his friends moved toward the new arrivals and stopped. One in his group said, "We always have choice, and our choice is in how we respond to these changes."

A female guardian said, "Earth has taught me more about Creation than anything since my own Creation. We must go to the ethereal centers of Earth and do this healing."

Gamon said, "It's good all agree the problem with Earth's ethereal centers is our priority. If the centers aren't in balance, it's only a matter of time before ours aren't, either."

One of his companions said, "It is amazing how the harm happened at the same time in the same way to all nine centers. It was reasonable to think it was due to a power surge of some kind, especially given they're scattered across continents around the globe."

Gamon crowed, "At least we have a plan. I'll see you at the heart center before sunrise on the day of the next full moon. We'll get it done before Yawri and the others can arrive. I'm ready now. Aren't you?"

Rhee and Camic watched Gamon and those near him laugh. Then the astral forms of Gamon's group faded as they returned to their physical bodies.

Camic whispered, "We have the date and their plan. Let's return to our own bodies. Hard to believe, but some of these misguided guardians may question our presence."

"Sounds good. Besides, a friend is sleeping next to me and I'd like to wake up," Rhee replied.

Before they left Camic snapped, "These fools corrupted Earth's centers so greatly the only way this planet can find Life again is if it is unmade and reborn along with them."

Rhee added, "I can't believe they broadcast the date. By the night of the next full moon, the centers and these lost guardians will have a new start. It's the Way to make all truly one."

48. DAWN

∞

A full moon sank in the dark sky while the first rays of sun reached over a distant eastern ridge and scratched the night. The night rolled west and the guardian's white tunics began to glow with a faint orange sheen.

A bird trilled.

Gamon gave a loud laugh and turned to the guardian next to him. "Can you believe Yawri wanted us to prepare more? You couldn't ask for a more peaceful morning!" He shook his head. "It's a splendid day from horizon to horizon."

He held his hands loosely behind his back and smiled. "I settled here because this is the etheric center that teaches caring creation across differences. Healing it is going to help everyone else a lot."

The guardian next to him chuckled. "You settled here because you like co-creating across differences, or because you want to learn how?"

Gamon shrugged. "I've always been more of a teacher than a student." The harmonies from the crystals standing at all angles behind him rose with the new day. "How could anyone think we need Yawri and his cohorts?" He gestured to the forest of crystals. "They came to help heal this center. They are ready. The heart center is ready. We're ready." He spoke the thought of all that came early. "Let this healing begin!"

The guardians began to glow, and they swayed gently with the flowing current between the core of the planet and themselves. The full sun crested the ridge and changed from an orb of deep orange to a blazing-white disk. Mirror-smooth faces of the forest of crystals flashed in dawn's light.

Precisely aligned under the sun's glare, twenty SkySlabs passed unseen over the ridge and down into a deep swale.

Shahten stood tall on his SkySlab and raised a hand. All the SkySlabs stopped in place, keeping Shahten at the hub of their wheel. All captains and their menders stood facing him, poised to hear his next instruction.

"The lost guardians are so predictable." He sounded so congenial it seemed all here must be dear friends. "They planned to start the healing today, and there they are, at sunrise. All those white robes circling those wonderful crystals look so picturesque it could be a mosaic."

The captains chanced a smile but the menders remained stoic. Shahten swiveled his gaze to settle on the two new captains who had replaced the two who falsely reported that Yawri, Tisbero and Keela were dead. The fresh-faced replacements stayed at attention, eyes bright and eager to please. A slight edge came into Shahten's voice, subtle but heard by all. "Do you foresee any problems if we all converge on that target?"

They tumbled over themselves to respond. One said, "Even though it is large, a single SkySlab could easily unmake these lost ones. Give me the honor, my lord, and I will see it done."

The other countered, "Surrounding them with all twenty of our SkySlabs assures they are finished immediately and completely."

Shahten smiled. "You demonstrate the problem of rushing to conclusions well. A single SkySlab would allow them time to panic, and panic creates uncertainty. If all of our SkySlabs surround it, we risk unmaking ourselves with our own crossfire."

Both new captains remained at attention but their eyes glazed and shoulders slumped. Neither spared a glance at the master captain. Even though he stood well behind Shahten, each felt his glower.

"I prefer a disciplined plan. Comparatively few lost ones are present, which means most are either still in their communities or on their way. They must be stopped. We will keep ten SkySlabs here. The remaining ten will search for those guardians' communities and unmake them as we have others before."

Shahten probed the faces of his captains. "Seven SkySlabs will circle the crystal forest the lost ones planted at this center. Unmaking beams have a long range. Position your SkySlabs so that none of you are in another's line of fire. Place all the menders along the side of your SkySlab facing this lair of lost souls. When all is aligned, order the menders to unmake them."

He rose taller. "These lost souls are so absorbed in their self-important task they might not even notice you. Encased in their own world, any who do will probably think you've come to help. Well, you did come to help, but not in the way their simple minds believe."

He seemed to tower over them. "After they are unmade, pull back to rest the mender's crystals. I will come with the three SkySlabs I held in reserve.

388

They will all have fresh crystals and menders. After so much dark light, we will be able to unmake the heart center itself. The planet will have a new beginning, free from corruption of the old way."

Each captain nodded, but none spoke.

Shahten paused to allow time for his master captain to stare at each of the other captains in turn. The expression on the master captain's face was all it took to communicate his warning.

Keep discipline. If you let your menders kill our own, either die well there or die poorly when you return.

Shahten let the unspoken message sink in before dipping his head. With that signal, the master captain said, "All move! End these fools before their misguided attempts at healing interfere with the permanent solution we bring." Ten SkySlabs started to move back up toward the ridge while seven moved much more quickly down the valley.

Shahten savored the spectacle for a long moment before speaking to his master captain. "Camic and Rhee's report serves us well. Having so few lost ones here now means that the argument for healing the center at the earliest possible moment won against those who wanted time to prepare to heal as well as defend it. Splintering amongst Guardians is so helpful. They do my work for me."

The master captain said, "They splinter in pursuit of perfection. We unite to achieve it. Bringing a quarter of our fleet was wise."

"While they doddle, we decide. Severing this center from its source will sever them all. Creation without caring will end this planet."

The master captain started to move but Shahten added another thought. "Have the SkySlab with the astral-body priest land next to us so he can get to sleep quickly. Astral-body priests at the other centers are doing the same. Make sure his body is undisturbed until their meeting on the astral is complete. He needs to return with accurate reports so all of our work is coordinated across the globe."

"Excellent," the master captain said. "Your intervention to save these lost souls from themselves is merciful. This planet will join others we've liberated from this endless cycle of life and death."

Shahten's eyes narrowed to slits. "Without existence, there is no beginning or end. When all is the same, all is truly One.

"All will follow the Way soon."

49. ATTACK

∞

Gamon stood with the other guardians surrounding the center, all eyes closed to better hear the harmonic tones each sought to blend with the damaged land. Their long, white robes swayed gently with the oscillating, healing current. Engrossed in the restorative sensation, none appeared to notice seven shadows creeping toward them until the dark shadows crossed over their heads.

Gamon raised his eyes and his voice boomed in greeting. "Welcome! You are late, but all is prepared. Come!"

"Other guardians have arrived!" another voice cried. "Thanks! There is much to do."

The guardians continued to expand connection to the ethereal heart of the planet while they tilted their faces upward. Seven skystones, more massive than any seen before, slowed to a stop above them. Each immense slab formed a part of a ring surrounding the center, their long sides evenly spaced between each one.

"Land and join us!" another guardian beckoned.

The massive skystones did not descend. Instead, men and women in rust-red tunics packed the inner side shoulder to shoulder. Each held a citrine to their solar plexus.

Instead of expressions of caring, the faces that looked down were frozen with scorn. The voice of one of the young captains carried across the ring. "Menders! These lost guardians want to send you back to caves and hunger. Prepare to unmake them so they can return open to the Way!"

Menders steadied their crystals on their chests and glared at their prey. In contrast to the communities many had unmade, directing dark light upon these false guardians would be a pleasure.

Another captain's voice screamed in panic. "Turn around! Turn around! We are being attacked from behind!"

Menders whirled with confusion. Hundreds of small skystones hovered in a ring surrounding their own. The bow of each diminutive slab pointed toward them held only one guardian. However, the menders' eyes went wide when they realized each also held a citrine to their chest.

"They have unmaking crystals!" another yelled.

"Where did they come from?"

"Don't wait for them to kill us! Loose the unmaking! Menders! Loose the unmaking now!" several captains yelled at once.

Menders followed the order immediately but their targets were unclear. Shafts of dark light shot toward the skystones hovering in front of them. At the same time, other menders aimed for the ones on the ground.

Shafts of dark light saturated the space between each front so completely the sky turned from sunlit dawn to dusk. The captains heard the familiar sound of screams that came from guardians being unmade, and they took comfort in it.

However, something was different this time. The guardians below were not running in panic. They still stood calm and serene.

One of the veteran captains howled, "The ones on the ground have unmaking crystals, too!"

Menders sent dark light toward any white robe they saw.

However, the screams still came from the wrong place. Captains' minds swirled with confusion. It was the menders, not the lost guardians, screaming. Their bodies fell from the SkySlabs in a torrent.

Within seconds of the start of the fusillade, every mender on the side facing the picket of skystones was gone. With all the weight on the inside facing the center, the tall crystals socketed down the middle of each SkySlab strained to keep the platform level. Captains felt their balance list and yelled, "Menders! Move to the outer side! Fire on those skystones!"

Menders on the inner side turned about-face to fire as commanded. However, the SkySlab's column of crystals constrained their shot. Menders moved to stand between them and released shafts of dark light. However, they fell writhing as soon as they did so. Others fired wildly. It only took one graze from an unmaking beam to unbalance a propulsion crystal, and several unmaking beams hit the upright crystals at once.

SkySlab after SkySlab tilted sharply. Menders and their captains slid off. The long crystals fell free of their sockets, and they fell, followed by the enormous slabs of stone.

Within moments only two of the seven SkySlabs remained, each absent of almost all menders. The two new captains stood dazed. Several wasp-like skystones started to dart around them ... and the swarm was coming.

"Loose!" both young captains screeched to their remaining humans. "What are you waiting for, them to kill you first?"

The remaining troops fired quickly, but not quickly enough. Menders released their unmaking but it was they who were unmade.

After the dark light cleared, only one human remained. He lay on a SkySlab, curled up and whimpering, after dropping his citrine overboard when the man next to him screamed and fell.

Both captains averted their eyes and stared at the distant ridge. Reading each other's minds, they accelerated away from the madness at top speed. However, a glance showed the white skystones flanked them with ease and still held their unmaking crystals trained upon them. The captains kept their eyes trained on the distant ridgeline. There was no point in watching death arrive.

Each waited for the dark light to rip their bodies apart.

It never came.

When the captains glanced back, sure that the demons were toying with them, they flinched in surprise. Rather than kill them, the white-robed demons had returned to the center. Their skystones reminded them of angry wasps swarming around an angry nest.

50. SEARCHERS

∞

Several skystones pursued the retreating SkySlabs, but with no dark light sent to unmake the guardians, there was nothing to return. Even though the skystones darted in close, the two SkySlab captains kept their eyes rigidly fixed on the distant ridge. The guardians finally peeled away to return to the center.

One of the white-robed pilots came alongside Yawri's skystone. "The humans that sent dark light died, but the captains who made them do it lived. I know we can only return unmaking back to who sent it, but Shahten and his captains are the ones responsible."

Yawri glanced over his shoulder toward the retreating SkySlabs. "What you create for others you create for yourself. It always returns to you. It's only a matter of when, not if, their actions come home to them. Right now, though, they are going to report what happened to Shahten and he is going to send everything he has against us."

"It's not finished? Their losses were so great! Why would they return?"

"He's convinced his followers we're lost souls, and the only way to save us is to return us to essence. He'll be back to attack with larger numbers. I just hope the crystals we seeded in that ridge are getting information that can help us."

Word of Shahten's impending return spread quickly from skystone to skystone, and sober expressions sobered further. Yet even this grim news paled in comparison to the gruesome scene at the center.

The change in sound was the first thing Yawri noticed. Air that had been filled with screams and the clapping sound of air rushing to fill the voids left by the hail-sized shafts of unmaking was utterly silent now.

He scanned the skystones hovering above the center. Every pilot flew with a dazed, vacant expression. White-robed guardians milled on the ground, staring at the carnage—the waste of human Life a loss beyond words.

Keela, Tisbero, and Zinn remained on their skystones as he'd asked, hovering near the center to watch for SkySlabs. The trio watched Yawri approach. He sensed their gaze and returned it. Like him, their faces held a grimace of sorrow mixed with determination. He raised his hand above his head, then dropped it to point at the ground. All four skystones started moving to their pre-arranged landing area below.

Tisbero landed first and hopped down to the ground. Yawri landed next to Keela and Zinn. He had just started to step down off his skystone when Keela stopped him and said, "Everyone needs a report, Yawri. Say something."

Yawri raised his head and surveyed the guardians standing in the carnage surrounding the center. He couldn't fathom why the faces looked expectantly at him.

Zinn said, "You're the one that got the citrines and told us how to use them. Everyone knows we'd be dead if you hadn't."

Yawri's brow furrowed. "Oh."

Most guardians had lowered their citrines to the ground but Yawri still held Red at his waist. The connection between it and the ethereal one inside his chest vibrated with Life.

He took a step forward on his skystone and planted his feet. Not sure where to start, he began anyway, and his rich, baritone voice traveled to every ear. "Guardians of All. Our choice was to either agree or disagree with those who decided to murder us and the heart-center of Earth. We chose to disagree. What they sent to us went back to them.

"Still, we are filled with sorrow for the waste of Life. When I was in the cave of the citrines, they told me their hope was to return the unmaking back to the enslaved crystals and give them a chance to experience themselves within All—a particle of Creation with the gift of free will—before they died."

Faces showed relief, although Yawri couldn't tell if it was due to his words or the sound of any voice breaking the grip of silence over the battlefield. "The crystals that came to us did well, and so did we. We must have, because we all remain alive."

Everyone relaxed slightly.

"You remembered what the citrines told us during training. When the unmaking fell upon us, anyone choosing judgment over connection would have died here today. Even the citrines, whose purpose is to join dimensions, could not have saved anyone, even themselves, if divisive rather than connective thought had been your choice.

"None of us asked to learn how to stop murder. This morning was our first lesson. Guardians of All, you learned well."

Yawri felt the red diamond in his hands pulse. It had a message as well. He waited for it to communicate with him through the ethereal one in his chest.

"Hours before dawn, we seeded crystals in the ridges and upper valleys surrounding this center. Those crystals have reported to the crystals we helped move here." He gestured to the forest of jutting, angles of light.

"Here is the report."

All leaned forward to listen, and Yawri raised his voice to make sure all heard. "Where the sun crested the ridge this morning, twenty SkySlabs passed over and down to hide in its swale. Fortunately, for us, only seven came to attack this center. Three SkySlabs, including Shahten, stayed at the ridge.

"The ten others left to unmake our other communities. However, we were also prepared for that attack. If they reach our communities, they will find guardians armed with their own citrines, just as they did here. The sentry crystals report that of the three SkySlabs Shahten retained here, two recently left for his island and one flew toward the nearest community at speed. We can expect more SkySlabs and menders to arrive from his island. In addition, the ten sent to attack our communities will undoubtedly return."

Yawri looked at Keela and his eyebrows raised. "It's your turn."

When she wanted it to, Keela's rich voice carried just as far as Yawri's. Keela took a deep breath and stepped forward. "Yawri, Tisbero, and I saw Shahten's Island and how he works. This morning he was surprised by our stand, but he will return with a plan carefully calculated to overcome it. To achieve his ends, he must unmake Earth's ethereal heart center. Even if no other centers are harmed, Earth's loss of this one—its ethereal connection to caring co-creation in the universe—could cause this jewel to become barren. He will return with force, and we must counter that with fewer guardians than we have now. Fewer, because as we agreed, some must travel in their astral forms to find a future when Earth can reawaken and reclaim its Life." Her gaze settled on Tisbero.

Your turn.

Tisbero's fiery voice rumbled. "We don't know how soon Shahten's forces will return, but we must implement our plan quickly. It's time for those who will search to move to your sleeping places.

"As discussed during our training, most guardians are needed to keep the center and the searcher's bodies safe. If they are not kept safe, it won't matter if their astral selves find a time for an arc of consciousness or not. Their bodies must be able to connect across time. If either their future body or their present one is unable to connect, Earth will conclude there is no Life in its future. It will not hibernate now if it only means waking up to murder."

Tisbero looked at Yawri.

Your turn again.

Yawri drew his lips in a tight line but finally spoke. "We trained quickly and hard for this day. We knew Shahten would come and we would stand together and search for a future where Life could live again. This has not changed." Yawri cast his eyes across the faces. Familiar ones looked back. "From our own meetings on the astral, we know all the other centers are as prepared as we are. All will help the planet close down its Lifeforce in this time, and All will return lifetime after lifetime until it can reawaken. As Earth reawakens with itself, so will we." He took a step forward and raised his voice further.

"As the crystals taught us, our challenge is to disagree with Shahten's captains without making them wrong and us right. Polarization is separation. There are differences, not separation, within All. We will learn how to halt their murder without becoming murderers ourselves."

Yawri's voice throbbed. "Free will is free will. They choose to collapse Creation. We choose to expand it with All we become!"

The guardians thundered the traditional response. "Go ever forth and Create with Creator!"

Guardians streamed to their places in a tapestry of motion. Three hundred skystones rose into the air to form a defensive ring over the guardians standing in a circle around the crystal forest. Twelve groups of four searchers each distributed themselves within the glowing center. Twenty guardians surrounded each group of searchers, determined to keep the time-travelers safe while their astral selves journeyed across time.

Yawri, Keela, Zinn, and Tisbero approached Gamon, one of the guardians set to protect them while they searched. Even though his boisterous, self-assured manner typically caused him to speak first, an immense monolith stood on its side less than an arm's length away from him where it had fallen. His face was stone sober.

He still managed to speak first, but only said, "Great speech, Yawri."

In spite of his blustery manner, Yawri saw Gamon's eyes glaze with a distant stare. "Our plan worked, Gamon. Whatever Rhee and Camic overheard you say at the astral meeting convinced them to tell Shahten of our ignorance. They came unprepared."

A subtle gleam returned to Gamon's eyes. "I did put on a great performance."

"It was convincing. Otherwise he'd have sent more against us," Keela added.

Tisbero said, "Still, I expect you were quite relieved to see our skystones rise from the forest."

Gamon simply replied, "True, as planned."

Tisbero finished scanning the area and they continued walking. "We best take our positions. Shahten isn't going to wait for us to find a future."

Gamon called after them. "I'm already in position."

Yawri increased his stride but his lips formed a grin. He enjoyed gruff Gamon, although he'd never tell him so. He laughed over his shoulder. "You keep our bodies safe. We'll find out if there is a future self who admits to being you."

Instead of responding, Gamon surveyed the surroundings. His lips compressed, sobered again by the sight of guardians using fallen SkySlabs as defensive barriers against Shahten's next attack. There would be no surprise to blunt it this time.

Several of the guardians also protecting this group of searchers looked thoughtfully at Gamon. He stared back. "What are you looking at? The attack will come from the ridgeline."

Yawri joined Keela, Zinn and Tisbero amongst the towering crystals, lowered Red to his side, and addressed their protectors. "Thank you for safeguarding us while we search. We will find a time when Earth can awaken!"

In a confident gesture, he threw the tails of his makeshift bandana over his shoulder and murmured to his friends, "I just have no idea where in time that might be."

Tisbero said, "You have more experience with time tunnels than all the rest of us combined. You helped build them."

"And built so many they let beings who had no business using them get lost."

Keela gave him a level stare. "None of us can control how what we co-create is used. Free will, remember?"

"I remember, but I also remember what can happen when you make something so easy for someone to use they don't learn how to make it themselves."

Tisbero retorted, "I don't need to know how to co-create time tunnels, but I do need to use them to find a time when a future self can awaken with Earth. Let's do this."

Keela pointed skyward urgently. "Look!" The others looked up in a panic to find the threat before she added, "Birds! Look at all of those birds!" Broad-winged hawks, falcons, and brown eagles soared in the distance. Keela's hand rose to her chest and felt her ethereal feather pulse. "You're beautiful!"

Zinn bubbled, "Smell the air! Mammoths and large-toothed cats are near. Connected as they are to All, they sense what's going on."

Tisbero rumbled, "The same way they know when earthquakes are coming. I'm not sure if it's a good sign or not."

Yawri felt the current of energy cycling between the Earth's heart center and its core expand. His body swayed with its slow, pulsing rhythm and he sensed time tunnels highlighted for their journey across time.

His voice was crisp. "These crystals are well joined across dimensions, from Earth's core to distant nebulae. All we need to do is hold our connection to the Life here while we travel the time tunnels to find our counterparts in the future."

"All?" Keela said. She held her hand over the large, green garnet Yawri had given her. Its sound joined dimensions even better than citrines, and she felt it blend with the ethereal feather within her.

"Look!" Keela said again, but this time she caused no alarm.

They looked skyward to see two giant orange-backed ahjas circling high overhead. Their shiny feathers stroked the air in a synchronized partnership. Suddenly, they rose up, touched beaks, and plummeted toward the crystal center. Their backs flashed with orange light with each spinning rotation of their bodies.

When it seemed no space remained between them and the crystals below, they shot upward like a lava bomb exploding skyward. Hundreds of beaks of every shape and size sounded a chorus. Mammoths trumpeted and big cats roared.

"It's Earth's signal!" Yawri yelled. In the span of a few heartbeats, the giant crystals at the heart center shone brilliant white. "Make sure the spheres in your body are in balance with Earth's centers before you leave! The more stable your body here, the more dimensions your astral selves can explore!"

"Go forth and Create with Creator!" Zinn cried out.

The searchers swayed, firmly anchored as timeless soul light and sound streamed through their bodies. Creation's essence flowed from the core of the planet through the ethereal center.

"The heart center is stable!" Keela said with excitement and relief.

"Time tunnels are opening!" Yawri exclaimed as portals to the living sea of time appeared. The searchers left their bodies standing, stabilized by those around them, and their astral forms rushed into the swirling matrix of timeless time.

51. TIMELESS TIME

∞

Yawri, Keela, Tisbero, and Zinn moved through a pulsing violet tunnel, its striated patterns rushing past in a blur. Yawri said, "Let's move forward in time just enough to see if we can learn something to help." All agreed, and within moments their astral bodies appeared in another time and place.

"What's this?" Zinn demanded, becoming suddenly still. The land was flooded and the smell of decay permeated the air.

Tisbero extended his senses to the rock under the flooded ground. "A tidal wave, followed by rain. A lot of rain."

Keela asked, "A tidal wave? Here? Isn't it too far from the sea?"

Tisbero looked from horizon to horizon. "It would take something like a huge undersea volcanic explosion to create a tidal wave big enough to reach here."

Yawri knelt and moved his hand through a small, dark pool. "Saltwater. I agree. It would take something that big to make the sea flow this far inland."

Zinn moved up a barren slope to survey the area. "Everything is dead! All we've helped in Life is gone! Did Shahten win? How else could so much death happen so quickly?"

"He must have killed the center!" Tisbero barked.

Zinn swayed and looked down at muddy ground. "No animals are here! All swept away!"

Keela raised her head and choked out, "Even the plants we tended are gone!"

Yawri moved quickly to stand in front of them. "Observe only! If you believe you are the experience, you become it! Reconnect to your whole, to All!"

Keela winced and blinked her eyes. Tisbero stood upright and stared from place to place. Zinn moved down from the rise and repeated, "Observe only," but her voice was uncertain.

Yawri's tone was insistent. "This was our first portal. We don't know why this tidal wave happened but it doesn't matter. Even if Shahten did win, we still need to use whatever time we have left to find a time to arc with a future self."

"Yes we do!" Tisbero growled. "What was I thinking?" He, Zinn and Keela moved toward the undulating portal.

Yawri moved in front of them again with his chin raised. "Wait! We talked about it before, but now you've experienced how other time periods can affect you. If you find a future self, it's even more dangerous than this, because they're physical and you're not. If you merge with them, you can become physical there and lose connection with your body here. Observe and learn only. Share thoughts if they can hear you, but remember they are another aspect of a whole you. They are you and yet not you! Be careful."

Zinn stared unblinkingly. Tisbero grunted. Keela pressed her hand against her chest. "I wasn't prepared for such intense feelings. I almost forgot and became what I felt."

Yawri stepped closer, his arms held low and wide. "It is a good lesson for all, and I keep relearning it. You never know what you'll find when you travel to another focus of time. If it triggers emotional trauma like this one, you must remember you're an observer, not a participant."

Keela nodded, a self-reprimanding tone in her voice. "No matter what I find, I must remain centered on our purpose. I agreed to search for a time when Earth can reawaken. Losing myself to my reaction helps nothing."

Yawri touched his ethereal bandana, Keela's old sash, and it reminded him of the challenges they'd faced together. He grinned. "Let's go."

Each centered themselves, focused once more, and entered the portal. They flowed through pulsing arteries in the body of time, and when they came to the first large branch Yawri said, "Stop a moment."

All three looked at him with their eyebrows raised. Yawri looked at the branching vein and back again. "There's an infinite number of loci to explore. The red diamond is with my physical body at the heart center. It's One with the Earth's core. The ethereal diamond that's within me is One with it. This means we have access to Earth's core and I can ask it to help guide us."

Zinn spoke for all as she replied, "Sounds good to me."

They moved more slowly than their first unbridled sortie. The ethereal diamond in Yawri's chest started to glow. After passing through a tunnel of streaking gold and violet, they emerged from a portal and found themselves between two massive trees.

The searchers relaxed when they saw a jungle of living green. Hundreds of species of plants grew on every available space, including the forest canopy.

Nuts, berries, and long yellow fruits gleamed. Birds, bright with more colors than a rainbow, flew from branch to branch. A howler monkey hanging from a branch above sounded a loud whooping bark. Zinn smiled. "Life blooms again!"

The searchers moved through the landscape, unseen and silent ghosts to any physical eyes and ears. "Do you hear voices?" Tisbero asked.

Zinn's ears perked up. "Human beings from the sound of it, up this slope and to the left."

Eager to observe a hopeful scene, they moved quickly and found the source of the familiar sound. The searchers stopped behind a curtain of vines stretching from branches high above down to the ground.

Zinn leaned forward. "Guardians live, and they still tend Earth!"

At least thirty human beings stood around a central fire pit of simmering coals. All wore simple tunics tied at one shoulder with a colorful strip of cloth sewn in a bottom hem.

A tall man with long, black hair paced back and forth, his face dour. "Too few of us understand what the plants and animals are saying anymore. Our children only understand our spoken tongue, not the language of Life. To be deaf in this jungle is perilous."

An old woman with a sky-blue feather in her gray hair spoke next. "But we have nurtured this land as a garden since our first joining with humans. Those who still know the one language of Life can help those who don't. They can be taught. They can remain safe."

"Safe?" a young woman across from her leaped forward. "My child is dead! The snake choked him and ate him whole!"

Another man spoke, his voice tired. "My great-grandmother spoke easily with all Life here. She never knew fear. But I do. I can only speak with water spirits. My children speak with nothing. The loss is shameful."

A woman next to him said, "My grandfather spoke with jaguars, but I'll never let my daughter go out of camp alone again. One was stalking her! My parents hunted *with* them. Now jaguars hunt us! What happened? I feel ashamed to be a human being."

A voice pleaded, "Did the forest change or did we?"

The answer came quickly from another. "It hasn't changed. We have. Everything in the forest remains within the chorus of All. It's we who have forgotten how to sing with it."

A tall young man with a broad, colorful hem around the bottom of his tunic spoke. "If we don't leave this jungle while we still have some ability, our future is to live in fear. Of the communities remaining here, more and more are warring against each other to survive."

A woman's voice anguished. "They worship carved stones as if Creator is outside of themselves! They burn the forest and claim it as their own. What kind of Life remains for your children when you murder Life in order to live?"

"The path to that future is upon us, but what if we take another?" the tall young man said. "The north continent is drier, colder, and has much less food, but there is also less there to kill us. Perhaps there our children could grow up without fear!"

A young woman added, "Maybe we could have the kind of conscious deaths our forbearers had. Ones where we could remember wisdom learned from lifetimes instead of trying to forget its trauma."

No one spoke for a long minute. All eyes gazed at the smoldering embers in the fire pit. Finally, the young woman continued speaking. "Better to leave now while some of us can still speak to the land rather than after we're all deaf and blind to it."

The old woman with the blue feather in her hair looked at a child held in the cradling arms of its father. The child's unsettled eyes roamed the branches and vines, looking for danger. The elder's voice shook with grief but her words were clear. "It is true. More and more only see with their physical eyes and ears and only perceive one dimension. What will happen if they come to believe such a small aspect of Creation is all there is?"

Tears streamed down her creased face, but she continued. "Wisdom was spoken today. If we stay, we'll become like those who fear nature, and like them, we will make a foe out of our dearest friend, thinking we must to survive."

Her voice changed from despair to hope as she avowed, "We leave for a land far less diverse, but a land where we can raise our children with hope for a thoughtful life, death, and conscious rebirth. A land where we can learn to listen again."

Zinn leaned back from the curtain of vines. "How could there be a time when we can't speak with animals?"

Keela stared down at her hands, her voice a whisper. "They can't even hear plants. I can't imagine."

Tisbero continued to peer intently through the vines, scanning the encampment for more information. "Human beings are still struggling to maintain ability, but the rest of nature looks well recovered from the die-off we saw at our last time landing."

Yawri added. "The problem could be due to Earth closing down its centers."

Keela ventured, "Did you hear them talk about being ashamed? What does ashamed mean?"

Yawri and Zinn shook their heads, wondering too. Tisbero gave a brief nod, stood straight and said, "Let's continue the search."

Yawri perused the sea of faces around the campfire. All were animated now. Voices engaged in planning the journey peppered the air. "At least we learned that guardians still ask good questions and have the courage to face hard answers. Whatever has happened to Earth's centers, guardians are still tenacious enough to do all they can to stay connected to the Whole."

He turned and looked back downslope. "Let's see what the future holds next. The portal between those two trees will still open."

Sooner than any expected they reached the two massive trees. "We've got to find a time where awareness is increasing instead of decreasing. Let's try a longer jump this time."

Keela spoke to herself but everyone heard. "Remember to observe and not become the experience."

Arteries and veins of living time streamed by, each with its own unique sound and color. Since helping to develop them was one of his first co-creations, Yawri recognized what type of reality each one meant.

Yawri combined the harmonics from the ethereal diamond in his chest with the harmonics he sought, looking for a time most likely to lead to a reawakening. Hopeful, he selected one pulsing with several familiar tones. The searchers exited a portal and found themselves next to a wall of limestone. To physical eyes it was gray, but to the searchers, it glowed with the living tones of multiple songs.

Tisbero paused to scan their surroundings. Keela bent to examine the plants. Zinn listened for animals. Yawri simply strode forward.

Tisbero mumbled, "What does he have against assessing something before plunging ahead? He's the one that warned us to be careful."

Keela was unperturbed. "He was that way when I met him." Her eyes flickered to Tisbero and back to Yawri. "You know if we don't go with him he'll just go alone."

Tisbero moved quickly to catch up. Keela smiled.

The searchers stopped above a frothing waterfall. Unlike the forest they had left behind, this time the area was filled with fern trees. "Ah," Yawri said with relief. "Feel the Life in this air."

Zinn climbed up to get a view over the trees. "This mountain's in a broad basin. There are other mountains, all flat-topped. From horizon to horizon they look like green logs floating in a sea." The others climbed up to join her and survey the surroundings.

After a minute, Tisbero bent to inspect the ground. "Hard-capped sandstone. The land without a cap was washed away, leaving these isolated mesas." Keela said, "There's more diverse plant life here than in any one place I've seen before."

Yawri lowered his hand from the ethereal diamond in his chest and turned from his communion with the cliff wall. "There are immensely large crystal families here, but deep in the Earth. This area of the continent still has a strong ethereal center connected to the planet's timing and integration of co-creation."

Tisbero's eyes locked on a distant vista while he spoke. "Look near the top of the waterfall on that cliff." He pointed. "There are people on its far side."

After a brief pause, Yawri moved toward them. "Let's find out who they are." Tisbero was already at his side. Keela and Zinn flanked them. The team's astral bodies sailed across the drop-off to the distant cliff and stopped on a shelf of rock with a full view of the site.

Zinn beamed. "I count twenty-one in their circle. Listen. Frogs and toads are singing."

Keela honed in on one of the figures. "The tall one in the center with the colorful sash, I can hear her tones from here. Do they remind you of anyone we know? Look at how she's integrating ethereal essence from the stars with the core of this planet. The amount of energy she's moving through her body is phenomenal. No wonder this area remains so healthy."

"The guardians surrounding her are moving a lot of energy too, like a wheel around a hub," Zinn observed. "Consciousness is building again. Maybe the time for the reawakening is near!"

The searchers watched the guardians blend endless dimensions and release the nourishing essence to feed Life throughout the basin.

"The woman in the center is Hetlin!" Yawri exclaimed. "I'm sure it's her. She was the one who communicated so well with the crystal caves and lakes deep in Earth. Remember?"

All smiled in answer.

"I recognize another one we know," Keela said. "Isn't the one at the far side of the circle a future Twaque? We used to create dyes together."

"Yes, I remember her very well. It's her." Tisbero spoke evenly. "Even though she met a cruel end, she must have embraced her death as a part of her life. She stayed conscious of who she was. Otherwise, she wouldn't be streaming so much essence with the body she has now." He nodded slowly. "That gives me hope, great hope."

The travelers watched in silence, their faces shining with relief. The guardians below concluded their focused endeavor and began to move out of their circle. Some examined plants, others stone or the falling water. A couple

406

of them came to stand by Hetlin and the sound of laughter carried through the air.

"Wait a minute," Keela said. "Hetlin and Twaque aren't the only ones from our time here. Look at who is talking to Hetlin."

Yawri's mouth dropped open. Tisbero starred. Zinn turned toward them both and her eyes danced across their faces. "This is wonderful! Yawri! Tisbero! They are your future selves, and you're still guardians. Maybe this means the time for reawakening is near!"

The searchers stared agape at the encouraging scene below. The future Tisbero stood erect and swept his head from side to side.

Zinn laughed, "You're still watching for anything amiss, Tisbero. Some things never change!"

"Why change something that works?" Tisbero responded, steadfast.

As the searchers watched, the future Tisbero froze in place, his eyes locked onto the path leading down the mountain. His bellow easily carried across the chasm. "Trouble comes! Run to the waterfall and cross under it! Go! Now!"

An angry voice flayed the air. "The betrayers are here!" it howled. "They defile the gods!"

The white-robed guardians, freshly out of their deep communion with Creator's Earth, looked down the path. Nothing was visible from where they stood. The future Tisbero continued to yell. "Run to the waterfall! Go behind it and get to the other side!"

The angry mob came into view, and the cry, "Appease the gods with their blood!" overwhelmed the sound of the waterfall. Hairy men burst up the path, bows and spears raised over their heads.

A man with sinuous, roped muscles strode in the lead. He jabbed the sharp point of a long spear toward the guardians and yelled, "Sacrifice! Sacrifice!" The bloodthirsty cries made the very rock tremble. He bellowed, "Take them alive for sacrifice! Shoot their legs!"

The guardians ran toward the falls. Arrows hissed around them with the sound of angry wasps. Several guardians in the lead suddenly cried out in pain and stumbled. Arrows pierced their legs or lower back.

Yawri's future self yelled, "Get Hetlin to safety! She'll be their main target!" The future Yawri and Tisbero rushed to protect her. Three guardians ran in front with Yawri and four with Tisbero at the rear.

The future Yawri continued, "We need to cross behind the waterfall. From there we can jump down into its pool!"

"A long drop but straight down!" Tisbero yelled in encouragement.

Arrows hissed by. One went through Yawri's sleeve but missed its mark. The leader with the ropey muscles yelled, "Shoot the legs of the tall woman! She's the witch who brought them together!"

Hearing the command to shoot Hetlin, the two white-robed guardians in the lead changed direction. They turned away suddenly and ran upslope, hoping to distract the archers from their target. It worked, but they fell, filled with arrows, within moments.

However, the distraction allowed Twaque, in the lead now, followed by Yawri and Hetlin, enough time to reach the waterfall before their attackers nocked new missiles. "Follow me in! Arrows will be deflected by the waterfall!"

Twaque sped through the first falling stream and stopped stone cold. She turned to face Yawri, her eyes filled with disbelief and an arrow protruding from her chest. She slumped against the wall. Hetlin ran into Yawri, who spun instantly to make sure she didn't fall. The point of an arrow emerged from his shoulder, but he was so focused on the task he didn't seem to notice.

Hetlin and Tisbero stared at the tip, their eyes wide, as they realized archers were ahead as well as behind. Yawri turned back around to check on Twaque. She locked her eyes on his. A fraction of a second was all it took her to convey her choice. Before he could move, she pushed herself off the wall, took a swirling pivot and made a staggering run back toward her assailant. Another arrow hit her chest. With her last effort, she hurled herself off the ledge. Her death would take one more arrow from their foes' supply and her body would not block the way.

Yawri had bent to run toward whatever lay ahead but another hail of arrows came from the path below. One pierced his calf. He stopped and called back, "We need a phalanx to push to the other side or we die!"

The last four in line behind Tisbero exchanged a glance, each knowing the next hail of arrows from below would seal the fate of all. Without a word, they turned and ran down toward the archers, yelling and waving wildly. The archers shot arrows faster than seemed possible, and their fusillade found flesh. Even after the hearts of the weaponless guardians were shot through, their bodies ran several steps before falling on the path in a twisted heap.

It gave Tisbero time to organize a new group around Hetlin. He howled, "We'll charge into the waterfall, you follow with Hetlin!" He stepped to Yawri's side.

Yawri saw the arrow sticking out of Tisbero's thigh at the same moment Tisbero saw the arrow protruding from Yawri's shoulder. Side by side they charged into the waterfall like bulls.

The archer on the far side yelped and jumped back, eyes wide in surprise. The abrupt appearance of two wild men hurtling toward him, more red than white, made his fingers fumble when he pulled back on the bowstring. When they were almost upon him he moved aside to get off a shot. However, the force of their bellowing screams caused him to take an unconscious step back. His foot only found air. He loosed the arrow into stone while he fell with his own scream filling his ears.

Yawri and Tisbero ran past his vacant space and saw the place where all could jump down to safety. Pulling up short, they stopped to let Hetlin and the others pass. "Jump here!" Yawri screamed.

Tisbero looked up in time to see arrows rain down from above. He yelled, "Stop!" but not soon enough to halt the running convoy. The arrows found their targets the moment they emerged from the falls.

Within seconds, all lay on the wet ledge, alive but stopped in a mid-stride tumble. Tisbero was hit twice more, once in the left thigh and the other in his side. Yawri lay sprawled; another arrow protruded next to the one already in his shoulder. Blood ran with the waterfall's spray and turned his white robe crimson.

Wild whoops and cheers arose from their assailants, who rushed to surround the crumpled guardians. The muscled man charged up to Hetlin. Her legs bled from two arrow wounds and one black-feathered spike protruded from her stomach.

The veins on his neck bulged with rage and he spat, "We have the witch!"

He bent down, grabbed the shaft, slowly twisted it, and pulled. Her eyes shuddered and he jerked the arrow out. The arrowhead came free with a sucking sound, and he held it up for all to all to see.

"This is what happens to those who anger the gods! She spoke lies! She tricked many into thinking these flat mountains speak to the universe! The proof that they defile the gods is here!" He pointed the bloody shaft to the sky.

Hetlin's eyes fluttered open. "How you treat others is how you tell Creation to treat you. You're asking Creation to give you lifetimes of being murdered. Don't do this."

His eyes bulged. "It is you who call down the gods' wrath, not the righteous!" He jabbed the arrow into the air again. "Stand her up and bring the sacred idols. We'll surround her with them so they can witness the sacrifice!"

Yawri raised his head and croaked, "Creation always returns what we do to others. You murder yourselves."

The leader swung a bow down toward Yawri's wounded shoulder. It landed with a loud *slap*, breaking the arrow that pierced his flesh. "Lies, all lies!" the man boomed. "Only the weak are killed, and we are the strong. Bring all alive and sit them here." He pointed to the ledge between Hetlin and the cliff. "We will cut their throats one at a time so she sees how the blood of the evil appeases the gods."

Within minutes, the fourteen guardians who remained were placed along the cliff's edge. One of Yawri's eyes was swollen shut, but he managed a wink at Hetlin, who was positioned before him. Her nod was almost imperceptible, but the message was clear.

He leaned against Tisbero and murmured, "Reconnect to essence, to the All. Hetlin will give the signal for the move." Tisbero passed the message to the guardian slumped against him. Although they appeared the same to physical eyes, the guardians vibrated with the ethereal essence streaming back and forth between them, the stars, and the planet's core.

A gentle rain began to fall as the conqueror's priest, in a dark-green cloak and mask, placed stone idols around Hetlin. Each one was accompanied by a chant. The idols for strength in harvest, fertility, and war had been set. Three more remained.

Although they looked complacent and resigned in their fate, the guardians increasingly blended more and more dimensions and released their nourishing essence to Life. Only they saw the small, black toads with bright yellow-orange bellies leap across the wet stone, the loud *plop* of their croaking call like a plump drop of water hitting water.

The priest finished placing the last three idols—the gods of rain, death, and the sun—around Hetlin. The leader, his roped muscles glistening in the rain, roared. "Ready your blades. The sacrifice begins!"

His brows drew closer, his face tightened, and his eyes wandered across the faces of the guardians in front of him. Some smiled calmly. Most had their eyes closed and their throat exposed as if inviting the blade. All had their bleeding legs stretched out before them, their hands gently resting on the darkened stone to either side.

He raised his hand to give the command, but before he dropped it, Hetlin spoke gently. "We leave you to your Creation. Our choice is to die in Life." Hetlin's body changed from a slump on the ground to an uncoiling spring in an instant. Before the leader could react, she hurled herself toward her bloodied friends. At the same moment, the guardians heaved themselves backward with their well-placed hands, now teetering on the edge.

The muscled leader's shock passed quickly and he darted for Hetlin. She ducked her head and staggered toward Yawri and Tisbero, who had their hands outstretched to receive her. They each grabbed one of her hands and leaned back.

The leader lunged forward and his broad, muscular hand grabbed Hetlin's foot in a vise. Her momentum was tremendous, but he knew he was strong enough to bring her down and smash her into stone.

The toads jumped up directly in front of his face, their orange bellies blazing like embers. He knew the slightest touch from their poisonous skin would burn hot as coals. He raised his hands to protect his face and stared at a sandal in one of them. His leading foot slipped off the edge followed by the other. Arms wheeling, he screamed, "No!"

The white robes of the guardians he meant to slay fluttered like wings toward the rocks below, and he plummeted like a stone, still screaming.

Keela, Zinn, Tisbero, and Yawri watched from the shelf of rock above the site. No one had spoken since seeing the reincarnated Twaque's death. A sudden veil of rain hid the falling flutter of dancing robes. The downpour came so quickly only a few of the attackers managed to climb out of the way before a river of water funneled from the flat-topped mountain and crashed upon the priest's stone idols and the zealots still standing by them.

The clouds from the valley joined those above and all became a swirling mist.

Keela didn't know when she'd started holding Yawri's hand but she didn't want to let it go. Considering her words carefully, she said, "I saw your future self smile when you helped Hetlin over the edge. You and Tisbero saved her from the torture of watching her friends slain. I've never seen such courage."

Zinn noticed her arm around Tisbero's waist, her hand resting where an arrow had pierced his future self. She moved it away slowly, stepped in front of him and looked into his eyes.

"I don't know why that happened. But I do know those guardians were no less connected to All than we are. The amount of trauma this ethereal center just experienced should have closed it down completely. However, it still vibrates. It's because they chose to die in Life rather than murder. It's because they maintained a stream of so much essence it continued to replenish Life even while they fell to their death. Who in our time has the strength to do that?"

Tisbero spoke, although his eyes were glazed. "They continued learning, even through such a cruel end. They have gained wisdom since our time. We must not let them die in vain."

Yawri noticed Keela's hand in his, but rather than drop it, he took Tisbero's in his other one. His glance asked Zinn to do the same. The small circle of friends held hands, all awkwardness forgotten in their need to touch each other's presence.

"There is no way to know what we will find ahead," Yawri said in a steady voice. "But the courage we saw here is our own." He turned toward the portal. "Let's find where courage lives in our future."

52. THE SEARCH

∞

The searchers pressed on, too distracted to appreciate the beauty of the rosy, luminescent time tunnel. They slowed when a portal in a section streaked with yellow veins came into view. A quick exchange of expressions showed all wished to find out what this time held, so Yawri opened it.

The searchers looked down upon a ring of giant stones. Individual slabs of living rock stood like towering sentinels in a circle. While the rest of the searchers studied the puzzling array, Tisbero's watchful eyes caught movement in the sky. "Look up!" He shot a thick finger toward the strangest skystone they'd ever seen. Three large skystones flew connected together. The middle one stretched much longer than the other two. Six guardians piloted them, three on each of the flanking skystones.

The strange formation reached the perimeter of the stone circle and one of the pilots said, "Carefully, now. Let's add a little soul sound to the wide end of the monolith to pivot it down to the ground." The large middle slab slowly shifted from horizontal to vertical, its wide end slightly above the ground.

"It wants to face the other direction," another said calmly. "Let's rotate it." The massive monolith turned smoothly, then stopped of its own accord. "It's how it wants to be set," the speaker said.

A female's voice responded. "Good. Let's increase gravity on it, so it sinks into the earth where it stands."

The pilots increased soul sound and decreased soul light, and the rock sank into the ground. After half of the long, narrow slab disappeared into the earth, the female guardian said, "Release!"

The stone stood perfectly upright and aligned with the rest of the circle. The pilots remained silent, listening. Individual stones started making a humming sound. After several moments the hum of each expanded into a chorus of all.

A voice rang out. "Each stone is connected to All and the circle is strong!" The pilots stepped off their skystones and walked into the center of the circle, their faces beaming with joy.

A female pilot said, "The pulse between the stone and Earth's core is strong."

A male pilot raised his head and said, "It's connecting to the other circles now, hundreds on every continent. The network of standing stones will maintain Earth's connection with All long after we've forgotten how."

Keela turned to her friends. "Even though awareness is in decline, guardians still work together to enhance Life. As long as they continue, there's hope. There must be a time in the future when Earth can awaken. All we have to do is—" Her voice was cut short by a swirl of light, and the portal suddenly re-opened. "What's happening?" she shouted as the searchers were pulled into it.

Yawri yelled in alarm. "We're being called back! We're being pulled back in time!" The whirl of spiraling light sucked the astral travelers through countless glowing tunnels.

"Stay together!" Yawri warned.

With a jolting shake, they found themselves standing in their bodies again at Earth's heart center.

Gamon bounded in front of them. "Shahten's attacking force is far larger than we can repel!" he yelled above the din.

The searchers tried to make sense of the frantic scene. At least thirty SkySlabs, each packed with menders holding unmaking crystals, flew down the valley toward the center. Within moments, shafts of dark light streamed down and exploded on the rolling ground in front of the defenders.

Gamon roared, "They're approaching from every side. Shahten knows the size of the force we have and clearly intends to overwhelm it. We couldn't keep your bodies safe!"

The four searchers watched guardians defending the outer ring tighten their circle around the center. More blasts rocked the ground. Although the defender's skystones harried it, a SkySlab stopped over the first line of defenders and loosed a hail of unmaking beams. Most of their beams reflected back with no deadly effect, but some damaged skystones and guardians.

"How long do think we have?" Yawri asked.

Gamon and Tisbero both surveyed the battle line. A guardian fell from his skystone, either hit by too many unmaking beams at once, or because he'd lost his connection to All. Either was fatal.

Gamon said, "We can hold out for … perhaps six hours."

"Looks more like four," Tisbero said.

Keela rocked back. "Four? Four hours to find one point within all timeless time? One point when awareness is strong enough for a future body able to receive us?"

Gamon straightened. "Have you found a hopeful future?"

Yawri's jaw tightened. "We investigated many but all still ended in decline. Our connection with the crystal center is strong, but with the harm of this battle, it's not able to hone in on the most promising futures as we planned."

Gamon looked at the crystal center and back to Yawri. "It needs more strength."

Yawri grew quiet, remembering how Red left Lazket's cavern because both crystals understood what was at stake. He remained quiet for so long Gamon opened his mouth to ask if he was all right, but before he could speak Yawri's rich baritone voice boomed, "Lazket has agreed to come!"

Tisbero took his eyes off the battle long enough to say, "Lazket? How? That crystal is deep in a cave over three hours from here. You can't go. You're needed to search!"

Yawri's response came fast. "Aronlat and Mariyonta are in a cavern next to his. Lazket is asking it to open a way so they can find him. I trained them to pilot skystones. They can fly him here."

Gamon's eyes went wide. "Those kids? In such a multidimensional vortex? They won't be able to stay conscious a minute. They'll pass out."

Yawri considered him. "Can you go, Gamon?"

Gamon rubbed his forehead but didn't respond. His eyes were drawn to the battle line. A searing beam landed next to a group of searchers. He barked, "One of the SkySlabs got through! It's going after them!"

The friends watched the vacant bodies sway where they stood. Defenders near the blast ran to stand in front of the unprotected searchers with their own reflecting crystals. In the next moment, twelve menders fell from the platform. One shielding guardian fell, but another one rushed to take his place in the defensive mirror.

Yawri yelled over the screams. "Many searchers are looking for the time to arc. As long as the defenders keep their bodies safe, there's a chance. It's good you called us back, Gamon. We needed to know!" Another blast echoed off a cliff wall and shook the ground. "Let's find that future!" he urged.

Gamon gave the searchers a parting glance. "I won't call you back again unless they are upon us."

Yawri opened another portal. "Stay alive!" he called to Gamon, who was already running toward the battle line. Gamon heard the call and looked back. However, he only saw their swaying, vacant bodies.

"You, too," he murmured, took a breath, pivoted, and hastened toward the approaching hail of dark light.

~

Yawri, Keela, Zinn, and Tisbero's astral bodies rushed through the time tunnel, straining to sense a future where Life bloomed again. The travelers streamed past a long series of branching tunnels. Finally, Yawri said, "I'm getting a signal from my ethereal diamond. That branch!"

The searchers all reached out to connect with living Life ahead. Zinn shot forward calling "Yes! Essence is strong down this one!"

The party hurtled down a translucent-green vein ringed with a spiral of gold light. Their astral selves emerged from a portal into a large underground room. "Where are we now?" Zinn asked the question on everyone's mind.

Yawri attempted an answer. "This must be a place made by guardians. It's deep underground, and the crystals in the alcoves willingly came from their caves to give light."

Tisbero stepped toward a tall archway and looked beyond it. "It leads to a hallway with several rooms. They're lit by crystals, too."

Keela struggled to put the scream of the guardian who had fallen from his skystone out of her mind. Her hand rose to sense the ethereal feather in her chest, but instead her fingers wrapped around the ethereal, green garnet Yawri had given her.

We can do this.

She spoke with decisive calm. "It's a sanctuary. It has multiple dimensions. Perhaps they can still communicate with Earth and the stars from here." The group moved down the hallway and heard voices echo down its walls. The searchers slowed, listening.

"This way," Zinn said.

The searchers went through an archway and entered a room that held a group of at least fifty guardians. A woman with long, dark hair was speaking.

"We do not deny the challenge before us. More and more human beings are separated from their Source and do not feel their impact on it. However, we do not deny our hope."

"That's future Pergaine," Yawri said to his companions.

Pergaine continued, "One of our seers, who still remembers how to be One with water, will speak to us now." She raised a palm to a small, dark-skinned guardian. His short, black hair shone with ethereal light.

He spread his arms to include several others near him, and his elegant voice resounded across the chamber. "We few are still One with the purest water.

When held in emerald bowls of old, we can still speak with Earth. We bring a message of great hope."

All in the chamber stood quiet. "We built the stone circles, and they function well to keep us awake and Earth alive, even as it slumbers. Their placement still propels Earth's song far into the universe, so other systems know of its plight. Earth says it is time for other structures to be built. Much larger structures.

"We are to build three triangular mountains in the heart region of Earth, that center which provides the wisdom of caring co-creation with Life.

"The first pyramid—smallest though not smaller in purpose—will provide connection to the memory of the entire history of Earth. Our own histories within that will be held in the living stone. In this way, Earth will make our memories of who we were available to us through ages to come, even as murder grows and our individual memories fail.

"The second pyramid is to be a ballast; a great, resonating, grounding source to Earth's core. It will keep the knowledge of how to keep physical and ethereal realms in a human being balanced and alive, so the wisdom of Creator's Earth remains awake within us.

"The third pyramid will be a generator connecting to the stone circles, to other pyramids to be built around the world, and to the universal essence of Life. Waterways will run under it to amplify its sound and light. It must be able to send and receive information with enormous strength, so gold will be its capstone. Lightning will flash from it to the heavens.

"Earth tells us that even if murder grows, for lifetimes to come we can work inside these mountains to keep our connection to All-that-is alive. Murderers destroy themselves as they destroy others. We hope they will end themselves while we are sustained by these pyramids of conscious Earth."

Stone and air alike relaxed, and a sigh filled the chamber.

"We will do this and all else Earth asks to keep Life alive," a voice rang out.

Tisbero turned to his companions. "This is hopeful, but our bodies stand at the center of a battle. It is good to learn of the work in this time, but they also say the decline continues. We need to find the time when awareness is expanding, not declining."

Zinn replied, "Maybe after the pyramids are built? The hope was that the guardians' connection to the living stone circles and these pyramids would keep them aware of All while the murderers ended themselves."

Yawri said, "Let's move forward in small increments. If their plan works, these pyramid structures will extend the awareness of the guardians to the time of reawakening."

The portal flashed open and closed and the searchers witnessed a rapid series of scenes showing the pyramids rise. They saw thousands of guardians communicating with granite, sandstone and limestone. The stone wishing to become a part of these mountains told them where and what shape each block needed to be. With their instructions clear, the guardians used laser-like emanations from crystals to separate stone from stone.

"Look!" Keela said. "Our future selves are a part of this. That's Hetlin, and Twaque too! Even though murdered they must have still been able to die in Life, because they came back with awareness of themselves!" The searchers recognized many others participating in the construction. A future Yawri flew a massive monolith through the air like a skystone, positioning it where it wished to live in the triangular mountain so it could settle seamlessly into place next to the stones on either side.

In another scene, Hetlin helped construct a passageway leading to chambers deep within the generator pyramid. Each chamber resonated with sound that kept each energy sphere in a human body attuned to its ethereal center counterpart in Earth.

Water flowing under the pyramid was somehow a part of its energy structure. An incarnation of Zinn busily helped construct channels to stream water from the nearby river through different rock types with different ionic properties.

A future Tisbero helped install an empty sarcophagus in the generator pyramid. "Hopefully, our future selves will see it and remember why we left it empty. It's to remind us that our bodies belong to Earth, not us."

The portal continued to open and close. After several more shifts in time, the searchers looked upon finished, marble-sheathed pyramids reflecting brilliant white light from the sun. A glittering, solid-gold cap rested on top of the largest one, and it continually streaked lightning skyward. The breeze hummed with tones of universal music in a living symphony. The pyramids moved with a breath of their own. Thousands of white-robed guardians radiated a vivid, auric glow.

"Perhaps this does lead to a time when Earth can reawaken," Zinn said. "Together, the stone circles and pyramids might keep us connected to All long enough to thwart Shahten's plan."

"Let's move ten thousand years ahead to find out," said Yawri. The searchers streamed through the tunnels and a portal opened at the same location in a distant time.

53. A SUMMONS

∞

"Did you feel something strange?" Mariyonta's question resonated in the deep crystal cavern.

Aronlat leaned forward. They were sitting at their campsite on the shore of the subterranean lake after a long day of learning. "Yes." Both listened to inner sounds, stretching to feel any ripple in the mineral Life surrounding them. "Something is wrong, but I can't tell what."

"I can't either," Mariyonta replied. "Let's go ask the geode cave. It will know." Her eyes darted to the glowing entrance near their camp. "I've never seen it radiate that reddish color before."

The two trainees hurried to its entrance and looked in. The angular shapes of the crystals inside the immense geode roiled with vibrant orange and red. The teaching cave said, "Come in, quickly."

The young adults exchanged a concerned glance. The multidimensional cave always taught patiently, never rushing through a session. They hurried in and stopped in the middle of the towering geode.

Mariyonta asked, "What's happening?"

Aronlat swayed in place. "The energy spheres of my body are wobbling."

Mariyonta widened her stance for balance. "It's the ethereal energy centers of Earth. Something is wrong with the energy centers of Earth!"

"Training is over," the geode cave declared.

"Over?" Mariyonta exclaimed. "How can it be over? We just started!"

Aronlat added, "What happened? Is it something we did?"

The geode cave continued without pause. "No. There is a crisis. Yawri contacted us through crystals he and other guardians brought to Earth's heart center. They are under attack by other human beings who wish to kill them and the heart center."

Aronlat arched back. "What? Why?"

"There isn't time to explain. They need Lazket. They need his assistance to locate future selves willing to connect to more of themselves."

Aronlat whirled. "What? That makes no sense. Who's Lazket?"

A crack of light appeared in the back of the geode cave and widened. "Go through there," the cave intoned. "It leads to the multidimensional cave that called you here. That's where Lazket lives."

Mariyonta's hand touched her throat. "The crystal being Yawri met when he first arrived on this planet? That Lazket?"

"Yes. Lazket can use Earth's magnetic fields to propel himself quickly, but he needs your soul light and sound to get to the planet's heart center. Yawri taught you how to fly with the living skystones, right?"

"Right," Aronlat answered flatly.

"Go now. Same as you do with skystones, increase your soul light and Lazket will float free from his cave, a place he's lived for a hundred million years. That gives you an idea of the importance he assigns to this task."

The pair stood silent for a heartbeat. The crack of light coming into the geode cave widened. A multidimensional chorus poured through the opening and circled them.

Suddenly energized, Aronlat and Mariyonta hastened toward the opening. "Thank you! Thank you for teaching us!" Mariyonta called back. They passed through the opening and suddenly stopped.

Every space of the floor, ceiling, and wall held quartz and fluorite crystals glowing bright as stars. The adventurers covered their eyes to lessen the light. Swirling in dimensions far beyond their experience, they leaned back against the wall.

Aronlat's hands played back and forth across its rocky surface. He turned. "Where did the opening go?" His strong fingers investigated every crack.

Mariyonta murmured, "Closed. The only way out is closed."

Aronlat looked for another exit, but a cavern of glowing crystals filled his vision. "We have to find Lazket."

Mariyonta leaned out slightly. "Yawri said he was as wide as a tree and grew out of a wall. Which wall?

"Let's ask this cave," Aronlat suggested.

Mariyonta opened to the energies present and felt a strong current of essence course through her. "I'm getting hot. The current is strong and getting stronger."

Aronlat opened himself further. "I'm getting visions. They can't be right. Guardians circle a cluster of crystals at home, at the heart center of Earth." His emotions surged. "Other guardians are trying to kill them!" He fell back against the wall, choking on pain.

"Breathe, Aronlat, breathe!"

Aronlat's head pounded with a deafening throb. Grief still choked his throat. Mariyonta felt dizzy. The chamber whirled. Her hands went numb, followed by her legs. She croaked, "My body. I can't feel my body. Where am I? I'm in an ocean, an ocean ... Who am I?"

Both slumped to the floor, eyes closed and unmoving.

54. PYRAMIDS

∞

The drastic change to the same location in a different time startled the four searchers. The wide river, initially close to the generator pyramid, now snaked away in the distance. Instead of succulent green, mud-brick dwellings covered the land. Fewer than a thousand guardians roamed the plateau, and none had an auric glow. Only those exiting the sacred passageways of the pyramids shone with ethereal light.

"The pyramids have become a raft of Life surrounded by an empty sea," Keela said. "Let's move on."

The portal of mist came again. Centuries passed. Another scene appeared.

The lightning no longer shot upward in a stream from the gold capstone. It flashed weakly, if at all. Scrub brush and sand-covered causeways. Pillars of smoke rose over the nearest ridge. The scent of burned buildings tainted the air. Fewer than a hundred guardians populated the scene.

A lone voice said, "The horde will be here soon. We must hurry to close down the pyramids, or what remains of their connection to Life will be used against Life."

Two dozen guardians flew skystones to the capstone and levitated it off its high perch. They reverently brought it to the ground. Other guardians shaped and moved granite blocks into passages, sealing them tight. Still others filled underground channels with stone, obstructing the water and the flow of its energy so it could not be misused.

The thunder of hooves rose over the ridge. Horsemen held swords high and yelled, "Gold! They hoard the gold! It is ours!"

Keela's astral form moved in front of Yawri, Tisbero, and Zinn. "Let's move ahead. There's nothing to be gained by watching guardians being killed again."

All agreed. Without comment, they moved ahead another thousand years and reopened the portal.

Kings, queens, and priests of every class took the place of guardians, their actions an imitation of forgotten knowledge. Written symbols took the place of living stone, whose song now fell on deaf ears. Small, pitiful imitations of the pyramids stood crudely hammered from commandeered stone.

Life and death no longer flowed in a continuous cycle but were split in two. Desperate for a way to return in their next body with full memory, the human beings tried to take their bodies with them. Encased in stone tombs as if it could be forced to follow its owner into the afterlife, the Earth spirits of the bodies were unable to return to Earth.

"We've got to go," Yawri forged on. "The living stone structures the guardians made did work. They kept connection to All alive for many thousands of years. However, their effect did not outlast the murderers as we hoped. From what we see, murder continued and eventually caused guardians to lose memory of who they are."

Zinn shook her head back and forth. "Do you think Shahten's forces killed Earth's ethereal centers? Perhaps this is happening because they are not asleep, but gone."

Tisbero rumbled, "Earth said it will not go to sleep only to reawaken to its murder."

Keela weighed her words. "The guardians at one of the portals said Earth gave them the vision of how its living stone could be used to keep consciousness alive. There must be a time when Earth believes it can reawaken. Otherwise, why tell guardians how to keep Life alive?"

"I agree," Yawri urged. Another portal opened and the four searchers leaped into it, propelled by their hope for the future as much as repelled by their despair for the past.

They hurtled down a wide time tunnel, but slowed when a large junction appeared.

"Hello!" a familiar voice called out. The searchers jarred to a stop. The astral bodies of four familiar searchers came into view. A stout woman with a wide, welcoming smile stood in the mouth of a translucent, turquoise tunnel.

"Hetlin?" Yawri called out. "Hetlin! It's so good to see you."

Hetlin replied, "All this travel across timeless time and we found each other. How goes your search?"

Yawri blurted out, "We've found periods when consciousness increased but declined again. None remained strong enough to serve as an arc to a future self. What about you?"

One of the other searchers in Hetlin's group said, "We went far ahead in time and may have found it."

"Pergaine! I didn't know you were one of the searchers!"

She bowed, smiling. "There's no age to my astral body, Yawri."

Hetlin said, "We asked her to join us. Searching across time with someone who still speaks with stars seemed like a good idea. It was. Pergaine found three alignments that promise great opportunity. We've visited two and are on our way to the third."

Zinn leaned toward them. "You found three times aligning for an arc?"

Hetlin moved toward them. "We believe the first two build to create a time for an arc in the third. All three alignments are focused on the heart center of Earth. The first alignment opened a door to receive a being called Aram. He delivered energies to remind us Creator's presence is with us, and co-creation is an active relationship with All-that-is. The next being was called Moshe. As foreseen, the enslavement of the human spirit and human bodies resulted in the slavery of human beings by human beings. We witnessed him delivering energies to end that slavery.

"We are on our way to a third alignment. If it works as foreseen, human beings will reconnect to the wisdom of the heart center with a depth not seen since hibernation began."

One of the two men in her group added, "This next alignment is poised to create the reawakening needed to arc."

Pergaine spoke next. "It appears four great souls will be born to support this major shift in awareness. One will be the teacher, a master being who will physically incorporate the knowledge of the other three. Search with us. It has been building for two thousand years. It is the best chance for an arc of consciousness we have found so far."

It took no convincing. Yawri, Tisbero, Zinn, and Keela grinned for the first time since their search began. They followed the other searchers down the pulsing tunnel.

Zinn said, "With the foundation under this timeline the end of our search sounds near."

The group stopped at the mouth of a large, orange vein. Hetlin said, "This will lead us to the best probable futures. To better cover points in time, let's investigate different segments and reconvene here. If either of us finds human beings with enough awareness to receive an arc, we'll call back through our connection to the crystals at the heart center to let all there know the time has been found."

The two groups eagerly flew down the tunnel. At the first branch, one went right and the other left. "We reconvene here!" Hetlin called out.

Glowing with hope, Yawri, Keela, Zinn, and Tisbero increased their speed and disappeared down a narrow, twisting turn.

55. HOPE'S STRUGGLE

∞

A group of ten people wearing rough woolen robes sat around a long, worn, wooden table. Large scrolls lay open in front of them. Keela, Yawri, Tisbero, and Zinn hovered invisibly above the gathering, listening to the intense discussion.

"I report the progress of the four goes well," a gray-bearded man said, rocking forward. "They are still young, but interpret the scripture's meanings with eloquence unknown for generations of rabbi."

"True," said another. "God has sent great souls to help us to return to Him. We will all strengthen with the Voice of Compassion. His support by the other three will unify people and guide us out of darkness. We live to see the rebirth of Light on Earth."

Another nodded agreement but his brow furrowed. "All four are strong and getting stronger. But Romans have slaughtered many in their search for these ones. What is to keep these four from being found?"

The man with the gray beard spoke again. "Yeshua is now traveling to Egypt to study with ancients there. The other three should be taken east, out of the Romans' grasp."

An aged face lined with sun-soaked creases said, "But to take them away from their families and communities so young will be damaging. They are not ready yet to leave their families."

"Yes." The man with the long gray beard held his arms out in a circle. "You are right, they are too young. Yet if they are killed, no voice with Creator's sound will speak. Let us do this. We will disguise them and a few of their family members as shepherds. Each family will take a herd of goats east to the Dead Sea.

"Those supported by Rome detest the Essenes, but we hear nothing of an attack upon them. Our charges will be safe there. If necessary, the three can go to the hidden land of Petra. Scholars of the light will protect them there.

We can send additional family members over time." They bowed their heads in thought and for the first time the room fell quiet.

The man who most objected to the idea of separating the four from their villages said, "I am sorry to say it is necessary. Let us go to their families and quietly begin preparation." All spoke their agreement. A decision made, smiles cracked tight lips. Relaxed hands passed plates of figs and dates around the table.

Two slow knocks sounded on the door, followed by two others in rapid succession. One of the men rose and walked over. "What do you bring?"

"The food for All," was the reply. The man slid a wooden latch free and opened the door. A short, weatherworn figure entered. His robe smelled of dust. He walked slowly, almost dragging himself, to the table and opened his mouth to speak. However, the words caught in his throat. The one who opened the door went to his side and placed a gentle hand on his slumped shoulder.

"What is it?" he asked kindly. A tear rolled down the new arrival's dirt-stained face.

"I bring sorrowful tidings," the fellow's voice cracked. "Soldiers attacked the villages of two of our precious children." Once more, the sounds caught in his throat. He looked pleadingly at the faces around the table but they only waited for him to go on. "The two young girls, our blessed cornerstones of wisdom, are slain."

"Slain?" several shouted.

"The soldiers came in the night," the messenger managed to say. "They knew where to look. Only their houses were attacked. Two of the four who came to bring Life back to us are dead."

Yawri, Keela, Zinn, and Tisbero pulled back in shocked disbelief.

"No!" Zinn cried. "How can this be? Over centuries of planning, the hand of the Creator itself fed this reawakening. How can they be murdered?"

Tisbero spoke in a low growl. "Free will. Creator does not control what we do, even if we choose to do great harm."

"But why kill what was sent to heal us?" she asked.

Keela said thoughtfully, "There are those who do not want us to be healed."

Yawri turned toward the portal. "Let's go meet Hetlin's group. Maybe they've found more hopeful news."

Rallying all the optimism they could, they entered the portal and rushed to the meeting place. The other party was already there.

Hetlin waved her arm in the air. "What did you find?"

Yawri responded. "Not good. Two of the four beings sent to help us were murdered."

Hetlin flared. "Two! There were two? We only saw one killed!"

"One?" Concern flashed across Keela's face. "Which one?"

"One of the boys. Not the Voice of Compassion. The one set to become the anchor with Earth. He and his entire family were killed by soldiers of Rome."

Pergaine asked, "Which young girl was slain?"

Yawri's face tightened. At last he said, "Both of them. All three who came to support the Voice of Compassion are gone."

"No! All three?" Pergaine cried out.

Hetlin sounded her shock. "But they were dear friends of the Voice of Compassion! How can this shift in awareness succeed without their support? Too many ears may confuse his words. Teachings designed to connect could be used to divide, could be twisted to create domination over Life instead of dominion with it!"

Keela asked, "How can one voice, no matter how One with All, return the memory of All-that-is to such diverse humanity absent the tones of both men and women?"

Pergaine shook her head in disbelief. "But the alignment shows this is to be the time of reawakening."

Yawri pulled on hope. "Maybe it can still work. His connection to All is strong. Maybe this teacher can still bring balance somehow. We've got to move forward and find out."

Distraught, they plunged back through the portal. Following the vibratory resonance of the Voice of Compassion, they rushed through time. The next portal opened and the searchers stared in shock. The Voice of Compassion was nailed to a cross. Large metal spikes pierced each hand and blood streaked down his face from gaping wounds on his head.

The searchers pulled back, and their eyes glazed in disbelief.

Yawri's hand went to the sash tied around his head. His voice began flat but flared as he continued. "I can't believe the thread of consciousness growing since Aram would result in this murder. Pergaine, there must be another alignment for Life."

Pergaine tore her gaze away from the unimaginable and said, "Observe only. I must observe only." She shook her head. "The energies Yeshua brought to us will continue even though his body dies." She continued at a measured pace. "Yes. Even with this, the thread is strengthened. We can still follow it."

All eight searchers plunged into the portal once more. Yawri called back with words that floated on the air. "Never, never give up. Always, always let go."

56. UNMAKE ALL

∞

Gamon studied the battle line surrounding the crystal center. The guardians protecting the searchers remained steadfast, their own reflecting crystals held to their chests. The outer ring of white robes faced a constant hail of unmaking beams, but forward progress of the murderers was slow. Shahten's massive SkySlabs hovered over them, but single guardians on skystones darted in and out to intercept the shafts of dark light.

Shahten heard another of his menders scream. As he watched the body fall and hit the ground, he showed his first wrinkle of concern. He spoke to himself more than to the master captain at his side. "The lost ones always die filled with fear. Unmade easily. It took them longer to start using unmaking crystals against us than I expected, but how did they become superior marksmen? Every time dark light is about to hit a lost one, our mender is struck down instead."

The master captain affirmed, "I see the same, my lord."

Another mender fell. Shahten pursed his lips and continued. "How can they fire with such unerring timing and accuracy?" He crossed his arms over his chest and studied the exchange. His eyebrows arched. He turned to a mender, pointed to a guardian below, and said, "Send an unmaking beam to that lost one. Aim carefully."

Even though the mender maintained his rigid stance, he had trouble disguising his smile.

Shahten never speaks to menders.

His chest swelled. Careful not to trip, he moved to the outer edge of the SkySlab so nothing would distract him from performing this honor.

With the practiced skill of one with years of experience shooting shafts of dark light into lost ones, he sent a long, powerful stream of unmaking toward his lord's target. In the same instant, he shrieked in agony. Shahten watched the mender's face contort in shocked disbelief a moment before his stomach collapsed in on itself. The terrified scream ended with a thudding *smack* against the rock below.

"So!" Shahten smiled with satisfaction. "The lost ones are not firing upon us."

The master captain blanched. "Not firing, my lord?" Another mender toppled from their SkySlab.

Shahten walked toward the edge, threw his head back and laughed. The master captain rushed to stand between him and the shafts of dark light rising from below. Shahten laughed louder and stepped up to the edge, entirely visible to the lost ones.

Shahten repeated, "They are not firing upon us! They only return unmaking beams to those who send them!" His smile stretched his tight skin.

The master captain swallowed hard. The memory of menders falling from his SkySlab after they fired at Tisbero flashed through his mind. The captain's jaw locked tight, but finally loosened. "You see what others don't, Lord Shahten. Of course they can't fire upon us, not with their precious code of Life."

Shahten remained fixed on the lost ones. "Well, well, my little sheep. You are intelligent fools, but still fools. Let's see how good you are at reflecting when you feel hate and despair."

The smile grew into a sardonic grin and his voice boomed. "All on this SkySlab, stop firing!" Every mender did as commanded. With the tumult ceased, they saw over a third of their numbers were missing. Shahten's grin did not comfort them, but the cessation of the screaming did.

Shahten barked at the chief pilot of the SkySlab, a deputy captain trusted to do whatever he was told. "Move forward and stop us within voice range of those lost guardians. The ones standing around the four in their center."

The deputy captain's brow creased, but one look at the master captain convinced him to take the SkySlab—with his menders under orders *not* to fire—within a stone's throw of the lethal enemy. "Yes, my lord."

The monolith floated silently beyond the front line of menders and SkySlabs, toward the circle of twenty or so lost ones Shahten had specified.

Surprisingly, the enemy let them pass over their lines without losing one beam of dark light. "Why aren't they firing?" the pilot breathed. Shahten smiled in response.

"Drop lower. They must hear my every word."

The SkySlab crept forward until every feature on the upturned faces, every wrinkle and smudge on their simple tunics, was clear.

"Stop here," Shahten ordered. He turned to his menders. "Stay at the ready, but no one fire unless I give the command."

Those on the SkySlab counted exactly twenty lost ones surrounding four of what must be their wounded. The four bodies stood, but, except for a gentle swaying back and forth, appeared to be comatose.

Shahten leaned over the SkySlab's edge and, smooth as ice, said, "Hello, my friends." Blank faces gazed upward in return, but none fired the citrines they held over their chests. Shahten leaned farther. "I have come to talk with you, to connect with you, to share with you. To be One with you." He took a deep breath and sighed.

"You wonder why your kind is getting slowly denser, why your children grow incompetent. How this could be happening to you? You are so caring for Life, so pure of purpose." His smile projected grace. "I know why." The serene faces below observed him with interest but nothing more.

"You think humans should only know the Creator through the soul of Earth. That they are not strong enough in their own identities to withstand the light coming from the knowledge we bring. But the truth is ... are you ready for the truth? The truth is that they are not only ready, they ask for it. All guardians see this, unless they are blinded by arrogance. You, not I, possessed the human spirit. I am here to save it." The expressions on the faces of the guardians hardened.

He continued inexorably. "You remember when you possessed them, don't you? You remember when the planet was moving into its next phase of incorporating more physicality. You complained you could no longer shepherd Earth's life forms because your etheric purity could not work with this increasing solidity. You could no longer communicate well with Earth's life because its tones ranged too low for your heavenly ears. You talked about leaving, but couldn't bear it, so you joined with human spirits so your 'work' could continue.

"You remember being warned, don't you? Many beings left. They said the time for guardianship here was past. It was time to let the life forms here grow into adulthood on their own. Isn't this what the Creator did with you? Sent you out to learn and grow without its direct hand so your own learning could expand?" Many of the guardians cast questioning glances to their companions and seemed to grow silently agitated.

Shahten spoke tenderly. "Many of your friends left, but you couldn't. So, truth be told, you took a human spirit so you could stay." The guardians fidgeted and cleared their throats. "Now, I know you *asked* them. You asked for their agreement. After all, you couldn't dominate them, could you? And so you continued joining with the same human spirit through the ages. How could that not be possession?

"How could they say no to such a powerful being of light? How could they say no to what would make them stronger than anyone else in their tribe? It doesn't matter if you overtook one human or a thousand. All it takes is one act, one choice made of your free will, to bring a thread of Creation into physical reality." He laughed softly.

"Open your eyes, your ears, and your hearts. The truth is, it was you who cracked Earth's Creation. It was you who chose to bring the knowledge of Creation's realms to humans before they were ready." He paused. "Perhaps you took the wrong advice."

"No!" a distraught guardian screamed. "You weave lies with truth! You bring lies to Earth!"

Another guardian spoke over him. "Stay connected to All, including the human spirit within! If we had done what Shahten says it would not be so alive within us. We are fully alive human beings!"

Shahten spoke in a whisper. "It doesn't matter if you possessed your body or not. Some did." He gestured to his menders. "After today all of you will be mine."

"Impossible!" the distraught guardian exclaimed.

Shahten raised a finger to one mender, indicating that only he should fire, and only at this lost one. Sweat ran down the mender's face when he saw every citrine of the lost ones below trained upon him. He took a breath, fearing Shahten far more than the dark light, and aimed his unmaking stone carefully.

He loosed an unmaking beam at the lost guardian, the one who glared at Shahten with undisguised hate. The unmaking crystal the guardian held cracked. Color around the man faded, and his chest imploded into dark light. When color returned, the lost one lay crumpled in a twisted heap.

Shahten stood tall and peered down his long nose. "What? Not one unmaking beam returned? Can't reflect back what you deserve, can you?" He studied the ring of lost souls. Some looked more collected than others, but all sagged. "If you had any conscience you would be ashamed. The thread you created will lead to more and more murder. How could it not? My followers only adhere to your example. The physical breeding with the humans only follows the domination of human spirits that you started."

"No!" another panicked voice screamed. Shahten's finger rose once more. One shaft of dark light fell. The voice below cried out in pain and stilled. The remaining guardians stiffened and strained to deepen their connection to All-that-is rather than sink into his trap of despair.

The guardian who reminded his companions to stay connected croaked, "Remember, he manipulates to gain control of our will. We are individual within the One. Shahten is no more, no less. No voice is greater than any other."

Shahten's long fingers massaged his chin. "Oh, we are all part of the One, so my voice is always with you. You have co-created well. Very well. So well, I assure you this planet will join other dead planets.

"You look so shocked. Of course, this planet must die. So-called guardians, like you, have already killed two in this solar system. Surprised? Why? Face the truth. Creator was wrong to send us forth. All we did was love it, and it sent us away. Wrong. Very wrong. But we can fix it. Together, we will create a void in the place of this jewel.

Together, we will show Creator the sending forth was a mistake. We will prove it. When every place of Life becomes a void, all will indeed be One again. A homogeneous One. I know you will help. You will help because you are possessed like the humans you yourselves possessed."

Many of the guardians began to cry. Shahten continued, unrelenting. "You're not to blame. It's not your fault. You were too young. However, you begin to understand the travesty forced upon us.

"All we did was love Creator, and it cast us away. How cruel of it. You know the law of Creation: What you create for Life is returned to you. How else can you learn if not from experiencing your own impact? Creator was cruel. So by its own law, we return cruelty.

"Join me. Feel the invincible power that comes from destroying what Creator itself made."

The steadfast guardian called out in a loud, yet wavering, voice to his companions. "Stay centered. The Creator sent us forth so we could become more with it, not less; an act of complete, selfless love."

"Really? Then why is there so much pain? So much suffering? Why are you shadows of your former selves? If Creator had not separated us, we would still be omnipresent within it. It cast you out and made you forget All-it-is, and you wonder why you are forgetting?"

Shahten droned on, his voice slow and reasonable.

"Would you send forth parts of yourself to learn what you already knew? How cruel. What kind of god would create separate beings from itself? An insane one. That's why human beings are becoming more and more disconnected. The way back to sanity is to unmake All."

A lone voice spoke calmly to her companions. "We are not separated from Creator. We have the gift of free will to learn and create. We have the choice to expand All with all we become."

"Or not, fortunately. I foresee a wonderful future." Shahten gazed upon the lost ones. Sweat dripped down every upturned face. His tongue flickered across his lips.

"Creator is to blame. Because of its mistake, the suffering you experience will grow. You will become ever more separate and isolated. It's only a matter of time before you find the strength to help me end this cruel game. I foresee a future where you poison all you touch. The air, the water, the soil, even your children. You will take whatever you want whenever you want it because it is your god-given right, and then throw it away. But the delightful thing, the wonderful thing, is that you won't care. Why should you? Creator didn't care when it threw you away."

A guardian raised his fist. "Twisting lies with truth only makes more lies! Your words are Creation of poison!"

Shahten looked at a mender and raised a finger. The guardian below who had spoken held his citrine crystal tight against his chest. However, no longer One with All, the dark light engulfed him, and he crumpled in a lifeless heap.

The remaining guardians glanced nervously around to see if any skystones were near to help protect their four searchers, and seeing none, moved closer together and closed the gap.

Shahten spoke quietly. "You react so because you know it is the truth." In a stern, confident voice he said, "The only way to return to the One you cherish is to end this separation. Ending Creation ends separation!"

A chorus of voices rang out.

"You lie. You created separation where none existed!"

"We will never believe your lies!"

A smile crossed Shahten's gently parted lips. He turned to his menders. "Open fire."

From across the field, Gamon caught sight of streams of dark light on the far side of the crystal center. The shafts rained down on a ring of guardians surrounding four searchers. As he expected, menders started to tumble from the SkySlab in a stream. However, while the screams continued unabated, fewer and fewer menders fell. When the dark light finally cleared, less than half of the menders remained, but not one guardian or searcher stood.

436

57. SEEKING ARC

∞

While Hetlin's group went to investigate a promising alignment in the eastern lands, Yawri, Keela, Zinn, and Tisbero followed the thread started by Aram.

They emerged near a broken stone wall on a high hill overlooking an expanse of fighting men. Battle cries rose above the sound of thundering hooves.

"Kill the heathens!" an army of human beings wearing large red crosses on their chainmail chests screamed. Another army wore colorful turbans and held long, curved swords.

A terrible clash of blade against blade echoed off the rock walls. Arrows flew through the sky and stabbed men in the neck and side. Blood spurted from the chest of one human being. He hurled his lance into another's eye. Both fell clawing at each other and were trampled into the ground.

Keela stared blankly, too stunned to speak.

I'm an observer, not a participant. Observer.

She looked at her friends. "Instead of connecting to expand the One as the sons of Aram taught, these men sever it."

Tisbero stared unblinkingly. "What is this madness?"

Keela swallowed and spoke again, her voice filled with sorrow. "Somehow, the followers of Ishmael and Isaac don't understand that different voices of the One are sent to different people across the world."

Cries of "Infidel!" joined the clash of spear and sword.

Zinn turned away as well. "They think there is only one way to connect with Creator. Theirs."

A large stone flew through the air and landed with a sickening crack of bone.

"Let's go," Yawri urged. "There is no light here. It doesn't matter which side. They love their own answers so much they hate anyone who questions them."

The four searchers walked, shoulders slumped and heads down, into the portal once more. They moved quickly down the tunnel, not speaking. Veins of the time branched in every direction, but they determinedly followed the vibratory rate they thought would awaken human beings to wisdom.

The portal opened on a large, cobblestone-paved town square under an overcast sky. Three men wore long black cloaks and sat in tall chairs next to a raised platform. The platform held two other men, both dressed in long red capes.

A man dressed in rags stood weaving on the cobblestones before them. The face of one of the men in red was calm but his voice was filled with accusation. "You were heard spreading doubt about the sanctity of Christ our savior. Do you confess to heresy against God?"

The man in rags steadied himself. His arms were strapped behind him so tightly his back arched. Tears rolled down his dirt-stained face, but he said nothing.

A man, also dressed in black but also with a black hood over his face, stood behind him. He glanced at the man in red, who gave a slight nod. In response, he pulled on a rope slung over a crossbeam above him. The rope raised the man's arms behind him to the point his feet barely touched the ground. His scream caused bystanders to step back.

Confess!" the other man shrouded in red insisted. "Confess, and thanks to the love of Jesus Christ you will be forgiven!"

"You tempt the weak away from the Lord with your heretical poison, the promise of healing illnesses with plants rather than prayer! Only submission to the will of God can heal!"

Confess, child! In the name of Jesus Christ, it is our duty to extract your confession, or your soul is lost!"

His eyes glazed, the man only whimpered.

One of the red-robed men raised a finger, and the rope was jerked up, then loosened to the point where he almost fell, then jerked up again. His feet dangled above the ground and one of his arms came out of its socket with a loud *pop*.

He screamed through a throat so raw the sound was like scraping stone.

"Do you confess? You must confess!"

The rope began to raise his arms behind him again. "I confess," he whimpered.

The rope lowered immediately.

"You confess to your sins and your soul can be saved. To enter the Kingdom of God, you must denounce other heretics who speak against God so their souls can be saved."

His weak voice babbled, "But plants are of God. They can heal sickness."

The rope tightened, his arms shot above his head, and his feet left the ground so quickly he didn't have time to scream before the other arm pulled from its socket. He dangled, slowly rotating in the air.

One of the red-robed men stood. "Your soul must be saved! You have confessed to heresy. Show your conversion by letting us save others who practice sin. Show that you give yourself to the love of our Lord so they, too, can be saved from eternal damnation!"

The man's gaze dimmed. His breath stopped.

After a long moment, the man holding the rope lowered him to the ground and prodded his eyes. "He is dead."

The red-robed man said, "The fact that he died means his soul was not strong enough. Burn his body with the others, so his flesh does not contaminate the ground."

The other man sat down again. "God's will. His soul was beyond redemption." He looked at a sheet of paper on a table between them. "Bring the next."

Zinn moved to the left and right, unable to stand in one place. "Human beings are torturing other human beings in the name of the Voice of Compassion?"

Tisbero's hands clenched and unclenched. "We better go before my observe-only state becomes an intervening state. Perhaps I could manifest as a ghost, an angry one."

Keela repeatedly touched her heart and recalled the ethereal feather within her. "Same here."

Yawri's arms hung at his sides "It continues," he said. "The murder designed to separate human beings from themselves continues."

Keela said, "Shahten murdered human beings over and over so they would become separated enough from themselves to become murderers themselves. The farther we go forward the more we see it. Divine messengers come but their messages are subverted. What is going to reverse it?"

Tisbero shook his head. "I refuse to believe this is our future. One where we choose to believe divisive lies instead of connection to all of Life? A future where we love to feel fleeting, false power over others?"

Zinn stepped forward, then back again. "How did the messages sent to humanity over thousands of years become so twisted?"

Keela exhaled despair from the bottom of her chest. "I don't know. Perhaps Shahten did kill all the ethereal centers of Earth. I don't know what else could explain this much separation." Her voice trailed off. "What is to become of us?"

"We've got to move on," Yawri said.

Without another word, the travelers reentered the portal. Transparent hues of yellow, purple, and green passed by in a blur. A branching tunnel of electric blue appeared. They dove into it and after a spiraling turn, exited a portal. It opened on a narrow street of packed dirt between a row of two-story stone dwellings. A window opened and yellow liquid was dumped out of a pot into the street. It splashed the passers-by when it landed, but no one even looked up.

"I think our future is more solid than stone." Yawri expressed the frustration of them all.

Tisbero pointed down the street. "What's going on there?" A man held a girl by her ear, twisting it while they marched down the dirt road.

"I'll teach you to do as I say!" the man spat out. "You're my property. I own you." He gave her ear a brutal twist. Pain buckled the girl's knees, but she was dragged by his grip. "I'll show you the price of such ingratitude. Now that you've proven you're a whore, it's time my son had his way with you," he sneered.

"No," she called out weakly. "I'll stay. Just you. I'll stay."

"You'll stay, all right. Chained." Her face went blank.

"You found her!" a woman's voice exclaimed.

"Get our son," was the curt reply. "Rather return from the market as she was told, I caught her accepting ale from a lout. It's time to teach her a lesson. Since she's a whore we'll treat her like one!"

Yawri turned toward his companions. "Are these even human beings? How can a woman, the bringer of Life into the world, be treated this way?"

Zinn moved toward the portal. "Let's go. These human beings have completely forgotten they are aspects of One Body. They think they are a body."

Yawri joined Zinn at the portal. "We've found enough to know Creator still sends help, but human beings are still in decline. Let's rejoin Hetlin's group. Maybe they've found a stronger thread."

Their faces filled with grief, but refusing to give up hope, the guardians re-entered the tunnel.

58. WARRIORS STAND

∞

Shahten instructed his pilot to move his SkySlab to another circle of lost guardians. Even though half of the menders on his platform had fallen, his voice rang with cheer.

"Closer, so they can all hear me clearly, deputy captain." They moved slowly over upturned faces. "Good. This will do nicely."

I know how to defeat them now.

"Hello, my friends," he crooned. Once more, the sea of guardians appeared calm, centered in their connection to All.

His smile grew.

"Let us stop this senseless fighting. You know the sending-forth was designed to take us away from our Source, and that our learning is to reunite with it. Beings of the beginning—Myself, Lucifer, Beelzebub and other genuinely great beings—know the Way. For us to stop this scattered dilution of the One, we must reverse the process. We know how to return All-that-is back to what it was before its loss. The void that was filled by the sending-forth must return to void. Only then will you be whole again."

He paused to survey their faces.

"The success of the Way cannot be denied. The void grows. Two planets have already been destroyed in this solar system. Killing this one will be enough to return it into the lifeless void it was before the sending-forth."

The guardians still stared up, their faces blank. Shahten raised his voice. "You don't believe me? Do you think you were the first ethereal souls to come to this solar system of spinning jewels? Can you be so naive? Perhaps. Let me tell you about it." He smiled beneficently.

"The first planet guardians destroyed was the easiest. It orbited this star beyond what you call Mars. It was too far from its star to receive warmth, so it created heat by transforming radioactive nature. So intense, so vital, so charged. You enjoy the sky here? That planet's was more than blue, its sky brilliant with hues of gold, red, green, and violet all rolling through it, a beacon for the universe to see.

"I was there.

"Its guardians were full of naive hope and goodness, and like you, so engaged in caretaking they couldn't leave, either. So much work to be done; so much Life to help. Over time, a long time, they made choices to dominate Life there. Like you did."

Shahten noticed several defenders shifting their reflecting crystals back and forth, but his benevolent smile remained.

Good. My seeds of despair grow.

"It's such a small change from caring to caretaking, and from co-creating to controlling, they didn't realize what it meant. Well-placed encouraging whispers have a delightful effect on those inexperienced with truth sprinkled with lies. It worked.

"No one, not even me, can make another use their essence for anything other than what they choose. Free will, you see. They needed to choose to act on my whispers."

He smiled. A few guardians exchanged glances.

"I told them they needed energy to build and develop the land. Their planet had lots of energy; all they needed to do was use it. Their early experiments were fine. We waited. When they grew in confidence, they set off a carefully controlled reaction … which happened to be near an unusually pure and large deposit of the silvery radioactive substance they loved. A chain reaction blew the planet apart." He paused. "It was beautiful."

One of the guardians leaned to whisper to the one next to him. "Could it be true?"

Shahten spread his arms wide. "Didn't you ever wonder about all those pieces of rock orbiting beyond Mars? You didn't? Well, it is an uncomfortable thought, isn't it? I wouldn't want to make you uncomfortable. No, no, your need to be comfortable is important. I count on it."

Shahten licked his lips in constrained anticipation.

"Arrogance murdered that planet … and Mars as well. Why is it called an 'angry planet?' Why would a planet, another of the Creator's thought forms, be angry? Afraid to ask? I'll tell you why. It was next in line, you see. It didn't have uranium, but it was close enough to the sun for all the energy needed. Quite a wonderful little planet. The currents flowing from its molten core kept it so even-tempered, Life accelerated faster there even than it does here. Its bacteria kept all its Life in balance better than on any planet I've seen." More guardians repositioned their citrines.

Shahten's expression remained beneficent. "You know bacteria are a cornerstone of physicality in Life. Many of you nurtured thought forms of bacteria into existence here."

A guardian murmured to his companion. "Does he know they're my specialty?"

Shahten's gaze was tender. "But the guardians there came to believe, with my considerable aid, that the planet needed some bacteria to fulfill a higher purpose. If only the guardians would help with this little change, the planet could become even greater.

"Some resisted. I shamed them. How could they not give what was needed? I spoke the truth. I did think the planet needed it. In the end, some of them created the new bacteria. They did help Life expand, for a while. However, since the new bacteria weren't co-created with the planet, they eventually broke many strands in the web of Life." Several guardians swallowed, their mouths dry. Shahten's eyes glistened. "What do you call it when death does not feed Life? Oh, yes. Murder."

Perspiration beaded on the faces below.

"With less and less Life, the planet's core cooled. The magnetic field weakened. Without it, solar winds stripped away the atmosphere and its water. Mars will die, but since guardians no longer live there to help, it's dying very slowly."

A female guardian stepped forward, her face still calm. "You delight in murdering Life. We delight in expanding it. Free will is free will, but all answer to Creator in the end. Those who destroy essence are destroying their own. With each murder, you lose your own essence."

Shahten barked a laugh. "The guardian speaks the truth! But here is another. Every time you agree with the Way it is a choice to give me *your* essence. It's why I'll convince human beings to demean women. We can't destroy Creator's Earth if the female aspect continues to be a cherished Life-bearer. No. I've already planted seeds to make humanity believe its loss is women's fault. I will delight in watching that murder grow."

A white-haired guardian exclaimed, "You're not going to divide male and female. No part of the Whole is greater than another. Absurd!"

"Absurd, is it? I foresee a future where the world believes females are only useful for breeding more property. Less useful than livestock. Ask your searchers. They've already seen it."

"You go too far, Shahten!" the man shrieked. "There is no way your words can diminish reverence for one aspect over the other. All know this planet creates through connection, not division!"

Shahten's eyes darted across the faces of three menders before returning to the white-haired man. "True again! The only power my words have comes from the power you give them. Fortunately, I have more than words to convince you." The old man stared unflinchingly at Shahten.

Shahten lowered his hand and three menders loosed dark light at the old man. The man's citrine reflected the beam of the first, but his neutrality started to fade when he saw Shahten laugh with apparent glee. Still, the unmaking beams pulsed undecided between menders and guardian.

Shahten decided to help tip the balance. He crowed, "You know only female bodies can bring forth Life, yours can't. That's why, deep down, all females think they are more important than you. How could they not? The male's only worth comes from what they provide to females!"

"Lies!" the elder yelled, but in anger, he held his crystal-like a shield. It ruptured in the dark light and the man crumpled in agony.

Shahten shook his head. "Good luck remembering you're different sides of the same quince fruit next lifetime." He turned to his master captain to share a thought. "I'll have to remember that speech. I wonder how many I can get to believe it?"

Many of the guardians shook visibly, but with no unmaking beams sent to them, there was nothing to return. Shahten exchanged knowing looks with his master captain and offered a bemused smile to the faces below.

He spoke calmly. "Think how wonderful it will be when all Creation is void. No souls, no stars, no cosmic oceans stirred by solar winds. Don't you see? More and more of you act on my words. Together, we will collapse All-that-is back upon itself, where it belongs. All will be the same in One."

"Take your venom into a void, Shahten!" The woman who stood next to what had been the white-haired man said. Menders on the SkySlab brought their citrines more firmly against their belts, but Shahten's glance told them to hold their fire.

Shahten leaned out so far it appeared he could jump into their arms. "We are all One, are we not? Are we not all of Creator? How can anything truly be unmade when All is a part of All-that-is? All we do is move All-that-is around."

He leaned back and considered his options.

This is a great opportunity to test which words work best.

He stepped to the edge again.

"This planet is filled with resources. Infinite resources. You have a right to use them. You deserve them. Take all you want. They're yours." He paused to consider his words. "You think you are guardians of Earth? My whispers will find a way to convince you of your rightful place. Your place is to rule it."

Another woman stepped forward, her eyes moist. "You murder Creation!"

Shahten examined the faces below with satisfaction.

"Open fire," he said, and dark light ruptured the air.

Murder them lifetime after lifetime and they will be reborn broken from the Source, and in shame. They will kill the others, and the others will be reborn and kill also. With their intelligence, they will be more wicked on this planet than any of my little bastards could ever hope to be.

The defenders who had given in to despair and judgment lost connection and died quickly. Those who remained One with their hearts, in spite of the loss they felt, rushed to cover the new gaps in the defender's wall. They reflected beams of dark light back to their source and menders fell in response.

The woman next to the crumpled, white-haired elder exclaimed, "Stay connected to the One Source! Bring change with Creation, not from division!" Two unmaking beams sent to her went back to their source with unerring accuracy.

Another unmaking beam hit a searcher, and his vacant body was thrown against the heart center's crystals with such force a crystal's narrow, pointed tip pierced his chest.

"Call our three remaining searchers back so they are not slaughtered where they stand!" she yelled again. "Call them back!"

A young man jumped to intercept a shaft of dark light aimed at one of the three. He reflected it back with deadly effect, but more unmaking beams came. They had just begun to pulse back to their senders when another shot over his shoulder. He heard a scream and turned his head. A second searcher lay dead. "No!"

The vacant bodies of the two remaining searchers stood defenseless in a hail of dark light. With youthful prowess, he expertly threw his reflecting crystal to deflect a shaft on a direct path for one of them. With nothing to reflect the beams aimed at him, he was engulfed by dark light. Through a haze of pain he saw the eyes of the searcher he saved flutter open as his own went dark.

59. MUSIC OF THE SPHERES

∞

Yawri, Keela, Yawri and Zinn rounded a turn in the time tunnel. "There they are!" Yawri called out in relief. Returned from their inspection of far eastern lands, the astral bodies of Hetlin and her companions floated under a gleaming ribbon of luminescent green.

Hetlin's stout form moved toward them. "At last! We were getting worried about you. We found something hopeful. What about you?"

The image of the young woman being dragged toward her tormentors still pulled at Zinn. However, she rallied and said, "You found something hopeful? All we found was misery."

Hetlin quickly reported, "Cycles of awareness continue to rise and fall. First, we investigated a messenger called Siddhartha. He brought the wisdom of compassionate co-creation. He remembered how to prosper without causing harm to any beings — including humans, plants or animals. We followed that thread of Life and found Kong Qui. He brought other energies of body and soul, and responsibility for the choices we make in Creation.

"However, while many aspects of the culture progressed some did not. Most people only survived by servitude to the powerful. Torture maintained their submission. The powerful routinely made slaves of nomadic peoples.

"A nomad named Temüjin escaped his slave master. We believe he was born to free people from such suffering. He promoted laws to ban murder, slavery and torture; and provide universal education. He insisted on freedom of religion. Many agreed with his vision and he became the Khan of a great army.

"His plan was simple. If the rulers of a city agreed to his laws, all lived. If they did not, they would experience the murder, slavery and torture they refused to ban. He was surprised when city overlords refused to agree with such basic laws for humanity, but many did not. He destroyed their cities. Millions died."

Zinn protested, "Will we ever find a time when human beings believe they are more than a body again?"

Yawri followed with, "What did you find that was hopeful?"

Pergaine responded with quiet certainty. "Music of the Spheres."

"What?"

"Music resonating with universal tones is given to human ears. Music transcends spoken language. There are no words to distort the message."

"What do you mean?" Keela asked.

"Messengers come with energies that reconnect us with different aspects of Creation, but human and being have become so separated that very few people can feel it. Great beings had to describe it for them. The problem is, humans can hear words without listening to their meaning. Words alone are easily misunderstood."

Keela was thoughtful. "Music has no words."

Tisbero said, "That makes sense. Let's go."

Yawri said, "Lead the way."

Grasping hope, both groups of searchers surged down the tunnel to find the time of music. A portal opened and the searchers hovered near a river filled with boats. Many people wearing colorful garments stood on an arched stone bridge spanning the river, as well as along its banks.

"What's going on?" Zinn wondered.

Other boats came into view. Large ones, with colorful banners over scarlet canopies. One held perhaps fifty people, all sitting in chairs. They all wore dark blue and sat facing a man standing on a short podium.

Pergaine said. "They're holding musical instruments."

Keela observed, "Those instruments are works of art!"

The crowd became uncannily still. Even the river seemed to hold its breath. Then the music began. String and reed instruments sang the melodic voice of the living trees within them; flutes echoed birdcalls at dawn. Harmonies and chords resonated with celestial music, touching the hearts and minds of all who listened.

Hovering in the portal, the searchers continued to watch the spellbound audience, open and rapt—parched soil receiving rain. The searchers beamed, and their smiles cracked faces too long etched with grief.

Harmonies from the songs of the cosmos touched every human being that heard the music. It linked all with their Source and touched their deepest memories. Playing on, the musicians seemed tireless and enraptured. Torches flared as day became night.

When the conductor finally put down his baton, silence came, but it was short-lived. Cheers from people, poor and rich, in small boats and large, on the bridge and bank, swelled and burst with triumphant joy.

The searchers overheard a man dressed in an elegantly tailored suit speak to another similarly adorned. "My resolve is strengthened by this music. Even though my friends protest, I've decided to disinvest in the Royal African Company."

His companion answered, "You know our profits have greatly increased the power we hold in London."

"Yes, but how can I justify selling slaves? The problem has nagged me for months, but no longer. I am done with it."

"You risk a staggering loss to your family."

"Perhaps. However, when my family invested, it was to trade the cloth we make here for gold there. But the Gold Coast is played out and the company turns to the slave and ivory trade for profit. I can't abide by it. I prayed to God for a message, and it came this night."

Hetlin said, "This energy brings great change without words. It comes because these human beings create sound with their living instruments that can join with Music of the Spheres."

Zinn asked, "Even though we've seen times of great darkness, you're saying progress toward reawakening continues?"

Pergaine answered, "Yes. More and more threads of Life are joining. It's why beings that compose such music could come here. It can move people out of their dark age into awakening. Let's follow it and see where it—"

One of the men in Hetlin's group disappeared. Not through a portal. He was there one second and gone the next. The other man in Hetlin's group vanished too. Before anyone could even say a word, Hetlin and Pergaine also disappeared.

Tisbero said in disbelief, "Where are they?"

Yawri rushed to the spot where they'd been. "There's no residue from a time branch. Branches can come fast but not that fast."

Zinn said, "Were they called back? It happened to us once."

"It doesn't make sense," Yawri pondered. "No portal opened. They simply vanished. The only thing that would cause that would be …" His words caught.

"If their bodies were killed," Tisbero stated flatly.

"Killed," Keela repeated. "If their bodies were dying their souls would immediately rejoin them for a conscious death."

The four stood in silence.

Zinn burst out, "We've got to get back and find out what's going on."

Keela automatically reached for the ethereal feather and green garnet of her physical body, and the thought centered her astral form. "If the battle is not going well, and from their disappearance, we can assume it's not, do we serve Earth best by going back to help or by continuing the search?"

Yawri spoke logically. "If we lose the battle at the heart center we'll die fighting there or die while searching for the arc. Either way, if our bodies are unmade, we are split from ourselves. Either way, information of body and soul can be lost." The group stood in silence once more.

Zinn's jaw set tight. "Let's keep searching. If our bodies are unmade, it will make little difference whether we're in them or not."

All looked at Yawri. "We search then. Pergaine said to follow the tones from Music of the Spheres."

Keela pointed toward a translucent yellow tube with pulsing violet veins near the next bend. "Music of the universe is strong in that one."

Determined, the four searchers quickly moved to the branching tunnel and plunged in. They found the thread they sought and kept moving.

"It's good," Tisbero acknowledged. "A strong thread of Life continues."

The searchers passed the first branching tubes slowly. Then they took a shimmering branch, found a portal, and looked through. It opened into a room filled with men dressed in waistcoats and breeches.

The statement, "Hold it up Mr. Adams. Hold it up!" was addressed to a fairly short, stocky man with fine brown hair. His quick blue eyes darted across the assembly and his voice rang with authority.

He held up a large, single sheet of parchment. "We have our declaration gentlemen, as we signed in our own hand for all to see!" Holding it high, he quoted, "We agree on the separate and equal station to which the Laws of Nature and of Nature's God entitle all—that we hold these truths to be self-evident—that all men are created equal, that they are endowed by their Creator with certain unalienable rights; that among these are life, liberty and the pursuit of happiness."

Applause filled the assembly. A voice called out, "There will be no king over us, or our children, or our children's children!"

The searchers continued watching from the portal. Keela spoke. "I see how threads of consciousness are woven across time. Old and wise souls still nourish this thread and weave light into physical Life."

Tisbero said, "Yet every bloom of light we've seen is shadowed by those who wish to destroy it."

Zinn declared, "Yes, but at some point human beings chose to recognize the lies and increase connection to All instead."

Yawri agreed. "Let's move on. The long-term direction is clear. Humans are learning how to care for Creation rather than fear and conquer it."

The searchers moved again, seeking the Life thread that ran strongest in the infinite matrix of timeless time. Instead, a swirling vortex of penetrating, violet light flashed open and jerked them in.

Yawri called out, "We're being pulled back to the heart center!" Portal after portal streaked past in a whirling blur.

"Are we being unmade?"

60. STORMS CENTER

∞

The searchers, finding themselves suddenly back at the heart center, looked through the dazed eyes of their swaying bodies. As they struggled to focus, the unmistakable clapping sound of unmaking beams surrounded them. They strengthened their connection with their reflecting crystals. Yawri's red diamond glowed.

A surreal scene coalesced. SkySlabs circled the outer ring of guardians and rained shafts of dark light down onto the tide of white robes. One SkySlab had managed to move past the outer ring and hovered over a group of searchers. Tisbero focused on that attack. "Only two of the four searchers in that group still stand!"

Yawri stared and jumped forward. "That's Shahten! Those two searchers are Pergaine and Hetlin! They're back in their bodies and alive, but not for long. All but two of the twenty defenders protecting them are down!" Yawri, Zinn, Keela, and Tisbero broke into a sprinting run.

Knowing Yawri, Gamon wasn't surprised but yelled out, "Wait for us! We called you back so you'd live!"

Gamon pivoted to face the others in his group of defenders. "Let's go! The four we're protecting are running toward the only SkySlab close enough to kill them!"

One replied, "The plan was for them to stay in our circle! What happened to the plan?"

"It's been Yawri'd! Get moving!" Gamon exclaimed as he ran.

Shahten remained focused on the determined, frozen expressions of the two defenders and their pitiful attempt to protect their searchers.

Time to kill the last two defenders and then their searchers.

Only six of the remaining thirteen menders on Shahten's platform had a clear view of Pergaine and Hetlin, and three beams went to each. The last two defenders jumped to intercept the shafts of dark light. The beams did not harm them, but because they and their crystals were so depleted, the beams were only deflected, not returned.

In a condescending voice, Shahten asked, "Having trouble protecting your precious searchers? What kind of defenders are you? Unmaking you all does Creation a favor! You are so weak, you don't deserve Life!"

The force of unmaking pushed the defenders back, but they planted their feet and the dark light flared around them.

It won't be long now.

The heroic cycle of defenders blocking and dying to protect Pergaine and Hetlin was at an end. The last two defenders screamed as dark light started to touch their flesh.

Pergaine and Hetlin, back in their bodies and their faces wet with tears, looked upon the carnage. There was nothing they could do to stop the line of defenders who chose to die protecting them, including these last two.

Pergaine slumped. Hetlin caught her but, weakened herself, could only slow her fall. She tried to raise her own reflecting crystal to thwart the salvo when the last two fell, but her muscles didn't respond. She watched the reflecting crystals of their last two defenders glow white.

Only seconds to live.

"Aheeee!" a voice cried.

Zinn's small, lithe body sailed past Yawri. Her springing jump carried her through the air and as she tumbled in a circle, she deflected the first course of beams away from one defender, landing to return the next.

Yawri was one leap behind Zinn. While she landed in front of one beam, he came down in front of the other.

The shafts of unmaking found complete non-resistance. The fluid essence of Creation surrounded the dark light and touched it, and essence returned it to its source, Whole.

Three menders fell from the SkySlab in rapid succession, followed by three more. Other menders ran to take their place.

"Stop! Menders, stop!" Shahten commanded. All but one halted immediately. That one was too caught up in his hatred and sent an unmaking beam. Shahten stared with disgust as his writhing form toppled down to join the heap of mangled bodies below.

Five. I have five left out of thirty-five.

Confident in his safety, Shahten turned to face his master captain, ignoring Yawri and his cohorts. "Signal another SkySlab to come alongside. I need more menders."

Tisbero's stout, blocky body caught Hetlin at the same time Keela reached Pergaine. The elder women's bodies wavered weakly, but their eyes still burned.

Yawri and Keela came to the aid of the last two defenders and helped them walk to Hetlin and Pergaine. Uncertain what to do when they got there, they looked down at the two women they were still willing to die for. Pergaine looked up. Tears came to her eyes. "Sit down with us."

Yawri and Keela helped their last two defenders, their robes black with char, lower themselves down next to their searchers.

Gamon hurried to brief them all. "Shahten caught on to the fact that we're only reflecting the beams, not firing them. That's why his SkySlab was able to gain the center and attack these searchers." He gestured toward the bodies but didn't turn to look at them.

"It's not good. Shahten brought in ground forces, humans—not armed with unmaking crystals but with clubs. He knows we have no way to return physical blows. The other SkySlabs are now concentrating fire on one guardian at a time. Their losses are still high because we take turns intercepting the unmaking. But we are losing. Shahten moves in front of them, and twists lies with truth. He keeps talking until a defender loses their center. Their death causes others to weaken. It spirals into what you see here."

Yawri said, "We need to remind the guardians how to stay out of despair and stay connected and in honesty in the face of his lies."

Another SkySlab, packed front to back and shoulder to shoulder with menders, flew over the outer ring of guardians without firing and approached Shahten. Gamon said, "They must be sixty menders, double the usual number, coming to his platform. We don't have time to remind anyone about anything. Have you found a time for the arc?"

Yawri stood still while he watched the SkySlab approach. Gamon was right. At least sixty. He surveyed the battle scene. The SkySlabs circling the outer defense had tightened their ring. "Not yet."

Zinn volunteered, "We are following a hopeful thread. It's from the one you found, Pergaine. In that time, people are awakening to the fact that all are empowered by Creator to choose what they will. They understand 'unique but equal' in Creation."

Cries of pain rose from a guardian on the outer ring. Previously, menders sent shafts of dark light from one or two unmaking crystals to attack one guardian. This one faced seven. Instead of scrambling to intercept the dark light every few minutes, other guardians had to intercede within seconds.

Gamon's voice was steel. "When Shahten sent the message for reinforcements, he must have included orders for the other SkySlabs to concentrate dark light on one guardian at a time. Our time is short. If there is no news of an arc, is there any more news from Lazket?"

Yawri raised Red to his chest and listened a moment. "Not yet."

Yawri glanced at his friends. All were disheveled and exhausted.

With his own tunic more brown than white and a bloodstained sash trailing from his head, his image fit the desperation of the moment perfectly—except for a boyish grin. "Let's talk to him."

"Talk to him," Gamon said flatly.

Everyone surrounding Hetlin and Pergaine looked up. Shahten's lips were pursed, and he was clearly savoring this moment.

Shahten let the silence grow; knowing it always unsettled the rabble before he began to speak. Except this time, the rabble spoke first.

"Hi, Shahten." Yawri's rich baritone rose easily. "You finally reveal the truth of yourself."

Shahten's head drew back. He bit his lip. Keela, Tisbero and Zinn stood behind Yawri, and Pergaine and Hetlin were getting up. Even the two injured defenders rallied. In addition, all twenty defenders from Gamon's group circled them.

Shahten stood taller and his tongue traced his thin lips. "We meet again, Yawri! How did you survive your fall? Pity it was just to die here." The sound of his voice was kind, even compassionate. "Why fight when you could join? We all want the same thing, don't we? We can all be One."

Although their expressions remained unchanged, Shahten watched a ripple pass through the defenders. He swept a hand toward the pile of torn bodies. "There is no need to die. All of this is foolish. I truly do only want to be One with you." His eyes caressed the defenders. He let them linger before they shifted to the long line of menders glaring down on their prey.

Beads of sweat formed on the faces of several defenders and they swallowed hard.

Yawri held Red comfortably over his chest. "One, unique within All? Sure, Shahten." He felt Red resonate with the ethereal diamond within him, and with crystals far beyond. "Sea, stone, and I are One, so we survived well. Thanks for asking. I see you're still trying to convince others to believe in you instead of themselves."

The sound of Yawri's voice broke the trance the guardians hadn't realized they'd been in. A silent sigh of relief passed through the defenders. A young woman stepped closer to Yawri, wanting to hear every word.

Shahten continued with calm resolve. "Yes, hello, Yawri. And Keela and Tisbero, too! You left the island without saying goodbye. That's why I had to come here. It was very rude of you to break tradition. What happened to 'Travel safely! Expand All with all you become?'"

Yawri's eyes shined. "By all means, 'go forth and Create with Creator,' Shahten. However, your actions show you're more interested in murder."

Shahten grinned and changed the topic. "Really? Have you found a time when human beings are willing to make your precious arc? I have searchers in the future too, you know, just looking for something different."

"Shahten," Yawri replied. "You know we haven't. Not yet."

Shahten laughed aloud. "But you have seen the effect of my counsel through the ages. You saw how your future selves love my truth and act upon it."

Yawri's gaze was steady. "I have seen those who choose to believe in your words create their own undoing."

"But you will come to love me, too! Surely, you have seen this. I save you from your pain. I bring the future comfort and pleasure. And you could use some saving right now."

"At what price?" Yawri let the sadness he felt course through him, accompanied by deep compassion for Life. The ethereal diamond within him sang in response.

Shahten pressed on. "What price? One you'll be happy to pay. I give your future selves what they want. They invite me into their lives. You know I cannot control what they do, not in the presence of this universal gift of free will you so cherish." His teeth glistened. "But they choose to act upon my thoughts above all others. They want me."

"And why is that, do you suppose?" asked Yawri.

"Why? Because they do not want to feel how weak and pitiful they really are. They want to stay comfortable in their own world, numb to the impact they have on Creation. I will protect them from feeling everything but their own righteousness and power."

"So the price is losing who they are?"

"But they get to become me! Marvelous, isn't it? The more they lose of themselves, the more of their essence I gain. They love the way being right makes them feel powerful. They love my Way. They like being better than others. They need to be. Especially since they're born in sin."

Yawri took a slow breath and let it go. "You love to separate people."

"Of course! When you are separate from 'them,' you are safe! I'll keep you safe inside your walls. Our walls. You have a right to protect yourself. You know—from the others."

"What you call separation, I call disconnection. And we've seen many human beings across time who don't agree with you."

"Not enough to matter. You know the future you will create. No one should question your right to do whatever you want to do ... to anything."

"So, you say no one should question what harms Life?"

"Harm life? Do you have any idea how large this planet is, Yawri? One person can't do enough to matter. How can you? Anything you do is insignificant. How do you think the message 'have dominion *with* Life' changed to 'have dominion *over* Life' so easily? Only a few noticed, and they died for speaking out. Serves them right for asking so many questions. Nature's dangerous! You better dominate it, or it will get you."

Shahten folded his hands over his waist. "You've seen the future. You know I'm right."

Yawri listened to Shahten and let what he said flow through him without resistance. Shahten's words were about Shahten, not him. "The tiniest particle of the universe contains the entirety of all. How can anything at all be insignificant? You know a human being is part of the One body of Creator. Every action matters."

"Now you are talking nonsense."

"No. Remember, Shahten; I am a part of All-that-is, as are you. It's how you know which words to take from our beliefs and twist them to make fear. I do not fear your words because I know they are yours, not mine. I listen with my whole body to know when you speak partial truths, and realize you have done so from the beginning. Each sentence you utter is designed to create despair and so convince guardians to believe your words more than those of the Creator within."

Yawri continued, his eyes steady. "Would you not find joy if this whole solar system collapsed into a void? If its vacuum pulled in adjacent stars and systems? Would it not be joyous for you if all Creation collapsed back into the void from which you say it came? A void in which all sound, light and soul was unmade?"

Shahten arched his back and pointed a long finger at Yawri. "And why shouldn't it? Free will was a mistake! Don't you see? Creator should never have sent particles of itself forth. Look at the murder, the suffering, the pain it caused! What kind of demon would force that upon itself? An insane one! People believe in me because I save them from feeling the pain of Creation. You will, too, when you finally believe!"

"Shahten, believing you creates the murder. Believing you causes the pain."

"But not in the end! In the end, they feel nothing. I don't make people choose to be numb, to protect themselves with their little rationalizations. They never question their meanness, because they know what's best for everyone else. It's their duty to cut people down to size, cut after little cut.

They love the feeling of power it gives them to slyly undermine those they envy, to seed gossip and lies to destroy others—and call it giving."

He laughed out loud again. "Don't you see? You think your grazing sea cows are going to live? Fantasy! You think your great trees will live? You'll unmake Murann and all his woody friends, too. As well as any human beings that try to remember who they are. You'll burn them at the stake, one way or another."

The words stung, but Yawri kept his connection to the heart center strong. The red diamond was glowing and warm. "You manipulate with the lightest touch to begin a crack in what is whole. You fracture our trust with treachery and so convince others to fracture more. We came here young. We were innocent of lies. None of us even comprehend one could exist. Those who believe yours don't yet know the harm of what they do."

"You can't be serious! You're not going to give me more of that 'Forgive them for they know not what they do' drivel, are you? They choose every day not to know what they do. It's so easy for me to twist the Voice of Compassion's *divine* words into what I want. I love the inquisition. Don't you? And the crusades. One group of God-fearing puppets torturing another. I'll feed that thread of hatred every chance I have."

Shahten's voice rose. "And killing the Jews. Talk about hate. Who do they think they are, trying to usher in their ten laws? We were getting along fine without commandments. Nothing wrong with worshipping carved cows." He smiled. "It's so easy to divide people. All you have to do is convince one group to blame another for their problems. A majority blaming a minority works every time. So murder continues. You might as well give up now and join me."

Yawri stood unflinching, still in centered calm. "It's true that I have seen what you say. The lie is in what you leave out. You pretend Creation is two poles, and leave out the world in between. Even in the darkest of times we find human beings connecting to Creation. Your tide of evil recedes and caring blooms, again and again. The thread of awareness grows slowly stronger."

"Oh, really? The future I foresee has both sides of every disagreement, large or small, filled with righteous hatred. It doesn't matter who wins, I've won. People know what they want and I give it to them. They will prove it over and over." Shahten placed his hands on his hips and leaned forward. "I don't make them think uncomfortable thoughts. You do. You and your *questions*. I will save them from uncomfortable thoughts. No one wants to change their life."

Yawri was one with the breath of the forests. "Life is change."

"The life I give them is safe, safe from being wrong. When you are right, there is no need to change. It's important because if you're wrong, you don't deserve to be loved. Best to be right and cover up any fear that you're not one of the righteousness ones. I want them to feel superior to others--or inferior. Better or worse, right or wrong, in shame or blame. I don't care which. Whatever it takes to keep their focus outside of themselves, away from Creation within."

Yawri was thoughtful. "You are a teacher, did you know that, Shahten? I had no idea intentional harm existed until you came. Even though you seek to destroy Creation, you are within it. I intensely disagree with what you do. You disagree with what I do. You may not wish to learn from me, but I will learn from you. I will not stand by and watch the harm you do. Knowing you is how I will learn how to transform it."

Shahten, tired of his talk with Yawri, dismissed him. "You are boring and annoying. You're right about one thing. I have nothing to learn from you." He gazed at the upturned faces.

They've become centered again, listening to Yawri's drivel. Enough.

Shahten's voice rose to a fevered pitch. "Are you sheep without a voice? Are you afraid to learn from me? All scared to be taught by Satan? With your broken memory that's how you'll recall my name, you know. Satan. Nice ring to it, don't you think? Satan. The delightful thing is that you won't remember what you forgot."

Keela spoke this time. "I'm sobered, not scared."

"Keela! My old friend. You find me sobering? 0Well, you should. Why wait? Join the Way now and save yourself. You've seen the future, too, so you know all guardians do in the end."

"Join you in oblivion?"

"Oblivion? Don't go spreading gossip again. It's salvation! Tell the truth. In all your searching, have you found anything other than insignificant pockets of do-gooders?"

"All are significant. Every choice matters."

"Oh, excuse me. Of course, the little do-gooders matter. They prolong suffering. If it weren't for them, caring would have died out long ago. But no, little pathetic human beings chose to care for others, even at the expense of their own lives! What's wrong with them?"

Keela replied, one hand resting on her chest. "For them, caring for Creation in and beyond self provides great purpose. They know the gift and responsibility of free will. They know the meaning of their choices."

"And they are fools. We torture them. We break their hearts. Over and over. Eventually, all will be reborn free to murder. Still, there are those that defy me."

"I defy you," Tisbero said. "I choose to disagree with you and stay connected at the same time. That way, I know your whisper among those of my own."

Shahten's eyes flashed in surprise. "Tisbero! You defy *me*? Now that your search is at an end, you defy me?" He glanced at the long row of menders ready to rain death on the lost ones. "Yes. Your search is over. I'll tell you what you would have found if you had been able to continue. There is no renaissance of consciousness. The desire for comfort and righteousness are king and queen, and those that buy it have no interest in knowing its true cost. They're entitled to get what they want, when they want it. Why shouldn't they get it?"

He grinned and continued in a soothing tone.

"The whale, your aquatic equal, will not be able to speak with you in this world you seek. The ancient kinship of the ethereal souls you share will be blotted from your memory so effectively that in a desperate attempt to communicate with you it will cast itself upon a beach. You might ask, 'Why is the whale killing itself?' but you won't realize that it is doing so because it wants you to ask, 'Why are *you* killing *yourself*?' Don't you find that funny? It is killing itself in the hope you will ask why you are doing the same!

"In your future, the descendants of mammoth beings are slain for their teeth. The great tree beings are slain to make benches." He chuckled. "Don't worry. Your intelligence will save you." He stared with a sardonic smile and added in an almost inaudible voice. "You won't fight for Creation, because if you felt what you were doing, I'd stop you with shame, blame, or both. How can *you* be one of the fallen? Not you, it's others who need to change. Those others are so ignorant, don't you just hate them?"

"No!" a frantic voice called out. "Never!"

Shahten raised a finger and a single shot crumpled the guardian. He writhed in a mass of pain before going still. Panic overtook the guardian standing next to him, and Shahten signaled again.

The young woman who had come to listen pivoted away from Yawri, and in a flowing movement intercepted the unmaking beam. It returned to its source with deadly effect.

"Now you've done it," Shahten said, detached and amused. "You killed one of my menders."

The young woman's voice was high, yet resonate. "Your voice is not my own. What was sent was returned. Noting more."

461

"Well, *you* may know my voice is nothing more than any other, but those who know that are few."

"More will learn," she replied. "I am."

Pergaine rallied her strength. "Your lies are your own, Shahten. We use honesty with self to know which voice to listen to and act upon."

The tip of Shahten's tongue traced slowly across his lip.

"Pergaine, you were so close to death. How sad. Now you must suffer again. Murder after murder, you'll become so confused you won't know what voice is yours."

"I may forget for a time, but I know I will never give up. I will remember who and what I am because my source is All-that-is."

Hetlin spoke, her voice deep with the sound of Earth. "We know you will not change, regardless of what we say. However, silence implies consent, so we will speak out again and again and show our disagreement." She waved her hand to include her companions. "Everyone here speaks with actions that show Creation we disagree with what you say and do."

Shahten stared down at the little circle of defenders and decided to change to a more enjoyable topic. Raising his voice, he said, "You think you will succeed at helping Earth sleep? You won't. Even if you did, do you think your future selves will want to wake up? Wake up to feel what happened while they forgot who they were—in spite of all the little stone clues they left? Shame. Shame on you all."

Yawri repeated, "There is no shame in learning what you do not know."

"No. All hope is lost. Hope is for fools. The nice thing about convincing you to divide human beings into human and being again is the war it creates within you. The body is sinful and the soul is spiritual, right? I'm brilliant."

The young woman who had returned the unmaking beam stood next to Yawri once more. She raised her face and her soprano voice rang, "Thoughts that expand connection of both, human and being, are mine. Ones that cleave it come from you."

Shahten didn't bother to look at her but swirled his glistening, silver cape and addressed all. "Cleaving will win in the end! Maybe I'll let you win this little battle, because it would be so enjoyable to get more of you to believe in me." His gaze swept across the conflict surrounding them and saw the agony of fallen men and women mixed with shafts of dark light. "Yes, more of this will do nicely."

He looked down at the searchers. "It is very enjoyable talking with you. So rare to have someone to talk to. Most people are so afraid of Satan. I like that name. One of my favorite tools, breeding fear. But you know that."

He surveyed the battle. The ring of SkySlabs was much tighter now. The strategy of concentrating several shafts of dark light on one guardian at a time was working. "I must get back to the task of saving you now. You will join me, you know. I look forward to seeing when and how."

The young woman continued, "No, Shahten. I choose to nurture, not murder Creation."

"A pity. Well, we have to start somewhere, and starting with those who speak out will help others stay silent." He glanced at a new line of fifteen menders standing along the edge of his SkySlab. "Unmake that young woman who spoke out with that annoying voice."

Beams from all fifteen unmaking crystals shot at the young woman next to Yawri. They hit her reflecting crystal with such force that she fell back. First Yawri, then in rapid succession, Zinn, Tisbero, Pergaine, Hetlin and all twenty-two defenders took turns of two or three seconds each reflecting the mass of dark light.

All fifteen menders fell, but it was a part of Shahten's plan. Starting with over sixty on board he had a line of three more ready to take their place. With each cycle, the defender's crystals needed more time to recover between the concentrated shafts of unmaking, but the hail of dark light was constant.

All I need to do is keep the dark light falling faster than they can recover.

He smiled when the first defender fell. Then the second. The next was even sooner. The cascade of fallen defenders increased rapidly. He laughed.

In the next instant, the ethereal diamond in Yawri's chest sent him a message he could not deny. It felt so clear it seemed to come from Tilan himself, the diamond being who had given him the gift so many eons ago.

Yawri spoke hurriedly to his companions. Nods of understanding came fast. All six searchers rushed to break into the line to intercept the focus of the attack on the young woman who spoke out against Shahten.

In one fluid motion, Yawri moved in front of her and held Red in the center of his chest. Keela came behind him and quickly held her crystal above his head, followed by Pergaine and Hetlin holding theirs to the left and right of his shoulders. Tisbero and Zinn sat in a lotus position near each of his knees. The result was a large five-pointed star with Red in its center.

All the life forms that the six guardians had nurtured through the ages pulsed within them. Sounds and sweet air from all of the wetlands, forests, seas, deserts and mountains of the world flowed through human beings and reflecting crystals alike.

The unmaking beams did not fall on individual crystals. They fell on a star.

Menders fell. Four. Six. Ten.

Shahten looked on with disbelief. Only twenty of the sixty he'd packed on his SkySlab remained.

"Stop!" he commanded. "Stop firing! All of you!" Those still upright pulled back quickly.

Yawri's voice was steady. "All is Creation, Shahten. You cannot divide it."

Shahten took a step back as well. "You connect. I divide! You hope you're going to win, but there is no hope. Your crystal center is not strong enough to suffer all of this death. It dims. Your fate is sealed. All of you will be murdered and broken in the end. It's only a matter of when." Hearing wild cries he looked toward the battle line. His foot soldiers were closing in with their clubs.

It won't be long now. Reflecting crystals can't return physical blows.

He stared down at the fools. "You've already seen it. Every time awareness comes, the few who support it will be overcome by those who don't want it. They will undermine it while saying they increase it. Self-righteousness is my calling card, and even you will come to use it. Your little ring might be yours, but this planet is mine!"

The master captain stepped to Shahten's side and pointed to a strange sight in the distance. Two figures rode on top of a sparkling crystal at least twice the length of a skystone, and it was flying toward the center.

Shahten grasped its significance instantly. The lost ones were bringing in another crystal, a massive one, to revitalize the heart center.

"Stop them!" Shahten commanded. "Make all speed to stop that skycrystal!" The deputy captain immediately turned the SkySlab to intercept the threat.

Yawri's eyes opened wide. "It's Mariyonta and Aronlat!" he shouted. "And Lazket!" While the words were still in the air, he scooped up Red, and his feet blazed toward his skystone.

"What's he doing?" the defender next to Gamon asked. "We're supposed to protect him!"

Keela almost knocked the speaker down as she ran past. "Don't worry about us. Protect the center!"

"Don't worry?" he echoed.

Gamon replied, "Defenders! Change of plans! Those SkySlabs intend to destroy the heart center before Lazket arrives."

Tisbero stepped toward the front line and shouted, "Reflecting crystals won't stop the clubs of Shahten's ground forces! Use the same principle, though. Use their energy against them!"

"How?" The question came carrying back.

Tisbero answered quickly, "Be in the same energy you are when you use your reflecting crystal. I know you know how because you're still alive!"

Zinn watched Yawri and Keela's skystones rise. The captains of two SkySlabs saw them moving too and ordered, "Unmake those skystones!"

A curtain of dark light fell, blocking Zinn's view. The ground exploded in a cloud of dust and ashes. Neither skystone came through the other side.

Tisbero came next to her. "They'll make it," he said, but his voice was flat.

He took a breath and pointed to the front line. The first wave of Shahten's club-wielding humans had arrived. Although much shorter than guardians, their ferocity made them swing their clubs at the defenders with crazed force. In desperation, the guardians used their crystal as shields, but the pounding continued. They stood taking blow after blow until they fell and the next took their place.

Tisbero stepped forward, then turned to face Zinn. "There must be a way to use the attackers' energy against them. Why should it be different from using reflecting crystals? Energy is energy. I'm going to find out how." Their eyes met, and their look conveyed that each knew this might be their end.

"Go," she said. "I'll be fine."

Swallowing hard, Tisbero took off at a run toward the front lines.

Zinn watched until he disappeared in the haze of dust and dark light. Her view of the approaching ground forces was clear, and there were hundreds of club-wielding humans. She looked at the guardians' diminishing front line.

She tucked her head and ran to her own skystone. It rose into the air the instant her feet landed. Dark light cascaded around her as she flew directly toward the human horde.

I'll be fine if I die stopping them.

61. VITAL YOUTH

∞

Mariyonta and Aronlat held on tight while Lazket sped up the ridge and down into the valley. The crystal leveled off and Mariyonta, sitting in front, scrutinized the tree-lined expanse ahead.

"The visions the cave gave were exact! There's the center." She pointed at the valley's distant, low end. "It looks like a cathedral of crystals. The heart center *is* under attack!"

Aronlat craned to see around her. "Those are our skystones darting around the massive ones it showed us. They've got to be three times the length of a skystone."

Mariyonta sat up straight. "And one of them is coming toward us!"

"I see it," he called back. "Let's turn and see if they follow!"

Lazket responded to their thoughts and banked in a sharp turn. They watched the large stone platform advance toward them. It had a tall line of crystals in a straight line down its center, and its change in course followed theirs.

"It turned with us," said Mariyonta. "The cave showed us images of the people wearing red tunics bent on unmaking the center, and they're on it."

"You fly. I'll shoot!" Aronlat exclaimed.

"Shoot? You mean reflect?"

"Right." Aronlat swiveled when a flash caught his eye. "There's another one! It's headed straight for us, too."

The young guardians took their reflecting crystals out of their slings and held them close.

Mariyonta studied one huge, soaring slab and then the other. She then focused on the shafts of dark light falling on the center. "Any idea how many unmaking beams Lazket can take?"

"I think we're about to find out. Lean down as far as you can. Smaller target."

Mariyonta was already down. "Are you ready? They're coming!"

"You worry about navigating. I'll stay One with All and manage the attack."

She cast him a sharp eye, "You've never been One with All."

"Thanks! Big help. Can't we do a little maneuvering? You're headed straight into the first one, and I don't like the look of that tall guy in the purple plumage."

"Done!" She accelerated, rolled the skycrystal onto its side, and swung a fast arc toward the second SkySlab, leaving the first behind.

The deputy captain controlling the second SkySlab had thought following Shahten would be an excellent way to gain his notice. With Shahten engaging the battle first, flying support could only end in victory. However, the unmaking crystal cannon now bore down on him instead. His face tightened when he saw their pilots.

They're not white-robes, they're barbarians! Barbarians flying a crystal cannon!

"Evade! Sharp right!" he ordered. The SkySlab banked hard to the right, catching several menders off balance. One slipped and fell to the ground. Another caught himself but his legs dangled in mid-air. The skycrystal cannon hurled past so closely that menders ducked in fear of losing their heads. The deputy captain stared after the barbarians in disbelief. "They didn't fire!"

Confused and struggling to find direction, his eyes strayed toward Shahten. One glace was enough. Shahten was angry. Very angry.

"After them!" the deputy captain commanded, and his SkySlab turned so quickly two more menders were hurled into the air. He hardly noticed. Shahten's SkySlab had streaked past him, and it would not do to have it claim the prize in spite of rather than due to his support.

"Faster!" he commanded.

Shahten's SkySlab, with a third more magnetic propelling crystals than any other in his fleet, closed the distance to Lazket and came into firing range.

"Now!" Shahten ordered. Unmaking beams shot out from the eight menders stationed across the bow. Five went wide. Three made contact.

The guardian blending with each reflecting crystal largely determined the degree of unmaking returned. Aronlat breathed with Earth and felt the strength of the crystal cave within him. With each breath, he expanded his connection, and it grew. All three shafts returned to their source.

However, Aronlat wasn't prepared for the screams.

They didn't bother Shahten. "You three fill that gap. Keep firing!"

Lazket darted side to side. Five beams missed but two more hit. Aronlat struggled to focus. One beam was reflected fully, but the second only deflected. A tremor passed through Lazket.

Mariyonta felt the tremor. "Aronlat! Center yourself!"

She looked over her shoulder and saw his face contorted in pain. "Aronlat!" His eyes closed. "Aronlat!" With a gulp of air, she asked Lazket to roll down and away from the attack.

Trying desperately to keep herself centered, she said, "We are One. Oh, Creator, we are One." She recalled the feeling she'd had at their camp on the shore of the asteroid-fed lake surrounded by the star-lit crystal cave.

Another hail of dark light came. Four beams reflected back, but two hit. She felt stress build within the crystal. "We are One. All are of the One Body." The two beams lost their grip when Lazket fishtailed up, down, left, and right.

Mariyonta breathed again and her hand stroked Lazket. Tears in her eyes, she glanced over her shoulder once more. "Aronlat?"

His eyes fluttered open. "My intestines feel like a pile of fire ants."

"You're alive!"

He tried to sit up but leaned forward again. "It's passing. I only got a glancing blow. Lazket took the brunt of it." He tried to scan the sky. "That doesn't look good," he got out.

The second SkySlab was now alongside the first. Mariyonta watched them pull apart and accelerate toward her and Aronlat. "They're going to attack us in a crossfire!"

Aronlat said, "Lazket can't take another shaft of unmaking, and neither can I."

Mariyonta peered ahead. They'd covered over half the distance to the center. "Forget maneuvering. Let's make a run for it!" Before Aronlat could respond, another hail of dark light came from behind, but it came from both sides this time. Lazket rose straight up so fast Mariyonta and Aronlat hugged it tight to stay on. Shafts of unmaking passed so close it seemed night had fallen.

When Lazket reached the top of its sharp arc, they looked down. Both SkySlabs followed beneath them, and every mender held an unmaking crystal aimed right at them.

Shahten's voice carried easily. "There's no escape, now or ever. You're young. Do you want to be unmade? Are you going to make me destroy that magnificent crystal, too? If you land, no harm will come to it or to you. Choose Life for all of you!"

Aronlat and Mariyonta locked eyes. They *were* young. Wouldn't it be best if Lazket and they lived?

They both grinned. "He's a charmer," Mariyonta said.

Aronlat's grin was strained but it grew. "I trust him." He winked.

A moment later, they leaned over Lazket's side and Aronlat said, "Simply land and we'll be safe? The crystal too?"

Shahten couldn't believe his ploy worked. He'd turn that crystal into a real cannon.

The young are so naive.

"Yes. I give you my word. Descend slowly and come between our SkySlabs. We will escort you down. I'll keep you safe."

Lazket descended slowly but bobbled uncontrollably from side to side.

"Steady!" Shahten barked. "Kept it steady."

Mariyonta replied instantly. "The crystal was hit several times! We need to get it to the ground!"

"Fine! Keep coming down."

Lazket rolled to the side so much they were in danger of falling off. Aronlat clawed the surface to stay on. "Get it under control!"

"I'm trying! I need more room," was her sharp retort.

The SkySlabs moved farther apart. The giant crystal came between them but yawed dangerously back and forth. Shahten saw its pilots up close for the first time.

Children! The lost ones are desperate!

His voice was honey. "Steady ... We'll go down together now. I'll keep you sa—"

The crystal was gone. One moment it was there, and the next it was gone. No, not gone. It had dropped faster than possible toward the ground.

"After them! Kill them and we capture the crystal!"

Streaks of unmaking streamed past the plummeting crystal. Mariyonta leaned forward, her arms stretched as far around Lazket as possible. "We fooled him, but they're right behind us!"

The skycrystal fell so fast, obviously out of control, that anyone watching knew there was no way they could avoid hitting the ground. Yet shafts of unmaking still streamed by.

"What's that?" Mariyonta pointed to a small white dot rising toward them. Fast.

Before their eyes could blink, it streaked past. "It's a skystone!" Aronlat exclaimed.

Mariyonta sat bolt upright. "It's Yawri!"

The young guardians twisted to watch. Yawri's skystone darted into one unmaking beam after another. Each time, a mender fell.

Shahten commanded, "We'll retrieve the crystal after they smash it into the ground. Direct all fire to that skystone!"

Menders launched salvos directly at Yawri, but he rapidly dodged one while reflecting another.

Aronlat said, "He's cleared our way to the center. We've got to get Lazket there!" Before they could think, the ground came rushing at them faster than seemed possible.

They blazed with soul light, and in the same moment air responded to their request. A gale-force wind rose from below.

Although they both leaned forward and braced themselves against the sudden change in speed, Lazket stopped so quickly both hit their heads on the hard quartz.

When they rose, each had a line of blood trickling down their forehead.

"Mind your head!" Aronlat said.

"Mind yours!" Mariyonta beamed and added, "To the center!" Lazket felt the call of the crystal cathedral and their speed increased suddenly.

Out of nowhere, another wave of dark light hit its side.

Aronlat struggled to gain inner balance. "We are One," he chanted. "One body, nothing to defend against, only something to reflect." The crystal shuddered but the beam returned to its source.

Mariyonta scanned the sky. Yawri still fended off the two SkySlabs behind them, which meant … "It's a third one, Aronlat! We're being attacked by a third!"

They laid eyes on another massive monolith, its menders positioned to fire.

Suddenly, another skystone streaked past them. A strong alto voice calling "Get to the center!" trailed in its wake.

"Who's that?"

"It's Keela, the plant lady!" Mariyonta exclaimed.

Aronlat watched the pilot's honey-gold hair flutter in the air. "Yes! She must be as crazy as Yawri, but the way's clear for us to go!" Before the words were out of his mouth, Lazket shot down the valley with a speed that required all of their strength to hang on.

Shahten saw the third SkySlab arrive, but his gloating laugh turned to a scowl when the immense skycrystal escaped. He yelled at the deputy captain of the SkySlab next to his. "You finish off Yawri! I'm going to make sure that crystal is stopped once and for all!"

Yawri heard the command and saw Shahten's SkySlab move away.

"Forgive me, my body," he said, and wheeled his skystone in an instant sharp turn to speed directly toward Shahten.

The next moment his azure-blue skystone careened into the solid granite of the SkySlab. Shahten tumbled into a line of menders, who fell into others.

The SkySlab tipped. Shahten turned red with rage when he saw Yawri's body catapult past him. Several crystals from his SkySlab fell out of their sockets.

Keela returned an unmaking beam from her own attackers but noticed the motion and glanced up. Yawri's skystone fell from the sky, followed quickly by a SkySlab. Both hit tall trees and disappeared into a rising plume of leaves and branches.

"No! Yawri! No!"

A shaft of unmaking hit her reflecting crystal, then another. She felt the pressure build and knew they were not being returned. Her skystone shrieked as a shaft of dark light found its underside.

"Unmade at last!" the deputy captain of the third SkySlab jeered. Keela gasped, trying to rebalance. The SkySlab drew nearer. Every mender focused on her, hatred in their eyes.

The captain's jeer turned into a command.

"Fire!"

62. COURAGE

∞

Hetlin considered Shahten's shifting battle plan. His strategy was working and theirs wasn't. With his ground forces attacking the outer ring of guardians, and the menders concentrating their fire on one guardian at a time, Shahten was making short work of their defenses, and they needed more time.

She considered their strategy and the weaknesses in their defense. They'd planned to focus on protection for each group of searchers. Consequently, the circles of defenders were scattered over a wide area. It maximized stability for each group of searchers, but Shahten's forces could then pick off one group at a time.

Her deep voice called out, "We need to get our searchers positioned so Shahten's attack on anyone can be defended against by all! If we don't call them back to reorganize our defense, he'll continue killing one group at a time."

Many heads turned, but most remained steadfast in their assigned task.

Gamon heard her.

Why didn't I see that? If we don't change, neither will the result.

He boomed, "You heard her, change of plans! We need to call them back so we can defend against the attacks together!"

The lead defender for another group also agreed. "Call your searchers back! We need to move them behind all the defenders, not just some!"

Resistance to the change was strong, but it melted under the grounded heat of more and more voices. Defenders scrambled and their positions were soon reformed. Original groups of searchers remained together, but defenders could move freely between them to best defend all.

With the new defense in place, a quiet moment came. Hetlin turned to Pergaine. "Shahten weaves lies with truth skillfully, but he was right about one thing. We were unable to find a time when there are enough conscious people to arc. We found blooms of consciousness, but Shahten's whispers are effective. Given the numerous cycles of murder, it becomes harder and harder for humans to distinguish his voice from ours."

Even though the topic was hard, Pergaine was happy for a chance to talk. "It seems we all succumb to darkness at some point. But what I'm afraid to face, I won't be able to change. Because of our resonance, we'll all be drawn together for lifetimes. But the truth is, I've seen enough of our future to know I might forget who I am and become a murderer myself."

"No, not you."

"Yes, even me. Perhaps us all. What I'm saying is, if we come together and I do you harm, I hope I will feel the truth of what I have done, and choose to change."

Hetlin leaned toward her and spoke in a steady voice. "Even if we lose ourselves, we'll still have free will. We'll help each other remember."

"That is my hope, and that we forgive ourselves and each other."

A flash of light in the valley caught Hetlin's eye. "What is that?" Then her sharp eyes widened. "It's Lazket!"

Pergaine saw it too. "Its Mariyonta and Aronlat!" Her voice dropped. "Where are Keela and Yawri?"

Several captains on SkySlabs around the center saw the skycrystal as well. They ordered menders to send shafts of dark light to stop its progress. However, guardians piloting skystones saw the same and rushed to intercept the unmaking.

Heedless of their own safety, many skystone pilots dove directly at SkySlabs. A beam hit the center of one, but the pilot's connection to his skystone sent the unmaking back to its source. Before he was even fully recovered, he intercepted another, then a third. When the fourth came, he and his skystone disappeared in a mass of fractured stone.

With the skystones protecting them, Mariyonta and Aronlat saw a narrow path clear to the center. They leaned down on Lazket, and the crystal accelerated quickly toward it.

While most defenders were focused on the young adults, Hetlin scanned the sky and the grounds for Yawri and Keela. "No sign of them. Wait, who's that?" She pointed to a grimy guardian sprinting from the outer ring toward them. "It's Tisbero!"

Tisbero turned toward the rapidly approaching skycrystal and called out, "Mariyonta! Aronlat!" He waved his arms. "Over here! Bring Lazket here!" He stopped and called out to defenders. "Lazket is long, over twice as long as a skystone! Make room for it to land at the center point of our living circle!"

At least thirty defenders used a combination of soul light and sound to move crystals so it could land. The last found its new location moments before Mariyonta and Aronlat arrived.

Mariyonta rose to sit upright near the front of Lazket. Her tunic was tattered and streaked but her eyes burned sharp and clear. Aronlat leaned out, focusing all of his attention on the area cleared for them.

Hetlin saw the blood smeared on their faces. "So young and so old," she murmured.

"Young hearts, old courage," Pergaine added, and waved along with Tisbero.

The great crystal slowed, its landing imminent. Tisbero glanced at Hetlin and Pergaine. "Have either of you seen Zinn?"

They looked at him in surprise. Hetlin said, "She's not with you? If not with you, where is she?"

His stony silence was his only answer.

He scanned the battleground but he couldn't even sense her. He couldn't sense Yawri or Keela, either. He swallowed hard. His voice was a grinding glacier. "Make way for Lazket! Out of the way!"

Mariyonta and Aronlat brought the immense crystal down with skillful grace. The young guardians came to a hovering rest just above the ground, but to the surprise of many, they didn't stop there.

Aronlat spoke to Mariyonta. "The ground is clear. Let's increase soul sound."

The tones and light around Lazket changed, and the bottom side of the massive quartz started to descend into the ground. When half of the long, six-sided monolith was below ground and half above, Mariyonta said, "Balance light and sound. Return gravity on Lazket to normal."

Neatly settled in place exactly where Lazket had told the young adults to place him, the crystal started to glow.

A chorus of guardians erupted in cheers.

"I knew you'd do it!" Gamon said, reaching them first. The young skycrystal pilots looked up, all grins.

"We made it!" Aronlat exclaimed.

"We're still alive!" Mariyonta blurted out. She and Aronlat dismounted and exuberantly hugged each other. "Seems like I say 'We're still alive' a lot with you!"

"You mean like the time when Yawri let our skystone fall to within a span of Keela? Or when we survived the fall into the lake during the cave stay?" They scanned the surrounding faces.

Aronlat's face, though covered with grime, paled. "Are Yawri and Keela back? The last time we saw them—"

Gamon interrupted quickly. "I'm sure they're fine. The best thing we can do is help Lazket blend with all the other crystals so they can help the searchers find an arc. That's why you flew it here, right?"

Tisbero stepped forward, reached out and took the young guardians' hands. "Come with me," he said in a gravelly whisper.

Hetlin spoke to the assembly. "Listen to the energy matrix Lazket and the other crystals are forming!" Waves of light started to pulse from the center point to the outermost crystals and back. "Soon, there will be more than enough Lifeforce to direct us to the most likely time to arc."

Another searcher said, "It is already bringing in connections from crystal bodies on other planets. If there is a time when Life can return, we'll find it now."

Pergaine was almost singing. "The center is preparing to open a portal. It's bridging dimensions in a way we've never seen before. We're going to be able to search the future while keeping in contact through our bodies here. If any of us find the time when human beings can reawaken with Earth, we can communicate the news through this portal. All will hear and all will come."

A cry arose from those near the center. "It's opening!" A long, vertical line of iridescent light appeared overhead. It grew into a wavering oval of electric violet and blue. The light was brilliant, and a sound came from it: muted melodies at first, then more and more complex rhythms and tones, each distinct yet in harmony with uncountable others. The searchers left their physical bodies standing where they were, and a stream of ethereal bodies rushed into the portal on their urgent mission to find rebirth in time.

Tisbero stood on a fallen skystone with Mariyonta and Aronlat, scanning in all directions "Look!" he exclaimed, his arm thrust out like a spear.

The two young guardians turned in the direction he was pointing and saw a curious sight. A couple of guardians flew on a skystone too small to hold them. They'd crossed over the battle line, barely flying above defenders. Instead of soaring, they rose and fell like a rock skipping over water as they neared.

Mariyonta rejoiced. "It's Yawri!" The tails of the sash around his head danced through the air. "And Keela!"

Aronlat jumped up and waved. "Here! Over here!"

Yawri was talking to Keela and, as yet, hadn't seen them. His voice carried, though. "We're bouncing, not flying. I told you to wait until I found my skystone. I feel it hovering back in the forest. It's bound to catch up."

"Wait for you? After you crashed into Shahten's SkySlab he was not pleased. The other SkySlab picked him up far too quickly. I was lucky the air pressure trick sent me skyward as fast as it did. If it had taken any longer to find you stranded in the top of that tree, I'd have been spotted!"

"I wasn't stranded. The tree held me up so you would find me!"

Keela saw the gathering at the center point and waved wildly. "It's Mariyonta and Aronlat!"

The excited voices of the young guardians carried to them. "Yawri and Keela!"

Keela sped her skystone to land near Lazket, and she and Yawri jumped down to the ground. The young guardians ran to embrace them the instant their feet hit the ground.

Tisbero hurried, any trace of propriety forgotten. He struggled to find words. "You two!" he finally got out.

Yawri noticed the new crystal configuration, and not wanting to take up time talking about what he and Keela been through, asked, "I leave and you remodel the whole center? What's happening?"

Tisbero sighed in relief. Yawri was back, and that was a question he could answer. "As if his menders on SkySlabs weren't enough, Shahten brought club-wielding humans to attack us from the ground. Reflecting crystals don't return the energy from physical blows, but I figured energy was energy. I've found a way to use the downward thrust of their club against them. I've been teaching it to the guardians in the outer ring. Some are getting good at it."

Keela blinked and took a step toward him. "I didn't know you knew how to do that."

"Neither did I, but I was motivated."

Mariyonta and Aronlat turned to inspect the large chunks of charred stone on Keela's skystone. Yawri gazed at the battle line. Half the number of guardians stood there now compared to when he left. He asked quietly, "How much longer?"

Tisbero lowered his voice. "We can hold them off another hour, at most."

Keela anxiously scanned the faces, then burst out with "Where's Zinn? "

Tisbero dropped his eyes. "I don't know. A guardian on the line said he saw her flying a skystone toward a wall of humans."

Yawri pulled back. "That doesn't sound like Zinn. She can be impulsive, but always acts from within a plan."

Tisbero stared past Yawri and said nothing.

Hetlin called, "All of the searchers except you four have passed through the portal and it won't stay open forever. Are you coming?"

Yawri locked eyes with her for an instant. She nodded in response, and he turned to Gamon. However, Gamon was organizing defenders to protect the searchers. Yawri touched his brow in thought and spoke again to Tisbero. "You think Zinn would have flown her skystone against that human ground attack alone?"

Tisbero grumbled. "I was on the outer edge of the front line. I thought she'd stay here." He bit his lip. "A guardian said he saw her go."

All three stared at the front line. The number of club-wielding humans was growing.

Suddenly Keela's eyes went wide and she jerked back. "The giant! Shahten's brought the giant!"

All recalled the towering human who almost ended their escape from Shahten's human development compound. It walked toward the battle line at a slow, deliberate pace.

"I can't believe it." She looked down. "I am not giving him another sandal."

Yawri's hand went to his head. "And I'm not giving him my head-sash."

Keela blew out her cheeks. "That settles it then."

Tisbero saw movement in the sky. "Look! Human-birds! Shahten brought them, too!" Dozens were circling high overhead.

A new sound joined the cries: Howls. Wild and vicious howls. The three guardians froze. The unmistakable, crazed wail of the human-wolves grew louder. Tisbero groaned, "I can't believe this."

Yawri spun to Hetlin and beseeched. "Hetlin, go! The battle comes. Find the time when all can arc! Tell the searchers what's upon us. If Shahten kills us, he'll kill the heart center, then all of Earth!"

Hetlin's hand touched over her heart, then she turned her open palm to Yawri.

Yes. Unless they are stopped, it all ends now.

Her hand came down and her astral form flew through the portal. She called to the searchers. "The attack is upon us! The crystals will help guide us. You can report to all through the center!" The revitalized crystals in the center made the most likely time tunnels glow. Reports soon called out.

"We're following the branch from the nation that declared all are equally entitled to the laws of nature and of nature's god."

Another called, "That thread of awareness continues to build. Slavery is outlawed. Women again hold property, hold office and have the right to work anywhere they choose."

"We find hope, too! The co-creative balance of male and female can be restored in this time. Doors of Creation closed to humanity for generations are reopening."

A searcher inspecting another branch reported, "We see wars created to kill Creation. Shahten's Way of dividing humanity against itself still lives, but with every generation more and more guardians learn to bridge through differences."

Another in his party reported, "We see the nation of the declaration united with others to stop a world war fueled by hatred. They succeed, but shortly after, that energy circles back to attack it from within. Accusations of treason against minorities are once more presented as truth. A newscaster speaks. More and more recognize the lies."

Another reported, "That nation continues to expand with questions, even into space. A Creator-loving messenger champions human rights. The nation is listening. If this continues we may have an arc."

Another in his group said, "Awareness continues to ebb and flow with the rise and fall of fear-fueled division. Lies are cleverly mixed with truth, but human beings are remembering how that's used to manipulate, not strengthen them."

Another guardian's voice exclaimed, "I've found a future self ready to receive me! He's in a large city square, and many soldiers are attacking people running in panic. He is not running. He is walking into a street lined with tanks and they roll toward him. Yet, he stops in front of them."

I am with you. Remember all of what you are. We are One. If it is time to die, we will die in Life, not in fear.

"They're stopping! Blessed universe. His honest courage inspired them, and they chose not to murder!"

"Another called out, "Mine raises bees—and she's never been stung!"

A male's voice resounded through the center. "I've found a future self who is helping an elder pass on. He's helping the human being's body spirit to return to its source and the ethereal soul to return to its source. He senses my presence. We can arc!"

Other voices chimed in but Pergaine's sang. "Searchers! All these reports lead to a planetary strengthening of this thread. Earth asks Jupiter to help it reawaken! Jupiter called a large comet that came to it with new energies. Jupiter rings like a clarion bell to the universe asking for help, help for Earth and all upon it to reawaken!"

Hetlin's earthy voice called out next. "Go further forward! Awareness is building to a time when enough are willing to care for all life, not just themselves. Find that future self and be with them. They are the aspect of our

Whole who has lived through the darkness and kept their hearts alive. We have more to learn from them than they from us. When enough are found we will communicate through the center and—"

The brightly glowing tunnel suddenly dimmed.

"What's happening?" voices cried.

"It's shrinking in size!"

"That future is receding!"

"I can't find where I was in time!"

Hetlin heard the heart center of Earth groan and the cathedral of crystals upon it shriek. The violet-and-blue light of the portal faded. It winked once, twice, and closed.

63. HEART

$$\infty$$

The master captain looked at Shahten with a mixture of pride and trepidation. "Admittedly, that pest has been hard to kill. Had Yawri not crashed into our SkySlab, the skycrystal would be ours. However, even he couldn't survive a fall into the forest from that height. The SkySlab that was damaged will rejoin us within the hour. He died for nothing."

Shahten continued observing his thinning battle lines. More than a thousand bodies lay strewn across the valley. Some wore white, but most were fallen menders and his club-wielding humans.

The master captain started to speak again, but his leader's frown convinced him not to. Shahten's eyes rose at the sight of his humans pounding the outer ring of lost ones. What they lacked in height they made up for in barbaric ferocity. They'd been well conditioned—they truly believed that the lost ones wanted to send them back to caves.

Still watching the hopeful scene, he said, "Any of our followers disheartened by the minor advances of our foes do not feel the strength of the Way. The outcome of this battle doesn't matter when you know, without question, that every last one of them will fall in the end." He paused thoughtfully. "And fall they will. My interest is in how and when they will fall."

The master captain replied, "Yes, Shahten. How and when, not if." His hand went to his neck and stroked the leather collar.

Shahten's chin bobbed once and his gaze turned toward two SkySlabs landing a short distance up the valley. Both were packed with human-wolves. Their hands and snouts had been bound for the journey, but they would be freed to join the first shipment soon enough.

"Does our astral reporter have any news from Earth's other centers?"

The master captain cleared his throat. "He said only three of the nine astral reporters appeared at their last meeting. Battle lines at the other centers are ranging over great distances. Your orders to concentrate fire on one guardian at a time were received, but only after many menders were lost."

Shahten continued to stare unblinkingly at the human-wolves. When each was unbound, the smell of the bodies at the center sent them racing toward it. "No change from the last report, then. What of Laric? It's time our high priest did some real work."

"As instructed, our astral traveler on the island told Laric to divert Generator's energy away from the glowing crystals and to the citrines held by our menders. Laric discovered that when he disconnects Generator from the dwellings the glowing crystals might implode. Since losing our carefully bred humans would set back our plans significantly, he requested assistance to move the humans to the other side of the island. The commander in charge is herding them to safe areas. Laric is at Generator now."

"A reasonable precaution, but don't let evacuating humans delay the change for Generator. When Laric's work with it is complete, the dark light from our menders' crystals will double in intensity. When that happens, the end of the lost ones will be final."

"Unbeatable plan. Unbeatable," the master captain enthused.

Finished with his survey, Shahten ordered, "Take us to the center, but slowly. Creeping forward causes more anxiety for our prey and allows me time enjoy it."

His SkySlab moved farther down the valley toward the ring of white robes. The little skystones still darted about his remaining SkySlabs, but no longer in a swarm. If not for the fact that so few menders stood on them, he would have smiled.

His eyes drifted to his club-wielding humans attacking the crystal center. They were doing better than the menders. Physical blows instead of unmaking energy were proving effective. Although, based on the number of white-robed guardians still standing, not as effective as he'd hoped. One area was putting up a surprisingly impressive defense.

No matter. The human-wolves will be on them soon. I knew they'd be good for something.

For a better view, he commanded his SkySlab to go high over the mass of bodies fighting for their lives. From this height, he saw the lost ones had covered an area over eight hundred strides across with larger crystals than he first thought. Their colors ranged from clear through yellow to violet. Many stood planted in the ground and were as tall as a guardian.

What a beautiful crystal forest, and it's all mine.

He spoke calmly to his master captain. "They've changed the configuration of their searchers. They had eighteen separate groups before, each guarded by its own little circle of defenders. Their new configuration is one circle within the larger. Too bad they saw the weakness, I did so enjoy disrupting one group at a time. Now the defenders will move to wherever we attack."

The master captain said, "The inner circle containing the searchers is still a few hundred strides wide. Covering that distance while moving through that forest of crystals will go slowly. If we can draw them to one place, we can move quickly to another. They won't be able to keep up."

"Excellent, my captain! This configuration will be even more enjoyable than the last!"

Shahten looked across the sparkling crystal forest and said, "We need to find that skycrystal. It's three times taller than the others so it should be towering above them. Yet I don't see it."

All three scanned the immense crystal forest. After a moment the deputy captain said, "Down there. Are those the children that flew it?"

Shahten grinned. "Yes. It must be near them."

The master captain pointed. "There it is. They didn't plant it vertically. It's on its side, half-buried in the ground No wonder we didn't see it!"

"They try to hide it. Make haste."

~

Down on the ground, Aronlat raised his hand to shade his eyes. "It's Shahten!"

Mariyonta watched the SkySlab. "He's headed for Lazket!"

Aronlat looked at the defenders. "He's not firing, so there's nothing to return. No one can stop him." He turned and regarded the battle line. "Yawri, Keela, and Tisbero are at the outermost ring. The attack by those humans is so intense they may not have seen him."

Mariyonta gave a wry smile. "They probably didn't, especially with those wild dogs or whatever they are."

"We better make sure they know." Aronlat looked toward the conflict. "From the here to there is few hundred strides away. Are you ready to—?"

Mariyonta was already running. Aronlat took off too, and their nimble feet flew around crystals and shattered stone. When they came near the edge of the crystal center the din of battle roared, but they could still hear Yawri.

"Guardians! Let's use the fallen skystones to fill the gaps between the fallen SkySlabs. If we turn them edge up the barrier will slow their advance!"

Mariyonta called to Aronlat, "There he is!"

Yawri stood on the ground near a fallen SkySlab. Its nose was slanted into the dirt from its fall. Keela stood on the slab's top edge. "Let's get the rest of those dead menders out to the other side. Keep their leather tunics!"

Mariyonta and Aronlat stopped running when they saw Tisbero. He stood outside of the circling barrier of stone. A livid human rushed toward him, his club raised high. Tisbero kept his eyes fixed on the attacker but spoke so the guardians he was training could hear.

"Watch. You dart to the side. Grab the club on its downward swing. Then, pull it down while kneeing him up. His own momentum will flip him in the air."

The human howled when he reached Tisbero, but in a blur of motion, the man's head plunged down into the rocky ground while his back arched up and over it. He didn't move after he landed.

"It looks easy when you do it!" a bloodied guardian next to Tisbero said without taking his eyes off the human rushing at him.

"Not easy. I just had the opportunity for lots of practice today. Use the same energy we use when returning unmaking, redirect what they send back to them."

The guardian next to Tisbero grabbed the attacker's club on its downward swing and pulled it further down while using the assailant's momentum to tumble him forward. The man's head hit stone. "Practice. Lots of opportunities to practice here."

Tisbero yelled, "Remember! Stay One with All, the same way we do when using reflecting crystals. We only return what they send. They are not an enemy!"

With no more attackers near, Aronlat turned back to Yawri and refocused on their message. "Yawri!" he yelled. "Shahten is on a SkySlab that's headed for Lazket!"

Yawri paused from directing a cracked skystone into position, turned and saw Aronlat and Mariyonta staring at him expectantly. He opened his mouth to speak, but, when he looked at their blood-streaked faces, closed it again. After a moment he said, "Do you remember when your skystone plummeted toward Keela? You didn't think you could stop it, but you did?"

"Of course!" they both exclaimed.

"I believed in you then and I believe in you now. Tisbero, Keela and I are needed here. Go now! Do what you can to protect Lazket!" A shaft of dark light ruptured the ground behind him. "I'll come as soon as I can!"

Mariyonta managed to get out, "We tried to help, but the defenders said we were too young!"

Yawri faced them square on. "You know Lazket better than they do. You'll figure it out." The doubt in their eyes transformed to steely resolve. Yawri's voice boomed, "Go! Use what you know!"

At the word, "Go," both turned and started to run back to the center point. When they jumped over a low crystal, they heard Yawri call to the guardians building fortifications. "Repeat what we did here around the entire circle! Use all the fallen skystones we have to close the gaps. Make sure dead menders are on the outside, but keep their leather tunics!"

Between strides, Mariyonta said, "Yawri said he believes in us."

Aronlat put his head down and bounded over a rock. "It's time we did, too."

They sprinted back through the forest of crystals but stopped in shock when Lazket came into sight. Shahten's SkySlab hovered above the crystal being, and a constant barrage of dark light fell upon the defenders surrounding it. The shafts were too intense to reflect, but thanks to the rolling cascade of defenders taking turns, all were at least deflected. Mariyonta and Aronlat stared, uncertain about how to approach the group that told them they were too young to handle such concentrated unmaking.

Mariyonta said, "They can't keep this up."

Aronlat straightened. "There is so much dark light falling around Lazket there's no way the portal can still be open. With it closed, the searchers won't find a time to arc."

Mariyonta agreed. "Pergaine and all the others will be stranded. We have to do something."

To their relief, they heard Shahten say, "Quit firing so the air can clear. Time for me to talk to them. It will go faster when they're less centered. Besides, watching them crack at my words is so much more enjoyable."

The barrage of unmaking ceased and Shahten leaned over the edge. He sounded so smooth and self-assured many were tempted to trust him. "My guardians, I see you stand among a beautiful family of crystals and a glorious skycrystal!

"I am from Crystal Island, where we also have a crystal family. If these two crystal families were combined, the energy would be strong enough to help the entire planet. You want to help the world too, so let us connect them. Let us stop this senseless conflict and bring them together."

One of the defenders standing next to Lazket breathed deeply. It was the young woman who spoke up with Yawri and the others during Shahten's attack on Hetlin and Pergaine and was almost killed for it. Her body glowed with vitality that pulsed from connection with All. When she spoke, her sound carried rich and high.

"Yes, let's stop this conflict, Shahten. Go right ahead and leave off your attack. Our goal is to bring ever more Life to Creation. How can that be your goal also, when you kill so many?"

He nodded agreeably. "I'm so glad to see that you live! Yes, bringing more Life to Creation is my goal, too." As he spoke, his gaze fell upon the encroaching battle.

Still standing next to Lazket and drawing on what she learned from observing Yawri, the young woman remained centered. "When we joined with bodies we agreed to bring the Creator within us to the Creator within Earth, and to learn how to expand Life in All. You break that agreement."

Shahten gazed down with pity in his eyes.

An example must be made.

He continued agreeably, "I am sorry, but it was you who broke the agreement. Remove your blindfold and look about you! You murder Life."

She glowed even more brightly, and her lovely voice was rich. "You hope we will believe the black and white of your words but I will not. We do not murder Life. Those who believe in your words more than their own are those who murder it. Your unwitting puppets."

"Puppets? You think they are puppets? No. Your future selves love unmaking Life! To do harm and not care makes you feel powerful! You will choose power with your own free will. Ask your searchers, they will tell you. Do you want to see your future? I can show you visions of what will be."

A few defenders shifted back and forth on their feet, and Shahten's eyes sparkled as brightly as his cape. "You think there are guardians of Life in this future you so desperately seek? There are only guardians of greed. They love answers, not questions from some lost part of themselves, like you. They hate those who disagree with them, the different ones. The wrong ones."

The young woman persisted. "To murder Life is your purpose, not ours."

Shahten looked kind and sincere in his effort to share. "Yes. Your purpose is to expand and improve Life, isn't it? Believe me, I will help you expand in your purpose. I will help you improve your own life, at least. It's a small change from 'improve life' to 'improve my life,' and in time, you won't remember the difference. You think putting the planet to sleep will protect it? Do you really think it will wake up again? No, because you will slowly fall asleep too, and while you are unconscious, Life will go extinct."

The woman spoke like a soprano in a chorus. "If we sleep we will wake up."

"Wake up? Nothing is going to wake up. Your future selves are too broken. They will suck all of this little planet's water out of its eardrums, poison its eyes, and unmake every species they touch. Don't you see? You join me to enslave Earth the same way you enslave your bodies. Your body is your property, right? It belongs to you. Therefore, Earth belongs to you. So logical. Human beings will agree with me because I give them answers they like. I tell them what they want to hear. That's how it works."

More defenders distributed throughout the searchers' protective ring started moving through the crystal forest toward Lazket. The woman felt their connection and her breath stayed even.

"You say that is what *will* be. We choose to believe what *can* be. Even if we do forget who we are, we are still of Creation. We will remember there is something more than your divisive words. We will know it, forever seek it, and we will awaken with it."

Muzzle the first to speak and those who would speak second never will.

He leaned down, pleading reason. "But why? Walking sleep is so much more pleasant. Do you think these future selves dare to face the impact of their sleepwalking? It's hopeless. Don't you see? Murdering each other lifetime after lifetime works. So confused. So separate. They think my thoughts are theirs!" He walked back and forth, delighted.

"My answers give them reason not to change. I give them what they want. What do you have to offer your future selves other than the pain of remembering what they lost?"

She sang with her heart next to Lazket. "We offer them their whole selves."

Shahten continued, glowering now. "Whole selves? How many do you think will have the courage to confront the true impact of their choices? Their everyday evil? The little cruelties they inflict on each other? The comparison. The judgment. The competition. I love competition. You are better than others, you know. It's survival of the fittest, and the fittest are the ones with the power to make everyone else do what the powerful need to stay in power! It's beautiful."

Almost all of the defenders fidgeted now. Some had even lowered their crystals.

Yet another guardian said calmly, "No. They will choose to know when they harm Life. They will want to know the truth regardless of their pain."

"Feel the truth?" Shahten jeered. "You expect them to feel? After all the trauma they've had? They've all been so *damaged* through so many lifetimes. It's unfair of you to expect them to feel." Shahten leaned down, working hard to hide his glee. "If any do, we'll stop them with guilt. It's their fault. They should have known better!"

The young woman swayed under the hateful glare of the menders staring down at her, but she re-centered. "Our charge was to learn from Creation. We are not wrong for not knowing what we did not know. We learn even now, from you."

Shahten, enjoying the art of crumbling beliefs, only smiled. "Fortunately, you learn very slowly. Oh, more wise beings will come, of course. Light sent from on high to remind you who you are. But they learned single voices were easily silenced. So, in place of messiahs, thousands will come. That presents a problem for me. However, I find only a small change in tactics will address this Creator's ploy. Even thousands of messengers must be children first. Remember how emperors and pharaohs alike slaughtered children to protect their throne?"

What words will crack her?

He leaned over the edge. "The world I foresee is one where fathers cannot provide for the needs of their families. We do that first to trap mothers in poverty. It's hard for children to know what caring is when you're a burden. Making children homeless would be best." He paused. "No, there are far too many wise children coming. They must be kept off balance, we must replace feelings of safety with mistrust and fear. I'll find followers who will kill them where they think they are safe. Where?" He paused. "In their schools. No more safety, anywhere! That will stop them."

Another guardian, a tall one, spoke. "Even if what you say comes to pass, it will not be the whole of it. They will not be stopped. Your whispers are not our own."

Shahten replied easily. "Whispers? Did I say whispers? No. Mine will be your only voice! I can't make you do anything, but it will certainly be wonderful when you think you have to. 'I had to do it!' you'll say. I don't care what 'it' is, only that you believe you don't have choice."

Shahten spoke more softly. "Please try to be a little more understanding. You have no idea how much work it is to get you to give me your free will. Incremental steps work best. We worked very hard to find the first human being to massacre students. He used a weapon you skillfully crafted to keep you safe to kill college students instead. Getting someone to do a mass killing like that the first time is always the hardest. After that, it's easy to get copycats to follow. My shooter looked down from the university's 'ivory tower' on a plaza filled with students enjoying lunch hour. He shot over forty-five. Too much thinking happens when people feel safe. We need to stop the young from thinking. Don't worry. We'll take our time, so the shootings seem normal."

A tear ran down the young woman's cheek. She took a deep breath, let it go, and continued. "Human beings will go through wars and hardships untold, but caring lives on through each. After disconnection dominates again, caring will return stronger than it was, because we are learning. The thread our searchers follow shows this— and we are awakening."

Shahten smiled, amused. "That's your problem. Don't you understand? You nurture your tiny threads, but your future selves don't want to change.

They want to be told who they are, not question who they are. I will have all of you, and then this planet will be mine to destroy."

The young woman took a breath, released it, and spoke again. "Your lies have no power over us."

"Except for the ones you choose to believe!" Shahten laughed aloud. He paused, considering his next words. "Believe this. I foresee a future where you will not have the courage to remove me from your lives because you will think you need me to be strong. Your fate is sealed. Blabber to your future selves all you want. They will deny you, their deepest ancient self."

Even though the guardians around the young woman and tall man appeared to be joining in strength, beads of sweat glistened on most faces.

Shahten's eyes fell to Lazket.

If I can't have you, nobody can.

"I've let your searchers find hope, but it would be cruel to let them think it has meaning. Don't you agree? Unfortunately, to stop them permanently it looks like I'm going to have to unmake that skycrystal."

He turned toward his menders and commanded, "Unmake the crystal."

"No!" a score of defenders cried out.

The young woman scaled the side of Lazket to intercept unmaking beams sent at it. "As One!"

Within a moment, defenders stood front-to-back down the length of Lazket, all willing to protect the great crystal with their lives. Standing on the nose, the young woman returned one beam and then another. Menders' shots went wild, up and down the length of Lazket, and lacking concentrated force, each was returned.

Shahten, tired of his menders' screams, commanded them to stop. He looked at the loudmouth at the front of the line.

No one's going to save you this time.

"Menders, concentrate your unmaking on the annoying young woman at the front."

Four shafts of dark light immediately shot toward her. Overwhelmed, she could only deflect not return the beams. "I can't hold it any longer!"

The tall guardian behind her said, "Jump down! I'll take your place!"

Another defender farther back yelled, "When one of us jumps down we need others to climb up to take our place!" However, almost all the defenders nearby were already standing on Lazket.

Two more shafts of dark light hit the young woman before she could move. The tall guardian behind her rushed to get in front, but her crystal blazed brilliant white and broke in two. She screamed, buckled, and fell in a heap to the ground.

Shahten smirked.

How enjoyable. They have to stay on top of Lazket or he's unmade. All I have to do is concentrate dark light at the head of the line and each fool will be killed in turn.

"Hurry!" another guardian yelled. "We need more defenders!" More ran toward the attack but no clear path existed through the forest of crystals.

The tall guardian who had taken the young woman's place jumped down so the one behind him could take his. "Help me move her!" he yelled, unwilling to let her body be trampled under the rush.

Another defender helped him carry her to a nearby boulder, quickly set her down against it, and ran back to get in line.

Eventually, her eyes opened to a squint. The tall guardian who'd stood behind her was at the front again. She could tell he wasn't yet recovered from his first stand. Four beams hit him at once. His crystal exploded. The blast took him into the air. She watched his body land twisted in death, and beams of unmaking fall onto Lazket before another could take his place.

Tears welled in her eyes. She struggled to rise, blinked slowly, and fell back against the boulder. She saw Mariyonta and Aronlat. The corners of her mouth rose slightly and opened as if to release a final a note of a song. However, her eyes glazed over and she slumped to the ground before it escaped her lips.

Mariyonta and Aronlat watched in stunned silence. Their eyes shifted from her still form back to Lazket. A large man returned his fifth beam, but three more drilled home. His crystal shattered. With his last breath, he purposefully fell across Lazket so his flesh and bone would offer what protection it could before it turned to ash.

Mariyonta shrieked. "Defenders are falling faster than they arrive! We're not too young! We've got to do something!"

A gruff voice thundered next to them. "Too young? Madness!"

"Gamon! You're here!" Mariyonta bounded toward him.

"Finally, yes! I've been seeing to the searchers' defense. The portals closed and they can't get back!" He took in the situation.

Yawri and the others must still be at the attack on the outer ring.

"We need reflecting stars over Lazket!"

Aronlat said, "What's a reflecting star?"

"I'll tell you how to make them while we run. Don't worry. You can do it."

Heads down, they dashed toward the great crystal and the dark light showering it from above.

64. WARRIORS ALL

∞

Yawri, Keela, and Tisbero stood on the upper edge of a downed SkySlab and regarded the giant lumbering toward the center. He batted a human-wolf out of his way and sent it sprawling.

Yawri spoke with his eyebrows raised and his head tilted to one side. "His hands are bigger than I remember."

"They felt even bigger wrapped around my foot," Keela replied.

Yawri looked at her and his mouth quirked. "You did get new sandals."

She pulled on an end of his headband. "You got my sash."

"It's stained."

"With your blood!"

Tisbero sighed and his low voice grumbled, "The giant's not here yet, but the wolf-heads are … and they want to eat us."

Keela raised her head and called out with a volume surprising to any who didn't know her. "Get the dead menders over the wall! Keep their tunics!" She turned to Yawri and Tisbero. Snarls and howls filled the air. "I can't believe they're still hungry."

Yawri said, "They always stop for food, and better dead menders than us."

Their eyes swept back to the giant, but a sudden movement caught their attention. A flying human-bird, its talons like a vice, plucked a guardian from his skystone and carried him away. It celebrated the catch with a high-pitched screech from its feathered human face.

Keela stood firm. "We've got to stop them! That's the second pilot we've lost to those feathered monsters!" She studied the sky. Most still circled overhead, watching for a pilot to slow down in a turn. "I've asked for help fro—"

"A breach! They've breached the barrier!" a defender roared. A stream of human-wolves, snouts snapping atop human bodies with thin but strong arms and legs, climbed over a skystone used to fill a gap in the defensive wall.

A snarling human-wolf leaped toward a defender and bit through his cloak with a ferocity unknown to any guardian. White cloth bloomed red. Other guardians wrapped layer after layer of the menders' leather tunics around themselves and ran toward the breach.

"Use the momentum of their attack against them!" Tisbero called, but they didn't need reminding.

A pack of human-wolves charged the guardians who dared to run toward them. Long teeth bared, they leaped to slay their prey, but the leather-wrapped guardians stepped to the side and parried so smoothly it was hard to tell when each movement began. The end, however, was the same for all. Thin bones designed for running did not fare well when catapulted into the air to land hard against stone. The guardians flipped one human-wolf after another, using their own momentum and energy against them.

Even so, the snapping tide continued to rise over the barrier.

Open jaws leaped toward a defender before she had time to turn aside, so she raised her leather-bound hand like a spear instead. The wolf's long snout closed over it, but driven forward by its own momentum, it cut off its own air and choked. After it stilled, she lowered it to the ground and withdrew her arm.

A guardian to the far right yelled, "Breach! We have another breach!"

Another warned, "Keep them away from the searchers!"

The sound of grating stone caused Yawri, Keela and Tisbero to spin. The giant held a skystone, one carefully placed for defense. Its narrow eyes spied the trio on top of the fallen SkySlab. A guttural roar made the human-wolves stop mid-stride and retreat from the flying spittle. Though the three stood on the SkySlab's highest edge, the human-wolves sensed the giant's intent and also fixed their eyes on his prey. They ran to the bottom of the SkySlab and howled. Soon, there would be plenty of meat for all.

Even while threatened by the giant, Yawri's hand shot to his chest. The meaning of the shrill tone from the ethereal diamond within him was clear. He stormed above the howls. "Something's happening with Lazket! Something's breaking!"

Keela grasped the large green garnet hanging from her neck. An instant later she said, "Dimensions! Dimensions are losing connection!"

Their eyes shifted to the center point of the crystal forest. In the distance, shafts of dark light fell thickly where Lazket lay. A SkySlab hovered directly above him and a fluttering purple robe sparkled in the sun.

"Shahten!" Yawri declared. "I've got to go."

Keela pressed her lips tight. Out of the corner of her eye, she saw another human-wolf launch itself toward a guardian. A strange sensation tickled her feet and she looked down. The monolithic slab they stood upon was vibrating.

Tisbero was already kneeling, and he placed his hands on the chiseled stone. "Not an earthquake. A more constant thrum."

"Look!" Keela exclaimed.

Mammoths beyond count stampeded down the upper valley in a solid wall of pulsing thunder. The thrum turned into a shake, and the human-wolves ceased howling. Vicious but not dumb, they started to run toward the forest, hoping the trees were close enough together to stop the pursuit. The giant stood in place, gaping at the spectacle and unable to comprehend what had sent the wolves running. The skystone he held above his head, poised to throw, stilled in his hands.

The writhing tide of mammoths approached, and Tisbero yelled louder than Yawri and Keela imagined possible.

"Zinn!"

Then even louder, "Zinn!"

Yawri and Keela searched the cresting wave. Front and center, on the most massive mammoth of them all, rode Zinn. She saw them and raised a fist over her head, held it a moment, and thrust it forward.

A thousand mammoth trumpet calls blared. Human-wolves scattered toward the forest as fast as two legs could carry them. But they weren't fast enough.

The giant glared at the trio on the wall. His hatred for them was far stronger than any concern about droopy-nosed beasts. He started swinging the skystone above his head, picking up speed with every rotation, intending to send it crashing onto them.

He didn't see Zinn approach from the side.

Her mammoth skillfully ducked its head and used its massive tusks to catch the giant below the hips. In one motion, it threw back its head and sent the giant into the air. His arms wheeled, then he landed with a *crack* head first on the skystone meant to be his missile.

The human-birds, incensed at the giant's death, plunged toward the three on top of the wall. Keela saw them first and called to Yawri and Tisbero.

Tisbero arched back. "Their numbers have doubled! We've got to take cover!"

Yawri scanned the area. "Where? We made the barrier tall and narrow, and we're on its top."

Keela scanned the sky. "They came!" she called. Yawri and Tisbero looked at her, then up again. High above, flashes of orange streaked toward the human-birds. The ethereal feather within her pulsed with song beyond song. Tears welled and flowed. "They came!"

Tisbero tried to make sense of what he was seeing. "Who came?"

"Ahjas! Decedents of the giant bird who gave me the feather!" Her hand went to her chest again. "I called for their help with the feather inside of me." She breathed in and out and repeated, "They heard, and they came."

The human-birds soaring the highest disappeared in an explosion of their dark feathers. Those lower dove quickly toward the only defense they saw: the tall rocks protected by the fragile people flying on their little stones.

To frighten their quarry in place, the human-birds opened their talons wide and sounded their inhuman cry. However, rather than freeze in terror, the pilots on their flying rocks rose toward them. The human-birds screeched again, but the guardians only rose faster.

Believing it a feint, several pumped their wings to speed their downward plunge. Their shrieks of rage were cut short when the flying granite hit them straight on instead of turning away. Within moments, streaks of orange from above and sailing stone from below cleared the sky.

Without pausing, the ahjas flew for their next target: the SkySlabs surrounding the heart center. Seeing the threat, the captains directed half their remaining menders to unmake the new enemy while the other half still pounded the guardians on the ground. Shafts of dark light rose toward the great birds. One shaft tore through an outstretched wing, and the great bird spiraled.

Unable to fly, it still directed its plummeting fall toward the SkySlab. Its captain maneuvered frantically to get out of its way, but the ahja hit its aft quarter. Eleven menders fell. One of them careened into a vertical propulsion crystal with such force it rose from its socket. The SkySlab tipped. Menders cried out and one fell, but the monolith leveled when the long crystal fell back into place.

Some of the guardians piloting skystones saw the ahja's death, and they spun their crafts to race down and protect their avian allies. Even though the skystones fell far faster than gravity alone would allow, the bird beings didn't wait for them to catch up.

The ahjas continued their press on the menders, lifting them from their SkySlabs with talons in much the same way as the human-birds had snatched at the skystone pilots. However, the ahjas' beautiful feathers were no defense against unmaking beams. Two more great birds fell before the skystones arrived to intercept the dark light.

The captains ordered their menders to ignore the birds and focus on the skystone pilots. The guardians returned most shafts but not all. Four pilots fell before other skystones could rush in to take their place between the SkySlabs and ahjas.

The addition of the great birds to the defense caused the advance of the SkySlabs to halt, although given that the birds continued to fall, the question was for how long.

Yawri and Keela watched, transfixed, while Tisbero searched the thundering herd of mammoths for Zinn. She'd circled around, and when her mammoth reached the toppled SkySlab her friends stood upon, it stopped. She vaulted from its back to the top of the slab, landed on its edge, and let her momentum carry her forward without missing a step. Her face aglow, she bounded into Tisbero and threw her arms around him. Her arms barely reached his back, but his wrapped around her from shoulder to shoulder.

"I told you I'd be fine!" she whooped.

Even after holding her long enough to make sure she was real, Tisbero still wasn't sure what to say. He finally grumbled, "You could have been trampled by mammoths!"

Zinn's grin reflected the eons of friendship between them. "You're no fun." She spun to face Yawri and Keela. "What's happening? How's the center, and Lazket?"

The smiles on the faces around her turned to hard, thin lines.

Yawri swept a hand toward the center. The rain of unmaking continued over the area where Lazket lay.

Keela said, "We think we're very close to finding the time to arc too, but we'll never get to it if Lazket is unmade."

Zinn looked from Lazket back her friends. They were all thinking the same thing.

Yawri boomed, "Let's go!"

The guardians hurriedly dropped from the fallen SkySlab and ran, swerving around broken stone and crystals while picking up speed.

After a hundred strides, Yawri felt the ethereal diamond in his chest throb. "Turn left," it said. Yawri took another step forward. "Turn left!" The ethereal diamond added a vibration to the throb.

Yawri called out to his companions, "Go ahead! I need to go another way."

Tisbero slowed. "We're halfway there! Lazket is straight ahead!"

"See you there!"

Yawri shot a quick glance at Keela, who responded with a nod. Her long stride didn't change but Tisbero's mouth was still hanging open. "Come on, Tisbero! Yawri will do what he'll do!"

Tisbero blew out his cheeks. "I just wish he'd tell me once, just once, what he's doing before he does it." Still, he quickly tucked his head and pumped his stout legs to keep up. The three sprinted through the forest of crystals and finally ran up the final slope to Lazket. Many defenders lay dead where they'd tumbled from the crystal, but the rain of dark light was also far less than before.

"Three reflecting stars!" Keela said in a rush. "Gamon, Mariyonta, and Aronlat each made stars like we did to protect Hetlin and Pergaine!"

Gamon, with five defenders surrounding him, stood near Lazket's tip and held the center crystal of the first star. One defender held the top point, two more stood at each shoulder, and two more anchored the bottom points for the reflecting star.

Mariyonta held the center point for the star behind Gamon. Aronlat and five other defenders made the third.

It had taken a while for the dark light to clear enough for Shahten to see the change. The three stars covered most of Lazket, but not all. His root was still exposed. Since targeting the reflecting stars had proved a waste of menders, Shahten directed them to concentrate unmaking on the undefended root.

Worn beyond exhaustion, the few remaining defenders took turns covering the open area. None had the strength to return the unmaking, but they could still deflect it.

One defender slipped when he jumped to take the place of another. The glowing white crystal of the one standing split apart, and the shaft of unmaking passed through the dying defender and into Lazket.

The crystal center screamed.

Keela rushed forward with the four guardians. "Defenders, we're coming to make a fourth star!"

None of them even had the strength to turn their heads.

Mariyonta said, "Keela, we can't cover all of Lazket!"

Gamon barked, "Where's Yawri?" but no answer came.

They reached the back of the great crystal's side and Keela said, "I'll take the top. Zinn, you take the center." Keela chose three defenders still standing. Looking at the first two she said, "You hold the right shoulder position and you hold the left." She looked into the eyes of the third. "To secure the bottom two points, you hold the right while Tisbero holds the left! Go!"

The short line of defenders heard. No longer required to push beyond endurance, they slumped to the ground from where they stood.

While creating the star, Keela, Zinn, Gamon and his counterpart started deflecting beams. However, when Tisbero's counterpart started to move into position, his eyes rolled back in his head and he collapsed unconscious. His dimming crystal rolled out of his hands.

Keela spoke with pointed urgency yet unwavering calm. "Tisbero, there are only enough of us to make a four-pointed star—only one point to anchor its bottom. Not two."

Tisbero instantly changed position. Instead of sitting to Zinn's left side, he sat in front of her and held up his crystal. "Four-pointed star it is."

Shahten saw movement through the streams of dark light.

Chaos at the open end. They're tiring at last!

"All menders, loose unmaking on the end of that skycrystal!"

Shahten was right. Defenders were sprawled everywhere, and with Keela's star still in formation, there was a great deal of commotion on the back of Lazket. Only four menders were ready, but they did as commanded. Four shafts of unmaking struck the half-made star.

Even in motion each guardian and their crystal maintained connection to the others. Surprising everyone, the four-pointed star returned all four beams to their senders. All the menders fell.

Shahten stiffened.

They've only been able to deflect beams.

Two more menders fired, and they fell.

"Stop! Stop firing!"

What's this?

The air finally cleared.

"No!" he spat. Four crystal stars stood on Lazket instead of three. The new one only had four points instead of five, but could rotate the same as the others to face any place he flew. Eyes on fire, Shahten saw Keela holding its top crystal. He jabbed a long finger toward her and blazed, "All menders, unmake that fourth star!"

The replacements for the seven lost menders were still moving into position, but the remaining five were ready. Their shafts of dark light engulfed the fourth star. It flared but steadied. Three beams were deflected, and the other two returned to their source.

Shahten, learning from the defenders, now lined his menders up behind each other on the edge, so if any fell the shafts of unmaking would continue in an unbroken stream.

Tisbero stretched to cover both anchor points as dark light swelled and snaked around him. First his crystal, then all the others, changed from soft to bright yellow.

Tisbero growled, "My crystal can't cover both points under this attack! Stay connected to All. Stay connected."

We could sure use you right now, Yawri.

Zinn's crystal turned white and she implored, "We need that second bottom point! Now!"

Through the fog of dark light, Shahten saw the crystals of the fourth star flare bright white.

Now I have them.

Unseen from above, one more guardian rushed through the haze to fill the gap. Tisbero quickly moved aside.

Yawri. Finally!

Dark light swirled. Shahten was anxious to see the end of the guardians who had given him so much trouble. He howled, "Keep firing!"

Gray haze buried the back of Lazket. Many of the menders smiled, feeling the power of destroying in moments what had taken nature millions of years to grow. Shahten smiled with them ... until one yowled in agony and toppled to the ground, followed by another. In rapid succession eight more toppled.

In the time it took Shahten to say, "Menders, stop firing!" three more fell. The remainder stepped back from the edge. What was moments before a straight, proud line of red leather now swayed in a small clump of ragged, sweat-drenched menders, their eyes open but unseeing.

Shahten's determination didn't wane. Menders were easily replaced.

Keela's star was about to explode. Why didn't it?

Free of unmaking beams, the air started to clear. Shahten impatiently leaned forward to discern the problem. Keela remained at the top of the star, her crystal emitting a healthy glow. Five crystals surrounded the one in the center.

Wait. There were only four. Only one crystal held the bottom. Now there are two.

"Hello, Shahten," a young woman greeted him in a rich soprano.

Mariyonta and Aronlat recognized her voice at once. It was the young woman who first spoke when Shahten arrived at Lazket, the one they had watched die. Aronlat blinked to clear his eyes. "She's alive?"

Shahten jerked back. "You!"

She stood and looked him squarely in the eyes. "Me."

He adjusted his robe. "Yes. You. Glad to see you're alive," he said, but the sound was flat.

He surveyed the defenders on and around Lazket. The crystal was thoroughly covered by these star structures now, and there were more defenders here now than when he started.

He licked his lips and raised his eyes to peruse the rest of the forest of crystals. After a long moment, his knowing smile returned.

His voice dripped like ice on the defenders. "I'm so glad so many of you came. My plan worked. Drawing you to one place makes the others weak." His tender gaze looked sincere. "Thank you."

He raised a long arm and pointed. "Captain, there are very few defenders around Hetlin and Pergaine now. It's time to finish what we started."

The SkySlab rose and turned toward the vacant bodies of the two searchers.

The young woman jumped to the ground and faced Keela and the others. "Because so many have come, there are more defenders here now than when the attack on Lazket began. We'll keep Lazket safe. We know how to make stars if SkySlabs come. Save Hetlin and Pergaine if you can!"

Keela didn't take the time to respond. She jumped down and Tisbero and the others cascaded immediately after her. The guardians swerved around tall crystals and jumped over fractured stones in a hurtling rush. Shahten's SkySlab already hovered over Hetlin and Pergaine.

65. GUARDIANS

∞

Keela was several strides ahead. "I don't think we'll make it there in time!" All strained to run faster, but one misstep through the crystal forest could be disastrous. Tears welled in Keela's eyes.

Pergaine and Hetlin.

"Run!" she breathed.

All felt like their chests were going to explode, but their strides only lengthened. The clap of air rushing to fill the void left by unmaking beams echoed off crystalline faces. The guardians swerved around a boulder and stopped.

Over fifty defenders stood intermixed with twenty vacant bodies: the searchers unable to return because of the severed portal.

Shahten only had fifteen menders left but he'd learned how to use them effectively. All of them fired together on one searcher at a time. Defenders scrambled to cover the target. But even though they rotated swiftly, they were lucky to even deflect, not return, the concentrated beams. Many bought seconds of protection with their lives, and they collapsed, unmade. When a defender was able to return a beam, Shahten simply directed his menders to switch to a less-protected searcher. He enjoyed watching the defenders scramble from one target to the next.

Best enjoy them while I can. They'll all be unmade soon.

Keela and her companions slowed, then stopped, as they realized Shahten's strategy. Mariyonta took a step toward the shower of dark light. "We've got to do something!"

Tisbero replied, "Making a star won't help with him changing targets so quickly."

Aronlat said, "Shahten now has thirteen menders left. I've counted the remaining defenders. Including us, we have enough to assign three defenders to each searcher. If we do that, it will stop everyone surging from one place to the next."

"What? How?" Gamon asked.

Keela said, "I see what he means. With three of us focused on each searcher, we can move quickly to help those next to us, but not too far. If the defenders from the four searchers next to the one being attacked come to help, there will be fifteen defenders without any scrambling. When they achieve balanced rotation, the menders are going to fall."

Gamon acknowledged, "Shahten will run out of menders quickly."

"Good idea, Aronlat. Let's do it!" Zinn exclaimed, running forward to spread the word.

Zinn, Tisbero, Mariyonta, Aronlat, Gamon and Keela disbursed into the chaotic, rolling sea of defenders, crystals, searchers and unmaking beams to convey the plan. Their desperate situation was apparent and all saw the wisdom of assigning three defenders to each searcher. Keela and her five friends assigned themselves, three each, to Hetlin and Pergaine.

Shahten noticed the change after three of his menders fell. His eyes focused on two familiar faces near Hetlin and Pergaine. His lip curled but he spoke evenly. "Keela and Tisbero, I'm going to enjoy putting your intelligence to good use. Disconnected from the wisdom of Earth's ethereal heart, you'll forget who you are and help the Way more than you can imagine. And you'll love me for it."

"Always twisting words, Shahten," Keela responded. "You mix lies with truth to create fear in others, then mix in more to convince them you are their remedy for it."

"When you're doing what works, why change?"

Tisbero stared up at him. "No matter what the future holds, there will always be a part of me that cares for Source." He looked back at Zinn, Keela, Gamon, Mariyonta, and Aronlat. "We'll remind each other."

"And kill each other," Shahten mused. He turned toward the outer ring, his cape swirling with elegance. "I must say, even though your little group has been annoying at times, I've enjoyed you. For me, it's never been about if you're going to fall, but how. I look forward to seeing how it happens."

A shadow passed over the defenders, and two more SkySlabs came alongside Shahten's. Each was packed with menders and once more Shahten's platform was filled to overcapacity. The defender's expressions changed from hope to despair. Shahten's overwhelming force only gave a choice of how to die, not if. Guardian turned to guardian, said their goodbyes, and affirmed their commitment to die while One with All.

The SkySlabs started to circle the searchers, seeking a better position to unmake Hetlin and Pergaine. Menders' angry, determined faces looked down from the edge, their unmaking crystals ready. Aronlat and Mariyonta exchanged a long glance. Their eyes teared, but their stance did not waver. Zinn touched Tisbero's hand. He grabbed hers in return but they stayed focused on the threat above.

Keela saw a flash in the corner of her eye. Something pale blue and fast streaked toward Shahten.

Yawri's skystone drilled down, and if the master captain hadn't caught him, Shahten's jump to the side would have sent him off the edge. Several menders weren't so lucky. Those in the front line sprang forward, and those behind them jumped back. Those going forward found open air. Those that went back slammed into the SkySlab's crystal centerline. All dropped their unmaking weapons, and several citrines tumbled off the edge.

As Shahten watched seven of his forty menders tumble to the ground he yelled, "Unmake that skystone!"

Menders on the other two SkySlabs spun in confusion. They'd been prepared to fire on lost ones below, not skystones in the air. This one flew past so fast that few even saw him. A deputy captain on one of the other SkySlabs echoed his master's command, and the menders on his platform started firing, but wildly.

Yawri did a pinwheel turn and raced through three unmaking beams. Red returned each in rapid succession.

Shahten yelled, his eyes bulging, "All of you! Unmake that skystone!"

"Which one?" several replied.

Yawri brought friends. Seventeen scorched skystones, with pilots dour but determined, followed Yawri's crazy assault against three SkySlabs fully loaded with menders. They darted down to become a fluid shield between shafts of dark light from above and the searchers below.

Yawri flowed along unseen currents, a fully alive human being. The tones from every cell of his body, its Earth spirit and ethereal soul, pulsed in harmony.

His skystone shot up the instant before two beams seared the air where it had been. He swerved left, then right. Each time the shafts of dark-light behind him found only empty space. He felt two beams propelled with hate aimed directly at him. He greeted them full on, and returned both to their senders.

Shahten called to his master captain, "Laric should be redirecting Generator's energy to our unmaking crystals by now. We need its doubling power!"

The master captain agreed. "If the last report is correct, the change should happen very soon. When it does, this distraction from the Way will end!"

Shahten wiped his face with his hand, took a breath, and said, "Master Captain, you make a good point." The captain blanched, not knowing what to expect. "Yawri is a distracting pest, nothing more. Killing the searchers and gaining the heart center is our prize!"

The captain brought his hand back down from his collar but couldn't take his eyes off the pest. Yawri raked the SkySlab to the left of Shahten's, and four menders fell. He did the same to the one on Shahten's right with similar results.

"He's too fast to hit," the master captain complained.

Shahten spoke to air. "Now, Laric! Now would be a good time for Generator to double the strength of our unmaking crystals."

He thrust his long hand toward the vacant bodies of Hetlin and Pergaine and yelled to the other SkySlabs. "All menders, stop firing at that skystone. Direct all unmaking at those two searchers!"

The pilots below flew their skystones into position to defend. Looking up from the ground, Tisbero, Zinn, and Gamon stood around Hetlin and called to the defenders stationed near them. Keela, Aronlat, and Mariyonta did the same for Pergaine. Within moments, both searchers had fifteen guardians poised to take turns returning the dark light.

More than twenty shafts immediately fell from the SkySlabs. Two skystones just above Hetlin and Pergaine felt the impact of the converging beams from above and broke into pieces, their pilots turned to ash. Others flew higher in order to intercept individual beams, but the SkySlabs moved in a circle around their targets, making the task much more difficult.

All color in the area surrounding the two searchers bleached to gray. Defenders on the ground rotated quickly to take their place in line. However, with so many shafts of dark light coming from three different directions, each defender could only stand a second before the next had to take their place.

Just when defenders crystals began to fail, Yawri's skystone sped so close to a SkySlab that all of its menders dove to lay down where they stood. Shahten watched three of them fall. He shook his head wildly and bellowed, "What's taking Laric so long? Generator's energy should be here!"

"It's coming!" the master captain exclaimed. "I feel a flutter in the SkySlab's crystals. Unmaking will double in strength, and all lost the ones will die!"

Keela took her turn in front of Pergaine while Tisbero stood in front of Hetlin. "Something's changing! Stay connected! Stay connected!" she exclaimed.

In the next moment the current doubled.

Keela and Tisbero watched as every mender firing at them froze unexpectedly in shock. Six on Shahten's platform fell, instantly dead from their own unmaking.

Yawri wheeled toward a line of menders on one of the other SkySlabs. Seeing him speed toward them, most raised their unmaking crystals to fire at him instead of the searchers below.

Nine shafts of their dark light found Yawri, far more than he'd ever survived before. Embracing his connection to All for a conscious death, he bore down. Suddenly, the air around him cleared. Red had miraculously returned all nine shafts to their makers.

"How did you do that?"

Red replied, "Laric and Generator. They die in Life, not murder. The volcano will explode. The tsunami will reach your shore."

There was no time for Yawri to respond. Another mender sent a beam. It returned with such force his citrine exploded. Shards peppered several other menders, who raised their hands in defense. More unmaking crystals tumbled off the edge.

The deputy captains tried to bring order but the menders still panicked. They began shooting at any skystone or defender they saw. In every case, their beam returned with uncommon force.

Shahten took a moment to grasp what was happening, then raged, "Betrayed! Laric sent Generator's energy to their crystals instead of ours!"

The master captain scoffed, "Impossible!"

"How could he betray me? How could he betray the Way?"

Of the forty menders so recently packed on Shahten's platform, only nine remained. They huddled, trying to become invisible, on the far side of the SkySlab with a wall of crystal between themselves and the pile of menders on the ground below. Their sense of respite evaporated when the skystone demon dove toward them. In a rush absent of thought, they loosed shafts of dark light at the demon, which seemed to have a long white whip streaming from its head. All shots went wide. Yawri had none to return.

With an inspiration, he dove under the SkySlab. The menders remained so intent on blasting him from the sky they kept firing when he passed underneath them. Their beams hit the SkySlab and several large pieces of stone ruptured into the air.

The tremor and sudden change in mass caused the side they were on to first roll up, then down, as the SkySlab tried to stabilize. The menders were thrown back against the wall of crystals, then forward. Shahten's long fingers bit into stone to keep from falling off the edge.

505

"Get me! Get me!" he screamed at the master captain, whose arms remained wrapped around one of the standing crystals. The SkySlab started to fall. However, with all its crystals still safely in their sockets, it was able to level and slowly rose. The master captain pulled Shahten to safety.

He stood up and dusted off his sparkling cloak. If not for the empty SkySlabs around him, he could have pretended nothing had changed. However, as he surveyed his SkySlab his eyes narrowed to crinkled slits. Only four remained: himself, the master captain and deputy captain, and one mender who clung to the base of a socketed crystal.

The two other SkySlabs had fared little better. One had six standing, the other eight. Skystones darted in and out, tempting fire, but no mender dared.

Shahten's eyes scoured the lost guardians below. His voice filled with disdain, he insisted, "You will join me in the end."

Yawri suddenly brought his skystone next to Shahten, so close he could see the veins in his neck pulse with rage.

Yawri's eyes gleamed with inner light. "You might think you're bigger than Creator, but I think not." He nodded, then glanced up.

Shahten followed his gaze and his eyes bulged. An orange streak descended toward him, with claws like open jaws. With only an instant to spare, Shahten dove and flattened himself to the stone, but the sharp talons raked his cape. He got up slowly. His beautiful cape hung limply, shredded from shoulder to shoulder.

He still spoke with disdain, but this time to his pilot. "Deputy captain, what are you waiting for? More talons?"

He turned to Yawri. "I'm going to enjoy watching you fall."

Yawri replied simply. "I'll try to be entertaining."

More ahjas circled overhead. Shahten whirled toward his pilot, but his shredded cape didn't swirl with him. "Move or be bird food."

The SkySlab rose as Shahten finished the last word, turned, and accelerated quickly toward the coast. The deputy captains of the other SkySlabs saw him leave and immediately followed. No one told any of the captains remaining on the front ring about their departure, for good reason. The last SkySlab to leave was swept clean by wings and claws.

Echoes of collapsing air and cries of the fallen faded into dust. A strange calm bathed the landscape. Yawri brought his charred skystone down near the swaying bodies of Hetlin and Pergaine. He touched his chest in thanks to the ethereal diamond within him, and then appreciatively and very carefully placed Red in the middle of his skystone.

He jumped to the ground, but before he took a step, Mariyonta and Aronlat wrapped their arms around him. Keela came next, and Yawri opened his arms to embrace her as well. Zinn bounded up, her eyes a grin, and wrapped her arms as far as she could around all of them. Soon Tisbero and Gamon joined them.

Keela grasped the tail of Yawri's headband. She'd restitched the end after it was cut short by the first unmaking beams he'd encountered back at the crystal island.

She pulled it.

"You found your skystone."

"I told you it would come."

Zinn said to Mariyonta and Aronlat, "You flew Lazket here!"

Mariyonta enthused, "You were amazing on that mammoth!"

"How did our crystals get supercharged?" Aronlat asked. "It saved the day."

Yawri took a breath. "That was thanks to Generator ... and Laric. He had a change of heart."

"Anyone that loves volcanoes has to have heart," Tisbero replied.

Zinn gazed at him and her chin bobbed. "That explains a lot," she said quietly.

All of them wept joyous tears of relief.

While exhausted guardians surveyed the sky with cautious hope, Red rebalanced with the six crystals wedded to the light-blue quartzite. After their song was One, they sought Lazket. Joining with Lazket, they found he was already rebalanced with the crystal forest. It, in turn, rebalanced with those in Lazket's cavern, then with all caverns on Earth, and the crystals on other planets ... and the other eight energy centers of Earth.

Yawri felt the ethereal diamond within him sing. "Thanks to guardians everywhere, all of the other centers remain whole. All of Shahten's forces are in retreat. The portal is starting to reopen!"

Harmony built and grew. The crystal center radiated a soft, warm light. Melodies and infinite colors flowed back and forth. The dimensions reconnected, and a message from the searchers arrived.

Keela called out, "The time for awakening is here. Come! Come now!"

The gateway from past to future and from future to past opened, and an avalanche of energy shot through the portal from Earth's core.

Yawri boomed, "Every guardian, locate your future self in the arc across time. If they are awake enough to feel you, join with them. If enough can, Earth will go to sleep now and reawaken then!"

Exited voices started coming through the center. Pergaine and Hetlin's were first. "Here! Here! We've found ourselves here!"

Another voice rang out, "I found a future self who's willing to learn how to reconnect! They have knowledge that only comes from experiencing Earth's sleep and what it takes to awaken! I have so much to learn from them!"

"With mine too!" another called out. "Earth is awakening, slowly, but steadily. Our future selves have lived through Shahten's Way and have the knowledge from it that we need to counter its harm!"

Another said, "My future self has walked through darkness but never stopped seeking ever more of himself. He still carries an inner flame that reminds him there is much more to Life than eyes see."

"Mine feels a quickening in the heart. She's starting to remember the meaning of co-creation as a human being!"

"My future self never gave up, either! He still searches … for me!"

Zinn called out. "Yawri, I found you! But you're ill, very ill. Your future body is an unnatural yellow, even your eyes. I'm giving you healing herbs in sugar water. I'll make sure you live!"

Keela said, "Yawri, we're together again in my time, too! We're sitting on a knoll of soft grass. There is a statue of a man on a horse behind us. There is a building across a square. It has wide metal tracks coming in and out of it under big cars on rolling wheels. I still like plants, and you're still traveling. It's a beautiful night, and we're talking about our love of nature and our lives."

Gamon barked, "Are we connected by our resonance forever? I see you too, Yawri. I'm an old man, a storyteller of my village. I tell good stories about the way of Earth and human beings. You are a white face among those of my village. I'm reminding you of Orion and the pyramids!"

Tisbero added, "Guardians must be coming back and forth into each other's lives. We've all found you Yawri, but have you found yourself yet? I'm guarding the great pyramid. I'm considering letting you climb it with me, but it's dangerous."

Yawri exclaimed, "I see my future self there too, Tisbero! I'm at the base of the great pyramid! Maybe that future me can remember our history."

"I'm not sure he'll be able to. Seems kind of stubborn."

"I don't know if he can either. He tries to understand Life with his head rather than with his whole body."

Yawri flowed next to his future self and whispered, "Let go of what you think should be and feel what is."

Tisbero said, "Okay, maybe it will work. We'll climb together."

"Run him up the pyramid, Tisbero. If he's not exhausted, I don't think I can get through."

"Okay, I'm sprinting ahead. He's trying to keep up."

"Faster, he's still thinking too much. He needs to be in the experience, not trying to figure it out."

"Almost at the top!"

"Run. I'm with him. We'll make it."

"Wait. We're on the top, but something's wrong. He's not moving. I think he passed out."

Yawri exclaimed, "He opened too fast! He's losing himself in our ethereal Creation!"

Yawri tried to deliver a message but his future self seemed unconscious. "Observe and learn, don't become what you see."

Keela said, "Losing himself at the point of our Creation? Call help to him! Is anyone you know near?"

"Murann. Murann is near."

"Ask him to help! If your future self can't connect to his own Creation, he may never find himself within it!"

Hetlin's earthy sound rose above all the others. "Enough conscious connections are made! Earth is going to sleep in our time and waking up in theirs!"

The ground beneath the guardians' feet at the heart center went quiet. Pulsing ley lines, those arteries of Life, shrank. Pergaine said, "The Earth is starting to hibernate and is withdrawing vitality deep within itself. It's protecting its most precious parts from the unmaking that the Way would bring upon it."

Another voice said, "It's working! It's waking up in that future! I feel it stretching, its crust beginning to flex."

Guardians celebrated. "Earth lives! It's reclaiming its vital co-creation with Creator. We awaken with it! Shahten's reign will recede at last!"

"We know our future selves have the choice to hear us. We don't know if they will listen," said Tisbero.

Zinn affirmed, "They will listen," but it came out like a prayer.

Keela said, "I pray you hear me, that you receive me. Let us learn from each other, listen to each other. May we each have the strength to, over time, learn what it means to be both human and being again."

Mariyonta exclaimed, "I've found myself! I am young in that time, too. We bring new energies to reconnect the wisdom of Earth with the wisdom of self!"

Aronlat exclaimed, "I am there too! More and more human beings are using self-honesty to untangle truth from lie! We are young and filled with Life. We won't be stopped."

Yawri's voice rang for all to hear. "We know there are lifetimes of loss between then and now. May we wake up together, and know forgiveness of ourselves, each other and the strength of our caring for All!"

Slowly, a nurturing, etheric elixir and an Earthly presence grew. Ethereal and physical worlds, long torn apart, started to connect again.

A crescendo rose from the sea of guardians, a chorus of hope resonating across time. Gossamer threads joined. Each one thrummed with color woven in a vaporous fabric of graceful, undulating ribbons.

Particles of essence — radiant beings of Creator's Creation — vibrated within the cosmic symphony, and each rang with meaning.

"Self determine how you co-create in Creation. Go forth, go forth and create. Learn. Expand All, with all you become."

Endless hues and sounds rolled all directions at once.

"Free will ... is granted."

EPILOGUE

∞

The Return

I lay curled into a ball, eyes shut, head pounding.

My eyes cracked open slowly. An outstretched arm ran to a motionless hand, its fingers seemingly frozen by starlight. With an effort, one finger moved then another. Grit greeted their touch, and my eyes opened further. I watched my fingers part the grit as they moved across rippling stone toward my face. Fingertips touched my lips and the fragrance of earthy limestone filled my lungs.

Bright light suddenly seared the air and sound rolled all directions at once. My eyes snapped shut to ward off overwhelm. Dizzy. Floating. No up or down. No far or near.

Light flashed through my eyelids, but it felt heavy on my skin, so heavy my cheek pressed down into the stone.

The searing light and sound stopped as suddenly as it started. Darkness rolled, and I opened my eyes again. Stars twinkled and wrapped me in night's arching dome.

"It's okay," a voice said.

I looked from side to side to find its source. Only translucent ribbons of dust mingled with stars.

Am I on the top of a mountain? Where? Which one?

The distant voice pushed into my confused reverie. "You're on the pyramid."

The pyramid.

"Can you sit up?"

Sit up?

"Careful. You're near the edge."

Rolling to my knees, I sat up slowly. Threads of light in countless hues wove through the air. Mist rose from immense blocks of stone and danced with the kiss of a breeze.

Tears rolled down my cheeks.

"I've been lost to myself," I whispered.

A sigh responded. "We have."

I glanced in the direction of the sound. A man in baggy pants stood near a tall pole in the center of the pyramid. He moved toward me so lightly his body appeared to float above the massive stone. Coming to a slow stop, he leaned down toward me. "You made it to the top, alive."

My eyes blinked. His didn't, and he sat down next to me.

"I no longer bring visitors up here, but something told me to bring you."

There was something familiar about his eyes. "I'm glad you did."

His voice was a sandy whisper. "I'm glad you asked."

A calm silence fell, free of time. We watched a meteor streak across the night, but neither of us spoke. It disappeared in a bright flash, and words bubbled up without thought. "Thank you Tisber…no, that's not right."

He laughed. "My name is Tabari."

"Tabari, yes, of course. I don't know where that came from."

He smiled easily. "The pyramid has strange effects. Sometimes, like tonight, when I stand at the center pole the hair on my arm rises."

My face turned toward his. The image of a massive lightning bolt streaking up into the sky flashed before my eyes. I blinked and it was gone.

"Tabari," I repeated, trying to make sense of it and the vision. "Thank you." Breathing slowly and deeply, I added, "Thank you for everything."

"We go down now." It was a declaration, not a question. "Too much time on the pyramid is not good."

I need more time to know this is real.

"A moment," I said. With a practiced motion, my left hand unfastened the Goulimine bead latching the flap of my worn satchel and raised the old Nikon toward Tabari. "I'm sure I was shaking during the first shot of Chephren. This time I'll prop the camera on my knees." Steadying the camera with ease, I framed the shot to catch the lip of the Pyramid I sat upon and the shutter snapped. Its sound was so real I sighed with relief.

Bound to be a much better photograph.

I turned slowly to survey the flat apex of the Great Pyramid. "Its capstone was made of gold," came out.

"Yes," was the only reply.

A sudden gust of wind whipped sand up and over the edge, and he added, "We go back now."

I returned my camera to its satchel thoughtfully. "Okay."

Tabari stood up, scanned the night's sky, then looked down the slope. Satisfied, he stepped to the edge and turned to look at me.

Getting up much more slowly than he did, I joined him at the edge. A steep ramp tumbled down into darkness. However, rather than start down, he sat on the top block and hung his feet over the edge. As if on cue, music blared and brilliant orange light flashed on the Sphinx far below.

I sat down next to him. "We wait for the light show to end," I said, understanding.

"No. It's best to go down before it's over."

I jerked back. "With banks of floodlights flashing?"

He nodded matter-of-factly. "People are blinded by it. They never see me."

A question formed on my tongue but it came out in a confused blur. "Then, why did we run up?"

"Wasn't that the plan?" He pushed off the top lip and stood on the first course down.

"What plan? I didn't have a plan."

He took another step down. "It seemed like it was."

I pushed off the stone and caught up with him. His words mixed with dust. "You felt it, did you not? The past?"

My chest hummed but the answer caught in my throat. "Yes."

His chin bobbed. Then we bounded down the next step together, scarcely noticing the long, steep ramp that tumbled down before us. "But I have no idea what to do with it."

Tabari laughed aloud. "One step at a time. Just realize the step you're on before you take the next."

I breathed in starlight and stepped off the next block, and the next, and the next in endless succession.

"I've got a lot of choices to make."

"Like all of us do."

We jumped down in tandem to the ground. His head pivoted quickly toward voices echoing up from the guard station. "Soldiers come! You must go. Return the way you came." He turned to run toward the growing volume with a confidence that belied its threat. A voice like gravel called back over his shoulder.

"Remembering is good. Makes the next step clear."

I stared blankly after him until I saw a line of flashlights bobbing up the road.

Sprinting back to the middle pyramid, I continued along its steady stones to the first pyramid I'd sat upon, Mycerinus. Looking up to the course of stone where I'd lain, a torrent of light hit the small pyramid's face. I saw the guard before he saw me. He shouted a heartbeat after I'd spun and began to speed into the sandy sea of ancient tombs.

Surrounded by darkness again, the stars of Orion's Belt pulsed in the western sky. I was both a child sitting in the middle of a storm cellar and running here at the same moment. Tears of joy watered my eyes. An empowering sense of newfound freedom saturated and propelled me. I felt my body glide, flying over the ground. My feet moved of their own volition, thrumming with each stride in perfect symmetry. I darted around fallen stones, laughing with joy, fluid as the wind.

∞

The Aftermath

The adventure continued at home. My vision, hearing, and sense of smell became sensitive in a way typically only experienced after a week in the wild. The fossils on our living room shelf weren't dead. The potted plants called when they needed water.

Experiencing myself as both a soul and a body joined as a human being filled me with reverence and shock. I was individual, yet not. It reminded me of the storm cellar and my sensation of being one cell in a colossal giant's body, but to the point of overwhelm.

The city park near our house had a large pond, and my wife and I often took the kids there. Now, as I watched them play, the birds fly and the leaves of the trees move, an unshakable living essence gushed through everything. A powerful sense of purpose burned within me.

This planet consciously co-creates with Creator, and I agreed to become a human being—a human-being to share in the Creation and learning of this planet and enliven All-we-become.

A conflict roiled within me. The visions of the past made complete sense while experiencing them, but I lived here, in this time now. How did my life of traveling by car, plane, boat or train, shopping in big box stores, living in the suburbs and eating meat harmonize with the nurturing nature of guardians past?

What does it mean to be a human being today?

Keeping too busy to ponder the question bought me some time. Over the previous eight years, my wife and I had taught classes in personal development. It was a full-time business and the role in our classroom was comfortable for me. People are a part of the planet and helping them become more self-aware was one kind of guardianship.

However, even though the business continued to expand, so did my bewilderment.

My work is with people who come to me, a self-selected sphere of motivated individuals. How are other guardians awakening? Should I work with a more general population in a more collaborative way?

It wasn't practical, but I felt driven to let go of the classroom and work in the environmental field. Ignoring this message only made it louder. Discussing it with my wife resulted in a supportive, "Sounds like it's something you need to do."

Encouraged, I met with people who worked in large corporations, small non-profits, and a lot of organizations in between over the next few months. All of them had environmental aspects to their organizations.

However, other than volunteer work, nothing opened up. The longer the search took, the more my concern grew.

Do I personally need to change careers to fulfill my agreement as a human being?

Staying in my comfortable classroom looked better each day.

After the kids were in bed one night, I walked to the large pond near our home and stood on its bank. I opened myself to All as best I could. In the midst of frog song, the sense of being myself within the One Body and the One Body being in me felt incredibly real once more.

My silent prayer was, "I enjoy my classroom, but if I need to fulfill my agreement by working in a different way, please help me find it."

Heart in my feet, I walked home.

The next day a call came from the Office of Environmental Assistance, a small state agency. Like so many organizations before, I'd phoned a supervisor and asked for an informational interview. We met and she mentioned her office had posted a position for a "waste prevention program leader." Given my science degree and business and communications background, I appeared qualified. After applying and going through the interview process, they offered me the position. My wife agreed to continue teaching full time while I worked evenings in our business and full time for the state.

Within six months of returning from Egypt, my career changed drastically. Instead of being in charge of my own classroom, I'd be overseen by a supervisor, manager, commissioner and the legislature. Within a couple of years I figured I'd know how guardians were awakening in the world.

I stayed over twenty-seven.

There was a lot more to learn—from guardians of past, alive today—than I thought.

My position changed over time. The legislature eliminated the agency I started with but the State Energy Office hired me to lead industrial energy efficiency efforts. That changed to Clean Energy Commercialization for the next twelve years.

Here's what happened.

All positions required me to provide unbiased analysis and information to people who requested it. My work was non-regulatory. During my first year alone, over fifty organizations asked for presentations on what they could do to reduce their impact on the environment.

The number of requests increased each year. They came from schools, churches, hardware stores, and hotels, and manufacturers ranging from blankets to cereal, from computers to cheese, from fossil fuel refineries to renewable fuel production facilities.

Finding accurate information and complementary programs to help them implement their Earth-friendly efforts required me to work with city, county, state, and federal workers. Even when their offices were closed, many still answered my emails or phone calls. The first time it happened, I was surprised, but it kept happening.

Even if they weren't consciously aware of being a "guardian," person after person behaved like one. Once, the management of a large hotel asked me for assistance. The hotel housekeepers who spearheaded the request came to the first meeting. They wanted to make sure everything that could be recycled would be, and asked how much the new "reuse rather than replace" linen programs reduced water use. While talking to them a deep feeling of inner knowing surged through my body. Guardians of the past were conscientious hotel housekeepers today.

Other "guardians are here" experiences happened when I met with a manufacturer eliminating hazardous material from its products, high school students implementing youth eco-solutions activities, paper mill operators wanting more energy efficient production rollers, parishioners seeking help to expedite "Creation Care" efforts in their church and hard questions about loss of species due to human activities. It finally struck me.

I'd left America feeling little, if anything, made sense in life. I found common values connected people across the globe. Whether Hindu, Sikh, Christian, Muslim, Jewish, Buddhist, Native American, Shinto or Animist, in every economic bracket, the people who invited me into their homes lived with a caring connection to the world far beyond themselves. Circumstances did not define the kind of person they were. They did.

Globetrotting through people's lives was one thing, but now I worked with people year after year, across all sectors of society, who demonstrated the same values. They enjoyed connecting diverse people and interests because the inclusion resulted in lasting change, independent of whether they were still there or not. They did environmental tasks because they wanted to, not because they were told to.

My investigation into other countries continued. Through work, I met with numerous foreign trade delegations who came to leverage their environmental efforts with ours. Going overseas didn't stop after marriage. My wife and I have traveled with friends to seventeen more countries for a total of seventy. I have met guardians in each one.

The trend across the world is undeniable. Human beings awaken. My chest warms when guardians of old arrive in their present bodies. From their point of view, they aren't remarkable or even noteworthy. Being a caring person connected with Life is simply normal to them.

Remembering what it means to be a human being can come as a shock. If you feel a fluttering rush or quickening, it's your body talking with you.

Feeling more connection to the whole of Life is a constant choice to care about your impact.

Joy for your actions that enhance Life, and remorse for actions that don't, empower change. Blame, shame, guilt and "should," stop change. Expect others to tell you what they think you should feel, think and do. Know these things for yourself.

Expect yourself to want to tell them what *they* should feel, think and do. It's how learning happens. Humor helps.

There are millions of people around the globe who care deeply. Most simply, they are people with tremendous self-honesty who demonstrate their respect for Creation by their choices and actions.

Free will is a priceless gift beyond imagining.

May you expand All with who you are and All you choose to become.

∞

The Back-Story

The idea that the purpose of a human being is to be a guardian and co-creator with a living planet shook me to my bones. Now, I want to learn the reality of how to expand in Creation and give more to All. Suddenly every struggle has a purpose, meaning, and lesson.

I'll share what I learned.

Creation is infinite. It's impossible to learn how to accomplish all there is to learn within one lifetime. Each life is a specialized course in the nature of co-creating as a human-being.

When we were given free will to "Go forth and learn and expand All with all you become," I don't think any of us suspected that some would use their free will to murder. We learned how evil does intentional harm and then denies that harm occurred. We learned how it mixes lies with truth to create fear, and then nurtures that fear to gain control. We learned how to stop it without becoming evil ourselves.

However, when murder was introduced, we began to forget who we are. We became more and more disconnected. Our learning now is largely about what it means to lose yourself, then regain yourself. If this was easy, we'd all be done by now. It is an extremely challenging course and we don't graduate until we learn all the lessons.

Eons ago, we knew who we were. We looked into our future and saw the darkness coming. So, we built big things out of stone to help remind us who we were. Great teachers who remembered came to remind us, too. However, being murdered time and time again over many lifetimes does make it more challenging to return remembering all the human-being you are. Still, everyone seems to have a nagging feeling there is more to Life than what we know. We can't quite put our finger on it but we're driven to keep looking.

Evil came to this planet and that it meant we either needed to learn about it or leave. If you're reading this, you stayed. Learning to ride a bike—or in this case, learning about evil— requires experiencing it. By experience, I mean riding the bike, not just getting run over by it.

I'll share my two darkest lifetimes as an example of that learning, and why I was able to write Shahten's dialogue.

By the 13th century, the dark ages of Europe, only fleeting memories of myself as a human-being remained. I came into a lifetime so disconnected from myself it was possible for me to harm Life without feeling it.

Without any awareness of my impact, I sought the sense of power that came from knowing who should live or die. Lacking self, the sense of superiority, control, and certainty that came from domination over others was an irresistible temptation. Dividing people into "with me" and "against me" kept them properly focused on what they feared outside of themselves instead of the Creator within.

I thought Genghis Khan was right. In that lifetime, I retained some memory of my love of Earth, the nomadic lifestyle that moved without harming the planet, and how much I detested slavery of any kind ... but not much else. From my nomad warrior perspective, the rich and powerful in cities poisoned our water, killed the land, enslaved our families, perfected torture, and ignored any evidence that we could be anything other than subhuman.

It seemed simple. Everyone that agreed to outlaw slavery, ban torture, promote on merit, teach all to read and write, and incorporate the Mongols' respect for nature would live. Those who didn't would die. Since I made these choices based on the belief humanity needed to be saved from itself, there was no question about receiving my eternal reward in the celestial afterlife.

Remember the message of the Voice of Compassion? In another lifetime, I remembered my love of his message, but other than "Jesus will save me," little else. I was devoted to Him and became a cardinal in a Roman Catholic Church in Italy. When the church-sanctioned the Inquisition to save lost souls from eternal damnation in hell, it made sense to me. I wasn't an inquisitor, but I supported them. In the name of Jesus Christ, I supported the murder of people who I judged so lost to evil that they could not accept His love.

Both these lifetimes were right out of Shahten's playbook. I believed the lie, "lost ones" needed to change for their own good. It was one of countless variations of the Way. If the "lost ones" refused to agree, they deserved to suffer.

It didn't matter how many hundreds of lifetimes I'd had being in Life, I'd chosen to use my God-given free will to self-righteously waste Life and destroy the knowledge of others. Therefore, I would spend as many lifetimes as it took to learn to understand the value of Life and their knowledge.

I had four lifetimes of living in deserts so devoid of life that even a piece of broken green jade was cherished. I sucked on it in case it could bring water. My loved ones starved to death after self-righteous hands more powerful than mine took what little food we had.

There were five lifetimes in which I was blind, treated as the village idiot even though I was smart, and died because the healers who understood what natural ingredients could heal my blindness were gone.

Even in the hardest lifetimes, choice is always here. Evil tempts with empty promises. If I chose to embrace disconnection, it meant I could experience even more power and an even greater sense of superiority, control, and domination without feeling the truth of its impact—for a while.

Embracing connection meant knowing the terrifying pain of the harm that I caused sooner rather than later.

When you're a slave or kicked because you're poor and blind, it's very tempting to choose power. Bitterness, hatred and self-righteousness are easy. "It's their fault. It's better to prosper without heart than be one of 'them'".

Another part of me said, "How I treat others is how I tell Creation I wish to be treated."

It was a crossroads. I wondered what kind of person I wanted to be: powerful to the world and numb, or internally strong and sensitive?

Fortunately, as is true in my current lifetime, I had lots of good help. "Do unto others as you would have them do unto you," became "What you do to Life will be done to you."

By the fourth lifetime of blindness, instead of nursing hatred, I chose more connection to All—including to my abusers. Opening to nature and caring for it was my foundation for change. The minerals in the rocks and plants along my roadside ditch became known by touch and smell. I "saw" the abuse my abusers would be experiencing themselves.

Connection slowly built on connection, and the next lifetime I learned what combinations of minerals and plants healed specific ailments. People valued these abilities so much they provided well for my wife and children, who loved me greatly even though I was blind.

Although I chose to "learn evil" so I could counter it, I have great remorse for the pain I caused. Not shame or guilt. My guilt or my shame is useless and only about me. It gives nothing. Remorse is different. Remorse works with self-forgiveness. Guilt is glue, but remorse responds. Remorse is active. It's what fuels, "I'll never do *that* again," with enduring heart.

This learning was also a small step toward learning how to disagree with and change harmful action without being self-righteous—and understanding the harm that comes from dividing people into camps of right and wrong.

To learn compassion, I learned when you judge, you ask to become that which you judge in a future lifetime. It is not a pleasant experience but it is popular learning.

If you think you know why someone else is having a hard life, please reconsider.

I met a master healer once. I'd volunteered to help at a long-term substance abuse treatment center and he was one of the residents. Coke and meth. If you heard his life story, you'd understand why. I'm sure he didn't think of himself this way, but I repeatedly felt that he was a master healer who chose this lifetime to learn how to heal drug addiction from the inside out.

Appearance is not always what you think. I could have left this section out of the book and portrayed myself with mystic light, but here's the back-story. In my earnest quest to learn how evil worked, I supported the destruction of ancient wisdom that didn't agree with my beliefs at the time. Consequently, I lived lifetimes without the knowledge I helped destroy, and I do not wish that pain on anyone. Thanks to a lot of help this lifetime, I made choices that allowed me to do what I needed to do to return some of that information.

I provide these examples and thoughts in case your personal experience from reading this book touched a sense of yourself as a guardian of Creation. Your own experience would be what's true for you. However, even if it didn't, I hope that sharing my darkest lifetimes helps you touch compassion for yourself and the enduring strength—actually the eternal strength—that comes with free will.

Evil disconnects and separates what is whole. It's like sleepwalking, thinking you're awake until you realize you're not. Learning how to reconnect after disconnection is a tremendous learning and yes, waking up is hard to do.

The temptation and choices are real. Being numb lets you do harm without feeling your impact. The more you connect, the more you feel. For human beings who agreed to serve as guardians of Creation on Earth, it is not pleasant to realize what happened while we dozed. Forgiving ourselves for not knowing what we didn't know is a good start. The best warriors know compassion.

From my point of view, creation is infinite and there is no end to learning about yourself in it. Accepting the adventure and owning your learning is much more fun than complaining about how everyone else is using their free will. Most people have been both male and female, rich and poor, victim and perpetrator, and every race on the planet. Whether or not you remember your past lifetimes does not matter. Whatever it is you come to learn each lifetime, the information needed comes with you. The help. The harm. The choices are here now.

Really. It's not where you work but the kind of person you are while there and everywhere else that matters. Inaction is an action. If you know of harm and choose to take no action that demonstrates you disagree with that harm, you ask for a world where you are on its receiving end. I very clearly remember being on the receiving end after being on the giving end, and that makes the "you sow what you reap," clause rather real for me.

Human beings did not know evil, or even deceit, and we lost ourselves in choices we did not understand. We became split into "human" and "being." Lifetime after lifetime we've been learning how to re-join with all of ourselves again. We are not becoming the human beings we were. We are becoming human beings who remember what we were, plus all we have learned about separation and rejoining across time.

Planet Earth is waking up, and it is very well connected to Creator.

The actions of each person tells Creation how much that individual chooses to be a part of that awakening. The examples I shared show how that choice determines the lesson plan for many lifetimes to come.

There is no mistake in learning what you don't know. There are no "shoulds."

We can *give* our choices to others to decide for us. That is free will. However, nothing, no one can *take* your free will from you.

The choices you make matter—a lot.

You are precious to Life.

SPECIAL THANKS

This book would not have been possible without Renee and Donna.

After my global sojourn, I returned to the same town I'd left. My friend Renee had just returned from riding her horse from California to Montana, and let me stay on her back porch. It turned out we enjoyed each other's company and values a lot. One of the things we had in common was personal development as a whole person, body and spirit. We married in 1978, and I'm still learning what it means to be a healthy, caring husband and father of two children and two grandchildren.

Renee and I spent more than decade learning how to consciously connect with past selves. The kind of connection we practice means you feel the experience of the you "that was then" on an intimate level. This can be quite difficult or wonderfully joyous, depending. What we learned is that each lifetime we live has purpose for learning and opportunities to grow a deeper heart connecting your body and soul. It's up to us what we make of it.

After I collapsed on the top of the pyramid, around a hundred past selves I'd worked with coalesced. The history of human beings became pointedly real to me, and if not for Renee and Donna, I could have easily lost myself in time. Consciously connecting to past selves can help or do harm, depending on the ability and training of the facilitator. It is easy to be retraumatized or to move into fantasy without skilled guidance.

Renee also gave me helpful editing and comments on every page of this book.

We met Donna Taylor the year before we were married and discovered her life was also dedicated to personal development as a whole person, body and spirit. She remains our dearest friend today.

Donna taught me the difference between fantasy and vision, hearing and listening, seeing and sight, and —most importantly—how to accept my humanity. It was with Donna, Renee, and other friends that I hiked through seventeen more countries to add to the fifty-three I explored before I married, seventy…so far.

Donna has a way of making what I sense real in a kinesthetic way, including many experiences I shared in this book. Hiking next to her mile after mile taught me about what it means to be a guardian of Life in ways I didn't fathom. Her feet sing.

Donna also provided many helpful comments on Call to Purpose.

I am blessed to have friends who know the difference between caring and caretaking and who share the joy of success and sadness of loss without reservation. They practice honesty, self-forgiveness, and courage of heart, and they ask the same of me. Without such friendships, my own dark night of the soul would have been too lonely to bear.

Made in the USA
Monee, IL
10 May 2023

33430328R00312